HERE, BOY!

O'Leary swung the ax at the window. Glass burst outward. He jumped down to the turf six feet below. So far, so good. Now, where was his mount? He gave a low whistle. There was an answering hiss from beyond the nearest clump of trees, only dimly visible thorough the fog.

He set off in that direction and saw the stir of a tall body among the trunks. A mighty figure stalked forth to meet him, looking bigger than ever through the mist. "That's the boy, right on the job," O'Leary called in a low voice. He trotted forward to meet the tremendous beast as it advanced, emitting a rumble like a dormant volcano stirring to life. O'Leary admired the play of the massive thigh muscles under the greenish hide, the great column of the neck, the jaws—

Jaws? He didn't remember a head the size of a Volkswagen, opening like a power shovel to reveal multiple rows of gleaming ivory daggers, nor did he recall talons like bone scimitars.

He turned, dropped the cumbersome ax and dashed for shelter. A huge foot struck the earth just beside him; and O'Leary caught a glimpse of a steaming red-lined cavern big enough to stable a pony. He dived; there was a tremendous boom! as the jaws met inches behind him; a blow set him spinning.

He rolled over, came to hands and knees, his shirt in shreds. With a crash of rending branches, a second, smaller reptile stepped into view, Dinny!

The herbivore took two steps forward. The meat-eater bellowed. Dinny gave a leap when he saw the tyrannosaur for the first time. He bleated, turned and made for cover.

"Smart dinosaur," O'Leary muttered as he readied himself for a desperate sprint. . . .

Baen Books by Keith Laumer

edited by Eric Flint
Retief!
Odyssey
Keith Laumer: The Lighter Side
A Plague of Demons & Other Stories
Future Imperfect
Legions of Space
Imperium
The Universe Twister

The Bolo series
The Compleat Bolo by Keith Laumer
Created by Keith Laumer:
The Triumphant by David Weber & Linda Evans
The Unconquerable
Last Stand
Old Guard
Cold Steel
Bob Brigade by William H. Keith, Jr.
Bolo Rising by William H. Keith, Jr.
Bolo Strike by William H. Keith, Jr.
Bolo! by David Weber
The Road to Damascus by John Ringo & Linda Evans
Old Soldiers by David Weber

THE UNIVERSE TWISTER

Keith Laumer

Edited by Eric Flint

THE UNIVERSE TWISTER

This is a work of fiction. All the characters and events portrayed in this book are fictional, and any resemblance to real people or incidents is purely coincidental.

A Baen Book

Baen Publishing Enterprises
P.O. Box 1403
Riverdale, NY 10471
www.baen.com

ISBN 10: 1-4165-5597-8
ISBN 13: 978-1-4165-5597-1

Cover art by Bob Eggleton

First printing in this combined format, October 2008

Distributed by Simon & Schuster
1230 Avenue of the Americas
New York, NY 10020

Printed in the United States of America

10 9 8 7 6 5 4 3 2 1

Table of Contents

The Time Bender   1
The World Shuffler   253
The Shape Changer   489

The Time Bender

Chapter One

Lafayette O'Leary came briskly up the cracked walk leading to Mrs. MacGlint's Clean Rooms and Board, reflecting on his plans for the evening: First, he'd grab a quick bite, then check to see how his plastics experiment was coming along; after that, a look in on his *penicillium notatum* NRRL 1249.B21 culture, and then . . . He hefted the weighty book under his arm. Professor Hans Joseph Schimmerkopf's book on mesmerism ought to be good for at least a week of evenings.

As O'Leary put foot on the sagging veranda, the front screen door popped wide open. A square figure five feet eleven in height confronted him, a heavy-duty broom held at port arms.

"Mr. O'Leary! What's that mess you've got percolating on my hot plate back in my third-best western exposure?"

Lafayette retreated a step. "Did I leave my polymers cooking, Mrs. MacGlint? I thought I turned them off—"

"Them fumes has faded the colors right out of the wallpaper! Not to say nothing about running up the electric bill! I'll put it on your bill, Mr. O'Leary!"

"But—"

"And all this reading at night! Burning light bulbs like they was free! My other boarders don't set up all hours, studying Lord knows what in them un-Christian books you got!" She eyed the volume under O'Leary's arm with unmistakable hostility.

"Say, Mrs. MacGlint," O'Leary edged back up on the porch, "a funny thing happened last night. I was running a little statistical study, using ball bearings, and I happened to drop a couple of them—three-quarter-inchers—and they all rolled right to the northwest corner of the room—"

"Prob'ly marked up my linoleum, too! And—"

"I knew the floors slanted but I hadn't noticed how much," Lafayette gained another foot. "So I made a few measurements. I'd say there's a two-inch discrepancy from wall to wall. I knew you'd want to know, because Section Four, Article 19 of the Building Code—the part that covers Hazardous Conditions Due to Settlement of Foundations—is pretty clear. Now, the inspector will have to check it, of course, and after the house is condemned and the roomers find other quarters, then maybe they can save the place by pumping in concrete.

That's pretty expensive, but it's better than breaking the law, eh, Mrs. MacGlint?"

"Law?" The landlady's voice squeaked. "Building Code? Why, I never heard such nonsense . . . "

"Do you want to report it, or shall I? I know you're awfully busy, keeping everybody's affairs in order, so . . . "

"Now, Mr. O'Leary, don't go to no trouble . . . " Mrs. MacGlint backed through the door; Lafayette followed into the gloom and cabbage aroma of the hall. "I know you got your science work you want to get to, so I won't keep you." She turned and puffed off along the hall. O'Leary let out a long breath and headed up the stairs.

On the shelf behind the curtain in the former broom closet which served Lafayette as kitchen alcove were a two-pound tin of salt-water taffy, a cardboard salt shaker, a ketchup bottle, a can of soup and two tins of preserved fish. He didn't really like sardines, he confessed to himself, unwrapping a succulent taffy. Too bad they didn't can *consommé au beurre blanc Hermitage*. Tend-R Nood-L Soup would have to do. He started warming a saucepan of soup, took a beer from the foot-square icebox and punched a triangular hole in the lid. He finished off the candy, then the beer, waiting for the pot to boil, then set out a bowl, poured the soup and put two sardines on a cracker. Munching, he picked up his book. It was a thick, dusty volume, bound in faded dark blue leather, the cramped gilt letters on the spine almost illegible. He blew the dust away and opened it with care; the old binding crackled. The title page announced:

Mesmerism, Its Proper Study and Practice; or The Secrets of the Ancients Unlocked.

By Herr Professor Doktor Hans Joseph Schimmerkopf, D.D., Ph.D., Litt. D., M. A., B. Sc., Associate Professor of Mental Sciences and Natural Philosophy, Homeopathic Institute of Vienna. 1888.

O'Leary riffled through the tissue-thin pages of fine print; pretty dry stuff, really. Still, it was the only book on hypnotism in the library that he hadn't already read, and what else was there to do? O'Leary looked out the narrow window at the sad late-afternoon light, yellowing into evening. He could go out and buy a newspaper; he might even stroll around the block. He could stop by the Elite Bar and Grill and have a cold beer. There were any number of ways a young, healthy, penniless draftsman in a town like Colby Corners could spend an evening in the sunshine of his happy youth.

A rattle of knuckles at the door announced a narrow-faced man with thin hair and a toothbrush mustache slid into the room.

"Hi, Laff, howza boy?" the newcomer rubbed knuckly hands together. He wore a purple shirt and white suspenders supporting trousers cut high above bony hips.

"Hello, Spender," O'Leary greeted him without enthusiasm.

"Say, Laff, you couldn't slip me a five until Tuesday?"

"I'm busted, Spender. Besides which, you owe me five."

"Hey, what's the book?" Spender edged in beside him and poked at the pages. "When do you get time to read all this stuff? Pretty deep, huh? You're a funny guy; always like studying."

"This is a racy one," O'Leary said. "The press it was printed on was smashed with crowbars by a crowd of aroused peasants. Then they ran the author down and gave him the full werewolf treatment—silver bullet, stake through the heart—the works."

"Wow!" Spender recoiled. "You studying to be a werewolf, O'Leary?"

"No, I'm more interested in the vampire angle. That's the one where you turn into a bat—"

"Look, Laff, that ain't funny. You know I'm kind of like superstitious. You shouldn't ought to read them books."

O'Leary looked at the other speculatively. "What I need now is some practical experience—"

"Yeah, well, I'll see you, boy." Spender backed out the door.

O'Leary finished his repast, then stretched out on the lumpy bed. The water stains on the ceiling hadn't changed since yesterday, he noted. The opalescent globe shielding the sixty-watt bulb dangling on its kinked cord still contained the same number of dead flies. The oleander bush still scraped restlessly on the screen.

He flipped open Schimmerkopf's book at random and skimmed the print-packed pages. The sections on mesmerism were routine stuff, but a passage on autohypnosis caught his eye:

" . . . this state may readily be induced by the adept practitioner of the art of Mesmeric influence, or of hypnotism, as it is latterly termed, requiring only a schooled effort of Will, supported by a concentration of Psychical Energies. Mastery of this Force not only offers instantaneous relief from sleep-lessness, night sweats, poor memory, sour bile, high chest, salivation, inner conflict, and other ills both of the flesh and of the spirit, but offers as well a veritable treasurehouse of rich sensation; for it is a commonplace of the auto-mesmerist's art that such scenes of remembered or imagined Delight as must be most highly esteemed by persons sensible of the lamentable drabness of Modern Life can in this fashion be evoked most freely for the delectation and adornment of the idle hour.

"This phenomenon may be likened to the hypno-gogic state, that condition of semi-awareness some-times achieved by a sleeping person who, partially awakened, is capable of perceiving the dream-state images, whilst at the same time enjoying conscious-ness of their illusory nature. Thus, he is rendered capable of examining the surface texture and detail of an imagined object as acutely as one might study the page of an actual book, throughout maintaining knowledge of the distinction between hallucinatory experience and real experience . . . "

That part made sense, O'Leary nodded. It had hap-pened to him just a few nights ago. It was almost as though his awareness had been attuned to a different channel of existence; as though he had emerged from half-sleep at the wrong floor, so to speak, and stepped off the elevator into a strange world, not totally different, but subtly rearranged—until the shock of realization had jarred him back to the familiar level of stained wallpaper and the lingering memory of Brussels sprouts boiled long ago. And if you could produce the effect at will . . .

O'Leary read on, looking for precise instructions. Three pages further on he found a line or two of specifics:

" . . . use of a bright object, such as a highly polished gem, as an aid to the Powers of Concentration, may, with profitable results, be employed by the earnest student of these pages . . . "

Lafayette considered. He owned no gems—not even glass ones. Perhaps a spoon would work. But no—his ring; just the thing. He tugged at the heavy silver ornament on the middle finger of his left hand. No use; the knuckle was too big. After all, he'd been wearing it for years now. But he didn't need to remove the ring; he could stare at it just as well where it was, on his hand.

Lying on his back in the twilit room, he looked up at ancient floral-patterned paper, faded now to an off-white. This would be a good place to start. Now, suppose the ceiling were high, spacious, painted a pale gold color . . .

O'Leary persevered, whispering persuasively to himself. It was easy, the professor had said; just a matter of focusing the Psychical Energies and attuning the Will . . .

Lafayette sighed, blinked through the gloom at the blotched nongolden ceiling; he rose and went to the icebox for another warm beer. The bed squeaked as he sat on its edge. He might have known it wouldn't work. Old Professor Schimmerkopf was a quack, after all. Nothing as delightful as what the old boy had described could have gone unnoticed all these years.

He lay back against the pillows at the head of the bed. It would have been nice if it *had* worked. He could have redecorated his shabby quarters and told himself that the room was twice as large, with a view of a skyline of towers and distant mountains. Music, too; with total recall, he could play back every piece of music he'd ever heard.

Not that any of it really mattered. He slept all right on the sagging bed—and taffy and sardines might get boring, but they went right on nourishing you. The room was dreary, but it kept off the rain and snow, and when the weather got cold, the radiator, with many thumps and wheezes, kept the temperature within the bearable range. The furniture wasn't fancy, but it was adequate. There was the bed, of course, and the table built from an orange crate and painted white, and the dresser, and the oval rag rug Miss Flinders at the library had given him.

And, oh yes, the tall locked cabinet in the corner. Funny he hadn't gotten around to opening it yet. It had been there ever since he had moved in, and he hadn't even wondered about it. Strange. But he could open it now. There was something wonderful in it, he remembered that much; but somehow he couldn't quite recall what.

He was standing in front of the cabinet, looking at the black-varnished door. A rich-grained wood showed faintly through the cracked glaze; the key hole was brass lined, and there were little scratches around it. Now, where was the key? Oh, yes . . .

Lafayette crossed the room to the closet and stepped inside. The light was dim here. He pulled a large box into position, stepped up on it, lifted the trapdoor in the ceiling, climbed up and emerged in an attic. Late afternoon sun gleamed through a dusty window. There was a faded rug on the floor, and large, brass-bound trunks were stacked everywhere. Lafayette tried the lids; all locked.

He remembered the keys. That was what he had come for. They were hanging on a nail, behind the door. He plucked them down, started for the trapdoor.

But why not take the stairs? Out in the hall, a white-painted banister gleamed. He went down, walked along a hall, found his room and stepped inside. The French windows were open, and a fresh breeze blew in. The curtains, billowy white, gleamed in the sun. Outside, a wide lawn, noble trees, a path leading somewhere.

But he had to open the cabinet, to see what was inside. He selected a key—a large, brassy one—and tried it in the keyhole. Too large. He tried another; also too big. There was only one more key, a long, thin one of black iron. It didn't fit. Then he noticed more keys, hidden under the last one, somehow. He tried them, one by one. None fitted. He eyed the keyhole, bright brass against the dark wood, scarred by near misses. He had to get the cabinet open. Inside there were treasures, marvelous things, stacked on shelves, waiting for him. He tried another key. It fit. He turned it carefully and heard a soft click!

A violent pounding shattered the stillness. The cabinet door glimmered, fading; only the keyhole was still visible. He tried to hold it—

"Mr. O'Leary, you open up this door this minute!" Mrs. MacGlint's voice cut through the dream like an ax. Lafayette sat up, hearing a buzzing in his head, still groping after something almost grasped, but lost forever now.

The door rattled in its frame. "You open this, you hear me?" Lafayette could hear voices, the scrape of feet from the neighboring rooms. He reached, pulled the string that switched on the ceiling light, went across to the door and jerked it open. The vengeful bulk of Mrs. MacGlint quivered before him.

"I heard voices, whispering like, and I wondered," she shrilled. "In there in the dark. Then I heard them bedsprings creak and then everything got quiet!" She thrust her head past Lafayette, scanning the room's interior.

"All right, where's she hid?" Behind her, Spender, from next door, and Mrs. Potts, in wrapper and curlers, hovered, trying for a glimpse of the source of the excitement.

"Where is who hid?" O'Leary oofed as the landlady's massive elbow took him in the short ribs. She bellied past him, stooping to stare under the spindle-legged bed, whirled, jerked the alcove curtain aside. She shot an accusing look at O'Leary, bustled to the window and dug at the hook holding the screen shut.

"Must of got her out the window," she puffed, whirling to confront Lafayette. "Fast on your feet, ain't you?"

"What are you looking for? That screen hasn't been opened for years—"

"You know well as I do, young Mr. O'Leary—that I give house space to for nigh to a year—"

"Laff, you got a *gal* in here?" Spender inquired, sidling into the room.

"A girl?" Lafayette shook his head. "No, there's no girl here, and not much of anything else."

"Well!" Mrs. MacGlint stared around the room. Her expression twitched to blankness. Then she tucked in her chins. "Anybody would've thought the same thing," she declared. "There's not a soul'd blame me . . . "

Mrs. Potts sniffed and withdrew. Spender snickered and sauntered out. Mrs. MacGlint moved past O'Leary, not quite looking at him.

"Respectable house," she muttered. "Setting in here in the dark, talking to hisself, *alone* . . . "

Lafayette closed the door behind her, feeling empty, cheated. He had almost gotten that cabinet door open, discovered what was inside that had promised such excitement. Ruefully he eyed the blank place beside the door where he had dreamed the mysterious locker. He hadn't had much luck with the professor's recipes for self-hypnosis, but his dreaming abilities were still impressive. If Mrs. MacGlint hadn't chosen that moment to burst in . . .

But the trunks upstairs! Lafayette thought with sudden excitement. He half-rose—

And sank back, with a weak smile. He had dreamed those, too; there was nothing upstairs but old Mr. Dinder's shabby room. But it had all seemed so real! As real as anything in the wide-awake world; more real, maybe.

But it was only a dream—a typical escape wish. Crawl through a trapdoor into another world. Too bad it wasn't really that easy. And the cabinet—obvious symbolism. The locked door represented all the excitement in life that he'd never been able to find. And all that fumbling with keys—that was a reflection of life's frustrations.

And yet that other world—the dim attic crowded with relics, the locked cabinet—had held a promise of things rich and strange. If only this humdrum world could be that way, with the feel of adventure in the air.

But it couldn't. Real life wasn't like that. Real life was getting up in the morning, working all day on the board, then the evening's chores, and sleep. Now it was time for the latter.

Lafayette lay in bed, aware of the gleam of light under the door, tiny night sounds, the distant stutter of an engine. It must be after midnight, and here he was, lying awake. He had to be up in six hours, hurrying off to the foundry in the gray morning light. Better get to sleep. And no more time wasted on dreams.

Lafayette opened his eyes, looked at a brick wall a yard or two away, warm and red in the late orange sunlight. The bricks were tarnished and chipped, and there was moss growing along one edge of each, and between them the mortar was crumbling and porous. At the base of the wall there was grass, vivid green, and little yellow flowers, hardly bigger than forget-me-nots. A small gray insect appeared over the curve of a petal, feelers waving, and then hurried away on important business. O'Leary had never seen a bug quite like it—or flowers like those, either. Or for that matter, a brick wall like this one . . .

Where was he, anyway? He groped for recollection, remembering Mrs. MacGlint's, the book he'd been reading, the landlady's invasion; then going to bed, lying awake . . . But how did he get *here*—and where was *here*?

Quite suddenly, O'Leary was aware of what was happening: he was asleep—or half-asleep—and he was dreaming the wall, each separate brick with its pattern of moss—a perfect example of hypnogogic illusion!

With an effort of will, Lafayette blanked out other thoughts; excitement thumped in his chest. *Concentrate!* the professor had said. *Focus the Psychic Energies!*

The bricks became clearer, gaining in solidity. Lafayette brushed aside vagrant wisps of distracting thought, giving his full attention to the image of the wall, holding it, building it, *believing* it. He had known dreams were vivid; they always seemed real as they happened. But this was perfect!

Carefully he worked on extending the range of the scene. He could see a flagstone path lying between him and the wall. The flat stones were grayish tan, flaking in flat laminae, almost buried in the soil, with tiny green blades sprouting between them. He followed the path with his eyes; it led away along the wall into the shadow of giant trees. Amazing how the mind supplied details; the trees were flawless conceptualizations, every branch and twig and leaf, every shaggy curl of bark as true as life. If he had a canvas now, he could paint them . . .

But suppose, instead of letting his subconscious supply the details, he filled them in himself? Suppose, for example, there were a rosebush, growing there beside the tree. He concentrated, trying to picture the blossoms.

The scene remained unchanged—and then abruptly began to fade, like water soaking into a blotter; the trees blurred and all around dim walls seemed to close in—

Dismayed, Lafayette grabbed for the illusion, fighting to hold the fading image intact. He switched his gaze back to the brick wall directly before him; it had shrunk to a patch of masonry a yard in diameter, thin and unconvincing. He fought, gradually rebuilding the solidity of the wall. These hypnogogic phenomena were fragile, it seemed; they couldn't stand much manipulation.

The wall was solidly back in place now, but, strangely, the flowers were gone. In their place was a cobbled pavement. There was a window in the wall now, shuttered by warped, unpainted boards. Above it, an expanse of white-washed plaster crisscrossed by heavy timbers extended up to an uneven eave line silhouetted against an evening sky of deep electric blue in which an early moon gleamed. It was a realistic enough scene, Lafayette thought, but a bit drab. It needed something to brighten it up; a drugstore, say, its windows cheery with neon and hearty laxative ads; something to lend a note of gaiety.

But he wasn't going to make the mistake of tampering, this time. He'd let well enough alone, and see what there was to see. Cautiously, Lafayette extended his field of vision. The narrow street—almost an alley—wound off into darkness, closed in by tall, overhanging houses. He noted the glisten of wet cobbles, a puddle of oily water, a scattering of rubbish. His subconscious, it appeared, lacked an instinct for neatness.

There was a sudden jar—a sense of an instant's discontinuity, like a bad splice in a movie film. O'Leary looked around for the source, but saw nothing. And yet, somehow, everything seemed subtly changed—more *convincing*, in some subtle way.

He shook off the faint feeling of uneasiness. It was a swell hallucination and he'd better enjoy it to the fullest, while it lasted.

The house across the way, he saw, was a squeezed-in, half-timbered structure like the one in front of which he was standing, with two windows at ground-floor level made from the round bottoms of bottles set in lead strips, glowing amber and green and gold from a light within. There was a low, wide door, iron-bound, with massive hinges; over it a wooden sign hung from an iron rod. It bore a crudely painted representation of the prow of a Viking ship and a two-handed battle-ax. Lafayette smiled; his subconscious had seized on the device from his ring: the ax and dragon. Probably everything in the scene went back to something he had seen, or heard of, or read about. It was a fine illusion, no doubt about that: but what was it that was changed?

Odors, that was it. Lafayette sniffed, caught a scent of mold, spilled wine, garbage—a rich, moist aroma, with undertones of passing horses.

Now, what about sound? There should be the honking of horns, the clashing of gears—motor-scooter gears, probably; the street was too narrow for any except midget cars. And there ought to be a few voices hallooing some-where, and, judging from the smell, the clash of garbage can lids. But all was silent. Except—Lafayette cupped a hand to his ear . . .

Somewhere, hooves clattered on pavement, retreating into the distance. A bell tolled far away, nine times. A door slammed. Faintly, Lafayette heard whistling, the clump of heavy footsteps. *People!* Lafayette thought with surprise. Well, why not? They should be as easy to imag-ine as anything else. It might be interesting to confront his creations face to face, engage them in conversation, discover all sorts of hidden aspects of his personality.

Would they think they were real? Would they remember a yesterday?

Quite abruptly, O'Leary was aware of his bare feet against the cold paving stones. He looked down, saw that he was wearing nothing but his purple pajamas with the yellow spots. Hardly suitable for meeting people; he'd better equip himself with an outfit a little more appropriate to a city street. He closed his eyes, picturing a nifty navy-blue trench coat with raglan sleeves, a black homburg—might as well go first class—and a cane—an ebony one with a silver head, for that man-about-town touch . . .

Something clanked against his leg. He looked down. He was wearing a coat of claret velvet, breeches of brown doeskin, gleaming, soft leather boots that came up to his thigh, a pair of jeweled pistols and an elaborate rapier with a worn hilt. Wonderingly, he gripped it, drew it halfway from the sheath; the sleek steel glittered in the light from the windows across the way.

Not quite what he'd ordered; he looked as though he were on his way to a fancy-dress ball. He still had a lot to learn about this business of self-hypnosis.

There was a startled yell from the dark street to O'Leary's right, then a string of curses. A man darted into view, clad in dingy white tights with a flap seat, no shoes. He shied as he saw O'Leary, turned and dashed off in the opposite direction. O'Leary gaped. A man! Rather an eccentric specimen, but still . . .

Other footsteps were approaching now. It was a boy, in wooden shoes and leather apron, a wool cap on his head. He wore tattered knee pants, and carried a basket from which the neck of a plucked goose dangled, and he was whistling *Alexander's Ragtime Band*.

Without a glance at O'Leary, the lad hurried by; the sound of the shoes and the whistling receded. O'Leary grinned. It seemed to be a sort of medieval scene he had cooked up, except for the anachronistic popular tune; somehow it was comforting to know that his subconscious wasn't above making a slip now and then.

From behind the tavern windows, he heard voices raised in song, a clash of crockery; he sniffed, caught the odors of wood smoke, candle wax, ale, roast fowl. He was hungry, he realized with a pang. Taffy and sardines weren't enough.

There was a new noise now: a snorting, huffing sound, accompanied by a grumbling, like a boulder rolling slowly over a pebbled beach. A bell dinged. A dark shape trundled into view, lanterns slung from its prow casting long shadows that fled along the street. A tall stack belched smoke; steam puffed from a massive piston at the side of the cumbersome vehicle. It moved past, its iron-bound wooden wheels thudding on the uneven stones. Lafayette caught a glimpse of a red-faced man in a tricorn hat, perched high up above the riveted boiler. The steam car rumbled on its way, a red lantern bobbing at its tail gate. O'Leary shook his head; he hadn't gotten *that* out of a history book. Grinning, he hitched up his belt.

The door of the Ax and Dragon swung open, spilling light on the cobbles. A fat man tottered out, waved an arm, staggered off up the narrow street, warbling tunelessly. Before the door shut, Lafayette caught a glimpse of a warm interior, a glowing fire, low beams, the gleam of polished copper and brass, heard the clamor of voices, the thump of beer mugs banged on plank tables.

He was cold, and he was hungry. Over there was warmth and food—to say nothing of beer.

In four steps he crossed the street. He paused for a moment to settle his French cocked hat on his forehead, adjust the bunch of lace at his chin; then he hauled open the door and stepped into the smoky interior of the Ax and Dragon.

Chapter Two

In the sudden warmth and rich odors of the room, O'Leary paused, blinking against the light shed by the lanterns pegged to the wooden posts supporting the sagging ceiling. Heads turned to stare; voices trailed off into silence as Lafayette looked around the room. There were wine and ale barrels ranked along one side; to their right was a vast fireplace in which a whole hog, a goose, and half a dozen chickens turned on a spit over a bed of red coals. Lafayette sniffed; the odors were delightful!

The texture and solidity of the scene were absolutely convincing—even better than Professor Schimmerkopf had described—full tactile, auditory, visual and olfactory stimulation. And coming inside hadn't disturbed things in the least; after all, why should it? He often dreamed of wandering through buildings; the only difference was that this time he *knew* he was dreaming, while a small part of his mind stayed awake, watching the show.

There was a vacant seat at the rear of the long room; O'Leary started toward it, nodding pleasantly at staring faces. A thin man in a patched tabard scrambled from his path; a fat woman with red cheeks muttered and drew a circle in the air. Those seated at the table toward which he was moving edged away. He sat down, put his hat beside him, looked around, smiled encouragingly at his creations.

"Uh, please go right ahead with what you were doing," he said in the silence. "Oh, bartender . . . " He signaled to a short, thick-necked man hovering behind a trestle between the beer kegs. "A bottle of the best in the house, please. Ale or wine, it doesn't matter."

The bartender said something; O'Leary cupped his ear.

"Eh? Speak up, I didn't get that."

"I says all we got is small beer and *vin ordinaire*," the man muttered. There was something odd about the way he spoke . . . Still, O'Leary reminded himself, he couldn't expect to get everything perfect the first time out.

"That'll do," he said, automatically making an effort to match the other's speech pattern.

The man gaped, closed his mouth with an audible gulp, stooped and plucked a dusty flagon from a stack on the floor, which, Lafayette noted idly, seemed to be of hardpacked dirt. A nice detail, he approved. Practical, too; it would soak up spilled booze.

Someone was muttering at the far end of the room. A barrel-shaped ruffian rose slowly, stepped out into the clear, flexed massive shoulders, then sauntered forward. He had a wild mop of unkempt red hair, a flattened nose, one cauliflowered ear, and huge, hairy fists, the thumbs of which were hooked in the rope tied around his waist. O'Leary noted the striped stockings below the patched knee breeches, the clumsy shoes, like loafers with large iron buckles. The man's shirt was a soiled white, open at the neck, with floppy sleeves. A foot-long sheath knife was strapped to his hip. He came up to Lafayette's table, planted himself and stared down at him.

"He don't look so tough," he announced to the silent room in a growl like a Kodiak bear.

Lafayette stared into the man's face, studying the mean, red-rimmed eyes, the white scar tissue marking the cheek bones, the massive jaw, the thick lips, lumpy from past batterings, the sprouting stubble. He smiled.

"Marvelous," he said. His eyes went to the barman. "Hubba hubba with that wine," he called cheerily. "And I'll have a chicken sandwich on rye; I'm hungry. All I had for dinner was a couple of sardines." He smiled encouragingly at his table mates, who crouched back, eyeing him fearfully. The redhead was still standing before him.

"Sit down," Lafayette invited. "How about a sandwich?"

The lout's small eyes narrowed. "I say he's some kind of a Nance," the rumbling voice stated.

Lafayette chuckled, shaking his head. This was as good as a psychoanalysis! This oaf, a personification of a sub-conscious virility symbol, had stated an opinion doubtless heretofore suppressed somewhere deep in the id or superego, where it had probably been causing all sorts of neuroses. Now, by getting it out in the open, he could face it, observe for himself the ludicrousness of it and thereafter dismiss it.

"Come on, sit down," he ordered. "Tell me just what you meant by that remark."

"Nuts to youse," the heavyweight grated, looking around for approval. "Yer mudduh wears ankle socks."

"Tsk, tsk." Lafayette looked at the fellow reproachfully. "Better do as I say, or I'll turn you into a fat lady."

"Huh?" Big Red's rusty eyebrows crawled like caterpillars on his low forehead. His mouth opened, revealing a row of chipped teeth.

The landlord sidled nervously around the redhead and placed a dusty bottle on the table with a roast fowl beside it *sans* plate.

"That'll be a buck fifty," he muttered. Lafayette patted his hip pocket, took out his familiar wallet, remembering belatedly that there was only a dollar in it. Hmmm. But why couldn't it have fifty dollars in it, instead? He pictured the impressive bill, crisp and green and reassuring. And why just one? Why not a whole stack of fifties? And maybe a few hundreds thrown in for good measure. He might as well dream big. He squinted, concentrating . . .

There was an almost silent pop! as though a vast soap bubble had burst. O'Leary frowned. Funny sensation; still, it might be normal in hallucination; it seemed to happen every so often. He opened the wallet, revealed a stack of crisp bills, withdrew one with a grand gesture; it was a fifty, just as specified.

But the lettering . . . The hen-tracks across the top of the bill looked incomplete, barely legible—. The first letter was like an O with a small x on top, followed by an upside-down u, a squiggle, some dots . . .

Then suddenly the strangeness faded. The letters seemed to come into focus, like a perspective diagram shifting orientation. The words were perfectly readable, O'Leary saw. But the first letter: it *did* look like an O with an x on top of it. He frowned at it thoughtfully. There wasn't any such letter—was there? But there must be: he was reading it—

He smiled at himself as the explanation dawned. His dream mechanism, always consistent, had cooked up a foreign language to go with the foreign setting. Naturally, since he'd invented it himself, he could read it. The same probably applied to the spoken tongue. If he could wake up and hear his conversation here, it would all probably come out as gibberish, like the poems people dreamed and wrote down to look at in the morning. They never made sense. But the words on the bill were clear enough: the legend "Royal Treasury of Artesia" was lettered above the familiar picture of Grant—or was it Grant? Lafayette saw with some surprise that he was wearing a tiny peruke and a lacy ruff. Play money, after all.

But what did it matter? He smiled at himself. He couldn't take it with him when he woke up. He handed the bill over to the barman who gaped and scratched his head.

"Geez, I can't break no fifty, yer lordship," he muttered. As the man spoke, O'Leary listened carefully. Yes, it was a strange language—but his mind was interpreting it as modified Brooklynese.

"Keep it," Lafayette said grandly. "Just keep the wine flowing—and how about bringing over a couple of glasses, and possibly a knife and fork?"

The barman hurried off. The redhead was still standing, glowering.

"Down in front," Lafayette said, indicating the seat opposite him. "You're blocking the view."

The big man shot a glance at the customers watching him and then threw out his chest.

"Duh Red Bull don't drink wit' no ribbon-counter Fancy-Dan," he announced.

"Better change your mind," O'Leary cautioned, blowing dust from the lopsided green bottle the waiter had brought. "Or I may have to just shrink you down to where I can see over you."

The redhead blinked at him; his mouth puckered uncertainly. The barman was back with two heavy glass mugs. He darted a look at the Red Bull, quickly removed the cork from the bottle, slopped an inch or two of the wine in one cup and shoved it toward Lafayette. He picked it up and sniffed. It smelled like vinegar. He tasted it. It was thin and sour. He pushed the mug away.

"Don't you have something better—" he paused. Just suppose, he mused, there was a bottle of a rare vintage—Chateau Lafitte-Rothschilde, '29, say—over there under that heap of dusty bottles . . . He narrowed his eyes, picturing the color of the glass, the label, willing it to be there—

His eyes popped open at the abrupt flicker in the smooth flow of—of whatever it was that flowed when time passed. That strange little blink in the sequence of the seconds! It had happened before, just as he was providing the reserves in his wallet, and before that, out in the street. Each time he had made a modification in things, he had felt the jar. A trifling flaw in his technique, no doubt. Nothing to worry about.

"—the best in the place, yer Lordship," the barman was protesting.

"Look under the other bottles," O'Leary said. "See if there isn't a big bottle there, shaped like this." He indicated the contours of a Burgundy bottle.

"We ain't got—"

"Ah—ah! Take a look first." Lafayette leaned back, smiling around at the others. My, what an inventive subconscious he had! Long faces, round ones, old men, young women, fat, thin, weathered, pink-and-white, bearded, clean-shaven, blonds, brunettes, baldies—

The barman was back, gaping at the bottle in his hand. He put it on the table, stepped back. "Is this here what yer lordship meant?"

O'Leary nodded complacently. The barman pulled the cork. This time a delicate aroma floated from the glass. O'Leary sampled it. The flavor was musty, rich, a symphony of summer sun and ancient cellars. He sighed contentedly. It might be imaginary wine, but the flavor was real enough. The redhead, watching open-mouthed, leaned forward slightly, sniffed. A thick tongue appeared, ran over the scarred lips. Lafayette poured the second glass half full.

"Sit down and drink up, Red," he said.

The big man hesitated, picked up the glass, sniffed, then gulped the contents. An amazed smile spread over the rugged features. He threw a leg over the bench and sat, shoving the mug toward Lafayette.

"Bo, that's good stuff you got there! I'll go fer another shot o' that!" He looked around belligerently. Lafayette refilled both glasses. A turkey-necked gaffer down the table edged closer, eyeing the bottle.

"Garçon," Lafayette called, "more glasses!" The man complied. Lafayette filled one for the oldster and passed it along. The old man sipped, gaped, gulped, licked toothless gums and grinned.

"Hey!" he cackled. "We ain't seen wine like this since the old king died."

A round-faced woman in a starched wimple with a broken corner shushed him with a look and thrust out a pewter mug. Lafayette filled it.

"Everybody drink up!" he invited. Clay cups, topless bottles, copper mugs came at him. He poured, pausing now and then to take a healing draft from his own mug. This was more like it!

"Let's sing!" he suggested. Merry voices chimed in, on *Old MacDonald*. The words were a little different than the ones O'Leary was accustomed to, but he managed, adding a fair baritone to the din. A hand touched the back of his neck; a buxom wench in a tight-laced blouse and peasant skirt slid into his lap, nibbled at his ear, bringing with her, O'Leary noted, a disconcerting odor of goat. He snorted, twisted to get a better look at the girl. She was cute enough, with red cheeks, a saucily turned-up nose, corn-yellow hair and pouty lips—but it seemed nobody had told her about soap. Still, there might be a remedy for that. Lafayette narrowed his eyes, trying to remember the odor of the perfume he had smelled once when a bottle broke at the drugstore when he was sweeping up just before closing time . . .

There was the familiar jog in the machinery. He sniffed cautiously. Nothing. Again—and he caught a whiff of Ivory soap; a third time, and the scent of Chanel No. 22 wafted to his nostrils. He smiled at the girl. She smiled back, apparently noticing nothing unusual. More glasses were thrust out. Lafayette disengaged himself from the soft and eager lips, poured, paused to swallow, refilled the girl's glass, then Red's pint mug, and another, and another . . .

The old man sitting next to the big redhead was frowning thoughtfully at the bottle in O'Leary's hand. He said something to the skinny grandma beside him. More frowns were appearing now. The singing was faltering, fading off into silence. The merry drinkers at the next table fell silent. People began crossing themselves—or rather, describing circles over their chests.

"What's the matter?" he inquired genially, lifting the bottle invitingly. Everyone jumped. Those nearest were rising hastily, moving back. A babble was growing—not the gay chatter of a moment before, but a fearful muttering.

Lafayette shrugged, pouring his glass full. As he moved to place the bottle on the table, a thought struck him. He hefted the flask. It seemed as heavy as ever. He reached over and poured the Red Bull's glass full. The big man hiccupped, made a wobbly circle before him with a finger like a Polish sausage, lifted the glass and drank. Lafayette tilted the bottle, peered inside the neck; a dark surface of deep red liquid gleamed an inch from the top. No wonder they were spooked, he thought disgustedly. He had carelessly decanted several gallons of wine from a one-liter bottle.

"Ah . . . look," he started, "that was just a trick, sort of . . ."

"Sorcerer!" someone yelled. "Warlock!" another charged. There was a general movement toward the door.

"Wait!" O'Leary called, rising. At that, there was a stampede. In thirty seconds the tavern was deserted—with the sole exception of the Red Bull. The big man—sweating heavily but still game, Lafayette observed approvingly—held his ground. He licked his lips, cleared his throat.

"Dem other slobs," he growled, "pantywaists."

"Sorry about the bottle," O'Leary said apologetically. "Just a slip on my part." He could hear the voices of a gathering mob outside. The word "sorcerer" seemed to ring out with distressing frequency.

"A little magic, that ain't nuttin'," Red said. "But they got a idear dat on account of you're a . . . like a phantom ya might stick a . . . you know, whammy, on 'em, er maybe split open duh ground and drag 'em down into duh Pit. Er—"

"That's enough," Lafayette cut in, noticing the increasing nervousness on the battered features as the man enumerated the possible fates of those who trafficked with spooks. "All I did was pour out a few drinks. Does that make me a ghost?"

Big Red smiled craftily, eyeing Lafayette's clothes. "Don't rib me, mister," he grated. "I know duh Phantom Highwayman when I see him."

O'Leary smiled. "You don't really believe in phantoms, do you?"

The Red Bull nodded vigorously. Lafayette noticed that he smelled of Chanel No. 22; apparently he'd overdone the perfume a trifle.

"On nights when duh moon is like a ghostly galleon," Red stated, "dat's when yuh ride."

"Nonsense," Lafayette said briskly. "My name is Lafayette O'Leary, and—"

"Now, what I got in mind, Bo, you and me, we could make a great team," Red bored on. "Wit' dem neat tricks you can do, like riding tru duh sky an all, and wit' my brains—"

"I'm afraid you're on the wrong track, Red." O'Leary refilled his glass for the fourth—or was it the fifth time? Lovely wine—and the glow was just as nice as though he hadn't dreamed up the whole thing. Would he have a hangover, he wondered, when he woke up in the morning? He hiccupped and refilled Red's glass.

" . . . cased a coupla joints dat I figger dey'll be a cinch to knock over," the rumbling voice was saying. "Duh way I got duh caper doped out, I keep duh eyeball peeled for duh city guardsmen. Dem guys is all over like fleas in a four-bit flop dese days. If youse ast me, duh country ain't no better'n a police state; it ain't like de old days when I was a nipper. Anyways, youse can pull duh job, an' pass duh swag to me, and while duh johns is busy tailing youse, I'll—"

"You're talking nonsense, Red," O'Leary interrupted. "Crime doesn't pay. I'm sure you're really an honest fellow at heart, but you've been influenced by evil companions. Why don't you get yourself a job—at a service station, maybe—"

The Red Bull's forehead furrowed ominously. "Youse try'na tell me I look like a grease monkey?"

Lafayette peered at his companion's rugged features through a light fog which seemed to have arisen. "Nooo," he said thoughtfully. "More of an ape, I think. An oil ape." He beamed, raising his glass. "Tha's pretty clever, don't ye agroo? I mean don't you agree?"

The Red Bull growled. "I gotta good mind tuh rip youse apart, spook er no spook—!"

"Ah—ah!" Lafayette wagged a finger at the other. "No threats, please."

The redhead was on his feet, swaying slightly. "I can bust a oak plank in two wit' one punch," he stated, displaying a fist like a flint ax.

"Sit down, Red," O'Leary ordered. "I want to talk to you. As a figment of my imagination, you should be able to tell me lots of interesting things about my psyche. Now, I've been wondering, what role has sibling rivalry played—"

"I can ben' a iron bar inta pretzel wit' one hand tied behind me," the Red Bull stated. "I can—"

"Red, if you don't sit down, I'll be forced to take steps," Lafayette warned. "Now tell me, how does it feel to start existing all of a sudden, just because I dreamed you—"

"I can tear duh head off a alligator," Red declaimed. "I can rip duh hind leg off a elephant . . . " As the redhead rambled on, Lafayette concentrated. Red's voice rose higher, from bass to baritone, through tenor to a high contralto. " . . . handle any ten guys at oncet," he shrilled, "wit' bot' hands tied behind me . . . "

Lafayette made a final effort, listened for the result:

" . . . I'm thimply a brute, when arouthed," Red squeaked. "Thomentimeth I jutht get tho mad I could thpit!" He broke off, an amazed look settling over his meaty features. "Thpit?" he chirped.

"Now, Red, drink your wine and pay attention," Lafayette said severely. "You're port of an impartent experiment. I mean you're pent of an apartment—you're portable part of—apart of port—an appointment of pit—ah, the hell with it!" He picked up his wine mug.

Then door burst open. A tall man with long curls slammed into view, gorgeously arrayed in a floppy hat with feathers, a purple and blue striped jacket, a wide sash, baggy pants above sloppily rolled boots. He whipped out a slender epée and advanced on the lone occupied table. Another ornately outfitted swordsman crowded in behind him, and a third, and a fourth. They spread out and ringed the table, blades at the ready.

"Hi, fellas." Lafayette waved his heavy glass. "How about a little snort?"

"In the King's name," the leading dandy roared. "You're under arrest! Will you come along quietly, or have we got to run you through?" A fierce black mustache curled up on each side of his face like a steer's horns.

O'Leary eyed the nearest sword point, six inches from his throat. Rolling his eyes sideways, he could see two more blades poised, aimed at his heart. Across from him, the Red Bull gaped, his mouth hanging open.

"You, there!" the mustached officer bellowed, eyeing the redhead. "Who're you?"

"Me, offither?" the big man chirped. "Why, I wath jutht thitting here, thipping my therry and waiting for my thupper."

The cop blinked, then guffawed. "The bum looks enough like the Red Bull to be his twin."

"Beat it, you," another ordered. The redhead scrambled from his place and hurried unsteadily to the door. Lafayette caught a glimpse of faces peering in as it opened. The mob was still noisy outside.

"All right, on your feet," the man on his left commanded. O'Leary smiled negligently at the man, focusing his attention on the swords. *Salamis*, he thought. *Swords into salamis, kazam!*

A sharp point prodded his side; he jumped. The bright steel blade was set against his ribs, just above the kidney. "Salami!" O'Leary commanded aloud. "Turn into a salami, damn it!"

The blade—still stubbornly steel—poked harder. "No spells now, or you won't make it to a cell!"

"Hey!" Lafayette yelled. "Careful! You'll break the skin!"

"Look, Mac, have I got to slit your weasand to convince you this is a pinch? We're musketeers of the city guard, see? We're putting the sneeze on for disturbing the peace!"

"You mean about the wine bottle," O'Leary said. "I can explain—"

"Tell it to the executioner," a three-striper snarled. "On your feet, bub!"

Lafayette got up. "This is ridiculous," he started.

A hard hand gripped his arm and propelled him doorward. He shook it off, grabbed his hat from the table and settled it over his eyes. No need to get excited, he reminded himself. The salami gambit hadn't worked, but that was because he hadn't had time to concentrate properly and get his Psychic Energies attuned—besides which, he had already discovered it was tricky trying to change anything in plain view. He was a little woozy from the wine, but as soon as he had a quiet moment, he would handle these fellows . . .

He stumbled through the door, out into the frosty night air. A rank of frightened faces gaped at him. Fists shook. A vegetable came flying and bounced off his shoulder.

"All right, clear the way there!" the tallest musketeer roared. "Make way, in the King's name!" He and two of his men laid about them with the flats of their blades, opening a route to a waiting steamcar.

"Watch it, Mac," said the musketeer detailed to guard O'Leary. "Us police aren't what you'd call popular." He ducked as a ripe tomato whizzed past. "Can't say as I blame 'em much, the way his Majesty has got us putting the screws on lately. Everything that ain't compulsory is illegal."

"Sounds like a totalitarian regime," O'Leary commented. "Why don't you start a revolution?"

"You kidding? King Goruble's got a army that would—" he broke off. "Never mind that," he said. He looked at O'Leary curiously and edged closer.

"Say, is that the straight dope?" he said from the side of his mouth. "I mean about you being a sorcerer?"

O'Leary eyed the man. "You mean an intelligent fellow like you believes in magic?"

"Naw—but, well—they got you on a 902–that's a necromancy rap; o'course that's just a standard charge we use to hold suspicious characters for twenty-four hours.

But I figure maybe where there's a frog there's a puddle—"

"Did you ever see anyone perform magic?" Lafayette demanded.

"No, but my wife's aunt's cousin claims he knew a fellow—"

"I'm no magician," Lafayette said. "As a matter of fact, I'm—but you wouldn't understand."

"Look, what I was wondering—well, my wife, she's kind of running to fat lately; stringy hair, no make-up; you know the routine. Only been married a year. Maybe you could give me something to slip into her martini to kind of like put the old zazzle back; warm her up a little, if you know what I mean . . . " He winked elaborately, and casually shoved an overeager spectator back into line.

"That's silly—" Lafayette started, then paused. Well, why not? Good practice. He squinted, pictured a popular movie starlet whose name he had forgotten, imagined her as married to the cop at his side, then pictured her hurrying along a street, attracted by the mob noise . . . The scene winked. O'Leary relaxed, feeling complacent. OK, now he could get back in command of the situation . . .

"Roy!" a girlish voice called above the clamor. "Oh, Roy!" The cop beside O'Leary jumped, looked around. A lovely girl with huge dark eyes and soft brown hair was pushing through the crowd.

"Gertrude! Is it you?" the cop bleated, a look of delighted astonishment spreading across his face.

"Oh, Roy! I was so worried!" The girl hurled herself at the cop, staggering him. His sword dropped. O'Leary retrieved it and handed it back.

"I heard there was a dangerous arrest, and you were on it, and I know how brave you are, and I was afraid—"

"Now, now, Gertrude, I'm in the pink. Everything's jake."

"You mean it was a false alarm? Oh, I'm so relieved."

"False alarm? Yeah—I mean . . . " The musketeer turned to blink at Lafayette. He swallowed hard. "Cripes!" he muttered. "This guy is the McCoy!" He thrust the girl aside. "Excuse me, baby!" He cupped a hand beside his mouth. "Hey, Sarge!"

The large musketeer loomed up beside him. "Yeah?"

"This guy—" the cop jerked a thumb at O'Leary. "He's the goods! I mean, he's a sorcerer, like they said!"

"You lose your marbles, Shorty? Get your pris'ner and let's move out!"

"But look at Gertrude!" He pointed. The big cop glanced, jumped, gaped. He swept his hat off, executed an elaborate bow.

"Holy Moses, Gertrude," he said, "you got a new hairdo or something?"

"Hairdo?" Shorty snorted. "She's lost fifty pounds o' lard, stacked what's left in the right places, developed a curl in her hair, and remembered how to smile! And *he* done it!" He pointed at O'Leary.

"Oh, it was nothing," Lafayette said modestly. "And now, if you fellows don't mind—"

Abruptly, steel rasped. Four sharp blades jumped out, poised, ringing O'Leary in. The sergeant mopped sweat from his forehead with his free hand.

"I'm warning you, mister, don't try nothing! I'll have twelve inches of steel into you before you get past the first abracadabra!"

Lafayette snorted. "The whole thing is getting silly," he said. "That's the trouble with dreams; just when they begin to get interesting, things start to go wrong. I may as well just wake up and start over tomorrow night."

He squinted, concentrating; he was getting pretty good at the trick now, he thought complacently. Just picture what you wanted, build it up in the mind's eye—

Someone was jerking at his arm. Damned nuisance. Hard to concentrate. *Mrs. MacGlint's; the old family wallpaper, the homey smells, the creaky floor* . . . He opened an eye and saw a ring of angry faces. He shut his eyes tight, seized on the fading visualization of his room, working to solidify it. *Wake up*, he commanded himself. *This is just a whacky dream* . . .

The sounds around were fading now; he could almost see the blotched walls, the curtained alcove, the orange-crate table—

The hand was hauling at his arm again. He stumbled, almost fell. His eyes snapped open. A voice yelled in his ear.

The mob sounds swelled back to normal. Lafayette's breath made a frosty cloud before his face. The musketeers were staring at him, mouths wide.

"Did you see that, Sarge?" Shorty choked. "Like he turned to smoke!" They were backing away. The three-striper stood his ground, swallowed hard.

"Look, pal," he said desperately, "be nice and come along quiet, huh? I mean, if you got to do a fade, do it in front of witnesses, you know what I mean? If I report in with a story like this—and no pinch—well, it's goodby retirement, and me with twenty-one years on the force."

For the moment, O'Leary saw, it seemed there was no help for it: he was stuck in the damned dream—at least until he could manage a moment of peace and quiet.

"Certainly, Sergeant," O'Leary said grandly, "I'll be glad to accompany you. Just keep it couth, if you don't mind."

"Sure, kid gloves all the way, buddy. Now, if you don't mind just stepping this way?" The sergeant indicated the lane to the waiting vehicle. O'Leary strolled to the car, stood by while one of the guardsmen opened the rear door and then clambered up, seating himself on the wooden bench.

"All clear," he said. "Button her up." As the cops hurried to close the door, O'Leary caught a glimpse of four nervous faces looking oddly different . . .

Then he saw it: The big sergeant was now clean-shaven; somehow in the reshuffling of scenes, his immense mustachios had been inadvertently transferred to the upper lip of Shorty. O'Leary smiled, relaxed. There was really no need to be in a crashing hurry to get back to reality; why not stay with it a bit longer, and see what his subconscious came up with next? He could always wake up later.

O'Leary braced himself with one foot against the opposite bench and settled down for the ride.

Chapter Three

It was a bumpy twenty-minute trip. Lafayette held on, feeling his teeth clack at each uneven cobble, regretting that he had neglected to provide padded seats and a window. The wagon swayed, mounted a slight incline and then halted with a jolt. Feet clattered; voices muttered. The door clanked and swung open. Lafayette stepped down, looked around interestedly at a wide, cobbled courtyard fronted on all four sides by elaborate façades of rusticated stone, ornate with columns, pilasters, niches with statues, bright-lit rows of high, Gothic-arched windows. Far above, the slopes of massive mansard roofs gleamed a dull green in the moonlight. There were flower beds and geometric shapes of manicured lawn; clumps of tall poplars shimmered their silvery leaves in the night breeze. Flaming lanterns atop tall poles lighted a cavernous colonnaded entry, beside which two brass-helmeted, ramrod-stiff guardsmen in baggy knickers of Bromo-Seltzer blue and puff-sleeved jackets in red and yellow stripes stood with arquebuses at order arms.

"Now, if you'll just step this way, ah, sir," the sergeant said nervously, "I'll turn you over to the household detachment. After that you can disappear any time you like, just so I get a receipt from the desk sergeant first, OK?"

"Be calm, Sergeant," O'Leary soothed. "I'm not going to vanish just yet." He shook his head admiringly. "This if the fanciest police station I ever saw."

"You kidding, mac? I mean," the noncom amended hastily, "uh, this is the palace. Where the King lives, you know. King Goruble the First."

"I didn't know," said Lafayette, starting in the indicated direction. He stumbled and grabbed for his hat. It was difficult, walking in unfamiliar boots across uneven paving stones, and the sword had a disconcerting way of attempting to get between his legs.

The rigid sentries snapped to as the detachment mounted the wide steps; one barked a challenge. The sergeant replied and urged O'Leary on into the well-lit interior of a high-vaulted, mirror-lined hall, with a floor of polished marble in red and black squares. Elaborate gilt chandeliers hung from the fretted ceiling; opposite the mirrors, vast, somber draperies reflected woodland scenes.

Lafayette followed his escort along to a desk where a man in a steel breastplate sat, picking his teeth with a dagger. He cocked an eyebrow at O'Leary as the party came up.

"Book this, uh, gentleman in, Sarge," Lafayette's escort said. "And give me a receipt."

"Gentleman?" The desk sergeant put the dagger away and picked up a quill. "What's the charge?"

"A 902." Lafayette's cop looked defiantly at the pained expression that appeared on the other's lined face.

"Are you kidding, Sarge?" the desk man growled "Grow up! You can use a 902 to hold a drunk overnight, but you don't book 'em into Royal Court—"

"This one's the real article."

"That's right, Sarge," Shorty chimed in. "You oughta see what he done to Gertrude!"

"Gertrude? What is this, an assault?"

"Naw, Gertrude's the wife. He took fifty pounds off'n her and put the old shake back in her hips. Wow!" Shorty made lines in the air indicating Gertrude's new contours, then looked guiltily at O'Leary.

"Sorry, Bud," he whispered behind his hand. "I appreciate the favor, but—"

"You guys are nuts," the desk man said. "Get out of here before I lose my temper and have the lot of you clapped into irons!"

The musketeer sergeant's face darkened. He half-drew his sword with a rasp of steel. "Book him and give me a receipt, or I'll tickle your backbone from the front, you paper-pushing son of a—"

The desk sergeant was on his feet, whipping a saber from the sheath hung on the back of his chair, which fell over with a clatter. "Draw on a member of the Queen's

Own Light Cavalry, will you, you flat-footed night watchman—"

"Quiet!" someone barked. Lafayette, who had been watching the action open-mouthed, turned to see a dapper, gray-haired man in short sleeves frowning from an open doorway, surrounded by half a dozen elaborately garbed men in fantastic powdered wigs.

"What's the meaning of this altercation, right outside our gaming room?" The newcomer aggrievedly waved the playing cards clutched in a hand heavy with rings.

Everyone came to attention with a multiple clack of heels.

"Ah, Your Majesty, sir, this police officer," the desk sergeant stumbled, "he was wising off, sir, and—"

"I beg your Majesty's pardon, Your Majesty," the arresting sergeant cut in, "but if Your Majesty would—"

"See here, can't you go somewhere else to argue?" the king demanded. "Confound it, things are coming to a pretty pass when we can't play a few quiet hands of stud without some unseemly interruption!" The monarch turned to re-enter the room, his courtiers scattering from his path.

"If it please your Majesty," the formerly mustached musketeer persisted, "this prisoner is—"

"It doesn't please us in the least!" The king thrust out his mustached lip. "Scat, we say! Begone! And silently!"

The sergeant's face grew stubborn. "Your Majesty, I got to have a receipt for my prisoner. He's a dangerous sorcerer."

The king opened his mouth, then closed it.

"Sorcerer?" He eyed O'Leary with interest. At close range, Lafayette noted, the king looked older, more careworn, but meticulously groomed, with fine lines around his eyes and mouth.

"Are you sure of this?" the king asked in a low voice.

"Absolutely, your Majesty," the arresting cop assured him.

The desk sergeant bustled around the desk. "Your Majesty, I'm sorry about this; these nut cases, we get 'em all the time—"

"*Are* you a magician?" The king pursed his mouth, raising one carefully arched eyebrow at Lafayette.

"Why does everyone ask the same question?" Lafayette shook his head. "It would all be lots more fun if you just accepted me as one of yourselves. Just consider me a . . . ah . . . scientist."

The king's frown returned. "You show less than proper respect for our person. And what in the name of the Seafield is a—what did you call yourself?"

"A scientist. Someone who knows things," O'Leary explained. "You see, I'm engaged in an experiment. Now, none of you fellows realize it, but none of you actually exist."

The king was sniffing loudly. "The fellow reeks of wine," he said. He sniffed again. "Smells like good stuff," he remarked to a satin-coated dandy at his elbow.

"Phaugh, Majesty," the courtier said in a high nasal, waving a hanky under his nose. "Methinks the scoundrel is well and truly snockered. Didst hear him but now? None of us exist, quoth he—including your Majesty!"

"Sire, he's a warlock, take my word for it!" the sergeant burst out. "Any minute he's liable to poof! Disappear!"

"Yeah, yer Majesty," Shorty added, wagging his head, making his curls flop. "The guy is terrific!"

"How say you, knave?" The courtier fixed O'Leary with a slightly blood-shot eye. "Art a dabbler in the Black Arts?"

"Actually, it's all very simple," Lafayette said. His head was beginning to throb slightly as the glow of the wine faded. "I just—ah—have this slight ability to manipulate the environment."

The king's forehead wrinkled. "What does that mean?"

"Well . . . " Lafayette considered. "Take wine, for example." He squinted his eyes, concentrated on the upper right drawer of the desk beside him. He felt a slight, reassuring jar. "Look in the drawer," he said. "The top one."

The king gestured. "Do as he says."

One of the perfumed flunkeys minced forward, drew open the drawer, glanced inside, then, looking surprised, lifted out a bottle and held it up.

"Hey!" The desk sergeant started.

"Drinking on duty, eh?" The king beetled an eyebrow at the unfortunate fellow. "Ten days in the dungeon on canned soup."

"B-but, your Majesty, it's not mine!"

"That's right," Lafayette put in. "He didn't even know it was there."

"Then it's ten days for not knowing the contents of his own desk," the king said blandly. He took the bottle, looked at the label, held it up to the light and squinted at it.

"Good color," he stated. "Who has a corkscrew?"

Four manicured hands shot out with four elaborate corkscrews. The king handed over the bottle and watched as the cork was drawn with a loud *whok*!

He took the bottle, sniffed, then tilted it and took a healthy drag. A delighted expression lifted his rather sharp features.

"Zounds! We like it! Damned good vintage, that! Better than we find at our own table!" He looked at Lafayette approvingly.

"Still say you're not a magician, eh?"

"No, 'fraid not. After all, magic's impossible." O'Leary wagged an admonitory finger. "I suppose I seem a little unusual to you, but there's a perfectly simple explanation. Now, in this dream—"

"Enough!" The king held up a manicured hand. "This talk of dreams, we like it not—and yet, this wine we like right well. 'Tis a matter for our council to consider." He turned to a slight, pasty-faced man with a large moist nose, who was dressed in powder-blue silk with ruffles at the throat.

"Summon my councilors, we shall look into this affair. Mayhap the fellow has a simple explanation for these, ah, irregularities." He smacked his lips, looked fondly at the bottle and handed it to O'Leary. As the latter reached for it, the monarch seemed to start suddenly, half withdrew the bottle, then held it out again, staring at O'Leary's hand as he took the flask.

"We'll meet—immediately," the king said, sounding shaken.

"Tonight, Majesty?" a fat man in pink velvet squeaked.

"Certainly! In the High Chamber in a quarter of an hour!" King Goruble waved a hand at the musketeers.

"Be there! And as for you—" he shot a sharp glance at O'Leary. "You come with us, lad. We have a few questions to put to you."

The king waved his retainers back and closed the heavy door behind himself and Lafayette, who stared around the richly decorated gaming room admiringly. There were huge gilt-framed pictures against the paneled walls, a well stocked bar, deep rugs, soft lights to supplement the bright luminaries hanging over the card and billiard tables.

"I see you have electric lights here," O'Leary commented. "I can't quite figure out just what sort of place this is I've wandered into."

"This is the kingdom of Artesia." The king pulled at his lower lip, watching O'Leary speculatively. "Have you lost your wits, boy? Perhaps, ah, forgotten your name, your station?"

"No; I'm Lafayette O'Leary. I don't have a station: It's just that I can't quite place the, ah, context. Swords, steam cars, knee breeches, electric lights . . ."

"O'Leary, eh? A curious name. You came from a far land, I wot; you know nothing of our fair realm of Artesia?"

"Ummm," said Lafayette. "I guess you could say that; but in another sense, I live here—or near here."

"Eh? What mean you?"

"Oh, nothing much. You wouldn't understand."

Goruble worried his lower lip with even, white, false-looking teeth. "What errand brought you hither?" He sounded worried, O'Leary thought.

"Oh, no errand. Just . . . looking around."

"Looking for what?"

"Nothing special. Just sight-seeing, you might say."

"You came not to, ah, crave audience with ourself, perchance?"

"No—not that I'm not honored."

"How came you here?" Goruble demanded abruptly.

"Well, it gets a little complicated. To tell you the truth, I don't really understand it myself."

"You have—friends in the capital?"

"Don't know a soul."

Goruble took three paces, turned, took three paces back. He stopped and eyed O'Leary's right hand.

"Your ring," he said. "An interesting bauble." His eyes cut to O'Leary's face. "You, ah, bought it here?"

"Oh, no, I've had it for years."

Goruble frowned. "Where did you get it?"

"I guess you could say it came with me. It was hanging around my neck on a string when they found me on the orphanage doorstep."

"Orphanage? A place for waifs and strays?"

O'Leary nodded.

Goruble became suddenly brisk. "Just slip it off, there's a good fellow; I'd fain have a look at it."

"Sorry; it's too small to get over the knuckle."

"Hmmm." The king looked at O'Leary sharply. "Yes, well, let us make a suggestion, my lad. Turn the ring so that the device is inward. Others, seeing the symbol of the ax and dragon, might place some bothersome interpretation on't."

"What kind of interpretation?"

Goruble spread his hands. "There's a tale, told in the taverns. A mystical hero, 'tis said, will appear one day bearing that symbol, to rid the land of, ah, certain encumbrances. Sheer balderdash, of course, but it might prove embarrassing to you to be taken for the warrior of the prophecy."

"Thanks for the tip." O'Leary twisted the ring on his finger. "Now, do you mind if *I* ask a few questions?"

"Ah, doubtless you're wondering why you were brought here to the palace, rather than being trussed in chains and cast into a dungeon along with the usual run of felons."

"No, I can't say that I am. Nothing around here seems to make any sense. But now that you mention it, why *am* I here?"

" 'Twas our royal command. We instructed the captain of the city garrison a fortnight since to comb the city and bring to us any person suspect of witchery."

Lafayette nodded, found himself yawning and patted his mouth. "Excuse me," he said. "Go on, I'm listening."

" 'Tis a most strange manner of deportment you affect," the king said snappishly. "Hast no respect for royalty?"

"Oh, sure, uh, your Majesty," O'Leary said. "I guess I'm just a little tired."

The monarch sat himself in a deep leather chair, and watched open-mouthed as Lafayette settled himself in another, crossing his legs comfortably.

"Here!" the king barked, "we've given you no leave to sit!"

O'Leary was yawning again. "Look, let's skip all that," he suggested in a reasonable tone. "I'm pooped. You know, I have an idea these dream adventures are just as fatiguing as real ones. After all your mind—part of it, anyway—thinks you're really awake, so it reacts—"

"Have done!" the king yelped. "Your prattle threatens to unhinge my wits!" He glared at O'Leary as though pondering a difficult decision. "Look here, young man, you are sure there isn't something you'd like to, well, tell us? A matter we might ah, discuss plainly?" He leaned forward, lowering his voice. "To our mutual advantage?"

"I'm afraid I don't know what you mean."

"Answer us plainly, yea or nay? Speak without fear; we offer you amnesty."

"Nay," Lafayette said flatly. "Absolutely nay."

"Nay?" the king's shoulders slumped. "Drat it, I was hoping . . . perhaps . . . "

"Look here," Lafayette said in a kindly tone, "why don't you tell me what your problem is? Maybe I can help you. I do have certain, ah, techniques—"

The king sat erect, looking wary. "We took you here aside to, ah, advise you privily that you'd have our royal pardon in advance for the practice of your forbidden arts in the service of the crown. You spurn our offer—and in the same breath hint at the possession of demonic power. Almost it seems you ask to have your bones stretched!"

"I wonder," O'Leary said. "If I went to sleep now, would I wake up here—or back at Mrs. MacGlint's house?"

"Bah!" the king exploded. "But for a certain mystery we sense about you, we'd banish you forthwith to the county jail on a charge of lunacy!" He eyed the wine bottle on the table. "Tell us," he said in a confidential tone, "how *did* the bottle get in the desk drawer?"

"It was always there," O'Leary said. "I just pointed it out."

"But how—" the king shook his head. "Enough." He went to a bell cord. "We'll hear your case in open court—if you're sure you have nothing to impart in confidence?" He looked at O'Leary expectantly.

"This is all nonsense," O'Leary protested. "Impart what? Why don't you tell me about yourself? I have an idea that you represent some sort of authority symbol."

"Symbol?" Goruble roared. "We'll show you whether we be symbol or sovereign!" He yanked the cord. The door opened; a squad of household troops stood waiting.

"Escort him to the bar of justice," Goruble ordered. "He stands accused of sorcery."

"Oh, well," O'Leary said airily, "I guess it's no use trying to be reasonable. It may be amusing at that. Lead on, my good man." He gestured sardonically at the bull-necked corporal as the squad moved to box him in.

It was a five-minute walk along echoing corridors to the chamber where the hearing was to be held. A crowd of gaudily clad men and a few women in full skirts and cleavage eyed O'Leary curiously as he came in under guard. The ceremonial sentries beside the double doors motioned him and his escort through into a domed chamber, a rococo composition in red and green marble and heavy hangings of green velvet with gold fringes that reminded Lafayette of the lobby of the Colby opera house. At one side of the room a vast chair occupied a raised dais. A row of boys in baggy shorts, long stockings, pointed shoes, sailor's shirts and bangs raised long horns and blew a discordant fanfare. Through doors at the opposite side of the room the figure of the king appeared, wearing a scarlet robe now, followed by the usual retinue of hangers-on. Everyone bowed low, the women curt-sying. Lafayette felt a smart kick in the shin.

"Bow, bumpkin!" hissed a bearded stranger in pea-green knickers. Lafayette bent over, rubbed the spot where the other's boot had bruised him. "How would you like a punch in the jaw?"

"Silence! Wouldst have me rub your nose on the floor, wittol!"

"You and what other six guys?" O'Leary came back. "Ever had a broken leg before?"

"Before what?"

"Before you had a broken arm. I may just cross your eyes, too, while I'm at it."

"Art daft, varlet?"

"Maybe you haven't heard. I'm here on a witchcraft rap."

"Ulp?" The man moved away hastily. The king was seated on his throne now, amid much bustling of court-iers stationing themselves in position according to an elaborate scheme of precedence, each elbowing for a spot a foot or two closer to the throne. There were more trumpetings; then an old dodderer in a long black robe stepped forward and pounded a heavy rod on the floor.

"The Court of Justice of His Majesty King Goruble is now in session," he quavered. "All those who crave boons, draw nigh." Then, without pausing: "Let those who have offended against the just laws of the realm be brought forward."

"That's you, bud," a black-haired guard muttered. "Let's go." O'Leary followed as the man pushed through the throng to a spot ten feet from the throne where King Goruble sat, nibbling a slice of orange.

"Well, how plead you, my man?"

"I don't know," O'Leary said. "What's the charge?"

"Sorcery! Guilty or not guilty?"

"Oh, that again. I was hoping you'd thought up something more original, like loitering at the post office."

An effeminate-looking fellow in parakeet green stepped from the ranks of the retainers grouped around the throne, made an elaborate leg and waved a bit of lace from which an odor of dime store perfume wafted.

"An't please your Majesty," he said, "the fellow's insolence gives him away. 'Tis plain to see, he has a powerful protector. The villain is, I doubt not, a paid spy in the hire of the rebel Lod!"

"Lod?" Lafayette raised his eyebrows. "Who's he?"

"As is doubtless well known to you, this creature, thus y-clept is the fearsome giant, the bandit who impertinently presses a suit for the hand of her highness, the Princess Adoranne."

"And dreams of the day he will usurp our throne," Goruble added. He slapped the carved arm of the throne, looking angry.

"Well, fellow, do you deny it?" the green-clad exquisite persisted.

"I never heard of this Lod," Lafayette said impatiently. "And I've already told you the sorcery business was silly. There isn't any such thing!"

Goruble narrowed his eyes at O'Leary, pinched his chin between jeweled fingers.

"No such thing, eh?" He gestured. "Let Nicodaeus come forward."

A tall, well muscled but slightly paunchy gray-haired man in yellow tights and a short cloak ornately appliquéd with stars and crescent moons stepped from the ranks, bowed medium low before the throne, took a pair of rimless glasses from a breast pocket, put them on, turned and studied Lafayette.

"You deny the existence of magic, eh?" he asked in a mellow baritone. "A skeptic." He wagged his head, smiling ruefully, reached up and took an egg from his mouth. A little murmur of wonder went through the crowd. The gray-haired man sauntered a few feet, paused before a plump lady-in-waiting, plucked a gaily-colored scarf from her well filled bodice, tossed it aside, drew out another, and another. The fat woman retreated, squealing and giggling as the onlookers tittered.

"Well done, Nicodaeus!" a fat man in pale purple puffed. "Oh, jolly well done!"

Nicodaeus strolled to the dais, and with a murmured apology took a mouse from the king's pocket. He dropped the tiny animal on the floor and it scurried away, amid dutiful squealing from the ladies. He plucked another from the king's shoe, a third from the royal ear. The monarch twitched, shot a sharp glance at O'Leary, waved the magician aside.

"Well, how say you now, O'Leary!" he demanded. "True, the feats of my faithful Nicodaeus are harmless white sorcery, blessed in the temple of Goop the Good and employed only in defense of our crown; but none can deny the ordinary laws of nature have here been set aside."

"Fooie," Lafayette said. "That's just sleight-of-hand. Any carnival sideshow prestidigitator has a better routine than that."

Nicodaeus looked thoughtfully at O'Leary, walked over to stand before him.

"Do you mind telling me," the magician said quietly, "just where you come from?"

"Well, I'm, ah, a traveler from a distant land, you might say," O'Leary improvised. Nicodaeus turned to face King Goruble.

"Majesty, when I heard your police had picked up a sorcerer, I looked over the report. The arrest was made in a tavern in the Street of the Alehouses, about eight P.M. All the witnesses agree that he performed some sort of hocus-pocus with a wine bottle. Then when the officers were taking him out to the wagon, he reportedly tried to vanish, but didn't quite have the skill to manage it. I also heard a story that he cast some sort of spell on a woman, the wife of one of the arresting officers; changed her appearance, it seems."

"Yes, yes, I know all that, Nicodaeus!"

"Your Majesty, in my opinion all this is meaningless gossip, the product of wine-lubricated imaginations."

"Eh?" Goruble sat forward. "You're saying the man is innocent?"

"Not at all, Majesty! The really important point hasn't been mentioned yet. The accused was first seen, as I said, in the alehouse . . . " He paused dramatically. "Before that—no one had caught a glimpse of him!"

"So?"

"Your Majesty doesn't seem to get the point," Nicodaeus said patiently. "The city guards say he wasn't observed to approach the street where he was taken. The sentries at the city gates swear he never passed that way. He came from a far land, he says. Did he come on horse back? If so, where are the stains of travel—and where's the animal itself? Did he walk? Look at his boots; the soles show no more dust than a stroll in a garden might account for!"

"Are you saying he flew here?" Goruble shot a sharp look at Lafayette.

"Flew?" Nicodaeus looked annoyed. "Of course not. I'm suggesting that he obviously slipped into the city by stealth—and that he has confederates who housed and clothed him."

"So you agree he's a spy?" Goruble sounded pleased.

Lafayette sighed. "If I wanted to sneak into town, why would I suddenly walk into a tavern in plain sight of the cops?"

"I think the costume explains that," Nicodaeus said, nodding. "You're tricked out as the Phantom Outlaw, I believe. You intended to convince the gullible patrons of the dive that you were this mythical ghost, and then force them to do your bidding by threats of supernatural vengeance."

Lafayette folded his arms. "I'm getting tired of this nonsense," he stated loudly. "Starting now, this dream is going the way *I* want it to, or I'm just going to wake up and to hell with it!" He pointed at Nicodaeus. "This phony, now; if you'll detail a couple of men to hold him down while somebody goes through his pockets, and the trick compartments in the dizzy-looking cloak, you'd find out where all those mice come from! And—"

The magician caught O'Leary's eye, shook his head. "Play along," he whispered from the corner of his mouth.

Lafayette ignored him. " . . . I'm getting just about fed up with nonsense about magic and torture chambers," he went on. Nicodaeus stepped close. "Trust me, I'll get you out of this." He turned to the king and bowed his head smoothly. "The king is wise—"

"Nuts to all of you," O'Leary said. "This is just like a dream I had a couple of weeks ago. I was in a garden with nice green grass and a little stream and fruit trees, and all I wanted to do was relax and smell the flowers, but people kept coming along, bothering me. There was a fat bishop on a bicycle and a fireman playing a banjo, and then two midgets with a pet skunk—"

"Your Majesty, a moment!" Nicodaeus cried out. He threw a comradely arm about Lafayette's shoulders, led him closer to the throne. "It just came to me!" he announced. "This man is no criminal! We've been making a terrible mistake! How stupid of me not to have realized sooner."

"What are you babbling about, Nicodaeus?" Goruble snapped. "One minute you're sewing up a watertight case, the next you're hugging the man like a long-lost brother!"

"My mistake, my liege!" Nicodaeus said hastily. "This is a fine young man, an upstanding subject of your Majesty, a model youth."

"What do you know about him?" Goruble's voice was sharp. "A moment since, you said you'd never seen him before!"

"Yes, well, as to that—"

There was a tinkle of bells, and a face like a gargoyle's appeared between the king's feet.

"What's afoot?" a deep bass voice rumbled. "Your patterings disturb my slumbers!"

"Be quiet, Yokabump!" King Goruble snapped. "We're conducting important business."

The face came farther out, a small body behind it. The dwarf, rising to bandy legs, looked around, scratching his chest.

"Solemn faces!" he bellowed. "Sour pusses! You're all a bunch of stick-in-the-muds!" He whipped out a harmonica, tapped it on his oversized palm and started a lively tune.

"Sticks-in-the-mud, you mean," Goruble corrected. "Go away now, Yokabump! We told you we're busy!" He glared at Nicodaeus. "Well, we're waiting! What do you know of the fellow that should prevent his hanging by his thumbs!"

Yokabump stopped playing.

"You mean," he boomed, pointing at O'Leary, "you don't recognize this hero?"

Goruble stared down at him. "Hero? Recognize? No, we don't."

Yokabump bounded forward and struck a pose.

"When the dragon came out of the west.
The worst ran away with the best;
But one man with an ax stopped the beast in his tracks
And came home with the hide of the pest."

King Goruble frowned darkly. "Nonsense!" he said flatly. He turned to the dwarf. "No interference from you, manikin; this is a matter of deepest import. Don't distract us with foolish stories."

"But he is, in very truth, sire, the dragon slayer of the prophecy!"

"Why, ah, as a matter of fact . . . " Nicodaeus patted O'Leary heartily on the shoulder. "I was just about to make the announcement."

Yokabump waddled up to O'Leary, threw back his head and stared at him.

"He doesn't *look* like a hero," he announced in his subcellar bass. "But a hero he is!" He turned his heavy head, winked grotesquely at the magician, faced O'Leary again. "Tell us, Sir Knight, how you'll face the foul monster, how you'll overcome those mighty jaws, those awful talons!"

Goruble chewed at his lip, staring at O'Leary.

"Jaws and talons, eh," Lafayette said, smiling condescendingly. "No wings? No fiery breath? No—"

"Scales, yes—I think," Nicodaeus said. "I haven't seen him myself, of course, but the reports—"

A slender fellow in a pale yellow suit with a starched ruff came forward, sniffing a snuff box. He closed it with a click, tucked it in a sleeve and eyed O'Leary curiously.

"How say you, fellow? Wilt dispatch the great beast that guards the approaches to the stronghold of Lod?"

There was a sudden silence. Goruble blinked at O'Leary, his lips thrust out.

"Well?" he demanded.

"Agree!" Nicodaeus muttered in O'Leary's ear.

"Certainly!" Lafayette made an expansive gesture. "I'll be only too pleased to attend to this little matter. My favorite sport, actually. I often kill half a dozen dragons before breakfast. I'll promise to annihilate any number of mythical beasts, if that will make you happy."

"Very well." Goruble looked grim. "A celebration is in order, we suppose," he said sardonically. "We hereby decree a fete for tonight in honor of our valiant new friend, O'Leary." He broke off and shot Lafayette a fierce look. "And you'd better deliver the goods, young fellow," he added in an undertone, "or we'll have the hide off you in strips!"

Chapter Four

The room that O'Leary was shown to was forty feet long, thirty wide, carpeted, tapestried and gilt decorated. There was an immense four-poster bed, a vast, carved wardrobe, a gaily decorated chamber pot in a rosewood stand, a tall mirror in a frame, and a row of curtained windows with a view of lanterns strung in a garden where fountains played among moonlit statues of nymphs and satyrs. He tried a door, looked into a cedar-lined closet filled with elaborate costumes on satin-covered hangers. Another door opened into a tiny chapel, complete with a wheel of Goop and a fresh package of sacrificial incense sticks. There was one more door. O'Leary paused to give thought to what would be behind it, picturing the details of a cozy tiled bath with heated floor, glassed-in shower stall, plenty of hot water . . . He reached for the knob, swung the door wide, stepped through.

There was a loud squeal. Lafayette halted, staring. In the center of the small room was a long wooden tub containing soapy water and a girl. Her dark hair was piled high on her head, a few bubbles provided inadequate concealment for her charms. She stared back at him, amazement on her pretty features.

"Wha . . . ?" Lafayette stammered. "Where . . . but I was just . . . " He waved a hand vaguely toward the door.

The girl gazed at him wide-eyed. "You—you must be the new wizard, sir!" She took the towel from the rack attached to the side of the tub and stood up, wrapping it around herself.

"I—I'm sorry!" O'Leary blurted, his eyes straying to the expanse of white thigh revealed by the skimpy towel. "I was just—I mean—" He stared around at shelves stacked with clean sheets and towels.

"Something's wrong here," he said protestingly. "This was supposed to be a bathroom!"

The girl giggled. "You can have my bath, sir, I'd hardly started."

"But it wasn't supposed to be like this! I had in mind a nice tile bath, and a shower and plenty of hot water and soap and shaving cream—"

"This water's just right, sir," the girl stepped out onto the rug, loosened the towel and began modestly drying her neck, holding the towel more or less in front of her. "I'm Daphne; I'm the upstairs chambermaid."

"Gosh, miss, I didn't mean to disturb you. I was just—"

"I've never met a real magician before," Daphne said. "It was so exciting! One minute I was right there in my room, looking at the crack in the plaster, and the next—zip! Here I was!"

"You were somewhere else—taking a bath?" Lafayette frowned. "I must have made a mistake. Probably distracted by all the excitement."

"I heard about the fete," the girl said. "It *is* exciting. There hasn't been a real affair in the palace for months, not since that horrible ogre Lod came with his men under a truce flag to woo Princess Adoranne."

"Look, ah, Daphne, I have to get ready; after all, I'm sort of the guest of honor, so—"

"Oh." Daphne looked disappointed. "You didn't summon me on purpose?"

"No. Ah, I mean, I have to take a bath now."

"Would you like me to scrub your back?"

"No, thanks." O'Leary felt himself blushing. "I'm sort of used to bathing myself. But thanks just the same. But, uh, maybe I'll see you at the party."

"Me, sir? But I'm only a chambermaid! They won't even let me watch from the kitchen door!"

"Nonsense! You're as pretty as any of them! Come as my guest."

"I couldn't, sir! And beside, I haven't a thing to wear." She tucked the towel demurely about her slender figure, smiling shyly.

"Well, I think that can be fixed." Lafayette turned to the clothes closet, considering. "What size do you wear, Daphne?"

"Size? Why, as you see, sir . . . " She held her arms from her sides, twirled slowly around. Lafayette took a deep, calming breath, fixed his eyes on the closet, concentrating. He opened the door, glanced over the array of finery, reached, pulled out a pink-and-gold-brocaded gown.

"How about this?"

She gasped. "It's lovely, sir! Is it really for me?"

"It certainly is. Now, just run along like a good girl; I'll be looking forward to seeing you at the party."

"I've never seen anything so pretty." She took the dress tenderly in her arms. "If you'll just lend me a robe, sir, I'll be off like a flash. I know just where I can borrow a pair of shoes to go with it, and . . . "

Lafayette found a terry-cloth robe, bundled it about her shoulders and saw her to the door.

"I'd like to apologize again about, ah, disturbing you in your bath," he said. "It was just an accident."

"Think nothing of it, sir." She smiled up at him. "This is the most exciting thing that ever happened to me. Who'd have ever thought magicians were so young—and so handsome?" She went to tiptoes, kissed him quickly on the end of the nose, then turned and darted away along the hall.

There was a rap at the door as Lafayette was buttoning the last gilt button on the dark blue coat he had selected from the dozens in the closet.

"Come in," he called. He heard the door open behind him.

"I hope you don't mind my barging in on you," a deep voice said. Lafayette turned. Nicodaeus, trim in a gray outfit, closed the door behind him. He took out a pack of cigarettes, offered them and lit up with what appeared to be a Ronson lighter.

"Say, you're the first one I've seen smoking cigarettes here," O'Leary said. "And that lighter—"

Nicodaeus fingered the lighter, looking at O'Leary. "Plenty of time for explanations later, my young friend. I just wanted to take a few minutes before the festivities begin to, er, have a little chat with you."

"I want to thank you for helping me out this evening." Lafayette buckled on his sword belt, paused to admire the cut of his new knee breeches in the mirror. "For a while there, it looked like old Goruble had his heart set on railroading me into the Iron Maiden. What's eating the old boy?"

"He had an idea that if you knew a little magic, you might be a big help in the upcoming war with Lod's rebels. He was a bit put out when you denied it. You must excuse him; he's rather naïve in some ways. I was glad to help you out; but frankly, I'm a little curious about you myself. Ah . . . if you don't mind telling me, why are you here?" In the mirror O'Leary watched the magician, still fiddling with the lighter.

"Just a sight-seeing trip."

"You've never visited Artesia before?"

"Nope. Not that I know of. There was one dream I remember, about a glass house and a telescope—but there's probably no connection." He turned suddenly. Close behind him, Nicodaeus started and dropped the lighter in his pocket.

"What's that you had in your hand?" O'Leary demanded. "What are you creeping up behind me for?"

"Oh, that . . ." Nicodaeus blinked, smiling weakly. "Why, it's, ah, a little camera; you see I have a hobby—candid shots—and I just—"

"Let me see it."

Nicodaeus hesitated, then dipped into the pocket of his weskit and fished it out. It was made in the shape of a lighter—even worked as one, O'Leary saw—but it was heavy. And there were tiny dials set in its back. He handed it back. "I guess I'm overly suspicious, after being threatened by a number of horrible fates in less than two hours."

"Think nothing of it, my dear O'Leary." Nicodaeus glanced at the other's hand. "Ah, I noticed your ring. Very interesting design. Mind if I have a closer look at it?"

O'Leary shook his head. "I can't take it off. What's so interesting about a ring?"

Nicodaeus looked grave. "The device of the ax and dragon happens to have a peculiar significance here in Artesia. It's the insignia of the old royal house. There's an old prophecy—you know how people pretend to believe in that sort of thing—to the effect that the kingdom will be saved in its darkest hour by a, ahem, hero, riding a dragon and wielding an ax. He was supposed to appear bearing a symbol of his identity. I suppose that annoying clown Yokabump spotted the ring—he has sharp eyes—and improvised the rest. Luckily for you, I might add. He *could* have set up a howl that it was an evil charm. Lod carried an ax, you see, and of course he owns a dragon."

Lafayette glanced sharply at Nicodaeus, then laughed. "You almost sound as though you believed in the monster yourself."

Nicodaeus chuckled comfortably. "A mere fable, of course. Still, I'd wear the ring reversed if I were you."

"I can't help wondering," O'Leary said, "why should you care what happens to me any more than the rest of them? They all seem to want to see me strung up by the ears."

"Just a natural desire to help a stranger in distress," Nicodaeus answered, smiling. "After all, having saved you from a session with the hot irons, I have a sort of proprietary interest in seeing you safely through."

"At one point you just about had Goruble convinced I was a spy."

"A red herring; I wanted to distract him from the sorcery aspect. Like all Artesians, he's prey to superstition."

"Then I was right; you're not native here."

"Actually, I'm not," the magician admitted. "I, ah, come from a country to the south, as a matter of fact. I—"

"They must be way ahead of Artesia, technologically speaking. That lighter, for example. I'll bet you're responsible for the electric lights in the palace."

Nicodaeus nodded, smiling. "That's correct. I do what I can do to add to the amenities of palace life."

"Just what *is* your position here?"

"I'm an adviser to his Majesty." Nicodaeus smiled blandly. "He thinks I'm a master of magic, of course, but among these feather-heads a little common sense is sufficient to earn one a reputation as a wise man." He smiled comfortably. "Look here, my young friend—and I think I have established that I am a friend—isn't there something that you'd care to, ah, confide in me? I could perhaps be of some assistance, in whatever it is you have in mind."

"Thanks, but I don't have anything in mind that I need help with."

"I'm sure we could work out some arrangement, to our mutual benefit," Nicodaeus went on. "I, with my established position here; you Mr. O'Leary, with your, ah, whatever you have . . . " He paused on an interrogative note.

"Call me Lafayette. I appreciate what you did for me, but I really don't need any help. Look, the party must be about to begin. Let's beat it downstairs. I don't want to miss anything."

"You're determined to pursue your course alone, I see," Nicodaeus said sadly. "Ah, well, just as you wish, Lafayette. I don't mind saying I'm disappointed. Frankly, I've gotten just a little bit bored lately. I thought—but never mind." He eyed Lafayette, nibbling his lower lip. "You know, I wonder if it wouldn't be safer for you to just slip away tonight, before the fete. If you wait until later, his Majesty is likely to start having second thoughts and send you along to the rack after all. Now, I can arrange to have a fast horse waiting—"

"I don't want to leave now, before the party," O'Leary said. "Besides," he added grinning, "I promised to kill off a dragon, remember?" Lafayette winked at Nicodaeus. "I think it might be a little difficult to kill a superstition. But I have to at least go through the motions. Meanwhile, I hear this Princess Adoranne is quite a dish."

"Careful, lad. The princess is Goruble's most jealously guarded treasure. Don't make the mistake of thinking—"

"Thinking—that's the one thing I've determined not to do, as long as I'm here," O'Leary said with finality. "Let's go, Nicodaeus. This is the first royal function I've ever been to; I'm looking forward to it."

"Well, then." Nicodaeus clapped O'Leary on the back. "On to the ball! Tonight, revelry, and tomorrow, the fight to the death!"

"Fight to the death?" O'Leary looked startled.

"You and the dragon," Nicodaeus reminded him.

"Oh, that." Lafayette smiled. Nicodaeus laughed.

"Yes, that," he said.

At the high-arched entry to the ballroom, O'Leary paused beside Nicodaeus and looked out over an expanse of mirror-polished white marble the size of a football field, crowded with the royal guests, splendid in laces and satins of every imaginable hue, gleaming in the light from the chandeliers that hung from the gold-ribbed vaults of the ceiling like vast bunches of sparkling grapes. Heads turned as the majordomo boomed out the name of Nicodaeus, then looked inquiringly at O'Leary.

"Better get on your toes, Humphries," the magician advised the beribboned official. "This is Lafayette O'Leary, the young champion who's here to rid the kingdom of Lod's monster."

"Oh, beg pardon, milord. An honor!" He bowed and pounded his staff on the floor.

"Sir Lafayette of Leary!" he trumpeted. "The King's champion!"

"I'm not a sir," Lafayette started.

"Never mind." Nicodaeus took his arm and led him along toward the nearest group. "We'll see about an earldom for you at the first opportunity. Now . . . " He nodded casually at the expectant faces that moved in to surround them. "Ladies, sirs, may I present my good friend, Sir Lafayette."

"Are you really going to fight that horrid monster?" a cuddly creature in pale blue flounces breathed, fluttering her fan. A tall, hollow-faced man with thin white hair raised a bony finger. "Ride in fast, smite the brute in the soft under-parts and get out. That's my advice, Sir Lafayette! I've always found that boldness pays."

"Will you cut off his head?" a plump blonde squeaked. "Ooooh, how terrible! Will there be much blood?"

"I'd like to be riding with you, lad," a stout gentleman with an imposing nose and a walrus mustache wheezed. "Unfortunately, my gout . . . "

Lafayette nodded, offered breezy comments, accepted a drink from a tray after giving a moment's thought to the contents and feeling the slight jar that signaled successful manipulation. No use drinking cheap booze. He tested the drink: Rémy-Martin. He tossed the first shot down and scooped up another glass. The cognac had a pleasant, warming effect. He took another from a passing tray.

A sudden murmur ran through the assemblage. Horns tootled a fanfare.

"The princess," murmured the crowd. Lafayette looked in the direction toward which necks were craning and saw a cluster of women entering through a wide archway.

"Which is Adoranne?" He nudged Nicodaeus.

"She'll appear next."

A girl strolled into view, leading a tiger cub on a leash. She was tall, slender, moving as gracefully as a swan in a gown of palest blue scattered over with tiny pearls. Her hair—the color of spring sunshine, Lafayette decided instantly—was straight, cut short in a charming style that complemented the coronet perched atop it. She had a short patrician nose—at least it was the kind of nose that suggested that word to O'Leary—large blue eyes, a perfectly modeled cheek and chin line. Her figure was that of a trained athlete: trim, slim, vibrant with health. Lafayette tried to take a deep breath, his lips puckering instinctively for a long low whistle of admiration, but managed only a gasp.

"What's the matter?" Nicodaeus whispered.

"Now I know what they mean by breathtaking," he muttered. "Come on." He started through the crowd.

"Where are you going?" Nicodaeus plucked at his sleeve.

"I want to meet the princess."

"But you can't approach royalty! You have to wait for her to summon you!"

"Oh, don't let's bother with all that protocol. I want to see if she looks as marvelous up close as she does from here."

He pushed through between two bony dowagers just rising from creaky curtseys and smiled at the girl as she turned inquiringly toward him.

"Hi," Lafayette said, looking her over admiringly. "They told me you were beautiful, but that was the understatement of the year. I didn't know I could imagine anything this nice."

A big young man with curly dark hair and cigarette-ad features stepped forward, flexing Herculean shoulders that threatened to burst his royal blue gold-braid-looped tunic. He inclined his head to the princess, then turned to give O'Leary a warning look.

"Withdraw, bumpkin," he said in a low voice.

O'Leary waved a hand. "Go play with your blocks." He started around the man, who took a quick step to bar his way.

"Are you deaf, oaf?" he rapped.

"No, I'm Lafayette O'Leary, and if you don't mind, I'd like to—"

The young Hercules put a finger against O'Leary's chest. "Begone!" he hissed fiercely.

"Now, now, no rough stuff in front of the princess," O'Leary admonished, brushing the hand aside.

"Count Alain," a cool feminine voice said. Both men turned. Princess Adoranne smiled an intimate little smile at the count and turned to Lafayette.

"This must be the brave man who's come to rid us of the dragon." She tugged at the leash as the tiger cub came snuffling around O'Leary's ankles. "Welcome to Artesia."

"Thanks." Lafayette nudged the count aside. "I didn't exactly come here to kill dragons, but since I'm here, I don't mind helping out."

"Have you slain many dragons, Sir Lafayette?" She smiled at him coolly.

"Nope, never even saw one." He winked. "Did you?"

"Adoranne's lips were parted in an expression of mild surprise. "No," she admitted. "There is but one, of course—the beast of the rebel Lod."

"I'll bring you his left ear—if dragons have ears."

The princess blushed prettily.

"Fellow, you're overbold," Alain snapped.

"If I'm going to go dragon hunting, that's a characteristic I've been advised to cultivate." Lafayette moved closer to the princess. "You know, Adoranne, I really should have demanded half the kingdom and your hand in marriage."

Count Alain's hand spun O'Leary around; his fist hovered under Lafayette's nose.

"I've warned you for the last time."

Lafayette disengaged his arm. "I sincerely hope so. By the way, isn't there a little matter you wanted to attend to?" Lafayette envisioned an urgent physiological need.

Count Alain looked uncomfortable. "Your pardon, Highness," he said in a strained voice. He turned hastily and hurried toward an inconspicuous door.

O'Leary smiled blandly at the princess. "Nice fellow," he said. "Good friend of yours?"

"One of my dearest companions since were played together as children."

"Amazing," Lafayette said. "You remember your childhood?"

"Very well, Sir Lafayette. Do you not?"

"Well, sure, but let's not get started on that. Would you like to dance?"

The princess' ladies, drawn up in a rank behind her, sniffed loudly and moved as if to close in. Adoranne looked at O'Leary thoughtfully.

"There's no music," she said.

Lafayette glanced toward the potted palms, envisioned a swinging five-man combo behind them. They were in tuxes, and the music was on the stands, and the instruments out. The leader was saying a word to the boys now, raising a hand . . . He felt the small thump.

"May I?" Lafayette held out a hand as the opening blast of the Royal Garden Blues rang across the ballroom. Adoranne smiled, handed the cub's leash to a lady standing by and took Lafayette's hand. He drew her close—a feather-light vision of sky-blue and pearls and a faint scent of night-blooming jasmine.

"Sir Lafayette!" she gasped. "You have a strange manner with a lady."

"I'll show you a quaint native dance we do at home."

She followed without apparent difficulty as he tried out one of the Arthur Murray steps he had so often practiced solo in his room with the instruction book in his left hand.

"You follow beautifully," O'Leary said. "But then, I guess that's to be expected."

"Of course. I've been well instructed in the arts of the ballroom. But tell me, why did you agree to go out against Lod's dragon?"

"Oh, I don't know. To keep from finding out if your pop really meant what he said about hot irons, maybe."

"You jest, sir!"

"Sure."

"Tell me, did you swear some great oath to do a mighty deed?"

"Well . . . "

"And an oath of secrecy as well," she nodded, bright-eyed. "Tell me," she asked in an excited whisper, "who are you—really? The name—Sir Lafayette—does it disguise some noble title in your own land of Leary?"

"Now where did you get that idea?"

"You comport yourself not as one accustomed to bending the knee," she said, looking at him expectantly.

"Well, now that you mention it, where I come from, I don't have to kneel to anybody."

Adoranne gasped. "I knew it! How exciting! Tell me, Lafayette, where is your country? Not to the east, for there's naught but ocean there, and to the west lies only the desert stronghold of Lod."

"No fair to try to worm my secrets out of me," Lafayette said waggishly. "It's more fun if I'm mysterious."

"Very well, but promise me that when you reveal yourself, it will be first to me."

"You can count on that, honey," Lafayette assured her.

"Honey?"

"You know, sweet stuff."

Adoranne giggled. "Lafayette, you have the cutest way of putting things!"

"That's one of the nice things about being here," he said. "Usually I'm pretty dumb when it comes to light conversation."

"Lafayette, you're trying to cozen me! I'll wager there's never a moment when you're at a loss for words."

"Oh, there have been some moments. When the musketeers came to arrest me, for example. I'd been having a few quick ones with somebody called the Red Bull—"

Adoranne gasped. "You mean the infamous cutpurse and smuggler?"

"He seemed to have some illegal ideas, all right. A reflection of the anarchist in me, I suppose."

"And they arrested you!" Adoranne giggled. "Lafayette, you might have been lodged in a dungeon!"

"Oh, well, I've been in worse places."

"What thrilling adventures you must have had! A prince, wandering incognito—"

The music stopped with a clatter as though the players had tossed their instruments into a pile. Everybody clapped, calling for more. Count Alain shouldered past O'Leary, ducking his head to the princess.

"Adoranne, dare I crave the honor of the next?"

"Sorry, Al, she's taken," Lafayette took the girl's hand, started past the count, who pivoted to face him.

" 'Twas not *your* leave I spoke for, witling!" he hissed. "I warn you, begone before I lose my temper!"

"Look, Al, I'm getting a little tired of this," Lafayette said. "Every time I'm on the verge of having an interesting chat with Adoranne, you butt in."

"Aye! a greater dullard even than yourself should see when his company's not wanted. Now get ye gone!" People were staring now as the count's voice rose.

"Alain!" Adoranne looked at him with a shocked expression. "You mustn't speak that way to . . . to . . . a guest," she finished.

"A guest? A hired adventurer, by all accounts! How dare you lay a hand on the person of the Princess Royal!"

"Alain, why can't you two be friends?" Adoranne appealed. "After all, Sir Lafayette is sworn to perform a great service to the crown."

"His kind finds it easy to talk of great deeds," Alain snapped, "but when the hour comes for action—"

"I notice you didn't volunteer, Al," O'Leary pointed out. "You look like a big strong boy—"

"Strong enough to break your head. As for dragon slaying, neither I nor any other man can face a monster bigger than a mountain, armored and fanged—"

"How do you know he's armored and fanged? Have you seen him?"

"No, but 'tis common knowledge—"

"Uh-huh. Well, Alain, you run along now. After I've killed this dragon I'll let you come out with a tape measure and see just how big he is—unless you're too shy, that is."

"Shy, eh!" The count's well chiseled features scowled two inches from Lafayette's nose. "I'm not too shy to play a tattoo on your ill-favored hide, a-horse or afoot!"

"Count Alain!" Adoranne's cool voice was low but it carried a snap of authority. "Mend your manners, sir!"

"My manners!" Alain glared at O'Leary. "This fellow has the manners of a swineherd! And the martial skill as well, I'll wager!"

"Oh, I don't know, Al," O'Leary said casually. "I've done a bit of reading on karate, aikido, judo—"

"These are weapons I know not," Alain grated. "What do you know of the broadsword, the poniard, the mace? Or the quarterstaff, the lance—"

"Crude," Lafayette said. "Very crude. I find the art of fencing a much more gentlemanly sport. I read a dandy book on it just last month. The emphasis on the point rather than the edge, you know. The saber and epée—"

"I'm not unfamiliar with rapier form," Alain said grimly. "In fact, I'd welcome an opportunity to give you lessons."

Lafayette laughed indulgently. "*You* teach *me*? Al, old fellow, if you only knew how foolish that sounds. After all, what could you possibly know that I don't, eh?" He chuckled.

"Then, Sir Nobody, perhaps your worship would condescend to undertake my instruction!"

"Alain!" Adoranne started.

"It's all right, Adoranne," O'Leary said. "Might be fun at that. How about tomorrow afternoon?"

"Tomorrow? Ha! And overnight you'd scuttle for safety, I doubt not, and we'd see no more of you and your pretensions! 'Tis not so easy as that, knave. The inner courtyard is moon-bright! Let's repair to our lessons without further chatter!"

Nicodaeus was at Lafayette's side. "Ah, Count Alain," he said smoothly. "May I suggest—"

"You may not!" Alain's eyes found O'Leary's. "I'll await you in the courtyard." He bobbed his head to the princess, turned on his heel and pushed his way through the gaping circle of onlookers who at once streamed away in his wake.

"All this excitement about a fencing lesson," O'Leary said. "These people are real sports fans."

"Sir Lafayette," Adoranne said breathlessly, "you need not heed the count's ill-natured outburst. I'll command that he beg your forgiveness."

"Oh, it's all right. The fresh air will do me good. I'm feeling those cognacs a little, I'm afraid."

"Lafayette, how cool you are in the face of danger. Here." She took a lacy handkerchief from somewhere and pressed it in Lafayette's hand. "Wear this and please, deal generously with him." Then she was gone.

"Adoranne—" O'Leary began. A hand took his arm.

"Lafayette," Nicodaeus said at his ear. "Do you know what you're doing? Alain is the top swordsman in the Guards Regiment."

"I'm just giving him a few tips on saber technique. He—"

"Tips? The man's a master fencer! He'll have his point under your ribs before you can say Sam Katzman!"

"Nonsense. It's all just good clean fun."

"Fun? The man is furious!"

Lafayette looked thoughtful. "Do you really think he's mad?"

"Just this side of frothing at the mouth," Nicodaeus assured him. "He's been number one with Adoranne for some time now—until you came along and cut him out of the pattern."

"Jealous, eh? Poor fellow, if he only knew . . . "

"Only knew what?" Nicodaeus asked sharply.

"Nothing." He slapped Nicodaeus heartily on the back. "Now let's go out and see what he can do."

Chapter Five

The courtyard was a grim rectangle of granite walled in by the looming rear elevations of the servants' residential wings of the palace, gleaming coldly in the light of a crescent moon. The chill in the air had sharpened; it was close to freezing now. Lafayette looked around at the crowd that had gathered to watch the fencing lesson. They formed a ring three or four deep around the circumference of the impromptu arena, bundled in cloaks, stamping their feet and conversing in low, excited mutters. The wagers being made, O'Leary noted, were two to one in favor of the opposition.

"I'll take your coat," Nicodaeus said briskly. O'Leary pulled it off, shivered as a blast of frigid wind flapped his shirt against his back. Twenty feet away, Count Alain, looking bigger than ever in shirt sleeves, chatted casually with two elegant-looking seconds, who glanced his way once, nodded coldly, and thereafter ignored him.

"Ah, I see the surgeon is on hand." Nicodaeus pointed out a portly man in a long gray cloak. "Not that there'll be much he can do. Count Alain always goes for the heart."

The count had accepted his blade from one of his aides now; he flexed it, tested its point with a finger and made a series of cuts at the air.

"I'd better warm up, too," O'Leary drew his rapier from its scabbard, finding it necessary to use both hands to get the point clear. "It's kind of long, isn't it?" he said. He waved the weapon, took up a stance.

"I hope your practice has been against skilled partners," Nicodaeus said.

"Oh, I just practice by myself." O'Leary tried a lunge, went a little too far, had to hop twice to get his balance.

"This thing's heavy," he commented, lowering the tip to the ground. "I'm used to a lighter weapon."

"Be grateful for its weight; Count Alain has a superb sword arm. He'll beat a light blade aside like a wooden lath."

"Hey," Lafayette said, nudging the magician. "Look over there, in the black cloak. That looks like—"

"It is," Nicodaeus said. "Don't stare. The cloak is accepted by all present as an effective disguise. It wouldn't do for a lady of her rank to witness an affair of this sort."

Lafayette fumbled out Adoranne's hanky, fluttered it at her and tucked it in his shirt pocket. Across the yard, Count Alain, watching the byplay, set his left fist on his hip, proceeded to whip his blade through a dazzling warmup pattern. O'Leary gaped at the whistling steel.

"Say, Nicodaeus," he murmured thoughtfully, "he's good!"

"I told you he was a winner, Lafayette. But if, as you said, you're better—"

"Look, ah, maybe I was hasty." He watched as the count described a lightning series of figure eights, finished with an elaborate *redoublement* and lowered his point with a calculating glance at O'Leary.

"Go ahead," Nicodaeus whispered. "Show him a little swordsmanship. It will give you a psychological advantage if you can slice yours a hair closer to the test pattern than he did."

"Ah, look here, Nicodaeus, I've been thinking; it wouldn't really be fair of me to show him up, in front of his friends."

"He'll have to take that chance. After all, he was the one who insisted on the meeting."

Alain's seconds were nodding now. They turned and started across toward O'Leary.

"Nicodaeus!" O'Leary grabbed his second's arm. "This isn't going just the way I'd figured. I mean, I assumed that since Alain—that is, I don't see how—"

"Later." Nicodaeus disengaged his arm, strode across, engaged in deep conversation with his two opposite numbers. Lafayette hefted the sword, executed a pair of awkward thrusts. The weapon felt as clumsy as a crowbar in his cold-numbed fingers. Now Alain stepped forward a few paces and stood waiting, his slim blade held in his bronzed fist as lightly as a bread stick.

"Come along, Lafayette." Nicodaeus was at his side. "Now, I'll hold a white handkerchief between your crossed blades . . ."

Lafayette hardly heard Nicodaeus, who was talking rapidly as he urged him forward. Perhaps if he fell down, pretended to hurt his knee . . . no, no good. Maybe if he sneezed—a sudden attack of asthma—

It wouldn't do. There was only one course left. Damn! And just when he'd started having a good time. But it couldn't be helped. And this time it had better work. O'Leary shut his eyes, conjured up the image of Mrs. MacGlint's Clean Rooms and Board, the crooked hall, the cramped bedroom, the peeling, stained wallpaper, the alcove, the sardines . . .

He opened his eyes. Nicodaeus was staring at him.

"What's the matter? You're not sick?"

O'Leary snapped his eyes shut, muttering to himself: *"You're asleep, dreaming all this. You're in bed, feeling that broken spring in the mattress—the one that catches you under the left shoulder blade. It's almost morning now, and if you just open your eyes slowly . . ."* He opened one eye, saw Count Alain waiting ten feet away, the rank of expectant faces behind him, the stone wall looming above.

"It's not real," he hissed under his breath. *"It's all a fake, an hallucination! It isn't really here!"* He stamped a boot against the stone paving. *"This isn't real stone, ha ha, just imaginary stone. I'm not really cold; it's a nice night in August! There's no wind blowing . . ."*

His voice trailed off. There was no use in kidding himself: The stone was solid as ever underfoot. The icy wind was still cutting at his face like a skinning knife and

Alain waited, light glinting on the naked steel in his hand.
Nicodaeus was looking at him concernedly.

" . . . instructions," he was saying. "Well, do the best
you can, my boy." He took out the white handkerchief
and flapped it.

"It's the distractions," O'Leary mumbled to himself.
"I can't concentrate, with all these people watching."

"Gentlemen, on guard!" Nicodaeus said sharply.
Count Alain raised his sword, held it at the *engagé*.
Dumbly, Lafayette stepped forward, lifted his heavy
blade, clanged it against the other. It was like hitting a
wrought iron fence.

"Say, just a minute!" O'Leary lowered his blade and
stepped back. Alain stared at him, his black eyes as cold
as outer space. O'Leary turned to Nicodaeus. "Look
here, if this is a real duel, and not just a friendly lesson—"

"Ha!" Alain interjected.

" . . . then as the challenged party, I have the choice
of weapons, right?"

Nicodaeus pulled at his lower lip. "I suppose so, but
the meeting has already begun."

"It's never too late to correct an error in form,"
O'Leary said firmly. "Now, you take these swords—
primitive weapons, really. We ought to use something
more up to date. Pistols, maybe; or—"

"You demand pistols?" Nicodaeus looked surprised.

"Why not pistols?" At least—O'Leary was thinking of
the princess's eyes on him—he wouldn't look as silly
missing with a pistol as he would with Alain chasing him
around the courtyard slashing at his heels.

"Pistols it is, then," Nicodaeus was saying. "I trust
suitable weapons are available?"

"In my room," O'Leary said. "A nice pair of weapons."

"As Sir Lafayette desires," one of Alain's seconds was saying. "Subject to Count Alain's agreement, of course."

"I'm sure the count won't want to chicken out at this point," O'Leary said. "Of course pistols are pretty lethal—" he broke off, suddenly aware of what he was saying. Pistols?

"On second thought, fellows—" he started.

"I've heard of them," Alain was nodding. "Like small muskets, held in the hand." He shot O'Leary a sharp look. "You spoke only of cold steel when you goaded me to this meeting, sirrah; now you raise the stakes."

"That's all right," O'Leary said hastily. "If you'd rather not—"

". . . but I accept the gage," Alain declared flatly. "You're a more bloodthirsty rogue than I judged by the look of you, but I'll not cavil. Bring on these firearms!"

"Couldn't we just cut cards?" But Nicodaeus was already speaking to a mop-haired page, who darted away, looking eager.

Alain turned his back, walked off a few paces, spoke tightlipped to his seconds, who shot back looks at O'Leary. He shrugged apologetically, got scowls in return.

Nicodaeus was chewing his lip. "I like this not, Lafayette," he said. "With a lucky shot, he could blow your head off, even if you nailed him at the same time."

Lafayette nodded absently, his eyes half shut. He was remembering the pistols, picturing them as they lay snug in their jeweled holsters. He envisioned their internal workings, visualized the parts . . . His ability to manipulate the environment seemed to come in spells, but it was worth a try. Tricky business, at this range. He felt a reassuring flicker, faint but unmistakable—or was it? Perhaps it had just been a gust of wind.

The boy was back, breathing hard, holding out the black leather belt with its elegant bright-work and its burden of long-barreled pistols.

"I'll take those." Nicodaeus lifted the guns from the page's hands, crossed to the waiting count and offered both pistol butts. Alain drew one from its holster, hefted it, passed it to his seconds, who turned it over, wagged their heads, muttered together and handed it back. O'Leary took his, noted distractedly that it was a clip-fed automatic with a filed front sight. It looked deadly enough.

"What distance is customary, Lafayette?" Nicodaeus enquired in a whisper.

"Oh, about three paces ought to be enough."

"What?" Nicodaeus stared at him. "At that range, no one could miss!"

"That's the idea," O'Leary pointed out. "Let's get on with it." He licked his lips nervously, hardly hearing as Nicodaeus instructed both combatants to stand back to back, their weapons held at their sides, and at the signal to take three paces, turn and fire.

Alain stepped into position and stood stiffly, waiting. Lafayette backed up to him.

"All right, go!" Nicodaeus said firmly. O'Leary gulped, took a step, another, a third and whirled, raising the gun.

Alain's weapon was already up, pointed straight at O'Leary's heart. He saw the count's finger tighten on the trigger at the same instant that he sighted on the white blob of the other's shirt front and squeezed.

A jet of purple ink squirted in a long arc, scoring a dead center hit as a stream of red fluid from Alain's gun spattered on his own shoulder.

"I got you first!" O'Leary called cheerily, snapping another shot that arched across to catch Alain on the ear. It was a good, high-pressure jet, O'Leary noted approvingly. It followed the haughty count as he reeled back, played over his face and down the already empurpled shirt, and piddled out just as Alain, in retreat, collided with his own startled seconds and went down. The crowd, in silent shock until then, burst out with a roar of laughter, above which a distinct titter from the direction of Princess Adoranne was clearly audible.

"Well, I guess I win," O'Leary lowered the gun, smiling and taking the accolade of the crowd. Alain was scrambling to his feet, scrubbing at his face with both hands. He stared at his violet palms, then with a roar leaped at his second, wrested the sword from the startled man's grip and charged.

"Lafayette!" Nicodaeus roared. O'Leary looked around in time to see his rapier flying toward him, hilt first. He grabbed it and brought it up just in time to receive Alain's onslaught.

"Hey!" O'Leary back-pedaled, frantically warding off the count's wild attack. Steel clanged on steel as the bigger man's fury drove O'Leary back, back. His feet stumbled on the uneven pavement and the heavy blows numbed his arm, threatening to knock his weapon from his grip. There was no question of counterattack.

A mighty chop sent Lafayette's blade spinning. He had a momentary glimpse of Alain's face, purple with ink and fury, as he brought back his blade, poised for the thrust.

There was a flash and a resounding clong! as something white shot down from above to strike the count's head, bound aside and smash against the wall. Alain dropped his sword, folded slowly, knees first, and slammed out flat on his face.

A fragment of the missile clattered to O'Leary's feet. He let out his breath in a hoarse gasp, stooped and brought up the shard. It bore a familiar pattern of angels and rosebuds: the chamber pot from his room.

He looked up quickly, caught a glimpse of a saucy face, ringed with dark curls, just withdrawing from a darkened window.

"Daphne," he muttered, "nice timing, girl."

* * *

Back in the ballroom there was a great deal of hearty laughter and congratulatory slapping of Lafayette's back.

"As pretty a piece of foolery as I've seen this twelve-month," chortled a grizzled old fellow in pale yellow knee pants and a monocle. "Young Alain's had it coming to him, what? Bit of a prig, but a trifle too stout a lad to bait!"

"You handled the situation nicely, my boy," Nicodaeus nodded sagely. "A fatality would have been in rather bad taste, and of course, you've made your point now, statuswise."

Adoranne came up, looking prettier than ever with her cheeks pink from the cold air. She put a hand on Lafayette's arm.

"I thank you, noble sir, for sparing the count's life. He's learned a lesson he'll not soon forget."

A sudden loud shriek rang out across the crowded ballroom floor, followed by the piercing accents of an angry female voice. At this new diversion, Lafayette's circle of admirers broke up and moved off craning their necks to make out the source of the outbursts.

"Whew!" O'Leary looked around for a waiter and lifted the ninth—or was it the tenth?—brandy of the evening from a passing tray. "Adoranne," he started, "now's our chance to get away from the mob for a minute. I noticed there's a nice garden outside."

"Oh, Lafayette, let's discover what it is that's set the duchess to clamoring like a fishwife spoiled of a copper!" She tugged at his hand playfully. He followed as Nicodaeus moved ahead, calling for way for her Highness.

"It's a chambermaid," someone was passing the word. "The saucy minx was mingling with her betters, wearing a stolen gown, mind you!"

O'Leary had a sudden sinking feeling. He'd forgotten all about his invitation to Daphne. The petite chambermaid, transformed in rose-colored silk set off by white gloves, silver slippers and a string of luminous white pearls, defiantly faced a bony matron buckled into stiff yellowish-white brocade like a suit of armor. The latter shook a finger heavenward, her neck tendons vibrating like cello strings, the coronet atop her mummified coiffure bouncing with the vigor of the verbal assault.

" . . . my girl, and I'll see to it that after the flogging, you're sent away to a workhouse where—"

"Ah, pardon me, Duchess," O'Leary stepped forward, winked encouragingly at Daphne and faced the incensed noblewoman. "I think there's been a slight misunderstanding here. This young lady—"

"Lady! I'll have you know this is a common servant girl! The audacity of the baggage appearing here—and in *my* gown! My seamstress completed it only today."

"You must be mistaken," O'Leary said firmly. "The dress was a gift from me and I invited her here."

Behind him there was a sharp gasp. He turned. Adoranne looked at him, wide-eyed, then managed a forced smile.

"Another of our good Sir Lafayette's jests," she said. "Be calm, Veronica dear; the girl will be dealt with."

"No, you don't understand," O'Leary protested. "There's been a mistake. I gave her the dress this evening."

"Please, noble sir," Daphne broke in. "I . . . I'm grateful for your chivalrous attempt to aid a poor servant girl, but it's no use. I . . . I stole the dress, just as her ladyship said."

"She did not!" Lafayette waved his arms. "Are you all out of your mind? I tell you—"

The duchess pointed a skeletal finger at a decorative motif on the bodice of the gown. "Is that, or is that not, the crest of the House of High Jersey?" Her voice was shrill with triumph.

"She's quite right of course," Nicodaeus muttered at O'Leary's side. "What's all this about giving her the dress?"

"I . . . I . . ." O'Leary stared from the duchess to Daphne, who stood now with downcast eyes. A suspicion was beginning to dawn: somehow, his ability to summon up artifacts at will wasn't quite as simple as he'd thought. When he had called for a bathroom, he'd gotten a tub—complete with occupant—transferred, the girl had

said, from her garret room. And when he had ordained
a dress in the closet, he hadn't created it from nothing;
he had merely shifted the nearest available substitute to
hand—in this case, from the wardrobe of the duchess.

"I'll pay for the dress," he blurted. "It's not her fault.
She didn't know it was stolen—that is, I didn't steal
it—not really. You see, I invited her to the party, and
she said . . . "

He trailed off. Interested smiles were fading. Adoranne tossed her head, turned and moved grandly away.
The duchess was glaring at him like a mother tyrannosau-
rus surprising an early mammal sucking eggs.

"Adoranne, wait a minute! I can explain—" He caught
Daphne's tear-brimmed eye.

"Come along, Lafayette," Nicodaeus tugged at his
sleeve. "The joke didn't go over; these people are pretty
stuffy about protocol."

"Daphne," O'Leary started. "I'm sorry—" The girl
raised her head, looked past him. "I do not know you,
sir," she said coldly, and turned away.

"Oh, dammit all!" O'Leary grimaced and let his arms
fall at his sides. "I wish I'd never thought of the infernal
dress in the first place."

There was a startled yelp from the duchess, a squeak
from Daphne, a delighted roar from the males in the
audience. Lafayette gasped and caught a fleeting glimpse
of a curvaceous white flank as Daphne, clad only in silver
slippers, a few bits of lace and blushes, vanished into the
crowd, followed by a rising storm of applause.

"Oh, capital, old fellow!" A stout gentleman in deep
red velvet slammed O'Leary's shoulder with a meaty
hand. "Done with mirrors, I suppose?"

"Ah, Sir Lafayette, you are a sly fox!" boomed another appreciative oldster. The duchess sniffed, glared, stalked away.

"Where's Adoranne gone?" Lafayette rose on his toes, staring across heads.

"This wasn't exactly the kind of prank to impress her Highness with," Nicodaeus said. "You won't see her again this evening, my boy."

Lafayette let out a long sigh. "I guess you're right. Oh, well; the party's breaking up, anyway. Maybe in the morning I can explain."

"Don't even try," the magician advised.

Lafayette eyed him glumly. "I need some time to figure out a few things before I try any more good deeds," he said. "Maybe if I sleep on it—but on the other hand, if I go to sleep—"

"Never mind, my boy. She won't stay angry forever. Go along and get some rest now. There are a few things I want to discuss with you in the morning."

Back in his room, Lafayette waited while a soft-footed servant lit a candle. In the dim light he pulled off his clothes, used the washbasin to slosh water over his head and toweled off. He blew out the taper, then went to the four-poster, pulled back the blankets and clambered in with a grateful sigh.

Something warm and smooth cuddled up against him. With a muffled yelp he bounded from the bed and whirled to stare at the bright-eyed face and bare shoulder of Daphne, looking up tousle-headed from under the covers.

"Count Alain gave you an awful drubbing, didn't he, sir? Come along and I'll rub your back."

"Uh, thanks for dropping that, uh, missile on him," O'Leary started. "But—"

"Never mind that," Daphne said. "It was nothing. But your poor bruises . . . "

"Lucky for me he used the edge." Lafayette moved his arm gingerly. "It is pretty sore, at that. But what in the world are you doing here?"

She gave him an impish smile. "Where else could I go, milord, in my condition?"

"Well . . . " O'Leary froze, listening for a sound. It had been a stealthy sort of creak.

"Hssst!" the voice came from across the dark room. O'Leary tensed, remembering his sword, across the room on the floor in a heap with his clothes.

"Sir Lafayette, come quickly," the voice hissed. "It concerns the welfare of her Highness. Make no outcry! Secrecy is vital!"

"Who are you?" O'Leary demanded. "How did you get in here?"

"No time to talk! Hurry!" The voice was a throaty rasp, unfamiliar. Lafayette squinted, trying to get a glimpse of the intruder. "What's happened?"

"No more talk! Follow me or not, as you choose! There's not a moment to lose."

"All right; wait until I get my pants on . . . " He fumbled his way across to his clothes, pulled on breeches and a shirt, jammed his feet into shoes and caught up a short cloak.

"All right, I'm ready."

"This way!" Lafayette made his way across toward the sound of the voice. As he passed the bed, Daphne's hand reached out, tugged him down.

"Lafayette," she breathed in his ear, "you must not go! Perhaps it is a trick!"

"I've got to," he whispered back, equally quietly. "It's—"

"Who's that?" the voice snapped sharply. "To whom do you speak?"

"Nobody," Lafayette pulled free, went toward the voice. "I always mutter to myself when I don't know what's going on. Look here, is she all right?"

"You'll see."

A line of faint light showed against the wall and widened as a four-foot rectangle of paneling slid aside. A cloaked silhouette showed against it for a moment and then slipped past. O'Leary followed, barely able in the deep gloom to make out a narrow low-ceilinged passage and the stealthy figure of his guide. He cracked his head on a low beam, swore, scraped aside cobwebs that clung to his face. There was an odor of dust and stale air and mice; somewhere wind whined in a cranny in the wall.

The passage led more or less straight, with an occasional jog around a massive masonry column, then turned right, continued another fifty feet and dead-ended at a coarsely mortared brick wall.

"We go up here," the hoarse voice said shortly. Lafayette groped until he found rough wooden slats nailed to a vertical post against the wall. He went up, stepped off into a new passage and hurried after his guide. He tried to estimate his position in the palace. He was on the third floor, about halfway along the east wing.

Just ahead there was a soft creak, a faint rusty squeal. A hand caught his arm, thrust a coarse-textured sack into his hand—a sack heavy with something that clinked.

"Hey, what's—" A hearty shove thrust Lafayette violently forward. He stumbled, struck something with his shoulder, felt a rug underfoot now and caught a scent of delicate perfume. He whirled, heard a panel slam in his face; his hands scraped fruitlessly across a solid-seeming wall. There was a stir behind him in the room, a sharp cry, quickly cut off. O'Leary flattened himself, trying desperately to see through the darkness. Someone called in the next room. There were hurried footsteps; a door opened across the room, fanning soft light across a wedge of rich-patterned rug, a slice of brocaded wall, an arch of gilded ceiling. O'Leary saw a window with dainty ruffles, a vast canopied four-poster. A short, fat woman in a flounced nightcap puffed through the open door, holding a candle high.

"Your Highness! You cried out!"

Lafayette stood frozen, staring at a vision of bare-shouldered femininity sitting up in the huge bed, staring across at him in astonishment. The fat woman followed Adoranne's gaze, saw Lafayette, screeched, clapped a hand to her broad bosom and screeched again, louder.

"Shhh! It's only me!" Lafayette started forward, shushing the woman frantically; she yelled again and backed against the bed.

"Stay back, villain! Touch not one hair of her Highness's head—!"

"It's all a mistake." O'Leary indicated the wall through which he had entered. "Somebody came into my room and told *me*—"

There was a pounding of feet, a clash of steel. Two immense guardsmen in flaring helmets, polished breastplates and greaves thundered into the room, took one eye-popping look at Adoranne, who quickly pulled the pink silk sheet up to her chin.

"There!" screamed the fat lady-in-waiting, pointing with a plump finger. "A murderer! A ravisher! A thief in the night!"

"Let me explain how I happened to be here, fellows—" Lafayette broke off as the two men rushed him, pinned him against the wall with six-foot-long doubleheaded pikes at his chest. "It was all a mistake! I was in my room, asleep, and all of a sudden—"

"—you took it into your head to violate the boudoir of her Highness!" the fat woman finished for him. "Look at the great wretch, half-dressed, burning with unholy lust—"

"I was only—"

"Silence, dog," one of the pikemen grated between set teeth. "Who thinks to harm our princess begs for bloody vengeance!"

"Did he—did he—" The other guard was glaring at O'Leary with eyes like hot coals.

"The monster had no time to achieve his evil purpose," the chubby woman bleated. "I placed my own body between him and that of her Highness, offering it gladly if need be to save her Highness from this fiend!"

"Has he taken anything?"

"Oh, for heaven's sake," O'Leary protested. "I'm no thief!" He waved his arms. "I—" The bag, still clutched in his hand, slammed the wall. He stared at it dumbly.

"What's he got there?" One of the men seized the sack, opened it, peered inside. Over his shoulder, Lafayette caught of glimpse of Adoranne, an expression of mischievous interest on her perfect features.

"Your Highness!" The man stepped to the bed and upended the contents of the pouch on the rosebud adorned coverlet—a sparkling array of rings, necklaces, bracelets, glinting red, green, diamond-white in the candle light.

The fat woman gasped. "Your Highness' jewels!" Lafayette made a move, felt the pike dig into his chest hard enough to draw blood. "Somebody shoved that into my hands," he called. "I was in the dark, in the passage, and—"

"Enough, thief!" the pike wielder snarled. "Move along now, you! I need little excuse to spit your gizzard!"

"Look, Adoranne, I was trying to help! He told me—"

"Who? Have you an accomplice in your felony?" The guard jabbed again to emphasize the question.

"No! I mean there was a man—a medium-sized man in a cloak; he came into my room—"

"How came the rogue here?" the fat woman shrilled. "Did you great louts sleep at your posts of duty?"

"I came in through some kind of sliding panel," O'Leary turned to the princess. "It's right over there. It closed up behind me, and—"

Adoranne's chin went up; she gave him a look of haughty contempt and turned away.

"I thank you, Martha," she said coolly to the fat lady-in-waiting. "And you, gentlemen, for your vigilance in my defenses. Leave me now."

"But, your Highness—" the fat woman started.

"Leave me!"

"Adoranne, if you'd just—" A painful prod in the solar plexus doubled O'Leary over. The pikemen caught his arms and hauled him from the room.

"Wait!" he managed. "Listen!"

"Tomorrow you can tell it to the headsman," the guard growled. "Another word outta you and by the three tails o'Goop I'll spare the crown the expense of an execution!"

In the corridor, Lafayette, still gasping, fixed his eye on the intersection ahead. *Just around the corner*, he improvised. *There's a . . . a policeman. He'll arrest these two.*

The pikemen shoved him roughly past the turn; the corridor was empty of cops. Too bad. Must be a spot he'd already seen and thus couldn't change. *But that door just ahead: it would open, and a python would come slithering out, and in the confusion—*

"Keep moving, you!" the pikeman pushed him roughly past the door, which failed to disgorge a snake.

A gun, then, in his hip pocket—

He reached, found nothing. He should have known *that* one wouldn't work; he had just put the trousers on a few minutes earlier, and there had been no armaments bagging the pockets then—beside which, how could he concentrate with these two plug-uglies hauling at him? A sharp jerk at his arm directed him down another side way. He stumbled on, assisted by frequent jabs and blows, down stairs and more stairs, into a dim malodorous passage between damp stone walls, past an iron gate into a low chamber lit by smoking flambeaux in black iron brackets. He leaned against a wall, trying to decide which of his bruises hurt worst, while his pike-wielding acquaintance explained his case in a few terse words to an untrimmed lout with thick lips, pale stubble and pimples.

"One o' them guys, huh?" The turnkey nodded knowingly. "I know how to handle them kind."

"Wait . . . till I get my breath," O'Leary said. "I'll . . . visit you . . . with a plague of boils . . . "

A blow slammed him toward a barred gate. Hard hands hustled him through to a moldy oak-plank door. Keys jangled. The blond jailer cuffed him aside and hauled the door open with a rasp of dry hinges. O'Leary caught a glimpse of a stone floor and a litter of rubbish.

Damn! If he'd just thought to picture something a trifle cozier, before he saw it.

"Kind of crummy quarters fer a dude like youse, Buster," the turnkey leered. "You got straw, but I'll give ye a clue: Use the bare floor instead. We got a few fleas and stuff, you know?" Then a foot in the seat sent O'Leary spinning inside and the door thudded behind him.

Chapter Six

O'Leary sat on the floor, blinking into total blackness. Some day he'd have to read up on Freudian dream symbolism. All this business of stumbling around in the dark being beaten by large men must be some sort of punishment wish, probably arising from guilt feelings due to the Adoranne and Daphne sequences—particularly the former.

O'Leary got to his feet, felt his way to a wall, made a circuit of the cell. There were no windows, unless they were above his reach; and just the one door, massive and unyielding. He heard a furtive scuttling. Rats, no doubt. Not a very nice place to spend the rest of his dream. He sighed, regretting again he had been too rattled to provide a few amenities before it was too late. But perhaps he could still manage something . . .

Light, first. A candle would do. He pictured a two-inch stub lying among the litter in the far corner . . . and a match in his pocket.

There was a thump, as though the universe had gone over a tar strip in the road. O'Leary groped among odds and ends, felt straw, small bones—and a greasy lump of wax with a stub of a wick. Aha! Now for a match. In his pocket, a small item like that could have passed unnoticed. He checked, felt the smooth cover of a match folder, pulled it out and lit up. The candle burned with a feeble yellow flame, its light confirming his first impression of the cramped cell. Well, that part couldn't be helped, but it would be wise to think carefully about his next move.

O'Leary settled himself on the driest spot on the floor. It looked as though he were stuck here unless he could manage to regain the sanctuary of his room back at Mrs. MacGlint's house. The last two tries hadn't worked out, but then that was to be expected. After all, who could focus the Psychic Energies with someone hauling him toward a paddy-wagon or threatening to stick a foot of razor-edged steel into his internal arrangements?

At least it was peaceful here in the cell. But going back was a last resort; he couldn't just vanish without even a chance to explain to Adoranne how he had happened to be in her bedroom with a sackful of loot.

What could he do? If things hadn't happened so fast, he could have dreamed up some way out, some last minute rescue. Maybe it still wasn't too late. Nicodaeus, maybe; *he* could get him out of here. Probably he hadn't heard about his protégé's arrest yet—or, O'Leary amended, he had just heard a few minutes ago. By now he'd be coming along the hall, passing the iron-barred door, ordering guards around, demanding O'Leary's immediate release—

There was a sound from the door. A tiny panel opened; light glared in. O'Leary jumped up as he saw the face at the opening.

"Daphne! What are you doing here?"

"Oh, Sir Lafayette, I knew something terrible would happen!"

"You were right; there's dirty work afoot. Look, Daphne, I have to get out of here! I'm worried about Adoranne; whoever led me to her room—"

"I tried to tell them, sir, but they think I'm your confederate."

"What? Nonsense! But don't worry, Daphne, Nicodaeus will be along soon."

"He tried, sir—but the king was furious! He said it was an open-and-shut case, that you were caught red-handed—"

"But it was a frame-up!"

"At least you won't have a long wait in that awful cell. It's only three hours till dawn; it comes early this time of year."

"They're letting me out at dawn?"

"For the execution," Daphne said sadly.

"Whose execution?"

"Y—yours, sir," Daphne sniffled. "I'm to get off with twenty years."

"But—but they *can't*! King Goruble needs me to kill the dragon, and—and—"

"OK," a guard's rough voice interrupted, "you seen him, kid. Now how about that smooch?" the panel slammed with a bang. O'Leary groaned and resumed his seat. He'd not only reduced his own credit to zero, but dragged an innocent girl down with him. It looked like the end of the line—the second time in the last few hours that imminent death had stared him in the face. Some dream! What if he failed to wake up in time, and the sentence were actually carried out? He'd heard of people dreaming they were falling, and hitting, and dying in their sleep of heart failure. A hard story to check, but that was one experiment he couldn't afford to try. There was no help for it; he'd have to wake up.

Sitting against the wall, he relaxed, closed his eyes. *Mrs. MacGlint's house*, he thought, picturing the front porch in the gray predawn light; *the dark hall, the creaky stairs, the warped, black-varnished door to his room with its chipped brown-enameled steel knob; and the room itself, the odor of stale cookery and ancient woodwork and dust . . .*

He opened an eye. The candle flame across the cell guttered, making shadows bob on the stone wall. Nothing had changed. O'Leary felt uneasiness rising like water in a leaky hold.

He tried again, picturing the cracked sidewalk in front of the boarding house, the dusty leaves of the trees that overhung it, the mailbox at the corner, the down-at-the-heels shops along the main street, the tarnished red brick of the Post Office . . .

That was real, not the ridiculous dream about princesses and dragons. He was Lafayette O'Leary, aged twenty-six, with a steady if not inspiring job at which he was due in a very few hours. Old Man Biteworse would be hopping mad if he showed up late, bleary-eyed from lack of sleep. There was no time to waste, idling in a fantasy world, while his real-life job waited, with its deadlines and eyestrain and competition for the next two-dollar raise.

O'Leary felt a faint jar. A breath of warmth touched his face. His eyes snapped open. He was staring into a bright mist that swirled and eddied. The air was hot, moist. Abruptly, he was aware of dampness soaking into the seat of his trousers. He scrambled up, saw vague pale shapes moving in the fog. Out of the steam, figures appeared—the pink bodies of young girls with wet hair, wearing damp towels, carelessly draped. Lafayette gaped. He had made his escape—not back to Mrs. Mac-Glint's, it appeared, but to a sort of Arabian paradise, complete with teen-age houris.

There were sudden startled yelps; the nearest girls fled, squealing. Others bobbed into view, saw O'Leary, hastily hitched up towels and dashed away, adding to the outcry.

"Oh, no," Lafayette muttered. "Not again . . . " He moved off quickly to his left, encountered a corner and the sound of running water. He tried the other direction, spotted the darker rectangle of a doorless arch, made for it—and collided with a vast bulk in bundlesome tweeds hurtling through from the room beyond. There was a bleat like the cry of an outraged cow hippo defending her young; a rolled umbrella whistled past O'Leary's ear. He ducked; the shadowy giantess charged again, emitting piercing shrieks against the background of lesser yelps. Lafayette backed away, warding off a rain of blows from the flailing implement.

"Madam, you don't understand!" he shouted over the din. "I just wandered in by mistake, and—" his foot slipped. He had a momentary impression of a square red face like a worn-out typist's cushion closing in, the mouth gaping, tiny eyes glaring. Then a bomb exploded and sent him hurtling into a bottomless darkness.

"The way I see it, chief," a meaty voice was saying, "this character hides out over on the men's side last night, see? Then after the joint's locked up, he goes up a rope, out the skylight, across the roof, in the other skylight, down another rope, and hides out in the shower room until Mrs. Prudlock's early-morning modern dance class gets there—"

"Yeah?" a voice like soft mud came back. "So what'd he do with them ropes? Eat 'em?"

"Huh? How could a guy eat forty feet o' rope, chief?"

"The same way he done all that other stuff you said, lamebrain!"

"Huh?"

"Look, I think I got it, chief," an eager voice announced. "He dresses up like a janitor—"

"Only one janitor at the Y. Ninety years old. Checks out clean. Turned in a complaint last year he seen a nood dame." *Then*: "You boys sure you checked that side door?"

"She was locked up tighter'n a card-sharp's money belt, chief."

"Now, my theory is," another voice put in, "he's come in dressed as a broad, like. And after he's inside—"

"—he puts on tight britches and a cape, and jumps out at old lady Prudlock. Yah!"

The discussion continued. O'Leary sat up, winced at a throb from the back of his head and others from various parts of his body representing blows from Alain's sword, jabs from the pikemen and a few assorted kicks, cuffs and falls. He looked around; he was in a small room with walls of white-washed cement, a bare concrete floor, a no-nonsense toilet minus a lid, a tiny washbowl with one water tap and a mirror above. Two bunks were bolted to the wall, on the lower of which he was sitting. Beyond a wide, steel-grilled door he could see a short stretch of two-tone brown-painted hallway, another barred door and beyond it a group of men in baggy dark blue suits with shiny seats and fat leather holsters strapped to wide hips.

O'Leary got to his feet, made it to the small barred window. Outside, early morning sunshine gleamed down on the drowsy view of the courthouse lawn, the park with the Civil War cannon and the second-best shopping street of Colby Corners. He stumbled back and sank down on the bunk. He was home—that much was clear—but how in the name of Goop had he gotten into the county jail? He had been in a dungeon under the palace—the present quarters were a marked improvement over their Artesian equivalent—and then . . .

Oh, yes. The houris and all that steam, and the big woman with the umbrella . . .

"Look, chief," a rubbery-voice cop was saying, "What's the rap we're hanging on this joker?"

"Whatta ya mean, what's the rap? Peeping Tom, trespasser, breaking and entering, larceny—"

"We didn't find no busted locks, chief. Illegal entry, maybe, but the Y is open to the public."

"Not the YW! Not to the *male* public, it ain't! Besides he probably swiped something!"

"Naw, he just come fer the scenery." Guffaws rewarded this sally. The eager one cleared his throat. "What's the penalty for looking at nood dames, chief?"

"Hey, chief, can we hang a peeping Tom on a guy if he's working in broad daylight?"

O'Leary tuned out the legal hassle. There was something very strange here. From what the cops were saying, it was clear enough that he'd actually *been* in the YW. That part hadn't been a dream, and the knot on the back of his head where the tile floor had come up and hit it confirmed it. The old battleaxe had called in the police, hence his presence in a cell. But how—and why—had he gotten into the shower room in the first place? It was a good five blocks from Mrs. MacGlint's; about the same distance, he realized with dawning comprehension, as that from the Ax and Dragon to the palace. Did that mean that he had actually covered the distances that he had dreamed of moving? Had he walked in his sleep? But he never wore pajamas, and—he looked down quickly, confirming that he was wearing pants—

Tight-fitting pants, of a deep blue, with tiny bows at the knee. And low-cut shoes, with thin soles and silver buckles.

He gulped, staring at himself. Excitement started up, like distant drums. There was something strange here, something more than a back-fired experiment with self-hypnosis.

Artesia was no dream; the clothes he had gotten there were real. And if the clothes were real—he tugged at the cloth, felt its reassuring toughness—then perhaps all of it . . . ?

But the whole thing was too idiotic! O'Leary came to his feet, grunted as his wounds throbbed—those were real enough, too—and took a quick turn up and down the cell. You *couldn't* go to bed and dream, and then wake up and find it had all really happened! Maybe he was at home, dreaming that he was in Artesia dreaming that he was in jail?

Hell, if that were so, he was already hopelessly skitzy. He put a hand against the wall; it was rough, cold, solid. If it wasn't real cement, it might as well be.

O'Leary went back to the bunk and sat down. This was all going to be very hard to explain to Mr. Biteworse. When the story got out that he had been arrested in the girl's shower at the Y, wearing funny pants and a shirt with ruffles—

Well, it was goodbye job—even if the police released him, which seemed unlikely, in view of the charges being discussed in the outer office. He had to do something—but what? If he were back in Artesia, he could simply conjure up a key to the door, and be on his way. Things weren't quite that simple here in Colby Corners. Solid objects had a way of staying solid. If you wanted a telephone, say, you had to go find one previously installed by the Bell Company. You couldn't just whistle it up . . .

Lafayette sat up, holding a tight rein on a racing imagination. After all, he'd dreamed up all of Artesia; why not just one little old telephone? It could be out in the hall, maybe—mounted on the wall. And if he reached through the bars—

It was worth a try. O'Leary rose, eased over to the barred door and stole a look. The coast was clear. He closed his eyes, pictured a phone bolted to the brick wall, surrounded by scribbled numbers, with a tattered book dangling below . . .

Cautiously, he reached, and found nothing. He drew a deep breath, gathered his resources. *It's there,* he hissed. *Just a little farther to the right . . .*

His groping hand encountered something hard, cool. He grasped it, brought it into view. It was an old-fashioned instrument with a brass mouthpiece. He lifted the dangling ear unit and paused. He hadn't seen a phone in Nicodaeus' lab, but that could be fixed. There had been a lot of locked cabinets with solid wood doors; the phone would be fitted inside one of them—the one just to the left as you entered the lab . . .

"Central," a bright voice said tinnily in his ear. "Number, please."

"Ah, nine five three four . . . nine oh oh . . . two one one," Lafayette said, noticing how the number seemed to spell itself out.

"Thank you. Hold the line, please."

He held the receiver, listening to the hum, punctuated by an occasional crackle, then a loud pop. There was a harsh buzz. Pause. Buzz. Pause. What if Nicodaeus wasn't home? The cops would notice him any minute now, and—

There was a clunk! and the sound of heavy breathing.

"Hello?" a deep voice said cautiously.

"Nicodaeus!" Lafayette gripped the earpiece.

"Lafayette! Is it you my boy? I thought—I feared—"

"Yeah, let's skip that for now. I seem to have made a couple of small errors, and now—"

"Lafayette! Where did you get my number? I didn't think—that is, it's unlisted. And—"

"I have my methods—but I'll go into all that later. I need help! What I want to know is, ah, where—I mean, how—oh, dammit, I don't know what I need! But—"

"Dear me, this is all very confusing, Lafayette. Where did you say you are now?"

"I'd tell you, but I'm afraid you wouldn't understand! You see, you don't actually exist—that is, I just thought of you—but then, when Goruble slapped me in the cell, I decided to wake up—and here I was!"

"Lafayette—you've hurt your head, poor lad. Now, about my telephone number—"

"To heck with your telephone number! Get me out of here! I've got half a dozen stupid cops debating which of six assorted felonies I'm to be held without bail for—"

"Dumb cops, huh?" an ominous voice growled. The phone was yanked from Lafayette's hand and he stared into the bovine countenance of a thick-lipped redhead with old boxing scars on his cheekbones.

"You don't talk to no mouthpiece without the chief says okay, see?" The cop put the phone out of sight. "An' that'll be a dime for the call."

"Put it on my bill," Lafayette said bitterly. The cop snorted and turned away.

With a groan, Lafayette stretched out on the hard bunk and closed his eyes. Maybe it was nutty, but his only chance seemed to be to try to get out of this idiotic situation the same way he'd gotten into it. All he had to do was slide back into some other dream; a nice, restful place this time, he decided; to hell with romantic old streets and cozy taverns and beautiful princesses . . . But Adoranne *had* been gorgeous—and that flimsy nightgown . . . Damn shame he had to go off like that, leaving her thinking he was a liar and a cheat.

The man—the one who had come for him—had there been something familiar about the fellow? Who had sent him—and why? Alain, maybe? No, the count was a stuffed shirt, but not really the devious type; he'd simply have run him through. Nicodaeus? But what motive would he have?

O'Leary's ruminations were cut short by a sudden sensation of sliding, as though the cell had silently skidded a foot in some undefined direction. He sat up, staring across at the window. There were red-checked curtains beside it and a potted geranium on the sill—

Curtains? Geranium? O'Leary jumped to his feet and stared around the room. It was low-ceilinged, crooked-floored, spotlessly clean, with a feather bed in a polished wooden frame, a three-legged stool and a door made of wooden planks. Gone were the iron-grilled door, the concrete walls, the barred window, the cops. He went to the window, looked out at a steep street filled with the ring of a blacksmith's hammer, the shouts of stall-keepers hawking their wares. Half-timbered fronts loomed up across the way, and behind and beyond he saw the pennant turrets of a castle. He was back in Artesia!

O'Leary felt himself smiling foolishly. In spite of himself, he was glad to be here. And now that he was, he might as well take the time to clear up his misunderstanding with Adoranne.

O'Leary washed up quickly at the basin on a stand in the corner, tucked in his shirt tail, smoothed back his hair, dropped on the bed one of the small gold pieces he found in his pocket and went down to the street. The hammering, he saw, was emanating from a shop with a sign announcing Flats Fixed While U Wait. A wooden steam cart was jacked up with two wheels on the sidewalk while the smith pounded out a new steel-strap tire for a massive oak wheel.

O'Leary turned down the first side street leading toward the palace, threading his way through a bustling throng of plump Artesian housewives doing their morning shopping at the food stalls. He sniffed and caught the aroma of fresh-baked bread. He hadn't realized how hungry he was. But then he hadn't eaten since—when?

The bake shop was just ahead—into a cozy room crowded by two tiny tables. He ordered pastries and a cup of coffee from a red-cheeked girl in starched white. He reached for his money, hesitated. The city guard just might be looking for him. It wouldn't do to leave a trail of gold pieces all over town, but if there were some smaller coins in among the sovereigns . . .

He concentrated, picturing silver pieces, then checked the contents of his pocket. Success! He selected a quarter, handed it to the girl, started for the door—

"Beg pardon, sir," the girl called after him. "Ye've give me furrin money—by mistake, I don't doubt . . . "

Sure enough, a U.S. two-bit piece. "Sorry," he muttered; he took out a gold piece and handed it over. "Keep the change." He flashed her a quick smile, started out—

"But sir! A whole sovereign! Wait here half a sec and I'll pop across to Master Samuel's stall and—"

"Never mind; I'm...ah...in a hurry." Lafayette went up the steps, the girl behind him.

"Ye must be daft, sir!" she called indignantly. "A sovereign fer tuppence 'orth o' cakes?"

People were staring. A lantern-jawed woman with a basket on her arm jerked as though someone had pulled a wire attached to her neck. She pointed.

"It's him!" she squawked. "Last night, at the grand ball. I seen the rascal, plain as I'm seeing him now, when I come in to trim the wicks!"

Lafayette plunged past her, rounded a corner at a full run. Behind him a shout was rising; feet pounded in pursuit. He glanced back, saw a big-chested man in an open vest round the corner, hair flying, legs pumping.

O'Leary sprinted, bowled over a cart loaded with gimcracks and miniature pink-and-white Artesian flags, skidded into a narrow alley, pounded up a cobbled way toward the looming wall of a church. Someone shot from a side alley ahead, whirled, arms spread; Lafayette straight-armed him, jumped the sprawling body, emerged into an open court. There was an eight-foot wall rimming the yard. He ran for it, leaped, caught the top, pulled himself up and over. He dropped into a tiny back yard where an old man trimming roses with a pair of heavy shears opened a toothless mouth as Lafayette bounded past him through a door, along a short dark hall redolent of wood smoke and burst out onto a quiet side street. He paused a moment, took a deep breath, looked left and right.

The hunt, rounding the corner half a block above, gave a shout as they saw him. He whirled, dashed off down

the slope. If he could make the turn ahead in time to
duck out of sight before they caught up . . .

The street curved, widened into a plaza with a fountain
surrounded by flower stalls and a dense throng of shop-
pers, vivid in the shafts of morning light pouring down
past the cathedral towers. An inviting street turned off
to the left just ahead. He ducked into a crouch as he
pushed in among the crowd; maybe they wouldn't pick
him out in the press if he didn't stick up so high. People
gave way before him as he worked his way through, back
curved, neck bent. A motherly woman handed him a
copper. A legless man seated under the lamp post on
the corner with a hat in his lap gave him a resentful look.

"Hey, buddy, you joined the union?"

O'Leary dodged past him, straightened, went up the
street at a lope. The geography of the town, it occurred
to him, was similar to that of Colby Corners. The main
difference was that back home they'd leveled the ground;
here the streets wound up and down over the little hills
and valleys that in a less romantic clime had been hammered into drab horizontality.

The street he was now in was analogous to the alley
running behind Pott's Drug Store and Hambanger's
Hardware. That being the case, if he took a right just
ahead, and another right, he'd hit the park—and maybe,
among the trees and underbrush, he could lose his pursu-
ers. He could hear them behind him, closing in again.
He caught a glimpse as he rounded the corner. A big
man with a pitchfork was in the lead now, running hard.
Lafayette ran for the next turn, skidded into it, pelted
uphill, saw the gap ahead where the buildings ended and
the open green began. He leaped for the grass, threw

himself flat behind a hedge, twisted to see the pursuit streaming past. Nobody, as far as he could tell, had noticed his dash for the park. Maybe he was safe here for a while.

He cautiously worked his way behind the shelter of the hedge to a clump of arbor vitae. He rested for a moment, then crawled inside the concealment of the ring of trees. It was quiet here, in a green gloom of leaf-filtered sunlight. He settled himself on a carpet of piney mold and prepared to wait until dark. Apparently the story of his having invaded the princess's bedroom was all over town. Until he cleared up that little misunderstanding, there'd be no peace and quiet for him here.

A large, peach-colored crescent moon had risen behind the church towers before O'Leary emerged from his sanctuary. The streets, inadequately illuminated by the yellow gaslights at the corners, were deserted. A few small windows gleamed warm yellow and orange against the dark facades, shedding patches of light on the cobbles below. O'Leary moved along quickly across the park and found the high wall that surrounded the palace grounds. The palace itself, of course, was located in the same relative position as the YMCA back in Plainview. The gate was half a block ahead; he could see the sentry in his bearskin shako standing stiffly at parade rest before the narrow sentry box. No use trying to get through there; he'd be recognized in an instant.

O'Leary turned in a direction opposite to that of the gate. Ten minutes later, in the deep shadow of a clump of tall elms growing just inside the wall, he looked carefully in both directions, then found fingerholds, scrambled up the wall and peered over the top. No guards were in sight. Cautiously, he pulled himself higher, threw a leg over and crouched astride the wall. The tree that provided the shadow was too high, he saw, craning his neck, to be of any help.

Below there was a sudden thump of feet, the unmistakable rasp of a blade sliding from a sheath.

"Hold, varlet!" a hostile voice barked. Lafayette, startled by the sudden interruption, grabbed to retain his balance, missed, went over sideways with a choked yell. He saw the flash of light along a bared blade, had just an instant to picture himself impaled on it as he twisted aside and landed full on the man with a impact that knocked the breath from him. He rolled free and saw the watchman stretched on his back, out cold. Someone shouted—from the left, O'Leary thought. He came to his feet, struggling to breathe, and staggered off in the direction of the deepest shadow. Running feet approached. O'Leary leaned against the three-foot trunk of the largest elm, drawing painful breaths.

"It's Morton," a squeaky voice piped. "Somebody clobbered him!"

"He couldn'a of went far," a deep voice boomed. "You check over that way, Hymie; I'll scout along here."

O'Leary tried to quiet his wheezing; he heard hoarse breathing, the whack of a sword blade beating the bushes against the wall. He eased around the trunk as the searcher passed six feet away. O'Leary then tiptoed toward some shrubbery across the path twenty feet distant.

"Grab him, Hymie!" the deep voice yelled from the other direction. Lafayette sprang into action, dived for cover, hit the dirt, wriggled through, rose to a crouch on

the far side, scuttled for the shelter of an ornamental
hedge.

Another man, looking tall in a floppy hat and boots,
sprang from nowhere into his path, brandished a sword
aloft and charged with a yell. O'Leary ducked aside and
dashed for the hedge, rounded right end, leaped to a
marble bench, veered barely in time to miss the lily pool.
There was a yell and splash behind him; the pursuer had
misjudged the water hazard.

In the clear for the moment, O'Leary sprinted for the
tall shadow of the palace, angling to the right to miss a
pavilion glowing with strung lanterns. Judging from the
yells, he had a dozen men on his trail now, mostly behind
him, but some ahead, off to the right. If he could reach
the shelter of the wall before they spotted him . . .

Two men dashed into view ahead and skidded to a halt.
"They went that way!" O'Leary shouted. The two new-
comers whirled and dashed back out of sight. O'Leary
veered sharply, reached a line of trees leading generally
palaceward and pounded ahead. A wing of the massive
building stretched out toward the trees. O'Leary cleared
the end of the row, raced for the refuge of the deep
shadows ahead and saw a man back into view fifty yards
distant, his attention on the bushes from which he had
emerged. Lafayette put on a spurt, dived for the tangle
of ivy against the palace wall just as the fellow turned.

"Hey! Here he is, boys!" the man yelled. O'Leary muttered curses and worked his way behind the trailing curtain of vines, forcing his way along against the rough-
hewn stone blocks. Feet pelted past and he froze; voices
called near at hand. There was the clang of a blade thrust
through the vines.

"We got him pinned down, men!" someone exulted. "Spread out and work that ivy!" More clashing of metal against stone, coming closer. O'Leary moved cautiously, gained another foot. Tricky work, trying not to shake the vines. But if he could just get past the corner.

A projecting buttress blocked his way. He felt along its edge; the vine cover ended two feet along it. He was trapped—cornered. Unless . . .

O'Leary closed his eyes, remembering the palace layout. This was the southwest face of the building. He'd never been on this side of the palace, so it ought to be safe.

He pictured a door, just a small one, set a foot or two above ground level. It was made of stout oak planks, weathered but sound, and it was secured by a hasp—a rusty one. Very rusty. It was concealed by the vines, of course, and opened into a forgotten passage which led—somewhere.

At the comforting jolt in the smooth flow of the universe, O'Leary opened his eyes, started feeling over the wall, as steel clashed less than ten feet away. His hands encountered wood, a rough frame, then the door, a squat entry four feet by five, with rust-scaled hinges and a massive padlock dangling from a corroded hasp. O'Leary let out his breath in a preliminary sigh of relief, pushed against the panel. It stirred, came up against the restraint of the hasp. He pushed harder; rusted screws tore out of the wood with a crunching sound.

"Hark, men! What's that?" Hands were tearing at the vines. O'Leary pushed at the resisting door, got it open a foot, slipped inside, forced it shut behind him. A moldering beam lay on the floor; brackets to fit it were mounted on either side of the doorway. He lifted the timber, grunting, settled it into place as a hand slammed the oak from the outside.

"Hey, Sarge! A door! Look!" a muffled voice came through the barrier. More talk, thumps, then a heavy blow.

"He couldn'a got through there, ya dummy, it's locked."

"Hey—if this guy's a like sorcerer . . ."

"Yeah, what's a locked door to a guy like that?"

O'Leary looked both ways along a narrow, low-ceilinged passage, closely resembling the one through which he had been led to Adoranne's room—less than twenty-four hours before, he realized with wonderment; it seemed like days. As for the passage, it was probably part of a system running all through the building. With a little luck, he'd be able to find his way back to the princess' apartment and explain what had happened without having to venture out into the open.

He moved off, barely able to see by random glints of dim light filtering through chinks in the crudely mortared walls. The passage ran straight for twenty feet, then right-angled. There was a door a few feet beyond the turn. O'Leary tried the latch; it opened, revealing a wide, clean room, smoothly floored, crowded with bulky dark shapes the size of upright pianos. Along the left wall there was a complex pattern of highlights from massed dial faces and polished metal fittings. To the right, more panels, like computer programmer's consoles, were set under wide TV-type screens.

The whole thing, O'Leary thought, looked like a block-house where a space shot was being readied. How did all this fit into the simple Artesian scene? True, there were a few electric lights in the palace, and he had seen a number of clumsy mechanical devices in use—but nothing approaching the technology implied here. It didn't make sense—unless Nicodaeus knew something about it. That had to be it. There was definitely something fishy about the court magician. That candid camera he'd used, disguised as a lighter, for example . . .

But that wasn't finding Adoranne. He closed the door, noting the thick metal plate bolted to it. It would take some doing to force your way past that. He went on along the passage, passed a heavy metal-clad door like a butcher's walk-in refrigerator. More modern devices; maybe Nicodaeus had set it up and stocked it with foods in season, which he later miraculously produced. There was nothing like fresh frozen strawberries in the dead of winter to endear a sorcerer to a gourmet king.

Thirty feet past the refrigerator, the passage dead-ended. O'Leary thumped the walls, looking for concealed doors, then started back the way he had come—and stopped dead at a sound from the darkness ahead.

He stood, head cocked, listening, aware of the musty odor of the dead air, the rasp of his own breathing. The sound came again—a soft scraping. He flattened himself against the wall. There was a movement—a stirring of shadows against the darkness. Something was coming toward him—something bulky, crouched, no more than waist-high. O'Leary tried twice, managed to swallow. No wonder the secret passages were deserted; ordinarily, he didn't believe in spectral ogres, but—

It was closer now, no more than two yards away, waiting there in the darkness. O'Leary pictured diabolical eyes studying him, goblin fangs gaping . . .

He fumbled in his pockets; he had no weapon—damned careless of him. But he couldn't just stand here and wait to be savaged; he'd rather attack in the blind, come to grips with whatever it was. He took a deep breath, set himself—

"Hiya, Sir Lafayette," a bass voice rumbled. "What you doing down here?"

O'Leary jumped violently, cracking his head, and slumped back against the wall, weak with relief.

"Yokabump," he managed. "Fancy meeting you here."

Chapter Seven

"You're lucky I run into you," Yokabump was saying. "Duck your head now; low bridge."

Behind him, Lafayette maneuvered around a massive timber that half blocked the cramped way. "You're so right," he agreed. "I never would have found that stairway. I wonder how many people know about all these hidden entrances into their rooms?"

"Not many."

"Well, next time I'm chased at least I'll have somewhere to hide."

"There's some folks around here might say I shouldn't be helping you out," the dwarf said.

"I can explain all that nonsense about me being in her Highness' room," O'Leary began.

"Never mind, Sir Lafayette. I'm just the court jester; I supply the boffs and let the gentry work out their own problems. But I got confidence in you."

"I suppose you mean because of my ring—the ax and dragon."

"Nay, I don't go for that legend jazz. Anyway, that's just a story old Gory cooked up himself, back when he was new on the job. Propaganda, you know; people were restless. They kind of liked the old king, and who ever heard of this Cousin Goruble? There's still lots of folk think her Highness ought to be setting on the throne right now."

"I take it King Goruble isn't too popular?"

"Ah, he's OK—kind of strict, I guess—but you can't blame him, since this bird Lod made the scene. Him and his pet dragon—"

"More folklore, I take it?"

"Well, I never actually *seen* this dragon."

"Hmmm. Funny how nobody I've met has seen it, but they all believe in it."

"Yeah—well, here we are." Yokabump had halted at a blank wall. "This here is the panel that opens into her Highness' bedroom. I guess you know what you're doing—and I ain't going to ask you why you're going in there. When I trust a guy, I trust him all the way."

"Well, that's very decent of you, Yokabump. I have her Highness' best interests at heart."

"Sure. But look, Sir Lafayette, give me about five minutes to do a fade, OK? I don't want to be nowhere around in case anything goes wrong."

"If I'm captured, I won't implicate you, if that's what you mean."

"Good luck, Sir Lafayette," the rumbling voice breathed. There was a soft rustle, and O'Leary was alone. He waited, counting slowly to three hundred, then felt over the panel, found an inconspicuous latch at one side; it clicked as he flipped it up. The panel moved smoothly aside. He peered out into the dark room. Only a few hours ago, a hand had propelled him violently through the same opening; now he was back, voluntarily.

He stepped through onto the deep pile rug. He could see the shape of the big canopied bed.

"Adoranne!" he whispered, moving forward softly. "Don't yell. It's me, Lafayette! I want to explain . . . " his voice trailed off. Even in the dim moonlight filtering through the gauzy curtains at the high windows, he could see that the bed was empty.

A five-minute search confirmed no one was in the apartment. O'Leary stood by the ornately carved gold and white dressing table, feeling unaccountably let down. But after all, why should he have blandly assumed she'd be here? Probably there was a big party going on, and she was there, dancing with Count Alain.

But never mind that train of thought. It was time to go—before the fat lady-in-waiting came in and set up a howl. He went back to the inner doorway leading to the bedroom—and stopped short at the sound of voices. The door on the far side of the bedroom opened, and O'Leary ducked back as the maid came in, accompanied by an old man with a mop. The girl sniffled.

"It . . . it ain't . . . the same . . . "

"Never mind that; tears won't help nothing . . . "

O'Leary ducked across the room and tried the hall door. It opened. He peeked cautiously out; the corridor was dim-lit, deserted. Strange. Usually, ceremonial—or perhaps not ceremonial—guards were posted every fifty feet along the hall. And it was a little early for Nicodaeus' fifty-volt lighting system to be turned down so far.

He went along the carpeted corridor to the wide, ornate door, white with gold carving, that separated Adoranne's private quarters from the public area. He tried the gleaming golden handle. It opened. He went through and started off toward the next room from which he could re-enter the secret passage system.

Someone was coming; low voices muttered. O'Leary ran for it, ducked down a side hallway, slid to a halt as he saw a guard posted as the next intersection. The man was yawning; he hadn't seen O'Leary.

Just ahead was a narrow door. O'Leary stepped quickly to it, opened it, ducked through. Steps led upward. He could go up or back out into the hall. He paused with a hand on the door, hearing soft footfalls just outside. That narrowed the choice down; he turned and started up the winding stairs.

Five minutes later, winded by the climb, O'Leary reached a heavy door opening from a tiny landing at the top of the stairs. He listened, then tried the latch. The door opened noiselessly. He poked his head in, wrinkling his nose at a heavy stench resembling burnt pork that accompanied a dense cloud of greenish fumes boiling from an open pan placed over a tripod. Through the smoke he saw the tall figure of Nicodaeus, bent over a workbench, absorbed, his back to the door.

O'Leary studied the narrow, granite-walled chamber, floored with vast stone slabs, lit by giant candles guttering on stands, its ceiling lost in shadows and cobwebs. There were cabinets, shelves, chests, all piled with stuffed owls, alarm clocks, old boots, bottles and jars and cans both full and empty; against the walls wooden crates were stacked, cryptic symbols stenciled on their sides in red and yellow and black. Along one side of the room ran a workbench, littered with tools, bits of wire, odd-shaped bits of metal and glass and plastic. Above it was a black crackle-finish panel, set with dozens of round glass dials against which needles trembled. Double doors at the far end of the room were half-concealed by a heavy hanging. From the ceiling, a gilded human skeleton dangled from a wire.

O'Leary slipped inside, closed the door behind him, silently shot the bolt. The stench was really terrible. Lafayette concentrated, remembering his success with the goaty girl at the tavern. Roasted coffee, say; that would be a marked improvement . . .

He felt the subtle jar that indicated success. The color of the smoke changed to a reddish brown; the greasy smell faded, to be replaced by the savory aroma of fresh-ground coffee beans.

Nicodaeus straightened, went across to the instrument display panel, jabbed at buttons. A small screen glowed pale green. The magician muttered, jotting notes—then paused, ballpoint posed. He sniffed, whirled suddenly—

"Lafayette! Where did—how—what?"

"One question at a time, Nicodaeus! I had a hell of a time getting to you; the whole town's gone crazy. You don't have anything to eat handy, do you? I've been lying under a bush in the park all day."

"Lafayette! My boy, you've repented! You've come to me to make a clean breast of it, to tell me where you've hidden her! I'll go to his Majesty—"

"Hold it!" O'Leary sank down on a wobbly stool. "I haven't repented of anything, Nicodaeus! I told you somebody came to my room, told me Adoranne was in trouble and led me into a secret passage. Then the double-crosser gave me a push and shoved some junk into my hand, and the lights went on."

"Certainly, lad, and now you've decided to throw yourself on his Majesty's mercy."

"You mean apologize for not letting him cut me into slices for something I didn't do? Ha! Look here, Nicodaeus, there's something funny going on around here. I went to see Adoranne and explain what happened. She thinks I stole her crown jewels or . . ." He broke off, seeing the expression on the other's face. "What's the matter?" He came to his feet in sudden alarm. "She hasn't been hurt?"

"You mean—you really don't know?" Nicodaeus blinked through his rimless glasses.

"Don't know what?" O'Leary yelled. "Where's Adoranne?"

Nicodaeus' shoulders slumped. "I had hoped you could tell *me* that, Lafayette. She's been missing since some time before dawn. And everyone thinks you, my boy, are the one who stole her."

"You're all out of your minds," O'Leary said, finishing off a cracker with sardines—the only rations, it appeared, that Nicodaeus kept handy. "I was locked in a cell. How could I have kidnapped her? And why?"

"But you escaped from the cell. And as to why . . . " Nicodaeus looked wise. "Need one ask?"

"Yes, one need ask! I'm not likely to drag a girl away in the middle of the night just to . . . just to . . . do whatever people do with girls they drag away in the middle of the night."

"But, Lafayette!" Nicodaeus twisted his hands together. "Everyone's assumed you were the kidnapper. So who kidnapped her? And why?"

"I don't know who! You're supposed to be some kind of a magician; can't you find out things?"

"*Now* who believes in magic?" Nicodaeus inquired sardonically. He shot Lafayette a keen look. "By the way, I noted a severe energy drain recorded in the beta scale at 6:15 this morning. Then about ten minutes later—the would be at 6:25–there was the first of a series of lesser disturbances, that have continued at intervals all day."

"What are you measuring? Is this some sort of seismograph?"

Nicodaeus studied O'Leary's face. "See here, Lafayette, isn't it time you spoke frankly to me? I confess I don't know just what the connection might be between you and the data I've been collecting ever since your arrival—but it's more than coincidence."

"That giant!" O'Leary interrupted suddenly. "Cludd, or whatever his name is! Is there really any such ogre, or is he somebody's pet superstition, like the Phantom Highwayman and Goruble's dragon?"

"Oh, Lod exists. I can vouch for that, my boy. He visited the city, not a month ago. Thousands of people saw him; three meters tall, as broad as I can reach with both arms wide, and ugly as a wart hog!"

"Then he must be the one! Didn't they say he came here courting Adoranne? Then, when he was turned down, he planned this kidnapping—"

"And how, dear lad, would Lod—enormous, ungainly, with a price on his head and known to every subject in the country—slip into town, remove the princess from the midst of her guards and get away clean?"

"Somebody did, and it wasn't me! There are secret passages in the palace—I wouldn't be surprised if one of them led to a tunnel that would take you right outside the city walls. I want a good horse—"

"But, Lafayette, where would I get a horse?"

"You've got one waiting at the postern gate, remember? Don't stall, Nicodaeus! This is serious!"

"Oh, *that* horse . . . Mmmmm. Yes, perhaps. But—"

"Stop saying 'but'! Get me the horse and stock the saddlebags with food and a change of socks and . . . and whatever I might need. And don't forget a road map."

"Umm. Yes. Look here, Lafayette, you may be right. Lod *could* be the kidnapper. A difficult trip, though. Do you really intend to try, single-handed?"

"Yes, and I need help! You've double-crossed me a few times, but maybe that was just misguided loyalty. You *are* fond of Adoranne, aren't you?"

"Double-crossed? Why, Lafayette—"

There was a thunderous hammering at the door. Lafayette jumped. Nicodaeus whirled to him, pointing to the heavy hangings at the narrow end of the room.

"Quickly!" he whispered. "Behind the drapes!"

Lafayette sprang to the hiding place Nicodaeus had indicated and slipped behind the heavy hangings. There was a cold draft on his back. He turned, saw double glass doors standing ajar. A tiny balcony was dimly visible in the darkness beyond them. He stepped out into cold night air and a light drizzle of icy rain.

"Swell," he muttered, huddling against the ivy-covered wall beside the door. Through a narrow gap in the draperies he could see the magician hurrying across the room, drawing the bolt. The door burst open and armed men pushed through—two, three, more. Word must have spread that he had gotten into the palace. Probably they were searching every room.

Two men were coming across toward the hangings behind which O'Leary had been hidden a minute before. He threw a leg over the iron railing, slid down, found a toehold in the tangled vines beneath the balcony, his eyes at floor level. Through the glass door, he saw a sword blade stabbing through the drapes. The point struck the door and glass broke with a light tinkle. O'Leary ducked down and clambered in close under the shelter of the overhang of the balcony, gripping the wet vines. Above, the doors crashed wide open. Boots crunched glass above his head.

"Not out here," a gruff voice said.

"I told you—" the rest of Nicodaeus's speech was cut off by the clump of boots, the slamming of doors. Lafayette held on, shivering in the cold wind; water dripped from the end of his nose. He looked down. Below, there was nothing but darkness and the drumming of rain, heavier now. Not a very enticing climb, but he couldn't stay here.

He started down, groping for footholds on the wet stone, clinging to the stiff vines with hands that were rapidly growing numb. Wet leaves jabbed at his face, dribbling water down inside his sodden jacket.

Twenty feet below the level of the balcony, he found a horizontal stone coping and followed it along to the corner. The wind was stronger here, buffeting him, driving stinging rain into his eyes. He retreated to the opposite side of the tower. He was about fifteen feet above the slanting, copper-green plates of the roof over the main residential wing now. He'd have to descend, get past the eaves, and then make it to the ground without being seen. Far below, torches moved about the gardens; faint shouts rang out. The palace guard was out in force tonight.

It was a tricky climb down from the ledge to the roof below; only the thick-growing vines made it possible. O'Leary reached the roof, braced himself with one foot in the heavy copper gutter, now gurgling with runoff from the gable above, and rested five minutes. Then he gripped the vines firmly and lowered himself out and over the wide overhang of the roof. He swung his legs, groping for support, but found nothing. The vines here were sparser than above; probably they had been thinned to clear the downspout.

He let himself down another foot; the edge of the roof was at chin level now. He tried again and again failed to find a foothold. The strain on his icy hands was getting a bit tiresome. He slipped farther down, hanging at arm's length now, and ducked his head under the overhang. The face of the building was a good three feet distant—and as bare of ivy as a billboard. There was a window there, six feet to the left—but it was dark, shuttered and out of reach even if it had been wide open.

O'Leary grunted, hitching himself along to the left. Quite suddenly, he was aware of the hundred feet of empty night air yawning below him. Was that where he was going to end, after all? His hands were stiffening; he couldn't tell if he was gripping the vines hard, or if his hold was weakening, slipping . . .

With a desperate surge, O'Leary swung his legs and managed to slam one toe against the boarded window. Out of reach; he couldn't make it. Could he go back? He struggled to pull himself up, felt the edge of the roof cutting into his wrists; he kicked his legs vainly, then hung slackly. *Maybe five minutes*, he thought. *Then my grip will loosen and down I'll go . . .*

Abruptly, the shutters on the window clanked open. A pale, frightened face looked out, framed by dark hair.

"Daphne!" O'Leary croaked. "Help!"

"Sir Lafayette!" Her voice was a gasp. She thrust the shutter back and the wind caught it, thumping it against the stone. Daphne stretched out her arms. "Can you—can you reach me?"

O'Leary summoned his strength, swung his foot; Daphne grabbed and the buckled shoe came off in her hand. She tossed it behind her, brushed back a strand of hair with the back of her hand and leaned farther out.

"Again!" she said. O'Leary sucked in air, swung himself back, kicked out; the chambermaid's strong fingers gripped his ankle. She leaned back, pulled his lower leg across the sill, then grabbed the other foot as it swung forward. O'Leary felt his grip going as the girl tugged.

He gave himself a last thrust; his hands came free, and he was swinging down.

His back slammed the wall with a thud that knocked the wind from his lungs. Dizzily, he groped upward, caught the sill with one hand. Daphne seized his arm and tumbled him inside.

"You're . . . strong for a . . . girl . . ." O'Leary managed. "Thanks."

"Comes of swinging a broom all day, sir," she said breathlessly. "Are you all right?"

"Fine. How'd you happen to be there at just the right moment?"

"I heard the outcry above; I ran up to Nicodaeus' tower to see what was afoot. The guardsmen were in a pet, dashing about and cursing. Nicodaeus whispered to me it was you—that you'd gone over the balcony rail. I thought maybe I could catch a glimpse of you from the window—if you hadn't fallen, that is . . . and—"

"Look, Daphne, you saved my life. But—" he frowned, remembering his last conversation with the girl. "Why aren't you in jail?"

"King Goruble pardoned me. He was quite sweet about it; said a child like me couldn't be guilty. He wouldn't even let them hold a hearing."

"Well, the old grouch has a few redeeming traits, after all." O'Leary got to his feet, rubbing his lacerated wrists. "Listen, I have to get out of here. It's a bit too hot for me right now. I've just heard about Adoranne's kidnapping, and I—" he broke off. "*You* didn't think I was mixed up in that, did you?"

"I . . . I didn't know, sir. I'm glad if you're not. Her Highness is so lovely, though, and a gentleman like you . . . " She looked at her feet.

"A gentleman like me doesn't resort to kidnapping to get a girl. But I think I may have a lead. If you'll get me to one of the entries to the hidden passage system, I'll try to follow it up."

"Hidden passages, sir?"

"Sure, they run all through the palace. There are entries from just about every room in the building. Where are we now?"

"This is an unused storeroom, just down the hall from the suite of the Earl of Nussex."

"Is he in?"

"No, sir; he's off with one of the troops searching for her Highness."

"That'll do, then."

He found his shoe, put it on and followed as Daphne checked the corridor. She led him along to a locked door which she opened with one of the keys on a ring at her waist. He took her hand.

"By the way, you don't happen to know where Lod's headquarters is, do you?"

"In the desert to the west."

"Um. That's all anyone seems to know. Thanks for everything, Daphne." He leaned and kissed her smooth cheek.

"Where will you go?" she asked, wide-eyed.

"To find Lod."

"Sir—will you be safe?"

"Sure. Wish me luck."

"G-good luck, sir."

He slid inside the room, crossed to the panel Yoka-bump had pointed out to him earlier and stepped through into close, musty darkness.

Two hours later, O'Leary was in a twisting alleyway under the shadow of the city wall three-quarters of a mile from the palace grounds. Sheltered in the lee of a tumble-down shack, he breathed hard from the climb, the dash from one covering shrub to another across the wide palace lawns, the sprint through the gate while the sentry investigated a sound made by a thrown pine cone, the rapid walk through the streets to this noisome corner of the city slum. He was soaked to the skin, shivering. His hands were cut and scratched, yesterday's bruises still ached. The scant meal Nicodaeus had given him hardly assuaged the pangs of a day's fast.

It was raining harder now. O'Leary felt his teeth clatter; his bones felt like something rudely chipped from ice. At this rate he'd have pneumonia before morning—particularly if he spent the night standing out in the chill, raw wind.

He couldn't knock at a door and ask for shelter; every citizen in town seemed to know him. The clever thing to do would be to abandon this foolishness, shift back to Colby Corners and his room, and get what sleep he could. Tomorrow he could call Mr. Biteworse and explain his absence as being due to a sudden attack of flu . . .

But what about Adoranne? He pictured her waking up to find someone's hand over her mouth. The villain must have gotten in via the secret passage, of course. He probably gagged her, bound her hand and foot, slung her over a hard shoulder and carted her off to some robber hideout.

O'Leary couldn't abandon her. He might fail, but he couldn't leave without trying. But what could he do? At the moment he was a hunted fugitive with no one to turn to. His only friend, Nicodaeus, had been suspiciously quick about letting the soldiers in—and they'd rushed directly to his hiding place. If he hadn't climbed outside, prompted by some obscure instinct, he'd have been run through. Had the magician deliberately betrayed him? What reason would he have? True, he'd been eager to see the last of O'Leary; all that talk about fast horses at the postern gate—but then Nicodaeus *had* helped him at the trial . . .

He'd been lucky to get clear of the palace. The outcry inside had drawn off most of the guard force, fortunately, so he hadn't had to lie low in the mud more than half a dozen times before reaching the gate. He wiped his muddy palms on sodden trousers and shivered again. Briefly, he thought of conjuring up the image of the princess locked in the nearest hut, say. He could break in the door, and there she'd be . . .

It was no use. He didn't believe it. He was too tired to conjure up the impossible. She was miles from here, and he knew it. He needed food, warmth, sleep; then perhaps he could make his mind work again. He looked at the sagging structure against which he huddled. It was a shed no more than six feet by eight, with a roof of sodden thatch. The door was a battered agglomeration of mismatched boards, held together by a pair of rusting iron straps and hanging crookedly from one rotten leather hinge. He prodded it and it slumped even farther; O'Leary caught a glimpse of a dark interior.

He looked away quickly; no point in making *that* mistake again. There was no telling what that rude exterior might house—or be made to house. Perhaps it was a secret hideaway, fitted out by some adventurer with a need for private quarters away from the hubbub of busy streets—well camouflaged, of course . . .

No use carrying the rationalization too far, O'Leary reminded himself. Firmly, he pictured sound walls under the moldering slabs, a snug, waterproof roof concealed by the defunct thatch, a weatherproof door, an adequate heating system—a gas fire with artificial logs, perhaps, fed by bottled propane. Add a rug—cold floors were rough on bare feet, a shower stall with plenty of hot water—there'd been a shortage of that, even in the palace, a tiny refrigerator, well-stocked, a bunk—a wide one, with a good quality mattress . . .

O'Leary completed his mental picture, filling in the details with loving attention. Of course, it was there, he told himself; he needed a hideout.

Time seemed to hesitate for an instant; then O'Leary smiled grimly and reached for the door . . .

Half an hour later, with the door locked firmly against intruders, clean and warm after a hot shower, O'Leary finished off his second Bavarian ham on Swiss rye, quaffed the last of the sixteen-ounce bottle of lager, pulled the feather comforter up snug about his ears and settled down to catch up on some much needed rest.

The alarm clock he had thoughtfully provided woke him with chimes at dawn. He stretched, yawned, blinked at the glass door to the shower stall, the pale green walls, the olive-carpeted floor, the dark green wall-mounted refrigerator, and cheery fire on the hearth. Now, just where was he? There was Mrs. MacGlint's—or had that been an evil dream? And his room at the palace, and the bunk in the cell at the police station, and a room with a flowerpot . . . and oh, yes, the converted hut here. Quite cozy. He nodded approvingly. He was always waking up in different places these days, it seemed.

O'Leary threw back the coverlet, checked the refrigerator, nibbled a cold chicken leg, then showered while sorting out kaleidoscopic impressions of the day before. It was getting harder and harder to recall just what had been a dream and what hadn't—or whether there was any distinction. The visit to the palace, now. Had that been real? He looked at his hands. They were badly scraped. Uh-huh, that had been real all right. Nicodaeus had nearly gotten him killed, the skunk—unless it was S.O.P. to run swords through curtains first thing when searching a room.

And Adoranne was gone, kidnapped. That was the important fact. He'd have to do something about that, right away. Funny how different everything seemed in the morning, with a meal and a night's sleep behind him. He wasn't worried. Somehow he'd recover Adoranne, explain the business of the midnight visit and the bag of loot, and then . . . Well, then he could play it by ear. And now to business.

He tried the door to the clothespress, discovered a handsome outfit consisting of modern-style whipcord riding breeches, a heavy gray flannel shirt, cordovan boots, a short lined windbreaker, a pair of pigskin driving gloves, and—incongruously—a rapier in a businesslike sheath attached to a Western-style leather belt. He dressed, quickly fried three eggs and half a dozen strips of bacon and washed up after breakfast.

The rain had stopped when O'Leary closed the door carefully behind him. The shack, he noted with approval, looked as derelict as ever. Now to action. The first step . . .

He paused, standing in the garbage-strewn, dawn-lit alley. What *was* the first step? Where did Lod stay when he wasn't off on a raid? What was it they had said? In the desert to the west? Not much in the way of travel directions. He had to have more information—and he couldn't just collar a passer-by. The first question put to a local citizen would have the pack howling on his heels again before he could say "post-hypnotic suggestion."

Heavy boots clumped along the alley, coming closer. O'Leary made a move to duck into concealment . . .

Too late; a heavily built man in a greasy sheepskin jacket hove into view and halted at sight of him. Under the damp brim of a wide, shapeless hat, a battered face stared truculently. Then it broke into a crafty, gap-toothed smile.

"Duh Phantom Highwayman!" the newcomer squeaked. "Thay, am I glad to thee *you*! I wanted to thay thanks fer handing the copperth a bum thteer the other night. I don't know how youse thwung it, but they didn't theem to know me from Adam'th off okth."

"Oh, it's the Red Bull," O'Leary said cautiously. "Ah, glad to help out. Well, I have to run along now."

"I hear you're duh one dat thnatched duh princeth. Ith dat tuh thtraight goodth?"

"What, you, too? I had nothing to do with it! I've got an idea this fellow Lod is the guilty party. Maybe you can tell me: exactly where are his headquarters?"

"Youse can level wit' me, bo. I got contacth; we'll work togedduh and thplit duh take."

"Forget it. Now about Lod's hideout—"

"I get it. Youse figger to thell her Highneth to duh Big Boy. What youse figger theyee'll bring?"

"Listen to me, you, you numbskull!" O'Leary shook a fist under the flattened nose. "I'm not involved in the kidnapping! I'm not selling her to anybody! And I'm not interested in any shady deals."

The Red Bull's thick finger prodded O'Leary's chest. "Oh, thtingy, huh? Well, lithen to me, bo—what'th duh idea of working my thection of town, anyway? You thtick to yer highwayth, and leave duh thity to me, thee? And I'm cutting mythelf in on duh thnatch caper, thee? And—"

"There ithn't any thnatch caper—oh, for heaven's sake stop lisping! You've got me doing it!"

"Huh? Look, bo . . . " the Red Bull's voice dropped abruptly to its accustomed bass. "Yuh split wit' me or I cave in yer mush—and den call copper fer duh reward an' a free pardon."

O'Leary slapped the prodding finger aside. "Tell me where Lod's hideout is, you dimwit, and stop babbling about—"

A large hand gathered in the front of O'Leary's new jacket, lifted him to his toes.

"Who yuh calling a dimwit, bo? I got as good a mind as duh next gazebo."

"I happen to be the next gazebo," O'Leary said in a voice somewhat choked by the pressure at his throat. "And I'm an idiot for standing here chinning with you while there's work to be done." He brought up a hand

and chopped down in a side-of-the-palm blow at the base of the Red Bull's thick neck. The grasp on his shirt relaxed as O'Leary delivered a second hearty stroke across the big man's throat that sent him stumbling back. The Red Bull shook his head, roared, started for O'Leary with apelike arms outstretched, and met a kick in the pit of the stomach that doubled him over with a grunt in time to intercept a hard knee coming up to meet his already blunted features. He stumbled aside, one hand on his stomach and the other grasping his bleeding nose.

"Hey, dat's no fair!" he stated. "I never seen duh udder two guys!"

"Sorry. That was in Lesson Three, Unarmed Counterattack. Worked quite well. Now, tell me where I can find Lod. And hurry up—this is important!"

"Lod, huh?" The Red Bull looked disapprovingly at the blood on his hand and moved his head gingerly, testing his neck. "What kind of a split yuh got in mind?"

"No split! I just want to rescue her Highness!"

"How about forty-sixty, and I t'row in a couple o' reliable boys to side yer play wit' Lod?"

"Forget it! I'll ask somebody else." O'Leary straightened his jacket, rubbed the bruised side of his hand, gave the Red Bull a disgusted look and started off up the alley.

"Hey!" The Red Bull trotted to his side. "I got a idea! We split thoidy-seventy; what could be more gennulmanly dan dat?"

"You amaze me; I didn't know you knew that much arithmetic."

"I taken a night course in business math. How about it?"

"No! Get lost! I have things to do! I'm conspicuous enough without Gargantua padding along at my heels!"

"I'll settle for a lousy ten percent, on account of you got such a neat left hand, and duh knee work was nice, too."

"Go away! Depart! Dangle! Be missing! Get hence! Avaunt thee, varlet! No deal!" A small man probing hopefully in a sodden garbage bin gave O'Leary a look as the two passed.

"You're attracting attention!" O'Leary halted. "Listen, I give in. You're just too smart for me. Now here's the plan: Meet me an hour before moonrise at, uh—"

"How about duh One-Eyed Man on duh West Post Road?"

"Sure—just the place I had in mind. Wear a red carnation and pretend you don't know me until I sneeze nine times and then blow my nose on a purple bandanna. Got it?"

"Dat's duh way to talk, bo! Nuttin' I like better'n a slick plan, all worked out wit' snazzy details an' all. Uh . . . by duh way, where do I get duh carnation, at dis time o' year?"

O'Leary closed his eyes, concentrated briefly. "Just around the next turn," he said. "On top of the first garbage bin on the left."

The Red Bull nodded, eyeing Lafayette a trifle warily.

"Sometimes when youse ain't in such a hurry, pal, I want youse should clue me how yuh work some of dese angles."

"Sure," O'Leary said. "Hurry along now, before someone steals your flower." The Red Bull hustled away along the street; O'Leary turned into a side alley to put distance between himself and his volunteer partner. He'd like to know himself how he worked the angles, he reflected. He was beginning to take all this as seriously as though it were really happening. It was becoming increasingly difficult to remember which was the illusion, Artesia or Colby Corners.

In a small café consisting of a faded striped awning over a patch of cracked sidewalk, Lafayette sipped a thick mug of strong coffee. He had to have the location of the rebel HQ—but any question on the subject would immediately point the finger at him. As a matter of fact, the girl behind the charcoal stove where the water boiled was giving him sidelong glances right now. Maybe it was just sex appeal, but he couldn't afford to take the chance. He rose abruptly and moved on. His best bet was to keep moving and hope to overhear something.

It was a long day. O'Leary spent it wandering idly through open-air markets, browsing in tiny crack-in-the-wall bookshops, watching the skillful gnarled hands of silversmiths and goldsmiths and leather and wood workers as they plied their crafts in stalls no bigger than the average hot-dog stand back home in Colby Corners. He ate a modest lunch of salami and ale at an inn where low-sagging foot-square beams black with soot crossed above an uneven packed-earth floor. An hour before sunset he was near the East Gate, pretending to eye the display in a tattoo artist's window, while keeping an eye on a lounging sentry who gave him no more than a casual glance. It would be no trick at all to slip through, if he just knew where to go from there . . .

A large man standing a few yards away was looking at him carefully from the corner of a red-rimmed eye.

O'Leary whistled a few bars of *Mairzey Doats* with suddenly dry lips. He eased around the corner into a dark alleylike passage. He stepped along briskly and when he looked back he saw only looming shadows. He went on, following twists and turns. The last of the light was rapidly fading from the sky.

The alley abruptly ended in a garbage-strewn court. He cast about, found another narrow way leading off into blackness, ducked into it and turned to see a dark figure, then another, step into dim view. He whirled silently and started off at a trot. He had gone twenty feet when he tripped over a tub of refuse and sent it clattering. At once, there was a rasp of feet breaking into a run. By instinct, O'Leary ducked, threw himself aside as a dark cloaked figure slammed past, tripped and fell with a clangor of steel and a choked-off curse. Lafayette crouched, squinting into the dark and saw the man rise to hands and knees, groping for a dropped weapon.

It was no time for niceties. He took a quick step and planted a solid kick in the side of the jaw. The man skidded to his face and lay still. O'Leary moved off up the alley, scanning the way for other members of the reception committee. There had been at least two of them—maybe more. This would be an excellent place to get away from—fast. But there was no point in running into the waiting arms of an assassin.

A shadow moved against deeper shadow ahead. One of the party, it seemed, had circled to cut him off. O'Leary stooped, picked up a hand-filling cobblestone and stood flat against the wall. The shadow came closer; he could hear hoarse breathing now. He waited; the man came on, staring into the shadows, not noticing O'Leary.

"Hold it right there," O'Leary hissed. "I've got a musket aimed at your left kidney. Put down your weapon and stand where you are."

The man stood like a wax figure illustrating Guilt Caught in the Act. He stooped slowly, put down something that glittered in the moonlight and took a hesitant step.

"That's close enough," O'Leary breathed. "How many of you are there?"

"Just me and Moe and, and Charlie, and Sam and Porkeye and Clarence—"

"Clarence?"

"Yeah; he's a new boy, just learning the trade."

"Where are they?"

"Spotted around front. Hey, how'd you get past 'em bud?"

"Easy. I went over them. How did you happen to be staked out here?"

"Well, after all, you had to try one of the gates if you planned to get clear of the city."

"How did you know I was still in the city?"

"Look here, fellow—you expect me to rat on my own chief? I'm not saying any more."

"All right, there's just one more thing I want from you: Where's Lod's headquarters located?"

"Lod? Out west someplace? How do I know?"

"You'd better know, or I'll be annoyed. When I get annoyed, my finger gets twitchy, very twitchy."

"What the heck, everybody knows where Lod hangs out, anyway. I guess if I don't tell you, somebody else will, so what's the percentage in me being a hero, know what I mean?"

"Last chance—the finger is getting nervous."

"Ride west—you'll hit the desert after a half a day's travel. Keep going; there'll be a line of mountains to your left. Follow the foothills till you come to the pass. That's all." O'Leary thought he heard a snicker.

"How far is Lod's stronghold from the pass?"

"Maybe five miles, maybe ten, due west. You can't miss it—if you get that far."

"Why shouldn't I get that far?"

"Let's face it, pal; we got you outnumbered five to one."

O'Leary took a quick step and slammed the five-pound stone in his hand against his informant's skull just above the ear. He folded silently and lay on his face, snoring gently. O'Leary stepped past him, moving off up the alley. He emerged five minutes later half a block from the East Gate. Ready to duck and run if necessary, he strolled past the guard just as the fellow yawned, showing cheap silver filling. Once past him, O'Leary let out a long breath and set out to circle the town. His feet were already getting sore; the new boots had a tendency to pinch. Too bad he hadn't taken the time to steal a horse. He had a long trek ahead; maybe three miles around the town walls, then ten to the desert, then another ten . . .

"Well, there was no help for it—and thinking about blisters didn't help. He settled down for the hike ahead, watching the moon rise above the castellated city wall.

There was a light ahead, glowing in the window of one of the buildings huddled against the wall near the West Gate. Lafayette made his way to it, clambered over a heap of rubbish and came around to the front that faced

the twenty-foot wide dirt road that led off to the west.
He was ready for a good meal and a bottle of stout ale
before he tackled the long night's walk ahead. The shack
with the light seemed to be an inn; a sign nailed to a
post bore a horrendous portrait of a bush-bearded pirate
with a patch over one eye. Not a prepossessing establishment, but it would have to do.

Lafayette pushed through the door and found himself
in a surprisingly cozy interior. There were tables to the
left, a bar straight ahead, a gaming area to the right
where half a dozen grizzled gaffers were arguing querulously over a checkerboard. Oil lanterns on the bar lent
a warm light to the scene. O'Leary rubbed his chilled
hands together and took a seat. A vastly fat woman wobbled from a shadowy corner and plunked a heavy pewter
mug down in front of him.

"What'll it be, love?" she demanded cheerfully.
O'Leary ordered roast beef and baked potato and then
sampled the beer. Not bad at all. He'd stumbled into a
pretty fair eating place, it seemed.

"Hey, youse is late, bo," a familiar voice rasped in
O'Leary's ear. He jerked around. A red face with flattened features looked at him reproachfully. "I been waiting around dis dump for an hour."

"Listen here, Red Bull," O'Leary said quickly. "I told
you not to speak to me until I blew my nose six times
and, uh, waved a red handkerchief."

"Naw, youse said you'd sneeze nine times and blew
yer schnozz on a poiple hanky. An' look, I got my red
carnation; kind uh wilted, but—"

"It's the coolest, Red. I can see our partnership is
going to be a fruitful one. Now, I have further instructions for you. Just go along to the palace; most of the

guard force is away, looking for the princess. You can sneak inside without much trouble, and gather in all kinds of loot before they get back."

"But duh city gates is locked."

"Climb over the wall."

"Yeah—dat's a nifty idear—but what about my horse? He ain't so good at climbing."

"Hmmm. Tell you what I'll do, Red. I'll take care of him for you."

"Say, dat's white of yuh, bub. He's hitched out back. Now, where'll we meet?"

"Well, just stick around the palace gardens; there's good cover there. We'll rendezvous under a white oleander at the second dawn."

"Duh scheme sounds slick, chum. By duh way, what'll youse be doing in duh meantime?"

"I'll be scouting some new jobs."

The Red Bull rose, gathered his cloak about his broad frame. "OK, I'll see youse in duh hoosegow." He turned and strode off. The waitress stared after as she clanked O'Leary's platter down before him.

"Hey, ain't that the well known cutpurse and footpad—"

"Shhh. He's a secret agent of his Majesty," O'Leary confided. The woman looked startled and withdrew. Half an hour later, well fed and with three large beers inside him, O'Leary mounted the Red Bull's horse—a solidly built bay with a new-looking saddle—and, keeping in mind all he'd read about the equestrian art, spurred out of the inn yard and off along the West Post Road.

Chapter Eight

By dawn, O'Leary had crossed the fertile miles of plain west of the capital, passing tiny villages and lonely farmhouses sleeping in the night. Far ahead, he could see a smoky-blue line of rocky peaks catching the first light of morning. The verdant green of tilled fields had given way to dry-looking pasture spotted with scrubby trees, under which a few lean cattle stood listlessly. He rode up a final slope, the dust of the road rising like stirred talcum powder now, leaned aside from the taking branches of thorn trees beside the trail, and looked out across an arid expanse of pale terra cotta colored clay. He halted, frowning.

Somehow he had expected to encounter some sort of warning before reaching the desert—a saloon with a sign reading "Last Chance Charlie's," or something of the sort, where he could buy some supplies for the long ride still ahead. Instead, here he was, already worn out from an unaccustomed night in the saddle—the book hadn't mentioned blisters on the thighs—facing the desert.

And he was getting hungry again. He jogged on, thinking of food. Taffy, now; that was nourishing, compact, durable. O'Leary felt the glands at the side of his jaws ache at the thought. Beautiful, tawny, delicious taffy. Funny how he'd never really gotten enough taffy. Back in Colby Corners you could buy it in any desired amount at Schrumph's Confectionary, but somehow he'd always felt a little foolish walking in and asking for it. That was one thing he'd correct as soon as he got back—he'd lay in a larger stock of taffy and eat it whenever he felt like it.

He squinted across the hazy flat ahead, concentrating on the idea of saddlebags well stocked with good, mouthwatering, nourishing food. All he had to do was dismount, open them up, and there it would be. Concentrated rations that wouldn't suffer from the desert heat, enough to last him for—oh, say, a week.

There was a tiny jar—the familiar sense of a slipped gear in the cosmic machinery. O'Leary smiled. OK, he was set now. He'd ride on a mile or so into the desert, just to give himself a clear view of the trail behind so that no one could sneak up on him, and then he'd enjoy a long-delayed meal.

*   *   *

It was hot out here. O'Leary twisted, riding in a semi-sidesaddle position to ease the pain in his seat. The early sun was beating on his back, reflecting into his eyes from every projecting rock and desert plant. Too bad he hadn't thought to equip himself with a pair of Ray-Bans—and a hat would have helped, too; a wide-brimmed cowboy model. He reined in, turned in the saddle and looked back, squinting into the sun. Aside from his own trail of hoofprints and the settling dust of his passage, no sign of human life marred the expanse of dusty sand. It was as though the world ended a mile or two behind, where the low plateau met the dazzle of the morning sky. Not a very choice spot for a picnic, but the pangs were getting bothersome.

He swung stiffly down from the saddle, unbuckled the strap securing the flap on the left-hand saddlebag, groped inside and brought out a cardboard box. A bright wrapper showed a plate of golden-brown goodies. *Aunt Hooty's Best Salt Water Taffy*, O'Leary read delightedly. Well, that would make a fine dessert but, first, the more staple portions of the feast. He dropped it back in, came out with a familiar-shaped tin. *Sailor Sam's Salt Water Sardines*, the purple print announced, and beneath in small red letters: Finest Pure Taffy Confections. The next container was a square box containing *Old-Fashioned Taffy, a Treat for Young and Old*. O'Leary swallowed hard, dropped the box, probed for another; came up with a dozen eggs—chocolate-covered, taffy inside.

The other saddle bag produced a five-pound tin of taffy—a large gob of taffy artfully shaped to resemble a small ham, three square cans of *Old Style Taffy Like Mother Used to Make*, a flat plug of *Country Taffy—Pulled by Contented Clods*, and a handful of loose taffies wrapped in cellophane lettered *Taffy Kisses: Sweet as a Lover's Lips*.

O'Leary looked over the loot ruefully. Not what you'd call a balanced diet; still, it could have been worse. After all, he *did* like taffy. He sat down in the shade of the horse and started in.

It was worse after that, riding on in the later morning sun. His soreness stiffened into pain that made him wince at every jolt of the animal's hoofs. His mouth puckered with the cloying taste of candy, his stomach feeling as though a dollop of warm mud had been dropped into it. His fingers were sticky with taffy, and the corners of his mouth were gummed with it. Ye Gods! Why hadn't he dwelt on the idea of ham sandwiches or fried chicken, or even good old Tend-R Nood-L! And it would have been clever of him to have supplied himself with a canteen while he had the chance.

Well, he was committed to the venture, ill-prepared though he was. There was no turning back now; the cops would be out in force after the fiasco in the alley. Nicodaeus had shown his colors; he could reduce the tally of his friends here in Artesia from one to zero. Still, when he came riding back with Adoranne before him, all would be forgiven. That part of the trip would be a little more fun than this. She'd have to sit snuggled up close, of course, and naturally he'd have to have at least one arm around her—to steady her. Her golden hair would nestle just under his chin, and he'd ride slowly, so as not to fatigue her Highness. It would take all day, and maybe they'd have to spend a night, rolled up in a blanket—if he had a blanket—by a little campfire, miles from anywhere . . .

But right now it was hot, dusty, itchy and exceedingly uncomfortable. Ahead, the line of peaks showed as a sawtoothed ridge, angling in from the left, marching on without a break to the horizon. Keep going until he reached the pass, the fellow had said back in the alley—not that he could depend on his directions. But there was nothing to do now but keep going and hope for the best.

The sun was low over the mountains to the west, a ball of dusty red in a sky of gaudy purple and pink, against which a clump of skinny palm trees stood out in stark silhouette. O'Leary rode the last few yards to the oasis and reined in under the parched trees. The horse moved impatiently under him, stepped on past a low, half-fallen wall, dropped his head to a dark pool, and drank thirstily. O'Leary eased an aching leg over the saddle and lowered himself to the ground. He felt, he decided, like an Egyptian mummy buried astride his favorite charger, and just now unearthed by nosy archaeologists. He hobbled to a spot on the bank of the pond, got awkwardly to his knees and plunged his head under the surface. The water was warm, a little brackish and not without a liberal sprinkling of foreign particles, but these trifles detracted hardly at all from the exquisite pleasure of the moment. He scrubbed his face, soaked his hair, swallowed a few gulps, then rose and tugged the horse away from the water.

"Can't have you foundering, old boy, whatever that is," he told the patient beast. "Too bad you can't enjoy taffy—or can you?" He rooted in the bag and unwrapped a Taffy Kiss; the horse nuzzled it from his palm.

"Bad for your teeth," O'Leary warned. "Still, since it's all there is, old fellow, it'll have to do."

He turned to the rolled bundle behind the saddle, unstrapped it, found that it consisted of a thin blanket with holes and a weather-beaten tent with four battered pegs and a jointed pole; the Red Bull's equipage left much to be desired. Fifteen minutes later, with the patched canvas erected and a final taffy eaten, O'Leary crawled inside, shaped a hollow in the sand for his hip, curled up on his side and was instantly asleep.

He awoke with a sudden sense of the ground sinking under him, a blip! as though a giant bubble had burst, followed by an abrupt silence broken only by a distant carrump! and the lonely *skriii* of a bird. O'Leary's eyes snapped open.

He was sitting alone on a tiny island with one palm tree in the center of a vast ocean.

Chapter Nine

From the top of the tree—a stunted specimen with half a dozen listless fronds bunched at the top of a skinny trunk—O'Leary gazed out to sea. Beyond the white breakers that ploughed across the bright green of the shoal to hiss on the flat beach, deep blue water stretched unbroken to the far horizon. A few small petrel-like birds wheeled and called, dropping to scoop up tidbits as the waves slid back from the shelf of sugar-white sand. Three or four small white clouds cruised high up in the sunny sky. It was a perfect spot for a quiet vacation, O'Leary conceded—wherever it was—though rather barren. His stomach gave a painful spasm as he thought of real food.

He slid to the ground, slumped against the trunk of the tree. This was a new form of disaster. Just when he'd though he had a few of the rules figured out—*zip!* Everything had gone to pieces. How had he gotten to *this* ridiculous place? He certainly hadn't wished himself here—he'd never even given a thought to inhabiting a desert isle as a population of one.

And, of course, his efforts to shift the scene back to the oasis and his horse failed. Somehow, he couldn't seem to keep his mind on the subject while his stomach was shooting out distress signals. Just when he needed his dreaming abilities most, they deserted him. He thought of Adoranne, her cool blue eyes, the curl of her golden hair, the entrancing swell of her girlish figure. He got to his feet, paced ten feet, reached the water's edge, paced back. Adoranne had given him a hanky and was doubtless expecting him to come charging to her rescue—and here he sat, marooned on this loony island. Damn!

Never mind. Pacing and chewing the inside of his lip wasn't going to help. This was a time to think constructively. He put his hands to his hollow stomach; the pangs interfered with his mental processes. He couldn't even think about escape until he'd had some food! The palm tree wouldn't help: it was devoid of coconuts. He eyed the water's edge. There might be fish there . . .

O'Leary took a deep breath, concentrated, pictured a box of matches, a package of fish hooks, and a salt shaker. Surely, that wouldn't overtax his power, a modest little hope like that . . . There was a silent thump. Quickly, O'Leary checked his capacious pockets, brought out from one a book of matches labeled *The Alcazar Roof Garden: Dancing Nitely*, and a miniature container of

Morton's salt with a perforated plastic top; the other produced a paper containing half a dozen straight pins.

"The Huck Finn bit, yet," he muttered, bending one of the pins into a rude hook. He remembered then that he had neglected to evoke a length of line to go with the hooks. That, however, could be easily remedied. He picked a thread loose from the inside of the beaded vest, unraveled four yards of tough nylon line. For bait . . . hmmmm . . . a cluster of the tiny pearls from his vest ought to attract some attention.

He looped the thread to the hook, pulled off his boots, waded out a few yards into the warm surf. A school of tiny fish darted past in the transparent crest of a breaking wave; a large blue crab waved ready claws at him and scuttled away sideways leaving a trail of cloudy sand. He cast his line out, picturing a two-pound trout cruising just below the surface . . .

Nearly two hours later O'Leary licked his fingers and lay back with a sigh of content to plan his next move. It had taken three tries to land his fish—the pins, he discovered, tended to straighten out at the first good tug. The sharp-edged rock had been a clumsy instrument for cleaning his catch but as a skillet, it had served well enough, laid in the driftwood fire that still glowed in the hollow he had scooped in the sand. All things considered, it hadn't been a bad meal, for something improvised in a hurry.

And now the time had come to think constructively about getting off the island. It would help if he knew where he was; it didn't seem to be any part of Artesia—and it certainly didn't look like Colby Corners. Suppose he tried to transfer back home now, and wound up in the humdrum world of foundries and boarding houses? Suppose Artesia, once lost, could never be regained?

But time was precious. Already the sun was sinking toward the orange horizon; another day nearly gone.

He closed his eyes, gritted his teeth and focused his thoughts on Artesia: the narrow, crooked streets, the tall, half-timbered houses, the spires of the palace, the cobbles and steam cars and forty-wall electric lights—and Adoranne, her patrician face, her smile . . .

He was aware of a sudden stress in the air, a sense of thunder impending, then a subtle jar, as though the universe had rolled over a crack in the sidewalk.

He felt himself drop two feet, and a gush of cold salt water engulfed him.

O'Leary sputtered, swallowed a mouthful, fought his way to the surface. He was immersed in a choppy, blue-black sea, riffled by a chilly breeze. The island was nowhere in sight, but off to the left—a mile or more, he estimated as a wave slapped him in the face—was a shoreline, with lights.

He was sinking, dragged down by the heavy sword and the sodden clothes. The belt buckle was stubborn; O'Leary wrenched at it, freed it, felt the weight fall away. His boots next . . . He got one off, surfaced, caught a quick breath; the clothes were dragging him down like a suit of armor. He tried to shrug out of the vest, snarled it around his left arm, nearly drowned before he got his head free of the surface for another gulp of air.

It was all he could do to hold his own; he was out of breath, tiring fast. The cold water seemed to paralyze

his arms. His hands felt like frozen cod. He managed a
glance shoreward, made out a familiar projection of land:
the blunt tower of the Kamoosa Point Light. He knew
where he was now: swimming in the Bay, twenty miles
west of Colby Corners!

He went under again, shipping more water. His arms
. . . so tired. His lungs ached. He'd have to breathe soon.
What a fool he'd been . . . shifted himself back to the
Colby Corners . . . and since he'd traveled twenty miles
to the west, naturally he'd wound up in the Bay . . . too
tired now . . . can't swim any longer . . . cold . . . going
down . . . too bad . . . if he could have just seen her
turned-up nose once more . . .

—and something slammed against his back. The cold
and pressure were gone, as though they had never been.
O'Leary gasped, coughed, spat salt water, rolled over and
coughed some more. After a while his breathing was
easier. He sat up, looked around at an expanse of twilit
sand—lots of it, stretching away to a line of jagged peaks
black against the blaze of sunset.

Apparently he was back in Artesia. He looked up at
the stars coming into view now in the darkening sky. The
best bet would be to get a few hours of sleep and then
start on. But he was too chilled to sleep. Perhaps if he
walked a bit first, he'd warm up and his clothes would
dry.

Wearily O'Leary put one foot in front of another—hay
foot, straw foot, hay foot—He stumbled over a bundle
half buried in the sand. Clothes, dry clothes—pants,
shirt, boots, a jacket; probably left behind by some pic-
nicker. He knew he'd been too tired to think of them,

and besides he hadn't had that universe-slipping feeling. Hastily, O'Leary put on the dry clothes. There, that was better. He felt in the pockets. Miraculously, if that was the word, they were filled with Taffy Kisses. He was too bushed to figure this one out now. He scraped a hollow in the sand, building the sand up on one side as a windbreak, and went to sleep.

By midmorning, O'Leary estimated, he had covered no more than five miles of loose sand, in which his feet floundered and slipped with the maddening sense of frustrated progress so familiar in dreams. At each step his boots sank in to the ankle, and when he thrust forward, they slid back. Every time he lifted his blistered feet, it was like hauling a cast-iron anchor out of soft mud. At this rate, he'd never reach the mountains.

He sat down heavily. He pulled loose the bandanna he had tied over his head as an ineffective shield against the increasingly hot sun and mopped his forehead. He wouldn't sweat much more today; there was no moisture left in his body. No hope of a drink in sight, either. He shaded his eyes, scanning the stretch of rippled sand ahead. There was a slight rise to a wind-sculptured crest three hundred yards distant. What if there should happen to be water on the far side of the hill . . . And why shouldn't there be? He envisioned the scene, marshaling what was left of his Psychic Energies. There—had he felt the slight jar that signaled success?

With a sudden sense of urgency, he scrambled up, made for the ridge, stumbling and falling. He was getting weak, he realized, as he rested on all fours before getting up and plowing on. But just over the rise would be an oasis, green palms, a pool of clear, cool water, blessed shade.

Only a few yards now; he lay flat, catching his breath. He was a little reluctant to top the rise; suppose the oasis wasn't there after all? But that was negative thinking, not the sort of thing Professor Schimmerkopf would approve of at all. He got up, tottered on, reached the hilltop and looked down across a gentle slope of sun-glared sand at the square bulk of a big red Coke machine.

It stood fifty feet away, slightly tilted, a small drift of sand against one side, all alone in the vast wasteland. O'Leary broke into an unsteady run, stumbled to a halt beside the monster and noted approvingly the soft hum of the compressor. But where did the power come from? The heavy-duty electric cable trailed off a few yards and disappeared into the sand. But never mind the nitpicking details!

O'Leary tried his left pants pocket, brought out a dime and dropped it with trembling fingers into the slot. There was a heart-stopping pause after the coin clattered down; then a deep interior rumble, a clank and the frosted end of a bottle banged into view in the delivery chute. O'Leary snatched it up, levered the cap off in the socket provided, and took a long, thirsty drag. It was real Coke, all right, just like uptown. Funny; it was a long way to the nearest bottling plant. Lafayette lifted the bottle, peered at its underside. *Dade City, Florida*, said the raised letters in the glass. Amazing! Civilization was penetrating even into the most primitive areas, it appeared.

But what about Artesia? Surely it wasn't included on the rounds of the soft-drink distributors. Ergo, it could only have come from the "real" world—transported here by the concentrated O'Leary will.

He had already established that, when he evoked conveniences like bathtubs and dresses, his subconscious merely reached out and grabbed the nearest to hand. The idea that he could reach them all the way from Dade City was a bit frightening. Still, it was a comfort in a way; it lent a note of some sort of rationality to what had heretofore seemed pure magic.

What it boiled down to was that he had somehow stumbled onto the trick of moving objects around from one spot to another—not dreaming them up out of whole cloth. But that seemed to imply that Artesia was a real place! If that were so, where was it?

O'Leary put the question aside.

Ten minutes later, refreshed and with two spare bottles tucked in his hip pockets, O'Leary resumed the march toward his distant objective.

* * *

It was late afternoon when he reached the foothills—bare angles and edges of broken, reddish rock, thrusting up from the sea of sand. Cool air moved here in the shadow of the peaks above, soothing his sunburned face. He rested on a flat ledge, finished his last Coke, emptied the sand from his boots for the twentieth time since dawn, then resumed his trek, bearing northwest now, following the line of the escarpment. Still a long way to go, but the footing was better here. The sand was firmer, and there were patches of pebbly ground and even a few stretches of flat rock—a real luxury. With luck he should make the pass by dark; then tomorrow the final leg to Lod's HQ. As for water, that was no problem; he'd just provide a nice spring up ahead somewhere—and while he was at it, why not a steed, too?

O'Leary stopped dead. Why hadn't he though of that sooner? Of course, it would have been a little difficult to convince himself that there was a horse standing by, all by himself, out in the desert. An animal wasn't like a Coke machine; he had to have food and water. A long extension cord wouldn't do the job.

But here, with plenty of opportunities for nice deep caves, and hidden fastnesses up in the hills, sure, a mount could be wandering around here. In fact, he'd find him, just around one of those outcroppings ahead. A fine, sturdy beast, adapted to the desert, strong, high-spirited, bright-eyed, and not too nervous to get close to . . .

Four outcroppings and two hours later, O'Leary's pace had flagged noticeably. No horse yet—but that didn't mean, he reminded himself, that he wouldn't find him soon. He hadn't said which outcropping he'd be behind. Probably this next one, just another half a mile ahead.

He plodded on. Getting thirsty again. He'd have to produce that spring pretty soon—but first, the mount. His boots had been designed for riding, not hiking. The sand inside his collar and under his belt was wearing the hide away, too. Not much fun, walking across a desert—but then, Adoranne probably hadn't enjoyed her crossing, either.

He reached the point of rock, thrusting out like the prow of a ship, a vertical escarpment looming up forty, fifty feet above the sands. He angled out to skirt the far end, rounded the point, and found himself looking along a canyonlike ravine, cut through the towering mass of rock. The pass! He had reached it!

He hurried out into the lane of late sunlight streaming down through the gap, his long shadow bobbing behind him. The sun was an orange disc above the flat horizon, reflecting bloodily from the walls of the defile. The sand here was disturbed, as though by the passing of many feet; the low sun etched the prints of boots and hoofs in sharp relief. A horse had passed this way not too long ago—several horses: Lod and his party, with Adoranne, no doubt. There were other prints, too, O'Leary noted—the trail of a small lizard, a row of catlike paw marks—and over there—what was that? O'Leary followed the tracks with his eye. They were large—impossibly large, great three-toed impressions like something made by a giant bird. But who ever heard of a bird with feet a yard across? He smiled at the whimsy. Probably just a trick of light on shifting sand. But where was his horse? He had definitely ordered it for delivery before clearing the pass . . .

There was a sound from ahead, startling in the stillness. Ah, there he was now! O'Leary stopped and cocked his head, listening. The sound came again, a scrape of hoof on rock. He smiled broadly and tried out the whistle Roy Rogers used for calling Trigger. With his parched lips, it came out a weak *tweet*. Far up the pass, a shadow moved.

Something grotesquely tall detached itself from the deep shadow of a buttress of stone at the side of the ravine—a shape that stood fifteen feet high, slender necked, great bodied, stalking on two massive legs like a monstrous parody of a Thanksgiving turkey, except that the knees bent forward. A head like a turtle's turned his way, eyed him with bright green eyes. The lipless mouth opened and emitted a whistling cry.

"Th-that wasn't exactly wh-what I had in mind," O'Leary announced to the landscape. It occurred to him to run, but somehow his feet seemed frozen to the spot. Through them he could feel a distinct tremor in the rock at each step of the titan. It came on, moving with ponderous grace, its relatively small forearms folded against a narrow chest, the great curve of the belly gleaming pink in the failing light. Fifty feet from O'Leary, it halted, staring over his head and out across the desert as though pondering some weighty problem unrelated to small, knee-high creatures who invaded its domain. O'Leary stared, rooted to the spot. The seconds were ticking past with agonizing slowness. In a moment, O'Leary knew, the iguanodon—he recognized the type from an admirable illustration he had seen in a recent book on dinosaurs—would notice him again, remember what had started it lumbering in his direction. He pictured it wandering on, an odd leg hanging carelessly from the corner of the horny mouth, half swallowed, already forgotten.

He caught himself. No point in helping disaster along with vivid imaginings. He wasn't dead yet. And maybe he wouldn't be, if he could just think of something—anything!

A second lizard, to engage the first in mortal combat while he scuttled away to safety? Too risky; he'd be squashed in the sparring. How about a tank—one of those German Tiger models, with the big 88mm. gun! No, too fantastic. A diversion, perhaps—a herd of nice fat goats wandering by. But there weren't any goats out here. Just himself and the dinosaur—Lod's dragon, the thought dawned suddenly! And he'd dismissed the whole thing as a superstitious fancy. He'd been wrong about that—and about a lot of other things. And now he'd never have a chance to correct his errors. But he couldn't give up yet. There had to be something.

The great reptile stirred, swung his head about; O'Leary clearly heard the creak of scaled hide as it moved. Now it was turning back, dropping its gaze, fixing on the small figure of the man before it. A low rumble sounded from its stomach; it raised a foot, came striding forward.

O'Leary reached to his back pocket and yanked out a handful of taffy kisses. With a roundhouse swing, he hurled them straight at the oncoming monster's snout. The mouth opened with the speed of a winking eye and engulfed the tidbits. O'Leary turned to run, twisted an ankle, fell full length. The shadow of the giant fell across him. He tried to evoke the image of Colby Corners, willing himself there. Even drowning in the bay was preferable to serving as hors d'oeuvre to an oversized Gila monster—but his mind was a shocked blank.

There was a peculiar, sucking sound from above, like a boot being withdrawn from particularly viscous mud. He turned his head, looked up; the monster was poised above him, chewing thoughtfully, strings of sticky taffy linking the working jaws. O'Leary hesitated. Should he lie still and hope the monster would forget him or try a retreat while it was occupied?

A pointed tongue flicked out, snagged a loop of taffy dangling by one horny cheek. The behemoth cocked its head and eyed O'Leary. It was a peculiarly unnerving scrutiny.

O'Leary edged away, scrabbling backward on hands and knees. The dinosaur watched; then it took a step, closing the gap. With a final snap, it downed the last of the candy. O'Leary scuttled faster; the titan followed. O'Leary reached the wall of the canyon and started along its base. The monster came after him, watching with the same sort of interest that a cat evinces in a wounded mouse.

Ten minutes of this race, O'Leary decided, flopping down to breathe, were enough. If the thing was going to eat him, it could go ahead. Unless he could banish it, somehow.

Go away, he thought frantically. *You've just remembered your—your mate, that's it—and you have to hurry off now.*

It wasn't going to work. The dinosaur was too close, too real, with its warty, crevassed hide, its cucumber smell, its glittering eye. He couldn't begin to concentrate. And now the big head was dropping lower, the jaws parting. This was it! O'Leary squeezed his eyes shut . . .

Nothing happened. He opened them. The vast reptilian face was hanging before him, not two yards away—and the look in the eyes was . . . hopeful?

O'Leary sat up. Maybe the thing wasn't a man-eater. Maybe it was tame. Maybe—

But of course! He had ordered a steed! This was it! Back in the palace, when he'd ordered a bath, he had gotten the next best thing. This time it seemed he had somehow summoned the neighborhood dragon—and it liked taffy!

O'Leary tossed another sample of Aunt Hooty's best to the monstrous beast. It caught it like a dog snapping at a fly, except that the clash as the jaws met was louder.

O'Leary tossed half a dozen together, then the rest of the handful. The dinosaur leaned back on its tremendous tail with a sigh like a contented submarine and munched the goodies. O'Leary sighed too, slumped back against the rock. That had been a harrowing quarter hour—and it wasn't over yet. If he could just sneak away now.

He started off, moving as unobtrusively as possible. The iguanodon watched him go. Twenty feet, thirty feet; just around that next turn now, and he'd bolt.

The reptile came to its feet and padded after him, dainty as an earthquake. O'Leary halted; the huge creature squatted, holding its head low, as though waiting.

"Go 'way," O'Leary squeaked. He made shooing motions. The dinosaur regarded him gravely—almost expectantly.

"Scram!" he shouted. "Who do you think I am, Alley Oop?"

Then an idea struck him. He'd already deduced that the monster had appeared in response to his yearnings for a steed. Could it be? What an impression he'd make on Adoranne if he came cantering up to Lod's hideout on *that!* And since it didn't appear that he'd ever shake the brute, he might as well give it a try. He wouldn't be any more vulnerable seated on its back than he was jumping around under its nose, and anyway—hadn't that book said the iguanodon was a vegetarian?

O'Leary straightened his shoulders, set his jaw and crept cautiously around to the side. The giant head swung, following him. He paused at a leg like the warty trunk of a tree. Not much chance of climbing that. He went on, reached the tail, thick as a fifty-gallon molasses drum, tapering away across the sand. He ought to be able to make it up that route. O'Leary followed the tail out to a point where he could swing aboard, then walked up its length. As he passed the juncture with the hind legs, he found it necessary to lean forward and use his hands, but it was easy going; the fissured hide offered excellent footholds. The saurian waited patiently while he scaled the stretch from haunch to shoulder; then it lowered its head. O'Leary straddled the neck behind the head and the monster straightened, lifting him up to ride fifteen feet clear of the floor of the pass. There was a magnificent view from up here, he noted; far away across the sands to the west he fancied he saw a smudge of vegetation, a tiny glint of light on windows. That would be Lod's hangout. He clacked his heels against the horny hide.

"Let's go, boy," he commanded. At once, the dinosaur set off at an easy canter—in the wrong direction. O'Leary yelled, kicked with one heel; the mighty mount veered, came about on the port tack and headed back up the pass. In five minutes, they were clear of the ravine, striding out across the parched plain at a mile-eating pace. The sun was gone now; deep twilight was settling across the desert. "Steady as she goes, boy," O'Leary commented aloud. "In about an hour we'll be giving this Lod character the surprise of his life."

Chapter Ten

It was dark night with no moon as O'Leary sat his mighty steed behind a dimly seen screen of tall eucalyptus that marked the edge of the grounds surrounding the great building that towered up against the stars—fifteen stories at least, O'Leary estimated. Faint starlight glinted on hundreds of windows; there was dim illumination behind three of them. Blazoned across a strip of what looked like dark plastic twelve-foot-high lavender neon letters spelled out *LAS VEGAS HILTON*. Between him and the nearest corner of a projecting flank of the structure, a ten-foot iron fence ornamented with spearheads thrust up.

"This isn't quite what I expected, fellow," O'Leary muttered. "I pictured a collection of tin shacks, or maybe some wooden huts we could walk right through. Wouldn't do to slam into that; it might fall on us. And Adoranne might get hurt."

The dinosaur stretched its neck across the fence. O'Leary looked down at the sharp points below.

"Wouldn't do to fall on those, Dinny," he said nervously. The iguanodon leaned against the bars; they creaked, bent like soda straws, went down.

"Nice going, boy. Hope nobody heard the clatter . . . "

The monster lowered its head to ground level. O'Leary jumped off onto a carpet of knee-deep grass which the reptile sniffed and began peacefully cropping.

"All right, boy," he whispered. "The place is big, all right, but it seems sparsely manned. Wait here while I reconnoiter—and keep out of sight."

There was a soft snort from the great head, now lifted far above him, investigating the lower branches of a big oak. O'Leary moved off silently, skirted a waterless fountain in the shape of an abstract female, crossed a stretch of pavement marked with faint white lines at ten-foot intervals, hopped a strung chain and entered the rustling, leaf-strewn shadow of a stand of poplars.

From here he had an excellent view of the building. Nothing stirred. He emerged from the trees, made his way around to the front. There was a broad, paved drive—concrete, by the feel of it—which swept past a flight of wide steps leading up to a rank of glass doors, above which a cantilevered marquee thrust out fifty feet. Great, unpruned gardenia bushes bunched up from planters set along the terrace; the warm night air wafted the heavy fragrance of their blossoms to O'Leary.

Inside, beyond the doors, he could see a plushly carpeted foyer, dimly lit, its pale fawn walls decorated by framed pictures and gilt and white lamp brackets. Large soft-looking divans and easy chairs were placed in conversational groups around low coffee tables.

The peaceful order of the scene was marred only by a scattering of papers, bones, empty tin cans and the charred ring of a small camp fire beside a potted yucca. Someone, it appeared, had desired more informal cooking arrangements than the hotel kitchens afforded.

O'Leary went up the steps, approached the doors and jumped as the one before him swung in with a whoosh of compressed air. Magic, after all? He felt the untrimmed hair at the nape of his neck rising. But then, maybe it was just electronics—magic rationalized. He edged through the door and looked around the two-acre lobby.

Adoranne was here—somewhere. It was going to be a long search through fifteen floors of rooms to find her, but he had to make a start somewhere. He picked a corridor at random, went along it in the eerie light to the first door, tried the knob . . .

An hour and a half later O'Leary was working his way through the southwest wing of the ninth floor. So far he had encountered nothing but empty rooms, most of them immaculately made up, with dusty dresser tops and vases of withered flowers the only signs of neglect, but a few with rumpled beds and muddy bootprints on the pastel carpets—like the one he was in. Some careless occupant had plucked a chicken in the bathroom, leaving a clot of feathers in the toilet bowl. A chair had been disassembled for some reason not clear; its component parts lay about the room. A smashed wastebasket was on its side half under the bed. Something bright showed among the rubbish—a key, attached to a turquoise plastic disc with the number 1281 impressed on it in gilt. O'Leary picked it up. Maybe this was a clue. It was worth checking out, anyway. So far he'd seen nothing to indicate that Adoranne was here. Perhaps Lod and his merry men were off on a raid; maybe they'd be back at any moment. He'd better hurry.

As he emerged from the stairwell at the twelfth floor, the sounds of voices came to his ears. He felt his heart thump in unpleasant excitement. He was getting warm, it seemed. He went along the hall in the direction indicated by a glowing arrow. When he rounded a corner the sounds were louder. Room 1281 would be at the end of the hall—beyond the room from which the loud conversation was coming. O'Leary approached the door standing half ajar with a stripe of light falling across the carpet from inside the room.

". . . seen him in the palace, two days ago," a rusty voice was complaining. "An' I says to him, look, I says, if you got some kind of idear we're doing all the dirty work while you grab the loot, your aggies is scrambled."

"But he give the boss a promise he'd get the broad—" a second voice started, cut off with a sound like a croquet mallet striking a side of beef. "It ain't perlite to call a dame a broad," the rusty voice cawed. "And I know what he promised. But it's up to us to collect. Don't worry. The boss's got his plans all doped out. He's got a couple surprises up his sleeve fer his high-and-mightiness."

"Chee, you can't buck *him!*" a third voice said. "Wit' his power—"

O'Leary, straining to catch every word, was suddenly aware of footsteps approaching along the corridor. He looked, dived for a door across the hall, slid inside and flattened himself against the wall.

"Hey!" a voice yelled. "Who ast you in?" A large man with lather on his face stood in the open door to the bathroom, glowering. "Go find yer own flop." His tone changed. "Who're you? I ain't seen you before."

"Ah—I'm a new man, just signed up," O'Leary improvised. "The lure of adventure, you know, the companionship of kindred spirits. Now, about the, ah, girl. What room's she in?"

"Huh?"

"I just wanted to nip up and make sure the door's locked. Our boss, Lod, wouldn't appreciate it if she flew the coop, eh?"

"What are ya, nuts or sumpthin'?" The big man was frowning darkly, working with a forefinger in a cauliflowered ear. "She—"

The door banged open. "Hey, Iron-bender," a peg-legged John Silver type in a torn undershirt growled out. "Could I borry yer second-best brass knucks?" The newcomer's gaze fell on O'Leary. "Who's this?" he demanded.

"A new guy; some kind of a ladies' maid. How's come yer always on the scrounge, Bones? You ain't give me back my thumbscrew yet, the one Ma give me."

"A *what* kind of a maid?" Bones was eyeing O'Leary.

"I dunno; he was asting about where the dame was. The dummy don't even know—"

"Never mind what he don't know. He's prob'ly one o' the new reinforcements. That right, bub?"

"Absolutely," O'Leary nodded. "But about the, er, prisoner. Just tell me her room number, and I'll be off. I don't want to trouble you gentlemen further."

"This dope thinks—" Iron-bender started.

"The room, huh?" Bones gave Iron-bender a look. "It's kind of hard to find. Me and him better show ya the way. Right, Iron-bender?"

The thug wrinkled his broad, flat face. "Look, I got things to do."

"You can spare a few minutes to take care o' the demands o' hospitality. Let's go."

"Oh, you needn't bother, fellows," O'Leary protested. "Just give me the room number."

"Not a chance, matey; we got to do this right. Come on. It ain't far."

"Well . . . " O'Leary followed the two out into the hall. It might help, at that, to have an escort. It would save some embarrassing questions if he encountered anyone else. He followed the two slope-shouldered heavyweights along the passage to a stairway and up two flights. They emerged in a corridor identical to all the others.

"Right this way, bud," Bones said with a smile like a benign crocodile.

They went along past silent doors and halted before one numbered 1407. Bones thumped with his knuckles.

A deep grunt sounded from inside.

"That doesn't sound like Adoranne," O'Leary said. "That sounds like—"

Bones jumped for him, missed as O'Leary spun aside and dropped a side-hand chop across the base of the thick neck. Iron-bender, slow on the uptake, watched his companion stagger past with a muffled yell before he turned on O'Leary, in time to take the latter's stiff fingers in a hard jab to the sternum. He doubled over and caught a smashing uppercut with his massive chin. He shook his head.

"Hey, what goes on?" he inquired in a pained voice, reaching for O'Leary, who caught his arm, whirled, levered it across his hip—and felt himself being lifted, tossed aside. He rolled away and saw Iron-bender rubbing his arm, a pained expression on his face.

"Ow," the heavyweight said. Bones was coming back now, a little hunched to the left, but an expression on his face which prompted O'Leary to leap to his feet, dash past Iron-bender and make for the stairwell at flank speed. He reached it, slammed through, hammered down one flight, plunged out into the corridor—and into the waiting arms of a grizzly bear.

It was impossible, O'Leary had discovered, to concentrate on escape schemes while in a position of extreme stress—such as now, for example. The man who had gathered him in—a seven-footer with hands like machinist's vises, shoulders like football armor, and a variety of muscles to match—held him in an awkward grip, his arms crossed behind him and raised until he danced along on tiptoe in an effort to relieve the pressure.

"I'll go quietly," he assured his captor. "How about just leaving my arms in the same old sockets they've been in all along; I like them that way."

The thick arm jerked him sideways, heading down along a new passage. O'Leary scrambled to keep the weight off his arms. Through open doors he glimpsed unmade beds, soiled garments on unswept floors, empty cracker boxes, sardine tins, bean cans. His captor came to a halt, struck a closed door two blows with his fist. The door slid back, revealing the interior of an elevator. O'Leary's jailor pushed him inside, worked a handle; the car rose one floor. They stepped out into the corridor where Iron-Bender and Bones stood in heated debate.

" . . . we tell him the guy pulls a knife, see, and—"

"Naw, we don't tell him nothing. I'll say you was drunk—" the conversation broke off as the two spotted O'Leary.

"Hey!" Bones said. "Crusher got him!"

"Gee, thanks, Crusher," Iron-bender said. "We'll take him off yer hands now."

Crusher made a low rumbling sound in his throat. The two lesser thugs withdrew hastily. Crusher marched O'Leary along to the door Bones had knocked on earlier. This time the knock shook the panel in its frame.

A deep voice called, "It's open, curse you!" Crusher twisted the knob, flung the door wide, and propelled O'Leary into the room.

A man sat in an immense chair placed under the window across the room. He was taller sitting down than Crusher was standing: that was O'Leary's first startled impression. The second was that the man was wider, thicker, heavier, more massive, than any human being he had ever seen before—by far. The third was a shocked wondering whether this *was* a man.

The massive head—carried at an angle as though the neck had been broken once and badly set—was adorned by a dark leathery face, like some heroic carving of a demon. The nose was sharply chiseled, with great flaring nostrils. The mouth was wide, thin-lipped, with a long sparsely bristled upper lip, over a massive jaw with a receding chin. Small, bright eyes stared from the over-sized face; deep brown eyes, with no white showing. Coarse hair, short-cropped, covered the wide, knobby skull; the leg-thick neck was muffled in a great scarf, and the ponderous body was draped in shimmering folds of a dark wine-colored stuff. The hands that rested on the arms of the chair were big enough to hold two footballs each, O'Leary estimated. Great jewels glistened on the thick, hairy fingers. The giant twitched one of the latter members, and Crusher released his grip and backed from the room.

"So you reach my citadel," a thickly accented voice near the lower level of the audible range rumbled. "I thought you might—though sage Nicodaeus think otherwise."

"You're—you're darn right," O'Leary said, trying had to control a quaver in his voice. "And if you know what's good for you, you'll turn Adoranne over to me right now and maybe I'll put in a good word for you with King Goruble."

"If I know what is good for me? Alas, little man, none ever know what is good for him. And if one knew, would he follow that path?"

"I'm warning you, Lod—you *are* Lod, aren't you? If you've hurt her Highness—"

"Yes, Lod is my name." The giant's voice rang with a harder note. "Undertake to offer me no warnings, small creature. Instead, speak to me of the errand that brought you hither."

"I came for Princess Adoranne . . . " O'Leary stopped to swallow. "I know you've got her, because who else—"

"At first lie, I give you pain," Lod said. "Like this." He leaned forward with a swift motion, gripped O'Leary's shoulder with one huge hand and squeezed. O'Leary yelped in agony.

Lod rolled back, eyeing him with a touch of amusement. "At second lie, I give disfigurement; the loss of an eye, perhaps, or a crushed limb. And at third, I condemn you to hang in the cage of tears, where you will die with a sloth that will surprise you."

"Who—who's lying?" O'Leary managed, blinking away pain tears. "I heard Adoranne was missing; everybody thought I did it, but that's nonsense. You're the one with the motive and the organization—"

"What? Must I inflict lesson two already?"

"He's telling the truth, you great ugly imbecile," a sharp, though muffled voice piped up from somewhere. Lod halted in mid-reach, looking disconcerted.

"Of course I'm telling the truth," O'Leary moved his shoulder. Nothing seemed to be broken. What a pity he hadn't equipped himself with a .45 automatic while he was at it; it would be a pleasure to plug this leering man-mountain.

"Who sent you here?" Lod barked. "Nicodaeus, I think, that sly traitor!"

"Nicodaeus tipped off the palace guard when I paid him a visit in his room," O'Leary said. "I'm no messenger of his."

"Ask him who *he* is, not the name of his master," the snappish voice came again. It seemed to O'Leary that it emanated from behind Lod. He craned to see who might be crouched behind the chair.

"Name yourself then, little man," Lod commanded.

"I'm Lafayette O'Leary. What's that got to do with it? I demand—"

"Where do you come from?"

"I left Artesia yesterday, if that's what you mean. Before that—well, it's kind of complicated—"

"I sense a strangeness in this man," the shrill voice piped. "Let him go, let him go!"

Lod's eyes narrowed. "You came alone and unarmed against mighty Lod. How did you pass dragon who guards my eastern gate? How—"

"As well ask the west wind why it blows," the shrewish voice shrilled. "You face power here, vile usurper! Have the wit to turn from it in humility!"

"Speak up!" Lod's voice was a snarl. "I think you fairly beg for torment!"

"Look, all I want is the girl and my freedom," O'Leary said desperately. "Tell your gorillas to release us, unharmed, and—"

Lod's immense hands jumped, caught O'Leary between them and lifted him off his feet, bruising his ribs.

"Must I tear you in two, stubborn mite?"

"Aye, kill him now—ere he tells you that which you fear to hear," the shrill voice snarled. "Shut off the voice of doom impending!"

Lod snarled, tossed O'Leary from him. He came to his feet, stood over O'Leary, ten feet tall, a mountainous, crook-backed ogre. "Must I boil you in pitch?" he boomed. "Impale you on a bed of thousand needles?

Drop you in the dark well of serpents? Bury you neck deep in broken bottles?"

O'Leary picked himself up, half-dazed by the blow his head had struck the floor. "No, thanks," he faced the giant towering over him. "Just . . . give me Princess Adoranne and a good dinner and . . . I'll let you off easy this time."

Lod roared; the other voice squealed in wild laughter. The giant whirled, stalked back to his chair, threw himself in it, his face working through a series of Halloween expressions before setting in a grim stare.

"Kindness avail nothing with you, I see," Lod grated in a tone of forced calm. "That being case, stern measures are called for." He twitched a wrist. The door opened. Crusher stood in it, looking like a dwarf in the shadow of Lod.

"Take him to interrogation room," the giant rumbled. "Prepare him. Then await my coming."

***

It seemed as though hours had passed. O'Leary felt himself swaying again, tried to catch himself; then the stabbing pain as the sharp spikes set in the cage stabbed at his right shoulder. He jerked away, struck his left elbow an agonizing crack on the neatly placed projection on that side. Then again he was huddled in the only position possible in the cage; half-bent, half-crouched, his head cocked sideways. His knees and back ached; the throb of a dozen shallow puncture wounds competed for attention. He shifted minutely to relieve the cramp developing in his thigh, felt the prod of the waiting needle points.

"This won't get you anything, Lod," he croaked. "I can't tell you who sent me, because nobody sent me. I'm operating on my own." The giant was lounging at ease in a vast chaise lounge, dressed in pale pink robes now, a voluminous scarf of purple silk wound around his grotesque neck. He waved a ringed hand as big as a briefcase.

"Be stubborn as you like, little man. It gives me pleasure to watch you fret there, surrounded by pain, weighing one punishment against another. An artful device, the cage of tears, for as it torments body with its spiked caresses, so does it agonize the mind with the need to make frequent, painful decisions." Lod chuckled contentedly, lifted a gallon-sized leather jack, quaffed deeply, then plucked a leg from a roast turkey-sized creature and sucked the meat from the bone in one gulp.

Moving only his eyes, O'Leary looked around the room for the fifteenth time, scanning the high, beamed ceiling, the damp earth floor, the rich rug on which Lod's chaise rested, the trophies hung carelessly on the rough, stone walls. There were heads of great reptiles—not cured and stuffed, merely rotting empty-eyed skulls—broken weapons twice normal size, a great ax with a leather-wrapped haft and a rusted, double-bitted head. There was nothing here he could work with—not that he could concentrate, with pain stabbing at him from every side. There was just one door, and he knew where that led. It was fruitless to try to imagine the U.S. cavalry charging in to the rescue. King Goruble's subjects, fond though they were of the princess, were too much in dread of Lod and his dragon to attempt to storm his citadel.

"I see you admire my little souvenirs," Lod rumbled cheerily. He was growing more talkative as he downed mug after mug of brown ale. "Mementoes of early years, before my elevation to present eminence."

"Eminence?" O'Leary put all the scorn he could manage into the word. "You're just an ordinary crook, Lod. A little uglier than most, maybe, but there's nothing special about kidnapping and torture. The dregs of humanity have been at that sort of thing for thousand of years."

"Still you pipe merry tune," Lod boomed, smiling genially as he chewed, showing immense, square teeth. "But pain and thirst and hunger are faithful servants; they do their work, aided by their ally, fear."

"Only the fool knows no fear!" the strange, shrill voice screeched suddenly. "You toy now with forces you know not of, foul tyrant!"

"Where's that voice coming from?" O'Leary croaked.

"Voice of my conscience," Lod growled, then guffawed and drank.

"Some conscience; I can hear it all the way over here. Why don't you pay some attention to it? It's smarter than you are."

Lod lifted his lip in a snarl. "One day I kill conscience," he muttered as though to himself. "And day grows close." A shriek of insane laughter answered him. He drank again, spilling the ale down his chin, slammed the jack to the table and eyed O'Leary balefully.

"You babble of her Highness, Princess Adoranne, my bride-to-be," he growled. "He swore to me: wench would be my prize! And now my agents bring word that he spirit her away. Time grows close; his plots ripen—and now he needs me not, thinks he! He do away with girl, threat to his grip on throne, and cast me aside—me, to whom he swore his oath!"

"You mean . . . Adoranne really isn't here?" O'Leary stared with pain-blurred eyes at the horrendous face.

"Aye, he is sly one," the giant went on, slurring his words now. "With his promises and his gifts and his treachery. But the fool fail to remember that in my own land, I was king!" Lod banged the mug again, sloshing ale. "By force of my arm and guile of my nature, I *made* myself king! My father was mighty one, but I slew him! I!"

"He trusted you, unnatural son and brother!" the voice piped. "You cut him down while he slept."

"To victor belong spoils!" Lod boomed. He refilled his mug, drank, tore a great chunk off the roast bird while the thin voice screamed curses.

"But—" Lod pointed a finger at O'Leary, as the latter twitched away from the stab of a spike digging into his thigh. "Does traitor who plots in palace deal fairly with me? Does he fear powers that made me king? No! He thrust me aside, think to confine me here in this parched land while richness of cities and fields goes to him!"

"Why not?" O'Leary heard himself taunting. His mind was fogging now; only the recurrent prick of the dagger points kept him from fainting. "Nicodaeus knows it's safe to cheat you, because you're stupid."

"Stupid?" Lod laughed, a sound like a stone tower falling. "Yet he sent you, a weakling, here."

"How did this weakling pass the guardian?" the voice piped. "Ask him that, mighty imbecile!"

"Yes, now you will talk!" Lod leaned forward unsteadily. "Why did the gray magician send you? Why *you*? Who are you? *What* are you? How—"

O'Leary managed a creditable Bronx cheer.

Lod started to his feet, then sank back heavily. "I exercise myself needlessly," he muttered. "But a little time, and the cage will do its work."

"But a little time, and you will die," the disembodied voice screeched. "Then will the foul ghosts of the ancestors rend your stinking corpse, and that of my father will be foremost."

"Silence!" Lod bellowed. He poured and drank, slopping the ale. "If I die, who then feed you, evil leech?" The giant slumped back in his chair, watching O'Leary with red-rimmed eyes. "I tire of this sport," he rumbled. "Speak now, little man! What are secret schemes of Nicodaeus? What double-dealing lies behind his promises? Why did he send you? Why? Why? Why?"

"Don't you . . . wish you knew . . . " O'Leary managed. If the cage were made of something soft, like taffy . . . or if he had thought to provide a small gun . . . or if someone—anyone—would burst in now, open the cage . . .

It was no use. He was stuck here. His powers didn't work under stress like this. True, when he'd been drowning, he had managed to jump back to Artesia at the last instant. But at least he had been drowning in comfort, and perhaps he hadn't yet reached the last minute. If he ever got out of this, he'd have to set up some controlled experiments, determine the extent and nature of his abilities.

But this time he wouldn't escape. He'd die here; and Adoranne would never know he'd tried.

" . . . now, before it's too late," the tiny voice was chanting. "Let him go, foul parricide, turn back from disasters you know not of."

"Almost," Lod rumbled blurrily, "I think stubborn runtling has suborned you, so merrily you cry his cause! But I am Lod, king and master, and I fear neither man nor devil nor caster of spells."

"Fool! Let him go! I see death, and rivers of blood, and all your vile plans fallen to ruin! I see the shadow of the Great Ax that hovers over your head!"

"Great Ax hangs there amid my trophies," Lod laughed wildly. "Who's to wield it against me here?" He finished off another gallon of ale and refilled the jack with unsteady hands.

"How say you, starveling?" he called to O'Leary. "Do you tire of game? Do red-hot knives of pain loosen your tongue?"

"I'm fine," O'Leary said blurrily. "I like it here. It's restful."

"Let him go!" the voice snarled. "Let him go, cretinous monster!"

Lod shook his head in drunken stubbornness. "You see, little man, what a burden even greatness must bear. Day and night, waking and sleeping, that foul voice ever shrilling at my ear! Is enough to drive lesser man mad, eh?" He peered owlishly at O'Leary.

"I . . . don't hear . . . anything," O'Leary got out. "You've already . . . gone nuts, I guess . . . "

Lod laughed again, hiccupped. "No ghostly voice, this," he rumbled. "It issues from hideous lips as ever body nourished."

"That's . . . the first sign," O'Leary gasped. "Hearing voices . . . "

Lod grinned. "And you, little man—you draw comfort from the impertinence you hear pass unpunished. You guess you gain an ally, eh?" Lod's chuckle was not an encouraging sound. "Small help you'll have from that quarter," he cried. "But I've been discourteous! I've not made introductions! An oversight, believe me! But I'll soon set that aright." Lod reached to his throat, fumbled at the scarf, tore it free.

From the base of his bull-neck, a second head grew—a shrunken, wizened, hollow-cheeked copy of the first, with eyes like live coals.

"Behold my brother!" Lod mumbled; then he fell back in his chair, mouth open, eyes shut, and snored.

Chapter Eleven

For a long minute, there was silence. Lod's snores grew louder, deeper. He stirred, flung out an arm that knocked over the ale mug. Dark fluid gushed, splashed on the floor, then settled down to a steady drip. O'Leary watched, wide-eyed, as Lod's second head stirred, staring across at him. The lips worked.

"The . . . great brute . . . sleeps," it whispered shrilly. "The strong ale tugs at my mind also . . . but I will not heed it."

O'Leary stared. The spilled ale dropped. Lod snuffled, snorted in his sleep.

"Hearken, small one," the head hissed. "Will you do my bidding, if I help you now?"

O'Leary tried to speak; his tongue seemed paralyzed. It was too much effort. He felt himself slumping against the spikes. He knew they were cutting in, but the blessed relief of a moment's rest . . .

"Don't die now, fool!" the head whispered harshly. "I can free you—but first your word that you will do the task I set you!"

"What—what is it?" O'Leary tried to keep his mind on what the head was saying. He knew it was important, but a great pit of soft blackness was waiting, and if he just let go, he would sink down, down . . .

"Listen to me! Freedom! If you swear to serve me!"

The voice penetrated the fog. His chest hurt—how it hurt! Spikes were digging in as he slumped against them. Something sharp was cutting into his cheek, and another against his jaw.

He gasped and pulled himself off the daggers. The eyes in the shrunken head caught him, glaring.

" . . . now, fool! Catch at the chance Fortune throws in your path! Give me your word and I'll set you free!"

"What—what do you . . . want me to . . . do?" O'Leary managed.

"See the great ax on the wall yonder? It was written—ah, long and long ago—that by its keen edge the betrayer would meet his doom! Take it! Raise it high! Strike off his head!"

"His . . . head?"

"The murderer of his king and father has sworn to do the like by me," the head hissed. "He swore that none should witness his nuptial revels when he makes the Princess Adoranne his bride! The finest surgeons in the land will he summon, and under their knives I'll suffer living decapitation. He hates me, and he fears me. Me, who has suffered with him through thick and thin, ever ready with a word of advice. And now he says I will shame him before her quaking loveliness! Ah, the vile creature! He'd remove me like a wart, cut me down in my prime! His brother!"

"How . . . can you . . . release me?"

"When he sleeps in drunken sottishness, as now, I can, a little, control the body; *our* body, soon to be mine alone. How say you, little man? Is it a bargain?"

"I . . . I'll try."

"Done!" The glittering eyes narrowed. O'Leary saw perspiration pop out on the brown and furrowed brow under a lock of giant's hair. One hair hand stirred, groped clumsily in the folds of the gown, crept inside. There was a jingle of metal. The hand emerged, holding a ring of keys. Lod snored on, his tongue lolling from his gaping mouth.

"The pain—the mortal pain of it," the second head whimpered. "But soon, soon victory is mine!"

O'Leary watched, goggle-eyed as the hand lifted the keys—then, with an awkward motion, tossed them. They struck the cage, caught on a spike, dangled inches from his hand.

"I can't reach them," he whispered.

"Try! Only a little pain stands between you and freedom! Try!"

O'Leary moved his hand an inch; spikes caught at his arm. He twisted his body sideways, feeling the thrust of other stiletto points against his ribs and hip. He inched the arm forward and up, gritting his teeth as the skin scraped, the blood started, joining the dried blood from earlier cuts. Another inch . . . almost there . . . His finger caught the key ring, teased it . . .

It dropped into his palm, and he clutched it, his heart thudding. Lod snorted, stirred. O'Leary watched him, holding his breath. The giant's breathing steadied once more. Painfully, O'Leary worked his arm back to his side, then forward, enduring the stab of the knives. His clothes were a bloody mess, he realized dimly. He was bleeding from dozens of separate small wounds; none deep, but all painful. He was losing a lot of blood.

"The key of black iron," the head keened softly. "Quickly, now! He sleeps but lightly!"

One more effort. O'Leary took a deep breath, gripping the key in slippery fingers. He reached, forgetting the damage he was doing to his hide, concentrating on the objective. The key touched the dangling lock; it swung away, clattering. The head cursed softly. O'Leary dropped the keys, pushed up on the lock with a finger. In the chair, Lod moved his feet, reached up to rub a thick finger under his nose. The second head watched, cracked lips parted.

The lock rose, teetered, fell with a clatter. Lod half-opened his eyes, smacked his lips noisily, relaxed again. O'Leary pushed against the hinged front of the cage. It swung wide. He stumbled out, stood swaying before the sleeping giant.

"Adoranne," he said thickly. "Was he lying? Is she here?"

"He spoke the truth, foolish man. Doubtless He-Who-Plots-in-the-Palace can tell you of her. There is no time to waste! Quickly, to your duty!"

O'Leary straightened his aching back, wiped his bloodied hands on his thighs, tottered to the wall. The ax hung high, out of reach. He turned, dragged a three-legged stool over to the wall, stood on it, nearly fell, clutched at the wall for support. The dizziness passed. The haft of the ax was as big around as his wrist, diagonally wrapped with tough animal hide, dry and hard. He gripped it, lifted it free from the rusted spike it dangled from.

The heavy weapon slipped from his grasp, came clanging down against the hard earth floor. Lod grunted; O'Leary scrambled down, reached, brought up the ax. It was heavy, awkward, too long by a yard. The broad steel head was red with fine rust, twelve inches wide at each blade, two feet from edge to edge, set in a notch in the wood and wrapped with leather strips.

"Haste, small man!" the thin voice screeched. Lod's eyes flew open. He stared blankly, then shook his head, muttering. His gaze fell on O'Leary as the latter gripped the ax at midpoint, brought it up across his shoulder. Lod roared, tried to rise, slipped, fell back, bellowing.

With a heave, O'Leary swung the ax from his shoulder, took two steps, brought it over and down with all the force of his arms behind it, square on the juncture of Lod's neck and chest. The great head leaped up six inches, like a grotesque beach ball balanced on a spurting column of crimson; then it fell aside, bounced once on the massive shoulder, struck the floor with a meaty thud, spun, came to a stop staring up at O'Leary with a hideous leer.

In the chair, the great body, still fountaining blood, rose unsteadily to its feet.

"Now I am master," the tiny head croaked.

Then the body toppled—dead.

O'Leary groped to the table, feeling blackness closing in; he found the ale jug with his hands, tilted it, drank, then leaned on the table and waited while the cool liquid burned away the fog. There was food here—a feast fit for a giant. He sank down on a stool, picked up a roast pigeon, fell to, oblivious of the immense body lying at his feet in a spreading pool of tar-black blood.

After eating, O'Leary pulled off his shirt and examined his wounds. He was cut, slashed, scraped in fifty places. None of the cuts were deep, but he'd look like a school-girl's embroidery project when the doctors finished stitching him up. Using a little of the ale, he cleaned the slashes, wincing at the sting. He wiped away the drying blood, then tore strips from Lod's voluminous scarf to bind up the worst cuts.

He went to the door—there was no sound from out-side. Was Crusher or another of Lod's bulky bodyguard standing by, awaiting a summons? He needed a weapon. There were plenty of them on the wall, but all were broken—war trophies, taken from fallen enemies, Lod had boasted. The ax was too big to be handy, but it would have to do—and maybe its bloody condition would impress the locals. He hefted it, got it across his shoulder, flung the door open. There was no one in sight in the dark tunnel.

The rough-hewn passage led upward at a slant, angled around a massive reinforced concrete footing, ended at a crude doorway hacked in the ceramic tile cellar wall, covered over by an un-tanned hide of some scaly animal. O'Leary thrust it aside, emerged into a gloomy basement crowded with vast air-conditioner and furnace units festooned with aluminum-wrapped duct work, piping, and heavy electrical cables. At one side, a 50 kw diesel generator chugged patiently—the source of the remaining electric power in the hotel, O'Leary deduced.

He crossed the wide room, went up stairs and came out into the kitchens, foul with a faint odor of rotted food. Windows at the far side showed the gray light of early dawn. They were sealed shut, he saw. Still, there was no point in venturing out into the frequented area of the building. His mission now was merely escape, and return to the capital as quickly as his pet dragon could canter. Nicodaeus had been clever, tricking him into setting off on a wild goose chase while he completed his plans for seizure of the kingdom undisturbed. Lod had said that the plotter planned to dispose of Adoranne. If he had hurt her—

Time to think about that later. O'Leary swung the ax at the window. Glass burst outward. He knocked free the jagged shards remaining in the frame, stepped up on a table, ducked through to a wide stone sill and jumped down to the untrimmed turf six feet below. So far, so good. Now, where was his mount? He gave a low whistle. There was an answering hiss from beyond the nearest clump of trees, only dimly visible through the early-morning fog. O'Leary set off in that direction and saw the stir of a tall body among the trunks. A mighty figure stalked forth to meet him, looking bigger than ever through the mist.

"That's the boy, right on the job," O'Leary called in a low voice. He trotted forward to meet the tremendous beast as it advanced, emitting a rumble like a dormant volcano stirring to life. O'Leary admired the play of the massive thigh muscles under the greenish hide, the great column of the neck, the jaws—

Jaws? He didn't remember a head the size of a Volkswagen, opening like a vast power shovel to reveal multiple rows of gleaming ivory daggers, nor did he recall red eyes, pinning him down like spears, or talons like curved bone scimitars.

He turned, dropped the cumbersome ax and dashed for shelter. A huge foot struck the earth just beside him; something immense swooped down and O'Leary caught a glimpse of a steaming red-lined cavern big enough to stable a pony. He dived; there was a tremendous boom! as the jaws met inches behind him; a blow sent him spinning.

He rolled over, came to hands and knees, his shirt in shreds. He saw the strange dinosaur whirl, a tatter of cloth dangling from its teeth, and come prancing back, jaws ready for a second try. O'Leary backed, met the solid resistance of thick-growing shrubbery—

With a crash of rending branches, a second, smaller reptile stepped into view. Dinny!

The herbivore took two steps into the clear. The meat-eater bellowed. Dinny gave a leap when he apparently saw the tyrannosaur for the first time. He bleated, took three hasty steps backward, turned and made for cover.

"Smart dinosaur," O'Leary muttered. He readied himself for a desperate sprint as the carnivore veered to plunge after the tame saurian, jaws gaping even wider. A few yards in the lead, the iguanodon skidded to a halt, rocked forward, swept his heavy fleshy tail to one side, and brought it around in a swipe that caught the meat-eater solidly across the knees. The tyrannosaur stumbled, crashed through a screen of trees in a tangle of broken boughs and trailing vines, and went down out of sight with an impact like a falling skyscraper. There was one terrific blast of sound, like a calliope gone mad; the unbelievable legs kicked out, subsided to a regular twitching, shuddered, were still. O'Leary tottered across the patch of lawn, peered through the fallen foliage; the spearheads of the steel fence across which the monster had fallen protruded through the massive neck. O'Leary stooped, recovered his ax.

"Nice placement, boy," O'Leary said. "Now let's saddle up and ride—and hope we're not too late."

It was a two hours' ride into the desert. O'Leary shaded his eyes, watching a moving caterpillar of dust approaching, miles away across the parched sands. The column had halted. Men on horseback were milling, fanning out. One or two deserters or couriers had turned and were cutting trails back toward the distant faint line of green that marked the desert's edge, fifteen miles away. Now a single horseman spurred forward, riding out alone in advance of the deployed troop. O'Leary slowed his mount to a walk. The lone rider was a tall man, buckled into black armor, a long sword slapping at his side, a long lance in its rest. He reined in his handsome black charger a hundred yards distant, and O'Leary saw the black hair and clean-cut features of Count Alain. The count raised a gauntleted hand to wipe the sweat from his forehead.

"As I expected, the traitor, Sir Lafayette!" he shouted. "I warned the king you were in Lod's pay, but he seemed to find the suggestion amusing."

"I don't blame him, it's a very funny idea," O'Leary called back. "What are you doing out here in the desert?"

"I've come with a hundred loyal men to demand the return of her Highness, unharmed. Will you yield now, villain, or must we attack?"

"Well, that's very nobly spoken, Al," O'Leary said. "And I admire your nerve in facing up to Dinny here. But I'm afraid you're barking up the wrong dinosaur. I don't have Adoranne."

"Then your master, the unspeakable Lod—"

"He's not my master. In fact, he's not anybody's master now. I killed him."

"You? Ha! I'm laughing!"

O'Leary held up the bloodied ax. "Then laugh this off. But let's cut the chatter. Adoranne isn't back there; she never was. Nicodaeus is the man we want. He's plotting to take over the kingdom. He had a deal with Lod, but it seems he's decided he doesn't need him any more, so he double-crossed him and instead of delivering her Highness to him as a consolation prize, he intends to do away with her."

"Lies!" Alain shouted, rising in his stirrups and shaking a mailed fist. "You're trying to drag red herrings across the trail. But if you think I'm fool enough to swallow that tale—"

"Go ahead—see for yourself. You'll find Lod in his private interrogation room, at the end of a tunnel from the cellar under the kitchens. He had fifty or more thugs hanging around the place, so be careful. Don't worry about his dragon, though; Dinny here killed it."

"You take me for an idiot? You're perched on the Lod's dragon at this moment, in living testimony to your false alliance!"

"OK. I can't wait around. I've got to get to the capital before it's too late. Too bad you can't see your way clear to join me." O'Leary kicked his heels against the saurian's skull: it obediently started forward. Alain spurred aside, watched as O'Leary rode past.

"First I ride to rescue her Highness," he shouted. "Then I settle accounts with you, Sir Lafayette!"

"I'll be waiting for you. Ta-ta!" O'Leary waved and then settled down for the long ride ahead.

The sun was high when he crossed the cactus-grown borderland and rode down the last slope into the green countryside of Artesia. News of his approach had spread ahead of him: his fifteen-foot-tall mount must have been visible for the last quarter hour as it tramped across the sandy waste. The road was deserted now; shops stood empty; the windows of the houses along the way were tight-shuttered. O'Leary's cuts and bruises were aching abominably and his reflections were gloomy.

By agreeing with his theory that Lod was the abductor, Nicodaeus had neatly set one nuisance against another, with a chance that O'Leary and the giant might manage to destroy each other. The magician had been a plausible scoundrel; poor King Goruble had given the schemer quarters right in the palace, where he could carry out his plot with the greatest convenience. The plan had been well worked out, O'Leary conceded; and only luck had given him this chance to thwart the would-be usurper—if he wasn't already too late.

He entered the suburbs—the collection of squatters' huts and merchants' stalls clustered outside the city wall proper. All was silent, the narrow alleys empty. A damned shame he couldn't find someone to spread the word that he was on their side, that he needed their help now in his attack on Nicodaeus. No telling what the magician might have rigged in the way of defenses. There might be a battery of artillery waiting just inside the palace walls. Well, if so, that was just a risk he'd have to run.

The city gates just ahead were closed tight. From his perch, O'Leary could see over the wall into empty streets beyond. Well, if they wouldn't let him in, he'd have to make his own way. He urged Dinny ahead; the saurian balked, sidled, then turned, lashed out with its tail. A twenty-foot section of the ancient wall went over with a crash and rumble of falling masonry. The dinosaur picked its way delicately through the rubble into the street of shuttered shops. Far away, O'Leary heard the sound of a church bell tolling out a warning. Except for that, and the scrape and clack of the iguanodon's horny bird-feet on the cobbles, the city was silent as death.

The palace gates were shut, O'Leary saw, as he rode up the avenue leading through the park toward the high iron grilles. Two frightened sentries stood their ground inside the wall, nervously fingering blunderbusses. One raised his weapon as O'Leary halted fifty yards from the gates.

"Don't shoot," he called, "I'm—"

There was a loud boom! and a jet of black smoke spurted from the flared muzzle of the gun. O'Leary heard a shape whack! against the dinosaur's hide. The latter turned his head casually and cropped a bale of leaves from an arching branch.

"Listen to me!" Lafayette tried again. "I've just escaped from Lod's fortress, and—"

The second guard fired; O'Leary heard the ball shriek past his head.

"Hey!" he yelled. "That could be dangerous! Why don't you listen to what I've got to say before you make a serious error?"

Both men threw their guns aside and bolted.

"Oh, well, I guess it's what you'd expect," O'Leary muttered. "All right, boy, here we go again." He urged the dinosaur forward; it stalked up to the gates, leaned on them, trampled them down without slowing, continued along the wide, graveled drive. Ahead the palace loomed, windows aglitter in the afternoon sun, silent. A movement caught O'Leary's eye at the top of one of the towers. He turned toward it across the lawn and waved an arm.

"Hello in there!" he shouted. "It's me, Lafayette O'Leary—"

All along the parapets, from the castellated tops of towers, from the archer's slits set in the stone walls, arrows sprang, arching up in sibilant flight, converging, dropping.

O'Leary ducked, closed his eyes and gritted his teeth. An arrow clacked off Dinny's snout, inches from his boot tip. Something plucked at his torn left sleeve. Other darts clattered down, glancing from the dino's tough hide, bounding off to fall in the grass. Then silence. He opened an eye; ranks of men were in view at the ramparts now, fitting new bolts to strings, bending bows.

"Let's get out of here, Dinny!" O'Leary dug in his heels; the big reptile started forward as a second flight of arrows swept past to thud into the turf and rattle off the iguanodon's tail. The balustraded grand entry was just ahead. The dinosaur took the graceful flight of wide steps at a stride and halted at O'Leary's command.

"No use knocking the wall down," he panted, sliding down to the smooth tiles of the terrace as Dinny lowered his head to investigate the geranium boxes along its edge. "You wait here."

Still carrying Lod's ax, O'Leary ran to the wide glass doors—less substantial than the oak panels opening from the courtyard side, he noted gratefully—kicked them in. The great hall echoed his steps. Somewhere in the distance he could hear a hoarse voice yelling commands. Those archers at the battlements would be arriving on the scene at any moment—and at close range, they could hardly miss.

The entrance from the great hall to the secret passage system was on the far side, he remembered; right about there, where the tall mirrors reflected gilt ceilings and a vast crystal chandelier. Feet were clattering above. O'Leary ran, reached the wall, felt quickly over it. To the left? No, more to the right.

There was a loud yell from above: O'Leary looked up, saw a beefy-faced household guardsman with three wide yellow stripes on his sleeve leaning over a gallery rail, pointing. More men crowded up behind him. Bows appeared, and muskets. O'Leary searched frantically. He had seen the chandelier when Yokabump had opened the panel for him to peek out—he remembered that. And the fountain there—

A section of wall slid aside, just as the roar of a shot boomed through the hall. Bowstrings twanged and an arrow struck the wall beside him as he ducked, stepped inside and hauled the ax in behind him. A second arrow shot between his knees and thumped into the wall inside the passage. O'Leary slammed the panel, heard half a dozen hammer blows as more bolts struck, just an instant late. He leaned against the rough brickwork and let out a long sigh.

Now for Nicodaeus.

***

The heavy door was closed and the tower room silent, as O'Leary stood before it listening. From below, he could hear shouts ringing back and forth as the agitated guardsmen scurried about, looking for the lost trail. They might start up the stairs at any moment and if they cornered him here, it was all over. An ax wasn't much good against guns and bows. He hammered on the door.

"Let me in, Nicodaeus," he called in a low voice, then put his ear to the panel. There might have been a faint rustle from within.

"Open up or I'll knock the door down!" This time he was sure; there was a soft thump from beyond the door. Perhaps there was another passage, one Yokabump hadn't known about; maybe the magician was making a backdoor escape while he stood here like a Fuller Brush man.

O'Leary raised the ax, swung it high.

The door creaked open six inches. There was a hoarse yell as the ax came down against the panel with a crash that slammed the door wide. O'Leary looked past it at Nicodaeus, backed against a table, making gulping motions.

"Dear boy," the magician managed to gasp out, "you startled me."

O'Leary wrenched the ax from the oak door. "You can skip all that 'dear boy' schmaltz," he said coldly. "I'm a little slow to think unkind thoughts about anybody I've shared a drink with, but in your case I managed. Where is she?"

"Where—where is who?"

"Adoranne. And don't bother with the innocence routine either. I know all about you. Your friend Lod spilled the beans just before I killed him."

"You *killed* Lod?" Nicodaeus' eyebrows shot up toward his receding hairline.

"With this." O'Leary hefted the ax. "And I'm prepared to use it again, if I have to. Now start talking. Where have you got her stashed? Right here in the palace, I suppose. It would be easy enough, with all these passages in the walls."

"You must believe me, Lafayette!" The magician straightened himself. "I know nothing of her Highness' disappearance, no more than any other—"

O'Leary advanced. "Don't stall; I have no time to waste. Talk fast, or I'll hack you into stew-sized chunks and find her myself. I know the back routes pretty well."

"Lafayette, you're making a mistake! I don't know what the rebel, Lod, said of me, but—"

"Never mind what he said. What about the way the cops pounced, five minutes after I came into your inner sanctum here, looking for help, a couple of evenings ago?"

"But—but—I had nothing to do with it! It was a routine search. I didn't have time to summon the guard, even if I'd wanted to. And they couldn't have responded that quickly if I had."

"I guess you have nothing to do with framing me with that silly episode in Adoranne's boudoir, either—to get me out of the way, so you could carry on with your schemes unmolested!"

"Of course not! I was as amazed as you were."

"And I should just disregard what Lod said about your plans."

"Lafayette, I did, I admit, approach Lod on one occasion, but only in an effort to learn certain facts. I offered to, ah, grant him certain compensations if he would tell me all he knew of, well, certain matters . . . " Nicodaeus' face was damp, his eyes bugging slightly as they followed the glint of light on the brown-crusted edge of the ax in O'Leary's hands.

"Uh-huh. Certain compensations—like Adoranne."

"No!" the magician yelped. "Did he say that? In his own crude way, Lod was a man of directness, not guile. Surely he didn't accuse me of such an act!"

"Well . . . " O'Leary went back over the conversation with Lod. "He called you a traitor—and he accused me of being your agent."

"But the other—did he say that *I* had promised him the person of her Highness?"

"He kept babbling about the plotter in the palace—how you were out to seize the throne, and do away with Adoranne."

"The plotter in the palace?" Nicodaeus frowned. "It wasn't *I* he was talking about, dear lad. I promise you that. What else did he say?"

"He said you didn't need him any more, so you were welching on your promises."

"Lafayette, I made the giant a promise—this I admit. But it was only that if he would tell me all he knows of—of the matters I spoke of—that I would confirm him in his local power, and see to it that he received a reward in cash—an offer which he promised to consider. But as for thrones, and murder—"

"Get specific, Nicodaeus! What were these certain matters?"

"I'm . . . not at liberty to say."

"All right, play it mysterious then. But if you think I'm going to let you talk your way out of this . . . " O'Leary advanced, bringing the ax up.

"Stop!" Nicodaeus raised both hands. "I'll tell you, Lafayette! But I'm warning you, it's a gross violation of security!"

"Make it good!" O'Leary waited, ax ready.

"I'm a . . . a representative of an organization of vast importance; a secret operative, you might say. I was assigned here to investigate certain irregularities."

"Don't give me that 'certain' routine!"

"Very well; I was sent here by Central. There was the matter of a highly localized Probability Stress. I was sent to clear it up."

"Not very good," O'Leary said, shaking his head. "Not very convincing. Try again."

"Look . . . " Nicodaeus groped inside his flowing robe, brought out a shiny shield-shaped object. "My badge. And if you'll let me get my lock box, I'll show you my full credentials . . . "

O'Leary leaned forward to look at the badge. There was a large 7–8–6 engraved in its center on a stylized representation of what appeared to be an onion. Around the edge O'Leary spelled out:

SUBINSPECTOR OF CONTINUA

He frowned at the older man and lowered the ax reluctantly. "What does that mean?"

"One of the jobs of Central is seeking out and neutralizing unauthorized stresses in the Probability Fabric. They can cause untold damage to the orderly progress of entropic evolution."

O'Leary hefted the ax. "That's over my head. Tell me in simple language what this is all about."

"I'll try, Lafayette—not that I'm at all sure I know myself. It seems that this coordinate level, this, ah, um, universe? Dimension? Aspect of multi-ordinate reality?"

"You mean world?" O'Leary waved a hand to encompass all of Artesia.

"Precisely! Very well put. This world was the scene, some decades ago, of a Probability Fault, resulting in a permanent stress in continuum. Naturally, this required clearing up, since all sorts of untoward events can occur along the stress line, particularly where matter displacement has occurred."

"OK, let's skip over that. I'd say you were nutty as a pecan roll except for a few things that have happened to me lately. Too bad we don't have more time to discuss it. But what's that got to do with Adoranne?"

"I was merely attempting to establish my bona fides, dear boy. Some sort of skullduggery took place here twenty or thirty years ago; the situation still remains unresolved. It's my job to find the center of the stress pattern, restore all anachronisms and extra-continual phenomena to their normal space-time-serial niches, and thus eliminate the anomaly. But I confess I've made no progress. The center is here, nearby. At one time, I even suspected you, Lafayette—after all, you appeared under rather mysterious circumstances—but, of course, you checked out as clean as a scrublady's knees." He smiled glassily.

"What do you mean, checked out?"

"I took readings on you when I visited you in your room, before the ball. The lighter, you know. You gave a neutral indication, of course. You see, only an outsider—a person native to another continuum—would elicit a positive indication. Since you're a native, you gave no such reading."

"Mmmmmm. You'd better have your dials checked. But look—this isn't finding Adoranne. I was sure you had her. If not . . . " O'Leary looked at Nicodaeus, feeling suddenly helpless. "Who does?"

Nicodaeus stroked his chin. "The plotter in the palace you say Lod spoke of?"

"I wasn't paying much attention; I thought he meant you. He was pretty drunk, but still cagey enough not to mention the name."

"Who would gain by the disappearance of her Highness? Someone with ambitions of usurpation, someone close to the throne, someone unsuspected," Nicodaeus mused. "Could it be one of Goruble's painted dandies?"

"Lod is the one who had his eye on the throne—and a yen for Adoranne, too. Maybe Alain—but somehow he strikes me as honest, in his blundering way. Then there's you—but for some reason I believe your story. But I'd still like to know who spread the word that I'd been here. They were staked out at the city gates, waiting for me. Are you sure you didn't spill the beans?"

"I assure you, I was discretion itself. Even King Goruble . . . " Nicodaeus paused, looking thoughtful.

"What about Goruble?" O'Leary said sharply.

"I had a few words with his Majesty, just after you were here. He questioned me closely. I wondered at the time what he was hinting at; he appeared to suspect I'd been shielding you."

"Did you tell him I'd been here?"

"No . . . and yet, now that you mention it, he seemed to know . . . " Nicodaeus' eyes were round. "Great heavens, Lafayette! Do you suppose? But how could it be? I've been looking for someone, an outsider—but the king—"

"Lod said someone who *wanted* to take over the throne; Goruble already has it."

Nicodaeus frowned. "In these cases there's usually some individual—often a renegade agent of Central, I confess—who sees his chance to establish himself comfortably in a subtechnical environment and make himself dictator. To which Central would have no particular objection, if it weren't for the resultant chain of anomalies. But it never occurred to me—"

" . . . that he'd already taken over," O'Leary finished for him. "I don't know much about the history of Artesia, but from a few hints dropped here and there, I've gotten the impression King Goruble is far from beloved, and that he came to power some twenty-odd years ago under rather vague circumstances."

"I've been blind!" Nicodaeus exclaimed. "I've never tested him, of course. Who would have suspected the king? But it fits, Lafayette! It fits! He had the opportunity. He could walk into the princess's apartment without an alarm, lure her away, then presto—pop her into a locked room, and raise the outcry!"

"But what for? She's his niece."

"Not if our theory is correct, lad! He's an outsider, an interloper, a usurper, with no more claim to the throne than you! And Adoranne, as the niece of the previous king, represents a very real threat to his security—particularly since he is himself unpopular, while the masses adore the princess!"

"Then *he* was the one who was doing business with Lod—the plotter in the palace!" O'Leary nibbled at his lip. "But hold it, Nicodaeus. There's one big flaw in the picture: Lod—from what I could guess—was brought in from . . . somewhere else. One of these other continua of yours, I'd say. The same goes for that dinosaur he kept in his front yard. And his HQ itself—it looked like something that had been plucked up by the roots and dumped in the desert for Lod's use. The plotter we're looking for was using Lod as a diversion, to keep the people's minds off his own power grab, and the fancy quarters and the personal dragon were part of the bargain. But the only one around here with outside resources—is *you!*"

"Me? But Lafayette! I'm an inspector! I can't go moving buildings and tyrannosauri about at will! My workshop here suffices for a few modest surveillance instruments, nothing more! You're forgetting that our culprit was himself an outsider. If he transported himself here, why couldn't he have manipulated the rest?"

"You're still holding out on me, Nicodaeus. What about your *real* workshop? I saw some pretty big machines down there; they aren't just for checking suspects' vibrations."

"Real workshop? I'm afraid I don't know what you mean, Lafayette."

"In the cellar—the big room with the iron door, and the smaller room that looks like a walk-in refrigerator."

"Like . . . like . . . ?" Nicodaeus' eyes bugged. "Lafayette —did you say—walk-in refrigerator?"

"Yes, and—"

"With a large door—with a big latch mechanism, like this?" He sketched in the air.

"Right. What's it for?"

Nicodaeus groaned. "I fear, Lafayette, we'll not see Adoranne again. The device you describe is a Traveler—used to transport small cargoes from one coordinate level to another. I was dropped here in one, and expect, in due course, to be picked up by another. If Goruble had one here—a stolen vehicle belonging to

Central, no doubt—then I fear Adoranne is already beyond our reach."

"You really think Goruble's our man?"

"None other. Alas, Lafayette, she was such a charming girl."

"Maybe it's not too late," O'Leary snapped. "Come on, we'll pay a call on His Majesty—and this time I won't be bluffing!"

The red-faced sergeant of the guard spotted them as they stepped off the main stairway at the third floor. He gave a yell and dashed up, gun in hand.

"Hold, my man!" Nicodaeus called. "I'm taking Sir Lafayette to interview his Majesty on a matter concerning the security of the realm! Kindly call your men in as an honor guard!"

"Honor guard?" The noncom raised his musket threateningly, "I'll honor-guard the louse, kidnapping our princess."

"I didn't," O'Leary cut in, "but I think I know who did. If you want to shoot me before I can tell, go ahead."

The sergeant hesitated. "Better lay down that ax, buster. Drop it right there."

"I'm keeping it," O'Leary said shortly. "Come with us or stay here, I don't care which, but don't get in my way." He turned, strode off toward the royal quarters. Behind him, after a moment of hesitation, there was a curse and a snapped order to fall in. A moment later the ten-man detail closed in around Lafayette and Nicodaeus, guns ready, eyes rolling ominously at the pair.

"Better not try nothing," the nearest man muttered. "I got a yen to clear my barrel."

O'Leary halted at the door to the king's chambers, ignoring the two gaping sentries. He tried the elaborate gold knob, pushed the door wide.

"Hey, you can't—" someone gasped.

"All right, Goruble, come on out!" O'Leary called. He looked around at cloth-of-gold hangings, high windows, rich rugs, spindle-legged furniture with the gleam of rare wood. The room was empty. He walked across to an inner door, threw it wide; it was an ornate bath, with a sunken tub and gold fittings.

The next door let into a vast bedroom with a canopied bed looking like a galleon under full sail. O'Leary checked two more rooms, Nicodaeus at his side, the troop of soldiers following, silent, awed by this rude invasion of the royal privacy.

"He's not here," Nicodaeus said as O'Leary prodded the hanging clothes in the closet of the last room.

"But—he's got to be here," a guardsman said. "He couldn'a left without we knew about it; after all, we're the royal bodyguard."

"I think I might know where he went," O'Leary said. "I'll go check."

"You ain't going no place, bud." The sergeant stepped forward to assert his damaged authority. "I'm taking you down to the dungeons, and when his Majesty shows up—"

"Sorry, no time." O'Leary brought the butt of the ax up in a swipe from the floor, caught the sergeant under the third button; he oofed and doubled over. O'Leary tossed the ax, handle-first, at the man behind him, straight-armed the next, ran for the door, whirled and slammed it behind him. There were shouts and loud thuds as he turned the key in the lock. In three jumps he was across the room, pulling aside the drapes that framed a portrait of the king as a frowning youth. He slapped panels; a section of wall tilted outward. He slipped through, clicked it shut behind him, turned—and froze at a scraping sound from the darkness.

"Nice footwork, O'Leary," the cavernous voice of Yokabump said. "I kind of figured you'd be taking to the woodwork soon. Where you headed?"

"I'm glad you're here," O'Leary said tensely. "You remember the rooms in the cellar? The ones with all the big machines?"

"Oh, you mean old Goruble's thinking rooms. Sure. What about 'em?"

"I need to get down there—fast!"

"Maybe you better stay clear o' that section for a while. The old boy himself walked right past me in the dark, not an hour ago, headed in the same direction—and I'd say he was in a lousy mood."

"An hour ago? Then maybe there's a chance! Come on, Yokabump! Lead the way as fast as you can, and hope it's fast enough!"

The polished slab door was closed tight as O'Leary came softly up to it, his tread muffled by the carpet of dust in the narrow passage.

"He's still in there," Yokabump whispered. There was a sound like a dynamo growling to a halt. "His footprints go in, and don't come out."

"You must have eyes like a cat," O'Leary said. "It's all I can do to see where I'm going." He put his ear to the door. Silence.

O'Leary narrowed his eyes. There was a keyhole, just there, near the edge, he told himself; a small inconspicuous aperture. And the key—it would be hanging from a nail on the beam . . .

There was the faintest of bumps in the smooth flow of the timestream. O'Leary smiled grimly, groped over the rough-hewn member, found the tiny key.

"Hey, O'Leary!" Yokabump rumbled. "How'd you know that was there?"

"Shhhh." O'Leary quietly fitted the key into the door; there was a tiny click. He leaned against the door; it swung silently inward, revealing the dim-lit interior of the room, the massed dials and indicator lights, the tall shapes of the massive equipment housings, the festooned conduits and, in the center of the room, King Goruble, seated in a chair, holding a compactly built machine gun across his knees.

"Come right in, Sir Lafayette," Goruble said grimly. "I've been awaiting you."

Chapter Twelve

O'Leary gauged the distance to the rotund monarch. If he jumped to one side, then hit him low—

"I wouldn't recommend it," Goruble said. "I'm quite adept at the use of firearms. Come away from the door. I don't want you to be tempted. Just take a chair there." The king nodded to a seat beside the panel. O'Leary moved across, sat down gingerly, his legs under him, ready to move fast when the moment came.

"You look a trifle uncomfortable," Goruble said. His voice was hard. "Just lean back, if you please, and stretch your legs out. That way I think you'll be less likely to attempt anything foolish."

O'Leary followed orders. This was a new Goruble; the theories that had seemed farfetched minutes before were taking on a new plausibility. The small eyes that stared at him now were those of a man capable of anything.

"Where's Adoranne?" O'Leary demanded abruptly.

"Speak when spoken to," Goruble said harshly. "There are a few facts I want from you—before I make disposition of you."

"With that?" O'Leary glanced at the gun.

"Nothing so gory—unless you force me to, of course, in which case I can put up with the inconvenience. No, I'll merely remove you to a place where you can cause me no trouble."

"And what place would that be?"

"Don't bother your head about that," Goruble retorted coldly. "Now, tell me how much you know. If I find you holding back, I'll consign you to a certain small island I know of—capable of sustaining life, but not offering much in the way of amusements. But for each fact you confide in me, I'll add another amenity to your exile."

"I think I know the place you mean, but I didn't like it there, so I left—if you'll recall." O'Leary watched the stout ruler for a reaction to the shot in the dark. Goruble's mouth twitched in a frown.

"This time you'll have no confederate to snatch you back. Now, kindly start your recital. How much is known at Central?"

O'Leary considered and rejected a number of snappy answers. "Enough," he said after the momentary pause.

"You, I take it, are fully in the confidence of Nicodaeus. How did he discover your identity?"

"I told him," O'Leary hazarded.

"Ah." Goruble looked crafty. "And how did you discover your identity?"

"Someone told me," O'Leary replied promptly.

Goruble's brow furrowed. "I suggest you speak plainly!" he rapped. "Tell me all you know!"

O'Leary said nothing.

"You'd best discover your tongue at once," Goruble snapped. "Remember, I have it in my power to make it highly uncomfortable for you—or, on the other hand, to leave you in a situation of comparative ease."

O'Leary was studying the half-open door of a cabinet on the wall behind the king. If there should be a small glass container lying just inside—and if it should be on its side, ready to roll out—and if there should be just the slightest jar, such as a sneeze . . .

"Surely you're not childish enough to imagine that you can distract me by eyeing some imaginary intruder behind me," Goruble smiled sourly. "I'm . . . " his nose twitched. "I'm far too . . . tooo . . . " He drew a sharp breath, blasted out a titanic sneeze, then grabbed for the gun, brought it back on target.

"It requires bore thad a bere sdeeze to distragd be." He fumbled for a handkerchief in his breast pocket. "I'm quite accustomed to the dust in these unused ways."

There was a soft creak as the cabinet door stirred in the faint gust of air raised by Goruble's explosion. Light glinted for an instant on something on the dark shelf; an eight-ounce beaker rolled into view, dropped—

At the impact of glass against concrete, Goruble leaped from the chair. The gun went off with a shattering roar, stitched a row of craters across the floor, blasted tufts of cotton from the chair seat as O'Leary dived from it, slamming Goruble aside with a shoulder. He snatched the gun as it flew from the king's hands and whirled, centered the sights on the monarch's paunch.

"Nice weapon," he said. "I'll bet a few of these made a lot of difference, back when you were stealing the throne."

Goruble made an unpleasant, snarling noise.

"Sit down over there," O'Leary ordered. "Now, let's cut the chatter. Where's Adoranne?" He was fingering the unfamiliar stock of the weapon, wondering which projecting button was the trigger. If Goruble had another gun stashed, and went for it now . . .

"Look here, you utter fool," Goruble snapped. "You don't know what you're doing."

"You wanted facts," Lafayette said. "Here are a few: You're sitting on somebody else's throne. You've kidnapped her Highness—who isn't your niece, by the way—because she's a potential threat to you. You brought Lod in from Outside, and his pet lizard, too. Unfortunately, I had to kill both of them."

"You—" Goruble dropped flat as O'Leary's questing finger touched a concave button on the breech of the gun and sent a round screeching past the king's ear to blast a pocket in the stone wall.

"Just a warning shot," O'Leary said hastily. "Now, open up, Goruble. Where is she?"

The king crouched on all fours, looking badly shaken; his jowls had lost their usual high color.

"Now, now, don't get excited," he babbled, coming shakily to his feet. "I'll tell you what you want to know. As a matter of fact, I'd intended all along to propose an arrangement with you." He slapped at the dust on his velvet doublet. "You didn't think I intended to hog it all, did you, my dear fellow? I merely wished to, ah, consolidate the improvements I've made, before summoning you—that is, inviting you—or—"

"Get to the point. Where is she?"

"Safe!" Goruble said hastily.

"If she's not, I'll blow your head off!"

"I assure you she's well! After all, *you* suffered no harm, eh? I'm not bloodthirsty, you know. The, ah, earlier incident was just an unfortunate accident."

O'Leary raised his eyebrows. "Tell me about the accident."

Goruble spread his hands. "It was the purest misfortune. I had come to his chambers late one evening, with a proposal, a perfectly reasonable proposal—"

"By 'he,' I suppose you mean your predecessor?"

"My, ah, yes, my predecessor. Hot-tempered man, you know. He had no reason to fly into a pet. After all, with my, ah, special resources, the contribution I would make would be well worth the consideration I sought. But he chose instead to pretend that I had insulted him—as though an offer of honorable marriage to his sister could be anything but an honor to the primitive—that is, underdeveloped—or—"

"Get on with it."

"I was a bit put out, of course; I spoke up frankly. He attempted to strike me. There was a struggle; in those days, I was a rather powerful man. He fell . . . "

"Hit his head, I suppose?"

"No, there was a sword—his own, of course—and somehow, in the excitement, he became, er, impaled. Through the heart. Dead, you know. Nothing I could do."

Goruble was sweating. He sank down in the bullet-pocked chair, dabbing at his temples with a lace hanky. "I was in an awkward spot. I could hardly be expected to summon the guard and tell them what had happened. The only course open to me was . . . to dispose of the body. I brought it down through the inner passage, and, ah, sent it away. Then what? I racked my brain, but I could evolve only one scheme: to assume supreme authority—temporarily, of course—until such time as more, ah, regular arrangements could be made. I made certain preparations, called in the members of the council, explained the situation and enlisted their support. There were one or two soreheads, of course, but they came around when the realities of their position were explained to them."

"I get the general idea." O'Leary moved up and pressed the muzzle of the machine gun against Goruble's chin. "Take me to Adoranne—right now. I'll get the rest of your confession later."

Goruble's eyes crossed as he stared down at the cold steel jabbing his throat. "Certainly. The dear child is perfectly well."

"Don't talk; just show me."

Goruble rose carefully and led the way into the passage. O'Leary glanced both ways, but saw no sign of Yokabump. The clown must have fled at the first inkling of the strange doings here in the palace catacombs. Goruble was picking his way in near-darkness, moving along toward the chamber O'Leary had likened to a walk-in refrigerator. The king fumbled out keys under O'Leary's watchful eye, manipulated locks; the heavy panel swung silently open. Goruble stepped back as bright light gleamed through the widening opening. He indicated the interior of the eight-by-ten cubby-hole.

O'Leary moved clear of the opening door, took in the dial-covered walls, the console installation like an all-electric kitchen—and at one side, Adoranne, bound hand and foot and gagged with a silken scarf and tied to a gold-brocaded easy chair. She tugged frantically at her bonds as she saw O'Leary, her blue eyes wide. She was wearing a pale blue nightgown, he saw, an imaginative garment as substantial as a spiderweb. O'Leary smiled encouragingly at the girl and motioned with the gun at Goruble.

"After you, your borrowed Majesty," he said. Goruble quickly stepped through the door, went to Adoranne's chair, skipped behind it and faced O'Leary.

"There are a few other matters I must mention to you," he said, looking unaccountably smug. "First—"

"Never mind that. Untie her."

Goruble held up a plump hand. "Patience, if you please. I hardly think you'd dare fire the shatter-gun in such intimate juxtaposition to the object of your anxieties . . . He put a palm familiarly on the bare, rounded shoulder of the princess. "And if you should feel impelled to some more animalistic assault, let me point out that the controls are within my easy reach." He nodded to a variety of levers set in the wall to his left. "True, you might manage to halt me—but the danger of ricochets . . . " he smirked. "I'd suggest you exercise caution."

O'Leary looked from Adoranne to the monarch, noting the close-set walls, the nearness to hand of the levers . . .

"All right," he said between his teeth, "spit it out."

"The Traveler here—as perhaps you're aware—is a standard utility model. It can place its cargo at predetermined triordinates and return to base setting, requiring a controller at the console, of course. But what you *don't* know is that I have made certain special arrangements, to fit my, ah, specialized needs here."

The king nodded to a point between himself and O'Leary just outside the half-open door. "If you'd take a step forward so that I can point out the modifications—ah, that's close enough," he said sharply as O'Leary reached the threshold. "I found it convenient to so arrange matters that I could dispatch useful loads to random locations without the necessity for my accompanying them."

He pointed to a number of heavy braided copper cables dangling across the panel. "My modifications were crude, perhaps, but effective. I was able to bring the entire area of the corridor there, to a distance of some fifteen feet, well within effective range." He smiled contentedly, reached for a lever. O'Leary jerked the gun up, had a quick mental image of the explosive pellets smacking into Adoranne's soft flesh; he tossed the gun aside, leaped—

—and landed on his face. He was lying in a drift of powdery snow packed against a rocky wall that rose from a gale-swept ledge of glittering ice. He gasped as a blast of arctic wind ripped at him; through a blur of tears he saw a small purple sun low in the black sky, a ragged line of ice peaks. His lungs caught at the thin air—like breathing razor blades.

He tried to scramble to his feet; the wind knocked him down. He stayed low then, rolled, reached the inadequate shelter of a drifted cranny. He wouldn't last long here. There had to be some place to get in out of the cold . . . He picked a spot ten feet distant, where the rock wall angled sharply. *Just out of sight around that outcropping*, he thought desperately, *there's a door set in the stone. All I have to do is reach it.* He pictured it, built the image, then . . . There!

Had he felt the familiar faint thump in the orderly flow of entropy? It was hard to tell, with this typhoon blasting at him. But it had to be! It must be a hundred below zero here. The stone at his back and the ice under his hands had burned like hot coals at first. Now everything was getting remote, as though he were encased in thick plastic.

He forced himself to move, crawled forward, almost went down on his face as the full force of the wind struck him. His hands were like wooden mallets now. He made another yard, skidded back as a particularly vicious gust slammed against him, tried again—and saw the soft glow of yellow light across the snow ahead, a cheery reflection in the ice. He rounded the shoulder of rock; there it was, a glass door in an aluminum frame, a tall rectangle of warmth against the cold and dark.

No point in dwelling on the incongruity of it—just reach it. The latch was a foot from his hand. He lunged, caught it, felt the door yield and swing in. He fell half-through the door into a sea of warmth.

He rested a moment, then pulled himself farther inside. The door whooshed shut behind him. Soft music was playing. He lay with his cheek against a rug, breathing in short, painful gasps. Then he sat up, looked around at oil-rubbed, wood-paneled walls, a built-in bar with gleaming glasses and a silver tray, a framed painting showing colors aswirl on a silvery field. He got to his feet, lurched across to the bar, found a bottle, poured a stiff drink, took it at a gulp.

OK, no time to waste; no time to wonder what sort of place this was he'd found, or where it was in the universe. It certainly wasn't anywhere on the familiar old planet Earth.

He had to get back. Goruble had obviously been all ready to travel, just waiting to finish off his enemy before he left. O'Leary closed his eyes. Ignoring the throb of returning sensation in his hands and feet and ears, he pictured the dark, musty passage under Goruble's palace. Adoranne was there; she needed him . . .

There was a thump as though the world had grounded on a sand bar. O'Leary's eyes flew open. He was standing in pitch darkness, in an odor of dust and mildewed wood. Had he made a mistake?

"Over this way, Sir Lafayette," a rumbling voice whispered. "Boy, you sure get around."

"Yokabump!" O'Leary groped toward the voice, felt a massive shoulder under his hand at belt height. "Where is he? I've got to get there before—"

"Wow! Your mitts are like a couple of ice bags!" Yokabump tugged O'Leary forward. "Just around the corner here, there's a door. I was staying out of sight and I couldn't see what was happening, but I heard you yell. Then old Goruble was snickering and talking to himself, and I sneaked a peek. I pretty near jumped him myself when I seen her Highness, tied to a chair. But then I figured—"

"Then they're still here?"

"Sure. His Majesty's working away like a one-man band, switching wires around. I'm glad you didn't stay away long."

"How did you know where I was?"

"I heard the air sort of whoosh. I noticed that before, when you did the fade from the dungeon—"

"Oh, you were hanging around then, were you?"

"Sure, I like to keep in touch."

"Shhh." O'Leary pushed through the rough wooden door into the passage he had vacated so precipitously five minutes earlier. He was fifteen feet from the open door to the Traveler—roughly the distance he had crawled on the ice ledge. Goruble was peering anxiously at dial faces; in the chair, Adoranne tugged futilely at the bell cord binding her arms. O'Leary eased out into the passage, started softly forward. He would reach the door, then in one jump, grab Goruble and hustle him away from the controls.

O'Leary's head cracked a low beam in the dark. Goruble looked up sharply at the sound, stood gaping for an instant as O'Leary, half-stunned, staggered toward him; then the usurper whirled and reached as O'Leary jumped—

—Light glared abruptly; something caught at O'Leary's foot, pitching him headlong into a mass of thorny shrubbery. Steamy air redolent of crushed foliage, rotted vegetation, humid soil and growing things closed around him like a Turkish bath. He floundered, fought his way clear of clinging tendrils of rubbery green, ducked as an inch-long insect buzzed his face. Sharp-edged red and green leaves scraped at him. Small flying midges swarmed about him, humming. There was a rasp of scales on bark; a wrist-thick snake of a vivid green hue slid into view on a leafy bough just ahead, raised a wedge-shaped head to stare. Somewhere above, birds were screeching back and forth from the tops of the towering trees.

O'Leary struggled upright, groped for footing in the tangle of fallen greenery. This time he'd fool Goruble: about ten feet in *that* direction, he estimated. The snake was still there, looking him over. He ducked aside from it, crawled over a fallen tree limb and fanned at the warming insects. About here, he decided . . .

A movement caught by the corner of his eye made him whirl. A great striped feline with a bushy yellowish mane was poised in the crotch of a yard-thick tree six feet above O'Leary's head, the green eyes fixed on him like stabbing spears. The jaws parted in a roar that fluttered leaves all around. The cat drew in its hind legs, gathering itself for a leap, roared again and sprang.

O'Leary squeezed his eyes shut, muttered a quick specification, threw himself to one side as the heavy body hurtled past. He slammed into an unyielding wall as a tremendous impact sounded behind him, followed by an ear-splitting yell, a ripping of cloth.

He staggered upright. He was back inside the Traveler, just behind Adoranne's chair. The big cat recovered from its first thwarted spring, whirled toward the fleeing figure of Goruble, whose velvet doublet had been split from top to bottom in the first near-miss, revealing a monogrammed silk undershirt.

O'Leary caught an instant's glimpse of Yokabump's bignosed face in the dark passage beyond the king. Then

Goruble was going down face-first as the attacking preda-
tor sailed over him, skidded to a halt, rounded to renew
the assault. O'Leary grabbed for the lever Goruble had
used and pulled it down as the half-lion, half-tiger
bounded across Goruble, sprang for the threshold—and
disappeared with a sharp whack! of displaced air.

O'Leary sagged and let out a long sigh. Yokabump
waddled to the door and bent to rub his shin.

"The old boy moves pretty good," he said. "I nearly
missed. He's down for the count, though."

O'Leary went to Adoranne, "I'll have you loose in a
minute." He started in on the knots. Yokabump produced a large clasp knife and sawed at the heavy cord
on her wrists. A moment later she rose out of the chair
and threw herself into O'Leary's arms.

"Oh, Sir Lafayette . . . " He felt hot tears on the side
of his neck and discovered that he was beaming broadly.
He patted her silken hip in a comforting way.

"Now, now, your Highness," he soothed, "it's all over
but the singing and dancing."

"Oh-oh, he's coming around." Yokabump indicated
the fallen monarch, stirring and groaning on the floor.

"Better tie him up," O'Leary suggested. "He's too
tricky to let wander around loose."

"By your leave, Sir Lafayette." The dwarf stepped to
Goruble's side and squatted down on bowed legs.

"Ah, there, your Majesty," he said in a lugubrious tone.
"Have you got any last words to say
before . . . before . . . "

"What . . . " the king gasped. "Where—"

"Just lie quiet, your Majesty; it's easier that way,
they say."

"Easier? Ow, my head . . . " Goruble tried to sit up. Yokabump pressed him back. "It was the beast, your Majesty; he got you. Tore your insides out. Don't look. It's too horrible."

"My insides? But—but I don't feel a thing, just my head."

"A merciful provision of nature. But about those last words—better hurry."

"Then—it's all over for me?" Goruble slumped back. "Ah, the pity of it, Yokabump. And all because I was too tender hearted. If I'd done away with the infant—"

"Tender hearted?" O'Leary cut in. "You killed the king, stole his throne, lived it up for twenty-odd years, then brought in a goon to terrorize your own would-be subjects, gave him a dinosaur to assist in the job, and finally tried to do away with her Highness. That's tender hearted?"

"One thing leads to another," Goruble gasped, "as you'll find for yourself. I needed a distraction; the people were grumbling about taxes and even after all these years, still asking too many questions about the former king's death. They weren't too happy with the story that I was his wandering cousin come home. So I made a number of trips in the Traveler, found Lod living in a cave and brought him here. Then I fetched along that great ugly reptile; it fitted in with the old legend of a dragon. Eventually, of course, I intended to do away with it and reap the plaudits of the yokels. But the scheme backfired. Lod grew stronger, while I heard the muttering daily grow louder. The people wanted Adoranne, and always there were rumors of the lost prince." He sighed. "And to think that I could have saved all this, if I could merely have brought myself to murder a tot."

"What's a tot got to do with it?"

"Eh? Why, I refer to the infant prince, of course. Exile was the most I could manage. And now see what it's brought me to."

"You . . . exiled the little prince?" Adoranne gasped. "You horrid, wicked man! And to think I thought you were my uncle! And all these years, you've known where the lost crown prince was."

"No, my dear, I didn't. He was crying in his crib, poor motherless tot—orphaned by my hand, though accidentally. I sent him—I didn't know where. But he thrived—ah, all too well. Cosmic justice, I suppose. And now—"

"How do you know he thrived?" Adoranne exclaimed.

"Just look at him for yourself," Goruble said. "There he is, standing over me, looking down at me with that accusing expression."

Adoranne gasped. O'Leary looked to left and right, puzzled. Yokabump nodded his heavy head wisely.

"Now you're seeing visions, eh?" O'Leary commented. "But it's a little late for regrets."

Goruble was staring up at O'Leary. "You mean—you didn't know?"

"Know what?"

"The prince—the child that I sent away, twenty-three years ago—is *you!*"

Beside O'Leary, Adoranne gasped aloud. "Then . . . then you, Sir Lafayette . . . are the rightful king of Artesia."

"Now, hold on," O'Leary protested. "Are you all crazy? I'm an American. I never saw this place until a week or so ago."

"I knew you by the ring," Goruble said weakly.

"What ring?" Adoranne asked quickly.

O'Leary held out his right hand. "You mean this?"

Adoranne seized his hand, turned the ring to show the device.

"The ax and dragon—the royal signet!" She looked at O'Leary wide-eyed. "Why didn't you show it sooner, Sir Lafayette—your Majesty?"

"He told me to reverse it," Lafayette said. "But—"

"I should have known then that my plans would come to naught," Goruble went on. "But I thought that by casting suspicion on you, I could dispose of you painlessly."

"Your jail's a long way from painless," O'Leary put in.

"Then you escaped somehow. Sterner measures were called for. I employed my specialized remote control equipment to send you away. How you returned, I still don't know. I followed your progress and waited here for the showdown, only to have it—alas—end in my defeat, disemboweled by a ravening monster unleashed by my own hand."

"Oh, that," Yokabump called from inside the Traveler, where he was gazing at dials and levers, "that was just a gag, your ex-Majesty. You're not hurt. On your feet now, and we'll toss you into your own dungeon until your trial comes up."

"Not hurt?" Goruble sat up, felt gingerly over his corpulent frame. "You mean . . . " His eyes went to the open door to his stolen machine. In an instant, he was on his feet, plunging between O'Leary and Adoranne, dashing for the entry.

Yokabump reached for a lever, waited, threw it just as the fat monarch sprang for the entry. There was a clap of air and Goruble was gone.

"I hope he lands in the same spot as the cat," the jester said, dusting his hands. "The skunk. Leaves me out of a job, I guess—unless your new Majesty wants to take me on?" He looked hopefully at O'Leary.

"Wait a minute," Lafayette protested. "Adoranne's the heir to the throne! I'm just a guy who wandered into the scene."

The princess took his arm and looked up at him warmly. "I know a way to solve the dilemma," she said softly. "The whole question will become merely academic if we . . . if I . . . if you . . . "

"Oh, boy," Yokabump chortled. "Wait'll I spread the word. There's nothing like a royal wedding to cheer everybody up!"

Chapter Thirteen

A glittering assemblage filled the ballroom, hanging back shyly from O'Leary in his new eminence.

"As I see it, Lafayette—that is, your Majesty," Nicodaeus was saying.

"Knock off the 'majesty' stuff," O'Leary said. "Adoranne's the queen. I already told you how I happened to come here."

"Remarkable," Nicodaeus shook his head. "Of course, you had a strong natural affinity for this tricoordinate universe, having lived here until the age of two. Odd that you have no recollection of palace life at all."

"It did seem familiar, in a way. But I thought it was just because I'd invented it. And I caught on to the language in a hurry. I guess it was all there, in my subconscious."

"Of course, and when you began consciously striving to break down the interplane barriers, it was only natural that you should revert to your natural world of origin, thus canceling out at last the Probability Stresses you'd been creating in the other continuum. But I don't think it's ever been done before without equipment. Quite an achievement."

"I still don't see how it works," Lafayette protested. "I just dreamed it up. How could it be real?"

"It was here all along, Lafayette. Your discontent with your drab existence was an expression of the unconscious yearning toward your native clime. As for your belonging—with all the infinite universes to choose from, surely for every man there must be one where he is king."

"But that doesn't explain how I can invent anything from a bathtub to an iguanodon—and find it waiting just around the next bend."

"You created nothing; those things existed—somewhere. You've merely been manipulating them along lines of weakness in the probability fabric. I'm afraid all that will have to come to an end, however, as soon as I've reported in. We can't have anyone—even yourself, your Majesty—mucking about the natural order of things."

O'Leary looked at his watch. "Where's Adoranne?" he inquired. "The party's due to begin any minute."

"She'll be along. Now I have to be going, Lafayette. It's time for my regular Friday evening report." The inspector of continua nodded and hurried away. The orchestra was playing what sounded like a Strauss waltz, except that O'Leary had been assured the number had been composed by someone named Cushman Y. Blatz.

He stepped through the tall glass doors to the terrace, sniffed the perfume of flowers on the warm night air. Not a bad place at all, this Artesia—king or no king. And with Adoranne as his intended bride—

There was a sudden rush of feet across the lawn below. O'Leary looked around in time to see Count Alain, dust-streaked and grim-faced, leap the balustrade, naked sword in hand. O'Leary dropped his glass with a crash.

"Hey, you startled me—" he started. Alain sprang to him, jammed the sword point against his new green velvet doublet.

"All right, where is she, you slimy schemer!" he rasped. "One yell, and I'll let you have it. Now speak up—and she'd better be unharmed!"

"Look, you've got the wrong slant on all this," O'Leary protested, backing away. Alain followed relentlessly.

"You're a bold scoundrel," the count snarled. "I take it you've done away with his Majesty—else you'd not be disporting yourself openly, here on his very terrace!"

"Well, we just sort of, ah, sent him away."

"And her Highness!" The sword jabbed harder.

"She's here—she'll be down in a minute! Look, Al, old boy, I can explain."

"As I thought; you had her all along. And I, dolt that I was, spent a day and a night on a fool's errand."

"I told you that was a dry run. Did you see what was left of Lod?"

"When thieves fall out . . . " Alain quoted. "You slew him by a trick, I suppose; but you'll have no chance to trick me."

There was a sharp cry from the direction of the open doors. O'Leary looked, saw Adoranne standing in the opening, indescribably lovely in a gown of white, with diamonds in her hair.

"Your Highness!" Count Alain said huskily. "You're safe! And as for this wretch . . . " He tensed his arm, looking O'Leary in the eye.

Adoranne screamed. A dark shadow moved behind Alain; there was a dull clunk! and the young nobleman dropped the sword with a clang and fell against O'Leary, who caught him, letting him down on the flagged pavement. The wide figure of the Red Bull stood grinning a vast, crooked grin.

"I seen duh slob about tuh ram duh iron to yuh, bo," he stated. He ducked his red-maned head at Adoranne. "Hi, yer Highness." He tugged at O'Leary's limp arm. "Look, I waited around like yuh said, and the pickin's was great." The thick red fingers lifted half a dozen gold watches from a baggy side pocket. "T'anks, pal. You and me make a great team. But, look, I got a idear fer a caper dat'll make dis stuff look like chicken feed."

Adoranne gave a long sigh and sagged against the doorframe. O'Leary jumped to her, caught her slender body, lifted her in his arms.

"She's fainted," he announced, in a cracking voice. "Somebody do something!"

"I got to do a fast fade, chum," the Red Bull announced. "How's about we rondyvooze at duh Ax and Dragon at midnight Tuesday? How's about I wear a yeller tulip dis time, OK?" He eased over the balustrade and was gone. People were rushing up now, emitting squeaks as they saw the limp princess.

"I'll take her to her room," O'Leary said. "The poor girl's had a shock." With a fussy chamberlain leading the way and half a dozen ladies-in-waiting clucking along-side, O'Leary puffed up three flights, staggered along the marble-floored corridor and waited while the door was opened. Then he pushed through, made for the wide, canopied bed, with its yellow silk coverlet and eased his burden gently down. Behind him, the door clicked softly. He turned. He was alone in the room with Adoranne. Damn the nitwits! Where were the smelling salts? Probably because he hadn't given his royal invitation, they were all hanging back. Well—

Adoranne's eyes fluttered. "Count Alain . . ." she breathed. "Is he . . . all right?"

O'Leary sat on the edge of the bed. "Sure, he's OK. The Red Bull just cracked him over the head. Are you feeling OK now?"

"Of course, Lafayette. But you—he threatened you with his sword."

"The poor guy still doesn't know the score. That's all right. He was just trying to help you."

"You'll not hold a grudge?" Adoranne's shapely arms reached up around Lafayette's neck and pulled his face down. Her lips were as soft as pink velvet. There were tiny diamond buttons up the front of her silvery dress. Lafayette's hand wandered to them . . .

"Your Majesty," Adoranne murmured.

"Do we have to wait until tomorrow?" O'Leary heard himself saying hoarsely.

"You are the king," Adoranne's hand went to the buttons. They parted easily: one, two . . . a curve of white throat . . . three, four, five . . . a bit of lace . . . six, and a tug at a ribbon, and—

There was a distinct thump! and the lights dimmed to a single bulb glaring fifty feet away over a dark door frame. O'Leary sat up, heard bedsprings squeak under him. "Adoranne?" His hand groped, finding only a coarse blanket stretched over a lumpy mattress.

"Hey, shaddup," a voice growled from six feet away. "Can't a guy get some sleep?"

"Where—where am I?" O'Leary choked out.

"Sleeping it off, hey? I didn't see youse when I come in. Yer in the Railroad Men's Y, second floor, a buck for the bed; four bits extra for a shower. But what I says is, who needs it?"

O'Leary stumbled from the bed, picked his way between bunks to the lighted door. He went down the stairs two at a time, pushed through the swinging door to the street, stared at dark shop windows, the blue gleam of mercury vapor lamps on tall steel poles. A few passers-by gave his clothes curious stares. He was back in Colby Corners.

It was an hour later. O'Leary stood on a corner, staring glumly at the gibbous moon hanging above Wienerbur-er's Gro. And Mkt. Just a little while ago he had seen that moon rise above a garden wall, gleaming through the poplars, reflecting in a fountain below the terrace where he and Nicodaeus had stood waiting for Adoranne. He swallowed an egg a passing goose had laid in his throat. Adoranne . . . and those buttons . . .

He straightened his back. One more try. He *had* to be able to get back. It wasn't fair to get stuck here, now, after all he'd gone through! He squeezed his eyes shut, again evoking the recollection of the garden, the French doors behind him, the music of the Blatz waltz. He sniffed, recalling the scent of jasmine, the fresh fragrance of the garden, hearing the murmur of wind through the trees . . .

There was a clatter of metal, a groaning wow-wow-wow; an engine blattered into life. O'Leary stared dismally at the jalopy parked across the way; it dug off with a squeal of rubber and roared away down the street in a cloud of exhaust fumes. So much for night-blooming jasmine and the wind in the willows.

Something was wrong. Always before, when he hadn't been distracted by something like a dinosaur snapping at his heels, he'd been able to make the shift, if he just tried hard enough. But now—a total blank. It was as though his abilities had suffered a paralytic stroke. He couldn't feel so much as a tentative stir even when he focused every erg of Psychic Energy he possessed.

But there had to be *some* way. If he could only get word to Nicodaeus, tell him—

O'Leary stood stock-still, balancing a fragile idea. Nicodaeus. He had talked to him before, from the phone in the jail. And the number—it had ten digits, he remembered that . . .

He screwed his eyes shut and tried for total recall. The reek of the cell, the chill of the morning air—Artesia was unaccountably cooler than Colby Corners—the white-washed wall. The phone had been an old-fashioned one, with a brass mouthpiece. And the number—

It started with a nine . . . five three four, that was it; then a nine, two oh's, and ended with—was it two eleven? Or one one two? . . .

Lafayette looked along the street. There was a phone booth there, half a block away. He tried his pocket; it yielded a dime. He set off at a run.

The phone booth was small, cramped, of an old-fashioned design, with a folding wooden door. Inside, an ancient instrument with a brass mouthpiece and a hand crank hung crookedly from a wall thick with carved initials and frank anatomical sketches accompanied by phone numbers. He held his breath, dropped the coin, twirled the crank. There was a long silence. Then a click. Then more silence. Then a sharp ping! and a hum.

"Central," a bright voice said tinnily in his ear. "Number, please."

"Uh—nine, five, three, four, nine, oh, oh, two, one, one," Lafayette got off breathlessly.

"That number is no longer in service. Please consult your directory."

"Wait!" O'Leary yelled. "I have to talk to you!"

"Yes, sir?"

"I have to get back—back to Artesia," O'Leary gulped, rallying his thoughts. "I was there, you see. I belong there and everything was going swell; then, for no reason—here I was! And now—"

"I'm sorry, sir, where did you say you were calling from?"

"What? Why, from this phone booth—here in Colby Corners, on the corner next to the Schrumph's candy shop—what's that got—"

"An error has been made, sir. Calls from that sector are not authorized—"

"Let me talk to the supervisor!" O'Leary demanded. "It's a matter of life or . . . or exile!"

"Well . . . one moment, please."

O'Leary waited, hearing his heart pound. Half a minute passed. Then a distinguished-sounding voice said, "Yes?"

"Hello! Look, I've been the victim of some sort of mistake; I was perfectly happy there in Artesia—"

"One moment, please," the voice interrupted. Then in an aside: "Operator, this seems to be some sort of eccentric; the call originates in one of the null sectors, I note. Probably an inebriated local, dialing in by mistake. Lucky to get a line, at that. With the circuits as busy as they are, a fifty-year wait isn't uncommon."

"I'm not drunk! I wish I were!" O'Leary yelled. "Somebody listen! I'm King Lafayette the First of Artesia! This is all some terrible mistake! I want to talk to Nicodaeus! He'll tell you! Come to think of it, it's probably all his fault. He went to make his report, and he probably mixed things up and forgot to tell you I belonged there, in spite of having arrived sort of informally."

"Nicodaeus? Yes, I heard of his remarkable report, half an hour ago. You say you were involved?"

"I was there! You can't send me back here! I don't belong here! My little bride is waiting for me, my people demand their king, Yokabump needs a job, and the thought of the foundry—"

"Oh, yes, you must be the fellow Fishnet or something of the sort; quite a merry chase you led our man. Do you know you've been creating a Probability Stress of .8 for weeks now? A remarkable technique you worked out, but I'm afraid we here at Central can't let it go on. You've caused a rather severe power drain on the Cosmic Energy Source. The dinosaur alone—"

"I didn't do that! He was already there!"

"One was, true, but you seem to have brought along another. At any rate, a Suppressor has now been focused on you. It will hold you firmly in place in your present continuum. It will even eliminate all dreaming, so you can look forward to sleep uninterrupted by bothersome fantasies from now on."

"I don't want to sleep uninterrupted by fantasies! I want to go home! Back to Artesia! I belong there, don't you understand?"

"No, my dear fellow; I can understand your desire to return—a rather pleasant, though backward, locus, or so our man states in his report—but we can't have you grasshoppering about all over the continua, now can we? But thank you for your interest, and now goodby—"

"Wait! Call Nicodaeus! He'll confirm what I said!"

"I'm a busy man, Mr. Fishnet; I have a backlog—"

"If you leave me here, there'll be a . . . a Probability Stress! And with the loused-up filing system you've got, it will be forty years before you remember what's causing it. And by then, I'll be a retired draftsman, still subsisting on sardines—and no dreams!"

"Well, I'll just make a check. Hold the line, please; if you ring off, you may never get through again."

O'Leary gripped the receiver, waiting. Through the glass in the door, he saw a fat woman approach along the street, digging in her purse for a coin. She seized the door handle, yanked, then caught sight of O'Leary and gave him an indignant look.

He covered the mouthpiece. "I'll be through in a minute," he muttered, mouthing the words through the glass. The woman snapped her jaw shut and glared at him.

Another minute ticked past. There was no sound on the line but a wavering hum. The fat woman rapped on the glass. O'Leary nodded, made motions indicating that he was waiting for a reply. The woman caught the door handle, pulled it half open. "See here, you, I'm in a hurry."

He jerked the door shut, and braced a foot against it as the invading female shook it furiously.

"Come on," O'Leary muttered. "What's keeping you?"

The fat woman stalked away. O'Leary relaxed. What was that fellow on the line doing? It had been a good five minutes now. What if he never came back? A fifty-year wait, he'd said. Lafayette pictured a pert face with jet-black hair, an impish smile. Never to see her again . . . He blinked. Jet-black hair? But Adoranne was a blonde—

O'Leary turned at a sound. The fat lady was back, a large cop in tow.

"That's him!" He heard the shrill screech through the door. "Half an hour already he's been sitting there, just to spite me, not even talking. Look at him!"

The cop stooped and peered inside, looking O'Leary up and down, taking in the green doublet, the long yellow hose, the ruff at the neck, the medals, ribbons, gold chain.

"All right, you," the cop said; he hauled at the door. O'Leary braced himself, foot against the panel. The cop set himself, heaved—

The booth seemed to shimmer, faded to a smoky outline, and was gone. O'Leary fell backward off a marble bench beside the graveled walk under the towering dark trees.

He scrambled up, looked around at the palace gardens, the tall, lighted windows above the terrace, the colored lights strung around the dancing pavilion. He was back—back in Artesia!

He started across the grass at a run, emerged from a screen of shrubs and skidded to a halt. By a tinkling fountain just ahead Adoranne stood—kissing Count Alain.

O'Leary ducked back out of sight. "Alain, it's all so strange," the princess was saying. "I can't believe he's gone—just like that—without even saying goodby."

"Now, Adoranne, don't fret. I guess he meant well. But after all, he *was* some kind of warlock."

"He was fine, and noble, and brave, and I—I'll never forget him," Adoranne said.

"Certainly; I'm grateful to him for rescuing you—even if he did leave that infernal dragon eating rosebushes in the side garden. When the legend said he'd bring back the thing's hide, I never expected the dragon would still be in it."

"I'm so . . . so glad you're here, Alain." Adoranne looked up into the young count's handsome face. "You won't flit off and leave me all alone, will you?"

"Never, your Highness . . . "

The couple resumed their stroll, hand in hand. As soon as they had passed, O'Leary crept out, crossed to the terrace, went along it to a small door leading to the kitchens. Inside, a startled cook looked up.

"Shhh!" O'Leary cautioned. "I'm traveling incognito." He wound his way past the hot ranges and the tables laden with food, went out by a rear door, took the service stair to the fourth floor. There was no one in sight, here in the servants' wing. He hurried along the corridor, rounded a corner.

A chambermaid in drab gray glanced up from her dusting; O'Leary looked into the tear-reddened eyes of Daphne.

"Oh!" A breath-taking smile took the place of the girl's heartbroken expression of a moment before. "Your Majesty!" she breathed.

"Lafayette to you, girl," O'Leary said as he swept her into his arms. "Princess Adoranne is an adorable cutie, and I had an obligation to do what I could for her. But when it got right down to it, it was your face that kept haunting me."

"But—but you're a king, sire, and I'm just—"

"Let's leave the title to Adoranne and Alain. We've got too many things to catch up on to be bothered running the country."

Epilogue

Abstract from the log of Nicodaeus, inspector, serial
number 786.
Ref: Locus Alpha Nine-three, Plane V-87, Fox 22 A-b
(Artesia)
Subj: Recruitment follow-up on L. O'Leary.
" . . . since the double wedding performed the following day, having abdicated his claim to the throne in favor
of the Princess Adoranne, subject appears mightily
content, living with his bride, the Lady Daphne, in a
comfortable apartment in the west palace annex. Com-
munication equipment is still in place in a locked cabinet
in the former laboratory of the present reporter. The
line will continue to be monitored twenty-four hours

daily. Qualified volunteers are in scarce supply, and a number of interesting assignments are waiting. On several occasions, subject has lifted the receiver and listened to the dial tone, but to date, he has not dialed."

The World Shuffler

One

It was a warm autumnal afternoon in Artesia. Lafayette O'Leary, late of the U.S.A., now *Sir* Lafayette O'Leary since his official investiture with knighthood by Princess Adoranne, was lounging at ease in a brocaded chair in his spacious library, beside a high, richly draped window overlooking the palace gardens. He was dressed in purple kneepants, a shirt of heavy white silk, gold-buckled shoes of glove-soft kid. A massive emerald winked on one finger beside the heavy silver ring bearing the device of the ax and dragon. A tall, cool drink stood at his elbow. From a battery of speakers concealed behind the hangings, a Debussy tone poem caressed the air.

O'Leary patted back a yawn and laid aside the book he had been idly leafing through. It was a thick, leatherbound volume on the Art of Bemusement, packed with fine print but, alas, deficient in specifics. For three years—ever since Central had relieved a bothersome probability stress among the continua by transferring him here from Colby Corners—he had been trying without visible success to regain his short-lived ability to focus the Psychical Energies, as Professor Doctor Hans Joseph Schimmerkopf had put it in his massive tome on the Practice of Mesmerism. Now *that* had been a book you could get your teeth into, Lafayette reflected ruefully. And he'd only read part of chapter one. What a pity he hadn't had time to bring it along to Artesia. But things had been rather rushed, there at the last—and faced with a choice between Mrs. MacGlint's Clean Rooms and Board and a palace suite with Daphne, who would have hesitated?

Ah, those had been exciting days, Lafayette thought fondly. All those years, back in Colby Corners, he had suspected that life held more in store for him than the career of a penniless draftsman, subsisting on sardines and dreams. And then he had run across Professor Schimmerkopf's massive tome. The prose had been a bit old-fashioned, but the message was clear: with a little concentration, you could make your dreams come true—or at least *seem* true. And if by self-hypnosis you could turn your shabby bedroom into a damask-draped chamber full of perfumed night air and distant music—why not try it?

And try it he had—with astonishing success. He had imagined a quaint old street in a quaint old town—and presto! There he was, surrounded by all the sights and sounds and smells that rounded out the illusion. Even knowing it was all a self-induced dream hadn't lessened the marvel of it. And then, when things got rough, he had made another startling discovery: if it was a dream, he was stuck in it. Artesia was real—as real as Colby Corners. In fact, there were those who could argue that Colby Corners was the dream, from which he had awakened to find himself back in Artesia, where he really belonged.

Of course, it had taken a while to discover that this was his true spiritual home. For a while it had appeared that he'd discover the answer to the old question as to whether a man who dreamed he'd fallen off a cliff would ever wake up. In his case it hadn't been a cliff, of course—but that was about the only form of demise he hadn't been threatened with. First there had been Count Alain's challenge, and the duel from the consequences of which Daphne had saved him with a carefully placed chamber pot dropped at the psychological moment from an upper window of the palace; then King Goruble's insistence that he hunt down a dragon—in return for his neck. And after that, a whole series of threats to life and limb, ending with his dispatch of Lod, the two-headed giant. And then the discovery that Lod had been transported into Artesia from another plane, along with his pet allosaur—the dragon with which he had terrorized the countryside—all at the order of the false King Goruble.

It had been more luck than wisdom, Lafayette conceded privately, that had enabled him to prove that the usurper had murdered the former king and transported his infant heir to another continuum by use of the unauthorized Traveler he had brought along when defecting from his post as an agent of Central—the supreme authority in interdimensional matters. And he had been just in time to thwart Goruble's last-ditch attempt to secure his position by ridding himself of Princess Adoranne. It had been pure accident that Goruble, thinking himself mortally wounded, had confessed to Lafayette that he—O'Leary—was the true king of Artesia.

For a few moments there, the situation had been awkward indeed—and then Goruble had solved the problem of his own disposition by stumbling into the Traveler—which had instantly whisked him out of their lives, after which Lafayette had abdicated in favor of the princess, and settled down to a life of bliss with the sweet and faithful Daphne.

Lafayette sighed and rose, stood gazing out the window. Down in the palace gardens, some sort of afternoon tea party was under way. At least it *had* been under way; now that he thought of it, he hadn't heard the chattering and laughter for several minutes; and the paths and lawns were almost empty. A few last-departing guests strolled toward the gates; a lone butler was hurrying toward the kitchen with a tray of empty cups and plates and crumpled napkins. A maid in a short skirt that revealed a neat pair of legs was whisking cake crumbs from a marble table beside the fountain. The sight of her saucy costume gave Lafayette a pang of nostalgia. If he squinted his eyes a little, he could almost imagine it was Daphne as he had first known her. Somehow, he thought with a touch of melancholy, it had all been gayer then, brighter, simpler. Of course, there had been a few drawbacks: Old King Goruble had been pretty intent on cutting his head off, and Lod the Giant had had similar ideas; and there had been the business of disposing of the dragon, to say nothing of the complicated problems of Count Alain and the Red Bull.

But now Lod and the dragon were dead—the bad dragon, that is. Lafayette's own pet iguanodon was still happily stabled in an abandoned powder house nearby, eating his usual twelve bales of fresh hay daily. Alain was married to Adoranne, and quite affable, now that there was nothing to be jealous about. And the Red Bull had published his memoirs and settled down to tavern-keeping in a quaint little inn called the One-Eyed Man at the edge of the capital. As for Goruble, there was no telling where he had ended up, since he had been so abruptly transported out of the dimension by his own Traveler. Daphne was still as cute and charming as ever, of course—what he saw of her. Her promotion from upstairs maid to countess hadn't gone to her head, precisely—but somehow these days it seemed that most of her time was taken up with the gay social whirl. It wasn't as if he actually wished he were a hunted fugitive again, and Daphne a palace servant with an unselfish passion for him, but . . .

Well, it did seem that nothing much ever happened these days—nothing except the usual schedule of gaiety, such as the formal dinner this evening. Lafayette sighed again. How nice it would be to just dine tête-à-tête with Daphne in some cozy hamburger joint, with a jukebox blaring comfortably in the background, shutting out the world . . .

He shook off the daydream. There were no hamburger joints in Artesia, no neon, no jukeboxes. But there *were* cozy little taverns with sooty beams and copper-bound ale kegs and roast haunches of venison, where a fellow could dine with his girl by the smoky light of tallow candles. And there was no reason they couldn't eat at one. They didn't *have* to participate in another glittering affair.

Suddenly excited, Lafayette started for the door, then turned into the next room, opened the closet door on a dazzling array of finery, grabbed a plum-colored coat with silver buttons. Not that he needed a coat in this weather, but protocol required it. If he appeared in public in shirtsleeves, people would stare, Daphne would be upset, Adoranne would raise her perfectly arched eyebrow . . .

That was what it had settled down to, Lafayette thought as he pulled on the coat and hurried down the hall: conventional routine. Dull conformity. Ye Gods, wasn't that what he had wanted to get away from when he had been a penniless draftsman back in the States? Not that he wasn't in the States now, geographically, at least, he reminded himself. Artesia was situated in the same spot on the map as Colby Corners. It was just that it was another dimension, where things were supposed to *happen!*

But what had been happening lately? The Royal Ball, the Royal Hunt, the Royal Regatta. An endless succession of brilliant events, attended by brilliant society, making brilliant conversation.

So . . . what was wrong? Wasn't that what he'd dreamed of, back in the boardinghouse, opening sardines for the evening repast?

It was, he confessed sadly. And yet . . . and yet he was bored.

Bored. In Artesia, land of his dreams. Bored.

"But . . . there's no sense in it!" he exclaimed aloud, descending the wide spiral staircase to the gilt-and-mirrored Grand Hall. "I've got everything I ever wanted—and what I haven't got, I can order sent up by Room Service! Daphne's as sweet a little bride as ever a man could imagine, and I have a choice of three spirited chargers in the Royal Stable, to say nothing of Dinny, and a two-hundred-suit wardrobe, and a banquet every night, and . . . and . . . "

He walked, echoing, across the polished red-and-black granite floor, filled with a sudden sense of weariness at the thought of tomorrow, of yet another banquet, yet another ball, another day and night of nonaccomplishment.

"But what do I want to accomplish?" he demanded aloud, striding past his reflection in the tall mirrors lining the hall. "The whole point in sweating over a job is to earn the cash to let you do what you want to do. And I'm already doing what I want to do." He glanced sideways at his image, splendid in plum and purple and gilt. "Aren't I?"

"We'll go away," he muttered as he hurried toward the garden. "Up into the mountains, or out into the desert, maybe. Or to the seashore. I'll bet Daphne's never gone skinny-dipping in the moonlight. At least not with me. And we'll take along some supplies, and cook our own meals, and fish and bird-watch, and take botanical notes, and . . . "

He paused on the wide terrace, scanning the green expanse below for a glimpse of Daphne's slender, curvaceous figure. The last of the partygoers had gone; the butler had disappeared, and the maid. A single aged gardener puttered in a far corner.

Lafayette slowed, mooched along the path, hardly aware of the scent of gardenia in blossom, of the lazy hum of bees, the soft sigh of the breeze through well-tended treetops. His enthusiasm had drained away. What good would going away do? He'd still be the same Lafayette O'Leary, and Daphne would be the same girl she was here. Probably after the first flush of enthusiasm he'd begin to miss his comfortable chair and well-stocked refrigerator, and Daphne would begin to fret over her hair-do and wonder what was going on in her absence from the party scene. And then there would be the insect bites and the hot sun and the cold nights and the burned food and all the other inconveniences he'd gotten used to doing without . . .

A tall figure appeared briefly at the end of the path: Count Alain, hurrying somewhere. Lafayette called after him, but when he reached the cross path, there was no one in sight. He turned back, feeling definitely depressed now, he admitted. For the first time in three years he had the same old feeling he used to have back in Colby Corners, where he'd go for his evening walk around the block and watch the yellow twilight fade to darkness, thinking of all the things he'd do, someday . . .

Lafayette straightened his back. He was acting like a nitwit. He had the best deal in the world—in any world—and all he had to do was enjoy it. Why rock the boat? Dinner was in an hour. He'd go, as he always went, listen to the conversation he always listened to. But he didn't feel like going back inside—not just yet; he wasn't quite up to making bright conversation. He'd sit on his favorite marble bench for a while and read a page or two of the current issue of *Popular Thaumaturgy*, and think himself into a proper mood for the gay banter at the dinner table. He'd make it a point to tell Daphne how stunning she looked in her latest Artesian mode, and after dinner they'd steal away to their apartment, and . . .

Now that he thought of it, it had been quite a while since he had whispered an abandoned suggestion in Daphne's cute little ear. He'd been so busy with his wine, and holding up his end of the conversation, and of course Daphne was quite content to sit with the other court wives, discussing their tatting or whatever it was the ladies discussed, while the gentlemen quaffed brandy and smoked cigars and exchanged racy anecdotes.

Lafayette paused, frowning at the azalea bush before him. He'd been so immersed in his thinking that he'd walked right past his favorite corner of the garden—the one with the bench placed just so beside the flowering arbutus, and the soft tinkle of the fountain, and the deep shade of the big elms, and the view of smooth lawn sloping down to the poplars beside the lake . . .

He walked back, found himself at the corner where he had glimpsed Alain. Funny. He'd passed it again. He looked both ways along the empty paths, then shook his head and set off determinedly. Ten paces brought him to the wide walk leading back to the terrace.

"I'm losing my grip," he muttered. "I *know* it's the first turn past the fountain . . . " He halted, staring uncertainly across the strangely narrowed law. Fountain? There was no fountain in sight; just the graveled path, littered with dead leaves, and the trees, and the brick wall at the other end. But the brick wall should be farther back, past several turns and a duck pond. Lafayette hurried on, around a turn . . . The path ran out, became a foot-worn strip of dirt across untended weeds. He turned—and encountered a solid wall of shrubbery. Sharp twigs raked at him, ripping at his lace cuffs as he fought his way through, to emerge in a small patch of dandelion-pocked grass. There were no flowerbeds in sight. No benches. No paths. The palace had a desolate, unoccupied look, looming against a suddenly dull sky. The shuttered windows were like blind eyes; dead leaves blew across the terrace.

O'Leary went quickly up the terrace steps, through the French doors into the mirrored hall. Dust lay thick on the marble floor. His feet echoed as he crossed quickly to the guardroom, threw open the door. Except for an odor of stale bedding and mildew, it was empty.

Back in the corridor, Lafayette shouted. There was no answer. He tried doors, looked into empty rooms. He paused, cocked his head, listened, heard only the faraway twitter of a bird call.

"This is ridiculous," he heard himself saying aloud, fighting down a sinking feeling in the stomach. "Everyone can't have just picked up and sneaked out without even telling me. Daphne would never do a thing like that . . ."

He started up the stairs, found himself taking them three at a time. The carpeting had been removed from the upper corridor, the walls stripped of the paintings of courtiers of bygone years. He flung wide his apartment door, stared at the unfurnished room, the drapeless windows.

"Good Lord, I've been robbed!" he gasped. He turned to the closet, almost banged his nose against the wall. There was no closet—and the wall was twelve feet closer than it should have been.

"Daphne!" he yelled, and dashed into the hall. It was definitely shorter than it had been, and the ceiling was lower. And it was dark; half the windows were missing. His shout echoed emptily. No one answered.

"Nicodaeus!" he gulped. "I'll have to telephone Nicodaeus at Central! He'll know what to do . . . " He darted along to the tower door, raced up the narrow, winding stone steps leading to the former Court Magician's laboratory. Nicodaeus was long gone, of course, recalled by Central for duty elsewhere; but there was still the telephone, locked in the cabinet on the wall; if only he could get there before . . . before . . . O'Leary thrust the thought aside. He didn't even want to think of the possibility that the cabinet might be empty.

Puffing hard, he reached the final landing and pushed through into the narrow, granite-walled chamber. There were the work benches, the shelves piled high with stuffed owls, alarm clocks, bottles, bits of wire, odd-shaped assemblies of copper and brass and crystal. Under the high, cobwebbed ceiling, the gilded skeleton, now mantled with dust, dangled on its wire before the long, black, crackle-finished panel set with dials and gauges, now dark and silent. Lafayette turned to the locked cabinet beside the door, fumbled out a small golden key, fitted it into the keyhole; he held his breath, and opened the door. With a hiss of relief, he grabbed up the old-fashioned brass-mounted telephone inside. Faint and far away came a wavering dial tone.

O'Leary moistened dry lips, frowning in concentration: "Nine, five, three, four, nine, oh, oh, two, one, one," he dialed, mouthing the numbers.

There were cracklings on the wire. Lafayette felt the floor stir under him. He looked down; the rough stone slabs had been replaced by equally rough-hewn wood planks.

"Ring, blast it," he groaned. He jiggled the hook, was rewarded by soft electrical poppings.

"Somebody answer!" he yelped. "You're my last hope!"

A draft of cool air riffled his hair. He whirled, saw that he now stood in a roofless chamber, empty of everything but scattered leaves and bird droppings. Even as he watched, the quality of the light changed; he whirled back; the wall against which the cabinet had been mounted was gone, replaced by a single post. There was a tug at his hand, and he continued the spin, made a frantic grab for the telephone, now resting precariously on one arm of a rickety windmill, at the top of which he seemed to be perched. Grabbing for support as the structure swayed in the chill wind, creaking, he looked down at what appeared to be a carelessly tended cabbage patch.

"Central!" he yelled through a throat suddenly as tight as though a hand had closed about it. "You can't leave me here like this!" He rattled the instrument frantically. Nothing happened.

After three more tries he hung the phone up with dazed care, as if it were made of eggshells. Clinging to his high perch, he stared out across the landscape of bramble-covered hillside toward a dilapidated town a quarter of a mile distant, no more than a sprawl of ram-shackle buildings around the lake. The topography, he noted, was the same as that of Artesia—or of Colby Corners, for that matter—but gone were the towers and avenues and parks.

"Vanished!" he whispered. "Everything I was complaining about . . . " He stopped the swallow. "And everything I wasn't complaining about along with it. Daphne—our apartment—the palace—and it was almost dinnertime . . . "

The thought was accompanied by a sharp pang just below the middle button of the handsomely cut coat he had donned less than half an hour ago. He shivered. It was cold now, with night falling fast. He couldn't just perch here beside the dead phone. The first trick would be to get down to the ground, and then . . .

That was as far as his numbed mind cared to go for the moment. *First I'll think about the immediate problem*, he told himself. *Then, later, I'll think about what to do next.*

He tried putting a foot on the open-work vane beside him; it seemed remarkably limber, his knees remarkably wobbly. The rough wood rasped his hands. As he started out, the framework sank slowly under him, with much creaking. He had already worked up a light sweat, in spite of the chill wind. No doubt about it, the easy living had taken its toll, condition-wise. Gone were the days when he could rise at dawn, breakfast on sardines, do a full day's work over a hot drawing board, dine on sardines, and still have the energy for an evening of plastics experiments and penicillium cultures. As soon as he got out of this—if he ever *got* out of this—he'd have to give serious thought to reviving his interest in body-building, long walks, pre-dawn calisthenics, karate, judo, and high-protein dieting . . .

The ring was a light tinkle, almost lost against the open sky. Lafayette froze, hearing the echo in his mind, wondering if he had imaged it, or if it had been merely the tolling of a bell down in the village; or possibly the distant *ding-dong* of a cowbell, if there were any cows in the vicinity and they wore bells that went *ding-dong* . . .

At the second ring, Lafayette broke two fingernails in his upward lunge; once his foot slipped, leaving him dangling momentarily by a one-handed grip, but he hardly noticed. A short instant later he had grabbed up the receiver, jammed it into his ear upside down.

"Hello?" he gasped. "Hello? Yes? Lafayette O'Leary speaking . . . " He quickly reversed the phone as a shrill squeaking came from the end near his mouth.

" . . . This is Pratwick, Sub-Inspector of Continua," the chirping voice was saying. "Sorry to break in on your leisure time in this fashion, but an emergency has arisen here at Central and we're recalling certain key personnel to active duty for the duration. Now, according to our records, you're on standby status at Locus Alpha Nine-three, Plane V-87, Fox 22 1-b, otherwise known as Artesia. Is that correct?"

"Yes," Lafayette blurted. "That is, no—not exactly. You see—"

"Now, this situation requires that you abandon your interim identity at once and commence to operate underground, posing as an inmate of a maximum-security penal camp, doing ninety-nine years for aggravated mopery. Got it?"

"Look, Mr. Pratwick, you don't quite grasp the situation," O'Leary broke in hastily. "At the moment, I'm perched in a windmill—which seems to be all that's left of the royal palace—"

"Now, you'll report at once to the Undercover station located at the intersection of the palace sanitary main and the central municipal outflow, twelve feet under the Royal sewage-processing plant, two miles north of town. Is that clear? You'll be in disguise, of course: rags, fleas, that sort of thing. Our man there will smuggle you into the labor camp, after fitting you out with the necessary artificial calluses, manacles, and simulated scurvy sores—"

"Hold on!" Lafayette cried. "I can't undertake an undercover assignment in Artesia!"

"Why not?" The voice sounded surprised.

"Because I'm not *in* Artesia, confound it! I've been trying to tell you! I'm hanging on for dear life, a hundred feet above a wasteland! I mean, I was just strolling in the garden, and all of a sudden the bench disappeared, and then the rest of the garden, and—"

"You say you're *not* in Artesia?"

"Why don't you listen! Something terrible has happened—"

"Kindly answer yes or no," the sharp voice snapped. "Maybe you don't know there's an emergency on that could affect the entire continuum, including Artesia!"

"That's just the point!" O'Leary howled. "No! I'm NOT in Artesia—"

"Oops," the voice said briskly. "In that case, excuse the call—"

"Pratwick! Don't hang up!" O'Leary yelled. "You're my sole link with everything! I've got to have help! They're all gone, understand? Daphne, Adoranne, everybody! The palace, the town, the whole kingdom, for all I know—"

"Look here, fellow, suppose I put you on to Lost and Found, and—"

"*You* look! I helped you out once! Now it's your turn! Get me out of this fix and back to Artesia!"

"Out of the question," the crackly voice rapped. "We're only handling priority-nine items tonight, and you rate a weak three. Now—"

"You can't just abandon me here! Where's Nicodaeus? He'll tell you—"

"Nicodaeus was transferred to Locus Beta Two-oh, with the cover identity of a Capuchin monk engaged in alchemical research. He'll be out of circulation for the next twenty-eight years, give or take six months."

Lafayette groaned. "Can't you do anything?"

"Well—look here, O'Leary: I've just leafed through your record. It seems you're on the books for unauthorized use of Psychical Energies, up until we focused a Suppressor on you. Still, I see you *did* render valuable services, once upon a time. Now, I have no authority to lift the Suppressor, but just between the two of us—off the record, mind you—I can drop you a hint which may help you to help yourself. But don't let on I told you."

"Well—go ahead and drop it!"

"Ah—let's see: O.K., here goes: Mid knackwurst and pig's knuckles tho you may grope/There's only one kind that's tough as a rope/The favorite of millions from the Bronx to Miami/The key to the riddle it—Oh-oh, that's it, O'Leary. Chief Inspector's coming! Got to go! Good luck! Let us hear from you—if you survive, that is!"

"Wait a minute! You didn't say what the key to the riddle was!" Lafayette rattled the hook madly, but only the derisive buzz of the dial tone answered him. Then, with a sputter, the phone went dead. Lafayette groaned and hung up the receiver.

"Pig's knuckles," he muttered. "Knackwurst. That's all the thanks I get for all these years of loyal service, pretending to be totally absorbed in living with Daphne and wining and dining and riding to hounds, all the while holding myself in readiness for instant action, any time that infernal phone rang . . . "

He drew a deep breath and blinked.

"You're talking nonsense again, O'Leary," he told himself sternly. "Admit it: you've been having the time of your life for three years. You could have dialed Central anytime and volunteered for a hardship post, but you didn't. Now that things look rough, don't whine. Pull in your belt, assess the situation, and decide on a plan of action."

He looked down. The ground, now pooled in dusk, looked a long way below him.

"So—how do I start?" he asked himself. "What's the first step to take to remove oneself from a world and into another dimension?"

"Of course, you boob!" he blurted with a sudden dawning hope. "The Psychical Energies! Isn't that how you got from Colby Corners to Artesia in the first place? And I'll have to cut out talking to myself," he added *sotto voce*. "People will think I've popped my cork."

Clinging to his perch, O'Leary closed his eyes, concentrated on recollecting Artesia, the smell and feel of the place, the romantic old streets clustered about the pennanted turrets of the palace, the taverns, the tall half-timbered houses and tiny, tidy shops, the cobbles and steam cars and forty-watt electric lights . . .

He opened one eye. No change. He was still in the top of a windmill; the barren slope below still led down to the bleak village by the lake. Back in Artesia, that lake was a mirror-surfaced pool on which swans floated among flowering lilies. Even in Colby Corners, it had been a neat enough pond, with only a few candy wrappers floating in it to remind you of civilization. Here, it had an oily, weed-grown look. As he watched, a woman waddled from the rear of a shack and tossed a bucket of slops into the water. Lafayette winced and tried again. He pictured Daphne's pert profile, the lumpy visage of Yokabump the Jester, Count Alain's square-cut shirt-ad features, Princess Adoranne's flawless patrician face and elegantly gowned figure . . .

Nothing. The telltale bump in the smooth flow of time failed to occur. Of course, he hadn't been able to make use of the Psychic Energies since Central had discovered that he was the culprit who had been creating probability stresses among the continua, and focused a Suppressor on him; but he had hoped that here he might have regained his former power. And—

What was it that bureaucrat on the phone had said? Something about a clue? And then that gibberish he'd spouted about a riddle just before he'd hung up. Nothing in that for him. He was on his own, and the sooner he faced it the better.

"So—now what?" he demanded of the chill night air.

"For a start, get down out of this nest," he counseled himself. "Before you stiffen up and freeze to the crossarm."

With a last, regretful look at the telephone, Lafayette began the long descent to the ground.

It was almost full dark when Lafayette dropped the last ten feet into a dry thicket. Sniffing vigorously, he detected a pleasing aroma of fried onions emanating from the direction of the town. He fingered the coins in his pocket; he could find a suitable tavern and have a bite to eat and possibly a small flagon of wine to restore the nerves, and then set about making inquiries— discreet ones, of course. Just what he'd ask, he didn't know—but he'd think of something. He set off down-slope, limping a bit from a slight sprain of the left ankle, twisted in the descent. He was getting fragile in his mature years. It seemed a long time ago that he had rushed about like an acrobat, climbing over roofs, swarm-ing up ropes, battling cutpurses, taming dragons—and wooing and winning the fair Daphne. At the thought of her piquant face, a pang of dismay struck through him. What would she think when he turned up missing? Poor girl, she'd be broken-hearted, frantic with worry . . .

Or would she? The way he'd been neglecting her lately, she might not even notice his absence for a few days. Probably at this moment she was being chattered at by one of the handsome young courtiers who hung around the palace, supposedly getting instruction in knightly ways, but actually spending their time idling over wine bottles, gambling, and wenching . . .

Lafayette's fists tightened. They'd swoop down on poor, unprotected little Daphne like vultures as soon as they realized he was out of the way. Poor, innocent girl; she wouldn't know how to fend off those wily snakes-in-the-grass; she'd probably listen to some smooth line of chatter and—

"None of that," Lafayette reproved himself sharply. "Daphne is as true-blue as they come, even if she is a little deficient in prudery. Why, she'd knock the ears off the first slicker who made an improper advance!" She'd swung a broom for enough years to have a solid punch, too, and she'd kept that trim little figure in shape by plenty of riding and tennis and swimming, once she was promoted to the ranks of the aristocracy. Lafayette remembered her, neat and curvaceous in a scant swimsuit, poised on the end of the diving board—

"None of that, either," he commanded. "Keep your mind on the immediate problem—just as soon as you figure out what the immediate problem is," he added.

The town's main street was a crooked, unpaved, pot-holed path barely wide enough for a cart to navigate, well dotted with garbage heaps featuring old fruit rinds and eggshells—no tin cans here yet, he noted. Dim lights shone from oiled-parchment windows. One or two furtive-looking locals eyed him from the shadows before slinking into alleymouths even narrower and darker than the main drag. Ahead, a crudely painted sign creaked in the chill wind before a sagging door set two steps below street level. The device was a misshapen man in gray robes and tonsure, holding out a pot. YE BEGGAR'S BOLE was lettered in crooked Gothic characters above the figure. Lafayette felt a pang of melancholy, comparing this mean dive with the cozy aspect of the Ax and Dragon back in Artesia, where he had once been wont to spend convivial evenings with a group of cronies . . .

Leaving Daphne at home alone, the realization struck him anew. "At least I *hope* she was alone," he groaned. "What a fool I was—but as soon as I get back, I'll make it all up to her . . . " He swallowed the lump in his throat, ducked his head, and pushed through the low door into the public house.

Greasy smoke fogged the air, stung his eyes. An odor of sour beer struck his nostrils, mingled with the effluvia of charcoal and burned potatoes, plus other, less pleasing additives. He made his way across the uneven dirt floor, ducking his head under the low beams from which strings of dried leeks depended, to a sagging counter behind which a slim female in gray homespun and a soiled headscarf stood with her back to him, rubbing at a soot-blackened pot with a rag and humming under her breath.

"Ah . . . do you suppose I could get a bite to eat?" he said. "Nothing elaborate, just a brace of partridge, a few artichoke hearts, and a nice light wine—say a Pouilly-Fuissé, about a fifty-nine . . . "

"Well," the woman said without turning. "At least you got a sense o' humor."

"Well, in that case just make it an omelet," Lafayette amended hastily. "Cheese and tuna will do nicely, I think—plus some hot toast and butter and a hearty ale."

"O.K.," the woman said. "Rib me. I'm laughing, ha-ha."

"Could you manage a ham sandwich?" Lafayette said, a hint of desperation in his voice. "Bavarian ham on Swiss rye is a favorite of mine—"

"Sausage and small beer," the serving wench said flatly. "Take it or leave it."

"I'll take it," Lafayette said quickly. "Well done, and no rind, please."

The woman turned, tucked a strand of pale hair behind her ear. "Hey, Hulk," she shouted. "Saw off a grunt, skin it, and burn it, the gent says."

Lafayette was staring at her wide blue eyes, her short, finely modeled nose, the uncombed but undoubtedly pale-blond curls on her forehead.

"Princess Adoranne!" he yelped. "How did *you* get here?"

Two

The barmaid gave Lafayette a tired look. "The name's Swinehild, mister," she said. "And how I got here's a long story."

"Adoranne—don't you know me? I'm Lafayette!" His voice rose to a squeak. "I talked to you just this morning, at breakfast!"

A sliding panel behind her banged open. An angry, square-jawed, regular-featured, but unshaven face peered out.

"Breakfast, hah?" it growled. "That calls for some explanation, bub!"

"Alain!" Lafayette cried. "You, too?"

"Whattya mean, me *too!*"

"I mean, I thought I was the only one—Adoranne and I, that is—of course I didn't realize until just now that she—I mean that you—"

"Two-timing me again, hey!" A long, muscular arm that went with the unshaven face made a grab for the girl, missed as she jumped aside and grabbed up a frying pan.

"Lay a hand on me, you big ape, and I'll scramble that grease spot you use for a brain," she screeched.

"Now, now, easy, Adoranne," Lafayette soothed. "This is no time for a lovers' spat—"

"Lovers! Ha! If you knew what I'd been through with that slob—" She broke off as the subject of the discourse slammed through the swinging door from the kitchen. She skipped aside from his lunge, brought up the iron skillet, and slammed it, with a meaty thud, against the side of his uncombed head. He took two rubbery steps and sagged against the counter, his face six inches from Lafayette's.

"What'll it be, sport?" he murmured, and slid down out of view with a prodigious clatter. The girl tossed the makeshift weapon aside and favored Lafayette with an irate look.

"What's the idea getting him all upset?" she demanded. She frowned, looking him up and down. "Anyway, I don't remember you, Sol. Who are you? I'll bet I never two-timed him with you at all!"

"Surely you'd remember?" Lafayette gulped. "I mean—what's happened? How did you and Alain get into this pig sty? Where's the palace? And Daphne—have you seen Daphne?"

"Daffy? There's a bum with a couple screws missing goes by that name, comes in here sometimes to cadge drinks. I ain't seen him in a couple weeks—"

"Not Daffy, *Daphne*. She's a girl—my wife, to be exact. She's small—but not too small, you understand—nice figure, cute face, dark, curly hair—"

"I'll go fer that," a deep voice said blurrily from the floor. "Just wait till I figure out which way this deck is slanting—"

The girl put her foot in Hulk's face and pushed. "Sleep it off, ya bum," she muttered. She gave Lafayette an arch look and patted her back hair. "This dame got anything I ain't?" she inquired coolly.

"Adoranne! I'm talking about Daphne—the countess—my wife!"

"Oh, yeah, the countess. Well, to tell you the truth, Clyde, we don't see a lot o' the countess these days. We're too busy counting our pearls, you know how it is. Now, if you got no objection, I got some garbage to drag out back."

"Let me help you," Lafayette volunteered quickly.

"Skip it. I can handle him."

"Is he all right?" Lafayette rose and leaned across the counter to look down at the fallen chef.

"Hulk? You couldn't bust his skull with a horseshoe, even if the horse was still wearing it." She grabbed his heels and started backward through the swinging door.

"Adoranne—wait—listen to me—" Lafayette called, scrambling around the counter.

"I told you—Swinehild's the name. What's this Adder Ann jazz all about?"

"You really don't remember?" Lafayette stared at the familiar, beautiful face, so unfamiliarly smeared with soot and grease.

"I'm leveling with you, bub. Now, if you're done clowning, how's about clearing out of here so's I can close the joint up?"

"Isn't it a little early?"

Swinehild cocked an eyebrow. "You got other ideas in mind?"

"I have to talk to you!" Lafayette said desperately.

"It'll cost you," Swinehild said flatly.

"H-how much?"

"By the hour, or all night?"

"Well, it won't take but a few minutes to explain matters," Lafayette said eagerly. "Now, to begin with—"

"Wait a minute." The girl dropped Hulk's heels. "I got to slip into my working clothes."

"You're fine just as you are," Lafayette said hastily. "Now, as I was saying—"

"Are you trying to tell me my business, stranger?"

"No—that is, I'm not a stranger! We've known each other for years! Don't you remember the first time we met, at the ball King Goruble decreed to celebrate my agreeing to take on a little chore of dragon-slaying? You were wearing a blue dress with little bitty pearls on it, and you had a tiger cub on a leash—"

"Aw—you poor sucker," Swinehild said in sudden comprehension. "Your marbles is scrambled, huh? Why didn't you say so? Hey," she added, "when you said you wanted to talk, you really meant talk, huh?"

"Of course, what else? Now, look here, Adoranne: I don't know what's happened—some kind of hypnotic suggestion, maybe—but I'm sure with a little effort you could remember. Try hard, now: Picture a big, pink quartz palace, lots of knights and ladies in fancy costumes, your apartments in the west wing, done in pink and gold, and with a view of the gardens, the gay round of parties and fetes—"

"Slow down, bub." Swinehild took a bottle from under the bar, selected two cloudy glasses from the mismatched collection heaped in the wooden sink, and poured out two stiff drinks. She lifted her glass and sighed.

"Here's to you, mister. You're nutty as a couple of dancing squirrels, but you got a nifty delusional system working there, I'll say that for you." She tossed the shot back with a practiced twist of the wrist. Lafayette sampled his, winced at the pain, then swallowed it whole. Swinehild watched sympathetically as he fought to draw breath.

"I guess life in these parlous times is enough to drive any kind of sensitive guy off his wire. Where you from, anyway? Not from around here. You dress too fancy for that."

"Well, the fact is," Lafayette started, and paused. "The fact is, I don't quite know how to explain it," he finished in a hopeless tone. Suddenly, he was acutely aware of the pain of scratches and the ache of unaccustomedly stretched muscles, conscious of his urgent need of a good dinner and a hot bath and a warm bed.

Swinehild patted his hand with a hard little palm. "Well, don't worry about it, sugar. Maybe tomorrow everything'll look brighter. But I doubt it," she added, suddenly brisk again. She refilled her glass, drained it, placed the cork in the bottle, and drove it home with a blow of her palm. "It ain't going to get no better as long as that old goat Rodolpho's sitting on the ducal chair."

Lafayette poured his glass full and gulped it without noticing until the fiery stuff seared his throat.

"Listen," he gasped, "maybe the best thing would be for you to fill me in a bit on the background. I mean, I'm obviously not in Artesia any longer. And yet there are certain obvious parallels, such as you and Alain, and the general lie of the land. Maybe I'll be able to detect some useful analog and take it from there."

Swinehild scratched absently at her ribs. "Well, what's to say? Up to a couple years ago, this used to be a pretty fair duchy. I mean, we didn't have much, but we got by, you know what I mean? Then everything just kind of went from bad to worse: taxes, regulations, rules. The cricket blight took out the tobacco and pot crops, then the plague of mildew spoiled the vintage two years running, then the yeast famine: that knocked out the ale. We squeaked by on imported rum until that ran out. Since then it's been small beer and groundhog sausage."

"Say, that reminds me," Lafayette said. "That groundhog sounds good."

"Brother, you *must* be hungry." Swinehild recovered the skillet from behind the door, shook up the coals in the grate, tossed a dubious-looking patty of grayish meat into the melting grease.

"Tell me more about this Duke Rodolpho you mentioned," Lafayette suggested.

"I only seen the bum once, as I was leaving the ducal-guard barracks about three at the A.M.; visiting a sick friend, you understand. The old boy was taking a little stroll in the garden, and being as it was early yet, I skinned over the fence and tried to strike up a conversation. Not that his type appeals to me. But I thought it

might be a valuable connection, like." Swinehild gave
Lafayette a look which might have been coy coming from
anyone else. "But the old goat gave me the swift heave-
ho," she finished, cracking an undersized egg with a
sharp rap on the edge of the skillet. "He said something
about me being young enough to be his niece, and yelled
for the johns. I ask you, what kind of administration can
you expect from an old buzzard with no more sporting
instinct than that?"

"Hmm," Lafayette said thoughtfully. "Tell me, ah,
Swinehild, how would I go about getting an audience
with this duke?"

"Don't try it," the girl advised. "He's got a nasty reputation for throwing pests to the lions."

"If anybody knows what's going on here, it ought to
be him," Lafayette mused. "You see, the way I have it
figured out, Artesia hasn't really disappeared: *I* have."

Swinehild looked at him over her shoulder, tsked, and
shook her head.

"And you not hardly more'n middle-aged," she said.

"Middle-aged? I'm not quite thirty," Lafayette pointed
out. "Although I admit that tonight I feel a hundred and
nine. Still, having a plan of action helps." He sniffed the
crisping patty as Swinehild lifted it onto a chipped plate,
added the brownish egg, and slid it in front of him.

"You *did* say groundhog?" he inquired dubiously, eyeing the offering askance.

"Groundhog is what I said. More power to you, mister.
I could never choke the stuff back, myself."

"Look here, why don't you call me Lafayette?" he suggested, sampling the fare. Aside from a slight resemblance

to library paste, it seemed to be tasteless—possibly a blessing in disguise.

"That's too long. How about Lafe?"

"Lafe sounds like some kind of hillbilly with one overall strap and no shoes," O'Leary protested.

"Listen, Lafe," Swinehild said sternly, planting an elbow in front of him and favoring him with a no-nonsense look. "The quicker you get over some o' them fancy ideas and kind of blend into the landscape around here, the better. If Rodolpho's men spot you as a stranger, they'll have you strung up on a curtain stretcher before you can say *habeas corpus*, tickling your secrets out of you with a cat-o'-nine tails."

"Secrets? What secrets? My life is an open book. I'm an innocent victim of circumstances—"

"Sure: you're just a harmless nut. But just try convincing Rodolpho of that. He's as suspicious as an old maid sniffing after-shave in the shower stall."

"I'm sure you're exaggerating," Lafayette said firmly, scraping his plate. "The straightforward approach is always best. I'll just go to him man to man, explain that I seem to have been accidentally shifted out of my proper universe by some unspecified circumstance, and ask him if he knows of anyone carrying on unauthorized experiments in psychical-energy manipulation. In fact," he went on, warming to his subject, "he might even be in touch with Central himself. In all likelihood there's a sub-inspector of continua on duty here, keeping an eye on things, and as soon as I explain matters—"

"You're going to tell him *that*?" Swinehild inquired. "Look, Lafe, it's nothing to me—but I wouldn't if I was you, get me?"

"I'll start first thing in the morning," Lafayette murmured, licking the plate. "Where did you say this duke maintains his establishment?"

"I didn't. But I might as well tell you, you'd find out anyway. The ducal keep is at the capital, about twenty miles west of here as the buzzard flies."

"Hmmm. That puts it at just about the position of Lod's H.Q. back in Artesia. Out in the desert, eh?" he asked the girl.

"Nix, bub. The city's on a island, in the middle o' Lonesome Lake."

"Fascinating how the water level varies from one continuum to another," Lafayette commented. "Back in Colby Corners, that whole area is under the bay. In Artesia, it's dry as the Sahara. Here, it seems to be somewhere between. Well, be that as it may, I'd better get some rest. Frankly, I'm not as used to all this excitement as I once was. Can you direct me to an inn, Swinehild? Nothing elaborate: a modest room with bath, preferably eastern exposure. I like waking up to a cheery dawn, you know—"

"I'll throw some fresh hay into the goat pen," Swinehild said. "Don't worry," she added at Lafayette's startled look. "It's empty since we ate the goat."

"You mean—there's no hotel in town?"

"For a guy with a chipped knob, you catch on quick. Come on." Swinehild led the way through the side door and along a rocky path that led back beside the sagging structure to a weed-choked gate. Lafayette followed, hugging himself as the cold wind cut at him.

"Just climb over," she suggested. "You can curl up in the shed if you want, no extra charge."

Lafayette peered through the gloom at the rusted scrap of sheet-metal roof slanting over a snarl of knee-high weeds, precariously supported by four rotting poles. He sniffed, detecting a distinct olfactory reminder of the former occupant.

"Couldn't you find me something a trifle more cozy?" Lafayette asked desperately. "I'd be forever in your debt."

"Not on your nickelodiodion, Jack," Swinehild said briskly. "Cash in advance. Two coppers for the meal, two more for the accommodations, and five for the conversation."

Lafayette dug in his pocket, came up with a handful of silver and gold coins. He handed over a fat Artesian fifty-cent piece. "Will that cover it?"

Swinehild eyed the coin on her palm, bit down on it, then stared at Lafayette.

"That's real silver," she whispered. "For sobbin' into your beer, why didn't you say you was loaded, Lafe—I mean Lafayette? Come on, dearie! For you, nothing but the best!"

O'Leary followed his guide back inside. She paused to light a candle, led the way up steep steps into a tiny room with a low ceiling, a patch-work-quilted cot, and a round window glazed with bottle bottoms, with a potted geranium on the sill. He sniffed cautiously, caught only a faint odor of Octagon soap.

"Capital," he beamed at the hostess. "This will do nicely. Now, if you'd just point out the bath? . . . "

"Tub under the bed. I'll fetch some hot water."

Lafayette dragged out the copper hip bath, pulled off his coat, sat on the bed to tug at his shoes. Beyond the window, the rising moon gleamed on the distant hills, so similar to the hills of home, and at the same time so different. Back in Artesia, Daphne was probably going in to dinner on the arm of some fast-talking dandy now, wondering where he was, possibly even dabbing away a few tears of loneliness . . .

He wrenched his thoughts away from the mental picture of her slim cuddliness and drew a calming lungful of air. No point in getting all emotional again. After all, he was doing all he could. Tomorrow things would seem brighter. Where there's a will there's a way. Absence makes the heart grow fonder . . .

"Of me?" he muttered. "Or of somebody closer to the scene? . . ."

The door opened and Swinehild appeared, a steaming bucket in each hand. She poured them in the bath, tested it with her elbow.

"Just right," she said. He closed the door behind her, pulled off his clothes—the rich cloth was sadly ripped and snagged, he saw—and settled himself in the grateful warmth. There was no washcloth visible, but a lump of brown soap was ready to hand. He sudsed up, used his cupped palms to sluice water over his head, washing soap into his eyes. He sloshed vigorously, muttering to himself, rose, groping for a towel.

"Damn," he said, "I forgot to ask—"

"Here." Swinehild's voice spoke beside him; a rough cloth was pressed into his hand. O'Leary grabbed it and whipped it around himself.

"What are you doing here?" he demanded, stepping out onto the cold floor. He used a corner of the towel to clear an eye. The girl was just shedding a coarse cotton shift. "Here," O'Leary blurted. "What are you doing?"

"If you're through with the bathwater," she said tartly, "I'm taking a bath."

O'Leary swiftly averted his eyes—not for aesthetic reasons: quite the opposite. The quick flash he had gotten of her slender body, one toe dipped tentatively in the soapy water, had been remarkably pleasant. For all her straggly hair and chipped nails, Swinehild had a figure like a princess—like Princess Adoranne, to be precise. He mopped his back and chest quickly, gave a quick dab at his legs, turned back the covers, and hopped into the bed, pulling the quilt up to his chin.

Swinehild was humming softly to herself, splashing in a carefree way.

"Hurry up," he said, facing the wall. "What if Alain—I mean Hulk—walks in?"

"He'll just have to wait his turn," Swinehild said. "Not that he ever washes below the chin, the slob."

"He *is* your husband, isn't he?"

"You could call him that. We never had no magic words said over us, or even a crummy civil ceremony at the county seat, but you know how it is. It might remind somebody to put us on the tax rolls, he says, the bum, but if you ask me—"

"Almost finished?" O'Leary squeaked, screwing his eyes shut against a rising temptation to open them.

"Uh-huh. All done but my—"

"Please—I need my sleep if I'm going to cover all that ground tomorrow!"

"Where's the towel?"

"On the foot of the bed."

Soft sounds of feminine breathing, of brisk friction between coarse cloth and firm feminine flesh, the pad of bare feminine feet—

"Move over," a soft feminine voice breathed in his ear.

"What?" Lafayette sat bolt upright. "Good Lord, Swinehild, you can't sleep here!"

"You're telling me I can't sleep in my own bed?" she demanded indignantly. "You expect me to bed down in the goat pen?"

"No—of course not—but . . . "

"Look, Lafe, it's share and share alike, or you can go sleep on the kitchen table, silver piece or no silver piece." He felt her warm, smooth body slide in next to him, lean across him to blow out the candle.

"That's not the point," Lafayette said weakly. "The point is . . . "

"Yeah?"

"Well, I can't seem to remember the point right now. All I know is that this is a very chancy situation, with your hubby snoring downstairs and only one way out of here."

"Speaking of snoring," Swinehild said suddenly. "I haven't heard a sound for the last five minutes—"

With a crash of splintering wood, the door burst open. By the light of an oil lantern held high, Lafayette saw the enraged visage of Hulk, rendered no less fierce by a well-blacked eye and a lump the size of a pullet egg swelling above his ear.

"Aha!" he yelled. "Right under my roof, you Jezebel!"

"*Your* roof!" Swinehild yelled back, as O'Leary recoiled against the wall. "My old man left the dump to me, as I remember, and out of the goodness of my heart

I took you in off the streets after the monkey ran away with your grind-organ or whatever that hard-luck story you gave me was!"

"I knew the second I set eyes on this slicked-up fancy-dancer, you and him had something cooking!" Hulk countered, aiming a finger like a horse pistol at O'Leary. He jammed the lantern on a hook by the door, pushed his sleeves up past biceps like summer squashes, and dived across the bed. Lafayette, with a desperate lunge, tore free of the confining coverlet and slipped down between the mattress and the wall. The impact as Hulk's head met the plaster was reminiscent of that produced by an enraged *toro* charging the *barrera*. The big man rebounded and slid to the floor like a two-hundred-pound bag of canned goods.

"Say, you've got quite a punch, Lafe," Swinehild said admiringly from somewhere above Lafayette. "He had it coming to him, the big side of beef!"

Lafayette, his arms and legs entangled in apparently endless swathes of blanket, fought his way clear, emerged from under the bed, to meet Swinehild's eyes peering down at him.

"You're a funny guy," she said. "First you knock him cold with one sock, and then you hide under the bed."

"I was just looking around for my contact lenses," Lafayette said haughtily, rising. "But never mind. I only need them for close work like writing my will." He grabbed for his clothes, began pulling them on at top speed.

"I guess you got the right idea at that," Swinehild sighed, tossing a lock of palest blond hair back over a shapely shoulder. "When Hulk wakes up, he's not going to be in his best mood." She sorted through the disarranged bedding for her clothes, began donning them.

"That's all right, you don't need to see me off," Lafayette said hastily. "I know the way."

"See you off? Are you kidding, Jack? You think I'm going to hang around here after this? Let's get out of here before he comes to, roaring, and you have to belt him again."

"Well—I suppose it might be a good idea if you went and stayed with your mother until Hulk cools down a little, so that you can explain that it wasn't what it looked like."

"It wasn't?" Swinehild looked puzzled. "Then what was it? But never mind answering. You're a funny guy, Lafe, but I guess you mean well—which is more than you could say for Hulk, the big baboon!" Lafayette thought he saw the gleam of a tear at the corner of one blue eye, but she turned away before he could be sure.

Swinehild did up the buttons on her bodice, pulled open the door to a rackety clothes press behind the door, and took out a heavy cloak.

"I'll just make up a snack to take along," she said, slipping out into the dark hall. Lafayette followed with the lantern. In the kitchen he stood by restlessly, shifting from one foot to the other and listening intently for sounds from upstairs while Swinehild packed a basket with a loaf of coarse bread, a link of blackish sausage, apples, and yellow cheese, added a paring knife and a hand-blown bottle of a dubious-looking purplish wine.

"That's very thoughtful of you," Lafayette said, taking the basket. "I hope you'll allow me to offer a small additional token of my esteem."

"Keep it," Swinehild said as he dug into his pocket. "We'll need it on the trip."

"We?" Lafayette's eyebrows went up. "How far away does your mother live?"

"What have you got, one of them mother fixations? My old lady died when I was a year old. Let's dust, Lafe. We've got ground to cover before himself gets on our trail." She pulled open the back door, allowing ingress to a gust of chill night air.

"B-but you can't come with me!"

"Why can't I? We're going to the same place."

"You want to see the duke too? I thought you said—"

"A pox on the duke! I just want to get to the big town, see the bright lights, get in on a little action before I'm too old. I've spent the best years o' my life washing out that big elephant's socks after I took 'em off him by force—and what do I get for it? A swell right-arm action from swinging a skillet in self-defense!"

"But—what will people think? I mean, Hulk isn't likely to understand that I have no interest in you—I mean no improper interest—"

Swinehild lifted her chin and thrust out her lower lip defiantly—an expression with which Princess Adoranne had broken hearts in job lots.

"My mistake, noble sir. Now that you mention it, I guess I'd slow you down. You go ahead. I'll make it on my own." She turned and strode off along the moon-bright street. This time O'Leary was sure he saw a tear wink on her cheek.

"Swinehild, wait!" He dashed after her, plucked at her cloak. "I mean—I didn't mean—"

"Skip it, if you don't mind," she said in a voice in which Lafayette detected a slight break, ruthlessly suppressed. "I got by O.K. before you showed up, and I'll get by after you're gone."

"Swinehild, to tell you the truth," O'Leary blurted, trotting beside her, "the reason I was, ah, hesitant about our traveling together was that I, ah, feel such a powerful attraction for you. I mean, I'm not sure I could promise to be a perfect gentleman at all times, and me being a married man, and you a married woman, and . . . and . . . " He paused to gulp air as Swinehild turned, looked searchingly into his face, then smiled brilliantly and threw her arms around his neck. Her velvet-smooth lips pressed hard against his; her admirable contours nestled against him . . .

"I was afraid I was losing my stuff," she confided, nibbling his ear. "You're a funny one, Lafe. But I guess it's just because you're such a gent, like you said, that you think you have to insult a girl."

"That's it exactly," Lafayette agreed hurriedly. "That and the thought of what my wife and your husband would say."

"If that's all that's worrying you, forget it." Swinehild tossed her head. "Come on; if we stretch a leg, we can be in Port Miasma by cockcrow."

Three

Topping a lose rise of stony ground, Lafayette looked down across a long slope of arid, moonlit countryside to the silvered expanse of a broad lake that stretched out to a horizon lost in distance, its smooth surface broken by a chain of islands that marched in a long curve that was an extension of the row of hills to his left. On the last island in line, the lights of a town sparkled distantly.

"It's hard to believe I made a hike across that same stretch of country once," he said. "If I hadn't found an oasis with a Coke machine, I'd have ended up a set of dry bones."

"My feet hurt," Swinehild groaned. "Let's take ten."

They settled themselves on the ground and O'Leary opened the lunch basket, from which a powerful aroma of garlic arose. He carved slices of sausage, and they chewed, looking up at the stars.

"Funny," Swinehild said. "When I was a kid, I used to imagine there was people on all those stars out there. They all lived in beautiful gardens and danced and played all day long. I had an idea I was an orphan, marooned from someplace like that, and that someday my real folks would come along and take me back."

"The curious thing about me," Lafayette said, "was that I didn't think anything like that at all. And then one day I discovered that all I had to do was focus my psychic energies, and zap! There I was in Artesia."

"Look, Lafe," Swinehild said, "you're too nice a guy to go around talking like a nut. It's one thing to dream pretty dreams, but it's something else when you start believing 'em. Why don't you forget all this sidekick-energy stuff and just face facts: you're stuck in humdrum old Melange, like it or not. It ain't much, but it's real."

"Artesia," Lafayette murmured. "I could have been king there—only I turned it down. Too demanding. But you were a princess, Swinehild. And Hulk was a count. A marvelous fellow, once you got to know him—"

"Me, a princess?" Swinehild laughed, not very merrily. "I'm a kitchen slavey, Lafe. It's all I'm cut out for. Can you picture me all dolled up in a fancy gown, snooting everybody and leading a poodle around on a leash?"

"A tiger cub," Lafayette corrected. "And you didn't snoot people; you had a perfectly charming personality. Of course you did get a little huffy once, when you thought I'd invited a chambermaid to the big dance—"

"Well, sure, why not?" Swinehild said. "If I was throwing a big shindig, I wouldn't want any grubby little serving wenches lousing up the atmosphere, would I?"

"Just a minute," O'Leary came back hotly. "Daphne was as pretty and sweet as any girl at the ball—except maybe you. All she needed to shine was a good bath and a nice dress."

"It would take more'n a new set of duds to make a lady out o' me," Swinehild said complacently.

"Nonsense," Lafayette contradicted. "If you just made a little effort, you could be as good as anyone—or better!"

"You think if I dress fancy and tiptoe around not getting my hands dirty, that'll make me any better than what I am?"

"That's not what I meant. I just meant—"

"Never mind, Lafe. The conversation is getting too deep. I got a nice little body on me, and I'm strong and willing. If I can't get by on that, to perdition with the lace pants, get me?"

"I'll tell you what: when we get to the capital, we'll go and have your hair done, and—"

"My hair's Jake with me like it is. Skip it, Lafe. Let's get moving. We still got a long way to go before we can flop—and getting across that lake won't be no picnic."

The lake shore in the lee of the rocky headland was marshy, odiferous of mud and rotted vegetables and expired fish. Lafayette and Swinehild stood shivering in ankle-deep muck, scanning the dark-curving strand for signs of commercial transportation facilities to ferry them out to the island city, the lights of which winked and sparkled cheerfully across the black waters.

"I guess the old tub sank," Swinehild said. "Used to be it ran out to the city every hour on the hour, a buck-fifty one way."

"It looks like we'll have to find an alternative mode of travel," O'Leary commented. "Come on. These huts along the shore are probably fishermen's shacks. We ought to be able to hire a man to row us out."

"I ought to warn you, Lafe, these fishermen got a kind of unsavory rep. Like as not they'd tap you over the head and clean out your pockets, and throw the remains in the lake."

"That's a chance we'll have to take. We can't stay here freezing to death."

"Listen, Lafe—" She caught at his arm. "Let's just scout along the shore and find us a rowboat that ain't tied down too good, and—"

"You mean steal some poor fellow's means of liveli-hood? Swinehild, I'm ashamed of you!"

"O.K., you wait here and *I'll* take care of getting the boat."

"Your attitude does you no credit, Swinehild," Lafa-yette said sternly. "We'll go about this in a straightfor-ward, aboveboard manner. Honesty is the best policy, remember that."

"You sure got some funny ideas, Lafe. But it's your neck."

He led the way across the mud to the nearest shack, a falling-down structure of water-rotted boards with a rusted stovepipe poking out the side, from which a mea-ger coil of smoke shredded into the brisk, icy wind. A faint gleam of light shone under the single boarded-up window. Lafayette rapped at the door. After a pause, bedsprings creaked inside.

"Yeah?" a hoarse voice responded without enthusiasm.

"Ah—we're a couple of travelers," Lafayette called. "We need transportation out to the capital. We're prepared to pay well—" he *oof*!ed as Swinehild's elbow drove into his side. "As well as we can, that is."

Muttering was audible, accompanied by the sound of a bolt being withdrawn. The door opened six inches, and a bleary, red-rimmed eye under a shaggy eyebrow peered forth at shoulder level.

"What are youse?" the voice that went with the eye said. "Nuts or something?"

"Mind your tone," Lafayette said sharply. "There's a lady present."

The bleary eye probed past O'Leary at Swinehild. The wide mouth visible below the eye stretched in a grin that revealed a surprising number of large, carious teeth.

"Whyncha say so, sport? That's different." The eye tracked appreciatively down, paused, up again. "Yeah, not bad at all. What did you say youse wanted, squire?"

"We have to get to Port Miasma," Lafayette said, sidling over to block the cabin dweller's view of Swinehild. "It's a matter of vast importance."

"Yeah. Well, in the morning—"

"We can't wait until morning," Lafayette cut in. "Aside from the fact that we have no intention of spending the night on this mud flat, it's essential that we get away—I mean reach the capital without delay."

"Well—I'll tell you what I'll do; outa the goodness of my heart I'll let the little lady spend the night inside. I'll throw you out a tarp, cap'n, to keep the wind off, and in the A.M.—"

"You don't seem to understand," O'Leary cut in. "We want to go now—at once—immediately."

"Uh-huh," the native said, covering a cavernous yawn with a large-knuckled hand matted on the back with dense black hairs. "Well, Cull, what youse need is a boat—"

"Look here," O'Leary snapped. "I'm standing out here in the cold wind offering you this"—he reached in his pocket and produced a second Artesian fifty-cent piece—"to ferry us out there! Are you interested, or aren't you?"

"Hey!" the man said. "That looks like solid silver."

"Naturally," Lafayette said. "Do you want it or don't you?"

"Geeze, thanks, bub—" The knuckly hand reached, but Lafayette snatched the coin back.

"Ah-ah," he reproved. "First you have to row us out to the city."

"Yeah." The hand went up to scratch at a rumpled head of coarse black hair with a sound like a carpenter filing a knot. "There's just one small problem area there, yer lordship. But maybe I got a solution," he added more briskly. "But the price will be the silver piece plus a sample o' the little lady's favors. I'll take a little o' that last on account." The hand poked at O'Leary as if to brush him aside. He gave it a sharp rap on the knuckles, at which the owner jerked it back and popped the wounded members into his mouth.

"Ouch!" he said, looking up at O'Leary reproachfully. "That hurt, guy!"

"It was meant to," Lafayette said coldly. "If I weren't in such a hurry, I'd haul you out of there and give you a sound thrashing!"

"Yeah? Well, you might run into a little trouble there, chief. I'm kind of a heavy guy to haul around." There was a stir, and the head thrust through the door, followed by a pair of shoulders no wider than a hay rick, a massive torso; on all fours, the owner of the hut emerged, climbed to a pair of feet the size of skate boards, and stood, towering a good seven-foot-six into the damp night air.

"So O.K., I'll wait and collect at the other end," the monster said. "Prob'ly a good idea if I work up a good sweat first anyway. Wait here. I'll be back in short order."

"I got to hand it to you, Lafe," Swinehild murmured as the giant strode away into the mist. "You don't let a little beef scare you." She looked lingeringly after the big man. "Not that he don't have a certain animal charm," she added.

"If he lays a hand on you, I'll tear his head off and stuff it down his throat!" Lafayette snapped.

"Hey, Lafe—you're jealous!" Swinehild said delightedly. "But don't let it get out of hand," she added. "I had enough of getting backhanded ears over teakettle every time some bum looks over my architecture."

"Jealous? Me? You're out of your mind." O'Leary jammed his hands in his pockets and began pacing up and down, while Swinehild hummed softly to herself and twiddled with her hair.

It was the better part of a quarter of an hour before the big man returned, moving with surprising softness for his bulk.

"All set," he called in a hoarse whisper. "Let's go."

"What's all the creeping around and whispering for?" O'Leary demanded loudly. "What—" With a swift move, the giant clapped a hand as hard as saddle leather across his mouth.

"Keep it down, Bo," he hissed. "We don't want to wake the neighbors. The boys need their sleep, the hours they work."

O'Leary squirmed free of the grip, snorting a sharp odor of tar and herring from his nostrils.

"Well, naturally, I don't want to commit a nuisance," he whispered. He took Swinehild's hand, led her in the wake of their guide down across the mucky beach to a crumbling stone jetty at the end of which a clumsy, flat-bottomed dory was tied up. It settled six inches lower in the water as the big man climbed in and settled himself on the rowing bench. Lafayette handed Swinehild down, gritting his teeth as the boatman picked her up by the waist and lifted her past him to the stern seat.

"You sit in the front, bub, and watch for floating logs," the big man said. Lafayette was barely in his place when the oars dipped in and sent the boat off with a surge that almost tipped him over the side. He hung on grimly, listening to the creak of the oarlocks, the splash of small waves under the bow, watching the deck recede swiftly, to disappear into the gathering mist. Twisting to look over his shoulder, he saw the distant city lights, haloed by fog, floating far away across the choppy black water. The damp wind seemed to penetrate his bones.

"How long will the trip take?" he called hoarsely, hugging himself.

"Shhh," the oarsman hissed over his shoulder.

"What's the matter now? Are you afraid you'll wake up the fish?" Lafayette snapped.

"Have a heart, pal," the big man whispered urgently. "Sound carries over water like nobody's business . . ." He cocked his head as if listening. Faintly, from the direction of the shore, Lafayette heard a shout.

"Well, it seems everybody isn't as scrupulous as we are," he said tartly. "Is it all right if we talk now? Or—"

"Can it, Buster!" the giant hissed. "They'll hear us!"

"Who?" Lafayette inquired loudly. "What's going on here? Why are we acting like fugitives?"

"On account of the guy I borrowed the boat from might not like the idea too good," the giant rumbled. "But I guess the fat's on the hotplate now. Some o' them guys got ears like bats."

"What idea might the fellow you borrowed the boat from not like?" Lafayette inquired in a puzzled tone.

"The idea I borrowed the boat."

"You mean you didn't have his permission?"

"I hate to wake a guy outa a sound sleep wit' a like frivolous request."

"Why, you . . . you . . ."

"Just call me Clutch, bub. Save the fancy names for the bums which are now undoubtedly pushing off in pursuit." Clutch bent his back to the oars, sending the boat leaping ahead.

"Great," Lafayette groaned. "Perfect. This is our reward for being honest: a race through the night with the police baying on our trail!"

"I'll level wit' youse," Clutch said. "These boys ain't no cops. And they ain't got what you'd call a whole lot o' inhibitions. If they catch us, what they'll hand us won't be no subpoena."

"Look," Lafayette said quickly, "we'll turn back, and explain that the whole thing was a misunderstanding—"

"Maybe you like the idea o' being fed to the fish, yer worship, but not me," Clutch stated. "And we got the little lady to think of, too. Them boys is a long time between gals."

"Don't waste breath," Lafayette said. "Save it for rowing."

"If I row any harder, the oars'll bust," Clutch said. "Sound like they're gaining on us, Cull. Looks like I'll have to lighten ship."

"Good idea," Lafayette agreed. "What can we throw overboard?"

"Well, there ain't no loose gear to jettison; and I got to stick wit' the craft in order to I should row. And naturally we can't toss the little lady over the side, except as a last resort, like. So I guess that leaves you, chum."

"Me?" Lafayette echoed. "Look here, Clutch—I'm the one who hired you, remember? You can't be serious—"

"Afraid so, Mac." The big man shipped oars, dusted his hands, and turned on his bench.

"But—who's going to pay you, if I'm in the lake?" O'Leary temporized, retreating to the farthermost angle of the bows.

"Yeah—there is that," Clutch agreed, stroking his Gibraltar-like chin. "Maybe you better hand over the poke first."

"Not a chance. If I go, it goes!"

"Well—I guess we ain't got room to like scuffle. So—since youse want to be petty about it, I'll just have to collect double from the little lady." Clutch rose in a smooth lunge, one massive arm reaching for Lafayette. The latter ducked under the closing hand and launched himself in a headfirst dive at the other's midriff, instead crashed into a brick wall that had suddenly replaced it. As he clawed at the floorboards, he was dimly aware of a swishing sound, a solid *thud!* as of a mallet striking a tent stake, followed a moment later by a marine earthquake which tossed the boat like a juggler's egg. A faceful of icy water brought him upright, striking out gamely.

"Easy, Lafe," Swinehild called. "I clipped him with the oar and he landed on his chin. Damn near swamped us. We better get him over the side fast."

Lafayette focused his eyes with difficulty, made out the inert form of the giant draped face down across the gunwale, one oak-root arm trailing in the water.

"We . . . we can't do that," Lafayette gasped. "He's unconscious; he'd drown." He took the oar from her, groped his way to the rower's bench, thrust Clutch's elephantine leg aside, dipped in, and pulled—

The oar snapped with a sharp report, sending Lafayette in a forward dive into the scuppers.

"I guess I swung it too hard," Swinehild said regretfully. "It's all that skillet-work done it."

Lafayette scrabbled back to the bench, ignoring the shooting pains in his head, neck, eyeballs, and elsewhere. "I'll have to scull with one oar," he panted. "Which direction?"

"Dunno," Swinehild said. "But I guess it don't matter much. Look."

O'Leary followed her pointing finger. A ghostly white patch, roughly triangular in shape, loomed off the port bow, rushing toward them out of the dense fog.

"It's a sailboat," Lafayette gasped as the pursuer hove into full view, cleaving the mist. He could see half a dozen men crouched on the deck of the vessel. They raised a shout as they saw the drifting rowboat, changed course to sweep up alongside. Lafayette shattered the remaining oar over the head of the first of the borders to leap the rail, before an iceberg he had failed to notice until that moment fell on him, burying him under a hundred tons of boulders and frozen mammoth bones . . .

O'Leary regained consciousness standing on his face in half an inch of iced cabbage broth with a temple gong echoing in his skull. The floor under him was rising up and up and over in a never-ending loop-the-loop, but when he attempted to clutch for support he discovered that both arms had been lopped off at the shoulder. He worked his legs, succeeded in driving his face farther into the bilge, which sloshed and gurgled merrily down between his collar and his neck before draining away with the next tilt of the deck. He threshed harder, flopped over on his back, and blinked his eyes clear. He was lying, it appeared, in the cockpit of the small sailing craft. His arms had not been amputated after all, he discovered as fiery pains lanced out from his tightly bound wrists.

"Hey, Fancy-pants is awake," a cheery voice called. "O.K. if I step on his mush a couple times?"

"Wait until we get through drawing straws fer the wench."

O'Leary shook his head, sending a whole new lexicon of aches swirling through it, but clearing his vision slightly. Half a dozen pairs of burly rubber-booted legs were grouped around the binnacle light, matching the burly bodies looming above them. Swinehild, standing by with her arms held behind her by a pock-marked man with a notched ear, drove a sudden kick into a handy shin. The recipient of the attention leaped and swore, while his fellows guffawed in hearty good fellowship.

"She's a lively 'un," a toothless fellow with greasy, shoulder-length hair stated. "Who's got the straws?"

"Ain't no straws aboard," another stated. "We'll have to use fish."

"I dunno," demurred a short, wide fellow with a blue-black beard which all but enveloped his eyes. "Never heard of drawing fish for a wench. We want to do this right, according to the rules and all."

"Skip the seafood, boys," Swinehild suggested. "I kind of got a habit of picking my own boyfriends. Now you, good-looking . . . " She gave a saucy glance to the biggest of the crew, a lantern-jawed chap with a sheaf of stiff wheat-colored hair and a porridgy complexion. "You're more my style. You going to let these rag-pickers come between us?"

The one thus singled out gaped, grinned, flexed massive, crooked shoulders, and threw out his chest.

"Well, boys, I guess that settles that—"

A marlinspike wielded by an unidentified hand described a short arc ending alongside the lantern jaw, the owner of which did a half-spin and sank out of sight.

"None o' that, wench," a gruff voice commanded. "Don't go trying to stir up no dissension. With us, it's share and share alike. Right, boys?"

As a chorus of assent rang out, Lafayette struggled to a sitting position, cracking his head on the tiller just above him. It was unattended, lashed in position, holding the craft on a sharply heeled into-the-wind course, the boom-mounted sail bellying tautly above the frothing waves. O'Leary tugged at his bonds; the ropes cutting into his wrists were as unyielding as cast-iron manacles. The crewmen were laughing merrily at a coarse jape, ogling Swinehild, while one of their number adjusted a row of kippered herring in his hand, his tongue protruding from the corner of his mouth with the intensity of his concentration. The object of the lottery stood, her wet garments plastered against her trim figure, her chin high, her lips blue with cold.

O'Leary groaned silently. A fine protector for a girl he'd turned out to be. If he hadn't pigheadedly insisted on doing things his own way, they'd never have gotten into this spot. And this was one mess from which he was unlikely to emerge alive. Swinehild had warned him the locals would cheerfully feed him to the fish. Probably they were keeping him alive until they could get around to robbing him of everything, including the clothes on his back, and then over he'd go, with or without a knife between his ribs. And Swinehild, poor creature—her dream of making it big in the big town would end right here with this crew of cutthroats. Lafayette twisted savagely at his bonds. If he could get one hand free; if he could just take one of these grinning apes to the bottom with him; if he only had one small remaining flicker of his old power over the psychic energies . . .

Lafayette drew a calming breath and forced himself to relax. No point in banging his head on any more stone walls. He couldn't break half-inch hemp ropes with his bare hands. But if he could, somehow, manage just one little miracle—nothing to compare with shifting himself to Artesia, of course, or summoning up a dragon on order, or even supplying himself with a box of Aunt Hooty's taffies on demand. He'd settle for just one tiny rearrangement of the situation, something—anything at all to give him a chance.

"That's all I ask," he murmured, squeezing his eyes shut. "Just a chance." *But I've got to be specific*, he reminded himself. *Focusing the psychic energies isn't magic, after all. It's just a matter of drawing on the entropic energy of the universe to manipulate things into a configuration nearer to my heart's desire. Like, for example, if the ropes were to be loose . . .*

"But they aren't loose," he told himself sternly. "You can't change any *known* element of the situation. At best, you can influence what happens next, that's all. And probably not even that."

Well, then—if there was a knife lying here on deck—an old rusty scaling knife, say, just carelessly tossed aside. I could get my hands on it, and—

"Lay down and sleep it off, landlubber," a voice boomed, accompanying the suggestion with a kick on the ear that produced a shower of small ringed planets whirling in a mad dance. Lafayette blinked them away, snorted a sharp aroma of aged cheese and garlic from his nostrils. Something with the texture of barbed wire was rasping the side of his neck. He twisted away from it, felt something round rolling under him. An apple, he realized as it crunched, releasing a fresh fruity odor. And the cheese and the sausage . . .

He held his breath. It was the lunch basket. The pirates had tossed it aboard along with the prisoners. And in the basket there had been a knife.

Lafayette opened one eye and checked the positions of his captors. Four of them stood heads together, intently studying the array of fishheads offered by the fifth. The sixth man lay snoring at their feet. Swinehild was huddled on the deck—knocked there by one of her would-be swains, no doubt.

Cautiously, O'Leary fingered the deck under him with his bound hands; inching sideways, he encountered the loaf of bread, reduced by soaking to a sodden paste, then a second apple, flattened by a boot. He reached the basket, felt over it, found it empty. The sausage lay half under it. Lafayette hitched himself forward another six inches, grinding the cheese under his shoulderblades. As the waves thumped the hull under him, his numb fingers closed over the haft of the knife.

It was small, the blade no more than four inches long—but it was big enough for his purpose. The crewmen were still busy with their lottery. Lafayette rolled over, struggled to his knees, maneuvered into position with his back against the tiller. Gripping the knife, he felt for the lashings, began sawing through the twisted rope.

It was an agonizing two minutes before a sharp musical *thong!* sounded; the suddenly freed tiller gouged Lafayette painfully in the ribs as it slammed around to a full starboard position. Instantly the boat heeled sharply, falling away downwind. The crewmen, caught by surprise, reeled against the rail, grabbing for support. The boat gave a wild plunge, the sail slatting as the breeze struck it dead astern. Cordage creaked; the sail bulged, then, with a report like a pistol shot, filled. The boom swept across the deck—precisely at head height, Lafayette noted, as it gathered in the four sailors and sent them flying over the side, where they struck with a tremendous quadruple splash as the pilotless craft went leaping ahead across the dark water.

Four

"Your poor head," Swinehild said, applying a cool compress made from a section of her skirt to one of the knots on O'Leary's skull. "Them boys throwed you around like a sack o' turnips."

"My ear feels the size of a baked potato, and about the same temperature," Lafayette said. "Not that I suppose it actually gleams in the dark." He peered across toward the misty glow in the middle distance toward which he was steering.

"In a way those hijackers did us a favor," he commented. "We'd never have made such good time rowing."

"You got kind of a irritating way o' looking on the bright side, Lafe," Swinehild sighed. "I wish you'd work on that."

"Now, Swinehild, this is no time to be discouraged," Lafayette jollied her. "True, we're cold and wet and so tired we ache all over; but the worst is over. We got out of an extremely tight spot with no more than a few bruises to my head and your dignity. In a few minutes we'll be tucking our feet under a table for a bowl of hot soup and a little drop of something to cut the chill, and then off to the best hotel in town."

"Sure, it's OK for *you* to talk. With that slick line o' chatter o' yours, you'll probably land a swell job with the duke, soothsaying or something."

"I don't want a job," Lafayette pointed out. "I just want to get out of Melange and back to the comfortable monotony I was fool enough to complain about a few hours ago."

O'Leary brought the boat smartly about on the starboard tack, closing in on the ever-widening spread of city lights ahead. They passed a bell-buoy dinging lonesomely in the mist, sailed past a shore lined with high-fronted buildings recalling the waterfront at Amsterdam, backed by rising tiers of houses clustered about the base of a massive keep of lead-colored granite, approached a lighted loading dock where a number of nondescript small craft were tied up, bobbing gently on the waves. As they came alongside, Swinehild threw a line to an urchin, who hauled it in and made it fast. Flickering gas lights on the quay above shed a queasy light on wet cobbles well strewn with refuse. A couple of dockside loafers watched incuriously as Lafayette assisted Swinehild from the boat, tossing a nickel to the lad. A stray dog with a down-curled tail slunk away past the darkened fronts of the marine-supply houses across the way as they started across the cobbles.

"Geeze—the big town," Swinehild said reverently, brushing a curl from her eyes. "Port Miasma—and it's even bigger and glamorouser than I expected."

"Um," Lafayette said noncommittally, leading the way toward the lighted entry of a down-at-heels grog shop just visible at an angle halfway up a steep side street, before which a weathered board announced YE GUT BUCKET.

Inside the smoky but warm room, they took a corner table. The sleepy-eyed tavern-keeper silently accepted their order and shuffled away.

"Well, this is more like it," Lafayette said with a sigh. "It's been a strenuous night, but with a hot meal and a good bed to look forward to, we can't complain."

"The big town scares me, Lafe," Swinehild said. "It's so kind of impersonal, all hustle-bustle, no time for them little personal touches that mean so much to a body."

"Hustle-bustle? It's as dead as a foreclosed mortuary," Lafayette muttered.

"Like this place," Swinehild continued. "Open in the middle o' the night. Never seen anything like it."

"It's hardly ten P.M.," Lafayette pointed out. "And—"

"And besides that, I got to go," Swinehild added. "And not a clump o' bushes in sight."

"There's a room for it," O'Leary said hastily. "Over there—where it says LADIES."

"You mean—*inside?*"

"Of course. You're in town now, Swinehild. You have to start getting used to a few amenities—"

"Never mind; I'll just duck out in the alley—"

"Swinehild! The ladies' room, please!"

"You come with me."

"I can't—it's for ladies only. There's another one for men."

"Well, think o' that!" Swinehild shook her head wonderingly.

"Now hurry along, our soup will be here in a minute."

"Wish me luck." Swinehild rose and moved off hesitantly. Lafayette sighed, turned back the soggy lace from his wrists, used the worn napkin beside his plate to mop the condensed moisture from his face, sniffing the bouquet of chicken and onions drifting in from the kitchen. His mouth watered at the prospect. Except for a chunk of salami, and that plate of dubious pork back at the Beggar's Bole, he hadn't eaten a bite since lunch . . .

Lunch, ten hours and a million years ago: the dainty table set up on the terrace, the snowy linen, the polished silver, the deft *sommelier* pouring the feather-light wine from the frosted and napkin-wrapped bottle, the delicate slices of savory ham, the angelfood cake with whipped cream, the paper-thin cup of steaming coffee—

"Hey—you!" a deep voice boomed across the room, shattering O'Leary's reverie. He looked around to see who was thus rudely addressed, saw a pair of tall fellows in gold-braided blue tailcoats, white knee breeches, buckled shoes, and tricorner hats bearing down on him from the door.

"Yeah—it's him," the smaller of the two said, grabbing for his sword hilt. "Boy oh boy, the pinch of the week, and it's ours, all ours, Snardley—so don't louse it up." The rapier cleared its sheath with a whistling rasp. Its owner waved it at O'Leary.

"Hold it right here, pal," he said in a flinty voice. "You're under arrest in the name of the duke!"

The second uniformed man had drawn a long-muzzled flintlock pistol of the type associated with Long John Silver; he flourished it in a careless manner at O'Leary's head.

"You going in quiet, rube, or have I gotta plug you, resisting arrest?"

"You've got the wrong rube," Lafayette replied impatiently. "I just arrived: I haven't had time to break any laws—unless you've got one against breathing."

"Not yet—but it's a thought, wise guy." The rapier-wielder jabbed sharply at him. "Better come along nice, Bo: Yockwell and me collect the same reward, dead or alive."

"I seen what you taken and done to a couple pals of mine, which they was snuck up on from behind," Yockwell warned. "I'm just itching for a excuse to get even." He thumbed back the hammer of the big pistol with an ominous click.

"You're out of your minds!" O'Leary protested. "I've never been to this water-logged slum before in my life!"

"Tell it to Duke Rodolpho." The sword poked Lafayette painfully. "Pick 'em up, Dude. We got a short walk ahead."

O'Leary glanced toward the ladies' room as he got to his feet: the door was closed and silent. The landlord stood furtive-eyed behind the bar, polishing a pewter tankard. Lafayette caught his eye, mouthed an urgent message. The man blinked and made a sign as if warding off the evil eye.

"You fellows are making a big mistake," Lafayette said as a push helped him toward the door. "Probably right now the man you're really after is making a fast getaway. Your bosses aren't going to like it—"

"You either, chum. Now button the chin."

A few furtive passersby gaped as the two cops herded O'Leary up the narrow, crooked street which wound sharply toward the grim pile towering over the town. They passed through a high iron gate guarded by a pair of sentries in uniforms like those of the arresting patrolmen, crossed a cobbled courtyard to a wooden door flanked by smoking flambeaux. It opened on a bright-lit room with hand-drawn WANTED posters on the walls, a wooden bench, a table stacked with curled papers in dusty bundles.

"Well, look who's here," a lean fellow with a yellowish complexion said, picking up a bedraggled quill and pulling a blank form toward him. "You made a mistake coming back, smart guy."

"Coming back wh—" A sharp jab in the back cut off O'Leary's objections. His captors grabbed his arms, hustled him through an iron-barred door and along a dark passage ending in a flight of steps that led downward into an odor like the gorilla house at the St. Louis zoo.

"Oh, no," Lafayette protested, digging in his heels. "You're not taking me down there!"

"Right," Yockwell confirmed. "See you later, joker!" A foot in the seat propelled Lafayette forward; he half-leaped, half-fell down the steps, landed in a heap in a low-ceilinged chamber lit by a single tallow candle and lined with barred cages from which shaggy, animal-like faces leered. At one side of the room a man wider than his height sat on a three-legged stool paring his nails with a sixteen-inch Bowie knife.

"Welcome to the group," the attendant called in a tone like a meat grinder gnawing through gristle. "Lucky fer you, we got a vacancy."

Lafayette leaped to his feet and made three steps before an iron grille crashed down across the steps, barely missing his toes.

"Close," the receptionist said. "Another six inches and I'd of been mopping brains off the floor."

"What's this all about?" Lafayette inquired in a broken voice.

"Easy," the jailer said, jangling keys. "You're back in stir, and this time you don't sneak out when I ain't looking."

"I demand a lawyer. I don't know what I'm accused of, but whatever it is, I'm innocent!"

"You never hit no guys over the head?" The jailer wrinkled his forehead in mock surprise.

"Well, as to that—"

"You never croaked nobody?"

"Not intentionally. You see—"

"Never conspired at a little larceny? Never wandered into the wrong bedroom by mistake?"

"I can explain—" Lafayette cried.

"Skip it," the turnkey yawned, selecting a key from the ring. "We already had the trial. You're guilty on all counts. Better relax and grab a few hours' sleep, so's you'll be in shape for the big day tomorrow."

"Tomorrow? What happens tomorrow?"

"Nothing much." The jailer grabbed Lafayette by the collar of his bedraggled plum coat and hustled him into a cell. "Just a small beheading at dawn, with you as the main attraction."

Lafayette huddled in the corner of the cramped cell, doing his best to ignore his various aches and pains, the itching occasioned by the insect life that shared his accommodations, the mice that ran across his feet, the thick, fudgy odor, and the deep, glottal snores of the other inmates. He also tried, with less success, to keep his mind off the grisly event scheduled for the next morning.

"Poor Swinehild," he muttered to his knees. "She'll think I ran off and deserted her. She'll never trust another ladies' room as long as she lives. Poor kid, alone in this miserable imitation of a medieval hell-town, with no money, no friends, no place to lay her head . . . "

"Hey, Lafe," a familiar voice hissed from the murk behind him. "This way. We got about six minutes to make it back up to the postern gate before the night watchman makes his next round!"

"Swinehild," Lafayette mumbled, gaping at the tousled blond head poking through the rectangular aperture in the back wall of the cell. "Where did you—how—what—?"

"Shh! You'll wake up the screw!" Lafayette glanced across toward the guard. He sat slumped on his stool like a dreaming Buddha, his fingers interlaced across his paunch, his head resting comfortably against the wall.

"I'll hafta back out," Swinehild said. "Come on; it's a long crawl." Her face disappeared. Lafayette tottered to his feet, started into the hole head first. It was a roughly mortared tunnel barely big enough to admit him. A cold draft blew through it.

"Put the stone back," Swinehild hissed.

"How? With my feet?"

"Well—let it go. Maybe nobody'll notice it for a while in that light."

His face bumped hers in the darkness; her lips nibbled his cheek. She giggled.

"If you don't beat all, Lafe, grabbing a smooch at a time like this. Anybody else'd be thinking o' nothing but putting distance between hisself and that basket party."

"How did you find out where I was?" Lafayette inquired, scrambling after her as she retreated.

"The tapman told me they'd put the sneeze on you. I followed along to the gate and made friends with the boys there. One of 'em let slip about this back way in. Seems like another feller escaped the same way, just a couple days back."

"They told you all that, on such short acquaintance?"

"Well, look at it their way, Lafe: low pay, long hours—and what's it to them if some poor sucker Rodolpho's got it in for cheats the headsman?"

"Well, that was certainly friendly of them."

"Yeah, but it was kinda tough on my back. Boy, them cold stone floors them boys has to stand on!"

"Swinehild—you don't mean—but never mind," Lafayette hurried on. "I'd rather not have it confirmed."

"Careful, now," Swinehild cautioned. "We go up a steep slant here and come out under a juniper bush. Just outside there's a guy pounding a beat."

Using elbows, toes, and fingernails, Lafayette crept up the incline. At the top, he waited while Swinehild listened.

"Here goes," she said. There was a soft creak, and dim light filtered in, along with a wisp of fog. A moment later, they were across the alley and over a low wall into a small park. They picked their way among trees and shrubs to a secluded spot in the center of a dense clump of myrtle.

"And I was worried about you," Lafayette said, flopping down on the ground. "Swinehild, it's a miracle; I still don't believe it. If it weren't for you, in another three hours I'd have been shorter by a head."

"And if it wasn't for you, I'd still be playing ring-around-the-rosy with them five deck-apes, Lafe." She snuggled close to him on the carpet of fragrant leaves.

"Yes, but it was me that got you into the situation in the first place, dragging you off in the middle of the night—"

"Yeah, but I was the one got you in bad with Hulk. He ain't really such a bad guy, but he ain't long on brains, always jumping to conclusions. Why, if he was to come along now, I bet the dummy'd try to make something of you and me here in the bushes together!"

"Er, yes." Lafayette edged away from the warm body beside him. "But right now we have to give some thought to our next move. I can't show my face around this place; either they've mistaken me for someone else, or those sailors we ditched are the world's fastest swimmers."

"We never did get nothing to eat," Swinehild said. "Or did they feed you in jail?"

"It must have been the caterer's day off," O'Leary said sadly. "I'd even welcome another slice of that leatherwurst we had in our lunch basket."

"You peeked," Swinehild said, and produced the sausage from a capacious reticule, along with the paring knife and the villainous-looking vintage Lafayette had last seen sliding about the bilge of the sailboat.

"Clever girl," Lafayette breathed. He used the knife to cut thick slices of the garlicky sausage, halved the apple, and dug the cork from the bottle.

"Nothing like a picnic under the stars," he said, chewing doggedly at the tough meat.

"Gee, this is the kind o' life I always pictured," Swinehild said, closing the distance between them and sliding her hand inside his shirt. "On the loose in the big town, meeting interesting people, seeing the sights . . . "

"A tour of the local dungeons isn't my idea of high living," Lafayette objected. "We can't stay here under this bush; it'll be dawn soon. Our best bet is to try to make it back down to the wharf and sneak aboard our boat, if it's still there."

"You mean you want to leave Port Miasma already? But we ain't even been through the wax museum yet!"

"A regrettable omission; but in view of the habit of the local cops to hang first and look at ID's later, I think I'll have to try to survive without it."

"Well—I guess you got a point there, Lafe. But I heard they got a statue o' Pavingale slaying the gore-worm that's so lifelike you could swear you heard the blood drip."

"It's tempting," O'Leary conceded, "but not quite as tempting as staying alive."

"Hulk ain't going to be glad to see us back," Swinehild predicted.

"You don't have to go," Lafayette said. "You seem to manage quite well here. I'm the one they want to hang on sight. Anyway, I have no intention of going back. What's on the other side of the lake?"

"Not much. Wastelands, the Chantspel Mountains, a bunch o' wild men, the Endless Forest, monsters. And the Glass Tree. You know."

"How about cities?"

"They say the Erl-king's got some kind o' layout under the mountains. Why?"

"I won't find the kind of help I need in an underground burrow," Lafayette said doubtfully. "Central wouldn't bother posting a representative anywhere but in a large population center."

"Then I guess you're stuck, Lafe. Port Miasma's the only town in this part o' Melange, as far as I know."

"That's ridiculous," Lafayette scoffed. "There has to be more than one city."

"Why?"

"Well—now that you mention it, I guess there doesn't." He sighed. "And I suppose that means I have to stay and make another try to see the duke. What I need is a disguise: different clothes, a false beard, maybe an eye patch . . . "

"Too bad I didn't pick up a soldier's uniform for you while I had the chance," Swinehild said. "There it was, laying right there on the chair . . . "

"All I need is something to get me through the gate. Once I gained the duke's ear and explained how vital it is I get back to Artesia, my troubles would be over."

"Better take it slow, Lafe. I heard Rodolpho's kind of careful who gets near him these days, ever since some intruder hit him over the head with a chair while he was sitting in it."

"I'll deal with that problem when I get to it," O'Leary said. "But this is all just a lot of air castle. Without a disguise, it's hopeless." He pared another slice from the sausage, chewed at it morosely.

"Don't be downhearted, Lafe," Swinehild cajoled. "Who knows what might turn up? Heck, you might just find what you need hanging on a bush; you never know."

"I wish it was that easy. It *used* to be that easy. All I had to do was focus the psychic energies and arrange matters as I pleased. Of course, there were limitations. I could only change things that hadn't happened yet, things I hadn't seen—like what was around the next corner."

"Sounds like a swell trick, Lafe," Swinehild said dreamily, joining in the mood. "You could conjure up jewels and black-satin pillers with MOTHER on 'em and Gorp knows what-all."

"I'd settle for a putty nose complete with spectacles, buck teeth, and a toothbrush moustache," Lafayette said. "And maybe a bushy red wig—and a monk's outfit, with a pillow for padding. It would just be lying there under the bushes where somebody lost it, and—" He broke off, his eyes wide open.

"Did you feel that?"

"Uh-uh. Do it again."

"Wasn't there a . . . a sort of . . . thump? As if the world went over a bump in the road?"

"Naw. Now, you was just saying, about the three wishes and all: I wish I had a pair o' them black-lace step-ins with a little pink ribbon—"

"Swinehild—shhh!" Lafayette interrupted abruptly. He cocked his head, listening. There was a muffled giggle from nearby, accompanied by threshings and puffings as of a friendly wrestling match.

"Wait here." Lafayette crept under the encircling boughs, skirted a stand of dwarf cedar. The sounds were coming from the deep shadows ahead. A dry twig snapped sharply under his hand.

"Hark, Pudelia—what's that?" a jowly voice whispered. The bushes trembled and a pouch-eyed face with a fringe of mouse-colored hair poked forth. For an instant the bulging blue eyes stared directly into O'Leary's paralyzed gaze. Then, with a muffled gobbling sound, it disappeared.

"Your husband!" the voice strangled. "Every man for himself!" There was a squeal, followed by the sound of rapid departures. Lafayette let out a long breath and turned away.

Something caught his eye, draped on the bush. It was a capacious gray robe of coarse wool, well matted with leaves on the underside. Beside it lay a black-satin cushion, lettered INCHON in pink and yellow.

"Great heavens," Lafayette breathed. "Do you suppose . . . ?" He scouted farther, encountered what felt like a small, furry animal. He held it up to the moonlight.

"A . . . a red wig!"

"Lafe—what's going on?" Swinehild whispered from behind him. "Where'd you get that?"

"It was—just lying here."

"And a monk's robe—and my piller!" Swinehild caught up the latter and hugged it. "Lafe—you seen all this stuff before! You was funning me about wishing for it!"

"There ought to be one more item," Lafayette said, scanning the ground. "Ah!" He plucked a false nose with attached spectacles, teeth, and moustache from under the bush.

"And my fancy underdrawers just like I always wanted!" Swinehild yelped in delight, catching a wispy garment. "Lafe, you old tease!" She flung her arms around his neck and kissed him warmly.

"Oh boy," Lafayette said, disengaging himself from her embrace. "I've got my old stuff back. I don't know why, or how, but—" He closed his eyes. "Right behind that tree," he murmured. "A Harley-Davidson, fire-engine-red." He paused expectantly, opened one eye, then walked over and looked behind the tree.

"That's funny." He tried again:

"Behind the bench: a Mauser seven-six-five automatic in a black-leather holster, with a spare clip—loaded." He hurried over and rooted unsuccessfully among the leaves.

"I don't get it—first it works and then it doesn't!"

"Aw, never mind, Lafe, it was a good joke, but now, like you said, we got to shake a leg. Lucky for you that local sport tricked hisself out in a friar's costume to meet his doxy. That get-up's better'n a soldier suit."

"Could it have been just coincidence?" O'Leary muttered as he tucked the pillow inside his belt, pulled on the robe, donned the wig and the nose. Swinehild snickered.

"How do I look?" He rotated before her.

"You look like one o' them strolling minstrels—the Spots Brothers, the smart one—Grumpo."

"Well, it will have to do."

"Sure; it's swell. Listen, Lafe: forget about seeing the duke. You can make like a strolling minstrel yourself. We'll find us a snug garret someplace and fix it up with curtains on the windows and a pot o' pinks, and—"

"Don't talk nonsense, Swinehild," Lafayette reproved her. "Duke Rodolpho's my only hope of getting out of this miserable place."

Swinehild caught at his hand. "Lafe—don't go back to the palace. If they catch you again, this time it'll be *zzzt!* for sure. Can't you just settle down here and be happy?"

"Happy? You think I enjoy being hit on the head and thrown in jail and hiding in the bushes?"

"I'll . . . I'll hide with you, Lafe."

"There, there, Swinehild, you're a nice girl and I appreciate all your help, but it's out of the question. I have a wife waiting for me, remember?"

"Yeah—but she's there—and I'm here."

He patted her hand. "Swinehild, you run along and pursue your career. I'm sure you're going to be a great success in the big city. As for me, I have more serious business to attend to—alone. Good-bye and good luck."

"D-don't you want to take the lunch?" She offered the bottle and what was left of the sausage. "In case you wind up back in the pokey?"

"Thanks—you keep it. I don't intend to eat again until I'm dining in style . . ."

There was a clip-clop of hooves on the street beyond the hedge. Lafayette ducked to the nearest gap and peered through. A party of mounted cuirassiers in lemon-colored coats and plumed helmets was cantering toward him, followed by a matched pair of gleaming black horses with silver-mounted harness drawing a gilt-and-pink coach.

At the open window of the vehicle, Lafayette glimpsed a gloved feminine hand, a sleeve of pale-blue velvet. A face leaned forward in profile, then turned toward him . . .

"Daphne!" he yelled. The coachman flicked his whip out over the horses; the coach rattled past, gaining speed. Lafayette burst through the hedge and dashed after it, raced alongside. The passenger stared down at him with a wide-eyed look of astonishment.

"Daphne!" O'Leary gasped, grabbing for the door handle. "It *is* you! Stop! Wait!"

There was a roar from the nearest of the escort; hooves clashed and thundered. A trooper galloped up beside him; Lafayette saw a saber descending in time to duck, trip over a loose cobblestone, and skid two yards on his jaw. He pried his face from the street and saw the coach bowling away across the plaza before his view was cut off by the legs of the prancing horses that had surrounded him. He looked up into the fiercely musta-chioed face of the captain of the escort.

"Throw this miserable bum in the dungeons!" he bellowed. "Truss him in chains! Stretch him on the rack! But don't spoil him! The Lady Andragorre will doubtless want to witness his death throes personally!"

"Daphne," Lafayette mumbled brokenly as a trooper prodded him to his feet with a lance. "And she didn't even look back . . . "

Five

Lafayette's new cell was somewhat less luxurious than the first he had occupied, featuring a damp floor the size of a card table and a set of leg irons which had been riveted to his ankles, not without occasioning a few bruises. Beyond the bars, a big-armed man in ominous black leathers whistled with more cheer than tune, poking up a merry blaze on a small grate beside which hung an array of curiously shaped tongs, pincers and oversized nutcrackers. To the right of the fireplace was a metal rack resembling an upended bedstead, but for a number of threaded rods running its full length, with crank handles at the ends. Balancing the composition on the left was an open, upended sarcophagus studded with rusted three-inch spikes.

"Listen to me," Lafayette was saying for the ninth time. "If you'll just get a message to the duke for me, this whole silly misunderstanding will be cleared up!"

"Have a heart, pal." The technician gave O'Leary a weary smile. "For you, this is all new; but I been through it a thousand times. Your best bet is to just relax and keep your mind on something else. Flowers, now. Flowers is nice. Just think about 'em poking up their purty little heads on a spring A.M., all bedewed wit' dew and all. You won't hardly notice what's happening."

"You have more confidence in my powers of contemplation than I do," Lafayette said. "Anyway, my case is different. I'm innocent, just an inoffensive tourist; all I want is a chance to explain matters to his Grace the duke, after which I'll put in a good word for you, and—"

"Tch. You're wasting your wind, fella. You goofed when you didn't ditch your mad-monk suit before you pulled the caper. Half the ducal guard's been combing the town for a week to apprehend that blackguard, which he's pulled ten jobs right under their noses. And you musta been consumed wit' unholy lusts or something to jump her ladyship's carriage right in front of the gate, not that I blame you. She's a looker, all right, all right."

"Is that, er, all they have on me?"

"Jeez, kid, ain't that enough? The duke hisself's got a eye on her Ladyship. He don't take kindly to mugs which they make a pass at her."

"I mean, there isn't any old charge left over from yesterday or anything silly like that? Anything they'd want to, say, cut my head off at dawn for?"

"A beheading rap? Naw, this is nothing like that, just the standard workout wit' the irons and then a nice clean garroting. There *was* a axing slated for dawn, but I heard the guy turned out to be a wizard: he turned into a bat and flew up the chimbley."

"How clever of him. I wish I knew his secret." Lafayette squeezed his eyes shut.

"I'm back in Artesia, out in the desert," he whispered urgently. "It's a nice night, and the stars are shining, and all I have to do is walk about twenty miles through loose sand and I'll be back at the palace and—"

"Hey, nix on the spells," the executioner broke in reproachfully. "You got enough on your plate wit'out a necromancy charge."

"It's no use, anyway," O'Leary groaned. "I thought I had it back, but I guess I was just kidding myself. I'm stuck here—unless I can talk to the duke," he finished on a note of desperation. "Won't you at least try? If I'm telling the truth, it could mean a nice promotion for you."

"I don't need no promotion, chum. I'm already at the top o' my profession; I'm happy wit' my work."

"You *enjoy* being a torturer?"

"That ain't a term us P.P.S.'s like, mister," the man said in a hurt tone. "What we are, we're Physical-Persuasion Specialists. You don't want to get us mixed up wit' these unlicensed quacks, which they're lousing up the good name of the profession."

"You mean it takes special training to raise a blister with a hot iron?"

"There's more to it than that. You take like the present assignment: I got strict instructions to keep you in what we call an undergraduate status until her Ladyship gets back. And since she figures to be gone a couple weeks, you can see I got a delicate fortnight ahead. Not any slob could do it."

"Say, I have a suggestion," Lafayette offered brightly. "Why not just kind of forget I'm here until maybe just before the deadline? Then you can paint on a few stripes with Mercurochrome and fake up some wax welts, and—"

"Hold it right there," the P.P.S. cut in sternly. "I'm gonna pretend like I never heard that. Why, if I pulled a stunt like that, I'd be drummed outa the guild."

"Tell you what," O'Leary said. "If you promise not to tell, I won't either."

"Cheese—it's a temptation—but no." The P.P.S. poked at the coals, rotating the iron he was holding to ensure an even cherry-red heat. "I got tradition to think of. The honor of the calling, all that stuff. I mean, it's thoughtful of you, bub, but I couldn't do it." He lifted the glowing poker and studied the color critically, licked a finger and touched it lightly, eliciting a sharp hiss.

"O.K., I guess we're ready. If you don't mind just stripping to the waist, we can get started."

"Oh, no hurry," Lafayette protested, retreating to the back wall of the cell, his hands searching frantically over the rough masonry. *Just one loose stone*, he pleaded silently. *One little old secret tunnel . . .*

"Candidly, I'm already behind," the P.P.S. said. "What say we warm up on a little light epidermal work, and then move into the pressure centers before we break for midnight snack? Hey, I forgot to ask: you want a box lunch? A buck-fifty, but I hear they got chicken salad tonight and a jelly roll."

"No thanks, I'm on a food-free diet for the duration. Did I mention I'm under a physician's care? No sudden shocks, particularly electrical ones, and—"

"If it was me, I'd throw the chow in free, you know, American plan. But—"

"What do you know about America?" Lafayette blurted.

"Everybody knows Luigi America, the big noodle and egg man. Too bad the duke's too tight to go along wit' the meal-ticket scheme—"

"I heard that, Groanwelt," a resonant baritone voice rang out. A tall, well-muscled but slightly paunchy man with smooth gray hair and rimless glasses had stepped through a door in the far wall. He wore tight-fitting yellow trousers, red-leather shoes with curled-up toes, a ruffled shirt, a short cloak trimmed with ermine. Jewels sparkled on his fingers. Lafayette looked at him, speechless.

"Oh, hi, your Grace," the torturer said casually. "Well, you know I never say anything behind your back I w'unt say to your face."

"One day you'll go too far," the newcomer snapped. "Leave us now. I'll have a word with the prisoner."

"Hey, no fair, your Grace; I just got my number-four iron up to operating temperature!"

"Need I point out that I would find it somewhat difficult to carry on a lucid conversation with your client amidst an odor of roasting callus?"

"Yeah—I guess you got a point." Groanwelt shoved the iron back into the coals and cast a regretful look at O'Leary. "Sorry, chum. But you see how it is."

The gray-haired man was studying O'Leary with narrowed eyes. As soon as the door had closed behind the P.P.S., he stepped close to the bars.

"So it *is* you," he said and broke off, frowning. "What's the matter with you?" he demanded sharply. "You look as if you'd seen a ghost."

"N-N-Nicodaeus?" O'Leary whispered.

"If that's supposed to be some kind of password, I don't recognize it," Duke Rodolpho barked.

"You're . . . not Nicodaeus? You aren't a sub-inspector of continua? You can't make a fast phone call and have me whisked back to Artesia?"

The duke glared at O'Leary.

"Enough of these obfuscations, Lancelot. First you burst into my audience chamber spouting nonsense; then you escape from my maximum-security dungeon under the very eyes of my alert guard staff. Next, you openly appear in a waterfront dive, fairly begging to be brought in again—whereupon you once more fly the coop—only to invite arrest a third time by accosting a certain great lady in full view of her guard. Very well, I may be a bit obtuse, but I think I get the message: you have something to sell."

"Oh?" Lafayette squealed. "That is, oh. So you finally caught on."

"And?" Rodolpho glared.

"And, uh . . . what?" O'Leary inquired brightly. The duke frowned.

"So you intend to keep me on tenterhooks, do you? Well, it won't wash, fellow! Disappear again, go ahead, amuse yourself! But don't expect me to come crawling to you begging for information regarding the Lady

Andragorre . . . " He finished on a semi-interrogative
note, almost a pleading look in his eyes.

"Lady Andragorre?" Lafayette mumbled. "Me, tell
you . . . ?"

"Very well," the duke sighed. "I can see I've handled
you wrongly from the beginning, Lancelot. All right, I
acknowledge my mistake. But you can hardly blame me,
considering the affair of the poached egg and the incident of the bladder of ink! Still, I'm ready to make
amends. I'll even apologize, though it goes against the
grain. Now will you consent to sit down with me and
discuss this matter in gentlemanly fashion?"

"Well, ah, of course I want to be reasonable," Lafayette ad-libbed desperately. "But a torture chamber is
hardly the proper surroundings for a heart-to-heart."

The duke grunted. He turned and yelled for
Groanwelt.

"See that this nobleman is released, washed, fed,
garbed as befits his station, and brought to my apartment
in half an hour," he commanded. He gave O'Leary a
sharp look. "No disappearing until then, Lancelot," he
said gruffly, and stalked from the room.

"Well, that's the breaks," Groanwelt said philosophi-
cally as he unlocked the door. "Looks like we don't get
together on a professional basis tonight after all. But it
was swell meeting you anyway, kid. Maybe some other
time."

"I wouldn't doubt it," Lafayette said. "Say, Groanwelt,
what do you know about this, er, Lady Andragorre?"

"Nothing special. Just that she's the richest, most
beautiful dame in Melange, is all, which the duke is carrying a torch the size of the Chicago fire for her."

"You know about the Chicago fire?"

"Sure. A beer joint. Burned down last week. Why?"

"Never mind. You were saying?"

"Too bad fer his Grace, he'll never get to first base wit' her Ladyship."

"Why not?"

Groanwelt leered and lowered his voice. "On account of there's another guy, natch. It's the talk of the locker rooms."

"Another guy?" Lafayette felt his heart lurch violently under his sternum.

Groanwelt dug an elbow into Lafayette's ribs. "Duke Rodolpho don't know it, but he's playing second fiddle to a rogue name of Lorenzo the Lanky—or is it Lancelot the Lucky?"

"Lorenzo the Lanky?" Lafayette croaked as Groanwelt struck off his gyves.

"As a matter of fact," the P.P.S. said in the tone of one who imparts a confidence, "right now milady is officially on her way to visit her old-maid aunt and twelve cats. But between you and me, the word is she's headed for a hunting lodge in the Chantspels for a trial honeymoon wit' the lucky geezer."

"T-trial honeymoon?"

"Yep. Now, let's go turn you over to the chamberlain, which he'll doll you up in shape for yer audience wit' his Grace."

Duke Rodolpho was sitting in a big soft-leather wing chair when Lafayette was shown in, clean and fragrant and dressed in a fresh outfit of spangled silk which almost fit.

"Sit down, Lancelot," the duke ordered with an air of forced cordiality. "Drink? Cigar?" He waved a hand, which took in a deep easy chair, a low table with a decanter and glasses, and a humidor.

"Thanks." Lafayette flopped gratefully, then yawned earcrackingly. "Sorry. I'm up past my bedtime. By the way, my name's Lafayette."

"You dined adequately?"

"As adequately as you can while six handmaidens are scrubbing your back, putting Band-Aids on your hurties, and massaging your bruises. Not that I didn't appreciate the attention."

"Excellent. Now let's not beat around the cactus bed, Lancelot. Just what is your, ah, connection with the Lady Andragorre?" The duke nipped at a hangnail, eyeing Lafayette sharply.

"My connection with the Lady Andragorre," Lafayette temporized. "Well, ah, as to that—the fact is, I'm her husband."

The duke's face went rigid. "Her husband?" His voice cracked like a snapped neck.

"Her estranged husband," O'Leary amended hurriedly. "As a matter of fact, we're practically strangers."

"I had never heard that milady had been married," Rodolpho said in a dangerous tone. He reached to pour himself a stiff jolt of brandy, tossed it back in a gulp. "Much less divorced."

"She's a charming girl," Lafayette hurried on. "Full of fun, lighthearted—"

"You may skip over the intimate revelations," Rodolpho snapped. He chewed his lip. "Perhaps this explains

Captain Ritzpaugh's report that you attempted to speak to her in the street and were repulsed with a riding crop."

"He's a"—Lafayette started—"a very perceptive fellow," he finished.

"One wonders what offense you committed to earn such detestation from so high-bred a lady."

"Well, I think it all started with crackers in bed," O'Leary began, then noted the black frown spreading over the ducal features. "Crackers is her cat," he improvised hastily. "She insisted on sleeping with her. And since I'm allergic to cats—well, you can see it wasn't much of a marriage."

"You mean—you never—you didn't—"

"Right." Lafayette used his lace cuff to wipe the dew from his brow and poured out a revivifying draft for himself.

"That's well for you, Lancelot," Rodolpho said in steely tones. "Otherwise I'd be forced to order your instant execution."

"Lafayette. And let's not start that again," O'Leary said, shuddering with the strong spirits. "You had me dusted off and brought up here for a reason. Let's get on with it."

The duke started to drum his fingers on the table, halted them abruptly. "I have conceived an infatuation for the lady," he said brusquely. "Accordingly, I invited her to spend a weekend with me at my winter palace. Instead of accepting the honor with alacrity, she pleaded a previous appointment with an aged relative."

"And?"

"Perhaps I'm overly sensitive, but I imagined just the faintest hint of coolness in her manner." The duke poured himself another peg.

"Maybe you're not her type," Lafayette suggested, following suit.

"Not her type? What do you mean?"

"Well, for one thing, you're old enough to be her father," O'Leary pointed out.

"That's unimportant!"

"Maybe not to her. Also, if you don't mind my saying so, you don't have what I'd call exactly a jolly manner about you. Daph—I mean the Lady Andragorre's a fun-loving kid—"

"A jolly manner? How can I be jolly, burdened as I am with affairs of state, indigestion, insomnia, and an unfavorable balance of payments?" The duke grabbed the bottle and poured, belatedly filled Lafayette's glass as he held it out.

"That's just it, your Grace. All work and no play makes Rodolpho a dull fellow."

"All work and no—by gad, sir, well put!" They clicked glasses and swallowed. The duke licked his lips thoughtfully. "I see it now. What an idiot I've been! Why didn't I just go to her openly, suggest a gay afternoon of mummy-viewing at the local museum, or possibly a wild, abandoned evening of canasta? But no: all I ever offered her was state dinners and tickets to the visitors' box at the weekly meetings of the Fiduciary Council."

"That's the idea, Rodolpho." Lafayette poured this time. "You might even go all out and propose a walk in the park, or a swim at the beach, or even a picnic on the lawn. There's nothing like a few ants in the potato salad to break down the barriers. Skål."

"Of course, my boy! Why didn't it occur to me sooner?" Rodolpho splashed brandy on the table in the process of filling the glasses. "I've been a fool. A stodgy, imperceptive idiot."

"Don't blame yourself, Rudy," Lafayette said, raising his glass. "After all, you had the duchy to run."

"True. But now everything's going to be different, thanks to you, lad. I'll ply her with my favorite viands, treat her to the music I like best, overwhelm her with my preference in wines, literature, and perfume, shower her with the kind of clothes I think she ought to wear—"

"Slow down, Rudy." Lafayette wagged an admonitory finger. "How about giving some thought to the little lady's tastes?"

"Eh? How could she object to chopped chicken livers washed down with Pepsi and Mogen David while a steel band plays variations on the theme from the 'Dead March from *Saul*'?"

"While wearing a Mother Hubbard reeking of *Nuit de Gimbel*'s? Hard to say, Rudy. But women are strange little beasts. You can never tell what they're thinking. Remind me to tell you about the princess I was once engaged to—"

"I'll do it now—tonight!" Rodolpho exclaimed, and banged his fist on the tray. "I'll—but hang it all, I can't! She's out of town, won't be back for a fortnight."

"She was a swell-looking girl, too," Lafayette said. "But the minute my back was turned—"

"But, blast it, what's the good in being duke if I can't have my own way?" Rodolpho looked triumphantly at Lafayette. "I'll have her brought back. A fast troop of cavalry can overtake her entourage in a couple of hours, which will just give me time to chill the Pepsi and—"

"Ah, ah, Rudy," O'Leary objected. "Cajolery, not force, remember?"

"But force is so much quicker."

"Do you want a whipped slave, sullenly doing your bidding—or a willing *petite amie*, charmed into your web by your munificence and consideration?"

"Hmmm. The slave approach is probably the more practical, now you mention it."

"Nonsense, Rudy. You want this lovely little piece of ripe fruit to drop into your hand, right? So instead of having a bunch of sweaty soldiers on lathered horses haul her back to you kicking and scratching, you need an envoy who can convey your wishes with the delicacy appropriate to so tender a mission." Lafayette hiccupped and upended the bottle over his glass.

"Egad, son, you're right, as usual." Rodolpho frowned thoughtfully. "But who among this collection of cretins and dullards who surround me can I entrust with the task?"

"You need a man of proven ability, ingenuity, and courage. Somebody who won't sell the horse and auction off the autograph on your letter as soon as he's out of sight of the castle walls. A gentleman-adventurer, resourceful, intrepid, dedicated—"

"What letter?"

"The one you're going to write, to tell her how you've been worshipping her from afar," O'Leary said. He shook the empty bottle and tossed it over his shoulder.

"A capital notion!" Rodolpho exclaimed, and banged the tray again, upsetting the glasses. "But—but what will I say?" He gnawed the outer corner of his left ring finger. "Candidly, my boy—"

"Just call me Lafayette, Rudy."

"I thought it was Lancelot," the duke said. "But never mind. Candidly, as I say, I've never been much of a one for writing flowery language—"

"Where did you get that idea?"

"Why, you suggested it."

"I didn't mean that, I meant the idea my name was Lancelot."

"Lancelot—what about it?" Rodolpho looked blank, then brightened. "Of course!" he exclaimed, expelling a scrap of fingernail from the tip of his tongue. "Just the man for it! You're ingenious, intrepid, and have a sound head on your shoulders. Do you drink?" he asked in an abruptly challenging tone.

"Not when the bottle's empty."

"Excellent. Never trust a man who can't handle his liquor. By the way, the bottle's empty." Rodolpho rose and made his way across the room, bucking powerful crosswinds, opened a cabinet, extracted a fresh fifth, and navigated back to his chair.

"Now, as I was saying: go to this person, Lancelot, pour out your heart to her, explain that it's woman's highest duty to fetch and carry for her lord and master, and that while you can offer her only the miserable life of a serf, she can draw comfort from the fact that she won't live forever."

"That's certainly a persuasive approach," Lafayette said, wrestling the cork from the bottle. "But I had a funny idea it was *you* that wanted the girl." He frowned, straining to focus his eyes. "Or am I confused?"

"By gad, Lancelot, you're right. I *am* the one who wants her." The duke shot Lafayette a hostile look. "I must say it's cheeky of you to attempt to try to come between us. The minx is mad about me, but being a trifle shy, I'm thinking of sending a trusted emissary to drag her back billing and cooing. I mean coax her back kicking and screaming."

"A capital idea," Lafayette agreed, pouring a stream of brandy between the two glasses. "Who do you have in mind?"

"Well—how about Groanwelt?"

"Positively not. No diplomatesse, if you know what I mean."

"Lancelot! I've a splendid notion. Why don't you go?"

"Not a chance, Rudy," Lafayette said. "You're just trying to distract me from my real mission."

"What mission?"

"To get you to send me after the Lady Andragorre."

"Out of the question! You presume too far!" Rodolpho grabbed the bottle and splashed brandy across the glasses.

"What about a compromise?" Lafayette suggested with a crafty look.

"What do you have in mind?"

"I'll deliver your letter to the lady—in return for which you appoint me your messenger. Or is it vice versa?"

"That seems fair. Now, when you catch up with her, you're to tell her of my deep attachment, explain in detail my many sterling qualities, and in short, overwhelm her with the picture of the good fortune which has befallen her."

"Anything else?"

"Absolutely not!" Rodolpho looked sternly at a point to the right of O'Leary's ear. "I'll handle the courtship from that point on."

"All right, Rudy—I'll undertake this assignment. You did right to come to me."

"I knew I could count on you," the duke said brokenly. He rose and handed over a massive ring. "This signet will secure the cooperation of my staff." He held out his hand. "I'll never forget this, old man. You've given me new hope."

"Think nothing of it, Rudy. Now you'd better run along. I'm pooped. Got a big day tomorrow."

"What's tomorrow?"

"Tuesday."

"Of course. And speaking of tomorrow, I may have a surprise in store for you. Don't tell anybody, but a little birdie told me a certain lady may be calling."

"Rudy! You lucky dog! Congratulations!"

"But don't bruit it about. Bad luck, you know. Well, I really must be going. Jolly evening and all that."

"Don't rush off. We were just getting started." Lafayette held up the half-full bottle and blinked at it. "Hardly touched it," he pointed out.

"I never go near alcohol," the duke said stiffly. "Rots the brain, I'm told. Good night, Lancelot." He tottered uncertainly to the door and out.

For a moment after Rodolpho had left, Lafayette stood swaying in the center of the room, which seemed to have developed a fairly rapid rotation. He made his way across to the bathroom, sluiced cold water over his face, toweled his head vigorously. In the duke's closet he found a capacious fleece-lined riding cloak. He helped himself to a handful of cigars from the ducal humidor, tucked a pair of riding gloves into his pocket, and let himself out into the corridor.

The head groom woke, knuckling his eyes as O'Leary demanded the best horse in the ducal stables. Five minutes later, reeling slightly in the saddle, O'Leary showed the ring at the gate. The guards grumbled but opened up for him. He cantered down through the dark street to the waterfront, used the ring to requisition the ducal barge, ignoring the bargeman's muttered complaints. An hour later, after a chilly crossing, with the first twinges of a hangover stabbing at his temples, he stepped ashore on the west bank of the lake. A narrow, rutted track led up from the jetty into the forest.

"Is that the way the Lady Andragorre's party went?" he inquired of the shivering boatman. "Up that cowpath?"

"Yeah—if you can call it a party, on a night like this." The man blew on his hands. "Snow'll fly before dawn, mark my words, squire."

"Swell," Lafayette said into his turned-up collar. "That's all I need to make this a perfect night." He set spurs to the horse and moved off into the blackness among the trees.

Six

For the next two hours Lafayette followed the winding trail steadily up among the giant trees, past looming boulders and small, rushing streams which spilled down over moss-grown rock formations. The marks of wheels were visible intermittently in the dust, overlain by the hoofprints of the escort. His head throbbed. The cold wind slashed at him through his cloak. As far as evidence to the contrary indicated, he was making no progress whatever.

"It's probably a wild-duck chase," he mumbled to himself. "I've done nothing but blunder from the beginning. First, by not insisting that that chap Pratwick put me through to his supervisor. But I was so rattled I hardly knew where I was—and still don't, for that matter.

Melange. Who's ever heard of it? And Port Miasma: a pesthole if there ever was one . . . "

And he'd goofed again by getting mixed up with Swinehild. Strange, her looking so much like Adoranne. Poor kid, she'd been badly enough off before he arrived. He'd only been here twelve hours or so, and already he'd broken up a home. And then being idiot enough to fall afoul of the cops; and then that supreme triumph of the blunderer's art, leaping at Daphne's—that is, Lady Andragorre's—carriage. He should have known she wouldn't know him; nobody around this insane place was what they seemed. And then all that persiflage with the duke . . .

"Why did I sit around half the night trying to drink Rodolpho under the table, while Lady Andragorre rode off into the distance?" he groaned. "In fact, why am I here at all? If I do find her, I'll probably end up getting that riding crop Rudy mentioned across the chops for my pains. But what else could I do? If she isn't Daphne, she's her twin. I can't very well let her fall into the clutches of this Lorenzo the Lanky character. Or is it Lancelot the Lucky?"

He shifted in the saddle. The cold had numbed his toes and ears and fingers. Was he gaining on the quarry or falling behind? The tracks looked no fresher than they had when he started.

He flapped the reins, urging his mount into a canter. The beast clattered up the trail, snorting steam, while Lafayette crouched low on its neck, ducking under the pine boughs that brushed his back. He rounded a turn, caught a glimpse of something bulky blocking the path ahead. He reined in sharply.

"Oh-oh," he said, feeling a sudden dryness in his mouth. "Dirty work's afoot . . . "

It was Lady Andragorre's pink coach, standing silent in the center of the track, one door swinging in the gusty wind. Lafayette dismounted, wincing at the ache behind his eyes, walked up beside it, glanced into the rose-velvet interior. A lacy handkerchief lay on the pink lamb's-wool rug. He picked it up, sniffed it.

"Moonlight Rose, Daphne's favorite," he groaned.

The traces, he found, had been cut. There was no sign of the four splendid blacks, or of the escort, other than a confused spoor leading on up the trail.

"Funny there are no bodies lying around," Lafayette muttered. "But I suppose the cowardly louses surrendered without a struggle." As he turned back toward his horse, there was a crackling in the underbrush beside the trail. Lafayette grabbed for the ornamental sword with which the duke's servants had provided him.

"Not another move, or I'll punch a hole through your treacherous weasand," a voice rasped behind him. He spun, looked into a scowling, mustachioed face, and the tip of a bared blade inches from his throat. Other men were emerging from concealment, swords in hand. Lafayette was just realizing that they wore the yellow livery of the Lady Andragorre's household, when rough hands seized his arms from behind.

"Came back to gloat, did you? Or was it loot you had in mind?" The captain poked the sword at Lafayette's midriff. "Where is she, miserable wretch?"

"I w-was just going to ask *you* that question!"

"Speak—or I may not be able to restrain my lads from ripping your carcass limb from limb!"

"*You* were escorting her," Lafayette found his voice. "Why ask *me* where she is? What did you do, run off and leave her?"

"Ah-hah, so that's the game, is it? Next I suppose you'll demand ransom for her return!" Lafayette yipped as the point pinked him again. "I'll ransom you, you sneaking snake in the underbrush! Talk! What have you done with the finest little mistress a squadron of cavalry ever had!"

"I'm on official business," Lafayette panted. "Take a look at the signet on my left hand."

Hard hands fumbled with the massive ring.

"It won't come off," a corporal reported. "Want me to cut it off?"

"You think to bribe us with this bauble?" the captain barked.

"Of course not! It belongs to Duke Rodolpho! But the finger's mine. Do you mind leaving it where it is?"

"Boy, what a nerve, to swipe the duke's ring and then have the gall to brag about it," the troop sergeant growled.

"I didn't steal it, he gave it to me!"

"Let's run the bum through, Cap'n," a trooper spoke up. "I got no use for guys which they're such lousy liars. Everybody knows his Grace is tighter than a thumb-screw."

"Can't you get it through your thick heads I'm not a kidnapper? I'm on an important mission, and—"

"What mission?"

"To catch up with the Lady Andragorre, and bring her back—"

"So you admit it!"

"But I had no intention of doing it," O'Leary amplified, struggling to force his throbbing head to function effectively. "I intended to head in the opposite direction, and—"

"And lingered a bit too long about the scene of your dastardly abduction!" the captain snarled. "Very well, fetch rope, men! His dangling corpse will serve as a warning to others!"

"Wait!" Lafayette shouted. "I give up, you're too smart for me. I'll . . . I'll talk!"

"Very well." The captain jabbed him. "Talk!"

"Well, let's see . . . where shall I begin," O'Leary stalled.

"Start with when Lou had to step into the bushes," the sergeant suggested.

"Yes, well, as soon as Lou stepped into the bushes, I, ah . . ."

"You hit him over the head, right?" a trooper contributed.

"Right. And then, er . . ."

"Then when we held up and sent a couple guys back to see what was taking Lou so long, you bopped *them* on the knob too, right?"

"That's it—"

"And then, while the rest of us was beating the brush for the boys which they hadn't come back, you nips in and whisks her Ladyship away from under the nose of Les, which he was holding the nags, right?"

"Who's telling this, you or me?" O'Leary inquired tartly.

"So where is she now?"

"How do I know? I was busy hitting Lou over the head and whisking around under Les's nose, remember?"

"How come you know the boys' names? You been casing this job a long time, hey?"

"Never mind that, Quackwell," the captain barked. "We're wasting time. The lady's whereabouts, you, or I'll stretch your neck i' the instant!"

"She's—she's at the hunting lodge of Lorenzo the Lanky!"

"Lorenzo the Lanky? And where might this lodge be found?"

"It's, er, right up this trail a few miles."

"Liar," the officer barked. "This road leads nowhere save to the château of milady's Aunt Prussic!"

"Are you sure of that?" Lafayette shot back.

"Certainly. Milady herself so informed me."

"Well, your intelligence apparatus needs overhauling," Lafayette snapped. "It's the talk of the locker rooms that Lorenzo the Lanky lives up this way. Or maybe Lochinvar—or is it Lothario? . . . "

"I fail to grasp the import of your slimy innuendos, varlet," the captain said in a deadly tone. "Wouldst have me believe that milady deliberately misled me? That she in fact had arranged some clandestine rendezvous with this Lorenzo, here in the depths of the Chantspels?"

"It wouldn't be very clandestine, with a dozen pony soldiers hanging around," O'Leary pointed out.

"You mean—you think she ditched us on purpose?" The N.C.O. scowled ferociously.

"Use your heads," Lafayette said. "If I'd taken her, do you think I'd leave her and come nosing back around here, just so you could catch me?"

"Enough of your vile implications, knave!" the captain barked. "Stand back, men! I'll deal with this blackguard!"

"Hey, hold it, Cap," the sergeant said, tugging at his forelock. "Begging the captain's pardon, but what the guy says makes sense. It was her Ladyship that said we ought to go back and look for Whitey and Fred, right?"

"Yeah, and also, come to think about it, I never heard before about her having no aunt living out in the boondocks," a trooper added.

"Preposterous," the captain said in a tone lacking in conviction. "Her Ladyship would never thus cozen me, her faithful liegeman, in such fashion!"

"I dunno, Cap. Dames. Who knows from dames, what they might do?"

"Mind your tongue!" The captain yanked at his tunic with a decisive gesture. "I'll soil my ears with no more of the knave's preposterous inventions. On with the hanging!"

"Now, don't be hasty, fellows," O'Leary yelled. "I'm telling you the truth! Lady Andragorre is probably just a few miles ahead; we ought to be galloping to overtake her instead of standing around here arguing!"

"He seeks to mislead us!" the captain snapped. "Doubtless milady lies trussed where he left her, mere yards from this spot!"

"He's out of his skull!" Lafayette protested. "He's afraid to go after her! This is just an excuse to muddy the waters and turn back!"

"Enough! Prepare the criminal for execution!"

"Wait!" Lafayette cried as the noose dropped around his neck. "Can't we settle this like gentlemen?"

A sudden silence fell. The sergeant was looking at the captain, who was frowning blackly at O'Leary.

"You demand the treatment accorded a gentleman? On what grounds?"

"I'm Sir Lafayette O'Leary, a—a charter member of the National Geographic Society!"

"Looks like he's got something, Cap," the sergeant said. "With credentials like them, you can't hardly accord the guy short shrift."

"He's right," Lafayette said hastily. "I'm sure that on sober reflection you can see it wouldn't look at all well if you lynched me."

" 'Tis a parlous waste of time," the captain growled. "But—very well. Remove the rope."

"Well, I'm glad we're all going to be friends," Lafayette said. "Now, I—"

"Out pistols!"

"Wha—what are you going to do with those?" Lafayette inquired as the troopers unlimbered foot-long horse pistols, busied themselves with flint and priming.

"Take up your stance against yon tree, sir knight," the captain barked. "And be quick about it. We haven't got all night!"

"Y-you mean this tree?" Lafayette half-stumbled over gnarly roots. "Why? What . . . ?"

"Ready, men! Aim!"

"Stop!" O'Leary called in a cracking voice. "You can't shoot me!"

"You demanded a gentleman's death, did you not? Aim—"

"But—you're not going to fire from *that* range?" Lafayette protested. "I thought you fellows were marksmen!"

"We took first place in the police tournament last June," the sergeant stated.

"Why don't I just move back a little farther?" Lafayette suggested. "Give you a chance to show your skill." He backed ten feet, bumped another tree.

"Ready!" the captain called. "Aim—"

"Still too close," Lafayette called, wagging a finger. "Let's make it a real challenge." He hastily scrambled back an additional four yards.

"That's far enough!" the captain bellowed. "Stand and receive your fate, sirrah!" He brandished his saber. "Ready! Aim!" As the officer's lips formed the final word, there was a sudden, shrill yowl from the dense brush behind him. All eyes snapped in the direction from which the nerve-shredding sound had come.

"Night cat!" a man blurted. Without waiting for a glimpse of the creature, Lafayette bounded sideways, dived behind the tree, scrambled to his feet, and pelted full speed into the forest, while shouts rang and guns boomed and lead balls screamed through the underbrush around him.

The moon was out, shining whitely on the split-log front of a small cabin situated in the center of a hollow ringed in by giant trees. Lafayette lay on his stomach under a bramble bush, aching all over from a combination of hangover, fatigue, and contusions. It had been thirty minutes since the last halloo had sounded from the troops beating the brush for him, twenty since he had topped the rim of the bowl and seen the dim-lit windows of the hut below. In that time nothing had stirred there, no sound had broken the stillness. And nothing, Lafayette added, had interfered with the development of a classic case of chilblains. The temperature had dropped steadily as the night wore on; now ice crystals glittered on the leaves. Lafayette blew on his hands and stared at the lighted window of the tiny dwelling below.

"She has to be down there," he assured himself. "Where else could she be, in this wilderness?" Of course, he continued the line of thought, whoever kidnapped her is probably there too, waiting with loaded pistols to see if anyone's following . . .

"On the other hand, if I stay here I'll freeze," O'Leary countered decisively. He tottered to his feet, beat his stiffening arms across his chest, eliciting a hacking cough, then began to make his way cautiously down the shadowy slope. At a distance he circled the house, pausing at intervals, alert for sounds of approaching horsemen or awakening householders; but the silence remained unbroken. The flowered curtains at the small windows blocked his view of the interior.

Lafayette slipped up close to the narrow back door, flanked by a pile of split wood and a rain barrel; he put an ear against the rough panels.

There was a faint creaking, an even fainter, intermittent popping sound. A low voice was moaning words too faint to distinguish. Lafayette felt a distinct chill creep up his backbone. Early memories of Hansel and Gretel and the witch's cottage rose to vivid clarity.

"Nonsense," he told himself sternly. "There's no such thing as a witch. There's nobody in there but this Lorenzo operator, and poor Lady Andragorre, probably tied hand and foot, scared to death, hoping against hope that someone will come along and rescue her, poor kid. So why am I standing around waiting? Why don't I kick the door down and drag this Lorenzo out by the scruff of the neck, and . . . "

The popping sound rose to a frantic crescendo and ceased abruptly. There was a soft *whoosh!*, a faint clank of metal. The creaking resumed, accompanied now by a stealthy crunching, as of a meat grinder crushing small bones.

"Maybe he's torturing her, the monster!" Lafayette took three steps back, braced himself, and hurled himself at the door. It flew wide at the impact, and he skidded to the center of a cozy room where a fire glowed on a grate, casting a rosy light on an elderly woman seated in a rocker on a hooked rug, a cat in her lap and a blue china bowl at her elbow.

"Why, Lorenzo, welcome back," she said in tones of mild surprise. She held out the bowl. "Have some popcorn."

Sitting by the fire with a bowl of crisp, lightly buttered and salted kernels on one knee and a cup of thick cocoa on the other, Lafayette attempted to bring his reeling thoughts to order. His hostess was stitching away at a quilt she had exhumed from a chest under the window, chattering in a scratchy monotone. He couldn't seem to follow just what it was she was saying—something about a little cuckoo fluttering from flower to flower and settling down in a big soft blossom to snooze . . .

Lafayette came awake with a start as his chin bumped his chest.

"Why, you're sleepy, poor lad. And no wonder, the hours you've been keeping. Oh, I almost forgot: your friends were here." She gave him a sharp sideways smile.

"Friends?" Lafayette yawned. How long had it been since he had slept? A week? Or only three days . . . or . . . was it possible it was only last night, curled up in the big bed with the silken sheets . . .

" . . . said not to bother telling you, they wanted to surprise you. But I thought you'd rather know." Her tone had a sharp edge, penetrating his drowsiness.

Lafayette forced his mind to focus on what the old lady was saying. Her voice seemed vaguely familiar. Had he met her before? Or . . .

"Rather know, ah, what?" He forced his thoughts back to the conversation.

"About them coming back."

"Er, who?"

"The nice gentlemen with the lovely horses."

Suddenly Lafayette was wide awake. "When were they here?"

"Why, you just missed them, Lorenzo—by about thirty minutes." Dim old eyes bored into him through thick glasses. Or were they dim and old? On second look, they were remarkably sharp. Where, Lafayette wondered, had he seen that gimlet gaze before? . . .

"Ma'am—you've been very kind, but I really must rush. And I think you ought to know: I'm not Lorenzo."

"Not Lorenzo? Whatever do you mean?" She peered over her lenses at him.

"I came here looking for a fellow named Lorenzo, or possibly Lothario or Lancelot. When you welcomed me so nicely, and offered me food and warmth, I, well—I was starving and freezing and I simply took advantage of your kindness. But now I'll be going—"

"Why, I wouldn't hear of it! A body could catch his death on a night like this—"

"I'm not sure you understand," Lafayette protested, sidling toward the door. "I'm a total stranger. I just wandered in here, and—"

"But surely you're the same charming young man who rented the spare bedroom?" The old lady peered nearsightedly at him.

Lafayette shook his head. "Afraid not. I came here looking for the Lady Andragorre—"

"Why, you're a friend of my niece! How delightful! Why didn't you tell me! Now you really must give up this silly idea of going back out in that icy wind. Oh, by the way, ah, where *is* dear Andi? I had a foolish notion you might be bringing her along?"

"You're Daph—I mean Lady Andragorre's aunt?"

"Why, yes, didn't you know? But you haven't said where she is . . . "

Lafayette was looking around the room. It was clean and comfortable enough, but decidedly on the primitive side. "I got the impression the Lady Andragorre is very well off," he said. "Is this the best she can do for you?"

"Why, foolish boy, I adore living here among the birds and flowers. So quaint and picturesque."

"Who chops the wood?"

"Why, ah, I have a man who comes in on Tuesdays. But you were saying about Lady Andragorre . . . ?"

"I wasn't saying. But I don't know where she is; I came alone. Well, thanks for the goodies—"

"You're not leaving," the old lady said sharply. She smiled. "I won't think of it."

Lafayette pulled on his cloak, went to the door. "I'm afraid I have to decline your hospitality—" He broke off at a sudden sound, turned in time to see the old lady behind him, her hand swinging down edge-on in a murderous chop at his temple. He ducked, took the blow on a forearm, yelled at the pain, countered a second vicious swing, aimed a stiff-fingered punch at his hostess's ribs, took a jab to the solar plexus, and fell backward over the rocker.

"Double-crosser!" the old lady yelled. "Selling out to that long-nosed Rodolpho, after all I've promised to do for you! Of all the cast-iron stitch-welded gall, to come waltzing in here pretending you never saw me before!" Lafayette rolled aside as the old lady bounded across the chair, barely fending her off with a kick to the short ribs as he scrambled to his feet.

"Where is she, curse you? Oh, I should have left you tending swine back in that bog I picked you out of—"

Abruptly the old girl halted in mid-swing, cupped an ear. Faintly, O'Leary heard the thud of approaching hooves.

"Blast!" The old woman bounded to the door, snatched a cloak from the peg, whirled it about herself.

"I'll get you for this, Lorenzo!" she keened in a voice that had dropped from a wheezy soprano to a ragged tenor. "Just you wait, my boy! I'll extract a vengeance from you that will make you curse the day you ever saw the Glass Tree!" She yanked the door open and was gone into the night.

Belatedly, O'Leary sprang after her. Ten feet from the door, she stood fiddling with her buttons. As O'Leary leaped, she emitted a loud buzzing hum, bounded into the air, and shot away toward the forest, rapidly gaining altitude, her cloak streaming behind her.

"Hey," Lafayette called weakly. Suddenly he was aware of the rising thunder of hooves. He dashed back inside, across the room, out the back door, and keeping the house between himself and the arriving cavalry, he sprinted for the shelter of the woods.

Dawn came, gray and blustery, hardly lessening the darkness. Lafayette sat in deep gloom under a tree big enough to cut a tunnel through, shivering. His head ached; his stomach had a slow fire in it; his eyeballs felt as if they had been taken out, rolled in corn meal, and Southern-fried. The taste in his mouth resembled pickled onions—spoiled ones. In the branches overhead, a bird squawked mournfully.

"This is it," Lafayette muttered, "the low point of my career. I'm sick, freezing, starving, hung-over, and dyspeptic. I've lost my horse, Lady Andragorre's trail—everything. I don't know where I'm going, or what to do when I get there. Also, I'm hallucinating. Flying old ladies, ha! I probably imagined the whole business about the cottage. A dying delirium, maybe I was actually shot by those bumbling incompetents in the yellow coats. Maybe I'm dead!"

He felt himself over, failed to find any bullet holes.

"But this is ridiculous. If I were dead, I wouldn't have a headache." He hitched up his sword belt, tottered a few feet to a small stream, knelt, and sluiced ice water over his face, scrubbed at it with the edge of his cloak, drank a few swallows.

"O.K.," he told himself sternly. "No use standing around talking to myself. This is a time for action."

"Swell," he replied. "What action?"

"I could start walking," he suggested. "It's only about twenty miles back to Port Miasma."

"Rodolpho isn't likely to be overjoyed to see me coming back empty-handed," he countered. "But I'll probably have a chance to explain my reasons—to Groanwelt. Anyway, I don't know which direction it is." Lafayette peered upward through the canopy of high foliage. Not even a faint glow against the visible patches of gray sky indicated the position of the sun.

"Besides which, I can't run off and leave the Lady Andragorre to her fate.

"All right, I'm convinced: I press on. Which way is on?"

He turned around three times, with his eyes shut, stopped, and pointed.

"That way."

"You know," O'Leary confided in himself as he started off in the indicated direction, "this talking to myself isn't such a bad idea. It opens up whole new vistas.

"And it certainly cuts down on the shilly-shally factor.

"Of course, it *is* a sign of insanity.

"Poof—what's a little touch of schizophrenia, among all my other ailments?"

He pushed on, limping alternately on the left and right ankles, both of which he had twisted during his several sprints, leaps, and falls of the night before. Gradually the trees thinned; the tangled vines and undergrowth thickened. Patches of bare rock showed through the greenery. As he emerged on a bare, wind-swept slope dotted with stunted, wind-twisted cedars, it began to rain, a needle-sharp spray that stung his eyes, numbed his face. Fifty feet farther, the slope ended in a sheer drop. O'Leary crept close to the edge, looked down a vertical face that disappeared into mistiness.

"Splendid," he commented to the airy abyss. "Perfect. Fits right in with everything else that's happened. No wonder the old lady flew off on a broomless broom. Not even a fly could climb down that.

"So—I simply continue along the edge until I come to a road, path, or stairway leading down," he advised.

"You left out a rope ladder or a funicular railway."

"A regrettable omission. Eenie, Meenie, Miney, Mo . . . that way." He set off, following the cliff line. Another hour passed, the monotony of fatigue, pain, and frostbite broken only by two or three slips that almost pitched him over the edge.

"You're losing your stuff, O'Leary," he panted, struggling back to his feet after the last spill. "Just a few years ago, a little hike like this would have been child's play.

"Well, I can't expect to live in luxury, with every whim attended, and stay as hard as I was when I lived by my wits.

"There must be a lesson in that for me, but I hate to admit it."

The wind had increased; a driving downpour sluiced across the rock. O'Leary staggered on. His fingers and toes and lips were numb. He covered another half-mile before he paused for another conference.

"Something's bound to turn up soon," he told himself in tones of false confidence, rubbing his stiff fingers against his aching ears. "A footprint, or a dropped hanky, say . . ."

BEE-beep, BEE-beep, BEE-beep . . . The tiny sound seemed to be right beside him. Lafayette looked all around, saw nothing.

"Look here," he said aloud. "Talking to myself is bad enough, but in Morse code?"

He resumed rubbing his ears.

BEE-beep, BEE-beep, BEE-beep, the tone sounded sharply. O'Leary looked at his hands. Duke Rodolpho's ring winked on his middle finger. The ruby light glowed, dimmed, glowed, dimmed . . .

"Hey," O'Leary said weakly. He put the ring cautiously to his ear. It beeped steadily on in time with the flashing light.

"It didn't do that before," he told himself suspiciously.

"Well, it's doing it now," he came back smartly. "And it must have some significance."

"Maybe—maybe it's a radio beam—a beacon, like the airlines use."

"Maybe. Let's test it." He slogged downslope, fifty feet—listened again.

Bee-BEEP, bee-BEEP, bee-BEEP . . .

"A-ha! That means I'm moving off course." He moved on, angling back upslope. Now the ring emitted a steady hum.

"On course," O'Leary breathed. "But on course for what?"

"What does it matter? Anyplace would be better than here."

"True." Head down, his eyes squinted against the freezing rain, O'Leary plowed on, the ring held to his ear. The hum grew steadily louder. A clump of sodden stalks barred his way. He pushed through—and was teetering over empty space. For a wild instant he clutched at the sky for nonexistent support. Then the wind was blasting past him like a hurricane. The cliff face flashing upward like the shaft of an express elevator; O'Leary noticed the large 21 painted in white as it shot past; the 20, the 19, a mere blur—

From somewhere, a giant baseball bat swung, knocked him over the fence for a home run amid a vast display of Roman candles, while thousands cheered.

Seven

Someone had used his back as a diving board; or possibly they had mistaken it for a Persian rug and given it a good flailing with steel rods. His stomach had been employed by a gang of road menders for brewing up a batch of hot tar; he could distinctly feel the bubbles swelling and popping. His head had been dribbled up and down a basketball court for several close-fought quarters; and his eyes—apparently they'd been extracted, used in a Ping-Pong tournament, and rudely jammed back into their sockets.

"Hey—I think he's coming around," a frog-deep voice said. "That last groan was a lot healthier-sounding."

"He's all yours, Roy. Let me know if he relapses." Footsteps clunked; a door opened and closed. Lafayette pried an eye open, looked up at a perforated acoustical ceiling with flush-mounted fluorescents. Ignoring the fish spear someone had carelessly left embedded in his neck, he turned his head, saw a stubby little man with a cheerful, big-nosed face peering at him anxiously.

"How are ya, pal?" the watcher inquired.

"Yokabump," O'Leary chirped feebly, and lay back to watch the lights whirl.

"Cripes, a foreigner," the froggy voice said. "Sorry, Slim—me no spikka Hungarisha, you savvy?"

"But I guess you're not really Yokabump," O'Leary managed a thin whisper. "You just look like him, like everybody else in this nightmare looks like somebody they aren't."

"Hey, you can talk after all! Boy, you had me worried. I never lost a customer yet, but I came close today. You were in some rush, Slim—couldn't even wait for the elevator." The little man mopped at his face with a green-monogrammed red bandanna.

Lafayette's eyes roved around the room. It was ivory-walled, tile-floored. The soft susurrus of air-conditioning whispered from a grille above the door.

"What happened?" He tried to sit up, flopped back.

"Don't worry, Slim," the little man said. "The doc says you're O.K., just shook up."

"I . . . I seem to have a sort of confused memory," O'Leary said, "of stepping down an elevator shaft—out in the wilderness?"

"Yeah. Fell two floors. Lucky at that, no busted bones."

"Isn't that a rather peculiar location for an elevator shaft?"

The little man looked surprised. "How else you figure we're gonna get up and down? Hey, you ain't got in mind filing no claim against the company, I hope? I mean, I picked up your beep, and was coming as fast as I could, right? You should of just held your horses."

"No doubt you're right. By the way—who are you?"

The little man thrust out a square, callused hand. "Sprawnroyal is the handle, Slim; Customer Service. Glad to make your acquaintance. You're a day early, you know. The order's not quite ready."

"Oh . . . the order," Lafayette temporized. "Frankly, I'm a little confused. By the fall, you know. Ah . . . what order was that?"

"Yeah, I guess you got a little concussion. Affects the memory." Sprawnroyal shook his heavy head sympathetically. "Your boss, Prince Krupkin, gave us a down payment on a two-passenger rug, a blackout cloak, and a dozen illusions, the number-seventy-eight assortment."

"Oh, a two-passenger assortment and a dozen rugs," O'Leary mumbled. "Splendid. Ready tomorrow, you say?"

"You better lay here awhile and get it together, kid," Sprawnroyal advised. "Your brains is still a little scrambled."

"No—no, I'm fine." O'Leary sat up shakily. He had been bathed, he saw, and shaved and bandaged here and there and dressed in baggy pajamas—yellow with purple dots.

"By the way," he said. "How did you . . . ah . . . know I was here about the, ah, prince's order?"

Sprawnroyal blinked at him. "Who else would be wearing one of the tight-beam signalers we made up for him?"

"Of course, how could I forget a thing like that?" O'Leary swung his legs over the side of the bed and got to his feet. His knees wobbled but held.

"I just need a little fog to clear the exercise out of my head," he said. "I mean some head, to for the clear . . . some clead. I mean the head—"

Sprawnroyal's hand grabbed for Lafayette's elbow. "Yeah. Take it easy, Slim. How's about some hot chow, hey? Good for what ails ya."

"Chow," Lafayette creaked. "Yes, by all means."

"Come on—if you're sure you can walk O.K." The little man handed him a bathrobe, led the way along a twisting corridor apparently cut from living rock and carpeted in pale nylon, into a low-ceilinged wood-paneled room with a long bar at one side backed by huge copper-bound kegs. At tables spread with checkered cloths other small, sturdily built men sat talking volubly over large coffee mugs. Several of them waved or nodded to O'Leary's guide as he steered him across to a table beside a curtained window beyond which rain swirled and beat against the glass. A jaw-aching aroma of fresh-ground coffee and fresh-baked bread filled the air. A plump little waitress with a turned-up nose, no taller than Lafayette's middle button, bustled over and slid cups in front of them, gave O'Leary a wink, and poised a pencil over her pad.

"What'll it be, boys? Hotcakes? Steak and eggs? Strawberries and cream? Toast and jam and honey-butter?"

"Right," O'Leary said eagerly. "And a big glass of milk."

"Sounds good, Gert," Sprawnroyal said. "Me, too."

"Coming up."

Sprawnroyal rubbed his hands together, grinning. "Well, this is more like it, eh, Slim? Nothing like a snack to brighten the outlook."

"It's a distinct improvement over that." O'Leary indicated the dreary downpour outside. "There's just one little point that bothers me: where am I?"

"I don't get you, Slim. You're right here, at the Ajax Specialty Works, Melange Branch, having a midmorning snack in the Yggdrasil Room."

"Oh, in a factory. Well, that's a relief. Don't laugh, but I had the silly idea I was inside a cliff."

"Yeah, sure. But it wasn't always a cliff, understand. When the branch was first set up, it was under level ground. But there was the usual geological activity, and the plain subsided on us. But we got used to the split-level layout. And the view ain't bad."

"Geological activity?" Lafayette frowned. "You mean an earthquake?"

"Naw, just a spell of mountain-building. Happens every now and then, you know. Next time, this place may wind up under half a mile of seawater, you can't tell."

"O.K., move the elbows," Gert called, arriving with a laden tray. Lafayette managed to restrain himself until she had laid out the food; then he pitched in with a will.

"Say, Slim," Sprawnroyal said with his mouth full. "How long you been on the prince's payroll?"

"Ah . . . not long," Lafayette said, chewing. "In fact, you might say no time at all."

"Say, just between the two of us—how's the old boy's credit rating holding up?"

"His credit?" Lafayette jammed his mouth full of hot-cake and made incoherent sounds.

"The Customer Service man held up a hand. "Not that we're worried, you understand," he said worriedly, "but he still owes us a bundle on the Glass Tree job."

Lafayette paused with his fork halfway to his mouth.

"Glass Tree job?" he mused. "Where have I heard of that before?"

"Say, Slim, you're *really* out of it."

"I've got an idea, Mr. Sprawnroyal," O'Leary said. "Why don't you just pretend that I haven't the faintest idea what's been happening, and just sort of fill me in? It will speed my recovery."

"Call me Roy. Well, where to start? We first hear from his Highness a few years back, when he drops around looking for a job. That was while he was still a commoner. He's got a few ideas, you know, so we put him to work in R & D. After a couple months the boss has to let him go. He's got the biggest light bill of anybody on the staff, but no production. The next we know, he's back flashing a fat purse and with a set of specs, wants to know can we knock out a few special-order items. We fix him up, he pays off in cut gemstones, and everybody's happy. Then he promotes himself to prince, and comes up with this construction job, wants to know if we'll take the contract. The price is right, so we go along. Do him a nifty job, too: the whole thing is formed-in-place silicone, microfiber-reinforced. A plush installation, believe you me."

"Yes—but where does this Glass Tree you mentioned come in?"

"That's what the construction-crew boys started calling it; the name caught on. Looks kind of like a tree at that, with all them turrets and minarets and stuff branching off the main keep. Shines real snazzy in the sun. Only it ain't paid for," Sprawnroyal finished on a glum note.

"Does this prince have an old lady on his payroll—one who flies on a broom—I mean without a broom?"

O'Leary's host eyed him solicitously. "Maybe you better go back and lay down, Slim—"

"Listen, Roy: last night an old lady mentioned the Glass Tree—just after she tried to kill me."

"Cripes! With a gun?"

"No. She—"

"Oh, used a knife, eh?"

"No, it was a vicious bare-handed attack—"

"While you were asleep, I bet!"

"Certainly not! But—"

"You *did* say an old lady?"

"Please, Roy—I'm trying to tell you—"

"Maybe you ought to go in for lifting, Slim, you know, weights. Get you in shape in no time, you wouldn't have to worry about no old ladies roughing you up. Now, I can make you a attractive price on our Atlas set number two-two-three, complete with a ear-link for pep talks and inspirational messages—"

"I don't need a pep talk! What I'm trying to say is, this old lady has something to do with the Lady Andragorre's disappearance!"

"Lady who?"

"Andragorre. She's my wife. I mean, she isn't *really* my wife, but—"

"Oh, I get it." Sprawnroyal winked. "You can rely on my discretion, Slim."

"That's not what I meant! She's a very beautiful girl, and she disappeared on her way to a kidnapping. I mean she was kidnapped on her way to a disappearance. Anyway, she's gone! And the old bat at the hut mentioned the Glass Tree!"

"So? Well, I guess everybody in these parts would know about it." Sprawnroyal frowned. "The only thing is, there ain't nobody *in* these parts."

"The old woman must work for this Prince Krupkin! She mistook me for someone else—she's nearsighted, I guess—and let slip that she was expecting her Ladyship to be delivered to her at her hut!"

"I don't get it. If this old dame is on the prince's payroll same as you, how come she jumps you?"

"She thought I'd double-crossed her, led Duke Rodolpho's men to her."

"Chee—you know Duke Rodolpho? His Grace fired in a inquiry some time back, wanted quotes on a Personal Aura Generator; but we couldn't get together on price."

"The point is—this Krupkin fellow must be behind the kidnapping. Only something went wrong, and Lady Andragorre was snatched out from under his nose before the old lady could take delivery."

"This Lady A is from Rodolpho's duchy, huh?" Sprawnroyal shook his head. "It don't make sense, Slim. That's a long way out of his territory for a strong-arm play."

"He lured her out of town first—she thought she was going to a rendezvous with some slicker named Lorenzo who'd insinuated himself into her good graces, not knowing the miserable sneak intended to hand her over to Krupkin." Lafayette rubbed the unbruised side of his face. "But who could have intercepted her?"

"Who indeed? It could of been anybody. The woods is full of cutpurses and footpads. Better forget it, Slim, and let's get back to business. Now, about that overdue payment—"

"Forget the most beautiful, wonderful, faithful, marvelous creature who ever wore a bikini? You don't seem to understand, Roy! At this very moment she may be in the most terrible danger—lonely, scared, maybe being tortured, or . . . or . . . "

"You said yourself she was on her way to a get-together with some guy name of Lorenzo, Slim," Sprawnroyal said in a reasonable tone, smearing jam on his third slice of golden-brown toast. "Looks like Krupkin's cut out of the pattern anyway, so why sweat it?"

"I told you, she was tricked!"

"Oh. You mean the guy told her he wanted her to look at some property, or take a test spin in a new model coach?"

"No, it was to be more of a trial honeymoon, as I understand it," O'Leary confessed. "But that's neither here nor there. Someone grabbed her, and I want to get her back!"

"How about this Lorenzo guy? You figure him for the snatch?"

"Well—I suppose he could have done it. Maybe he changed his mind at the last moment and couldn't go through with Krupkin's plan. In fact, the more I think of it, the likelier it seems. He probably abducted her from the coach as planned, and then instead of taking her to the hut, he took her . . . somewhere else."

"Nice piece of deductive reasoning, Slim. So I guess the best man won—and they live happily ever after. Well, maybe not really the best man, who knows, maybe he's scared of old ladies too; what I mean is—"

"I know what you mean!" Lafayette snapped. "Listen, Roy: I have to find her!"

"I've got to admire your loyalty to your boss, Slim—but I'm afraid he'll have to line up something else—"

"To heck with my boss! Anyway, I may as well tell you: he's not my boss."

"You mean—you quit?"

"I never worked for him. You leaped to a faulty conclusion. I'm sorry."

"Then—where'd you get his signaler?"

"If you mean this ring—" Lafayette held up the sparkling red stone. "Duke Rodolpho gave it to me."

"Huh?" Sprawnroyal grabbed O'Leary's finger and gave the gem a careful scrutiny.

"It's Krupkin's, all right." The little man lowered his voice. "On the level, Slim, what'd you do, slit his throat to get it?"

"Certainly not! I've never even seen the fellow!"

Sprawnroyal shook his head, his eyes hard on O'Leary. "It don't figure, Slim. How would the duke get the prince's ring? His Highness set a lot of store by that gimcrack—I know!"

"All *I* know is, the duke had it—and he gave it to me." Lafayette tugged at the ring, slipped it over his knuckle. "Here," he said, "you can have it back. I don't want it. I'm only interested in finding Lady Andragorre."

His host weighed the ring on his palm, looking grim.

"Slim, you're in trouble," he said; he pushed back his chair. "Come on; you and me better go see Flimbert, our security chief, trial judge, one-man jury, and enforcer. He won't like this development at all, at all. And on the way you better think up a better story than the one you told me. Otherwise, I'm afraid we'll have to invoke the full rigor of Ajax Commercial Regulations."

"What does that mean?" O'Leary snapped. "You'll cut off my credit?"

"Not quite, Slim. More like your head."

Flimbert was a round-faced, hairless gnome with half-inch-thick lenses which looked as though they were permanently set in his head. He drummed his pudgy fingers on his desktop as Sprawnroyal gave his account of O'Leary's appearance. "I checked: the ring's one of the ones we made up for Prince Krupkin, all right," he finished.

"It looks like a clear case of murder and grand larceny, compounded by unauthorized entry, false pretenses, and perjury," Flimbert piped in a voice like a peanut whistle. "Any last words, you?" He looked at O'Leary like an angry goldfish peering through its bowl.

"Last words? I haven't even had my first ones yet! All I know is I was crawling along peacefully, minding my own business, when I fell down that lift shaft of yours! And I didn't say I was from Krupkin—that was Roy's idea. And where do you get that murder charge? Talk about conclusions of the witness—"

"Prince Krupkin would never have let his personal signaler out of his sight. Ergo, you must have killed him to get it. Open and shut. By the power vested in me—"

"I told you, I got the ring from Rodolpho!"

"Equally unlikely. Krupkin wouldn't have given it to Rodolpho either—"

"But he did! Why don't you check my story, instead of railroading me!"

"Hey, Bert," Roy said, rubbing his massive chin. "I been wondering: why would Slim here come up with a story as screwy as this unless it was true? And if he was trying to pull something, how come he told me himself he wasn't from Krupkin? He could've fooled me: the guy has a fantastic grasp of the prince's affairs."

"Hey," Lafayette protested.

"It's an old trick," the security chief said. "Reverse cunning, we call it in the security game; indistinguishable from utter stupidity."

"Welcome to the club," Lafayette said. "Look, Krupkin gave the ring to Rodolpho; Rodolpho gave it to me. I came here by accident, and all I want now is to leave—"

"Impossible. You've been caught red-handed, fellow. Unauthorized possession is the worst crime on the books. You're going to spend the next three hundred years chained to a treadmill in level twelve—"

"I'm afraid I'll have to disappoint you," Lafayette snapped. "I won't live three hundred years."

"Oh. Sorry, I didn't realize you were sick. We'll just make it a life sentence then; don't feel badly if you can't go the whole route."

"That's thoughtful of you. Say, just as a sort of intellectual exercise, why don't you spend thirty seconds or so considering the possibility that Rodolpho *did* have Krupkin's ring?"

"His Grace with his Highness's ring?" Flimbert put his fingertips together and looked grave. "Well, first, it would be a gross breach of the conditions of sale. Secondly, it would be quite unlike Krupkin, who never does anything without a good reason."

"So—he had a reason! Aren't you curious as to what the reason was?"

"I wonder." Sprawnroyal picked up the ring, held it to his nose, and studied it. "He couldn't've tinkered with it . . . ?"

"Nonsense; only a man trained in our shops—" Flimbert broke off. "Now that you mention it, Krupkin *was* trained in our shops . . . "

"Yeah—and he's a top man, microengineeringwise," Sprawnroyal put in. "Cripes, but—could the guy have had a angle he was working?"

The security chief whipped out a jeweler's loupe, examined the ring.

"Just as I thought," he said crisply. "Tool marks." He laid the ring aside, poked a button on his desk. "Security to lab," he barked.

"Pinchcraft here," a testy voice responded. "What do you want, I'm in the midst of a delicate operation."

"Oh—the gnat-borne miniaturized-TV-camera project?"

"No, I was fishing the olive out of my martini with a paper straw. I almost had it when you made me jiggle it!"

"Forget the olive; I'm on my way down with a little item I want you to take a look at before I carry out the death sentence on a spy!"

The laboratory was a rough-hewn cavern crowded with apparatus as complex and incomprehensible to O'Leary as a Chinese joke book. They found the research boss perched on a high stool before a formica-topped bench poking at a glittering construction of coils and loops of glass tubing through which pink and green and yellow fluids bubbled, violet vapors curled.

Security Chief Flimbert handed over the ring. The research chief spun on his stool, snapped on a powerful light, flipped out a magnifying lens, bent over the ring.

"A-ha," he said. "Seal's broken." He pursed his lips, gave O'Leary a sharp look. With a needle-pointed instrument, he prodded the bezel of the ruby, flipped open a tiny cover, revealing an interior hollow packed with intricate components.

"Well, well," he said. "Haven't we been a busy boy?" He put the ring down and quickly placed an empty coffee cup over it.

"Find somethin'?" Roy asked anxiously.

"Nothing much—just that the entire device has been rewired," Pinchcraft snapped. "It's been rigged to act as a spy-eye." He glared at O'Leary. "What did you hope to learn? Our trade secrets? They're freely available to the public: hard work and common sense."

"Don't look at me," O'Leary said. "I haven't tampered with it."

"Uh—the ring was made up for Prince Krupkin," Roy pointed out.

"Krupkin, eh? Never did trust that jumped-up jack-in-office. Sneaky eyes."

"Yeah—but Slim here says he didn't get the bauble from Krupkin. He claims it was given to him by Duke Rodolpho."

"Nonsense. I remember this order now: I designed the circuits myself, in accordance with Krupkin's specs. Yes, and now I see why he insisted there be no modifications! The thing was shrewdly designed for easy conversion. All he had to do was switch the A wire to ground, the B wire to contact A, the C wire to contact D, reverse wires D and E, shunt wire F off to resistance X, and throw in the odd little black box. Nothing to it."

"I still got it from Rodolpho," Lafayette said hotly. "He gave it to me as a safe-conduct for a mission I undertook for him."

"You'll have to think up a better story," Flimbert said. "That ring wouldn't get you through a schoolboy patrol line."

"Say," Roy put in, "maybe he meant to give you the ducal signet—I saw him wearing it when we were dickering. It's got a ruby, too, with a big RR carved on it. Maybe he grabbed the wrong one. How was the light?"

"Wet, as I recall," Lafayette said. "Look, gentlemen, we're wasting time. Now that the misunderstanding is cleared up, if I could have my clothes back, I'll be on my way—"

"Not so fast, you!" Pinchcraft said. "We have methods of dealing with those who renege on the solemn fine print in a contract!"

"Then see Krupkin, he's the one who signed it."

"He has a point," Pinchcraft said. "Krupkin, as contracting party, is ultimately responsible. This fellow is merely an accessory."

"What's the penalty for that?"

"Much less severe," Flimbert said grudgingly. "Only one hundred years on the treadmill."

"Hey, that's a break, hey, Slim?" Roy congratulated him.

"I'm overwhelmed," Lafayette said. "Look, fellows, couldn't we work something out? A suspended sentence, maybe?"

"Hey, maybe we could give him a feat to perform," Roy proposed. "We got a couple lines of hand-painted neckties that ain't been moving. Maybe he could go on the road with 'em—"

"This is all wrong!" O'Leary protested. "Krupkin is the one behind this—I'm just an innocent bystander. And I think he's also behind the Lady Andragorre's kidnapping."

"That's no concern of ours."

"Maybe not—but I thought you had dire penalties for anybody who tinkered with your products."

"Hmmm." Flimbert fingered his nose. "We do, at that."

"Listen," O'Leary said urgently. "If Krupkin could convert a personal signaler to a spy-eye, why couldn't you rewire the ring to reverse the action?"

"Eh?"

"Rig it so that instead of relaying sounds from the vicinity of the ring back to Krupkin, it would transmit sounds from Krupkin to you."

Pinchcraft frowned. "Possibly. Possibly." He signaled for silence, lifted the cup. Holding the ring in the light, he went to work. The others watched silently as he probed inside the case, murmuring " . . . wire B to Contact D . . . conductor E to remitter X . . . red . . . blue . . . green . . . " After ten minutes, he said "Ha!," closed the back of the ring, and held it to his ear. He smiled broadly.

"I can hear him," he said. "No doubt this ring is tuned to its twin, which Krupkin keeps on his person." He handed the ring to Flimbert.

"Ummm. That's his voice, all right."

"Well—what's he saying?" O'Leary demanded.

"He's singing. Something about a road to Mandalay."

"Let me listen." Flimbert gave him the ring; he held it to his ear: " . . . *Bloomin' idol made of mu-ud . . . what they called the great god Buddd . . .* " The words came indistinctly through the sound of running water. Lafayette frowned. The voice seemed to have a half-familiar note. Abruptly, the singing cut off. Lafayette heard a faint tapping, followed by a muttered curse, footsteps, the sound of a door opening.

"Well?" the voice that had been singing said testily.

"Highness . . . the pris—that is to say, your guest declines to join you for breakfast—with, ah, appropriate apologies, of course."

"Blast the wench, can't she see I'm trying to make her comfortable, nothing more? And don't bother lying to me, Haunch. That little baggage doesn't know the meaning of the word 'apology.' She's done nothing but stamp her foot and make demands since the moment she arrived. I tell you, there are times when I wonder if it's worth all the maneuvering involved, trying to set up shop as a benevolent despot."

"Shall I, er, convey your Highness's invitation to lunch?"

"Don't bother, just see that she has whatever she wants served in her room. Keep her as content as possible. I don't want her developing frown lines or chapped knuckles while in my care."

"Of course, Highness." Footsteps, a closing door; a few bars of under-the-breath whistling; then sudden silence, with heavy breathing.

"Damn!" the voice muttered. "Could those little—?" The voice broke off. There were loud, rasping sounds, then a dull *clunk!* followed by total silence.

"Oh-oh," Lafayette said. "He's stopped transmitting."

The others listened in turn. "He must have realized something was amiss," Pinchcraft said. "Probably stuffed the ring in a box and closed the lid. So much for counter-intelligence."

"Too bad," O'Leary said brightly. "Just as it was getting interesting."

"Yes; well, let's be going, fellow," Flimbert said. "The treadmill is waiting."

"Well—good-bye, Roy," O'Leary said. "I wouldn't want to default on my debt to society, of course—but I certainly will hate missing all the excitement."

"Oh, life around the Ajax Works is pretty quiet, Slim; you won't be missing much."

"Just the invasion," Lafayette said. "It ought to be quite spectacular when Krupkin arrives with his army, navy, and air force."

"What's that?" Flimbert snapped. "What are you talking about?"

"Oh—I forgot I was the only one who heard him. But never mind. Maybe he was only fooling."

"Who?"

"Prince Krupkin. He was closeted with his War Cabinet, laying on the strategy for the takeover. He cut off just as he was about to announce the timetable for the three-pronged assault."

"Nonsense! Krupkin wouldn't attack Ajax!"

"Probably not. Just his idea of a joke. Of course, he didn't know we were listening—but then maybe he's an eccentric and was just reading off logistical schedules for the fun of it."

"He couldn't be so base as to use our own equipment against us?" Flimbert inquired, aghast.

"I wouldn't put it past him!" Pinchcraft said.

"Well, I'd better get started treading that mill," Lafayette said. "You gentlemen will be pretty busy for the next twenty-four hours, I suppose, making out wills and burying your valuables—"

"Just a moment. What else did he say? When does he plan to hit us? How many troops has he under arms? What will his primary objectives be? What kind of armaments—"

"Sorry, that was the part he was just coming to."

"Drat it! Why couldn't we have tuned in sooner!"

"Look here—can't you rig up something else, Pinchcraft?" Flimbert demanded. "We have to know what's going on over there!"

"Not without a pickup planted at that end, I can't."

"What about sending over a robot bird to scatter a few bugs around the premises?"

"Useless. The range on these micro-micro jobs is very short. The pickup has to be planted on or near the person of the subject to do us any good."

"We'll have to send a man in."

"Nonsense. None of our boys are as tall as those bean-poles; anyone we sent would be spotted instantly. Unless—"

All eyes turned to O'Leary.

"What, me stick my head in the lion's den?" he said with raised eyebrows. "Not a chance. I'm on my way to a nice, safe treadmill, remember?"

"Now, now, my boy," Flimbert said with a smile like the father of a pauper's bride, "don't worry about the treadmill. You can always serve out your sentence after you get back—"

"Forget the sentence," Pinchcraft said. "This is more important. Don't you want to do your bit, fellow, to assist the forces of righteousness?"

"What have the forces of righteousness done for me lately?" O'Leary inquired rhetorically. "No, thanks, men, you can just carry on without me as you did before I came along."

"See here, Slim," Roy said. "I didn't think you were the kind of fellow who'd let the side down when the pinch came."

"The pinch came half an hour ago, remember? You did the pinching."

"Sir," Pinchcraft spoke up, "we appeal to your nobler instincts! Assist us now, and earn our undying gratitude!"

O'Leary patted back a yawn. "Thanks—I'm overstocked on gratitude."

"Possibly some more negotiable form of payment . . . ?" Flimbert suggested.

O'Leary raised an eyebrow, pursed his lips.

"You'll have the best equipment from our labs," Pinchcraft said quickly. "I'm just finishing up a blackout cloak in your size, as it happens, and—"

"We'll drop you onto a balcony on the main turret of the Glass Tree on a fast one-place rug," Flimbert chimed in. "The trip won't take an hour."

"Are you out of your minds?" O'Leary demanded. "My only chance would be to sneak up after dark and try for an unlocked door."

"Not with this on!" Pinchcraft hopped from his stool, grabbed up a long, red-lined green-velvet cape from a worktable, and swirled it around himself. The heavy fabric whirled, shimmered—and disappeared, along with the small technician.

"Huh?" O'Leary said.

"Not bad, eh?" Pinchcraft's voice spoke from the emptiness where he had stood a moment before.

"M-magic?" Lafayette stuttered.

"Nonsense. Electronics." Pinchcraft's face appeared, framed by nothingness. "Well, how about it?"

O'Leary forced the astounded look from his face.

"Well—I *might* go," he said, "provided you make that a two-man rug."

"Whatever you want, Slim," Roy spoke up. "For a volunteer hero like you, nothing but the best!"

"Don't worry, we'll get you in," Pinchcraft said.

"And out again?" O'Leary countered.

"One thing at a time," Flimbert said. "Come along, fellow, let's get you fitted out. I want you inside the Glass Tree by sundown."

Eight

It was late afternoon, Lafayette saw, when Sprawnroyal led him along a twisting passage to a double door opening on a tiny balcony overlooking the vast sweep of the valley below.

"Now, you want to be careful of the carpet, Slim," the Customer Relations man said as he rolled out the six-by-eight-foot rectangle of what looked like ordinary dark-blue Wilton carpet. "The circuits are tuned to your personal emanations, so nobody can hijack her. She's voice-operated, so be careful what you say. And remember, there's no railings, so watch those banked turns. The coordination's built in, naturally, but if you're careless—well, keep in mind you've got no parachute."

"That's all very encouraging," Lafayette said, adjusting the hang of the blackout cloak and fighting down a quivering sensation in his stomach. "With all this gear Pinchcraft loaded on me, I feel as maneuverable as a garbage scow."

"Frankly, he sees this as a swell chance to field-test a lot of the offbeat items he and his boys cook up on those long winter nights. Like the sneeze generator: top management wouldn't let him call for volunteers, even. And the flatwalker: it's a dandy idea, but if it doesn't work—*blooie!* There goes your research worker and a big chunk of lab."

"Fill me in with a little more data, and the flight is off," O'Leary said. "Just point me in the right direction before common sense overwhelms my instinct for making mistakes."

"Just steer due west, Slim. You can't miss it."

"You'd be amazed at some of the things I've missed," Lafayette said. "By the way, my name's not really Slim, you know. It's Lafayette O'Leary."

"Yeah? Say, that's a coincidence—but never mind that. Bon voyage, kid, and don't forget to flip the switch before you drop the bug in the target's pocket."

"Well," Lafayette said, easing into a sitting position on the dark rug, legs folded. "Here goes . . . "

He closed his eyes, thought about the coordinates Flimbert had drilled him in for half an hour. Under him, the thick wool nap seemed to vibrate minutely. He resisted an impulse to grab for support as the rug stirred, twitched, tightened; forced himself to sit limply.

"Like a sack of potatoes," he reminded himself while sweat ran down behind his head. "A big burlap bag of good old Idaho baking potatoes . . . "

The tugging, swaying sensation went on; a breeze that had sprung up blew gustily at him, riffling his hair, making the cloak flap.

"Come on, lift!" he hissed. "Before that Flimbert sharpy realizes they've been conned!"

Nothing changed. The wind whipped briskly about him; the rug felt passive under him.

"Oh, great," Lafayette said. "I should have known this idea wouldn't work." He opened his eyes, gazed blankly for a moment at the vista of open blue sky ahead, then turned, looked back . . .

On the tiny balcony scabbed to the face of the immense cliff receding rapidly behind him, a tiny figure waved a scarf. O'Leary forced his eyes down, saw the rolling grassy landscape sliding swiftly behind him. He closed his eyes tightly.

"Mamma mia," he muttered. "And me without even a paper bag, in case I get airsick!"

The palace-fortress known as the Glass Tree rose out of the west like a star caught on the peak of a mountain. Dazzling in the rays of the setting sun, it scintillated red and green and yellow and violet, materializing gradually into a cluster of sparkling, crystalline shafts. A branching structure of tall towers, dazzling bright minarets, glittering spires, clustered on the tip of the highest peak of the range.

"O.K., cloak, do your stuff," O'Leary murmured, gathering the garment about him, arranging the wide skirts so as to encompass as much as possible of the carpet itself. Sprawnroyal had assured him that Prince Krupkin was in possession of no antiaircraft facilities, but Lafayette nonetheless scrunched down on the rug to provide the minimum possible target as he swooped toward the looming structure ahead.

At half a mile he ordered the rug to slow. If there was any change in the speed—too fast—and the direction— dead at the tallest tower—Lafayette was unable to detect it. With frightening speed, the slim, glittering minaret rushed closer . . .

At the last possible instant, the rug braked, banked—almost pitching a petrified O'Leary over the side—and circled the tower.

"Like a sack of Idaho number-ones," O'Leary whispered urgently to himself. "Please, up there, just let me get out of this one alive, and I promise to tithe regularly . . ."

The rug slewed to a halt, hung quivering in the air before a tall, Moorish-arched window.

"OK, all ahead, dead slow," Lafayette whispered. The rug drifted closer to the translucent, mirror-polished wall. When it nudged the crystal rail, he reached cautiously, grabbed, and held on. The rug bobbled and swayed under him as he climbed over; relieved of his weight, it began to drift away, rippling slightly in the breeze. Lafayette caught a corner, pulled the carpet to him, rolled it into a tight cylinder, and propped it in a corner.

"Just wait here until I get back," he whispered to it. He took a moment to tuck in the tail of the embroidered shirt Sprawnroyal had supplied, and tug his jeweled sword into line, then pressed the button set in the pommel of the latter.

"Flapjack to Butterfly," he whispered. "O.K., I'm down, in one piece."

"*Very good*," a shrill whisper rasped from the two-way comm rig installed in the weapon's hilt. "*Proceed inside, and make your way to the royal apartments. They're on the twelfth floor of the main keep. Watch your step; don't give yourself away by knocking over a vase or stepping on somebody's foot.*"

"Glad you mentioned that," Lafayette snapped. "I intended to come on strumming a ukulele and singing 'Short'nin' Bread.'"

He tried the door, stepped into a dim-lit, softly carpeted chamber hung with rose-and-silver drapes. A pink-and-silver four-poster stood opposite the balcony. Silver cupids disported themselves at the corners of the dusty-rose ceiling. A wide crystal chandelier sparkled in the center of the room, tinkling with the breeze from the open door. Lafayette started toward a wide silver-and-white door at the far side of the room, halted at the sound of voices beyond it.

". . . just for a nightcap," a wheedling male voice said. "And besides," it went on with an audible leer, "you might need a little help with those buttons."

"You're impertinent, sir," a familiar feminine voice said in a playful tone. "But I suppose it will be all right—for a few minutes."

"*Daphne?*" Lafayette mumbled. As a key clattered in the lock, he dived for the shelter of the four-poster. He had no more than gained the darkness behind the brocaded skirt when the door opened. Lying with his face to the rug, Lafayette could see a pair of trim ankles in tiny black patent-leather pumps with silver buckles, closely attended by a pair of shiny black boots with jingling jeweled spurs. The two sets of feet moved across the room, out of Lafayette's line of sight. There were soft sounds as of gentle scuffling, a low laugh.

"Avaunt thee, sirrah!" the female voice said mildly. "You'll muss my coiffure."

As Lafayette stretched to get a glimpse of the action from behind the carved claw-and-ball foot of the bed, his sword clanked against the floor. Instantly there was silence.

"Milord Chauncy—didst hear that?"

"Well, I really must be going," the male voice said loudly, with a slight quaver. "As you know, his Highness—the best boss a fellow ever had—gave orders you were to have whatever you wanted, milady—but I'm afraid that if I lingered any longer attending to your whims, it might be susceptible of misinterpretation—"

"Why, of all the nerve!" There was a sharp *smack!* as of a wrathful feminine hand striking an arrogant male cheek. "As if I invited you here!"

"So . . . if you'll excuse me—"

"Not until you've searched the room! It might be a horrid big bristly rat!"

"Yes, but—"

A dainty foot stamped. "At once, Chauncy, or I'll report that you tried to force your lustful will on me!"

"Who, me, your Ladyship?"

"You heard me!"

"Well . . . " Lafayette saw the boots cross the room, pause before the closet; the door opened and shut. The feet went on to the bathroom, disappeared inside, reemerged. They went to the balcony, stepped out, came back.

"Nothing at all. Probably just your imagination—"

"You heard it too! And you haven't looked under the bed!"

Lafayette froze as the feet crossed to the bed, halted two feet from the tip of his nose. The skirt was lifted; a narrow face with fierce, spiked mustachios and a pair of small, beady eyes peered directly into his face.

"Nothing here," the man said and let the skirt drop. Lafayette let out a breath he hadn't noticed he was holding. "Sure, I forgot the cloak," he chided himself.

"That being the case," the male voice continued, "what's my rush?"

"Art related to an octopus on thy father's side?" the Daphne-like voice was inquiring with a suppressed giggle. "Aroint thee, milord, thou'll break the zipper."

"Why, you . . . " Lafayette muttered, and froze as conversation again cut off abruptly.

"Chauncy—there's someone here!" the feminine voice said. "I . . . I sense it!"

"Yes, well, as I was saying, I have my sheet-and-towel inventory to check over, so I really can't linger—"

"Pooh, Chauncy, at this hour? Surely you're not afraid?"

"Me? Afraid?" Chauncy's voice broke on the word. "Of course not, it's just that I've always loved inventories, and this is my chance to steal a march by working on it all night, so—"

"Chauncy—we were going to take a moonlight walk, remember? Just you and me . . . "

"Yes, well—"

"Just wait while I slip into something more comfortable. Now, don't go 'way . . ."

"Hey," Lafayette murmured weakly.

"The acoustics in this room are terrible," Chauncy said nervously. "I would have sworn someone whispered 'hey' just then."

"Silly boy," the other voice replied. There was a soft rustling sound, followed by a sharp intake of masculine breath. The feminine feet reappeared; they paused before the closet; slim, ringed fingers appeared, to pull off one shoe, then the other. The feet went to tiptoe, and a voluminously skirted garment collapsed on the floor. A moment later, a filmy nothing floated down beside the dress.

"Really, milady," Chauncy's voice squeaked, "his Highness . . . but to perdition with his Highness!" The booted feet rushed across the floor, trod on a small, bare foot. There was a sharp yelp, followed by the second sharp *smack!* of the evening.

"You big, clumsy idiot!" the female voice wailed. "I'd rather stay cooped up here forever than put up with—"

"Oh, so that was your scheme, you slick little minx!" Chauncy cried. "You inveigled me here with promise of goodies to come—planning all the while to dupe me into abetting your escape! Well, this is one time the old skin game won't work, milady! I'm collecting right now—"

Lafayette emerged from under the bed in a rush. As he leaped to his feet, the owner of the boots—a tall, lean, courtier type in the pre-middle-aged group—spun, grabbing for his sword hilt, staring wildly over, past, and through O'Leary. Behind Chauncy, Daphne—or Lady Andragorre—bare-shouldered in a petticoat, stood on one shapely leg, massaging the toes of the other foot. Lafayette reached out, lifted the man's chin to the optimum angle, and delivered a sizzling right hook which sent the fellow staggering back to bounce off the wall and pitch forward on his face.

"Chauncy!" the lady whispered, watching his trajectory. "What—how—why—?"

"I'll teach that lecher to sneak around ladies' bedrooms helping them with their buttons," Lafayette said, advancing on the half-clad girl. "And as for you, I'm ashamed of you, leading that gigolo on!"

"I hear your voice . . . oh, beloved—I can hear you—but I can't see you! Where are you? You're not . . . you're not a ghost?"

"Far from it!" Lafayette pulled the cloak back from his back. "I'm flesh and blood, all right, and all I have to say about this spectacle is—"

The lady stared for a moment into O'Leary's face; then her eyes turned up. With a sigh, she crumpled onto the old rose rug.

"Daphne!" Lafayette blurted. "Wake up! I forgive you! But we have to get out of here in a hurry!" As O'Leary bent over her, there was a thunderous pounding at the door.

"There's a man in there!" an irate voice yelled from outside. "All right, men—break it down!"

"Hold your horses, Sarge—I got a key—"

"You heard me!" There was a thunderous crash that shook the door in its frame, the sound of heavy bodies rebounding.

"So, OK, we use the key." Lafayette slipped his arms under the unconscious girl and lifted her, staggered to the heavy hangings against the wall, and slid behind them as the lock clicked, the latch turned, the door banged wide. Three large men in cerise coats with lace at wrist and chin, tight cream-colored pants, and drawn swords plunged into the room and skidded to a halt.

They stared, then cautiously prowled the room.

"Hey! The place is empty," a man said.

"There's ain't nobody here," a second added.

"Yeah, but we heard voices, remember?"

"So we made a mistake."

"Either that, or . . ."

"Or we're all going crackers."

"Or else the joint is haunted."

"Well, I got to be getting back to my pinochle game," a private said, backing toward the door.

"Stand fast, you," the NCO barked. "I'll say when we get back to the pinochle game!"

"Yeah? You want to wait around and shake hands with the Headless Hostler?"

"And like you said, it's time we was getting back to the pinochle game," the sergeant finished sternly. "Let's go."

Three sets of footsteps retreated cautiously toward the door. As they reached it, Lafayette, standing behind the curtain inhaling the perfume of the girl in his arms, heard a preliminary crackle from his sword hilt.

"Oh, no," he breathed.

"Butterfly to Flapjack," a testy voice sounded from near his left elbow. *"What's going on, Flapjack? You haven't reported for over five minutes now!"*

"Over there," a tense voice said. "Behind them drapes."

"Flapjack? Report!"

"Shut up, you blabbermouth!" Lafayette hissed in the general direction of his left hip, and sidestepped as the curtains were rudely torn aside.

"Chee!" the man who stood there said, staring wide-eyed at Lafayette's burden.

"Coo," said the comrade peering over his shoulder, and ran a thick pink tongue along his lower lip like one recovering a crumb of icing.

"Holy Moses," said the third. "She's . . . she's floating in midair, like!"

"She—she got little teeny rosebuds embroidered on her undies," the first man said. "Think o' that, fellers!"

"Walking or floating, them are the neatest curves a guy ever seen," his comrade stated.

"Hey—she's floating toward the balcony doors, boys!" a man blurted as O'Leary edged sideways. "Block the way!"

As the three palace guards spread out, O'Leary tried a play around left end, gained two yards, delivered a sharp kick to a kneecap as the owner reached a tentative hand toward milady's dangling arm. He dodged aside as the fellow yelled and clutched at the injured member, hopping on one foot. For the moment, the way to the door was clear; Lafayette lunged, felt the cloak tug at his back as the hopper trod on the hem; before he could halt his plunge, it was ripped from his back.

"Hey! A guy! He just popped out o' the air, like!" a man yelled. "Take him, Renfrew!" Lafayette made a desperate leap, ducked the haymaker, felt hard hands grab his ankles, saw other hands seize the girl as he went down, banging his head against the baseboard. Half-dazed, he was dragged to his feet and flung against the wall.

"Well, look who's here," the grinning face hovering before him said in tones of pleased surprise as hands slapped his pockets, relieving him of the gadgets pressed on him by Pinchcraft. "You get around, bub. But you should of thought twice before you tried this one, which his Nibs ain't going to like it much, you in here with her Ladyship, and her in the altogether!"

"She's not altogether in the altogether," O'Leary mumbled, attempting to focus his eyes. "She's wearing her rosebuds."

"Hey, look!" another of the new arrivals called. "Lord Chauncy's over here back o' the divan! Boy oh boy, will you look at the size o' the mouse on his jaw!"

"Add assaulting his Lordship to the charges on this joker," the sergeant in charge said. "Kid, you should of stayed where you was. You didn't know when you was well off."

Two men were holding Lafayette's arms. The third had placed the unconscious girl on the bed.

"O.K., Mel, don't stand back to admire your work," the NCO growled. "Let's hustle this joker back to the cell block before somebody finds out he's gone and starts criticizing the guard force."

"Can't I . . . can't I just say a word to her?" O'Leary appealed as his captors hustled him past the bed.

"Well—what the heck, kid, I guess you paid for the privilege. Make it fast."

"Daphne," Lafayette said urgently as her eyelids quivered open. "Daphne! Are you all right?"

For a moment, the girl looked dazedly around. Her eyes fell on Lafayette.

"Lancelot?" she whispered. "Lancelot . . . dearest . . . "

"OK, let's go," the NCO growled. Lafayette stared despairingly back as they escorted him from the room.

Nine

Lafayette sat in pitch darkness, slumped against a damp stone wall, shivering. The tomblike silence was broken only by the soft rustlings of mice frisking in the moldy straw and the rasp of heavy breathing from the far corner of the dank chamber. His fellow prisoner had not wakened when he was thrown into the cell, nor in the gloomy hours since. The aroma of Moonlight Rose still lingered in O'Leary's nostrils, in spite of the goaty stench of the dungeon. The memory of those soft, warm contours he had held briefly in his arms sent renewed pangs through him every time he let his thoughts rove back over the events since his arrival at the Glass Tree.

"I really handled it brilliantly," he muttered. "I had every break—even stumbled right into her room, first try—and I still muffed it. I've done everything wrong since the second I found myself perched on the windmill. I've let down everybody, from Swinehild to Rodolpho to Pinchcraft, not to mention Daph—I mean Lady Andragorre." He got to his feet, took the four paces his exploration of the dark chamber had indicated were possible before bumping a wall, paced back.

"There's got to be *some*thing I can do!" he hissed to himself. "Maybe . . . " He closed his eyes—an action which made very little difference under the circumstances—and concentrated his psychic energies.

"I'm back in Artesia," he muttered. "I've just stepped outside for a breath of air in the midst of a costume ball—that's why I'm wearing this fancy outfit Sprawnroyal gave me—and in a second or two I'll open my eyes and go back inside, and . . . "

His words trailed off. With the stench of the cell in his nostrils, it was impossible to convince himself that he was strolling in a garden where nothing more odiferous than a gardenia was to be found.

"Well, then—I'm inspecting the slums," he amended "—except that there aren't any slums in Artesia," he recalled. "But how about Colby Corners? We had a swell little slum back there, created and maintained by as determined a crew of slum dwellers as ever put coal in a bathtub." He squinted harder, marshaling his psychic forces. "I'm in a Federal Aid to Undesirables project," he assured himself, "doing research for a book on how long it takes the average family of ne'er-do-wells to convert a clean, new, modern welfare-supplied apartment into the kind of homey chaos they're used to . . . "

"Say, would you mind hallucinating a little more quietly?" a querulous voice with an edge like a gnawed fingernail inquired from the far corner of the room. "I'm trying to catch a few winks."

"Oh, so you're alive after all," Lafayette replied. "I certainly admire your ability to doss down in comfort in the midst of this mare's nest."

"What do you suggest?" came the snappish reply. "That I huddle here with every nerve a-tingle to monitor each nuance of total boredom and discomfort?"

"How do we get out?" Lafayette said tersely. "That's the question we ought to be thinking about."

"You're good at questions, how are you at answers?" The voice, O'Leary thought, was a nerve-abrading combination of petulant arrogance and whining self-pity. He suppressed the impulse to snap back.

"I've tried the door," he said in tones of forced optimism. "It's a single slab of cast iron, as far as I can determine, which seems to limit the possibilities in that direction."

"You're not going to let a little thing like a cast-iron door slow you down, surely? From your tone of voice, I assumed you'd just twist it off its hinges and hit someone over the head with it."

" . . . which means we'll have to look for some other mode of egress," O'Leary finished, gritting his teeth.

"Splendid. You work at that. As for me, I'm catching up on my sleep. I've had a pretty strenuous forty-eight hours—"

"Oh, have you? Well, it can't begin to compare with *my* last forty-eight hours. I started off on top of a windmill, worked my way through a homicidal giant and a set of pirates, two jail cells, an execution, a fall down an elevator shaft, a trial for espionage, and a trip on a flying carpet, to say nothing of the present contretemps."

"Uuuum-ha!" Lafayette's cellmate yawned. "Lucky you. As for myself, I've been busy: I've parlayed with a mad prince, dickered with a duke, carried out a daring rescue, double-crossed a sorcerer, and been beaten, kicked, hit on the head, slugged, and thrown in a dungeon."

"I see. And what are you doing about it?"

"Nothing. You see, it's actually all a dream. After a while I'll wake up and you'll be gone, and I can get back to my regular routine."

"Oh, I see. The solitude has driven you off your hinge. Rather ironic, actually," he added with a hollow chuckle. "You, imagining I'm a figment of your nightmare. I remember when I had similar ideas about a lot of things that turned out to be painfully real."

"So if you'll stop chattering, so I can go back to sleep, I'll be grateful," the abrasive voice remarked.

"Listen to me, Sleeping Beauty," O'Leary said sharply. "This is real—as real as anything that ever happened to you. Maybe hardship has driven you out of whatever wits you may once have had, but try to grasp the concept: you're in a cell—a real, live, three-dee cell, complete with mice. And unless you want to stay here until you rot—or the hangman comes for you—you'd better stir your stumps!"

"Go 'way. I haven't finished my nap."

"Gladly—if I could! Wake up, numbskull! Maybe between the two of us we can do something!"

"Poo. You're nothing but a figment. All I have to do is go back to sleep, and I'll wake up back in Hatcher's Crossroads, bagging groceries at Bowser's."

Lafayette laughed hollowly. "You remind me of a poor innocent nincompoop I used to know," he said. "By the way, where's this Hatcher's Crossroads located?"

"In the Oklahoma Territory. But you wouldn't know about that. It's not part of this dream."

"Oklahoma—you mean you're from the States?"

"Oh, so you do know about the States? Well, why not! I suppose in theory you could know anything I know, eh? Well, ta-ta, I'm off to dreamland again—"

"Wait a minute," O'Leary said urgently. "Are you saying you were brought here from the U.S.? That you're not a native of Melange?"

"The U.S.? What's that? And of course I'm not a native. Do I look as though I'd run around in a G-string, waving an assegai?"

"I don't know, I can't see in the dark. But if you come from Oklahoma, you must know what the U.S. is!"

"You don't mean the U.C.?"

"What's that?"

"The United Colonies, of course. But look, be a good imaginary character and let me catch a few winks now, all right? This was all rather lark at first, but I'm getting tired of it, and I have a hard day ahead tomorrow. Mr. Bowser's running a special on pickled walnuts, and the whole county will be there—"

"Try to get this through your thick skull," Lafayette snarled. "You're here, in Melange, like it or not! It's real—whatever real is! If they hang you or cut your head off, you suffer the consequences, get it? Now, look, we have to talk about this. It sounds as if you were shanghaied here the same way I was—"

"I never knew my subconscious could be so persuasive. If I didn't know you were just a subjective phenomenon, I'd swear you were real."

"Look, let's skip that part for now. Just act as if I were real. Now, tell me: how did you get here?"

"Easy. A troop of Prince Krupkin's cavalry grabbed me by the back of the neck and threw me in here. Satisfied?"

"I mean before that—when you first arrived—"

"Oh, you mean when I focused the cosmic currents?" Lafayette's cellmate laughed hollowly. "If I'd known what I was getting into, I'd have stuck to my tinned kippers and jelly doughnuts. But no, I had to go intellectually questing, searching for the meaning of it all. And then I had the bad luck to stumble on Professor Hozzleshrumph's book, *Modern Spellbinding, or Self-Delusion Made Easy*. I tried out his formulae, and—well, one second I was in my room at Mrs. Ginsberg's, and the next—I was in the middle of a vast desert, with the sun glaring in my face."

"Yes? Go on."

"Well, I started hiking east—that way the sun wasn't in my eyes—and after a while I reached the hills. It was cooler there, and I found a stream, and some nuts and berries. I kept on, and came out in a tilled field, near a town. I found a lunch counter, and just as I was about to take my first bite of grilled Parmesan cheese on rye, the local police force arrived. They took me in to the prince, and he offered me a job. It all seemed pretty jolly, so I went along. I was doing all right, too—until I got a look at the Lady Andragorre."

"Lady Andragorre? What do you know about Lady Andragorre?" Lafayette barked.

"I have to keep reminding myself this is just a dream," the unseen voice said agitatedly. "Otherwise, I'd be tearing my hair out!" Lafayette heard a deep breath drawn and slowly let out. "But it's all a dream, an illusion. Beverly really isn't in the clutches of that slimy little Krupkin; I haven't really been double-crossed and thrown in a cell. These aren't real hunger pangs I feel. And if you'd just shut up and go away, I could get back to my career at Bowser's!"

"Let's get back to Lady Andragorre!"

"Wouldn't I love to? Those sweet, soft lips, that curvy little frame—"

"Why, you—" Lafayette caught himself. "Listen to me, whoever you are! You've got to face up to reality! You have to help me! Right now Lady Andragorre's in the hands of these lechers—and I do mean hands—"

"Just last week Mr. Bowser was saying to me: Lorenzo, my boy, you have a great future ahead in the provisions game . . . "

"Lorenzo! Then you're the one that sold out Lady Andragorre!" Lafayette lunged in the direction from which the voice came, slammed into the wall, acquiring a new contusion to add to those already marring his head. "Where are you?" he panted, making grabs at the air. "You dirty, scheming, double-crossing, kidnapping, conniving snake-in-the-grass!"

"What are you getting so excited about?" the voice yelped from the opposite corner. "What's Bever—I mean Lady Andragorre to you, you jailbird?"

"Jailbird, eh?" Lafayette panted, stalking the detestable voice. "You're a swell one to talk, sitting here in your cell—" He jumped, almost got a grip on an arm, saw stars as a fist connected with his eye.

"Keep your distance, you!" the voice barked. "Troubles enough I didn't have, they had to toss a homicidal maniac in with me!"

"You lured her out of the city with your sweet talk, just so you could turn her over to her aunt! I mean to the old bat who was fronting for Krupkin!"

"That's what Rodolpho thought—but once I'd seen her, I had no intention of taking her there, of course—not that it's any of your business!"

"Where *were* you taking her? To some little love-nest of your own?"

"As a matter of fact, yes, big nose. And I'd have made it, too, if something hadn't set that gang of mounted police swarming through the woods. We had to run for it, and as luck would have it, that long-legged sheik, Lord Chauncy, was out hunting and nabbed us."

"Oh. Well, maybe it's just as well. At least here she has a decent bed."

"Oh? What do you know about Bever—I mean, Lady Andragorre's bed?"

"Plenty. I just spent an exciting half-hour under it."

"You did say—*under* it?"

"Exactly. I overheard her fending off the advances of that Chauncy character. I had my flying carpet—I mean my Mark IV personnel carrier—waiting right outside on the balcony. Just as I was about to whisk her away, the palace guard arrived."

"Yes, I warned Krupkin to keep an eye on Chauncy. Looks like they got there just in time, too!"

"Just too soon! I had her in my arms when they burst in on us—"

"Why, you—" An unseen body hurtled past O'Leary; he thrust out a foot and had the satisfaction of hooking an ankle solidly. The resultant crash went far to assuage the pain of his swelling eye.

"Listen, Lorenzo," Lafayette said, "there's no point in our flailing away at each other in the dark. Apparently we both have an interest in the welfare of Lady Andragorre. Neither of us wants to see her in Krupkin's clutches. Why don't we work together until she's safe and then settle our differences?"

"Work together, ha," Lafayette's unseen cellmate muttered from a point near the floor. "What's to work? We're penned in, empty-handed, in the dark. Unless," he went on, "you have something up your sleeve?"

"They cleaned me out," Lafayette said. "I had some dandy items: a two-way intercom sword, a blackout cloak, a fast-key, a fast-walker . . . " He paused, quickly felt for his belt. It was still in place. He unbuckled it, pulled it free, felt over the back, found the zipper tag there, pulled it.

"Hold everything, Lorenzo," he said tensely. "Maybe we're in business."

"What are you talking about?" the other came back in his pettish voice. "Swords? Keys? What we need is a charge of dynamite, or a couple of stout crowbars."

"I may have something better," Lafayette said, extracting a flat two-inch by one-inch rectangle of what felt like flexible plastic from its hiding place under the zipper. "They missed the flat-walker."

"What's a flat-walker?"

"According to Pinchcraft, it generates a field which has the effect of modifying the spatial relationships of whatever it's tuned to, vis-à-vis the exocosm. It converts any one-linear dimension into the equivalent displacement along the perpendicular volumetric axis, at the same time setting up a harmonic which causes a reciprocal epicentric effect, and—"

"How would you go about explaining that to an ordinary mortal?" Lorenzo interrupted.

"Well, it reduces one of the user's physical dimensions to near zero, and compensates by a corresponding increase in the density of the matter field in the remaining quasi-two-dimensional state."

"Better try the idiot version."

"It makes you flat."

"How is wearing a corset going to help us?" Lorenzo yelped.

"I mean *really* flat! You can slide right between the molecules of ordinary matter—walk through walls, in other words. That's why it's called a flat-walker."

"Good grief, and I was practically outside, sneaking up on that long-legged son of a Schnauzer who pitched me in here."

"That's the spirit! Now stand fast, Lorenzo, and I'll try this thing out. Let's see, Pinchcraft said to orient it with the long axis coinciding with my long axis, and the smooth face parallel to the widest plane of my body, or vice versa . . . "

"I suppose this was all part of their torture plan," Lorenzo muttered, "to lock me in with a mental case. I should have known better than to get my hopes up. Poor Beverly. With me put away, there's no one to help her. She'll hold out for as long as she can, but in the end the ceaseless importuning of her captor combined with the prospects of ruling this benighted principality will erode her will, and—"

"I read the same book," Lafayette said. "It was lousy. How about bottling up your pessimism while I conduct a test." Lafayette fingered the flat-walker, found the small bump at the center, and pressed it.

Nothing happened. He peered disappointedly into the surrounding blackness.

"Damn!" Lafayette said with feeling. "But I guess that would have been too easy. We'll have to think of something else. Listen, Lorenzo: how high is this room? Maybe there's a hatch in the ceiling, and if one of us stood on the other's shoulders, we could reach it." He stood on tiptoes and reached as far overhead as he could, but touched nothing. He jumped, still found no ceiling.

"How about it?" he snapped. "Do you want to climb up on my shoulders, or shall I get on yours?"

There was no answer. Even the mice had stopped rustling.

"Speak up, Lorenzo! Or have you gone back to sleep?" He moved across toward the other's corner, feeling for the wall. After he had taken ten steps, he slowed, advancing cautiously. After five more steps, he halted.

"That's funny," he said in the circumambient darkness. "I thought the cell was only ten paces wide . . . "

He turned and retraced his steps, counting off fifteen paces, then went on another five, ten, fifteen steps. Abruptly, blinding light glared in his eyes. He blinked, squinting at what appeared to be a wall of featureless illumination, like the frosted glass over a light fixture. As he turned, the wall seemed to flow together; lines and flecks and blots of color appeared, coalesced into a normal though somewhat distorted scene: a dim-lit corridor, glass-walled, glass-floored, lined by heavy doors of black glass.

"I'm outside the cell!" he blurted. "It worked! Lorenzo—!" He turned, saw the walls expand as he did, stretching out into featurelessness, like a reflection in a convex mirror.

"Must be some effect of two dimensionality," he murmured. "Now, let's see—what direction did I come from?"

Squinting, he stepped hesitantly forward; the glare winked out to total darkness. He took fifteen paces and halted.

"Lorenzo," he hissed. "I made it!"

There was no answer.

"Oh—he probably can't hear me—or I can't hear him—with this gadget turned on . . . " Lafayette pressed the deactivating switch. There was no apparent change, except for the almost imperceptible sounds of moving air—and a muffled sob.

"Oh, for heaven's sake, buck up," Lafayette snapped. "Crying won't help!"

There was a startled intake of air.

"Lafe?" a familiar voice whispered. "Is it really you?"

Lafayette sniffed: garlic? "Swinehild!" he gasped. "How did *you* get here?"

"Y-you told me not to follow you," Swinehild was saying five minutes later, having enjoyed a good cry while O'Leary patted her soothingly. "But I watched the gate and seen you come through. Happened there was a horse tied in front of a beer joint, so I ups and takes off after you. The feller on the ferry showed me which way you went. When I caught up with you, you was smack in the middle of a necktie party—"

"It was *you* that yowled like a panther!"

"It was all I could think of in a hurry."

"You saved my life, Swinehild!"

"Yeah. Well, I beat it out of there, and next thing I knew I was lost. I spent some time wandering around, and then my horse shied at something and tossed me off in a berry bush. When I crawled out of that, here was this old lady sitting on a stump, lighting up a cigar. I was so glad to see a human face, I waltzed right over and said how-do. She jumped like she'd set on a cactus and give me a look like I was somebody's ghost. 'Good Lord,' she says. 'Incredible! But after all—why not?' I was just starting to ask her if she'd seen the big bird or whatever that'd spooked my critter, and she outs with a tin can with a button on top and jams it in my face, and I get a whiff of mothballs, and that's all I know for a while."

"I believe I know the lady in question," Lafayette said grimly. "That's three scores I have to settle with her—if not more."

"After that I had some crazy dreams about flying through the air. I woke up in a nice room with a smooth-looking little buzzard that must have been the old dame's brother or something; they favored a lot. He asked me a lot of screwy questions, and I try to leave and he grabs me, and naturally, I swat him a couple and the next thing I know a strong-arm squad is bum's-rushing me down here." Swinehild sighed. "Maybe I shouldn't of been so fast with that right hook—but the slob had cold hands. But I should of known I didn't have to worry. I knew you'd find me, Lafe." Her lips nuzzled his ear.

"By the way," she whispered, "I brought the lunch. How about a nice hunk o' sausage and cheese? It's a little crumbly—I been carrying it tucked in my bodice—"

"No, thanks," Lafayette said hastily, disengaging himself. "We have to get out of here right away. I'm going to go back outside and find a key—"

"Hey, how'd you get in here, Lafe? I never heard the door open . . . "

"I came through the wall. Nothing to it, just a trick I'll tell you about later. But I can't take you out that way. I'll have to get the door open. So if you'll just wait here—"

"You're going to leave me alone again?"

"It can't be helped, Swinehild. Just sit quietly and wait. I'll be back as soon as possible. It shouldn't take too long."

"I . . . I guess you know best, Lafe. But hurry. I never did like being alone in the dark."

"Never fear, there's a good girl." He patted her shoulder. "Try to think about something nice, and I'll be back before you know it."

"G-g'bye, Lafe. Take care."

Lafayette groped his way to the wall, reactivated the flat-walker, waded forward into the glare of the corridor. Again he adjusted his eyes to the light and to the alternately stretched-out and compressed nature of visual phenomena. The narrow passage was still empty. He deactivated the flat-walker, saw the view slide into normality. He made his way stealthily along to the nearest cross-corridor. Two men in scarlet coats lounged in a lighted doorway twenty feet from the intersection. One of them, a paunchy, pasty-faced fellow with untrimmed hair, wore a large ring of keys dangling from his belt. There was no chance to approach them openly. Again O'Leary pressed the control switch of the flat-walker, saw the sides of the passage rush together while the solid glass walls beside him stretched out to a shimmering, opalescent blankness.

"Don't lose your bearings," he instructed himself sternly. "Straight ahead, about twenty paces; then rematerialize—and while they're catching their breath, grab the keys and go flat. Got it?"

"Got it," he replied, and started forward.

At the first step, the lighted corridor shifted, collapsed, became a cloudy veil. Lafayette felt about him; nothing tangible met his hands.

"Must be some kind of orientation effect," he suggested to himself. "Just keep going."

It was confusing, pushing forward into the milky glare. By turning his head sideways, O'Leary could see an alternate pattern of glass bricks which revolved away from him as he passed, like walking past an endless curved mirror. After five paces, he was dizzy. After ten, he halted and took deep breaths through his nose to combat the sensation of seasickness.

"Pinchcraft has a few bugs to iron out," he muttered, swallowing hard, "before the flat-walker is ready for the market." He forged on another five paces. How far had he come now? Ten paces? Or twenty? Or . . .

Something flashed and twinkled in front of him, surrounding him. There was a swirl of scarlet, a glitter of brass. Then he was staring directly into a set of what were unmistakably vertebrae, mere inches from his eyes, topped by a jellylike mass of pinkish material . . .

With a lunge, Lafayette leaped clear, gave a whinny of gratitude as darkness closed about him.

"Pinchcraft didn't warn me," he panted, "about walking through a man . . ."

It was a good five minutes before Lafayette felt equal to resuming his stalk. He picked a direction at random, took five more paces, two more for good measure, then halted and switched off the flat-walker.

"How'd you get out?" a surprised voice said as blazing sunlight flooded his retinas. Lafayette caught a swift impression of an open courtyard etched in light like a scene revealed by a flash of lightning, a grinning face under a feathered hat, a swinging billy-club—then the nearest tower fell on his head, and the world exploded into darkness.

Ten

"All I know is, yer Highness, the mug shows up in the exercise yard, blinking like a owl." The voice boomed and receded like surf on a tropical beach. "I ask him nice to come along, and he pulls a knife on me. Well, I plead wit' him to hand it over, no violence, like you said, and he tries a run fer it and slips on a banana peel and cracks hisself on the knob. So I lift him up real easy-like and bring him along, knowing yer Highness's interest in the bum, and frankly it beats me what all the excitement is about, after twenty-one years on the force—"

"Silence, you blithering idiot! I told you this subject was to receive kid-glove treatment! And you bring him to me with a knot on his skull the size of the royal seal!

One more word and I'll have you thrown to the piranhas!"

Lafayette made an effort, groped for the floor, found it under his feet. He wrestled an eye open, discovered that he was standing, supported by a painful grip on his upper arms, in a large, high-ceilinged room adorned by tapestries, chandeliers, rugs, gilt mirrors, polished furniture of rich, dark wood. In a comfortable-looking armchair before him sat a small, dapper man wearing a ferocious frown on his familiar, well-chiseled features.

"Go-go-go-go," Lafayette babbled, and paused for breath.

"Sergeant, if you've scrambled his wits, it's your head!" the gray-haired man yelped, rising and coming forward. "Lorenzo!" he addressed Lafayette. "Lorenzo, it's me, your friend, Prince Krupkin! Can you understand me?" He peered anxiously into O'Leary's face.

"I . . . I understand you," Lafayette managed. "But—but—you—you're—"

"Good lad! Here, you cretins, seat my guest here, on this pile of cushions. Bring wine! How's your head, my boy?"

"Terrible," Lafayette said, cringing at each pulsebeat. "I was almost over my hangover when I fell down the elevator, and I was almost over that when this lout clubbed me down. I must have three concussions running concurrently. I need a doctor. I need sleep. I need food. I need an aspirin—"

"You shall have it, dear lad. Along with my abject apologies for this dreadful misunderstanding. I hope you'll excuse my remarks at our last meeting, I was overwrought. I was just on the point of sending for you to make amends when the sergeant reported he'd encountered you wandering in the courtyard. Ah, by the way, how did you happen to be in the courtyard, if you don't mind my asking?"

"I walked through the wall—I think. It's all a little hazy now."

"Oh. To be sure. Well, don't worry about it, just relax, have a drink. A nap will fix you up nicely—just as soon as we've had a talk, that is."

"I don't want to talk, I want to sleep. I need an anesthetic. I probably need a blood transfusion, and possibly a kidney transplant. Actually I'm dying, so it's probably wasted effort—"

"Nonsense, Lorenzo! You'll soon be right as rain. Now, the point I wanted to inquire about—or about which I wanted to inquire, we must be grammatically correct, ha-ha—the point, I say, is—where is she?"

"Who?"

"Don't play the noddy, my lad," Prince Krupkin came back in a sharper tone. "You know whom."

"Tell me anyway."

Krupkin leaned forward. "The Lady Andragorre!" he snapped. "What have you done with her?"

"What makes you think I did anything with her?"

His Highness glared at O'Leary. He gripped his knuckles and cracked them with a sound that sent new waves of pain lancing through O'Leary's head.

"Who else would have had the audacity to spirit her away from the luxurious chambers in which I, from the goodness of my heart, installed the thankless creature?"

"Good question," O'Leary mumbled. "Lorenzo would be the likeliest suspect if he weren't in a cell . . ."

"Exactly! Which brings us back to the original query: where is she!"

"Beats me. But if she got away from you, good for her."

"I'll have the truth out of you if I have to extract it with red-hot pincers, you miserable ingrate!"

"I thought the kid-glove treatment was the prescription," Lafayette said. His eyes were closed, watching the pattern of red blobs that pulsed in time with his heartbeat.

"I'll kid-glove you! I'll have the hide off your back under a cat-o'-nine-tails—" Krupkin broke off, took a deep breath, let it out between his teeth.

"Such are the burdens of empire," he muttered. "You try to give a vile wretch of a double-crossing sneak an even break, and what happens? He throws it in your face . . ."

Lafayette forced both eyes open, looked long into the irate features of the prince.

"It's amazing," he muttered. "You talk just like him. If I hadn't already met Swinehild and Hulk and Lady Andragorre and Sprawnroyal, and Duke Rodolpho, I'd swear you were—"

"Ah, that slippery eel, Rodolpho! He seduced you from the path of duty, eh? What did he promise you? I'll double it! I'll triple it!"

"Well, let's see: as I recall, he said something about undying gratitude—"

"I'll give you ten times the gratitude that petty baron can bring to bear!"

"I wish you'd make up your mind," Lafayette said. "What's it to be, the red carpet or the rack?"

"Now, now, my boy, I was just having my little jest. We have great things to accomplish together, you and I! A whole world to whip into shape! The riches of all the mines and seas and forests, the fabled loot of the East!" Krupkin leaned forward, his eyes bright with plans. "Consider: no one here knows the location of the great diamond mines—the richest gold deposits—the rarest beds of emeralds! But you and I do—eh?" He winked. "We'll work together. With my genius for planning, and your special talents"—he winked again—"there's no limit to what we can accomplish!"

"Special talents? I play the harmonica a little—learned it via correspondence course—"

"Now, now, don't twit me, lad," Krupkin waggled a finger good-naturedly.

"Look, Krupkin—you're wasting your time. If the lady's not in her chambers, I don't know where she is." Lafayette held his head in his hands, supporting it delicately, like a cracked melon. Through his fingers he saw Krupkin open his mouth to speak, and suddenly freeze, lean forward, staring at him with an expression of total amazement.

"Of course!" the prince breathed. "Of course!"

"See something green?" Lafayette snapped.

"No. No, not at all. Not green at all. Amazing. That is to say, I don't notice a thing. I mean to say I didn't see anything at all. But it suddenly comes to me that you're tired, poor lad. Surely you'd like a hot tub and a few handmaidens to scrub your back, and a cozy bed to snuggle down in? And after you've rested, we can have a long chat about your further needs, eh? Splendid. Here!" The prince snapped his fingers at an attendant. "Prepare the imperial suite for my honored guest! A scented bath, my most exquisite personal masseuses—and let the royal surgeon attend with balms and unguents for this nobleman's hurts."

Lafayette yawned hugely. "Rest," he mumbled. "Sleep. Oh, yes . . . "

He was only half-aware of being led from the room, along a wide corridor, up a grand staircase. In a big, soft-carpeted chamber, gentle hands helped him out of his grimy garments, lowered him to a vast, foamy tub, scrubbed him, dried him, laid him away between crisp sheets. As the rosy light faded to sweet-scented gloom, he snuggled down with a sigh of utter contentment . . .

Abruptly, his eyes were wide open, staring into the darkness.

"You and I know the location of the diamond mines . . . the gold deposits," he seemed to hear Krupkin's unctuous voice saying. *"With your special talents . . . "*

"Only someone from outside Melange—someone from a more highly developed parallel world—would know anything about gold mines and emerald beds," he muttered. "The geology is very much the same from world to world—and an outsider could dig into the Kimberley Hills or the Sutter's Mill area and be dead sure of a strike. Which means Krupkin is an outsider—like me. And not only that—" Lafayette sat bolt upright. "He *knows I'm* an outsider! Which means he knew me before, which means he's who he looks like: Goruble, ex-king of Artesia! Which means he has a method of shifting from here to there, and maybe he can get me back to Artesia, and—"

Lafayette was out of bed, standing in the middle of the room. He groped, found a lamp, switched it on, went to the closet, extracted his clothes—including the innocent-looking blackout cloak—neatly cleaned and pressed.

"But why is he interested in Lady Andragorre?" he ruminated as he dressed quickly. "And Swinehild? But—of course! Being who he is, he realizes that Swinehild is the double of Princess Adoranne, and that Lady Andragorre is Daphne's twin . . . "

"Never mind that right now," he advised himself crisply. "Your first move is to get Daph—that is, Lady Andragorre—out of his clutches. And Swinehild too, of course. Then, when they're safely tucked away, you can talk from a position of strength, make some kind of deal to get home in return for not turning him into Central.

"Right," he agreed with himself. "Now, which way to the tower?" He went to the window, pulled aside the hangings, looked out at deep twilight, against which the minarets of the Glass Tree glittered like spires of varicolored ice. He visually traced the interconnecting walls and walkways and airy bridges linking the keep in which he found himself with the tall tower. "If I can just keep my sense of direction . . . "

Silently he let himself from the room. A lone guard under a light at the far end of the passage failed to look around as he eased off along the deep-carpeted hall.

Three times in the next half-hour O'Leary reached a dead end, was forced to turn back and find another route. But at last he gained the circular stair down which the guards had dragged him some hours earlier, on the way to the dungeons. On the landing above, he could see an armed guard in scarlet and white, yawning at his post. O'Leary went up silently, invisible inside his cloak, carefully cracked the man over the head, and laid him out on the floor. He tried the door. It was locked. He tapped.

"Lady Andragorre! Open up! I'm a friend! I came to help you escape!"

There was no answer, no sound from inside. He checked the guard, found a ring of keys, tried four before finding the correct one. The doors swung in on a dark, untenanted room.

"Daphne?" he called softly. He checked the bathroom, the closet, the adjacent sitting room.

"It figures," he said. "Krupkin/Goruble said she was gone. But where could she have gotten to?"

He stepped out onto the balcony. The Mark IV was missing from the spot where he had left it propped against the wall. He groaned.

"Why didn't I hide it? But no, I was so loaded with gadgets and confidence, I thought I'd be back in ten minutes with Daphne, and off we'd go. So now I'm stuck—even if I found her, there'd be no way out." Lafayette left the room, closed the door behind him. The guard was just coming to, mumbling to himself. As Lafayette stepped over him, he caught the blurred words.

" . . . not my fault, Sarge, I mean, how could anybody get loose outa a room at the top of a tower with only one way down, except if they jumped? And there ain't no remains in the courtyard down below, so my theory is the dame was never here in the first place . . . "

"Huh?" O'Leary said. "That's a good point. How could she have gotten away? Unless she took the Mark IV. But that's impossible. It's just an ordinary rug to anybody but me."

"Hey." The guard was sitting up, feeling of the back of his head. "I need a long furlough. First, I got these fainting spells, and now I hear voices . . . "

"Nonsense," O'Leary snapped. "You don't hear a thing."

"Oh. Well, that's a relief." The guard slumped back against the wall. "For a minute there I was worried."

"There's nothing I can do for Lady Andragorre now," Lafayette told himself, keeping his thought subvocal now. "But—good night, I've been forgetting all about Swinehild, poor kid, all alone down there in the dark . . . " He hurried down the stairs, headed for the dungeons.

The passage was dark, narrow, twisting and turning its way downward to keep within the narrow confines of the spire of rock from which it had been hollowed. Lafayette passed barred doors behind which forlorn-looking prisoners in grimy rags and lengthening beards slumped dejectedly on straw bunks. The meager light came from unshielded fifteen-watt bulbs set in sockets at intervals along the way. The doors in the final, deepest section of the subterranean installation were solid slabs secured by heavy hasps and massive, rusted locks.

"The solitary-confinement wing," Lafayette murmured. "Close to paydirt now. Let's see . . . it must have been about here . . . " He placed himself in the approximate spot at which he had emerged from the cell in which he had been confined with Lorenzo. As he studied the wall to orient himself—it wouldn't help to get the direction wrong again and wind up hanging in space, or back out in the courtyard—he heard stealthy footsteps approaching from around a curve above, down which he had just come. At once, he activated the flat-walker, waded forward into pitch darkness, switched back to natural density.

"Swinehild?" he called. "Swinehild?"

There was a soft clank and rasp of tumblers from behind him. A line of light appeared, widened. A male figure in a floppy hat with a broken, curling plume stood silhouetted there, holding a ring of keys in his hand.

"Lafayette!" an irritating voice hissed. "Are you here?"

"Lorenzo!" Lafayette said. "What are you doing here? I thought—"

"Well, so you did come back!" Lorenzo said in a relieved tone. "It's about time! This is the third time I've checked this pesthole! Let's go! This luck can't hold out forever!"

"I left you locked in; how did you get out?"

"Well—when I discovered you'd left without even saying good-bye, I knew there had to be a way—so I searched until I found the trapdoor in the ceiling. Since then I've had nothing but narrow escapes. Still, I suppose you were right about acting as if all this were real. At least it's more fun playing hide-and-seek around the palace with the guards than it was trying to sleep in here with the mice. Now, let's go—"

"Not without Lady A! She's disappeared—"

"I've got her. She's just outside the landing window, on your Mark IV. Nice little gadget, that. Lucky this is just a dream, or I'd never have believed it when you described it. Now, let's get moving!"

"Swell," Lafayette grumbled. "It was supposed to be tuned to my personal wavelength . . . "

"Keep it quiet! The guards are playing pinochle at the head of the stairs."

"Wait a minute!" Lafayette called urgently. "Give me those keys. I have another detail to attend to—"

"Are you kidding? I risk everything on the off-chance you came back to the cell for me—out of a misguided feeling that I couldn't take your Mark IV and go off and leave you stranded—and you start babbling about errands you have to do!" He tossed the keys. "Do as you like; I'm on my way!"

Lafayette botched the catch. By the time he had retrieved the ring and jumped after Lorenzo, the latter was already disappearing around the tight curve of the passage.

"Hold the carpet for me!" O'Leary hissed. Hastily he examined the doors, picked one, tried keys. The door opened. From the darkness came a growl like a grizzly bear. O'Leary slammed it hurriedly, an instant before a heavy body struck the panel. He tried the next door—opened it a crack.

"Swinehild?" he called. This time he was rewarded by a quick intake of breath and a glad cry. There was a rustling near at hand, a faint whiff of garlic, and a warm, firm body hurled itself against O'Leary.

"Lafe—I figgered you'd went off without me!" Soft-skinned, hard-muscled arms encircled his neck. Eager lips found his.

"Mmmmhhhnnnmmm," O'Leary tried to mumble, then discovered that the sensation of kissing Swinehild was not at all unpleasant—besides which, the poor girl's feelings would be hurt if he spurned her friendly advance, he reminded himself. He gave his attention to the matter for the next thirty seconds . . .

"But looky here, Lafe, we can't get involved in no serious spooning now," Swinehild said breathlessly, coming up for air. "Let's blow outa this place pronto. It reminds me o' home. Here, you hold the lunch. It's rubbing a blister on my chest."

He stuffed the greasy parcel in his side pocket, took her hand, led her on tiptoe along the upward-slanting passage. Suddenly, from ahead, there was a sharp outbreak of voices: a deep, rasping challenge, a sharp yelp which sounded like Lorenzo, a feminine scream.

"Come on!" Lafayette broke into a run, dashed on ahead. The sounds of scuffling, gasps, blows grew rapidly louder. He skidded around the final turn to see two large men grappling with his former cellmate, while a third held the Lady Andragorre in a secure grip with one arm around her slender waist. At that moment one of the men kicked Lorenzo's feet from under him, threw him on his face, planted a foot on his back to hold him down. The man holding the girl saw O'Leary, goggled, opened his mouth—

Lafayette whipped the cloak around himself, took two quick steps forward, delivered a devastating punch to the solar plexus of the nearest guard, swung a hearty kick with his sharp-toed boot to the calf of the next. Dodging both victims' wild swings, he sprang to the Lady Andragorre's side and drove a knuckle blow to her captor's left kidney, grabbed her hand as the man yelled and released his grip.

"Don't be afraid! I'm on your side!" he hissed in her ear, and towed her quickly past the two whooping and cursing men. One made a grab at her, was rewarded with a clean chop across the side of the jaw that sent him to his knees with glazed eyes. Swinehild appeared, stared with wide-open eyes at Lady Andragorre, past O'Leary at something behind him.

"Lafe," she breathed. "Where'd you get that hat?"

"Quick! Get Lady Andragorre onto the rug outside the window at the next landing down," Lafayette barked, and thrust the girl forward.

"Gee, Lafe, I never knew you was a ventriloquist," Swinehild blurted as he turned back to see Lorenzo, just coming to all fours, his plumed cap awry, one eye black, a smear of blood under his nose. Lafayette hauled the dazed man to his feet, sent him staggering after the women.

"I'll hold these clowns off until you're aboard," he barked. "Make it fast!" He stepped forward to intercept one of the redcoats as he lunged after Lorenzo, tripped him, gave a side-handed chop to another, then whirled, raced down the passage after the others.

Swinehild's face was visible in the window ahead as she tugged at the still-dazed Lorenzo's hand.

"Who're you?" he said blurrily. "Aspira Fondell, the Music Hall Queen? Bu' I don' love you. I love Bev—I mean Lady Andragorre—or do I mean Beverly?"

"Sure, she's already aboard," Swinehild gasped. "Come on!" She hauled backward, and Lorenzo disappeared through the window with a wild leap. Muffled cries came from the darkness as Lafayette reached the open sash. Six feet away, the Mark IV carpet sagged in the air, sinking under the weight of the three figures huddled on it.

"She's overloaded." Swinehild's voice seemed thin and far away. "I guess we got one too many, Lafe—so—so—I guess I won't be seeing you no more. Good-bye—and thanks for everything . . . " Before Lafayette's horrified gaze, she slipped over the side and dropped into the darkness below, while the carpet, quickly righting itself, slid away into the night.

"On, no!" Lafayette prayed. "She won't be killed—she'll land on a balcony just below here!" He thrust his head out the window. In the deep gloom he barely made out a slim figure clinging to a straggly bush growing from the solid rock fifteen feet below.

"Swinehild! Hang on!" He threw a leg over the sill, scrambled quickly down the uneven rock face, reached the girl, caught her wrist, tugged her upward to a narrow foothold beside him.

"You little idiot!" he panted. "Why in the world did you do that?"

"Lafe . . . you . . . you come back for me," she quavered, her pale face smiling wanly up at him. "But . . . but that means her Ladyship is all alone . . . "

"Lorenzo's with her, blast him," Lafayette reassured her, aware suddenly of his precarious position, of the cold wind whipping at him out of the surrounding night.

"Lorenzo? Who's he?"

"The clown in the floppy hat. He has some fantastic notion that the Lady Andragorre is his girl friend, some creature named Beverly. He's probably bound for that love-nest he was on his way to when Krupkin's men grabbed him."

"Gee, Lafe—I'm getting kind of mixed up. Things have been happening too fast for me. I guess I wasn't cut out for a life in the big time."

"Me too," Lafayette said, looking up at the glassy wall above, then at the sheer drop below. He clutched his meager handholds tighter and squeezed his eyes shut.

"Which way do we go, Lafe?" Swinehild inquired. "Up or down?"

He tried a tentative move, slipped, grabbed, and clung, breathing shallowly so as not to disturb any boulders which might be delicately poised. The icy wind buffeted at him, whipped Swinehild's skirt against her legs.

"What we need," he said in a muffled voice, his face against the stone, "is a convenient door in the side of the mountain."

"How about that one over there?" Swinehild suggested as a tremor went through the rock under O'Leary.

"Where?" He moved his head cautiously, saw the small oak-plank door with heavy wrought-iron strap hinges set in a niche in the solid-rock wall ten feet to his left.

"We'll have to try," he gulped. "It's our only chance." He unclamped his aching fingers, edged a toe sideways, gained six inches. Five minutes of this painful progress gave him a grip on a tuft of weeds directly beside the door. He reached with infinite care, got his fingers on the latch.

"Hurry up, Lafe," Swinehild said calmly from behind him. "I'm slipping."

He tugged, lifted, pulled, twisted, pushed, rattled. The door was locked tight. He groaned.

"Why didn't I wish for an open door while I was at it?"

"Try knocking," Swinehild suggested in a strained voice.

Lafayette banged on the door with his fist, careless now of the pebbles dribbling away under his toe.

"No need to say good-bye again, I guess, Lafe," Swinehild said in a small voice. "I already done that. But it was sure nice knowing ya. You were the first fella that ever treated me like a lady . . . "

"Swinehild!" As her grip slipped, Lafayette lunged, caught her hand, clung. His own grip was crumbling—

There was a click and a creak from beside him; a draft of warm air flowed outward as the door swung in. A small, stocky figure stood there, hands on hips, frowning.

"Well, for Bloob's sake, come in!" Pinchcraft snapped. A calloused hand grabbed Lafayette, hauled him to safety; a moment later Swinehild tumbled in after him.

"H-h-how did you happen to be here?" O'Leary gasped, leaning against the chipped stone wall of the torchlit passage.

"I came with a crew to do a repossession." The Ajax tech chief bit the words off like hangnails. "The idea was to sneak up and grab before he knew what hit him."

"Sure glad you did, Cutie-pie," Swinehild said.

"Don't call me Cutie-pie, girl," Pinchcraft barked. He took out a large bandanna and mopped his forehead, then blew his nose. "I told Gronsnart he was an idiot to keep on making deliveries on an arrears account. But no: too greedy for a quick profit, that's the business office for you."

"You're taking over the Glass Tree?"

"This white brontosaur? Not until the last hope of payment has faded. I was after the last consignment of portable goods we were so naïve as to deliver."

"Well, I'm glad you came. Look, we have to grab Krupkin at once! He's not what he seems! I mean, he *is* what he seems! He recognized me, you see—which means he's actually ex-King Goruble and not his double, but he doesn't know I know that, of course, so—"

"Calmly, sir, calmly!" Pinchcraft cut into the spate of words. "I was too late! The check-kiting fast-shuffler and his private army have flown the coop! He packed up bag and baggage and left here minutes before I arrived!"

Eleven

"Late again," Lafayette groaned. He was sitting, head in hands, at a table in the glittering, deserted dining room of the glass palace. A few servants and guards had eyed the party uncertainly as they invaded the building, but the sudden absence of their master combined with the rugged appearance of the repossession squad had discouraged interference. The well-equipped kitchens had been deserted by the cooks, but Swinehild had quickly rustled up ham and eggs and coffee. Now Pinchcraft's group sat around the table morosely, looking at the furniture and décor and mentally tallying up the probable loss on the job.

The Ajax representative said petulantly, "What about me? For the past three years this swindling confidence man who called himself Krupkin has been gathering resources—largely at the expense of Ajax—for some grandiose scheme. Now, abruptly, he decamps minutes before my arrival, abandoning all this!" Pinchcraft waved a hand to take in the installment-plan luxury all around them. "*Now* who's going to pay the bills?"

"Why did he suddenly abandon his plans?" Lafayette inquired. "Could he have been afraid of me—afraid I'd tip Central off to his takeover bid?"

Pinchcraft was frowning in deep puzzlement. "Are you saying, lad, that you know about Central? But that's—that's the second most closely guarded secret of the Ajax Specialty Works!"

"Sure—I'm a sort of parttime Central agent myself," Lafayette said. "But Goruble knew me; and that must be why he packed up and left in the middle of the night—after first bundling me off to bed to get me out of the way. He was afraid I'd recognize him; but I was so dopey with lack of sleep I didn't know what I was doing. By the time I realized—it was too late." He sat down heavily and groaned again. "If I'd just gone straight to his apartment, instead of wasting time trying to find Lady Andragorre, I'd be back home by now."

"Don't take it too hard, Lafe," Swinehild said. "You done your best."

"Not yet, I haven't!" Lafayette smacked a fist into his palm. "Maybe I can still get ahead of him. He doesn't know I know what I know—not that I know much. But I still have an ace or two: Goruble doesn't know I know who and what he is. And he doesn't know I have a line of credit with Ajax!"

"Who says you have a line of credit with Ajax?" Pinch-craft cut in.

"Well—under the circumstances—since you and I are interested in the same thing: laying Krupkin/Goruble by the heels . . ."

"Well—all right," Pinchcraft muttered. "Within limits. What do you have in mind?"

"I need to get back to Port Miasma and tip Rodolpho off. Maybe between us we can throw a stillson wrench into Goruble's plans. How about it, Pinchcraft? Will you help me?"

"I suppose it can be arranged—but you already owe us for a number of items—"

"We'll settle all that later. Let's get moving; it's a long walk, and time's of the essence and all that."

"I suppose I can crowd you into the tunnel car we came in," Pinchcraft said reluctantly. "Even though it's supposed to be for official use only."

"Tunnel car? You mean there's a tunnel all the way from here to the Ajax plant?"

"Certainly. I told you I never trusted this fellow—"

"Then why," Lafayette demanded, "was I sent out here on that flimsy little Mark IV carpet? I could have broken my neck!"

"All's well that ends well," Pinchcraft pointed out. "I needed a diversion to cover my repossession. And when would I ever have a better chance to field-test the equipment? Let's go, men. The night's work's not over yet!"

It was a fast, noisy, dusty ride in a child-sized subway train that hurtled along the tracks laid through the twisting series of caverns underlying the miles of desert over which O'Leary had flitted so nervously the previous night. Swinehild cuddled next to him in the cramped seat and slept soundly until the car docked at their destination. She oohed and ahhed at the sights as they left the terminus and made their way through vast workshops, foundries, stamping plants, refineries, the odors and tumult of a busy underground manufacturing operation.

"I've always heard about elves toiling away under the mountain," Lafayette confided in his guide as they emerged into the comparative quiet of the admin level. "But I always pictured little fellows with beards pounding out gold arm rings at a hand forge."

"We modernized a while back," Sprawnroyal told him. "Production's up eight hundred percent in the last fiscal century alone."

In the retail-sales department, Swinehild watched in silence as a bustling crew of electronics men rolled out a small, dark-green carpet at Pinchcraft's instruction.

"This is our Mark XIII, the latest model," the production chief stated proudly. "Windscreen, air and music, safety belt, and hand-loomed deep pile as soft as goofer feathers."

"It's cute," Swinehild said, "But where do I sit?"

"You can't go," O'Leary said shortly. "Too dangerous."

"I am too going," she came back sharply. "Just try and stop me!"

"You think I'd risk your neck on this contraption? Out of the question!"

"You think I'm going to sit around this marble factory ducking my head under the ceiling while you go off and get yourself killed?"

"Not on your life, lady," Sprawnroyal said. "Fitz-bloomer, roll out a Mark XIII—a two-seater." He gave O'Leary a challenging look. "Anybody thinks I'm going to get myself saddled with the care and feeding of a broad two feet higher'n me's got wrong ideas."

"Well . . . in that case," O'Leary subsided.

It was the work of ten minutes to check circuits, carry the Mark XIII to a launching platform on the face of the cliff, and balance out the lift system for a smooth, level ride.

"Contraption, eh?" Pinchcraft snorted under his breath. "She'll handle like an ocean liner. Just hold her under sixty for the first few miles, until you get the feel of her."

"Sure," Lafayette said, tucking his fur-lined blackout cloak around him against the bitter night wind. Swinehild settled herself behind him, with her arms around his waist.

"Here we go," O'Leary said. There was the familiar lifting surge, a vertiginous moment as the rug oriented itself on the correct course line. Then the wind was whistling past their faces as the lights of the Ajax Specialty Works receded behind them.

"I hope you ain't mad at me for coming along," Swinehild whispered in Lafayette's rapidly numbing ear.

"No, not really," O'Leary called over his shoulder. "Just don't get in my way when the action starts to hot up. Krupkin beat it because he was afraid I'd realize who he was and unleash my psychic energies on him." He gave a humorless chuckle. "I recognized him, all right—but what he doesn't know is that I haven't got a psychic erg to my name anymore."

"You've got luck," Swinehild pointed out. "Like finding that door into the tunnel just when you did. That's just about as good, I guess."

"There's something strange about my luck," O'Leary said. "It's either unbelievably bad, or unbelievably good. Like finding that disguise in the park—and before that, in the boat, coming up with a knife just when I need it: sometimes it's almost as if my psychic energies were back at work. But then I try again, and draw a goose egg. It's very unsettling."

"Don't worry bout it, Lafe. Just take it as it comes. That's what I do—and somehow I always get by."

"That's all very well for you," O'Leary countered. "All you're interested in is getting to the big town and living high; as for me—there are times when I almost wish I was still back at Mrs. MacGlint's, with nothing to worry about but earning enough to keep me in sardines and taffy."

"Yeah—you got it rough, all right, Lafe, being a hero and everything."

"Hero? Me?" O'Leary laughed modestly. "Oh, I'm not really a hero," he assured his companion. "I mean, heroes love danger: they're always dashing around looking for adventure, and that sort of thing. Whereas all I want is peace and quiet."

"You could have peace and quiet easy enough, Lafe. Just turn this rug around and head for the south. I hear there's some nice islands down that way where we could build us a grass hut and live on coconuts and fresh fish—"

"Would that I could, Swinehild. But it's not that easy. First I have to deal with Krupkin/Goruble, the skunk! I just wish I could get my hands on him right now! I'd like to see the look on his face when I tell him I know who he is and what he's up to, and—"

The rug bumped, as if hitting an updraft.

"Look out!" Swinehild cried as something white loomed directly before them. Lafayette yelled a command to the Mark XIII—too late. The carpet banked sharply to the left, struck, plowed through a drift of snow as fine as confectioner's sugar, upended, and went cartwheeling downslope in a cloud of ice crystals. Lafayette was aware of Swinehild's arms clinging to him, of the safety belt cutting into his ribs, of flying snow slashing at him like a sand blaster . . .

With a final sickening drop, the rug came to rest half-buried in loose ice. Lafayette struggled upright, saw moving lights, blurred figures, heard gruff voices, the stamp of hooves . . .

"It's *you*," a familiar voice blurted. "How—what—when—but most of all, *why*? I left you snoozing soundly in sybaritic luxury. What are you doing out here in the snow?"

O'Leary blinked away the slush from his eyelashes, gazed blearily up at the anxious visage of Goruble/Krupkin. Behind him, uniformed men stood gaping.

"Thought you'd steal a march, eh?" Lafayette said brokenly. "Well, you won't get away with it, your Former Majesty. I know you—and I know what you're planning . . . " He tugged at the rug, which had somehow wrapped itself around him, but he was bound as tightly as if by ropes.

"S-see here, my boy," Goruble stammered, waving his men back. "Can't we work something out? I mean, you have your cushy spot, why begrudge me mine? It's not easy, you know, having been a king, to revert to mere commonerhood. Why not take the charitable view? With your help, I can be back on the Artesian throne in a lightning coup, after which you'll have your pick of the spoils—or better yet, I'll give you all of Melange, to do with as you will—"

"Forget it," O'Leary said, surreptitiously striving to free an arm. "I have everything I want, back in Artesia. Why would I want to help you?"

"But here you can be absolute owner of everything—the real estate, wildlife, natural resources . . . women . . ."

"Stay in Melange? Are you crazy? I can't wait to get home. I've had nothing but misery since I got here!"

Goruble opened his mouth to speak, hesitated, looked suddenly thoughtful.

"In that case," he asked carefully, "why haven't you done something about it?"

"Well—"

"You were, as I recall, in rather difficult straits when my chaps first apprehended you. And now—well, from the mode of your arrival, it appears that you are perhaps somewhat less than master of your fate." The ex-king rubbed his chin. "You *are* Lafayette O'Leary—I saw your ring. Only *you* wear the ax and dragon. But . . . can it be, dear lad"—his voice took on a purr like a tiger about to dine—"that you have in some way lost your valuable ability to manipulate the probabilities at will? Eh?"

"Of course not. I . . . I was just wishing I could have a chat with you, and . . . and here I am."

"Yes—with a mouthful of snow and a number of new contusions that are already beginning to swell, no doubt.

Very well, Sir Lafayette: before we discuss matters further, just demonstrate your puissance by, oh, summoning up a cozy little tent, say, complete with camp stove and liquor cabinet, in which we can complete our negotiation."

"Phooey," Lafayette said weakly. "I wouldn't waste my time."

"Something simpler, then: what about a small, cheery blaze in the shelter of the rocks, there . . . " Goruble waved a hand at the curtain of falling snow.

"Why bother?" O'Leary gulped. "Why don't you just surrender, and I'll put in a good word for you with Mr. Pratwick . . . "

"Admit it!" Goruble leaned close to hiss the words. "You're impotent to interfere! You're as helpless as the clod you appear to be!"

"I am not," Lafayette said desperately. "I have all kinds of resources at my disposal!"

"Then let's see you get yourself extricated from that piece of rug you seem to be ensnarled in."

Lafayette pulled, twisted, wrenched; but it was no use. He was wrapped as tightly as a caterpillar in a cocoon. Goruble laughed happily.

"Capital! Oh, capital! I've had a nervous night for nothing! I don't know how it is you happen to have stumbled on my little base of operations here, Sir Lafayette, but there's no harm done after all. In fact . . . " He sobered suddenly, nodding. "I can see that a whole new dimension might be added to my plans, so to speak. Yes, why not? With the new data this development places at my disposal, why stop with Melange? Why not move on—expand my empire to encompass a whole matched set of worlds, eh? In the meantime—where's the elusive doxy you stole from me?"

"Where you'll never find her," Lafayette said.

"Reticent eh? Well, we'll soon correct that. Oh, we'll have long talks, my lad. My liegeman, Duke Rodolpho, retains a skilled interrogator in his employ, one Groanwelt by name, who'll soon wring your secrets from you!" Goruble whirled, bawled orders; red-coated men with ice in their eyelashes leaped forward to lift Lafayette to his feet, peel the frozen rug away—

"Hey—a dame!" a man blurted as Swinehild appeared from the folds of the Mark XIII, dazed and shivering.

Goruble laughed merrily. "My luck has turned at last!" he cried. "The fates smile on my enterprise! I take this as a sign—a sign, do you hear?" He looked on, beaming as the grinning men pulled the girl to her feet, keeping a stout grip on her arms. For the moment, the carpet lay in an unattended heap. Lafayette made a sudden lunge for it, but was quickly grabbed, but with a final surge, he managed to plant a foot on the snow-covered nap.

"Go home!" He addressed the yell to the receiver's verbal input circuitry. "Top speed and no detours!"

In response the carpet flopped, sending up a spray of ice crystals, leaped six feet into the air, hung for a moment rippling, then, as one of the men made a belated grab, shot away into the gathering storm.

" 'Tis enchanted, by crikey!" a man yelled, recoiling.

"Nonsense," Goruble snapped. "It's undoubtedly another gadget from Ajax. So you're working with those sharpies, eh, Sir Lafayette? But no matter: I have my plans for them, as well as the rest of this benighted land!"

"You've sprung your seams," Lafayette snapped. "Your last takeover bid flopped, and so will this one."

"Truss them and hoist them on horseback," Goruble commanded the captain of his guard. "We'll see what a night in the cold followed by a day on the rack does for this upstart's manners."

"Well, back again, hey, pal?" Rodolpho's physical-persuasion specialist greeted O'Leary cheerfully as four guards dumped him, more dead than alive, on a wooden bench near the fireplace in which half a dozen sets of tongs and pincers were glowing a cozy cherry red.

"Mnnnrrgghhh," O'Leary mumbled through stiff lips, crouching nearer the blaze. "Just give me heat, even if it's my own feet burning."

"Anything to oblige, chum. Now, lessee, where were we?" Groanwelt rubbed a hand over his bristled chin with a sound like tearing canvas. "We could start out wit' a little iron work, like you suggested, then move on to a few strokes o' the cat, just to get the old circulation going good, and wind up the session wit' a good stretch on the rack to take the kinks out. How's it sound?"

"A well-balanced program, no doubt," Lafayette mumbled. "Could you stoke up this fire a little first?"

"That's the spirit, kid. Say, on the other hand, maybe you'd like to try the new equipment I just got in since you was here: a swell hydraulic-type joint press, roller bearings throughout. A versatile outfit: handles everything from hip sockets to knuckles. But maybe we better save that and the automatic skinning machine for last; they're kind of permanent, if you know what I mean. We don't want you graduating on us before we get the dope, which the duke wants it pretty bad."

"It's not the duke, it's that sneaky little Krupkin who thinks I'm going to spill a lot of secrets," Lafayette corrected the P.P.S. "Listen, Groanwelt, as a loyal Melanger, you should be fighting Krupkin, not helping him. His scheme is to take over the whole country and use it as a base of operations to launch an attack on Artesia!"

"Politics," Groanwelt said apologetically, "was never a big hobby wit' me. I mean, administrations come and go, but the need for a skilled specialist remains constant—"

"Don't you have any patriotism?" O'Leary challenged. "This man's a maniac! He'll loot Melange of everything useful: food, weapons, raw materials—and—"

"Sure, fella. But look, OK if we get started? You can talk while I work. How's about getting the shirt off and stepping over here so's I can buckle you up in working position?"

"C-couldn't I just toast my toes for a few minutes longer?"

"Good notion. I'll help you off wit' the boots, and we'll strap the ankles up nice to hold 'em in optimum position. Too close, and you get a lot o' smoke; too far, and you don't get the full effect, like—"

"On second thought, why don't I tell you whatever you want to know right now, and save you all that effort?" O'Leary suggested hurriedly. "Where shall I start? With my arrival on top of the windmill, two weeks ago? Or was it three? Or should I go farther back, to when I had everything in the world a sane man could want, and it wasn't enough? Or—"

"Hey, hey, hold on, pal!" Groanwelt lowered his voice, looking around nervously. "What you trying to do, put me out o' business?"

"Not at all, but it just happens I'm in a talkative mood this evening—"

"It's morning. Geeze, kid, you're out o' touch."

"Yes, morning, evening, it doesn't matter, I love to talk night and day. Now, as I was saying—"

"Shhhh!" The P.P.S. laid a thick finger across his pooched-out lips. "Have a heart! You want to lose me the best post on the ducal staff? You go blowing your gaff wit'out me even laying a iron to you, and somebody's going to start getting ideas about redundant personnel. At my age, I can't take no RIF, kid. So be a sweet guy and button it up, hah?"

"I . . . I'll tell you what," Lafayette proposed, eyeing the smoking forceps in the technician's hairy fist. "You hold off with the irons for a few minutes—just until I do a few yoga exercises to heighten my appreciation of your virtuosity—and I'll try to bottle up the speech I want to make."

"Say, that's white o' you, neighbor!"

"Think nothing of it, Groanwelt. Glad to be helpful. By the way, do you have any idea what became of the young lady who arrived when I did?"

"Oh, her? Yeah. Say, cleaned up, she wouldn't be a bad-looking little piece, you know? I think I seen the boys handing her over to the housekeeper. Seems like your pal Prince Krupkin's got some kind o' special plans for her." Groanwelt winked.

"The rat," Lafayette snarled between his teeth. "Groanwelt, you seem like a decent sort of chap: are you going to sit quietly by while that unprincipled crook carries out his plans right over your head, without a word?"

The P.P.S. sighed. "Yeah, I know, the idealism o' yout'. You young guys think you can cure the world o' its ills. But as you get a little older, you find out it ain't so easy. Me, I've settled for the pride o' craftsmanship: the integrity o' the skilled technician. I give every job the best that's in me, no shoddy work to have to be ashamed of later. I mean, when people are looking at a project o' mine, I want to be able to hold my head up, right? Speaking o' which, maybe we better start in; old Rodolpho's likely to show up any minute to check on progress—"

"He just did," a cold voice spoke up. The P.P.S. whirled to see Duke Rodolpho glowering at him from the doorway.

"Geeze!" he exclaimed. "I sure wish you wouldn't come pussyfooting up on a guy that way, y'er Grace! You give me such a start, I ain't sure I can go on wit' my work." He held up his hands, studying them for tremors.

"Never mind that," Rodolpho snapped. "You're about to be honored by a visit from his Highness. Now tighten up here and try to make a good impression . . . " The duke turned as bustlings sounded from the corridor behind him.

"Ah, right this way, my dear prince," he said through a forced smile. "A modest installation, but fully equipped—"

"Yes, yes, I'm sure," Krupkin cut him off, sauntering into view attended by a pair of lackeys who seemed to be trying to shine his shoes at full gallop. His sharp eyes swept the chamber, fell on Lafayette. He grunted.

"Leave us, Rudy," he ordered offhandedly. "And take these pests with you," he added, kicking at the fellow attempting to adjust the hang of his robes. "You stay," he addressed Groanwelt.

"But I haven't had a chance to show you the newly equipped forcing vats yet—" Rodolpho protested.

"You have our leave to withdraw!" Krupkin/Goruble barked. As the rest of the party hastily evacuated the room, the prince came over to O'Leary, who rose to face him. The ex-king looked him up and down, glanced at the ring on his finger. He hooked his thumbs in the broad, bejeweled belt encircling his middle and thrust out his lower lip.

"All right, Sir Lafayette," he said in a tone inaudible to the P.P.S., who hovered uncomfortably in the background, polishing an iron boot. "Last chance. Your value to me, minus your former abilities, is small, but still, your cooperation might smooth my path a trifle. I've spent the last few hours reviewing my plans, and have realized that I've been thinking too small. Conquer Melange, indeed! As you pointed out, the place is a pesthole. But new vistas have opened themselves. Your presence here shows me the way. It was your meddling that lost me my throne in Artesia. Now you'll help me recover it."

"Don't talk like a boob," O'Leary said tiredly. "After what you tried to do to Adoranne, the people would throw stones at you if you ever showed your face in Artesia, even if you could get back there, which I doubt."

Goruble poked O'Leary's chest. "Cast aside your doubts, Sir Lafayette! That part is simplicity itself. Less than an hour ago I dispatched a set of specifications to our mutual friends at the Ajax Specialty Works, and expect delivery of a functioning Traveler in a matter of days."

"You're going to be disappointed. Your credit's shot. They won't deliver."

"Indeed?" Goruble/Krupkin purred, fingering a large jewel pinned to his collar. "I have reason to expect the early acquisition of new resources, courtesy of my good friend Duke Rodolpho. As for the possible animosity of the Artesians—I feel sure it will dissipate as the morning mist before a public declaration by Princess Adoranne that the previous canards spread regarding me were a tissue of lies homologated by enemies of the state; that I am in fact her sole benefactor, and that she wishes to relinquish the crown to me as an older and wiser monarch, solely out of her selfless concern for the well-being of the state."

"She'll never do it," O'Leary declared flatly.

"Perhaps not," Goruble said calmly, nodding. He poked O'Leary again, as one imparting the punch line of a joke. "But the wench Swinehild will."

"What's Swinehild got to do with it . . . " O'Leary's voice trailed off. "You mean—you intend to use her to impersonate Adoranne?" He smiled pityingly. "Wake up, Goruble; Swinehild's a nice kid, but she'd never fool anyone."

Goruble turned, barked an order at Groanwelt. The P.P.S. went to the door, thrust his head out, passed on the command. There was a stir of feet. Groanwelt stepped back, gaping, then executed a sweeping bow as a slim, dainty figure entered the room hesitantly. Lafayette stared openmouthed at the vision of feminine enchantment who stood there, gowned, jeweled, perfumed, elegant, her golden hair a gleaming aura about her perfect face.

"P-Princess Adoranne!" he gulped. "Wha—how—"

"Lafe! Are you O.K., sugar?" Swinehild's familiar voice inquired worriedly.

"I confess we need to do a little work on her diction before she makes her public appearance," Goruble said blandly. "But that's a mere detail."

"Swinehild—you wouldn't help this fiend with his dirty schemes—would you?" O'Leary implored.

"He . . . he said if I didn't—he'd slice you up into sandwich meat, Lafe—so—"

"Enough! Take her away!" Goruble roared, red-faced. He whirled on O'Leary as Groanwelt bowed Swinehild out.

"The doxy is merely attempting to save face," he snarled. "She leaped at the chance to play princess, as well she might, kitchen slavey that she is! To sleep on silken sheets, dine from dishes of gold—"

"And what about the real Adoranne?"

"There appears to be a certain symmetry in these matters of intercontinual transfer," Goruble said with a foxy smile. "The former princess will find herself here in Melange in the role of scullery wench, a fitting comeuppance in return for her arrogant assumption of my throne." Goruble rubbed his hands together. "Yes, you opened new vistas, lad, once I realized you were who you are. My original plan in decoying the Lady Andragorre into my hands was designed merely to place me in an advantageous position, trump-wise, vis-à-vis Rodolpho, who'd been recalcitrant in seeing the wisdom of my plans. But now wide vistas open. She'll be a useful pawn in the vast new game I'll play, as will the feckless Rodolpho, lending their countenances to my pronouncements. And you, too, have your little role to perform." His face hardened. "Assist me—willingly—and you'll retain your comfortable Artesian sinecure as palace hanger-on. Refuse, and I'll arrange a fate for you to make strong men shudder!"

"You've lost what wits you ever had if you think I'd help you with your miserable plot!"

"So? A pity. I had in mind that after their usefulness to me had ended, I might hand the females along to you to use as you will. But in your absence, alas, I fear they'll end up in the harem of some more devoted servant."

"You wouldn't!"

"Oh, but I would." Goruble wagged a finger. "That's the true secret of success, my boy: total ruthlessness. I've learned my lesson now. Had I disposed of the infant Princess Adoranne in the beginning—and of a certain infant Prince Lafayette as well—none of this unfortunate business would have occurred."

"I won't help you," Lafayette gulped. "Do you worst. Central will catch up with you and—"

Goruble laughed. "That's the true beauty of the plan, my dear boy! I admit that for long the threat of Central's meddling inhibited the free play of my imagination—but the new equation of power renders that prospect nugatory. The reciprocal transfer of personnel will maintain the net energy equations; there will be no imbalance in the probability matrix, nothing to attract Central's attention to peaceful Artesia, one locus among a myriad. No, look for no assistance from that direction. As a former inspector of continua, please be assured that I know whereof I speak. Now, be sensible: throw in with me, and share in the rewards of success."

"Go hang yourself," O'Leary suggested sharply. "Without me, Swinehild will never cooperate—and without her, the whole thing flops."

"As you will." Goruble smiled a crafty smile. "My offer to you was based on sentiment, my lad, nothing more. I have more than one string to my bow—or should I say more than one beau to my string?"

"You're bluffing," Lafayette said. "You talk about using Lady Andragorre to impersonate Daphne—but I happen to know she got away clean!"

"Did she?" Goruble yawned comfortably, turned to Groanwelt. "By the way, my man," he said. "It won't be necessary to extract the whereabouts of the Lady Andragorre from this treacher. She and her companion were nabbed half an hour ago, and will be arriving within minutes. Just throw him in the pit with Gorog the Voracious, who I'm informed hasn't been fed for several days, and will appreciate a good meal."

"The breaks of the game, buddy," Groanwelt said sorrowfully as he led Lafayette, chains clanking, along the dim passage. "I got enemies around this place, that's plain to see. Me, a inoffensive guy that never stepped on a toe in his life except in line o' duty. But that goes to show you what years o' faithful service do for a guy." He peered through the inch-thick bars of a vast, barred door. "Good; he's in his den, sleeping. I won't have to use the electric prod to keep him back while I slip you in. I hate to be cruel to dumb beasts, you know?"

"Listen, Groanwelt," Lafayette said hastily, recoiling from the dank odor and the bone-littered straw of the monster's cage. "In view of our long-standing relationship, couldn't you see your way clear to just slip me out the back way? I mean, the duke need never know—"

"And leave Gorog to miss another meal? I'm ashamed o' you, pal. The suggestion does youse no credit."

The P.P.S. unlocked the door, swung it open just far enough to admit O'Leary, whom he helped forward with a hand like a winepress clamped to his shoulder. Lafayette dug in his heels, but Groanwelt's thrust propelled him into the noisome cage and the door clanged behind him.

"So long, kid," the P.P.S. said, resecuring the lock. "You would have been a swell client. Too bad I never really got to the nitty wit' you." As his footsteps died away, a low, rumbling growl sounded from the dark opening cut in the side wall of the den. Lafayette whirled to face the mouth of the lair, a ragged arch wide enough to pass a full-grown tiger. A pair of bleary, reddish eyes glinted from the deep gloom there. A head thrust forth—not the fanged visage of a cat or a bear, but a low-browed, tangle-haired subhuman face, smeared with dirt and matted with black stubble. The low, rumbling growl sounded again.

"Excuse me," a hoarse, bass voice said. "I ain't eaten in so long my insides is starting to chew on theirselfs."

O'Leary backed. The head advanced, followed by massive shoulders, a barrellike torso. The huge creature stood, dusted off its knees, eyeing Lafayette speculatively.

"Hey," the deep voice rumbled. "I know you! You're the guy was with the cute little trick that laid me out with a oar!"

"Crunch!" Lafayette gasped. "How—how did you get here? I thought this was the den of Gorog the Voracious . . ."

"Yeah, that's the name I usta fight under. The duke's boys picked me up on a bum rap when I come looking for ya. I cleaned up a couple blocks o' city street with the slobs, but after a while I got tired and they felled me with a sneak attack from bot' flanks at oncet, plus they dropped a cannonball on my dome." The giant fingered the back of his massive skull tenderly.

"L-looking for me?" O'Leary was backed against the wall; his breath seemed to be constricted by a bowling ball that had dropped into his throat. "W-whatever for?"

"I got a little score to settle with you, chum. And I ain't a guy to leave no unfinished business laying around."

"Look here, Crunch, I'm the sole support of twin maiden aunts," O'Leary stated in a voice with a regrettable tendency to break into a falsetto. "And after all I've been through, it wouldn't be fair for it all to end here, like this!"

"End? Heck, bub, this is just the beginning," Crunch growled. "A score like I got with you'll take a while to pay off."

"What did I do to deserve this?" O'Leary groaned.

"It ain't what you done, sport, it's what you didn't do."

"Didn't do?"

"Yeah. You didn't put me over the side o' the boat when you had the chanct. I was groggy but still listening; I heard the little dolly make the suggestion, which you nixed it on account of you didn't think it was cricket to toss a unconscious guy to the sharks."

"So this is my r-reward?"

"Right, palsy." The giant put a hand to his midriff as his stomach emitted another volcanic growl. "Boy, I ain't had a good feed in a bear's age."

Lafayette squeezed his eyes shut. "All right," he gasped. "Hurry up and get it over with before I lose my nerve and start yelling to Groanwelt that I've changed my mind . . . "

"Get what over with, feller?"

"E-eating me." Lafayette managed to force the words out.

"Me—eat you?" Crunch echoed. "Hey, you got me wrong, pal. I wouldn't eat no guy which he saved my neck like you done."

O'Leary opened one eye. "You mean—you're not going to tear me limb from limb?"

"Why would I wanta do a thing like that?"

"Never mind," Lafayette said, sinking down to the floor with a deep sigh of relief. "Some subjects are better left uninvestigated." He drew a deep breath and pulled himself together, looked up at the tall figure peering down at him concernedly.

"Look—if you want to do me a favor, let's start by figuring out a way out of here."

Crunch scratched at his scalp with a forefinger the size of a hammer handle.

"Well, lessee . . . "

"We might try to tunnel through the wall," O'Leary said, poking at the mortar between the massive stone blocks. "But that would take steel tools and several years." He scanned the dark interior of the cell. "There might be a trapdoor in the ceiling . . . "

Crunch shook his head. "I been ducked under that ceiling for a week. It's solid oak, four inches thick."

"Well . . . maybe the floor . . . "

"Solid rock, six inches thick."

Lafayette spent ten minutes examining floor, walls, and door. He leaned disconsolately against the bars. "I may as well admit it," he said. "I'm licked. Krupkin will force Swinehild to do his bidding, Adoranne will wind up scraping grease off pots here in Port Miasma, Goruble will take over Artesia, and Daphne—Daphne will probably be dumped here when Lady Andragorre goes to Artesia, and if Rodolpho doesn't get her, Lorenzo the Lucky—or is it Lancelot the Lanky?—will."

"Hey—I got a idear," Crunch said.

"Just lie down and take a nap, Crunch," O'Leary said listlessly. "There's nothing else to do."

"Yeah, but—"

"It's just self-torture to go on thinking about it. Maybe the best bet would be for you to disassemble me after all."

"Hey, how's about if—"

"I should have known it would end up here. After all, I've been bouncing in and out of jails ever since I got to Melange; it was inevitable that I'd end in one eventually."

"I mean, it ain't a fancy scheme, but what the heck," Crunch said.

"What scheme?" O'Leary inquired dully.

"What I was trying to tell you. My plan."

"All right. Tell me."

"Well, what I was thinking—but naw, I guess you want something with a little more class—like with secret tunnels and all."

"You may as well get it off your chest, Crunch."

"Well, I'm just spitballing, mind youse—but, ah, how's about if I rip the door off its hinges?"

"If you ri—" Lafayette turned to gaze at the massive welded-steel construction. He laughed hollowly.

"Sure, go ahead."

"O.K." Crunch stepped past him, gripped the thick bars. He set his size seventeens, took a deep breath, and heaved. There was a tentative screech of metal, followed by sharp snapping sounds. A lump of stone popped from the wall and dropped to the floor. With a rending sound comparable to that which might be produced by two Rolls-Royces sideswiping each other, the grating buckled, bent inward, and tore free of its mountings. Crunch tossed it aside with a deafening crash and wiped his palms on the seat of his leather pants.

"Nothing to it, chum," he said. "What's next?"

There was no one in the torture chamber when Lafayette, freed of his manacles by a deft twist of Crunch's wrists, and his large companion made their way there along the torchlit passage, past cells through the barred doors of which wild-haired and wild-eyed inmates gaped, gibbered, or grabbed.

"That's bad," Lafayette said. "I was counting on Groanwelt helping us."

"Hey, this is kinda cute," Crunch said, hefting a set of razor-edged cutters designed for trimming up ears and noses. "I been needing some cuticle scissors."

"Listen, Crunch, we need a plan of action," O'Leary said. "It won't do us any good to just go blundering out of here and wind up back in chains. The palace is swarming with guards, Rodolpho's regular staff plus Goruble's strongarm squad. We need a diversion—something to distract attention while I sneak in and whisk Swinehild and Lady Andragorre out from under his nose."

"Hey!" a reedy voice yelled from a side passage. "I demand a lawyer! I want to see the American consul! I have a right to make a phone call!"

"That sounds like Lorenzo . . . "

Lafayette trotted along to the cell from which the shouts had come. A nattily Vandycked and moustached fellow with an Edgar Allan Poe haircut and a high, stiff collar by Hoover out of Napoleon was gripping the bars with well-manicured hands.

"You, there . . . " His voice trailed off. "Say, don't I know you?"

"Lorenzo?" Lafayette eyed the other. "Got caught after all, eh? The last I saw of you, you were leaving me in the lurch with a free run ahead, but of course you blew it. And where'd you get the beaver and the fancy outfit?"

"Don't babble," the prisoner snapped in the same annoying fashion Lafayette had listened to in the dark cell under the Glass Tree. "My name's Lafcadio, not that it's any of your business. Say, who are you, anyway? I'd swear we've met somewhere . . . "

"This is no time to play games," Lafayette snapped. "Crunch and I broke out. I'm going to make a try for the Lady Andragorre, but—"

"You mean Cynthia, I suppose. Are you in on this fantastic plot too? Well, you won't get away with it! And stay away from my fiancée—"

"I thought her name was Beverly. But let's skip that. If I get you out, will you help create a diversion to cover my movements?"

"Just get me out," the bearded inmate yelped. "We can talk about terms later."

"Crunch!" Lafayette called. "See to this door, will you?" He went on along the passage. Most of the prisoners slumped on their straw pallets, but a few watched him with alert eyes.

"Listen, men," he called. "We're breaking out! If I free you, will you promise to run amok in the corridors, attack the guards, smash things, yell, and generally commit a nuisance?"

"Hey—you're on, mister!"

"That's for me!"

"Count me in!"

"Swell." Lafayette hurried back to instruct Crunch. Moments later the giant was busily dismantling the cellblock. Bushy-bearded villains of all degrees of dishevelment crowded into the torture chamber. Lafayette caught a glimpse of Lorenzo, now minus his disguise. He pushed through to him.

"Listen, why don't you and I work together . . . " He paused, staring at his former roommate, who was staring back with a puzzled expression on his features—features which O'Leary was seeing clearly in an adequate light for the first time.

"Hey," Crunch boomed. "I thought you went thataway, palsy . . . " He broke off. "Uh . . . " He hesitated, looking from Lafayette to the other man. "Say, maybe I'm losing my bite—but which one o' youse birds is my pal which we just sprung out together?"

"I'm Lafayette," O'Leary spoke up. "This is Lorenzo—"

"Nonsense, my name is Lothario—and I never saw *this* pithecanthropus before in my life." He looked Crunch up and down.

"Why'n'cha say youse had a twin brother?" Crunch inquired.

"Twin brother?" both men said as one.

"Yeah. And listen, little chum: what was you doing dressed up in buckskins and knee boots? What are youse, a quick-change artist?"

Lafayette was staring at Lorenzo's—or Lothario's —clothing: a skin-tight doublet and hose, topped by a brocaded tailcoat and a ruffled shirt, all much the worse for wear.

"He doesn't look like me," he said indignantly. "Oh, there might be some superficial resemblance—but I don't have that feckless look, that irresponsible expression—"

"Me look like you?" the other was exclaiming. "You haven't known me long enough to be handing out insults. Now, where's the nearest imperial transfer booth? You can depend on it, I'm turning in a report to my PR rep that will clean out this whole nest of hebephrenics before you can say 'noblesse oblige!' "

"You there!" A shout cut through the hubbub. "Lafayette!" He turned. A man identical but for clothing to the one with whom he was conversing was pushing through the press toward him, waving his arm. Lafayette whirled. The man who had called himself Lothario was gone in the milling crowd.

"How did *you* get here?" Lorenzo was demanding as he came up. "I'm glad to see you got clear. Say, I never got a chance to thank you for saving me from Krupkin's men. Beverly told me what happened, poor kid. She was so confused by everything that she didn't even remember my name—"

"What *is* your name?" Lafayette cut in with a rising sense of imminent paranoia.

"Huh? Why, it's Lorenzo, of course!"

Lafayette stared at the face before him, noting the set of the blue eyes, the untamed lock of brownish-blond hair over the forehead, the well-shaped mouth marred by a certain petulance . . .

"What's . . . " He stopped to swallow. "What's your last name?"

"O'Leary, why?" Lorenzo said.

"Lorenzo O'Leary," Lafayette mumbled. "I should have known. If Adoranne and Daphne and Yokabump and Nicodaeus all had doubles here—why not me?"

Twelve

"Hey, chums!" Crunch's subcellar voice shattered the paralysis that gripped the two O'Learys. "It's time to blow, if we don't want to miss all the fun." Lafayette looked around, saw that the room was rapidly emptying as the shouting mob of released prisoners streamed away along the passage, brandishing rude implements pressed into service from the array racked around the walls.

"Look, Lorenzo—we can sort out who's who later," he said over the fading clamor. "Right now the important thing is to save poor Swinehild and the Lady Andragorre from Goruble—Krupkin, to you. He's hatched a mad plot to take over Artesia, and the lousy part of it is, it looks as though he may be able to do it. No wonder he didn't care much whether I helped him or not: He can ring you in for me and force Swinehild to cooperate, and—but never mind that. I'm going to try to reach Rodolpho's apartment and tell him what's going on. Maybe it's still not too late to nip the whole thing in the bud. Why don't you come with me? Maybe between the two of us, one will get through. I'll brief you on the way. How about it?"

"Well—since you seem to have some notion of what's going on in this cackle factory, I may as well—but keep your meat hooks off Beverly!"

"I thought her name was Cynthia," Lafayette muttered as they selected stout clubs from a handy club stand and set off behind Crunch in the wake of the mob. Ahead, startled yells and a rising roar of enthusiasm indicated first contact with the palace guard.

"Down here," Lafayette called, indicating a side passage. "We'll go around, try for the back stairs."

"Look here, where do you fit into all this?" Lorenzo panted as they raced along the winding corridor.

"I don't," Lafayette assured his double. "I was back in Artesia, minding my own business, when suddenly here I was in Melange. The next thing I knew, I was up to my neck in accusations—" He veered aside into a stairway leading up. "I guess that was your doing; they mistook me for you, apparently. You must have been pretty busy, judging from the way the cops jumped me."

"It looked like a fairly straightforward proposition," Lorenzo puffed, keeping pace as they bounded up the steps, Crunch slogging along in the rear. "Krupkin . . . offered me a free trip home . . . plus other inducements such as staying alive . . . if I'd carry out a mission for him. I was supposed to sneak myself into . . . this Lady

Andragorre's chamber . . . and set up a tryst. Well . . . I climbed a few walls . . . and paid a few bribes . . . I got in, all right. But then . . . I saw it was Beverly. We didn't have time to talk much . . . but I did slip her a note . . . proposing a rendezvous at the cottage—as Krupkin had planned. But from there on I intended to introduce . . . some changes . . . in the script . . . "

"He suckered you," Lafayette panted. "I don't know how he got you here . . . but I doubt if he had any intention . . . of sending you back to your United Colonies . . . "

They emerged from the stairhead into a wide corridor, from both ends of which sounds of mob violence rose.

"Let's see—I think it's that way," Lafayette pointed. As they sprang forward, there was a bellow from behind them. Crunch was rubbing his head and looking back down the stairway.

"Why, the lousy bums—" he roared, and dived back down the steps.

"Crunch!" Lafayette yelled, but the giant was gone. A moment later, a tremendous crash sounded from the stairwell, followed by sounds of hand-to-hand combat.

"Let's get out of here," Lorenzo proposed, and dashed for the grand staircase ahead. Lafayette followed. A guard in crimson popped into view above, brought up a blunderbuss to firing position—

"Don't shoot that thing, you idiot!" Lorenzo yelled. "You'll louse up the wallpaper!" While the confused sentry was still blinking, the two fugitives struck him amidships; as he went down, the piece discharged a load of birdshot into the floral-patterned ceiling.

"I *told* you not to spoil the wallpaper," Lorenzo said as he bounced the man's head on the floor and bounded on. They ascended another two flights, pelted along a carpeted passage happily deserted of guards, to the door Lafayette remembered from his last visit. The sounds of battle were faint here. They skidded to a halt, drew a few gulps of air.

"Now, let me do the talking, Lorenzo," Lafayette panted. "Rodolpho and I are old drinking buddies—"

A door twenty feet along the hall flew open; flanked by four burly crimson-uniformed men, the short, imperious figure of Krupkin/Goruble strutted forth, turned to speak back over his shoulder: "That's an order, not a suggestion, Rudy! Present yourself and your chief ministers in the Grand Ballroom in half an hour, prepared to rubber-stamp my mobilization, curfew, rationing, and martial-law proclamations, or find yourself dangling from your own castle walls!" The former usurper of Artesia twitched his ermine-edged robes into line and strode off along the passage, conveyed by his bodyguard.

"So much for Rodolpho's help," Lorenzo muttered. "Any other ideas?"

Lafayette frowned, nibbled his lip. "You know where this ballroom is?"

"Two flights up, on the south side."

"It would be; that's where the riot's centered, to judge from the sounds of shattering glass."

"So what?" Lorenzo inquired. "It sounds like a swell place to stay clear of. We can dodge around to Beverly's apartment and grab her off while the big shots are playing politics."

"I have reason to believe Daph—I mean Lady Andragorre will be in the ballroom, along with Swinehild. It's all part of Goruble's big plan. We have to stop him now, before things go any farther."

"How? There's just the two of us. What can we do against a whole palace of armed men?"

"I don't know—but we have to try! Come on! If we can't get through one way, we'll find another—and time's a-wasting!"

Twenty-five of the allotted thirty minutes had passed. Lafayette and Lorenzo crouched on the palace roof, thirty feet above the high windows of the ballroom two floors below. Already the murmur of nervous conversation rose to them from the chamber where great events were about to occur.

"All right," Lafayette said. "Who goes first, you or me?"

"We'll both be killed," Lorenzo said, peering over the parapet. "The cornice overhangs about three feet. It's impossible—"

"All right, I'll go first. If I . . . " Lafayette paused to swallow. "If I fall, take up where I left off. Remember, Lady Andragorre—I mean Beverly's counting on you." He mounted the low wall rimming the roof, and carefully avoiding looking down, prepared to lower himself over the edge.

"Hold it!" Lorenzo said. "That metal edging looks sharp. It might cut the rope. We'll have to pad it . . . "

"Here, use my coat." Lafayette stripped off the gaudy garment given to him by the employees of the Ajax works, folded it, tucked it under the rope they had purloined from a utility room under the eaves.

"And we really need some stout leather gauntlets," Lorenzo pointed out. "And shin guards. And spiked shoes would help."

"Sure—and it would be nice if we had large insurance policies," Lafayette cut him off. "Since we don't, we'd better get moving before our resolve stiffens up on us." He gripped the rope, gritted his teeth, and slid down into windy darkness.

The wind clawed at his coatless back. His feet pawed for nonexistent purchase on the wall three feet away. The fibers of the heavy rope rasped at his palms like barbed wire. The lighted window below slid closer. His foot touched the wall with a noise which seemed loud enough to rouse the county. Ignoring the ache in his arms, the quivering in his stomach, the sense of bottom-less depths yawning below, Lafayette inched down the last few feet, came to rest dangling against the four-foot section of blank wall between two windows. From inside came a restless susurrus of voices, the shuffle of feet.

" . . . can't imagine what it's about," a male tenor was exclaiming. "Unless it's my investiture as Squire of Honor to the Ducal Manicure coming through at last . . . "

"Gracious knows it's about time *my* appointment as Second Honorary Tonsorial Artist in Attendance on the Ducal Moustache was confirmed," a fruity baritone averred. "But what a curious hour for the ceremony . . . "

"Since his Grace has no moustache, you may be wait-ing quite a while, Fauntley," an acid voice suggested. "But—hark—they're coming . . . "

"Sst! Are you all right?" Lorenzo's call hissed from above. Lafayette craned upward, could see nothing but the dark bulk of the overhanging cornice.

From inside sounded a flourish of trumpets. There was a spatter of polite handclapping, followed by a sonorous announcement in an incomprehensible nasal. Then Duke Rodolpho's reedy voice spoke up faintly: " . . . gathered here . . . this auspicious occasion . . . pleasure and honor to present . . . a few words . . . careful attention . . . "

More polite applause, then a sudden hush.

"I'll not mince words," Goruble's voice rang out. "A state of dire emergency exists. Prompt measures are called for . . . " As the voice droned on, the rope to which O'Leary clung began to shake. Seconds later, Lorenzo appeared, descending rapidly.

"Slow down!" Lafayette hissed, as a pair of sharp-cornered boots slammed against his clavicles.

"Hssst, Lafayette! Where are you?"

"You're standing on me, you idiot!" Lafayette managed between teeth clenched in agony. "Get off!"

"Get off?" Lorenzo hissed back. "Onto what?"

"I don't care what! Just do it—before I lose my grip and we both go down!"

There were huffings and puffings from above. One foot lifted from O'Leary's pained flesh, then the other.

"All right—I'm clinging like a human fly to a crack you couldn't hide a dime in," Lorenzo whispered shakily. "Now what?"

"Shut up and listen!"

" . . . for this reason, I have decided to honor the lady in question by making her my bride," Goruble was announcing in unctuous tones. "You have been chosen to witness this felicitous event as an indication of my high esteem for your loyalty, to say nothing of your keen judgment, which tells you when to join in the spirit of the occasion." He paused ominously. "Now, is there anyone present who knows of any reason why I should not be instantly joined in holy matrimony to the Lady Andragorre?"

"Why, the dirty, double-crossing rat!" Lafayette burst out.

"Why, you dirty, double-crossing rat!" an angry shout sounded from within—in the unmistakable tones of Duke Rodolpho. "This wasn't part of our agreement, you slimy little upstart!"

"Seize the traitor!" Goruble bellowed.

"What's happening?" Lorenzo whispered as bedlam broke out within.

"Krupkin plans to marry Lady Andragorre, the swindler! Rodolpho is objecting, and Krupkin's objecting to his objecting!"

The babble from within had risen to a clamor reminiscent of a traffic jam. Goruble's shouted orders mingled with screams, curses, Rodolpho's bellows of outrage. There was a scrape and a crunch, and Lorenzo was jostling Lafayette on his fragile perch.

"Out of the way," he yelled. "Just wait until I get my hands on that kidnapping, confidence-betraying, bride-stealing son of a rachitic fry cook!"

"Hey," Lafayette yelled as his fellow eavesdropper thrust against him, nearly dislodging him from his grip. "Hold on!"

"I'll hold on—onto his neck, the lousy little claim-jumper!" Lorenzo's swinging boot contacted glass; it burst in with an explosive crash. An instant later the enraged Lorenzo had disappeared through the swirling drapes.

"The poor idiot!" Lafayette groaned. "He'll be torn to bits—and without helping Daphne—I mean Beverly—I mean Cynthia—or Lady Andragorre at all!" He craned, caught a glimpse of the surging crowd, the red-uniformed men moving among the gowns and cravats, of Lorenzo, charging through—

At the last moment, Goruble turned—in time to receive a jolting roundhouse punch in the right eye. As the assaulted prince staggered back, large uniforms loomed, closed in on Lorenzo.

"That did it," Lafayette muttered. "But at least he landed one good one . . . " He leaned for another look.

"So," Goruble was roaring, dabbing at his injured eye with a large lace-edged hanky, "it's you, is it, Lorenzo? I have plans for you, lad! Gorog's been fed once this evening, but he'll savor another snack, no doubt! And before you die, you'll have the pleasure of witnessing my union with the lady whom you've had the audacity to molest with your unwanted attentions!"

"M-M-Milady Andragorre," the shaken voice of a palace footman announced in the sudden hush. The crowd parted. A dark-haired, dark-eyed vision of loveliness appeared, clad in bridal white, accompanied by a pair of angular females in bridesmaid's costumes which failed to conceal their police-matronly physiques.

"On with the ceremony," Goruble shouted, all pretense of courtliness gone now. "Tonight, my nuptials; tomorrow, the conquest of the known universe!"

Lafayette clung to the wall, shivering violently as the icy wind whipped at his shirt. His hands were as numb as grappling hooks, though far less secure. His toes felt like frozen shrimp. Any moment now, his clutch would fail, and down he would go, into the depths below. He pressed his chin against the cold stone, listening to the droning voice of the ecclesiastic beyond the window, intoning the marriage ceremony.

"Why did it have to end like this?" he muttered. "Why did I have to get mixed up in it in the first place? Why didn't Pratwick help me instead of torturing me with that idiotic jingle—that meaningless rhyme that doesn't rhyme? " . . . the favorite of millions from the Bronx to Miami / The key to the riddle is . . . what? What rhymes with 'Miami'? 'Mammy'? 'Bon Ami'? 'Clammy'? The favorite of millions from the Bronx to Miami—the key to the riddle is . . . is . . . "

There was a sudden outburst inside: "Beverly—tell him no! Even if he does promise to slit my throat if you don't go through with it!" Lorenzo's shout was cut off by a meaty smack followed by a thud.

"He's merely stunned, my dear," Goruble said unctuously. "Carry on, you!"

"D-do you . . . Lady Andragorre . . . take this . . . this Prince . . . "

"No," Lafayette moaned. "This is too terrible. It couldn't be happening! Total, utter failure—and I've always been such a lucky fellow—like finding the door in the cliff when I needed it, and the Mad Monk costume, and . . . and . . . " He froze, groping for a ghostly idea floating just beyond his grasp.

"Think," he commanded himself. "Luck, I've been calling it. But that's fantastic. You don't have that kind of luck. That's the kind of thing that happens when you manipulate the probability fabric. So—the conclusion is that you were manipulating the cosmic energies. It worked—those times. But other times it didn't. But what was the difference? What did those occasions have in common that was lacking when I tried and failed?"

"Smelling salts," Goruble was bellowing from inside. "The poor creature's fainted, no doubt from the sheer thrill of her good fortune . . ."

"Nothing," Lafayette groaned. "I can't think of a thing. All I can think of is poor Daphne, and Swinehild, a sweet kid even if she did smell like garlic . . ."

Garlic . . .

"Garlic's always been associated with thaumaturgy and spells," Lafayette babbled, grasping at straws. "And spells are just amateur efforts to manipulate the cosmic energies! Could it be garlic? Or maybe Swinehild herself—but 'Swinehild' doesn't rhyme with 'Miami.' Neither does 'garlic.' Anyway, she only smelled like garlic because she was always making sandwiches out of that kosher salami—

"*Kosher salami!*" Lafayette shouted. "That's it! The favorite of millions from the Bronx to Miami—the key to the riddle is kosher salami!" He gulped, almost lost his grip, and held on.

"The salami was under me when I conjured up the knife—and we were eating it when I managed the costumes—and it was in my pocket on the cliff. So all I have to do is—"

O'Leary felt a cold hand clutch his heart.

"My pocket. It was in the pocket of my coat—and I left it up above, padding the rope!"

"All right," he answered. "So that means you have a climb ahead, that's all."

"Climb up there? My hands are like ice, and I'm weak as a kitten, and freezing, and anyway—it will take too long—"

"Get moving."

"I . . . I'll try." With vast effort, O'Leary unclamped a hand, groped for a grip higher up on the rope. He was dangling free of the wall now. His arms were like bread dough, he realized, his weight like a lead effigy.

"It's no use . . ."

"Try!"

Somehow he pulled up another foot. Somehow he managed another six inches. He clung, resting, inches upward. The wind banged him against the wall. He looked up; something dark lay on the parapet, flapping in the wind.

"It's too far," he gasped. "And anyway—" As he watched with horrified fascination, the coat, having gradually worked free of the rope under which it had been pinned, flopped over, the brocaded tails dangling down the outer face of the parapet. The wind plucked at the garment, nudged it closer to the edge. It hung for a moment; a new gust stirred it—

It was falling, the empty sleeves waving a hectic farewell, dropping toward him. Wind-tossed, it whirled out away from the building.

With a wild lunge, Lafayette threw himself into space. His outstretched fingertips brushed the coat, snatched, caught the heavy cloth. As wild wind screamed past him, O'Leary groped for the pocket; his fingers closed over the greasy lump of salami Swinehild had placed there—

"A miracle! Any miracle! But make it fast!"

A terrific blow smashed at O'Leary; out of the darkness he went spinning end over end into fire-shot darkness filled with shatterings and smashing and screams. Then blackness closed in like a filled grave.

"It was a miracle," a voice that Lafayette remembered from another lifetime, ages before, was saying. "As I reconstruct events, he fell from the roof, struck the flagpole, and was catapulted back up and through the window, to land squarely atop his Highness, who was rushing to discover the source of the curious sounds outside."

"Give him air," another voice snapped.

Lafayette found his eyes open, looking up at the frowning visage of Lorenzo, somewhat bruised but as truculent as ever.

"You could at least have let me in on your plan," the other O'Leary said. "I was getting worried there at the last, just before you arrived."

"You . . . you were marvelous, sir," a sweet voice murmured. With an effort like pushing boulders, Lafayette shifted his eyes, was looking into the smiling face of Daphne—of Lady Andragorre, he corrected himself with a pang of homesickness.

"You . . . really don't know me, do you?" O'Leary managed to chirp weakly.

"You're wondrous like one I know well, yclept Lancelot," the lady said softly. "I ween 'twas you I saw from my coach as I rode forth to my tryst in the forest. But—no, fair sir. We are strangers . . . and I am all the more in your debt."

"As am I," another voice spoke up. A man stood beside Lady Andragorre, his arm familiarly around her girlish waist. He wore a short, trimmed beard and a curling moustache under a floppy hat. "Methought I'd languish till doomsday in his Grace's dungeons—until you arrived to spring me." He studied Lafayette's face, frowning. "Though I cannot for my life see this fancied resemblance of which my bride prates."

"Face it, Lafayette," Lorenzo spoke. "This character's in on the ground floor. He belongs here in Melange, it seems. He used to be duke, before Krupkin came along and stuck Rodolpho up in his place. Now he's in charge again, and Krupkin's in the dungeon. And the lady isn't Beverly after all. She finally convinced me." He sighed. "So—I guess we lose out."

"Swinehild," Lafayette muttered, and managed to sit up. "Is she all right?"

"I'm here—and in the pink, thanks to you, Lafe," the former barmaid cried, elbowing a nervous-looking medico aside. "Gee, sugar, you look terrible." She smiled down at him, radiant in her court costume.

"I just want to talk to her!" a shrill male voice was yelling in the background. A ruffled figure in tight silks thrust through the circle, shot Lafayette a hot look, confronted Lady Andragorre.

"What's this all about, Eronne? Who's this bewhiskered Don Juan who's fingering your hipbone? And where did you get that get-up? What is this place? What's going on—"

"Hold it, chum," Lorenzo said, taking the stranger's elbow. "This is going to take a little explaining, but it seems we're all in the same boat—"

"Get lost, junior; who asked you to meddle?" The newcomer jerked his sleeve free. "Well, what about it, Eronne?" he addressed Lady Andragorre. "You act as if you'd never seen me before! It's me, Lothario O'Leary, your intended, remember?"

"The lady's name is Andragorre," the moustached Duke Lancelot spoke up harshly. "And she happens to be my intended, not yours!"

"Oh, yeah?"

"Absolutely! Wouldst dispute me?"

As peacemakers moved in to soothe the ruffled disputants, Lafayette rose unsteadily, and, supported by Swinehild, tottered away.

"I have to get out of here," he said. "Look, Swinehild—I've had a stroke of luck at last. I've recovered my ability to manipulate the cosmic energies—so I'm going home, where I belong. And I wonder—well, I have Daphne waiting for me, so I don't want you to misunderstand my motives—but wouldn't you like to come with me? I can pass you off as a long-lost cousin of Adoranne's, and with a little tutoring in how to walk and talk, you can soon fit right in—"

"Gee, Lafe—you really gotta go?"

"Certainly! But as I said, you may come too. So if you're ready—"

"Uh, say, excuse me, ma'am," a deep voice said hesitantly. "Begging your ladyship's pardon, but I was looking for—I mean, I hear tell my, er, wife—what I mean to say is, I plan to get around to marrying her as soon as . . . "

"Hulk!" Swinehild cried. "You come looking for me! You must care!"

"Swinehild?" Hulk quavered incredulously. "H-holy jumping Georgie Jessel—you're—you're plumb beautiful!"

"Hmmmphh," Lafayette said as the pair moved off, grabbing at each other. He managed to work his way across the room unnoticed, slipped out into a small cloakroom off the grand ballroom.

"Home," he said, patting his pockets. "Home sweet home . . . " He frowned, patted his pockets again, in turn. "Damn! I've lost the salami . . . must have dropped it somewhere between the flagstaff and Goruble's head." He reemerged, encountered Lorenzo.

"There you are!" his double exclaimed. "Look here, Lafayette—we have to talk! Maybe between the two of us we can summon up enough cosmic power to get back where we belong! I'm going crackers watching Duke Lancelot squeeze Andragorre—"

"Just help me find my salami," Lafayette countered. "Then I'll see what I can do."

"Food, at a time like this?" But he followed as Lafayette led the way down into the courtyard directly below the scene of his miraculous coup of an hour before.

"It should be lying around here someplace . . . "

"For heaven's sake, why not go to the kitchen?"

"Look, Lorenzo, I know it sounds silly, but this salami is vital to my psychic-energy-harnessing. Don't ask me why—ask a bureaucrat named Pratwick."

Ten minutes' diligent search of the enclosed space yielded no salami.

"Listen, was I holding it in my hand when I came through the window?" he inquired urgently of Lorenzo.

"How would I know, I had two bruisers sitting on my chest at the time. I didn't know what was happening until that Lancelot character came charging in and demanded the return of his ducal estates."

"We'll have to go back up and ask." Back in the ball-room, now only sparsely crowded as the former adherents of the now-imprisoned Rodolpho maneuvered for position in the entourage of their new master, Lafayette went about plucking at sleeves, repeating his question. He netted nothing but blank stares and a few polite laughs.

"A blank," he said as Lorenzo, equally luckless, rejoined him. "To think I had it that close—and let it get away."

"What's up, Lafe," Swinehild spoke behind him. "Lost something?"

"Swinehild—the kosher salami from our lunch—have you seen it?"

"Nope. But wait a minute, I'll see if Hulk's got some. He loves the stuff."

Hulk sauntered over, wiping his mouth. "Somebody call me?" he inquired, and belched. "Par'me," he said. "Kosher salami gives me gas."

Lafayette sniffed. "You didn't—you didn't *eat* it?"

"Was that yours, Mister O'Leary? Sorry about that. Can't get any more just like it, but we got plenty liver-wurst back at Ye Beggar's Bole."

"That does it," Lafayette moaned. "I'm sunk. I'm stuck here forever." He slumped in a chair, put his face in his hands. "Daphne," he muttered. "Will I ever see you again?" He groaned, remembering her as he had seen her last, her voice, the way she moved, the touch of her hand . . .

The room had grown curiously still. Lafayette opened his eyes. A few dropped hankies and smeared cigar butts on the polished floor were all that remained to indicate that a few moments before a noisy crowd had thronged the room. Faintly, voices floated from the passage outside. Lafayette sprang up, ran to the high, ornately carved, silver-handled door, pushed through into the red-carpeted hall. A figure—he thought it was Lothario, or possibly Lorenzo—was just disappearing around the shadowy corner. He called but no one answered. He hurried along the empty passage, looked into rooms.

"Swinehild!" he called. "Lorenzo! Anybody!"

Only echoes answered him.

"It's happened again," he whispered. "Everyone's disappeared, and left me marooned. Why? How?"

A sound of padding feet approaching along a side passage. A small, rotund figure in green-leather pants and a plaid sportcoat appeared at the head of a band of Ajax men.

"Sprawnroyal!" O'Leary greeted the customer-service man. "Thank Grunk someone's left alive here!"

"Hello, Slim. Boy, you get around. Me and the boys are here to see Krupkin—"

"He's in the dungeon—"

"Say, we're operating a half-phase out of sync with Melange; we usually duck over here for jobs like this to avoid the crowd, you know. But how'd *you* get here? When your Mark XIII came back empty, we thought you'd bought the farm! And—"

"It's a long story—but listen. I just had a thought of blinding brilliance! Krupkin gave you plans for a Traveler. Will you build it—for me—so I can go back to Artesia, and—"

"Not a chance, friend." Sprawnroyal held up both hands in negation. "If we pulled a trick like that, Central would land on us like a ton of twenty-two-karat uranium bricks!"

"Central! That's it! Put me in touch with Central, so I can explain what happened, and—"

"Nix again, Slim. Pinchcraft just got through going round and round with some paper-pusher named Fernwick or something about an allegation Ajax had let slip some cosmic-total-secret info to Krupkin. We barely managed to square matters; we won't reopen that can of worms for a while, believe me!"

"But—where is everybody?"

"We told Central about some of the monkey business going on here. Seems like Krupkin used stuff we sold him to make up a gadget to meddle with the probability fabric. He used it to yank a fellow named Lorenzo here. Wanted to use him as bait to get his hands on Lady A, so he could trade her back for Rodolpho's help. But when he did, he started a chain reaction; he got Lorenzo, and a couple dozen other troublemakers from alternate realities. What a hassle! But Central pulled a few strings and whisked a lot of displaced characters back to where they belonged. I don't know how it is they left you stranded here in half-phase. There's no life here at all, you know."

Lafayette leaned against the wall and closed his eyes. "I'm doomed," he muttered. "They're all against me. But maybe—maybe if I go back to Ajax with you, and explain matters directly to Pinchcraft and the others, they'll think of something."

Suddenly the silence was suspicious. O'Leary snapped his eyes open. Sprawnroyal was gone. The corridor was empty. There was not even an impress of feet in the deep-pile blue carpet to show where he had stood.

"Blue carpet?" he muttered dazedly. "But I thought it was red. The only place I've seen a blue carpet like this was in Lod's palace . . . "

He whirled and ran along the corridor, leaped down stairs, sprinted across a wide lobby, dashed out onto an expanse of sand-drifted lawn, turned to look back. Broken lavender neon letters spelled out LAS VEGAS HILTON.

"It's it," he gobbled. "The building Goruble supplied to Lod. And that means—I'm back in Artesia . . . doesn't it?" He looked out across the dark expanse of desert. "Or am I still in some kind of never-never land?"

"There's just one way to find out," he told himself. "There's twenty miles of loose sand between here and the capital. Start walking."

Dawn was bleaching the sky ahead as Lafayette tottered the last few yards to the door of the One-Eyed Man tavern on the west post road.

"Red Bull," he whispered hoarsely, thumping feebly at the heavy panel. "Let me in . . . "

There was no response from behind the shuttered windows. An icy chill stirred in Lafayette's midsection.

"It's deserted," he muttered. "A ghost city, an empty continuum. They shifted me out of Melange, because I was unbalancing the probability equation, but instead of sending me home—they marooned me . . . "

He hobbled on through the empty streets. Ahead was the high wall surrounding the palace grounds. He clung for a moment to the small service gate, then, with fear in his heart, thrust it open.

Morning mist hung among brooding trees. Dew glistened on silent grass. Far away, an early bird called. Beyond the manicured flower beds, the rose-marble palace loomed, soundless. No curtain fluttered from an open window. No cheery voices cried greetings. No footstep sounded on the flagged walks.

"Gone," O'Leary whispered. "All gone . . ."

He walked like a man in a dream across the wet grass, past the fountain, where a tiny trickle of water tinkled. His favorite bench was just ahead. He would sit there awhile, and then . . .

And then . . . he didn't know.

There was the flowering arbutus; the bench was just beyond. He rounded it—

She was sitting on the bench, a silvery shawl about her slim shoulders, holding a rosebud in her fingers. She turned, looked up at him. The prettiest face in the known universe opened into a smile like a flower bursting into blossom.

"Lafayette! You've come back!"

"Daphne . . . I . . . I . . . you . . ."

Then she was in his arms.

The Shape Changer

Out of the world, away and beyond
Borne on the wings of the magic song . . .

—*Chant of the Thallathlonians*

The Shape Changer

Chapter One

1

The moon shone bright on the palace gardens as Sir Lafayette O'Leary stepped stealthily forth from the scullery entrance. Silently, he tiptoed along the graveled path which led beneath a rhododendron hedge, skirting the royal Artesian vegetable garden and winding past the chicken yard, where a sleepy hen clucked irritably at his passing. At the street gate he paused to glance back at the dark towers looming against the cloud-bright sky. A faint light shone behind the windows of his third floor apartment. Up there Daphne was curled between silken sheets, waiting for him. He had sent her off to bed alone, telling her he'd join her as soon as he'd perused another chapter of his newest book on mesmeric science; instead, here he was, creeping out like a thief in the night, on his way to a stealthy rendezvous with a person or persons unknown—all because of that ridiculous note he'd found tucked under the napkin accompanying his after-dinner drink.

He pulled the grubby scrap of paper from his pocket, reread it by the dim glow from a lamp in a bracket on the wall.

> "Dear Sir Laffeyet,
> I doant sea you in kwite a wile, but you bin on my mind plenty. The reezin I rite you this letter is, I got holt of a item witch its two big to handle aloan. I cant sa no more now, wich some fink mite get holt of it and steel a march on us. But meat me at midnite at Ye Axe and Draggin, an I will fill you in. X (His mark)"

"It must be from the Red Bull," Lafayette told him. "Nobody else could spell as creatively as this. But why the cloak-and-poniard approach? You'd think he was still cutting purses for a living, instead of being a lionized hero with the royal pardon and the Order of the Dragon for his services to the crown. Which suggests that he's up to his old tricks. It's probably some wild scheme for counterfeiting quarters, or turning base metal into gold. If I had good sense, I'd turn around right now and forget the whole thing . . . "

But instead of turning back, he thrust the note into his pocket and let himself out the gate. Here in the narrow side street, the wind seemed chiller, bearing with it a whiff from the palace sty, where a pair of prize China pigs awaited the next feast day. Lafayette heard a mournful snort as he passed. In the far corner of the enclosure, George, the four-hundred-pound boar, huddled against the wall, as if recoiling from the advances of the scarcely less bulky Jemimah.

"Poor George," Lafayette murmured. "Maybe you've been cursed with too much imagination—like me."

At that moment, George seemed to catch his eye. With a frantic lunge he eluded the amorous sow, scrambled toward Lafayette, making piteous gobbling sounds.

"Don't make the same mistake I do, George, of not appreciating what you've got while you've got it," Lafayette advised the giant hog as it attempted unsuccessfully to rear up against the fence only to fall back with a loud *squelch!* into the mud.

"Go to Jemimah, tell her you're sorry, and forget the inevitable barbecue—" Lafayette broke off as George hurled himself at the fence, eliciting an ominous creak from the stout boards.

"Shhh!" he hissed. "You'll rouse the palace guards! Be sensible, George. Gather ye rosebuds while ye may . . . " But as he hurried off along the dark street, the mournful sounds followed him.

Few of the leaded glass windows set in the half-timbered gables overhanging the cobbled street showed lights; the honest folk of the capital were abed at this hour. Only dubious characters like himself—and the man he was going to meet—were abroad now, Lafayette reflected guiltily. In the distance he heard the *haloo* of a city watchman making his rounds, the barking of a dog, the tinkle of a bell. A steam-carriage rumbled past the intersection ahead, a red lantern swaying at its tailgate, its iron-shod wheels groaning against the paving blocks. Beyond, he saw a signboard bearing a familiar device: the prow of a Viking ship and a two-handed battle-ax. Below it was a low, wide, oaken door, iron bound, with heavy strap hinges. The sight brought back piquant memories. The Axe and Dragon had been the scene of his arrival in Artesia some years before—transported instantaneously from Colby Corners, USA, by the Psychic Energies focused by the Hypnotic Art, as described by Professor Doktor Hans Joseph Schimmerkopf in his massive volume on Mesmeric Science. It had also been the scene of his immediate arrest by the King's musketeers on a charge of sorcery, brought about by his careless decanting of several gallons of vintage wine from a one-liter bottle. He had managed to quash the indictment only by the desperate expedient of promising to slay a dragon. Well, in the end he had slain the dragon—one of them. The other had become his pet and favorite steed. He had also eliminated the fearsome two-headed giant Lod, which was rather a shame in a way; one of the heads hadn't been a bad sort of chap at all. Lafayette had gone on to depose the usurper, Goruble, and restore the throne to Princess Adoranne. Ever since, he—and his charming former chambermaid, Daphne—had been honored citizens of the quaint kingdom of Artesia, occupying a spacious apartment in the West Palace Annex, and on the closest terms with Adoranne and Prince Alain, her consort.

And now, here he was, back out in the cold, dark street, again approaching the door that had led him to such adventures, so long ago.

But there'd be no adventures this time, he told himself sternly. He had learned his lesson the last time he had found himself impatient with the peaceful life. His meddling had gotten him involved on a mad assignment from Central—head office of the Inter-dimensional Monitor Service—which had almost left him stranded in a deserted parallel world. No, this time he would know better. He had just come as a lark, actually. In a way it was rather jolly shivering in the cold, remembering his early days as a penniless draftsman, holed up in Mrs. McGlint's Clean Rooms and Board, subsisting on sardines and daydreams—but only because he had a cozy bed waiting for him back in the palace. Wouldn't it be ghastly, he thought, to *really* be some homeless gypsy, out on the tiles at this hour, chilled to the bone and hungry, with no relief in sight?

"That's enough gloomy thinking," he told himself firmly as he reached the tavern door. "In an hour I'll be snuggled up with Daphne, all the better for a brisk stroll in the night air." He adjusted a look of amused complacency on his face, shook out his cloak, and stepped into the warmth and beery aroma of the Axe and Dragon.

2

A bed of coals glowing in the ox-sized fireplace dimly illuminated the long, low room, the plank tables ranked along one side, the wine and ale kegs along the other. But for the silent bartender behind the trestle bar, the place seemed deserted, until a large figure rose among the shadows at the rear.

"Over dis way, bub!" a hearty voice growled. "Take a load off duh dogs, an' we'll hoist a few in membry o' duh old days!"

"Red Bull!" Lafayette exclaimed, ducking his head under the low, age-blackened beams. "I thought it would be you!" He clasped the calloused hand of the big man who beamed at him, his little red-rimmed eyes agleam in his lumped, scarred face. There was a little gray now, Lafayette noticed, in the bristly red thatch above the cauliflowered ears. Otherwise the soft life hadn't changed the former outlaw.

"Where've you been keeping yourself?" Lafayette demanded as he took the proffered chair. "I haven't seen you in a year or more."

"Take a tip from a pal," the Red Bull said sadly as he poured wine into O'Leary's glass. "Stay away from dem hick jails."

"You haven't been up to your old tricks?" Lafayette demanded in a severe tone. "I thought you'd reformed, Red Bull."

"Naw—dey nabs me on account of I was astride a nag which it had some udder mug's brand on. But, geeze, youse know how all dese bay mares look alike on duh parking lot."

"I warned you about your casual view of property rights," Lafayette said. "The first night we met—right here at this very table."

"Yeah—I picked duh spot for duh sentimental associations," the big man acknowledged. He sighed. "Youse had duh right idear, chum: youse give up duh cutpurse racket and went straight, and now—"

"Are you back on that old idea?" Lafayette said sharply. "I was never a cutpurse. I don't know how you got that impression—"

"Dat's right, pal, don't admit nothing." The Red Bull winked, a grotesque twisting of battered features. "It'll be our little secret dat youse used to be duh Phantom Highwayman, duh dream spector o' duh moors."

"That's a lot of rubbish, Red Bull," Lafayette said, sampling his wine. "Just because the first time you saw me I was wearing a coat of claret velvet and breeches of brown doeskin—"

"Yeah, an' dey fitted wit' never a wrinkle, right? An' dey come up to your thigh. An' yuh had a French cocked hat on your forehead, and a bunch of lace at your chin—"

"That doesn't mean a thing! It just happened to be what I conjured up—I mean," he corrected, seeing that he was about to complicate matters: the Red Bull would never understand the Focusing of the Psychic Energies. "I mean, I actually intended to wear a gray suit and a Homburg, but something went a little awry, and—"

"Sure, sure, I heard all dat sweet jazz before, pal. Anyways, I seen by duh papers dis would be a night when duh moon would be like a ghostly galleon, and duh wind would be a torrent o' darkness, an' all, so I sez—"

"Will you come to the point?" Lafayette snapped. "It's actually long after my bedtime, and—"

"Sure, chum. Drink your wine whilst I fill youse in. It's like dis, see? I'm ankling along duh pike, on my way back from duh burg where dey hung duh frame on me, an' I'm overtook by nightfall. So I seeks shelter in a cave an' in duh morning what was my surprise to find duh rock I was using fer a piller was ackshully a neat little cask like, you know, a safety deposit box."

"Oh?"

"Yeah. So, I'm shaking it around a little, and duh lids falls open. And guess what's inside?"

"Money? Jewels?" Lafayette hazarded, swallowing more wine. It was poor stuff, thin and sour. Too bad Central was keeping that Supressor focused on him; otherwise they could have just as easily been drinking Château Lafite-Rothschild . . .

"Naw," the Red Bull said disgustedly. "Dere was just some kind o' gadget, like a combination can opener and hot-patch kit. Only it looks like it's broke. I'm about to t'row it away, when I notice duh lettering on duh bottom."

"What did it say?" Lafayette inquired, yawning. " 'Made in Japan'?"

"Take a look fer yourself, pal." The Red Bull dipped a set of scarred knuckles inside his grimy leather jerkin, withdrew a small apparatus of the approximate appearance of a six-inch-high patent coffee maker—or possibly a miniature jukebox, Lafayette corrected himself. There was a round base, painted a dark red, surmounted by a clear plastic box inside which were visible a maze of wires, wheels, levers, gears, tiny bits of colored glass and plastic.

"What in the world is it?" he inquired. "Why, those look like condensers and transistors—but that's silly. No one's invented transistors yet, in Artesia."

"Great, chum!" the Red Bull exclaimed. "I knowed youse would have duh straight dope!"

"I don't have any dope, straight or otherwise," O'Leary objected. "I haven't the faintest idea what the thing is." He turned it around, frowning at it. "What does it do, Red Bull?"

"Huh? Beats me, bub. But what I figger is, it's gotta do *some*thing nifty—and all we got to do is dope out what, and we're in business!"

"Nonsense." Lafayette pushed the apparatus away. "Red Bull, it was nice seeing you again, but I'm afraid you're wasting my time with this Rube Goldberg. Are you sure you didn't cobble it up yourself? I never saw mechanical and electronic components jumbled together like that—"

"Whom, I?" the Red Bull said indignantly. "Pal, I wouldn't string youse! Like I says, I find duh gimcrack in duh cave, an'—"

"Phooey, Red Bull." Lafayette finished his wine and pushed the mug back. "I'm going home and to bed, where I belong. Drop around some evening and we'll talk over the good old days when I was a poor, homeless boob, with no friends, no money, and a death sentence hanging over me."

"Hey, wait, pal! You ain't seen what's wrote on duh bottom, which I din't t'row it away when I seen it!"

Lafayette grunted impatiently, picked up the gadget and peered at the underside of the base. He frowned, held it in a better light.

"Well," he exclaimed. "Why didn't you say so? This could be something important. Where did you say you found it?"

"Buried in duh cave. And as soon as I seen duh royal coat of arms, I glommed I was onto something big, right, pal?"

"Goruble's personal cartouche," Lafayette muttered. "But it looks as if it were stamped in the metal with a hand-punch. There's something else . . . "

"What does it say, chum?" The Red Bull leaned forward eagerly.

"Haven't you read it?" Lafayette inquired in surprise.

"Uh—I didn't go in much fer duh scholar bit when I was a nipper," the big man said abashedly.

"It's difficult to read in this light—but I can make out . . . PROPERTY OF CENTRAL PROBABILITY LABORATORY." He rubbed a finger at the tarnished surface; more letters appeared:

FOCAL   REFERENT—VARIABLE   (FULL RANGE) MARK III

WARNING—EXPERIMENTAL MODEL

FOR USE BY AUTHORIZED PERSONNEL ONLY

"Chee," the Red Bull said reverently.

"Why, good lord," Lafayette said, "I'll bet this is part of the loot Goruble brought along to Artesia when he defected from the Central Monitor Service, twenty-five years ago! I remember that Nicodaeus said they'd recovered a Traveler-load of stuff from the lab he'd rigged up in the palace catacombs, but that the records seemed to indicate there was more that they couldn't find—" He broke off. "Red Bull—that cave—could you find it again? There might be a whole trove of other items there!"

"Dat's what I been tryna tell youse, pal," the former second-story man said aggrievedly. "Oncet I seen I was onto duh real goods, I dig around and come up wit' a whole bunch o' wild-looking gear under duh floor! I can't carry all duh stuff, so I bury it again, and come hot-footing to youse wit' duh whole story."

"Ye gods, Red Bull—this stuff is dynamite! If it fell into the wrong hands—"

"Right, bub! Dat's why I think of youse! Now, duh way I got duh caper doped, I bring in duh stuff a couple choice items at a time, see, and wit' your old contacts from when youse was in duh game, we could soon retire on duh take!"

"Take! Are you out of your mind? This stuff is experimental equipment from a temporal laboratory—where they run experiments in probability, time travel, interdimensional relationships! Start messing with this, and heaven only knows what kind of probability stresses you'd set up! You might shift half of Artesia into some other phase of existence—or even worse!"

The Red Bull was frowning darkly. "What's duh proposition got to do wit' timetables? And you can skip duh cracks about my relationships. I been keeping company wit' duh same frail for five years now, and all we ever do—"

"You don't understand, Red Bull! We can't sell this stuff! It belongs to Central! Goruble stole it! We have to get it back to them at once, before something terrible happens!"

"Listen, pal," the Red Bull said earnestly. "Duh worst t'ing I can see happening is fer some udder slob to latch onto duh gravy, see?"

"Red Bull, try to fix this thought in your mind," Lafayette said tautly. "This thing is potentially more dangerous than an atom bomb—not that you know what an atom bomb is. Just take my word for it that I have to turn it over to the Central authorities at once—if I can get hold of the authorities," he added doubtfully.

"Nix, pal." The Red Bull's immense hand closed around the device resting on the scarred table. "Turn duh goods over to duh bulls, and dey pocket duh spoils fer demselves. Nuts to dat. If youse don't want a slice o' duh action, I'll work duh play solo!"

"No, Red Bull, you still don't get it! Listen—I promise you there'll be a fat reward for turning this in. Say—a hundred gold pieces."

"What about duh rest o' duh trove?" the Red Bull inquired suspiciously, rubbing a calloused hand across his stubbled chin with a sound like frying fat.

"We can't touch it. I'll use the special phone in Nicodaeus' old lab to put a call through to Central, and get an Inspector of Continua in here to take charge—"

"Youse was saying about duh reward. What say to ten grand, cash on duh line?"

"I'm sure it can be arranged. What about it, Red Bull? I'll see that your interests are protected."

"Well—it ain't like duh old days, bub. I still think youse and me would have been a great team, wit' my brains an' your neat tricks, like riding t'rough duh sky an' turning to smoke under duh very noses o' duh Johns—"

"You're talking nonsense, Red Bull. Just trust me: I'll see it to you don't lose by it. Now tell me—where is this cave, exactly?"

"Well . . . I dunno, pal," the Red Bull said doubtfully. "Youse is a square mug, an' all, but dis is duh biggest career opportunity dat ever come my way." He rose. "I got to go to duh can," he confided. "Gimme a minute to consider duh angles." He swaggered off toward the rear of the tavern. Lafayette picked up the Focal Referent, Mark III, and stared into the complexities of its interior.

It resembled no machine he had ever seen before; it was as though the components of an eight-day clock and a portable TV had been mixed thoroughly and packed into the same restricted space. There was a small, flat button on one side, near the bottom, glowing with a faint, enticing glow. Lafayette poked at it . . .

The Universe turned inside out. Lafayette—clinging to the interior of the vast solid that surrounded the hollow bubble that was the earth—was dimly aware that his body now filled a void of infinite extent, while his eyes, situated at the exact center of reality, stared directly into each other, probing a bottomless nothingness that whirled, expanded, and—

The walls of the room were sailing past, like a merry-go-round running down. Lafayette blinked dizzily, grabbed for his wine glass, took a hearty gulp, sat trembling and drawing deep, restorative breaths. He swallowed a lump the approximate size of a hard-boiled egg, edging as far as possible away from the innocent-looking apparatus sitting on the table before him.

"Oh, you're a genius, O'Leary," he muttered to himself, patting his pocket for a handkerchief with which to mop the cold sweat from his brow. "You give the Red Bull a lecture on the danger of meddling with experimental temporal lab equipment, and then you poke a button yourself, and nearly . . . nearly . . . do whatever I nearly did!"

There was a sudden sound of scuffling, emanating from the direction of the alley behind the tavern. The tapman came around the bar with a stout cudgel in his hand. He halted abruptly, staring at Lafayette.

"We're closed, you," he said roughly. "How'd ye get in here, anyway?"

"Through the door, Tom, as usual," Lafayette snapped. "What about it?"

"Haul ye'r freight, ye scurvy knave." The barman hooked a thick thumb over his shoulder. "Out!"

"What's got into you, Tom?" O'Leary said testily. "Go polish a glass or something—"

"Look, crum-bum—so I open the joint so me old mate the Red Bull could have a quiet rondy-vooz with a nobleman; that don't mean every varlet on the pavement gets to warm hisself at me fire—"

"Some fire," Lafayette snapped. "The A & D used to be a fairly nice dive, as dives go—but I can see it's deteriorated—" He broke off with an *oof!* as Tom rammed the club into his short ribs, grasped him by the back of the neck, and assisted him from the bench.

"I says out, rogue, and out is what I mean!"

As the landlord sent him staggering toward the door, Lafayette caught at one of the posts supporting the sagging beams, whirled around it, and drove a straight right punch to the barman's chin, sending him bounding backward to end up on the packed-earth floor with his head under a table.

"I was just leaving, thanks," Lafayette said, noting as he seized the Mark III from the table that his voice had developed a hoarse, croaking sound. But no wonder, after the scare he'd had, followed by the unexpected attack by an old acquaintance.

"I think you'd better lay off sampling the stock, Tom. It does nothing for your personality." He paused at the door to straight his coat, smooth his lapels. The cloth felt unaccountably greasy. He looked down, stared aghast at grimy breeches, torn stockings, and run-over shoes.

"All that from one little scuffle?" he wondered aloud. The landlord was crawling painfully forth from under the table.

"Stick around, mister," he said blurrily. "It's two falls out o' three, remember?" As he came to his feet with a lurch, Lafayette slipped out into the dark street. A chill drizzle of rain had started up, driven by the gusty wind. The Red Bull was nowhere in sight.

"Now, where's he gotten to?" Lafayette wondered aloud as he reached to draw his cloak about him, only to discover that the warm garment was gone.

"Drat!" he said, turning back to the tavern door.

"Tom! I forgot something!" he shouted; but even as he spoke, the light faded inside. He rattled and pounded in vain. The oak panel was locked tight.

"Oh, perfect," he groaned aloud. "Now he's mad at me—and it was my second-best cloak, too, the one Daphne's Aunt Lardie made for me." He turned up his jacket collar—of stiff, coarse wool, he noted absently; funny, he'd grabbed a coat from the closet in the dark, but he didn't remember owning anything *this* disreputable. Maybe it belonged to the man who had come to clear the swallows' nest out of the chimney . . .

"But never mind that," he reminded himself firmly. "Getting this infernal machine into safe hands is the important thing. I'll lock it in the palace vault, and then try to get in touch with Central, and . . . " His train of thought was interrupted by the clank of heavy boots on the pavement of an alley which debouched from between narrow buildings a few yards ahead. O'Leary shied, reaching instinctively for his sword-hilt—

But of course he wasn't wearing a sword, he realized as his fingers closed on nothing. Hadn't worn one in years, except on gala occasions, and then just a light, bejeweled model that was strictly for show. But then, he hadn't been out in the midnight streets alone for quite a while. And it had never occurred to him tonight to do anything as melodramatic as buckling on the worn blade he'd used in the old days . . .

As he hastily tucked the Mark III away out of sight, three men emerged from the alley mouth, all in floppy feathered hats, green-and-yellow-striped jackets— Adoranne's colors—wide scarlet sashes, baggy pants above carelessly rolled boots: The Royal City Guard.

"Oh, boy, am I glad to see you fellows," Lafayette greeted the trio. "I thought you were footpads or worse. Look, I need an escort back to the palace, and—"

"Stay, rogue!" the leading musketeer barked. "Up against the wall!"

"Turn around and put your hands against it, over your head, you know the routine!" a second guardsman commanded, hand on épée hilt.

"This is no time for jokes," O'Leary announced in some asperity. "I've got some hot cargo for the royal vault—high-priority stuff. Shorty"—he addressed the smallest of the trio, a plump sergeant with fiercely curled mustachios—"you lead the way, and you other two chaps fall in behind—"

"Don't go calling me by my nickname!" the short cop roared, whipping out his blade. "And we ain't no chaps!"

"What's got into you, Shorty?" Lafayette demanded in astonishment. "You're not mad because I won two-fifty from you playing at skittles the other night—"

The sword leaped to prick his throat. "Jest you button the lip, Clyde, 'fore I pin you to the wall!" Shorty motioned curtly. "You boys frisk him. I got a funny feeling this bozo here's more'n a routine vagrant."

"Are you all out of your minds?" O'Leary yelled as the guardsmen flung him roughly against the wall, began patting his pockets none too gently. "Shorty, do you really mean you don't recognize me?"

"Hey—hold it, boys," Shorty said. "Uh—turn around, you," he addressed Lafayette in a more uncertain tone. "You claim I know you, hah?" He frowned at him searchingly. "Well, maybe you went downhill since I seen you last . . . but I wouldn't want to turn my back on an old pal. What was the name again?"

"O'Leary!" Lafayette yelled. "Lafayette O'Leary. *Sir* Lafayette O'Leary, if you want to get technical!"

"OK," Shorty rasped with a return to his gravelly voice. "You picked the wrong pigeon! It just so happens that me and Sir Lafayette are just like that!" He held up two fingers, close together, to indicate the intimacy of the relationship. "Why, on his first night in town, five years ago, Sir Lafayette done me a favor which I'll never forget it—me and Gertrude neither!"

"Right!" Lafayette cried. "That was just before I went all wivery and almost disappeared back to Mrs. McGlint's —and as a favor to you boys, I stuck around, just so you wouldn't have anything inexplicable to explain to the desk sergeant, right?"

"Hey," one of the troopers said. "Lookit what I found, Sarge!" He held up a fat gold watch, shaped like a yellow turnip.

"W-where did that come from?" Lafayette faltered.

"And how about this?" A second man produced a jeweled pendant from O'Leary's other pocket. "And this!" He displayed a silver inlaid Elk's tooth, an ornate snuffbox with a diamond-studded crest, a fistful of lesser baubles. "Looks like your old pal has been working, Sarge!"

"I've been framed!" Lafayette cried. "Somebody planted that stuff on me!"

"That cuts it," the NCO snarled. "Try to make a monkey out o' me, will you? You'll be on maggoty bread and green water for thirty days before your trial even comes up, wittold!"

"Let's just go back to the palace," Lafayette shouted. "We'll ask Daphne—Countess Daphne, to you, you moron—she'll confirm what I say! And after this is straightened out—"

"Put the cuffs on him, Fred," Shorty said. "Hubba hubba. We go off duty in ten minutes."

"Oh, no," Lafayette said, half to himself. "This isn't going to turn into one of those idiotic farces where everything goes from bad to worse just because no one has sense enough to explain matters. All I have to do is just speak calmly and firmly to these perfectly reasonable officers of the law, and—"

From the nearby alley there was a sudden rasp of shoe leather on cobbles. Shorty whirled, grabbing for his sword-hilt as dark figures loomed. There was a dull *thunk!* as of a ball bat striking a saddle; the stubby sergeant's feathered hat fell off, as its owner stumbled backward and went down. Even as their blades cleared their scabbards, the other three musketeers received matching blows to the skull. They collapsed in a flutter of plumes, a flapping of silk, a clatter of steel. Three tall, dark men in the jeweled leathers and gaudy silks of a Wayfarers Tribe closed in about Lafayette.

"Let's get going, Zorro," one of them whispered in a voice that was obviously the product of damaged vocal chords, substantiating the testimony of the welted scar across his brown throat, only partially concealed by a greasy scarf knotted there. A second member of the band—a one-eyed villain with a massive gold earring—was swiftly going through the pockets of the felled policemen.

"Hey—wait just a minute," O'Leary blurted, in confusion. "What's going on here? Who are you? Why did you slug the cops? What—"

"Losing your greep, Zorro?" the leader cut him off brusquely. "You could have knocked me over weeth a feather wheen I see you in the clutches of the *Roumi* dogs." He stooped, with a quick slash of a foot-long knife freed a dagger in an ornately worked sheath from the belt of the nearest musketeer. "Queek, compadres," he rasped. "Someone's coming theese way." He caught O'Leary's arm, began hauling him toward the alley mouth from which the raiders had pounced.

"Hold on, fellows!" Lafayette protested. "Look, I appreciate the gesture and all that, but it isn't necessary. I'll just turn myself in and make a clean breast of it, explain that it was all a general misunderstanding, and—"

"Poor Zorro, a blow on the head has meexed up his weets, Luppo," a short, swarthy man with a full beard grunted.

"Don't you understand?" Lafayette yelped sharply as he was hustled along the alley. "I *want* to go to court! You're just making it worse! And stop calling me Zorro! My name's O'Leary!"

The leader of the band swung Lafayette around to glare down into his face from a height of close to seven feet of leather, bone and muscle. "Worse? What does theese mean, Zorro? That you deedn't come through on your beeg brag, eh?" He gave O'Leary a bone-rattling shake. "And so you theenk instead of facing up to King Shosto, you'll do a leetle time in the *Roumi* breeg, ees that eet?"

"No, you big ape!" Lafayette yelled, and landed a solid kick to the bulky Wayfarer's shin. As the victim yelled and bent to massage the injury, Lafayette jerked free, whirled—and was facing half a dozen bowie knives gripped in as many large, brown fists.

"Look, fellows, let's talk it over," Lafayette started. At that moment, there was a yell from the street where they had left the three musketeers. Lafayette opened his mouth to respond, caught only a glimpse of a cloak as it whirled at his head; then he was muffled in its sour-smelling folds, lifted from his feet, slung over a bony shoulder, and carried, jolting, from the scene.

Chapter Two

1

Bundled in the reeking cloak and trussed with ropes, Lafayette lay in what he deduced to be the bed of a wagon, judging from the sounds and odors of horse, the rumble of unshod wheels on cobbles, and the creak of harness. His attempts to shout for air had netted him painful blows, after which he had subsided and concentrated his efforts on avoiding suffocation. Now he lay quietly, his bruises throbbing with every jolt of the cumbersome vehicle.

At length the sound of cobbles gave way to the softer texture of an unpaved surface. Leather groaned as the wagon bed took on a tilt that testified to the ascent of a grade. The air grew cooler. At last, with a final lurch, all motion ceased. Lafayette struggled to sit up, was promptly seized and pitched over the side where waiting hands caught him, amid a guttural exchange of questions and answers in a staccato dialect. The ropes were stripped away, then the muffling cloak. Lafayette sneezed, spat dust from his mouth, dug grit from his eyes and ears, and took a hearty breath of cool, resin-scented air.

He was standing in a clearing in the forest. Bright moonlight dazzled down through the high boughs of lofty pines on patched tents and high-wheeled wagons with once-garish paint jobs now faded to chipped and peeling pastel tones. A motley crowd of black-haired, olive-skinned men, women, and children, all dressed in soiled garments of bright, mismatched colors, stared solemnly at him. From tent flaps and the dim-lit windows of wagons more curious faces gazed. Except for the soft sigh of wind through the trees and the clop of a swaybacked horse shifting his hooves, the silence was total.

"Well," Lafayette began, but a spasm of coughing detracted from the tone of indignation. "I suppose (cough) you've kidnapped me (cough-cough) for a reason . . ."

"Steeck around, Zorro. Don't get impatient," the one-eyed man said. "You'll geet the message queeck enough."

There was a stir in the ranks; the crowd parted.

An elderly man, still powerful-looking in spite of his grizzled hair and weather-beaten face, came forward. He was dressed in a purple satin shirt with pink armbands, baggy chartreuse pants above short red boots with curled toes. There were rings on each of his thick fingers; a string of beads hung around his corded neck. Through his wide green alligator belt were thrust a bulky pistol and a big-bladed knife with glass emeralds and rubies set in the plastic handle. He planted himself before Lafayette, looking him up and down with an expression of sour disapproval on his not-recently-shaved mahogany-dark face.

"Ha!" he said. "So Meester Beeg-mouth Zorro, he not so hot like he theenk, hey!" He grasped a long hair curling from his nose, yanked it out, held it up, looking at it, let his narrowed eyes slide past it to Lafayette.

"Look, I don't know what this Zorro business is," O'Leary said, "but if you're in charge of this menagerie, how about detailing someone to take me back to town before matters get entirely out of hand? I can square things by saying a word to a chap in the records department and have the whole thing scratched off the blotter, and—"

"Ha!" the oldster cut Lafayette's speech short. "You theenk you weegle out of the seetuation by pretending you got bats een the belfry! But eet's no use, Zorro! Theese is not the way the ancient Law of the Tribe, she works!"

A mutter of agreement rose from the bystanders. There were a few snickers; a single muffled sob came from a dark-eyed young creature in the front rank.

"What's your tribal law got to do with me?" Lafayette said hotly. "I was going quietly about my business when your gang of thugs grabbed me—"

"OK, I streeng along weeth the gag," the fierce-eyed old man interrupted with an ominous grin. "Last night, you dreenk a few bottles of Old Sulphuric, and you geet beeg ideas: you have the nerve to make a pass at the niece of the King! By the rule of the Tribe, theese offer, she cannot be ignored—even from a seemple-minded nobody like you! So—poor old King Shosto—he geeves you your chance!" The swarthy man smote himself on the chest.

"Look, you've got me mixed up with somebody else," Lafayette said. "My name is O'Leary, and—"

"But naturally, before you can have the preevilege of wooing Gizelle, you got to breeng home a trophy to qualify. For theese reason, you sleep eento the ceety under cover of darkness. I seend Luppo and a few of the boys along to keep an eye on you. And—the first theeng—the *Roumi* cops peek you up. Beeg deal! Ha!"

"This seems to be a case of mistaken identity," Lafayette said reasonably. "I've never seen you before in my life. My name is O'Leary and I live in the palace with my wife, Countess Daphne, and I don't know what you're talking about!"

"Oh?" the old chieftain said with a sly smile. "O'Leary, eh? You got any ideentification?"

"Certainly," Lafayette said promptly, patting his pockets. "I have any number of . . . documents . . . only . . . " With a sinking feeling, he surveyed the soiled red bandanna his hip pocket had produced. "Only I seem to have left my wallet in my other suit."

"Oh, too bad." King Shosto wagged his head, grinning at his lieutenants. "He left eet een hees other suit." His smile disappeared. "Well, let's see what you've got een *theese* suit to show for a night's work! Show us the trophy that proves your skeel weeth your feengers!"

With all eyes on him, Lafayette rummaged dubiously, came up with a crumpled pack of poisonous-looking black cigarettes, an imitation pearl-handled penknife, a worn set of brass knuckles, a second soiled handkerchief of a virulent shade of green, and a gnawed ivory toothpick.

"I, er, seem to have gotten hold of someone else's coat," he ad-libbed.

"And somebody else's pants," King Shosto grated. "And that somebody ees Zorro!" Suddenly the giant knife was in the old man's hand, being brandished under O'Leary's nose. "Now I cut your heart out!" he roared. "Only eet would be too queek!"

"Just a minute!" Lafayette back-pedaled, was grabbed and held in a rigid grip by eager volunteers.

"The penalty for failure to breeng home the bacon ees the Death of the Thousand Hooks!" Shosto announced loudly. "I decree a night of loafing and dreenking to get eento the mood, so we do the job right!"

"Zorro! What about your treeck pockets?" a tearful feminine voice cried. The girl who had been showing signs of distress ever since Lafayette's arrival rushed forward and seized his arm as if to tug him from the grip of the men. "Show them, Zorito! Show them you are as beeg a thief as any of them!"

"Gizelle, go bake a pizza!" the old man roared. "Theese is none of your beezness! Theese cowardly peeg, he dies!"

"Eet ees too!" she wailed defiantly. "Theese ees the cowardly peeg I love!"

"*Zut alors!*" Shosto yelled. "You . . . and theese four-flusher! Theese viper een my bosom! Theese upstart! Never weel he have you!"

"Zorito!" she wailed. "Don't you remember how I steetched all those secret pockets for you, and how you were going to feel theem weeth goodies? Don't you have one leetle souvenir of your treep to show theem?"

"Secret pockets?" Shosto rumbled. "What's theese nonsense?"

"Een his sleeves!" Gizelle seized Lafayette's cuff, turned it back, explored with her brown fingers. With a yelp of delight she drew forth a slim, silvery watch dangling from a glittering chain.

"You see? Zorito, my hero!" As she flung her arms around Lafayette's neck, Shosto grabbed the watch, stared at it.

"Hey!" the man called Luppo blurted. "You can stuff me for an owl eef that eesn't the solid platinum watch of the Lord Mayor of Artesia Ceety!"

"Where deed you get theese?" Shosto demanded.

"Why, I, ah . . . " Lafayette faltered.

"He stole eet, you brute," Gizelle cried. "What do you theenk, he bought eet een a pawnshop?"

"Well, Shosto, eet looks like Zorro fooled you theese time," someone spoke up.

"He not only leefted the Lord Mayor's watch—but what an actor!" another said admiringly. "I would have sworn he deedn't have the proverbial weendow to throw eet out of—and all the while he had the beegest heist of the decade stashed een hees coat lining!"

"Come on, Shosto—be a sport!" another challenged. "Admeet he has made the team!"

"Well—maybe I geev heem another chance." Shosto dealt himself a blow on the chest that would have staggered a lesser man, grinned a sudden, flashing grin. "Ten

thousand thundering devils on a teen roof!" he roared.
"Theese ees an occasion for celebration! We proceed
weeth the loafing and dreenking as planned! Too bad we
have to do weethout the diversion of the Death of the
Thousand Hooks," he added, with a regretful glance at
Lafayette. "But I can always reschedule eet, eef he
doesn't treat my leetle Gizelle right!" He gestured
grandly and the men holding Lafayette released him.

The Wayfarers gathered around him, slapping him on
the back and pumping his hand. Someone struck up a
tune on a concertina; others joined in. Jugs appeared, to
be passed from hand to hand. As soon as he could, Lafayette disengaged himself, used the green handkerchief
to wipe the sweat from his forehead.

"Thanks very much," he said to Gizelle. "I, uh,
appreciate your speaking up for me, miss."

She hugged his arm, looked up at him with a flashing
smile. Her eyes were immense, glistening dark, her nose
delightfully retroussé, her lips sweetly curved, her
cheeks dimpled.

"Theenk nothing of it, Zorito. After all, I couldn't let
theem cut you in beets, could I?"

"I'm glad somebody around here feels that way. But
I still have the problem of getting home. Could I arrange
to borrow a horse—just overnight, of course—"

A burst of laughter from the gallery greeted this
request. Gizelle compressed her lips, took Lafayette's
arm possessively.

"You are a beeg joker, Zorito," she said sternly; then
she smiled. "But eet ees no matter; I love you anyway!
Now—on weeth the festeevities!" She seized his hand
and whirled him away toward the sound of music.

2

It was three hours later. The twenty-gallon punch-tank contained only half an inch of pulpy dregs; the roast ox had been stripped to the bones. The musicians had long since slid, snoring, under their benches. Only a few determined drinkers still raised raucous voices in old Wayfarer songs. Gizelle had disappeared momentarily on some personal errand. It was now or never.

Lafayette put down the leathern cup he had been nursing, eased silently back into the shadows. No one called after him. He crossed a moonlit strip of grassy meadow, waited again in the shelter of the trees. The drunken song continued undisturbed. He turned and slipped away between the trees.

A hundred feet up the trail, with the sounds and smells of the celebration already lost in the spicy scent of pine and the soughing of wind through the heavy boughs, Lafayette halted, peering back down-trail for signs of followers. Seeing no one, he tiptoed off the trail, setting a direct course for the capital—about ten miles due south, he estimated. A long hike, but well worth it to get clear of this bunch of maniacs. Little Gizelle was the only sane person in camp—and even she had some serious hang-ups. Well, he'd send her a nice memento once he was safely back in town; a string of beads say, or possibly a party dress. It would be nice to see her dolled up. He pictured her garbed in formal court wear, with jewels in her hair and her fingernails polished, and just a touch of perfume back of the ear.

"I might even invite her down to a rout or ball," he mused. "She'd be a sensation, cleaned up a little; she might even meet some nice young fellow who'd put a ring on her finger, and—"

Ducking under a low-spreading branch, Lafayette halted, frowning at a large pair of boots visible under a bush. His gaze traveled upward along a matching pair of legs, surmounted by the torso and unfriendly features of Luppo, standing fists on hips, smiling crookedly down at him.

"Looking for sometheeng, Zorro?" the big man growled in his husky voice.

"I was just taking a little constitutional," Lafayette said, getting to his feet with as much dignity as he could muster.

"Eef I was the suspeeciuos type," Luppo growled, "I might theenk you were trying to sneak out on my seester like a feelthy double-crossing rat."

With a muttered "Hmphff," Lafayette turned and made his way back down the path, followed by the big tribesman's sardonic chuckle. Judging that he had put sufficient distance between himself and Luppo, he picked a spot where the undergrowth thinned, again left the path, striking off to the left. A dense stand of brambles barred his path; he angled uphill to avoid it, crawled under a clump of thorn, scaled an outcropping of rock, turned to take his bearings, and saw a large man named Borako leaning against a tree, casually whittling a stick. The Wayfarer looked up, spat.

"Another shortcut?" he inquired with a sly smile.

"Actually," Lafayette said haughtily, "I thought I spotted a rare variety of coot over this way."

"Not a coot," Borako said. "A wild goose, I theenk."

"Well, I can't stand here nattering," Lafayette said loftily. "Gizelle will be wondering where I am."

He made his way back down into camp, Borako's boots clumping behind him. Gizelle met him as he reached the clearing.

"Zorito! Come! Eet's time to get ready for the wedding."

"Oh, is someone getting married?" Lafayette said. "Well, I'm sure it will be a jolly occasion, and I appreciate the invitation, but—" His remonstrances were cut short as Gizelle threw her arms around his neck.

"Uh—Gizelle," he started, "there's something I should tell you—"

"Zorito! Stop talking! How can I keess you?"

"Are you sure you know me well enough?" He temporized as she clung to him.

"Eet ees an old tribal custom," she murmured, nibbling his ear, "to sneak a leetle sample of the goods before buying . . . "

"Buying?" Lafayette stalled. "You mean stealing, don't you?"

Gizelle giggled. "Sure—you get the idea. Come on." She caught his hand and pulled him toward her wagon. As they approached it, a large man stepped forth from the shadows.

"Well—what do you want, you beeg bum?" Gizelle said spiritedly, with a toss of her head.

"The Ancient Law don't say notheeng about geeving the veectim a beeg smooch before the wedding," the man said sullenly.

"So—what's eet to you, Borako?"

"You know I got the hots for you, Gizelle!"

"Get lost, you," Lafayette spoke up. "Can't you see you're disturbing the lady?"

"You want to come out een the alley and say that?" Borako demanded, stepping forward truculently.

"No!" Gizelle cried, hurling herself at him; he knocked her roughly aside.

"Here!" Lafayette exclaimed. "You can't do that!"

"Let's see you stop me!" Borako yanked the broad knife from his belt, advanced on Lafayette in a crouch. As he slashed out with the blade, Lafayette leaned aside, clamped a complicated two-handed grip on the man's wrist and with a heave, levered him over his hip. Borako executed a flip and landed heavily on his jaw and lay still, while the knife went skittering across the grass.

"Zorito! My hero!" Gizelle squealed, throwing her arms around Lafayette's neck. "For a meenute there I theenk eet ees all over! But you protected me, at the reesk of your life! You *do* love me, my hero!"

"You did the same for me," Lafayette mumbled, his vocal apparatus somewhat encumbered by the kisses of the grateful girl. "That was queek theenking—I mean, quick thinking—"

"Aha—you sleeped! You forgot your phony accent!" Gizelle hugged him tighter. "Frankly, I was begeening to wonder a leetle . . . "

"Look here," Lafayette said, holding her at arm's length. "Look at me! Do I really look like this Zorro character?"

"Zorito, you are a beeg comeec!" Gizelle grabbed his ears, nibbled his cheek. "Of course you look like yourself, seely! Why shouldn't you?"

"Because I'm *not* myself! I mean, I'm not anyone named Zorito! I'm Lafayette O'Leary! I'm a peaceful *Roumi*, who just happened to be skulking around in the dark and got picked up by the City Guard, and rescued by mistake by Luppo and his thugs! And now everybody seems to think I'm somebody I'm not!"

Gizelle looked at him doubtfully. "Nobody could look theese much like my Zorito and not be Zorito . . . unless you got maybe a tween brother?"

"No, I'm not twins," Lafayette said firmly. "At least," he started, "not unless you want to count certain characters like Lorenzo and Lothario O'Leary, and of course Lohengrin O'Leary, and Lafcadio and Lancelot—" he caught himself. "But I'm just obfuscating the issue. They don't really exist—at least not in this continuum."

"You sure talk a bunch of nonseense, Zorito," Gizelle said. "Hey—I know! Take off your clothes!"

"Er—do you think we have time?" Lafayette hedged. "I mean—"

"You got a leetle birthmark on your heep," Gizelle explained. "Let me see, queek!"

"Just a minute, somebody might come along and get the wrong idea!" Lafayette protested; but the girl had already grabbed his shirt, yanked the tails clear of his belt, dragged his waistband down to expose his hipbone.

"See? Just like I remeember!" She pointed in triumph to the butterfly-shaped blemish on the olive skin. "I knew you were keeding all along, Zorito!"

"That's impossible," Lafayette said, staring at the mark. He poked at it experimentally. "I never had a birthmark in my life! I . . . " his voice faltered as his gaze focused on his fingertip. It was a long, slender finger, with a grimy, well-chewed nail.

"That," O'Leary said, swallowing hard, "is not *my* finger!"

3

"I'm perfectly fine," Lafayette said calmly, addressing the backs of his eyelids. "Pulse sixty, blood pressure normal, temperature 98.6°F., sensory impressions coming in loud and clear, memory excellent—"

"Zorito," Gizelle said, "why are you standeeng there weeth your eyes closed, talking to yourself?"

"I'm not talking to myself, my dear. I'm talking to whoever I've turned into—*whom*ever, I should say—object of the preposition, you know—"

"Zorito—you don't turn into eenybody—you are steel you!"

"I can see we're going to have a little trouble with definitions," Lafayette said, feeling the fine edge of hysteria creeping higher, ready to leap. With an effort, he pulled himself together.

"But as I tried to tell your uncle, I have important business in the capital—"

"More important than your wedding night?"

"*My* wedding night?" Lafayette repeated, dumbfounded.

"Yours—and mine," Gizelle said grimly.

"Wait a minute," Lafayette said, "this has gone far enough. In the first place, I don't even know you, and in the second place, I've already got a wife, and—" He leaped back just in time as a slim blade flashed in the girl's hand.

"So—eet's like theese, eh?" she hissed, advancing. "You theenk you can play games weeth the heart of Gizelle? You theenk you can keess and run away, hey? I'll feex you so you never break a poor girl's heart again, you worm-in-the-grass!" She leaped, Lafayette bumped against the side of a wagon; the blade came up—

But instead of striking, Gizelle hesitated. Sudden tears spilled from her long-lashed eyes. She let the stiletto fall from her fingers, covered her face with her hands.

"I can't do eet," she sobbed. "Now they weel all speet on me, b-b-but I don't care. I weel keel myself instead . . . " She groped for the knife; Lafayette grabbed her hands.

"No!" he blurted. "Gizelle! Stop! Listen to me! I . . . I—"

"You . . . you do care for me theen?" Gizelle said in a quavering tone, blinking away the tears.

"Of course I care for you! I mean . . . " He paused at the succession of expressions that crossed the girl's piquant face.

"You remember now how much you love me?" she demanded eagerly.

"No—I mean—I don't remember, but . . . "

"You poor darleeng!" Sudden contrition transformed Gizelle's features into those of an angel of mercy. "Luppo said you got heet on the head! Theese geeves you amnesia, no? That's why you don't remember our great love!"

"That . . . that must be it," Lafayette temporized.

"My Zorito," Gizelle cooed. "It was for me you got knocked on the head; come, we go eenside; soon eet

weel all come back to you." She turned him toward the
wagon door.

"But—what if your uncle sees us—"

"Let heem eat hees heart out," Gizelle said callously.

"Fine—but what if he decides to cut *my* heart out
instead?"

"You don't have to play cheecken any longer, Zorito;
you made your point. Now you get your reward." She
lifted a heavy latch and pushed open the door; a candle
on a table shed a romantic light on tapestries, icons, rugs,
a beaded hanging beyond which was visible a high-sided
bed with a red and black satin coverlet and a scattering
of pink and green cushions, a tarnished oval mirror. Lafayette stared in fascination at the narrow, swarthy, black-
eyed face reflected there. Glossy blue-black hair grew to
a widow's peak above high-arched brows. The nose was
long and aquiline, the mouth well-molded if a trifle weak,
the teeth china-white except for a gold filling in the
upper left incisor. It wasn't a bad-looking face, Lafayette
thought numbly, if you liked them flashy and heavy on
the hair oil.

Hesitantly, he fingered an ear, poked at his cheek,
writhed his lips. The mirrored face aped every action.

"Zorito, why are you weegling your leeps?" Gizelle
inquired anxiously. "You aren't goeeing to have a feet,
are you?"

"Who knows?" he said, with a hollow laugh, fingering
a lean but tough biceps. "I seem to be stuck with someone else's body; it might have anything from paresis to
angina pectoris. I suppose I'll find out as soon as the first
attack strikes."

"You are a naughty boy, Zorito, not to tell me you are a seek man," Gizelle said reproachfully. "But eet's OK—I'll marry you eenyway. Eet weel be fun while you last." She kissed him warmly. "I won't be a meenute," she breathed as she slid through into the next room with a soft clash of beads.

Dimly through the curtain he saw her toss a garment aside with a deft motion; saw the soft ivory glow of her skin in the colored light.

"Why don't you get comfortable?" she called softly. "And pour us a glass of blackberry wine. Eet's een the cupboard over the Ouija board."

"I've got to get out of here," Lafayette mumbled, averting his eyes from the alluring vision. "Daphne would never understand the Law of the Tribe." He tiptoed to the door, had his hand on the knob when Gizelle's soft voice spoke behind him:

"Seely—that's not the cupboard. The door beside eet!" He turned; she stood in the doorway, clad in an invisible negligee.

"Oh, of course. My amnesia, you know," he jerked his hand back.

"Amnesia, nothing," she snapped. "You don't theenk I eve let eeny man eento my bedroom before, do you?"

"No offense," Lafayette said quickly, forcing his gaze from her figure to the corner of the room.

Gizelle giggled. "Oh, boy, what a surprise eef you'd stepped out there and run eento Borako. The sight of you would drive heem mad weeth jealousy."

"Maybe I'd better just go out and have a word with him," Lafayette suggested.

"Don't overdo the hero routine, my Zorito. Borako ees steel the tribal champ weeth a knife, even eef you deed accidentally treep heem up. Better geev heem time to cool off . . . " She came to him, slipped her arms around his neck. "Now you better kees me, before I cool off, my lover!"

"Ah . . . mmnnn," Lafayette said as their lips met. "I just remembered something I have to do—"

Gizelle made a swift movement; the knife glittered under Lafayette's nose.

"I theenk you remember the wrong theengs at the wrong time, beeg boy," she said in a tone like torn metal. "Better geet weeth the program!"

"Do you . . . carry that knife all the time?" O'Leary inquired, edging away from it.

"As long as I have one leetle wisp on to hide eet een," she said sweetly.

"Oh," Lafayette said. "In that case—I mean, ah . . . "

"You forgot the wine," Gizelle said. She brushed past him, took out a purple bottle and two long-stemmed glasses, poured them full.

"To our wedded blees," she murmured and sipped. "What's the matter, you don't dreenk?" she asked sharply as Lafayette hesitated.

"Uh—to wedded bliss," he said, and drank. "And now, why don't we, ah, repair to the, er, nuptial couch?"

Gizelle giggled.

"I'll turn off the light," Lafayette said, and quickly snuffed the candle.

"What's the matter, you don't like to look at me?" Gizelle pouted. "You theenk I'm ugly?"

"I'm afraid of a heart attack," Lafayette said. "Can I, ah, help you with your, er, garment?"

"As you weesh, carissimo," she breathed. Lafayette's fingers brushed satin skin; then he was holding the wispy negligee. Something heavier than sheer silk thumped against his knee; the knife, in a thin leather sheath.

"Now—take me, my Zorito—I am yours!"

"Uh, I'd better make sure the door's locked," Lafayette said, backing away from the sound of her voice.

"Don't worry about trifles at a time like theese!" she whispered urgently. "Where are you, Zorito?"

"How about the back door?" Lafayette persisted, groping in the dark for the doorknob.

"There ees no back door!"

"I'll just make one last check," Lafayette said as his fingers found the latch. He jerked the door open, slid through into bright moonlight, slammed the door and shot home the bolt. From beyond the panel, Gizelle's voice called his name in a puzzled tone. As Lafayette hastily descended the three steps, the bulky figure of Borako separated itself from the shadow of a giant tree fifty feet away.

"Ha!" he growled; in the moonlight his teeth flashed white in a wide and unfriendly grin. "Threw you out, deed she? Eet feegures. And now I feex you, permanently." Borako jerked the knife from his belt, whetted it on a hairy forearm, advancing toward Lafayette.

"Look here, Borako," Lafayette said, edging sideways. "I bounced you on your head once today; am I going to have to do it again?"

"Last time you treecked me," Borako snarled. "Theese time I've got a few freends along to referee." As he spoke, three large men materialized from the deep shadows behind him.

"Well, now that you have a foursome, you can play a few holes of golf," Lafayette snapped. As he spoke, the door of the wagon rattled; a sharp, furious shriek sounded, followed by the pounding of irate feminine fists on the panels.

"Hey—what deed you do to her?" Borako grunted.

"Nothing," Lafayette said. "That's what she's mad about."

As his cohorts rushed to the locked door, Borako uttered a roar and charged. Lafayette feinted, ducked aside and thrust out a foot, hooked Borako's ankle. The Wayfarer plunged headfirst into a wagon wheel, wedging his head firmly between the big wooden spokes.

The other three men were fully occupied in impeding each other's efforts to unbar the door. Lafayette faded back between wagons, turned, and sprinted for the shelter of the deep forest.

Chapter Three

1

For half an hour, the sounds of men beating the brush waxed and waned around O'Leary where he lay facedown in the concealment of what he had belatedly realized was a patch of berry bramble. At length the activity dwindled, a last voice called a final curse. Silence fell. Lafayette crawled forth, dusted himself off, wincing at the impressive variety of aches and pains he had acquired thus far in the night's adventures. He groped inside his coat; the Mark III was still in place. He scanned the dark slope below. Terraced formations of crumbling rock strata led precariously downward.

He started down, keeping his eyes carefully averted from the vista of black treetops beneath him. It was a stiff twenty-minute climb to a wide ledge where he flopped down to rest.

"Out of condition," he told himself disgustedly. "Lying around the palace with no more exercise than a set of lawn tennis now and then is making an old man of me. When I get back, I'll have to start a regimen of dieting and regular workouts. I'll jog early in the morning—say ten laps around the gardens while the dew is still on the roses—then a nice light breakfast—no champagne for a while—then a light workout on the weights before lunch . . . " He paused, hearing a faint sound in the underbrush. A hunting cat? Or Borako and his men, still on the prowl . . .

Lafayette got to his feet, resumed his cautious descent. The moon went behind a cloud. In pitch darkness, his feet groped for purchase. A rock moved underfoot; he slid, caught at wiry roots, slithered down a sudden steep declivity, fetched up with a painful thump while small stones rattled down around him.

For a moment he lay still, listening for alarums and excursions from above. Except for a high, faint humming as of a trapped insect, the night silence was unbroken.

Lafayette got cautiously to his feet. Inches from the spot where he had fallen, the ledge dropped vertically away; a yard or so on either side of him it curved back in to meet the cliff face.

"Nice going, O'Leary; you've got yourself trapped like a mouse in a wastebasket."

His eyes, accustoming themselves to the darkness, were caught by a faint hint of light emanating from a vertical cleft in the rock face, two feet to the right of the ledge. He leaned out, peered into a narrow, shadowy passage cutting back into the rock, barely visible in the pale glow from an unseen source.

There might be room to squeeze through, he decided. "And maybe there'll be a rear entrance. It's either that, or spend the rest of the night waiting for Borako and Luppo to find me when the sun comes up."

Without further debate, he swung himself out, found a foothold, and squeezed through the narrow opening. A narrow passage led inward ten feet, turned sharply to the right, and debouched into a wide, cool cave bathed in a ghostly blue light.

2

The rock chamber in which Lafayette found himself was high-vaulted, smooth-floored, with rough-hewn walls. The eerie glow came from an object resting on a pair of trestles in the center of the room—an object that bore an uncomfortable resemblance to a coffin. It was seven feet long, a foot deep, tapering toward each end from the three-foot breadth of its widest point. A remarkable assemblage of wires and pipes led from the foot of the sarcophagus—if it was a sarcophagus—down to a heavy baseplate where an array of dials glowed a bilious yellow from their own inner illumination.

"Just take it easy," Lafayette soothed himself. "There's nothing spooky about it. It's all perfectly natural. Outside the sun will soon be shining. It just happens to be a cave with a box in it, that's all . . ."

O'Leary circled the coffin—if it *was* a coffin, he reminded himself doggedly, suppressing a tendency for the hair on the nape of his neck to stand erect. There was nothing else in the chamber; no other passage led from it; there was no sound but the soft hum, like that of a heavy-duty freezer, Lafayette thought.

"A coffin-shaped freezer? Why would anyone want a coffin-shaped freezer?" he inquired aloud in a breezy tone; but the hollow, echoic quality of his words robbed them of the cheeriness he had intended. In silence he approached the box; it was covered by a thick lid, sealed with a strip of sponge rubber. At close range he saw that a layer of dust overlay the smooth, gray-green plastic. Lafayette drew a finger across the surface, leaving a distinct mark that glowed more brightly than the surrounding area.

"The accumulation of a few days—or a few weeks," he assessed. "So whatever this is, it hasn't been here long . . . "

There was a small nameplate attached to the side of the box. Lafayette could barely make out the lettering in the weak light:

STASIS POD, MARK XXIV
220v., 50 amp, 12 HP

Below this terse legend, other words had been carefully defaced, the metal scraped bare. Lafayette felt a deeper excitement stir within him.

"More Central equipment," he murmured. "First the Focal Referent—plus rumors of more of the same in a cave; then this—in another cave. There has to be a connection—and the connection has to tie in with me being somebody I'm not . . . "

He felt over the plastic case for further clues to its nature; under his hands he could feel a minute vibration, plus a barely perceptible sensation as of electrical current flowing over the surface. His finger encountered a small depression; as he explored it, a soft *click!* sounded from deep inside the container.

At once, the humming sound took on a deeper tone. Lafayette stepped back, startled. Further clickings and snickings as of closing relays came from the box. A sound remarkably like that of a blower motor started up. Lights winked on the panel. Needles stirred and jumped on dials, moving toward red lines.

Lafayette grabbed for the switch he had tripped, poked and prodded at it frantically; but the process he had set in motion proceeded serenely. He searched for another switch; there wasn't one. On all fours, he peered at the instrument faces, but their readings were cryptic:

97.1 SBT; BM 176 . . . 77 . . . 78; NF 1.02; 1AP 15 kpsc.

"Now I've done it," he muttered. Scrambling to his feet, he cracked his head a dizzying blow on the underside of the container. Through the momentary haze, it seemed that the top of the case was slowly sliding back, revealing an interior lined with padded red satin.

"It looks like Dracula's coffin," he mumbled, holding his head in both hands. "It even has . . . " His voice faltered as the retracting cover revealed a pair of feet clad in pointed black shoes. "It even has feet like Dracula . . . and . . . "

Now a pair of purple-clad legs were visible. A long cloak swathed the knees and upper legs. There was a heavy gold chain at the waist. A pair of long-fingered, knuckly hands were folded on the broad chest. From them, rings winked in the gloom. A white beard appeared, clothing an age-lined but powerful chin. A great hawk nose came into view, closed eyes under bushy black eyebrows, a noble sweep of forehead, a purple velvet skullcap atop backswept white locks.

"Not Dracula after all," O'Leary managed. "It's Merlin . . . " He watched in total fascination as the sleeper's chest rose and fell. A finger stirred. The lips parted, uttered a sigh. The eyelids fluttered, opened. Lafayette stared into a pair of immense, violet-pale eyes which fixed on him in a piercing stare.

"I, ah, I'm sorry, sir," O'Leary said hastily. "I just happened along, and I, ah, accidentally seem to have, er, interfered with your arrangements. I hope I haven't caused you any serious inconvenience . . . " As he spoke he backed away, followed by those hypnotic eyes.

"I'll go for help," he said, edging toward the exit, "and before you know it . . . " His voice trailed off as the staring eyes bored fixedly into his. The old man sat up suddenly, an expression of ferocity contorting his noble features. He drew a deep breath, uttered a snorting roar, and lunged—

As if released from paralysis, O'Leary gained the entry in a bound, squeezed into the narrow passage, lost skin thrusting through the cleft. His foot trod air. He grabbed, slipped, yelled—

And was falling through space. For a long moment he was aware of the rush of wind, of the starry canopy wheeling above him—

Then a silent explosion filled the world with Roman candles.

3

How lovely, Lafayette thought dreamily, *to be lying in a big, soft bed, warm and cozy and without a problem in the world.*

Yes, indeed, a whispery voice said soothingly. *Now, just relax and let your mind rove back over the events of the last few weeks. Back to your first meeting with him. That was . . . where—*

With who? Lafayette inquired offhandedly. *Or with whom?* He wasn't greatly interested. It was so much nicer just to let it all slide away on a sea of black whipped cream . . .

Tell me! the voice persisted, more urgently. *Where is he now? And where is it? Speak!*

Sorry, Lafayette replied. *I'm not in the mood for riddles right now. Why not go find someone else to play with? I just want to doze a little longer, and then Daphne will bring me a cup of coffee and tell me about all the nice things planned for the day, starting with breakfast on the balcony . . .*

He paused for a moment in these pleasant reflections to wonder what day it was. Sunday? Possibly—but it didn't seem like Sunday, somehow. And there was something else nagging at the corner of his mind, now that he thought about it. Something he was supposed to do—

He tried to ignore the intruding thought and snuggle back into the dream; but the damage had been done. He was waking up in spite of himself, in spite of a subconscious instinct that told him that the longer he slept the better he'd like it . . .

He opened his eyes, was looking up at a canopy of what appeared to be woven grass and leaves.

"Ah, awake so soon?" a brisk, cheery voice inquired at close range. "What about a spot of breakfast, then?"

Lafayette turned his head; a round, wizened face beamed down at him.

"Who—" Lafayette croaked, and cleared his throat, occasioning a sharp throb at the back of his skull. "Who are you?"

"I? Well, as to that—you may call me Lom. Quite. Good a name as any, what? And what do you say to Bavarian ham, eggs Benedict, oatmeal bread—lightly toasted—with unsalted Danish butter and a spot of lime marmalade; and coffee, of course. It's New Orleans style: I hope you don't mind a bit of chicory?"

"Don't tell me," Lafayette whispered, salivating profusely. "I've died and gone to wherever well-intentioned sinners go."

"Not at all, my dear sir." Lafayette's host chuckled gently. "You've taken a bit of a tumble, but we'll soon have you right as rain."

"Fine—but . . . where am I?" Lafayette raised his head, saw the rough walls of a lean-to made of sticks, and beyond the doorway the bright sunshine of a spring morning.

"Why, you're sharing my humble quarters," Lom said. "I apologize for the somewhat primitive accommodations, but one does the best one can with the resources at hand, eh?"

"Haven't we met before? Your voice seems familiar."

"I doubt it—though one can never be sure, eh?" Lom looked quizzically at O'Leary.

"The last thing I remember," Lafayette said, "was falling off a cliff . . . " He made a move to sit up; pain lanced through his right arm.

"Oh, best you don't move about," the old fellow said quickly. "You've had a nasty fall, you know. But you were fortunate in descending through the tops of a number of trees before coming to rest in a dense fern thicket."

"What time is it?" O'Leary asked. "What day is it?"

"Oh, I should say it's half past ten," Lom said cheerfully. "As for the day . . . ummm. I fear I've lost count. But it was just last night—or more properly, early this morning that I found you. My, what a din you made!"

"Ten thirty. Ye gods, I'm wasting time—" O'Leary made another move to sit up; but Lom pressed him back.

"My dear chap, you mustn't think of venturing out yet! The consequences, I fear, would be most serious!"

"Not half as serious as they'll be if I don't get on my way," O'Leary protested; but he sank back, and Lom turned, lifted a laden tray onto his lap.

"There now. A bite or two and you'll feel much better."

"Yes, but," Lafayette said, and took a mouthful of softly steaming eggs. "Mmnnn hnngg mrrlnggg."

"That's a good chap. Now a bit of the ham, eh?"

"Delicious," Lafayette said, chewing. "But you don't understand, Mr. Lom. I'm not actually what I seem. I mean, things of vast importance are waiting for me to do them." He took a large bite of the hot buttered toast.

"You see, I have to—" he paused; under the mild gaze of the amiable old man, the disclosure he had been about to make sounded too fantastic to voice.

" . . . to, ah, attend to certain matters," he said. "After which, I have to, uh, attend to certain *other* matters."

"Of course," the old man nodded in sympathy. "A bit of the marmalade?"

"I don't mean to be mysterious," Lafayette said, accepting the pale-green jelly. "But it's highly classified, you see."

"Ah. Quite candidly, I wondered a bit as to just why you were abroad on the heights; but if you're on official business . . . " Lom smiled understandingly.

"Exactly. Now, how far from town am I?" Lafayette craned to look out through the gaps in the wall. The setting seemed to be one of wild-growing foliage.

"Not far—as the crow flies," Lom said. "But the country between here and the city is somewhat difficult to negotiate, I must confess."

"If you don't mind my asking," Lafayette said, taking a hearty gulp of coffee, "how do you happen to live here all alone?"

The old man sighed. "True, it's lonely here. But peaceful. The contemplative life has its compensations."

"What do you do when it rains?" Lafayette persisted, noting the gaps in the fronded roof through which patches of bright-blue sky were visible.

"Oh, I take appropriate measures." Lom dismissed the problem with an airy wave of his hand.

"You seem to do very well," Lafayette agreed.

"One becomes accustomed to certain small comforts," Lom said almost apologetically.

"Certainly—I don't mean to pry, Mr. Lom—"

"Just Lom—no Mister. I make no pretensions to worldly titles."

"Oh. Well, Lom, I certainly enjoyed my breakfast, but now I really have to be getting started."

"Nonsense, my boy. You can't stir for at least a week."

"You still don't get the Big Picture, Lom. The future of the kingdom depends on my getting the word through at once."

"I have an idea," Lom said brightly. "Suppose I carry the message for you?"

"That's very kind of you, Lom, but this is much too important to entrust to anyone else." Lafayette lifted the tray aside, sat up, ignoring a swarm of little bright lights that swam into view before him. He swung his legs over the side of the narrow pallet on which he lay, and watched with detached interest as the floor tilted up and struck him a ghastly blow on the head.

" . . . really mustn't!" Lom's voice faded back in. Lafayette was back on the cot, blinking away the obscuring haze. "I can't be responsible for the results!"

"Guess I'm . . . little weaker . . . than I thought," Lafayette panted.

"Indeed, yes. Now about the message: what did you wish me to say?"

"This is noble of you, Lom," Lafayette said weakly. "But you won't regret it. Go directly to Princess

Adoranne—or, no, better if you see Daphne first. That's Countess Daphne O'Leary. The poor girl will be frantic. Tell her where I am, and that—" O'Leary paused. "That, ah, there are certain artifacts—"

"What sort of artifacts?" Lom murmured.

"Sorry, I can't tell you. But anyway, there are these artifacts; tell her they're items Nicodaeus would be especially interested in. And they're hidden . . . "

"Yes?" Lom prompted.

"Well, I can't tell you where. It's sensitive information, you understand. But if she'll get in touch with a . . . a certain party, he can show her where."

"May I ask the name of the certain party?"

"Classified," O'Leary said. "That's about it. Can you remember all that?"

"I think so," Lom said. "Something's hidden somewhere, and someone can tell her where to find it."

"Hmmm. When you put it that way, it doesn't sound like much."

"My boy, face the facts: it sounds like gibberish."

"In that case—I'll have to go myself, ready or not."

"If you'd just be a trifle more explicit . . . "

"Impossible."

"It's equally impossible for you to set out on a journey until you're regained your strength."

"Nevertheless, I'm going."

Lom stroked his chin thoughtfully. "Hmmm. See here, my boy—if you're determined . . . and I see you are . . . of course I wouldn't dream of standing in your way. Now, why don't you give yourself another few minutes' rest—time for your breakfast to digest, can't have you getting stomach cramps—and then I'll speed you on your way."

"All right. I admit I feel a little rocky . . . " Lafayette leaned back and closed his eyes.

"Can't afford to go to sleep," he told himself. "The dizziness will pass as soon as I get on my feet and start moving. Can't be far—should reach a farmhouse in an hour or two—get a ride—be at the palace by early afternoon . . . put a call through . . . "

"Yes?" said the operator. *"Central here. Your report, please."*

"This is Lafayette O'Leary. I'm calling from Artesia—Locus Alpha Nine-three—"

"I'm sorry, sir. No such locus is listed in the Central Directory. Kindly re-dial—"

"Wait a minute! Don't ring off! It might take me years to get through to you again! There's an emergency here! It involves a cache of illegal equipment, stolen from Central—"

"No report of missing equipment has been filed, sir. I must now ask you to hang up; the circuits are needed—"

"I've seen it! There's a thing called a Focal Referent—and something else, labeled Stasis Pod! And I have a report of a whole cave full of more of the same!"

"Highly unlikely, sir. You must have made a mistake—"

"I tell you I saw it! In fact, I have the Mark III tucked in a secret pocket inside my coat right now! I know what I'm talking about! I'm an accredited part-time agent of Central! If you don't believe me, talk to Nicodaeus! He'll tell you!"

"Our records indicate no one of that name in the service."

"Then your records are wrong! He's the one who helped me uncover Goruble's plot to take over the country!"

"Indeed, sir? And what is your name?"

"O'Leary! Lafayette O'Leary! Sir Lafayette O'Leary!"

"Ah, yes. I have a record of that name . . . But your voice does not agree with the coded pattern listed for Mr. O'Leary—and a visual scan indicates that your face doesn't match the photo of Mr. O'Leary in our files. I must therefore conclude that you are an imposter. The penalty—"

"I'm not an imposter! I just look like one! I can explain!"

"Very well. Explain."

"Well—I can't actually explain, but—"

"If you have nothing further to add, sir, I must conclude this conversation now. Thank you for calling . . . "

"No! Wait! You have to get the information into the right hands before it's too late! Hello! Hello? Central?"

Lafayette struggled up from the dream, his shouts echoing in his ears. "Must have dozed off," he mumbled, looking around the hut. Lom was nowhere to be seen. Outside, the light seemed to have taken on a different quality: a late-afternoon quality.

"How long did I sleep?" O'Leary mumbled. He struggled up; he was light-headed, but his legs supported his weight.

"Lom! Where are you—" he called. There was no answer. He stepped outside. The hut—a flimsy shack of sticks and leaves, he saw—was surrounded by a flat clearing no more than a dozen yards in diameter, ringed in by high bushes, beyond which distant peaks rose high into the dusk-tinged sky.

"Ye gods—it's almost dark. I must have slept for hours." Lafayette thrust through the encircling shrubbery—and stopped short. At his feet, a vertical cliff dropped away into dizzying depths. He backed off, checked at another point. In five minutes he knew the worst:

"Marooned," he groaned. "Stuck on top of a mesa. I should have known better than to trust anyone who lives in a grass hut and subsists on Bavarian ham."

Far below, the valley spread, green and orderly, a pattern of tilled fields and winding roads. In the distance, the towers of the palace sparkled, ruddy in the late sun. The nearest of the peaks looming beyond the airy gulf surrounding his eyrie were at least five miles away, he estimated.

"I fell here, eh? From where? And how did that frail little old man carry my one-hundred and seventy-five pounds into his hut unassisted? I must have been crazy not to have smelled treachery." At a sudden thought, Lafayette clutched at his coat.

The Mark III was gone.

4

"Beautifully handled, O'Leary," he congratulated himself half an hour later, after a fruitless search of the half-acre mesa. "You really came on like a champ every inch of the way. From the minute you got that idiotic note, you've been shrewdness personified. You couldn't have worked yourself into a tighter pocket if it had been planned that way . . ."

He paused to listen to the echo of his own words.

"Planned that way? Of course it was planned that way—but not by you, you dumbbell! The Red Bull must have been in on it; probably someone paid him to con me, and then . . ." his train of thought faltered. "And then—what? Why hijack me, give me somebody else's face, and strand me on a mountaintop?"

"I don't know," he answered. "But let's skip that for now. The important thing is to get off this peak. Lom managed it. I ought to be able to do the same."

"Maybe he used ropes."

"And maybe I'm a kangaroo!"

"Possibly. Have you looked lately?"

Lafayette examined his hands, felt of his features.

"I'm still Zorro," he concluded. "Worse luck."

"And down there, someone is still on the loose with enough Probability gear to shift Artesia into the next continuum. And what are you going to do about it?"

As if in answer to his question, the sky seemed to flicker—like a bad splice in a movie film—and darken; not gradually, but with an abrupt transition from gathering twilight to deep dusk. Some small, fluffy-pink clouds that had been cruising near the adjacent peak were gone, whisked out of sight like dust under a rug. And that wasn't all, O'Leary realized in that same dizzying instant: the peak itself was gone—as were the neighboring peaks. He saw that much before the last of the light drained away, leaving him in total darkness. He took a step back, felt the ground *softening* under his feet. He was sinking down—dropping faster—then falling through black emptiness.

Chapter Four

1

The wind shrieked past Lafayette's face, buffeted his body. Instinctively, he spread his arms as if to slow his headlong fall. The streaming air tugged tentatively, then with a powerful surge that made the bones creak in his shoulders. In automatic response, he stroked, angling his hands to cup the air. He felt the tug of gravity, the answering lift of giant pinions, sensed the sure, clean speed with which he soared over darkness.

"Good lord!" he burst out. "I'm flying!"

2

The moon came out, revealing a forested landscape far below. For an instant, Lafayette felt a frantic impulse to grab for support; but the instincts he had acquired along with the wings checked his convulsive motion with no more than a sudden, heart-stopping dip in his glide.

"Keep calm," a semi-hysterical voice screamed silently at him from the back of his head. "As long as you keep calm, you'll be all right."

"Fine—but how do I land?"

"Worry about that later."

A lone bird—an owl, Lafayette thought—sailed close, looked him over with cold avian eyes, drifted off on owl business.

"Maybe I can stretch my glide," he thought. "If I can make it back to the capital and reach Daphne . . ." He scanned the horizon in vain for the city lights. Cautiously, he tried to turn, executed a graceful orbit to the left. The dark land below spread to the horizon, unrelieved by so much as a glimmer.

"I'm lost," O'Leary muttered. "Nobody has ever been as lost as this!"

He tried a tentative stroke of his arms, instantly stalled, fell off in a flat spin. He fought for balance, gradually spiraled out into straight and level gliding.

"It's trickier than it looks," he gasped, feeing his heart hammering at high speed under his sternum—or was it just the rush of air? It was hard to tell. Hard to tell anything, drifting around up here in darkness. *Have to get down, get my feet on the ground . . .*

He angled his wings; the horizon slowly rose; the note of the wind in his ears rose to a higher pitch; the buffeting of the air increased.

"So far, so good," he congratulated himself. "I'll just hold my course until I've built up speed, then pull out and . . . " The horizon, he noted, had risen still higher. In fact, he had to bend his neck to see it—and even as he rolled his eyes upward, it receded still further.

"Ye gods, I'm in a vertical dive!" he pressed with his outspread fingers—but it was like thrusting a hand into Niagara Falls.

"There was nothing in *How to Solo Solo* about this," he mumbled, gritting his teeth with the effort. "Why in the world didn't I sprout inherently stable wings while I was at it—"

A tree-covered ridge was rushing toward him with unbelievable swiftness; Lafayette put all his strength in a last-ditch effort. His overstrained wings creaked and fluttered. A dark mass of foliage reared up before him—

With a shattering crash, he plunged into a wall of leaves, felt branches snapping—or were they bones?

Something struck him a booming blow on the head, tumbled him down into a bottomless silence.

How lovely, Lafayette thought dreamily, *to be lying in a snow bank, dreaming you're in a big, soft bed, warm and cozy, with an aroma of ham and eggs and coffee drifting in from the middle distance . . .*

He paused for a moment in these pleasant reflections to wonder why it all seemed so familiar. Something was nagging at the corner of his mind: a vague feeling that he'd been through all this before—

Oh, no, you don't, he cut the train of thought short. *I know when I'm well off. This is a swell hallucination, and I'm not giving it up without a struggle . . .*

"You've had that thought before, too," the flat voice of experience told him. "It didn't work last time, and it won't work now. You've got problems, O'Leary. Wake up and get started solving them."

Well, there's one consolation, he countered. *Whatever my problems are, they're not as silly as what I was dreaming. Wings, already. And a gang of Wayfarers on my trail. And a mummy that came to life, and—*

"Don't look now, O'Leary . . . but you've got a shock coming."

Lafayette pried an eye open. He was looking out through a screen of oversized leaves at a vista of treetops—treetops the size of circus tents, spreading on and on—

He clutched convulsively for support as his eye fell on the curving expanses of rough-textured chocolate-brown bark on which he lay.

"Oh, no," he said. "You've got to be kidding. I didn't *really* crash-land in a treetop after turning into a birdman . . . "

He started to scramble to his feet, felt a stab of pain that started at least ten feet beyond his fingertip and shot like a hot wire all the way up to his neck. Turning his head, he saw a great, sorrel-feathered pinion spread along the wide bough on which he lay, its feathers bedraggled and in disarray. He twitched his shoulder blades tentatively, saw a corresponding twitch of the unfamiliar members, accompanied by another sharp jab of pain—reminiscent of that occasioned by biting down on a bone-chip with a sensitive tooth.

"It's real," he said wonderingly. He sat up carefully, leaned over, looked down through level after level of foot-wide leaves. The ground was down there, somewhere.

"And I'm up here. With a broken wing, Zorp only knows how high in the air. Which means I have to get down the hard way." He studied the two-yard-wide branch under him, saw how it led back among leafy caverns to the shadow-obscured pillar of the trunk.

"It must be fifty feet in diameter. And that's impossible. There are no trees that big in Artesia—or anywhere else, for that matter, especially with leaves like an overgrown sycamore."

"Right," he replied promptly. "Nicely reasoned. The tree's impossible, your wings are impossible, the whole thing's impossible. So what do we do now?"

"Start climbing."

"Dragging a broken wing?"

"Unless you have a better idea."

"Take your choice, O'Leary," he muttered. "Try it, and fall to your death, or stay here and die in comparative comfort."

"Correction," he reminded himself. "You can't afford to be dead—not while the Red Bull is itching to sell Goruble's hoard to any unsavory character with the price of a chicken dinner."

"Besides which," he agreed, "I have a few chicken dinners to eat yet myself."

"That's the spirit. Up and at 'em. *I saye and I doe.*"

Painfully, Lafayette got to his feet, favoring the injured member. The wings, he saw by craning his neck, sprouted from his back between his normal shoulders and the base of his neck. His chest was puffed out like that of a pigeon; hard muscle, he found, prodding himself with the long, lean fingers he now possessed. His face—insofar as he could determine by feeling it over—was narrow, high cheek-boned, with small, close-set eyes and a widow's peak of bushy hair. Somehow, without a mirror, he knew that it was glossy black, that his eyes were a lambent green, his teeth snowy white in a sun-dark face.

"Good-bye, Zorro," he muttered. "It was a mixed pleasure being you. I wonder who I am now? Or what?"

There was a flutter among the leaves, a sharp *kwee, kwee!* A small white bird swooped on him. Lafayette batted at it in surprise, almost lost his balance, yelped aloud at the stab from his wing as he grabbed for support. The bird hovered, *kwee!*ing in a puzzled way. A moment later two more joined in. Lafayette put his back to a branch, fended off their repeated attempts to dart in close.

"Get away, blast you!" he yelped. "Don't I have enough trouble without being pecked by meat-eating cockatoos?"

More birds arrived; squawking indignantly, they circled Lafayette's head. He backed along the branch; they followed. He reached the giant bole. A dozen or more of the birds fluttered around him now.

"At least wait till I'm dead!" he yelled.

There was a sudden, shrill whistle from near at hand.

Abruptly, the birds flew up, scattering. The branch trembled minutely under Lafayette's feet. Leaves stirred; a small, slender figure stepped into view, swathed in a cloak of feathers—

No, not a cloak, O'Leary corrected his first startled impression.

Wings.

It was another flying man who stood facing him from ten feet away.

4

The man was narrow-shouldered, narrow-faced, with a long, pointed nose, tight lips, peaked eyebrows above pale, glistening eyes. He was dressed in close-fitting green trousers, a loose tunic of scarlet decorated with gold loops at the cuffs. His feet were bare; his long, slim toes clutched the rough bark.

"It ik ikik;riz izit tiz tizzik ik?" the newcomer said in a musical voice.

"Sorry," Lafayette said, and felt the awkwardness of the word on his lips. "I don't, uh, savvy your lingo . . ."

"Thib, it ik ikik;riz izit tiz tizzik ik, izyik!" The flying man's tone was impatient—but Lafayette hardly noticed that. With one part of his mind he had registered only a series of whistling, staccato sounds—but with another, he had heard words:

"I said, what's the matter? Been eating snik berries?"

"No," Lafayette said, and felt his mouth shape the sound: *"Nif."*

"I thought maybe the zik-zik's had spotted a zazz-worm," the message came clearly through the buzzing and clicking.

"I thought they were trying to eat me alive," O'Leary said—and heard himself mouthing the same twittering sounds.

"Do you feel all right, Haz?" The flying man came forward, moving quickly, with a precise, mincing gait. "You sound as if you had a mouthful of mush."

"As a matter of fact," O'Leary said, "I don't feel too well. I'm afraid heights make me dizzy. Could you, ah, show me the quickest way down?"

"Over the side, what else?" The flying man stared curiously at Lafayette; his eyes strayed to O'Leary's wing, which he had propped against the bole for support.

"Hey—it looks like—good night, fella, why didn't you say so? That's a broken freeble-bone, or I'm a landlubber!"

"I guess," Lafayette said, hearing his voice echo from far away. "I guess . . . it is . . . at that . . . "

He was only dimly aware of hands that caught him, voices that chirped and whistled around him, of being assisted along the rough-textured path, of being lifted, pulled, of twinges from his injury, faint and far away; and then of a moment of pressure—pressure inside his bones, inside his mind, an instant of a curious vertigo, of the world turned inside out . . .

Then he was in cool darkness and an odor of camphor, sinking down on a soft couch amid murmurings that faded into a soft green sleep.

5

"That's three times," he was saying as he awoke. "My skull can't take much more of it."

"Of what, Tazlo darling?" a soft, sweet voice whispered.

"Of being hit with a blunt instrument," O'Leary said. He forced his eyes open, gazed up at a piquant feminine face that looked down at him with an expression of tender concern.

"Poor Tazlo. How did it happen? You were always such a skillful flier . . ."

"Are you really here?" Lafayette asked. "Or are you part of the dream?"

"I am here, my Tazlo." A soft, slim-fingered hand touched Lafayette's cheek gently. "Are you in much pain?"

"A reasonable amount, considering what I've been through. Strange. I go along for months at a time—even years—without so much as a mild concussion—and then bam—slam—bash! They start using my head for a practice dummy. That's how I can tell I'm having an adventure. But I really can't take much more of it."

"But you're safe now, Tazlo dear."

"Ummmnn." He smiled lazily up at the girl. "That's one of the compensations of an active life; these delightful fantasies I have while I'm waking up."

He looked around the room: it was circular, with vertical-grained wood-paneled walls, a dark, polished floor; a lofty ceiling, lost in shadows, through which a single shaft of sunlight struck. The bed on which he lay had a carved footboard, a downy mattress, comfortable as a cloud.

"I suppose in a minute I'll discover I'm impaled on a sharp branch a hundred yards over a gorge filled with cacti or crocodiles," he said resignedly, "but at the moment, I have no complaints whatever."

"Tazlo—please . . ." There was a stifled sob in her voice. "Speak sensibly; tell me you know me—your own little Sisli Pim."

"Are you a Sisli Pim, my dear?"

"I'm Sisli Pim, your Intended! You don't remember me!" The elfin face puckered tearfully; but with an effort, she checked the flood, managed a small smile. "But you can't help that, I know. It's the bump on your head that makes you so strange."

"Me, strange?" Lafayette smiled indulgently. "I'm the only normal thing in this whole silly dream—not that you're silly, er, Sisli. You're quite adorable—"

"Do you really think so?" She smiled enchantingly. In the dim light Lafayette thought her hair looked like feathery plumes, pale violet, around her heart-shaped face.

"I certainly do. But everything else is typical of these fantasies I have when I'm waking up. Like this alleged language I'm speaking: it's just something my subconscious made up, to fit in with the surroundings—just gibberish, but at the moment it seems to make perfectly good sense. Too bad I can't get a tape recording of it. It would be interesting to know if it's actually a self-consistent system, or just a bunch of random sounds."

"Tazlo—please don't! You frighten me! You . . . you don't even sound like yourself!"

"Actually, I'm not," O'Leary said. "I'm actually a fellow named Lafayette O'Leary. But don't be frightened, I'm harmless."

"Tazlo—you mustn't!" Sisli whispered. "What if Wizner Hiz hears you?"

"Who's he?"

"Tazlo—Wizner Hiz is the Visioner of Thallathlone! He might not understand that you're just raving because of a blow on the head! He might take this talk of being someone else seriously! Remember what happened to Fufli Hun!"

"I'm afraid it's slipped my mind. What did happen to poor old Fufli?"

"They . . . Sang him Out."

Lafayette chuckled. "Sisli, anyone who's sat through a concert of the Royal Artesian Philharmonic isn't afraid of any mere choral group." Lafayette sat up, felt a sharp pain in the small of his back—a pain that seemed to originate from a point in midair, two feet above and to the left of his shoulder blade. He twisted his head, saw a bale of white bandages from which rather bedraggled russet feathers protruded.

"What—are *you* still here?"

"Who?" Sisli said in alarm. "Tazlo, you're not seeing invisible enemies, are you?"

"I'm talking about these infernal wings," Lafayette said. "I dreamed I flew through the air with the greatest of ease—until I crash-landed in a treetop. Then there was something about being attacked by meat-eating pigeons—and then a birdman arrived, and . . . and that's all I remember." He rubbed his head. "Funny—by now I should be waking up and having a good laugh about the whole thing . . . "

"Tazlo—you *are* awake! Can't you tell? You're here—in Thallathlone, with me!"

"And before the flying sequence," Lafayette went on, frowning in deep thought, "there was the business of being marooned on a mountaintop. A pretty obvious symbolism, reflecting my feeling of isolation with my problem. You see, I'd found this Focal Referent—some kind of probability gadget, I think, stolen from Central—and I was having a terrible time trying to get word to the authorities—"

"Tazlo—forget all that! It was just a nightmare! Now you're awake! You're going to be fine—just as soon as your wing heals!"

"I find that if you run over a dream in your mind as soon as you wake up, you can fix it in your conscious memory. Now, let's see: there was the man in the cave—*that* was spooky! He was under an enchantment, I suppose—except that the logical part of my mind cooked up something called a Stasis Pod to rationalize things. He represents Wisdom, I suppose—but the way he attacked me suggests that I must have a suppressed fear of knowledge."

"Tazlo—why don't we step outside and get a little sunlight, maybe that will dispel these morbid fancies—"

"Just a minute; this is pretty interesting. I never knew you could psychoanalyze yourself just by dissecting your dreams. I always thought I approved of Science—but apparently it's a secret bugaboo of mine. Now, let's see—there was a little old man, too—a cherubic type, he found me after I fell over the cliff, and brought me home and gave me a marvelous breakfast." Lafayette smiled at the recollection. "At the time it didn't even seem strange that someone living in a grass hut would have a refrigerator full of gourmet items—"

"Are you hungry, Tazlo? I have a lovely big boolfruit, just picked."

"Sure, why not?" Lafayette grinned indulgently at the girl. "I may as well sample everything this dream provides—including you . . . " He caught her hand, pulled her to him, kissed her warmly on the mouth.

"Tazlo!" She stared into his eyes with a look of amazed delight. At close range he could see the velvety-smooth texture of her cheek, the long lashes that adorned her pale-green eyes, the downy feathers that curled on her smooth forehead . . . "You mean—you really mean—"

"Mean what?" Lafayette said absently, noting for the first time the graceful white pinions which enfolded Sisli like a glistening feather cloak.

"That—you want to marry me!"

"Wait a minute," Lafayette said, smiling. "Where did you get that idea?"

"Why, you . . . you kissed me, didn't you?"

"Well, certainly, who wouldn't? But—"

"Oh, Tazlo—this is the most wonderful moment of my life! I must tell Father at once!" She jumped up, a slim, elfin creature aglow with happiness.

"Wait a minute—let's not bring anyone else into this dream. I like it just the way it is!"

"Father will be so happy! He's always hoped for this day! Good-bye for a moment, my dearest—I'll be right back!" Sisli turned, was gone. Lafayette tottered to his feet, grunted at a pang from his bandaged wing, stumbled after her—and slammed into a solid wall.

He backed off, groped over the rough-hewn wood surface, looking for the door through which Sisli had left.

"It's got to be here," he muttered. "I saw her with my own eyes—or at least with the eyes I happen to be using at the moment . . . " But five minutes' search disclosed no opening whatever in the seamless walls.

"My boy!" a whistling nasal voice exclaimed behind him; he whirled; a gnarled, wizened ancient stood in the center of the room, his face beaming in a toothless smile. "My little girl has just given me the happy tidings! Congratulations! I give my consent, of course, dear lad! Come to my arms!" The old boy rushed forward to embrace Lafayette, who stared in bewilderment over the old fellow's featherless skull at a pair of muscular youths who had appeared silently and stood with folded arms and expressions of slightly bored indulgence, flanking Sisli Pim.

"Father says we can have the ceremony this very evening, Tazlo!" she cried. "Isn't that marvelous?"

"Things are going too fast," Lafayette said. "You're leaping to conclusions," he paused, noting the sudden hostility in the expressions of the two young fellows—probably her brothers, O'Leary decided.

"About what?" one of them demanded.

"I mean—I'm very fond of Sisli, of course—but—"

"But what?" the other youth snapped.

"But I can't—I mean—well, confound it, I can't marry her—or anyone else!"

"Eh? What's this?" the oldster chirped, rearing back to gaze up at Lafayette with eyes as sharp as talons. "Can't marry my daughter?" Sisli Pim uttered a wailing cry. The two brothers stepped forward threateningly.

"What I mean is—I'm not eligible!" Lafayette blurted, backing a step.

"Not eligible—how?" the old man inquired, his gaze impaling O'Leary.

"You own the requisite number of acorns, right?" one of the young men demanded.

"And you have an adequate nest, right?" the other pressed.

"And you *did* kiss her," the first pointed out.

"And she didn't knife you," said his companion. "Which means she accepts you, right?"

"So what could possibly stand in your way?" the old man crowed, as if the problem were solved.

"It's just that . . . that . . . "

"Tazlo—you haven't . . . haven't . . . you didn't—"

"You don't mean, I suppose, that you've contracted an understanding with some other maid of Thallathlone?" the larger brother asked in an ominous tone.

"Certainly not! But I can't ask Sisli Pim to marry me," Lafayette said flatly. "I'm sorry I kissed her. I didn't mean it."

There was a sudden movement, a whistle of steel on leather, and a knife was poking Lafayette's throat, gripped in the hard, brown fist of the smaller of the brothers.

"Sorry you kissed my sister, eh?" he hissed.

"No—as a matter of fact I'm *not* sorry," Lafayette snapped, and stamped down hard on the knife-wielder's instep, at the same time chopping outward at the offending wrist, while ramming a fist into the youth's ribs. The lad doubled over, coughing and hopping on one foot.

"As a matter of fact I enjoyed it a lot," O'Leary said defiantly. "But the fact is, I never saw Sisli in my life before ten minutes ago. How can you want her to marry a stranger?"

"Never saw—" the old man quavered, waving back the other brother. "What can you mean? You were raised together! You've seen each other almost daily for the past twenty-one years!"

"Father—I think I understand," Sisli cried, thrusting herself between Lafayette and her male relatives. "Poor Tazlo feels it wouldn't be fair to marry me, in his condition!"

"Condition? What condition?" Father said querulously.

"In the fall—when he broke his wing—he suffered a blow on the head, and he's lost his memory!"

"A likely tale," the elder brother growled.

"How did he happen . . . unh . . . to fall in the first place?" the younger brother grunted, massaging his stomach, wrist and shin simultaneously.

"Yes—how did you happen to fall, Tazlo—you of all people?" the old man asked. "An expert wingsman like you."

"It's a long story," Lafayette said shortly. "You wouldn't understand—"

"Please—how can he tell you?" Sisli protested. "He remembers nothing."

"He remembered how to kiss unsuspecting young females," the younger brother growled.

"Look, fellows—why don't you just forget that? It was a mistake, I admit it. I'm sorry if I caused any misunderstanding—"

"Misunderstanding? This silly goose came rushing up to us, blurted out the glad tidings where half the eyrie heard her! We'll all be a laughingstock—especially if we go off and leave you here in her chamber, unchaperoned!"

"Well, then, I'll go elsewhere. I'm not looking for trouble. Just direct me to the nearest telephone—"

"Nearest what?" three voices chimed as one.

"Well, telegraph station, then. Or police station. Or bus station. I have to get a message through—"

"What's he talking about?"

"He must be raving."

"I think Wizner Hiz ought to know about this."

"No! Tazlo hasn't done anything!" Sisli spoke up. "He'll be fine—just as soon as you go away and leave us alone!"

"Not likely," Younger Brother said grimly. "You come with us, girl—and I'll see to it Haz is moved to a bachelor nest—"

"He needs me! Now get out—both of you—and Father, if you side with them—"

"I never take sides," the old man said quickly. "Calmly, my child. We'll take the matter under advisement. Something will have to be done. In the meantime—suppose we simply keep the entire matter, ah, confidential, eh? No need to give sharp tongues fodder to gnaw on."

"Then you'll have to leave Tazlo here," Sisli said flatly. "If he leaves, everyone will know that . . . that something's amiss."

"Bah, the chit is right," Younger Brother said.

"Tazlo—hadn't you best lie down?" Sisli said, taking Lafayette's hand.

"I'm fine," Lafayette said. "But they're right. I can't stay here." He turned to the three male members of the family—except for himself and Sisli, the room was empty.

"Where did they go?"

"Umm." Sisli looked thoughtful. "Father's hurrying along to his uncle Timro's perch, probably to discuss the situation over a cup or two of bool cider; and Vugli and Hinky are standing about twenty feet away, talking. I don't think they're too well pleased. But you know that as well as I, Tazlo."

"How did they get out?"

"They just . . . went, of course. What do you mean?"

"I looked for a . . . door," Lafayette stumbled over the word. "I can't find one."

"What's a *door*, Tazlo?"

"You know: the part of the wall that moves—swings out, or slides sideways. I can't seem to think of the word for it in Thallathlonian."

Sisli looked interested. "What's it for, Tazlo? Just decoration, I suppose—"

"It's to get in and out by. You know. A *door!*"

"Tazlo—you don't need a *dooor*—whatever that is—to go out. I think that bump on your head—"

"All right then: how do you go out without a door?"

"Why—like this . . . " Sisli turned to the wall, and stepped to it—*through* it. Lafayette saw her advancing foot sink into the solid wood, followed by her body, the tips of her trailing wings disappearing last, leaving the wall as unbroken as before. He jumped after her, ran his hands over the grainy wood. It was solid, slightly warm to touch—

Sisli reappeared just under his chin, bumped him lightly as he jumped back. She laughed, rather uncertainly.

"How—how in the world did you do that?" he gasped.

"Tazlo—you *are* just playing a game, aren't you—"

"Game? The game of going out of my mind—" Lafayette caught himself, drew a breath, managed a shaky laugh of his own.

"I keep forgetting. I'd just about decided this was all real instead of a dream. Then you walk through a wall and spoil the illusion. But it's really time I woke up." He slapped his cheeks lightly. "Come on, O'Leary—wake up! Wake up!"

"Tazlo!" Sisli caught his wrists. "Please—stop acting like one who's lost his wits! If Wizner Hiz should see you—terrible things would happen!"

"I've always had this trouble with too-vivid dreams," Lafayette said. "And it's been worse since I read all those books on mesmerism and hypnogogia. If Central didn't have a Suppressor focused on me, I'd be tempted to think I'd been transferred into another probability continuum—"

"Please, Tazlo," Sisli wailed. "Why don't you lie down and have another nice nap—"

"That's just the trouble, Sisli: I'm asleep now, and dreaming you. I have to wake up and get busy saving the kingdom—"

"Save what kingdom? Thallathlone isn't a kingdom—it's a limited mythocracy!"

"I'm talking about Artesia. It's a bit old-fashioned in some ways, but all in all a very nice place. I used to be a king there—at least I was for a few days, until I could abdicate in favor of Princess Adoranne. That was after I killed Lod, the two-headed giant, and his pet dragon. It wasn't really a dragon, of course, just an allosaurus Goruble had transferred in from a primitive locus—and—"

"Tazlo—lie down, just close your eyes and all these wild fancies will evaporate!"

"They're not wild fancies. *This* is the wild fancy. Don't you see how ridiculous it all is? People with wings, who walk through walls? Typical dream-images, probably reflecting a subconscious wish on my part to be freed of all restraints—"

"Tazlo—*think!* Of course we have wings! Otherwise how could we fly? And of course we walk through walls; how else would we get outside?"

"That's just it—it has all the illogical internal logic of a well-organized dream."

"All that talk about giants and dragons—*that's* the fantasy, Tazlo—don't you see that? They're symbols of the obstacles you feel you have to overcome; and that bit about being a king—a transparent wish-fulfillment. By imagining you abdicated, you have all the prestige of royalty without the responsibilities."

"Say—you know the jargon pretty well yourself. But I suppose that's to be expected, if you're a creation of my subconscious."

Sisli stamped her foot. "*Your* subconscious! Tazlo Haz, I'll have you know that I'm a real, live, three-D, living-color female, and your subconscious has nothing to do with it!" She threw her arms around Lafayette's neck, kissed him long and warmly.

"There!" she gasped. "Now tell me I'm your imagination!"

"But—but if you're real," Lafayette stammered, "then . . . what about Artesia—and the Red Bull and the cave full of gimmicks, and the old man in the coffin, and Lom, and—"

"Just something you dreamed, Tazlo dear," Sisli murmured. "Now lie down and let me feed you some cold boolfruit, and we'll talk about our future."

"Well . . . " Lafayette hesitated. "There's just one thing." He eyed the blank walls that encircled him. "It's all very well for you to walk through solid wood—and your pop and brothers, too, it seems. But what about me? How do *I* get outside?"

"Tazlo, Tazlo—you've been walking through walls since you were a year and a half old!"

"I guess that's about when I learned to walk—but not through teak paneling."

"Silly boy. Come . . . I'll show you." She took his hand, led him to the wall, slid into it. Lafayette watched as the wood engulfed her flesh, her body merging with the wall as if she were sinking into opaque water. Only her arm protruded, holding his hand. It withdrew swiftly, the wood closing around her forearm, her wrist—

Lafayette's fingers rammed the wood with a painful impact. Sisli's hand still gripped his; she tugged again. He pulled away, was rubbing his skinned knuckles as she reappeared, a worried expression in her wide eyes.

"Tazlo—what's the matter?"

"I told you I couldn't walk through walls!"

"But—but, Tazlo—you *have* to be able to!"

"Facts are facts, Sisli."

"But—if you can't walk through the wall . . . " Her expression was frightened.

"Then I guess I'll have to chop my way out. Can you get me an axe?"

"An *axe*?"

He described an axe.

"There's nothing like that in Thallathlone. And if there were—how long would it take you to cut through six feet of solid kreewood? It's harder than iron!"

Lafayette sank down on the bed. "Great. I'm trapped here. But—how did they get me inside—"

Before Sisli could answer, Vugli—the younger brother—stepped through the wall.

"I've just had a chat with Wizner Hiz," he said. "Now don't get upset with me," he added as Sisli whirled on him. "He sought me out, asked me how Haz was. I told him he was all right. So . . . he wants to see him."

"Vugli—how could you?" Sisli wailed.

"He'll have to face him sooner or later. And the sooner the better. If Haz does anything to rouse the old devil's suspicions—well, you know how Wizner is."

"How . . . how soon does he want to see him?"

"He said right now; tonight."

"No!"

"But I stalled him off—until tomorrow morning. I said he had a headache." Vugli gave Lafayette a sour look. "I didn't tell him his headache is nothing compared with the headache I've got."

After Vugli had left, Sisli looked at Lafayette with wide, fearful eyes.

"Tazlo—what can we do?"

"I don't know, kid," Lafayette said grimly. "But we'd better get busy doing it."

Chapter Five

1

"Let's start at the beginning and see if we can make some sense out of this," Lafayette said in a calm, reasonable tone. "Now, I was safe at home, perfectly contented, when I got the note from the Red Bull—"

"Wrong," Sisli said with a shake of her head that made the violet plumes wave adorably. "You were off on one of your hunting expeditions, determined to bring home a pair of gold-crested wiwi-birds to be our hearth-companions after we've set up our nest."

"Very well—if you say so. So I *dreamed* I was in Artesia, getting a note from the Red Bull. And on impulse I did as he asked; went out alone, in the middle of the night, for a mysterious rendezvous at the Axe and Dragon."

"If you were so content—in this dream," Sisli said, "why did you do anything as silly as that?"

Lafayette sighed. "I guess I've always had a romantic streak," he confessed. "Just when everything is at its best, I get this restless urge to adventure. And I suppose the idea of going back to the Axe and Dragon had something to do with it. That's where it all started, you know—"

"No—I don't know. Tell me."

"Well—where should I begin? Back in Colby Corners, USA, I suppose. I was a draftsman. I worked at the foundry. It wasn't very challenging work. But I used to do a lot of reading. I read up on hypnotism. One evening I was trying out a few of the techniques I'd picked up from Professor Shimmerkopf's book, and . . . well, there I was, in Artesia, walking down a cobbled street in the twilight, with the smell of roast goose and stout ale coming from this tavern—the Axe and Dragon."

"In other words—you admit Artesia was imaginary!" Sisli said triumphantly.

"Well . . . I suppose in terms of Colby Corners and the foundry and Mrs. MacGlint's Clean Rooms and Board it was a dream—but once I was there, it was as real as Colby Corner had ever been—realer! I was having adventures, doing all the things I'd always dreamed of doing, having the kind of adventures I'd always wanted—"

"Wish-fulfillment—"

"Please—stop saying 'wish-fulfillment.' I can't remember wishing I was accused of kidnapping the Princess and thrown in jail—or lost in the desert—or locked in a torture cage by Lod."

"But you escaped from all these dilemmas?"

"Well—certainly. If I hadn't, I wouldn't be here. In fact, I'm not sure I *am* here. How can I be sure? A dream seems real while you're dreaming it. You can pinch yourself—but you can dream you pinched yourself—and even dream you woke up, and—"

"Tazlo—please—don't let yourself get so excited. You were telling me about your dream-world of Artesia . . . "

"Yes. Well, I ended up living in the palace as a sort of permanent guest of Princess Adoranne—"

"This Princess—was she pretty?"

"Incredible. Golden hair, big blue eyes—"

"Blue eyes? How grotesque."

"Not at all; on the contrary. And a figure like an angel—"

"You—you were in love with this creature?"

"Well—I thought I was for a while—but . . . "

"But? But what?"

"But," Lafayette temporized, suddenly noting the edge Sisli's voice had acquired, "but of course in the end I realized I wasn't really in love with her—so she married Count Alain and lived happily ever after—at least for a while."

"While you occupied luxury quarters in her palace. How cozy."

"Believe me, she and I were good friends, that's all. And Count Alain was rated the top swordsman in the kingdom, by the way—"

"So—it was only fear of this redoubtable warrior that kept you from her?"

"Who, Alain? Nonsense. I fought a duel with him once and won—with a little help from Daphne, of course—"

"Who," Sisli said coldly, "is Daphne?"

"Why, Daphne is . . . is the former upstairs maid," Lafayette amended his statement. "But I mustn't get distracted from trying to figure out what's real and what isn't," he hurried on. "Anyway, there I was in Artesia, meeting the Red Bull. I thought—well, I thought it would be like old times, but somehow it wasn't. Even the Red Bull seemed different, somehow—he didn't seem to have any conscience anymore—"

"Things are always changed around in dreams, Tazlo."

"I suppose so. But that wasn't the biggest change. The Red Bull stepped out back for a moment, and suddenly—well, this part if very hard to explain. But suddenly—I was somebody else."

"It happens all the time in dreams," Sisli said sympathetically. "But now you're awake, and yourself, the same dear Tazlo Haz you've always been—"

"But I haven't always been Tazlo Haz! I was Zorro the Wayfarer!"

"I thought you said you were Lafayette Something, ex-king of Artesia! You see, Tazlo, how these different hallucinations keep shifting around?"

"You don't understand. It's all perfectly simple. First I was Lafayette O'Leary—then I was Zorro—and now I'm Tazlo Haz—only I'm still Lafayette O'Leary, if you know what I mean."

"No," Sisli sighed. "I don't. And this isn't helping our problem, Tazlo. You still have to remember how to walk."

Lafayette sat on the edge of the bed, gripping his head in both hands, ignoring the curious feel of short, curled feathers where his hair should have been.

"I have to come to grips with this," he told himself firmly. "Either I'm awake, and this is real, and I have amnesia—in which case I've always been able to walk through walls—or I'm asleep and dreaming—and if I'm dreaming, I ought to be able to dream anything I want to—such as the ability to walk through walls!" He looked up with a pleased expression.

"Ergo—either way, I can do it." He stood, eyed the wall defiantly, strode to it—and banged his nose hard enough to bring out a shower of little bright lights.

"Oh, Tazlo—not like that!" Sisli wailed. She clung to him, making soothing sounds. "Is it my itty bitty boy, can't even walk, poor Taz, there, there, Auntie Sissy will help . . ."

"I can walk through walls!" Lafayette snapped. "It's a perfectly natural thing to do in this crazy mixed-up place! All I have to do is hold my mouth right, and—" As he spoke, he had disengaged himself from the girl, advanced on the wall—and thumped it hard enough to stagger him.

"Tazlo—you're going about it all wrong!" Sisli cried. "There's really nothing difficult about it, once you get the feel of *merging*."

"Merging, eh?" Lafayette said grimly. "All right, Sisli—you want to help—teach me how to merge . . . !"

2

Lafayette had lost count of the hours. Twice Sisli had gone out for food—birdseed cakes and cups of sweet juices which in spite of their insubstantiality seemed to satisfy the inner man—or the inner whatever-he-was, Lafayette thought sourly. Once Vugli had appeared, ready to lay down the law, but Sisli had driven him off with a flash of temper that surprised O'Leary. But he was no nearer to pushing his body through six feet of kreewood than he had been at the start.

"Now, Tazlo," the girl said with a gentle persistence that Lafayette found touching even in his frustration, "relax, and we'll try again. Remember, *it's not difficult*. It's not anything that requires a tremendous effort, or any special skill. It's all . . . all just a matter of thinking about it in the right way."

"Sure," Lafayette said dully. "Like describing the difference between mauve and puce to a blind man."

"I can remember—just barely—the first time I did it," she said, musingly. Lafayette could sense the bone-deep fatigue in her, see it in the deep shadows under his eyes, the slump of her slim shoulders. But in the soft light from the glow-jar on the table, she still smiled lovingly at him.

"I was almost two. Father and Mother had planned a treetop picnic. They'd told me so many times how it would be to see the outdoors for the first time—"

"The first time? At age two?"

"Of course, my Tazlo. An infant can't leave the nest in which it's born until it learns to merge."

"Ye gods. What if the kid can't learn—like me?"

"Then—then it remains a prisoner for life. But that won't happen. Tazlo—it can't happen to you—to us!" Her voice broke into a sob.

"Now, now, take it easy, kid," Lafayette soothed, holding her frail, feather-like figure close to him and patting her back. "I'll catch on after a while—"

"Of . . . of course you will. I'm being silly." She brushed a tear away and smiled up at him. "Now, let's start again . . . "

3

The gray light of dawn was filtering through the light-aperture high in the wooden wall against which Lafayette slumped, fingering the newest bruise on his jaw.

"I guess maybe I wasn't meant for merging," he said wearily. "I'm sorry, Sisli. I tried. And you tried. You tried as hard as anyone could try—but—"

"Tazlo—if you don't appear for your appointment with Wizner Hiz, he'll know something is wrong. He'll come here—he'll question you—and when he learns you remember nothing of your life—that you have these strange delusions of other worlds—then he'll—he'll—" Her voice broke.

"Maybe not. Maybe I can convince him I'm just a nut case. That my brains are scrambled. Maybe he'll give me more time—"

"Never! You know how he is about anything that even hints of a Possession!"

"No—how is he?"

"Tazlo—you can't have forgotten *every*thing!" Sisli sat beside him, caught his hands, clasped them tightly. "In his Visioning, if he sees anything—just the faintest hint that a Mind-gobbler has gotten a foothold in someone—Out he goes!"

"Out where?"

"Out—outside. Into the Emptiness. *You* know."

"Sisli, could we accept it as a working hypothesis that I *don't* know? You tell me."

"Well . . . it seems so silly to be telling you what everyone knows—but—once, many years ago, Thallathlone was invaded by creatures too horrible to describe. They took people's minds—grabbed them when they had lowered the Barriers so they could merge—and possessed them. At first, the victim would simply seem a little strange—as if he'd . . . lost his memory. But little by little, they began to . . . change. First, they'd start to lose their feathers; their bones would begin to grow; their plumage fell out, and wiry, thin hairs grew in its place. Finally, their wings would—would wither away, and . . . and drop off!"

"It sounds awful," Lafayette said. "But surely that's just a myth. People don't just turn into other people—" he broke off abruptly at the import of what he was saying. "I mean—not usually . . . "

"Exactly," Sisli said. "*I* know you're still really you, Tazlo dear—but . . . but it does look rather . . . rather strange—and to Wizner Hiz, it will look more than strange! He'll be sure you're a Mind-gobbler—and he'll . . . he'll Sing you Through! And then you'll be lost . . . gone forever . . . " She burst into tears.

"There, there, Sisli, don't cry," Lafayette soothed, holding her in his arms. "Things aren't all that bad. We still have a little time. Maybe I'll get the knack of it yet—or maybe he won't come after all—or—"

"I'll . . . I'll try to be brave." Sisli brushed away her tears and smiled up at Lafayette. "You're right. There's still time. We can't give up. Now try again: close your eyes, think of the wall as being woven of little lines of light. And the lines of light are only tiny specks that move very fast—so fast they aren't really there—and you reach out . . . you feel them, you match the pattern of your mind to them, and—"

"All right," Vugli's blunt voice spoke suddenly beside them. "Wizner Hiz is waiting. Let's go, Haz."

The glowering youth stood just inside the impervious wall—impervious to O'Leary, at least, he thought disgustedly. Around here, every man, woman, and child over eighteen months had freedom to come and go—all but him!

"He's not ready," Sisli had jumped up, stood facing her brother. "Hiz will have to wait."

"You know better than that."

"Go away! You're spoiling everything! If you'd just give us more time—"

"It's not me—it's Wizner Hiz—"

"Yes, indeed, it *is* Wizner Hiz," a new voice spoke, a sharp, thin-edged voice that seemed to slice between Lafayette's bones. He turned to see a lean, leathery-faced old Wingman, with a few gray plumes still clinging to his withered scalp, a nose like an eagle's beak, eyes like bits of glowing coal.

"And I am here," Wizner Hiz said in an ominous hiss, "to discover the truth of this curious matter!"

"There's nothing to discover," Sisli spoke up defiantly, facing the Visioner. "Tazlo had a fall; he hit his head.

Naturally, he was a bit confused. But now . . . he remembers everything—don't you, Tazlo?" She turned to face him, her eyes bright with fear, and with determination.

"Well—there may be a few details I haven't quite remembered yet," he temporized.

"So? That is good news indeed," Wizner snapped. "But of course the matter is not one which can be settled so casually. The interests of all Thallathlone are concerned. People are afraid of the worst. They require reassurance. I'm sure you'll willingly join me in laying all fears at rest."

"Of course he will," Sisli spoke up quickly. "But he needs more rest. He hasn't recovered—"

"I have no intention of overstraining an honest invalid," Wizner cut in harshly. "A few questions, a few tests, publicly given—nothing more. Then honest Tazlo—if indeed the subject *is* Tazlo—can return to his sickbed—if—he is still in need of special attention."

"Tomorrow! He'll feel much better tomorrow—"

"Tomorrow may be too late, girl!"

"He might have a relapse if he has to go out now—"

"Suppose—" Wizner pointed a taloned finger at Sisli. "Suppose this man we call Tazlo Haz is in truth Invaded by a parasite from the dark spaces between the worlds! Would you nurture him here, assist him to prepare a place for others of his fell breed?"

"He isn't! I know he isn't!"

"Sisli—he has to be put to the test," Hinky interrupted. "Fighting it will only make it look worse for him. If he *is* Tazlo, it will all be over in a few minutes! It can't hurt to answer a few questions, even if he is still a little weak—and he looks strong enough to me," he added, giving Lafayette a look that was far from cordial.

"He'll come with you now," Vugli stated flatly. "Won't you, Tazlo?"

Lafayette looked at the wingman. He looked at Wizner Hiz. He looked at Sisli. He drew a breath.

"No," he said. "I'm afraid I can't oblige, fellows."

"No, you say?" the Visioner shrilled. "But I say *yes!* Vugli—Hinky—take him!"

"Come on you—" Vugli caught Lafayette's arm; Hinky seized his injured wing in a secure grip, twisted as Lafayette held back. Sisli screamed. Her father made distressed sounds. Lafayette braced his feet, but the pain in the broken member was like a hot sword under his shoulder blade. They hustled him forward, slammed him against the unyielding wall with stunning force.

"What's that?" said Vugli, who stood half in, half out of the wall, gaping at O'Leary. "Merge, man! Merge! This resistance is foolish!"

"Sorry," Lafayette said. "No can do. I seem to have forgotten how."

"Aha!" Wizner crowed. "You see? Proof! Proof positive! That was how we dealt with them last time, how we trapped them in the end! The Mind-gobblers had not our skill in merging! A wall of kreewood trapped them like weeki birds in a cage! And so we caged them, starved them—"

"No! It's not true!" Sisli wailed. "He's simply forgotten!"

"Silence, foolish chit! Would you shield the monster in our midst?"

"He's not a monster!"

"So? How can you be sure?"

"Because . . . because I've looked into his eyes—and he's *good*!"

"Then let him step forth—and prove himself a Wingman!"

"It's no use, Sisli," Lafayette said. "I can't, and that's that."

"Then you admit you're a Mind-gobbler!" Wizner Hiz screeched, backing away. Vugli and Hinky retreated, staring at him. Only Sisli still clung to his arm, until her father dragged her away.

"No," Lafayette said. "I don't admit anything of the sort."

"Come, let him prove himself," Wizner Hiz snarled. "We'll withdraw and leave him to himself. If he's a true man and not possessed, he'll emerge. If not—then let him be sealed up forever as a warning to others of his dread kind!"

In silence, except for Sisli's sobbing, Sisli's father and brothers trooped out through the wall as through a veil of dark-brown smoke. Wizner Hiz took the girl's arm, dragged her with him, still protesting.

Lafayette was alone in the sealed room.

4

There was a little of the fruit juice left in the cups; O'Leary drank half, preserving the rest for later. He circled the room, vainly prodding and poking in search of some overlooked egress.

"Don't waste your time," he advised himself, slumping on the bed. "There's no way out—except through the wall. You're trapped. You've had it. This is where it all ends . . . trapped by a silly superstition . . . "

"But," his thoughts ran on, "maybe it's not a superstition at that. In a way Wizner's right: I *am* an Invader. Apparently, this fellow Tazlo Haz is a real person—at least as real as any of this world. I haven't simply sprouted wings—I've taken over someone else's body. And it was the same when I was Zorro!" He rose, pacing the cell.

"Zorro really existed; he was a Wayfarer, with a girl-friend named Gizelle, and a big career ahead as a pick-pocket. Until I came along and swiped his identity. And then . . . " O'Leary paused, rubbing his chin thoughtfully. "Then I switched identities again—with Tazlo Haz. And this time, I switched worlds along with bodies. Why not? I've done it before, more than once. The USA—Artesia—then half a dozen continua that Goruble dumped me into when he was trying to get rid of me—then Melange. And now Thallathlone."

He sat on the bed again. "But why? At first I thought it was the Focal Referent. I pushed the button, and the next thing I knew no one recognized me. But this time I didn't have the Mark III. I was just standing there. And another thing: always before the parallel worlds I've stumbled into had the same geography as Colby Corners. There were a few variables—such as the desert in Artesia where the bay was back home—but that was relatively minor. But here—nothing's the same. It's a totally different setup, with a valley where the mountain was. And the people aren't analogs of the ones I knew—like Swinehild being Adoranne's double, and Hulk, Count Alain's . . . "

He rose again, paced restlessly. "I have to make a few assumptions: one, that I really did get a note from the Red Bull, I really did meet him at the A & D, and that somehow I changed places with Zorro—" He stopped dead. "Which implies . . . that Zorro changed places with *me!*"

5

"Oh, boy," Lafayette was still muttering half an hour later. "This changes everything. Nobody will be out looking for me. Or if they do, they'll find me wandering in a dazed condition, claiming I'm somebody named Zorro the Pig. Or they've already found me. I'm probably back home now, with Daphne fussing over me, feeding me soup. Or feeding Zorro soup!" He threw himself down on the bunk. "Just wait till I get my hands on that slimy character! Posing as me, insinuating himself into Daphne's good graces . . . " He paused while a startled expression fixed itself on his face. "Why, that dirty, underhanded, sneaking louse! Taking advantage of poor Daphne that way! I've got to get out of here! I have to get home!" He sprang up, hammered on the wall, shouted.

The silence was total. Lafayette slumped against the wall. "Great," he muttered. "Pound some more. Yell a lot. All that will do is convince Wizner Hiz you're just what he claims—if anyone can hear you, which is doubtful. That wood's as hard as armor plate." He sat on the bed, rubbing his bruised fists. "And he's probably right.

Thallathlone is obviously some kind of offbeat plane of existence, not a regular parallel continuum. Maybe it's on some kind of diagonal with the serial universes Central controls. Maybe people like me have accidentally wound up here before, just the way I did; maybe there's some kind of probability fault line you can slip through . . . "

He lay back with a sigh. The ray of sunlight from above made a bright spot on the dark, polished floor. The perfume of Sisli still lingered in the air.

"Maybe a lot of things," he murmured. "Maybe I'd better get some sleep. Maybe I'll be able to think better then . . . "

6

The dream was a pleasant one: he was lying on the bank of a river, under the spreading branches of a sycamore, with Daphne beside him, murmuring to him in a soft and loving voice.

. . . try, please, for me . . . you can do it, I know you can do it . . .

"Try what?" Lafayette said genially, and moved to put his arm about her shoulders. But somehow she was gone now; he was alone under the tree . . . and the light had faded. He was in darkness, still hearing her call, faint, as from a great distance:

. . . just for me, my Tazlo . . . please try . . . please . . .

"Daphne? Where are you?" He rose, groping in the pitch darkness. "Where did you go?"

Come to me . . . come . . . you can if you try . . . try . . . try . . . try . . .

"Certainly—but where are you? Daphne?"

Try, Tazlo! You are trying! I can feel you trying! Like this! You see? Hold your mind this way . . . and move like this . . .

He felt ephemeral hands touch his mind. He felt the lattice work of thought turned gently, aligned, steered. There was a gentle tugging, as if a cotton thread pulled at him. He moved forward, listening, listening to her voice. Cobwebs brushed his face, dragged back over his body, *through* his body . . .

Cool, fresh air around him, filled with a soft, rustling sound. He smelled green, growing things; he opened his eyes, saw the twinkle of stars through the filigree of foliage above, saw lights that gleamed through leaves, saw—

"Sisli!" he blurted. "How . . . what—"

She was in his arms. "Tazlo—my Tazlo—I knew you could do it! I knew!"

He turned, looked at the corrugated surface of shaggy bark behind him. He ran his hand over it, feeling the solidity of it, the denseness.

"Well, what do you know," he said wonderingly. "I walked through a wall."

Chapter Six

1

Wizner Hiz was still scowling; but even Vugli had taken Sisli's side—and Lafayette's.

"You were the one that set up the test, Wizner Hiz," Hinky shrugged. "Don't complain when he passes it."

"Come along, Tazlo," Sisli said with a toss of her head. "The party is about to begin."

Lafayette hesitated, looking out along the yard-thick branch with the shiny path worn along its upper surface, leading toward the lighted dancing pavilion. "What happens," he inquired, "if you slip?"

"Why should you slip?" Sisli walked out a few feet, stood on one toe and pirouetted, spreading her white wings just enough to make a sighing sound and stir the leaves around her.

"I've got a broken wing, remember?" O'Leary improvised. "I've got an idea: why don't we stay here, and just sort of listen in from a distance?"

"Silly boy." She caught his hand, led him out on the precarious path. "Just close your eyes and I'll lead you," she said with an impish smile. "I think you just want to be babied," she added.

"Let's go," Vugli said, jostling past Lafayette, almost sending him from the branch. "I have some drinking to catch up on, after the day I've been through."

O'Leary clung to a cluster of leaves he had grabbed for support; Sisli pulled him back.

"For heaven's sake, Tazlo—stop behaving as if you weren't one of Thallathlone's top athletes. You're embarrassing me."

"Sure; just give me time to get my sky-legs." He closed his eyes and concentrated. "It's funny, Sisli," he said, "but if I just relax and sort of clear my mind—fit myself into the Tazlo bag—I start remembering things. Little bits and pieces, like, oh, sailing through the air on a sunny day—and doing power dives over Yawning Abyss—and even walking branches . . ."

"Well, of course, Tazlo; you've done them often enough."

"And . . . even with my eyes closed, I can feel you, standing there, six feet away. I can sense Vugli, he's about thirty feet away now, talking to someone. And I think Hinky has gone back . . . in that direction." He pointed.

"Well, of course we can sense each other." Sisli sounded puzzled. "How else would we manage to find our way back to the eyrie after a long flight?"

"I guess it figures. And all I have to do to walk these branches is just hold my mind right, right?"

"Right." Sisli giggled. "You look so solemn and determined, as if you were going to have to do something terribly brave and terribly important—all just to take a stroll down the front walk."

"All things are relative, I guess," Lafayette, and stepped boldly out behind her toward the sounds of music.

2

Life in Thallathlone was pretty nice, all things considered, O'Leary reflected hazily, relaxing at the nightly fete. If it wasn't one occasion for joy, it was another. Tonight's ball, for example, had been in celebration of the second week's anniversary of his vindication. The fermented booljuice had flowed freely; the air dancers had been skilled and graceful in their wispy scarves and veils, the toasted birdseed had tasted better than broiled steak—and Sisli, at his side every minute, had been as loving and attentive a prospective bride as a man could want.

That was the only thought that dampened his enthusiasm momentarily.

"But actually, everything will turn out fine," he reminded himself for the tenth time. "As soon as I figure out how to get back into my own body, Tazlo Haz will be back in his. He may have a pretty wild story to tell, but it can all be blamed on the bump on my head. And he and Sisli will live happily ever after."

Swell, he answered himself. *Just as long as you don't get carried away and spend the wedding night with the bride.*

"Which reminds me—that feathered four-flusher is probably romancing Daphne right now!"

Not any more than you're romancing Sisli.

"You mean he's kissed her?"

Wouldn't you?

"Certainly—but that's different. When I kiss Sisli, it's just . . . just friendly."

So is he. You can count on that.

"I'll break his other wing, that bird in wolf's clothing!"

Not until he's back inside the birdskin, I hope.

"Tazlo—who are you talking to?" Sisli inquired.

"Ah—just a fellow named O'Leary. A sort of figment of my imagination. Or maybe I'm a figment of his. It's a question for the philosophers."

"Isn't that who you said you were when you were still delirious?"

"I may have mentioned the name. But I'm much better now, right?" He blinked away the double images and focused a smile on the girl's inquiring face. "After all—I *did* merge—and I walked the branches—and ate birdseed—and—"

"Tazlo—you frighten me when you talk like this. It's as though—as though you were playing a role instead of just being yourself."

"Think nothing of it, m'dear," Lafayette said solemnly. "You're letting what old Wizzy said bug you. Lot of nonsense. Mind-grabbers indeed. Probably just some poor Central agent with a short circuit in his probability wiring, meaning no harm at all."

"Harmless, eh?" an unfriendly voice snapped from near at hand. Wizner Hiz glowered from his perch a few feet above and to one side of the tiny table where Lafayette sat with Sisli. "I've been watching you, Haz—or whoever you are. You don't behave normally. You don't feel right—"

"Of course he's still a little strange," Sisli burst out. "He hasn't fully recovered from the blow on his head!"

"Go away, Wiggy Hig," Lafayette called carelessly. "Or Higgly Wig. Your sour puss bothers me. The night was made for love. Especially tonight, up here in a treetop. Back home they'll never believe all this . . . " He waved a hand to include the paper lanterns strung in the branches, the gaily dressed wingmen and women fluttering gaily about, the high moon riding above.

"Back home? And where might that be?" the Visioner said sharply.

"It's just a figure of speech," Sisli said quickly. "Leave him alone, Wizner Hiz! He's not hurting anyone!"

"Neither did the others—at first. Then they started . . . changing. You don't remember, girl; you were too young. But I saw it! I saw Boolbo Biz start turning into a monster before our eyes!"

"Well, Tazlo's not turning into a monster," Sisli said, and took his arm possessively.

"Course not," Lafayette said, and wagged a finger at the old Wingman. "Just the same old me—whoever that is. Get lost, Wiz—I mean Hiz—" He paused as something fluttered past his face. Twisting on his wicker stool, he saw a large russet feather drifting down through the foliage below.

"Someone shedding?" he asked genially. A second feather followed the first. Something touched his arm: a third feather. He made brushing motions. "What's going on here?" he inquired as more feathers swirled around him. He stood, caught sight of Sisli's horror-stricken expression.

"Wha's . . . what's the matter?" he asked, and blew a downy feather from his upper lip.

"Oh, no—Tazlo, no!" Sisli yelped.

"Aha!" Wizner Hiz screeched.

"Grab him!" Vugli bellowed.

"Grab who?" Lafayette demanded, looking around for the victim. His question was answered as hands caught at him, clamped on his arms, dragged him to the center of the dancing pavilion, amid a cloud of feathers.

"What's this all about?" he yelled. "I've passed your test, haven't I . . . " His voice trailed away as he caught sight of his unbroken wing, held in the grasp of half a dozen wide-eyed Thallathlonians. Even as he stared, another handful of feathers came free to swirl away in a sudden gust of wind.

"Not quite, Mind-grabber," Wizner Hiz rasped. "Not quite!"

3

Four sturdily muscled Wingmen prodded at Lafayette with stout ten-foot poles, keeping him immobilized at the center of the cleared open-work pavilion. All around, the ranked population of the eyrie clustered in a circle, ten deep, all eyes on him. Sisli was gone, borne away weeping by her brothers. So far O'Leary as could tell, there was not a friendly expression in sight.

"Don't do anything hasty," he urged as the pole-tip poked him painfully in the ribs. "I can't fly, remember? I know it looks bad, but I'll think of an explanation if you'll just—*ooof!*" His appeal was cut short by a hearty jab to the abdomen.

"Never fear, we know how to deal with your kind," Wizner Hiz crowed. He rubbed his hands together, skipping about beyond the pole-wielders with the agility of a ten-year-old, shaping up the crowd.

"You there—back a few feet! Hold it! Now you, ladies—just move in here, fill up this gap. You—the tall one—move back! Now, Pivlo Poo, you and Quigli step in here . . . close it up . . . "

"This looks like . . . a public execution," O'Leary pushed the words out painfully. "I hope you're not planning anything so barbaric—"

"All together, now," Wizner Hiz commanded, raising his hands for silence. He whistled a shrill note—like a pitch pipe—and gestured. An answering note came from the massed voices of the eyrie.

"Choir practice? At a time like this!" Lafayette wondered aloud.

"It will be the last choir you'll hear in this world," Wizner Hiz shrilled, fixing Lafayette with a beady eye filled with triumph. "You're about to be Sung Out! Out of the world! Back to the dark spaces you came from, foul Invader!"

"Oh, really?" Lafayette smiled painfully. "What happens if I fail to disappear? Does that prove I'm innocent?"

"Never fear—the Chant of Exorcism has never failed," one of the strong-arm men assured him. "But if it does—we'll think of something else."

"Actually, it's just a simple case of falling feathers, fellows," Lafayette said. "It could happen to anyone—"

At a sweeping gesture from Wizner Hiz, a chorus of sound burst from the choir, drowning Lafayette's appeal.

> Out of the World
>> Away and beyond
> Back through the veil
>> Stranger begone
> Afloat on a sea
>> Wider than night
> Deeper and deeper
>> Sinking from sight
> Back where you came from
>> Grabber of souls
> Back to the depths
>> Where the great bell tolls
> Out of the world
>> Far from the sun
> Of fair Thallathlone
>> Forever begone
> Borne on the wings
>> Of the magic song
> Forever begone
>> From fair Thallathlone . . .

The chant went on and on, waves of sound that waxed and waned, rolling at Lafayette from all sides, beating at him like the waves of the sea. There was a tune: an eerie, groaning melody repeated over and over.

> ... *Out* of the *world*
> *Away* and *beyond* ...
> For*ever* be*gone*
> From *fair* Thallath*lone* ...

The mouths of the singers seemed to move silently, like fish gaping in water, while the moaning chant, independent of them, rose and fell, rose and fell. The faces were blurring, running together.

> ... *Far and away* ...
> *Stranger begone* ...
> *Forever begone*
> *From fair Thallathlone* ...

The words seemed to come from a remote distance now. The lights had faded and winked out; O'Leary could no longer see the faces of the singers, could no longer feel the wicker floor under his feet. Only the song remained—a palpable force that enfolded him, lifted him, floated him away into lightless depths, then faded, dwindled, became a ghostly echo fading in utter darkness, utter emptiness.

4

Lafayette stared into the inky blackness, making vague swimming motions. Something that glowed faintly appeared in the distance, sailed closer in a great spiral, goggled at him with yard-wide eyes, spiraled off into the darkness.

"Which way is up?" O'Leary inquired; but there was no sound. In fact, he realized there was no mouth, no tongue, no lungs.

Good lord! I'm not breathing . . . The thought seemed to jump forth and hang in space, glowing like a neon sign. Other bits and pieces of mind-stuff came swirling around him, like flotsam in a millrace:

. . . oother-boober of the umber-wumber . . .

. . . try a section ooty-toot, or maybe a number tot noodle . . .

. . . told him to drop dead, the louse . . .

. . . eemie-weemie-squeemie pip-pip . . .

. . . so I says to him . . .

. . . to the right, hold it, hold it . . . don't move . . .

. . . HEY—I GOT A ROGUE BOGIE ON NUMBER TWELVE!

. . . smarmy parmy, wiffly niffly, weeky squeaky . . .

. . . aw, come on, baby . . .

. . . HEY—YOU—IDENTIFY!

. . . poom-poom-poom . . .

. . . so I ups to him and he ups to me and I ups to him . . .

YOU! WHAT'S YOUR SNAG NUMBER!

. . . poopie-poopie-poopie . . .

. . . HELLO, NARK NINE. I'VE GOT A SPOOK READING IN NUMBER TWELVE STAGING AREA.

UH-HUH. I READ IT. JUST GARBAGE, DUMP IT, BARF ONE.

NIX—I PICKED UP A BEEP ON OH SIX OH, NARK NINE. COULD BE A ROGUE.

. . . NIK-NIK-NIK . . .

DUMP IT, BARF ONE. WE GOT TRAFFIC TO HANDLE, REMEMBER?

HEY—YOU! GIVE ME A BEEP ON OH SIX OH OR I DUMP, YOU READ?

Something that resembled a tangle of glowing coat-hanger wire sailed purposefully up to O'Leary, hovered before him, rotating slowly.

"It looks like a disembodied migraine," he said. "I wonder if it would go away if I closed my eyes . . . if I had any eyes to close."

OK, THAT'S BETTER. NOW LET'S HAVE THAT SNAG NUMBER.

"Since I don't have eyes, obviously I'm not actually seeing things," Lafayette advised himself. "Still, some kind of impressions are impinging on me—and my brain is interpreting them as sight and sound. But—"

ANSWER ME, BUSTER!

"Who," Lafayette said. "Me?"

FLIPPIN A! SNAG NUMBER, PRONTO! YOU GOT TRAFFIC BACKED UP SIX HEXAMETERS ON NINE LEVELS!

"Who are you? Where are you? Where am *I*? Get me out of here!" Lafayette blurted, twisting to look all around him.

SURE—AS SOON AS YOU GIVE ME A SNAG NUMBER TO LATCH ONTO!

"I don't know what a snag number is! It looks as if I'm floating in some sort of luminous alphabet soup. Not the soup, the alphabet, you understand—"

A man came tumbling slowly out of the darkness toward Lafayette, end over end. He was dressed in what appeared to be a sequined leotard, and he glowed with a greenish light; Lafayette leaped toward him with a glad cry. Too far; he braced himself for the collision, caught a glimpse of a startled face twisting to stare at him in the instant before contact.

There was no impact; only a sense of diving into a cloud of whirling particles, tugged at by surging forces—

What in the name of two dozen dancing devils on a bass drum! a strange voice roared.

Light and sound burst upon O'Leary. He was staring at a plastic plate attached to his wrist, with the stamped legend:

SNAG NUMBER 1705.

LAST CHANGE, BUSTER! GOING ... GOING ...

"Snag number one thousand seven hundred and five!" O'Leary yelled.

From somewhere, a giant, unseen hook came, caught him by the back of the neck, and threw him across the Universe.

5

When Lafayette's head stopped whirling, he was standing in a chamber no bigger than an elevator, with opalescent, softly glowing walls, ceiling, and floor. A red light blinked on one wall; there was a soft *snick!*; the panel facing him opened like a revolving door on a large, pale-green room with a carpeted floor, a sound-absorbent ceiling, and a desk behind which sat an immaculately groomed woman of indeterminate age, extremely good-looking in spite of pale-green hair and a total lack of eyebrows. She gave him a crisp look, waved to a chair, poked a button on her desk.

"Rough one?" she asked in a tone of businesslike sympathy.

"Ah . . . just average," Lafayette said cautiously, looking around the room, which was furnished with easy chairs, potted palms, sporting prints, and softly murmuring air-conditioner grilles.

"You want a stretcher, or can you make it under your own power?" the green-haired receptionist inquired briskly as Lafayette edged into the room.

"What? Oh, I suppose you mean my bandaged wing. Actually it doesn't bother me all that much, thanks."

The woman frowned. "Psycho damage?"

"Well—frankly, I'm a little confused. I know it must sound silly, but . . . who are you? Where am I?"

"Oh, brother." The woman poked another button, spoke toward an unseen intercom. "Frink, get a trog team up here; and a stretcher. I've got a 984 for you, and it looks like a doozie." She gave Lafayette a look of weary sympathy. "Might as well sit down and take it easy, fellow." She wagged her head like one subjected to trials above and beyond the call of Job Description.

"Thanks." O'Leary sat gingerly on the edge of a low, olive-leather chair. "You, uh, know me?" he inquired.

The woman spread her hands in a noncommittal gesture. "How can I keep track of over twelve hundred ops?" She blinked as if an idea had just occurred to her. "You're not amnac?"

"Who's he?"

"Mama mia. Amnac means no memory. Loss of identity. In other words, you don't remember your own name."

"Frankly, there does seem to be a little uncertainty about that."

"Right hand, index finger," she said wearily. Lafayette approached the desk and offered the digit, which the woman grasped and pressed against a glass plate set in the desk top, one of an array of similar plates interspersed with counter-sunk buttons. A light winked, fluttered, blinked off. Letters appeared on a ground-glass screen in front of the receptionist.

"Raunchini," she said. "Dink 9, Franchet 43, undercategory Gimmel. Ring a bell?" She looked at him hopefully.

"Not deafeningly," Lafayette temporized. "Look here, ma'am—I may as well be frank with you. I seem to have stumbled into something that's over my head—"

"Hold it, Raunchini. You can cover all that in your debriefing. I'm strictly admin myself."

"You don't understand. The fact is, I don't know what's going on. I mean, I started off in perfect innocence to have a drink with an old associate, and when I saw what he'd stumbled on, I realized right away that it was a matter for—for higher authorities to handle. But . . . " He looked around the room. "I have a distinct feeling I'm not in Artesia; there's nothing like this there. So the question naturally occurs—where am I?"

"You're at Central Casting, naturally. Look, just take a chair over there, and—"

"Central? I thought so! Thank Groot! Then all my problems are solved!" Lafayette sank down gratefully on the corner of the desk. "Look, I have some vital data to transmit to the proper quarter. I've discovered that when Goruble defected, he stashed away a whole armory of stolen gear—"

A door across the room swung open and a pair of husky young men in crisp, pale-blue hospital garb stepped into the room, guiding between them a flat, six-foot slab of what looked like foam rubber. The latter floated without support two feet above the floor, bobbing slightly like an air mattress on water.

"OK, fella," one of them said, unlimbering a large and complicated-looking hypodermic, "we'll have you comfy in two and a half demisecs. Just hop up here and stretch out, face down—"

"I don't need a stretcher," Lafayette snapped. "I need someone to listen to what I have to say."

"Sure, you'll get your chance, fella," the orderly said soothingly, advancing. "Simmer down—"

Lafayette scrambled around behind the desk. "Listen —get Nicodaeus! He knows me! What I've got to report is triple X-UTS priority! I demand a hearing, or heads will be rolling around here like spilled marbles!"

The orderly looked uncertain, glanced at the woman for support. She waved her hands helplessly. "Don't look at me," she said. "I'm just the flunky on the front desk. Stand by one; Belarius is Duty Officer; I'll get him up here and let him stick his neck out." She pushed buttons and spoke briefly. The orderly flipped a switch at the head of the stretcher; it sank to the floor.

Three minutes passed in a tense silence, with Lafayette hovering behind the desk, the stretcher-bearers yawning and scratching, and the green-haired woman furiously filing her iridescent-green nails. Then a tall, wide-shouldered man with smooth gray hair and a professional air strode into the room. He glanced around, pursed his lips at Lafayette.

"Well, Miss Dorch?" he said in a mellow baritone.

"This is Agent Raunchini, sir. He's apparently a 984 case; but he won't accept sedation—"

"I'm not Agent Raunchini," Lafayette snapped. "And I have priority information to report!"

"A contradiction in terms, eh?" The newcomer gave Lafayette a glassy smile. "Just go along, there's a good fellow—"

"I want to talk to Inspector Nicodaeus!"

"Impossible. He's on a field assignment, won't be back for six months."

"I'll make a deal," O'Leary said. "Listen to what I have to say, and then I'll go quietly, fair enough? Spurd knows I could use a nap." He yawned.

Belarius looked at his wristwatch. "Young man, I don't lightly upset the routine of this Center—"

"What about a Focal Referent in unauthorized hands?" Lafayette cut in. "Is that worth missing a coffee break for?"

Belarius' urbane expression drained away.

"Did you say—don't say it!" He held up a well-manicured hand, shot a nervous glance at the others in the room.

"Possibly I'd best have a chat with Agent Raunchini after all," he said. "A private chat. Suppose we go along to my office, eh?" He gave Lafayette a smile like a warning blinker and turned to the door.

"Well, now we're getting somewhere," Lafayette murmured as he followed.

6

The gray-haired man led Lafayette along a silent corridor to a small room, unadorned except for a row of framed photographs of determined faces lining the walls. Belarius seated himself behind an impressive bleached oak desk, gestured Lafayette to a chair.

"Now, just make a clean breast of the whole matter," he said in a sternly avuncular tone. "And I'll undertake to put in a word for you."

"Sure, fine," Lafayette hitched his chair closer. "It was a Mark III. And according to—to a reliable source, there's more where that came from. With luck, he won't have had time to cart all the stuff into town and sell it—"

"Kindly begin at the beginning, Agent. When were you first approached?"

"Two weeks ago. I found the note rolled up in a pair of socks, and—"

"Who was your contact?"

"Let's leave his name out of it; he didn't know what he was getting into. As I was saying, the note told me he had to see me—"

"The name, Raunchini. Don't attempt to shield your confederates!"

"Will you let me get on with it? And my name's not Raunchini!"

"Now you're claiming to be a prep, eh? That would imply a conspiracy of considerable scope. What do you allege to have done with the real Raunchini?"

"Nothing! Stop changing the subject! The important thing is to grab the loot before the Red Bu—before anyone else gets their hands on it—and to recover the Mark III!"

"Mark II. You may leave that aspect of the matter to me. I want names, dates, drop points, amounts paid—"

"You're all mixed up," Lafayette cut in. "I don't know a thing about all that. All I know is the Mark III was stolen from me while I was asleep, and—" He paused, looking at one of the photos, showing an elderly gentleman with a vague smile and a pince-nez.

"How? With a derrick?" Belarius asked querulously.

"What? How do I know? I had it in my secret pocket, and—"

"Pocket! Look here, Raunchini—don't attempt to make a fool of me! Your only hope for clemency is strict veracity and total recall!"

"My name's not Raunchini!"

Belarius glared, then turned to a small console at his elbow and jabbed at a button.

"Full dossier on Agent Raunchini," he ordered. "And double-check the ID."

"Look here, Mr. Belarius," Lafayette said. "You can play with your buttons later. Right now you need to get a squad in there to collect the stuff and find that Mark III before Lom uses it!"

Belarius turned as the panel behind him *beep!*ed.

"Definite confirmation of Raunchini ID," a crisp voice said.

"Retinal and palm prints check out too. Junior Field Agent, assigned to Locus Beta Two-Four, Plane P-122, Charlie 381–f."

"Your wires are crossed," Lafayette said. "I'm Lafayette O'Leary—or I used to be. Right now I'm Tazlo Haz—"

"Stop babbling, man! An insanity plea won't help you!"

"Who's insane? Why don't you listen to me? I'm trying to save your bacon for you!"

"I doubt if you've ever seen a Focal Referent," Belarius snapped. "You obviously haven't the faintest notion of the machine's physical characteristics."

"Oh, no? It's about six inches high, with a plastic case with a bunch of wires and wheels inside!"

"That does it," Belarius said flatly. "The Mark II is a great improvement over earlier models; but it still weighs four and a half tons, and occupies three cubic yards of space!"

"Oh, yeah?" O'Leary came back. "You obviously don't know what you're talking about!"

"I happen," Belarius rasped, "to be Chief of Research, and Project Officer for the Focal Referent program—which happens to be classified *Unthinkable Secret!*"

"Well—I'm thinking about it—"

With a quick motion, Belarius lifted what was obviously a hand weapon from beneath the desk.

"Send a squad of enforcers to Trog 87 on the double," he said over his shoulder to the intercom.

"Just a minute," Lafayette protested. "You're making a big mistake! I admit it looks a little strange, my having wings—"

"Wings?" Belarius edged backward in his chair. "Hurry up with that enforcer squad," he said over his shoulder. "He may get violent at any moment, and I'd dislike to be forced to vaporize him before we get to the bottom of this."

"I can explain," Lafayette insisted. "Or—well, I can't explain it, but I can assure you it's all perfectly normal, in an abnormal sort of way."

"Never mind the protestations," Belarius said grimly. "Sane or otherwise, I'll soon have the truth out of you via brain-scrape. It may leave your cerebrum a trifle soggy, but in matters of Continuum security, there's no room for half measures!"

"Why don't you check my story out?" Lafayette protested. "What makes you so sure you know it all?"

"If there were one hard datum to check, Raunchini, I'd gladly do so!"

"Listen," O'Leary said desperately, "check on me: O'Leary, Lafayette O'Leary, part-time agent from Artesia!"

Belarius pushed out his lips, gave a curt order to the intercom. As they waited, Lafayette's eyes strayed back to the photo which had caught his eye. He had seen that face somewhere . . .

"Who's he?" he asked, pointing.

Belarius raised an eyebrow, following O'Leary's pointing finger. His expression flickered.

"Why do you ask?" he inquired casually.

"I've seen him—somewhere. Recently."

"Where?" Belarius came back crisply.

Lafayette shook his head. "I don't remember. All those blows on the head—"

"So—you're going to play it cagey, eh?" Belarius snarled. "What's your price for selling out? Immunity? Cash? Relocation?"

"I don't know what you're talking about," O'Leary snapped. "I just—"

"All right, you've got me over a barrel! You know how badly we want to get our hands on Jorlemagne! I won't hassle! Immunity, a million in cash, and the Locus of your choice. Is it a deal?"

O'Leary frowned in puzzlement. "Maybe you've been wearing tight hats," he said. "You don't seem to grasp the idea—"

"Raunchini—I'll have the full story out of you if it's the last thing I do!"

"O'Leary!" Lafayette matched the other's shout.

"O'Leary. Got it right here, Chief," the intercom blatted suddenly.

"Well, thank heaven," Lafayette sighed.

"Would that be Lorenzo, Lafcadio, Lothario, Lancelot, Leopold, or Ludwig?" the voice came back, businesslike.

"Lafayette," he supplied.

"Uh-huh. Here it is. Reserve appointment to classified Locus. Inactive."

"Physical description?" Belarius snapped.

"Six feet, one-seventy, light-brown hair, blue eyes, harmless appearance—"

"Hey," Lafayette protested.

Belarius swiveled to face him. "Ready to come clean now?"

"Look, I can explain," Lafayette said, feeling the sweat start on his forehead. "You see, I accidentally activated the Focal Referent. It was unintentional, you understand —"

"And—"

"And—well, I . . . I changed shape! Apparently I turned into this Tazlo Haz person, and—"

"You were transformed from O'Leary into Haz, is that it?" Belarius said wearily, passing a hand over his face. "Your story grows steadily more remarkable."

"Not exactly," Lafayette demurred. "Before I was Haz I was a fellow named Zorro."

Belarius sighed. "Doesn't this sound a trifle idiotic—even to *your* fevered brain?"

"All right! I can't help how it sounds; what matters is that there's a truckload of stolen Probability Lab gear lying there in the cave waiting for anybody who happens along, and—"

"And where might this alleged cave be located?"

"In Artesia—just outside the city of the same name!"

"Never heard of it." Belarius turned and snapped a question at the intercom, glared at O'Leary as he waited for an answer.

"Right, chief," the voice at the other end came back. "Here it is: Plane V-87, Fox 22 1–b, Alpha Nine-three."

"Are we carrying out any operations there?"

"No, sir. We closed the file out last year."

There was a short pause. "Well, I'll be graunched, sir. The classified Locus this Agent O'Leary was assigned to checks out as this same V-87, Fox 22 1–b, Alpha Nine-three. I'll have to post that to the file—" the voice broke off. "Odd, sir—it seems we have a new recruit on the roster, from the Locus in question, just arrived yesterday."

"Name?"

"O'Leary. Say, that's funny; O'Leary is coded inactive in the main bank—"

"You say O'Leary is here at Central Casting—now?"

"Affirmative, sir."

"Send O'Leary up to Trog 87 immediately." Belarius frowned bleakly at O'Leary. "We'll get to the bottom of this matter," he muttered.

"I don't get it," Lafayette said. "I'm down in your records as having arrived here yesterday?"

"Not you, Raunchini: O'Leary." Belarius drummed on the desk. There was a brief buzz from the door and four uniformed men entered with drawn handguns.

"Stand by, men," Belarius ordered, waving them back.

"I'll bet it's Lorenzo," Lafayette said. "Or possibly Lothario. But how could they have gotten to Artesia? They belong in completely different loci . . . "

A harassed-looking junior official entered, turned to usher in a second new arrival—a small, trim, feminine figure, neatly dressed in a plain white tunic and white knee-boots; she scanned the room with immense, dark eyes, a slight, anxious smile on her delicately modeled lips.

"Good lord," Lafayette blurted, jumping to his feet. "Daphne!"

Chapter Seven

1

For a moment there was total silence. Belarius looked from Lafayette to the girl and back again. She stared at Lafayette; he grinned a vast and foolish grin and started toward her.

"How in the world did you get here, girl? When they told me they had an O'Leary here, it never occurred to me it might be—"

"How do you know my name?" Daphne cut in with surprising sharpness. She spun to face Belarius. "Who is this man? Does he know anything about Lafayette?"

"Do I know anything about Lafayette?" O'Leary cried. "Daphne, I guess the wings fooled you. Don't you know me?"

"I never saw you before in my life! What have you done to my husband?"

"I haven't done anything to your husband! I *am* your husband!"

"Stay away from me!" She took refuge behind a large cop, who put a protective arm around her shoulders.

"Get your greasy paws off her, you flatfoot!" Lafayette yelled.

"One moment!" Belarius thundered. "You, Raunchini! Stand where you are! You, Recruit O'Leary: for the record: do you know this Agent?"

"I never saw him before in my life!"

"Why waste time and breath, Raunchini?" Belarius grated. "You heard O'Leary's description: six feet, one-seventy, blue eyes. You're five-five, two-ten, black eyes, swarthy complected."

"I know I'm—huh?" O'Leary paused, looked over his left shoulder, then his right. "The wings!" he blurted. "They're gone!" He looked down at himself, saw a barrel chest, generous paunch, bandy legs, pudgy-fingered hands with a dense growth of black hair on their backs. He stepped to one of the framed photos, stared at his face reflected in the glass. It was round, olive-skinned, with a flat nose and a wide mouth crowded with crooked teeth.

"Ye gods—it's happened again!" he groaned. "No wonder you thought I was crazy, talking about my wings!"

"May I go now?" Recruit O'Leary requested.

"Daphne!" Lafayette yelled. "Surely *you* know me, no matter what I look like!"

Daphne looked puzzled.

"There was this note," Lafayette went on in tones of desperation. "It was from the Red Bull; he wanted me to meet him at the A & D Tavern. I went down there, and he had this gimmick—something that Goruble had stashed in a cave. Anyway, I was looking at it, and my finger slipped, and *whap!* I turned into somebody else!"

"Is he . . . is he—" Daphne looked questioningly at Belarius, circling a shell-like ear with a slim forefinger.

"No, I'm not nuts! I tried to get back to the palace to report what I'd discovered, and the City Guard grabbed me! And before I could explain matters, Luppo and a mob of Wayfarers butted in and carted me off to their camp, but Gizelle helped me get away, and—"

"Gizelle?" Daphne pounced with unerring feminine instinct.

"Yes, uh, a fine girl, you'll love her. Anyway, she took me to her wagon, and—"

"Hmmph!" Daphne sniffed, turning away. "I'm really not interested in this person's *amours*, whoever he is!"

"It wasn't like that! It was purely platonic."

"That's enough, Raunchini!" Belarius bellowed. "O'Leary, you can go. Men, take Raunchini down to Trog Twelve and prep him for brain-scrape!"

"What's . . . what's brain-scrape?" Daphne paused at the door, casting a hesitant look at Lafayette.

"A technique for getting at the truth," Belarius growled. "Something like peeling a grape."

"Well it . . . hurt him?"

"Eh? Well, it will more or less spoil him for future use. Leaves the subject a babbling idiot in stubborn cases. But don't concern yourself, O'Leary; he'll receive his full pension, never fear."

"Daphne!" Lafayette called after him. "If you have any influence with this bunch of maniacs, tell them to listen to me!" Belarius gestured; two men stepped forward, seized Lafayette's arms, helped him toward the door.

"Tough luck, pal," one of the cops said. "I'd act nuts too, if I thought it'd get me next to a dish like that."

"I'll say," another of the escort agreed. "Brother, you don't see it stacked up like that every day—"

"That's enough out of you, Buster!" Lafayette roared, and delivered a solid kick to the shin of the luckless girl-watcher. As the man stumbled back with a yell, Lafayette jerked free, ducked under a grab, and leaped for the door. Belarius rounded his desk in time to receive a straight-arm to the mouth. O'Leary sidestepped a tackle, plunged into the corridor.

"Daphne!" O'Leary shouted as she turned and stared, wide-eyed. "If I never see you again—remember I love you! And don't forget to feed Dinny!"

"Hey—grab him!" one of the waiting stretcher-bearers yelled. Lafayette ducked aside from his reach, thrust out a foot, sending the fellow sprawling. Two more men erupted from the room. More men were advancing at a run, closing in from both directions.

"The stretcher!" Daphne cried suddenly. "Use the stretcher!"

Lafayette ducked a wild swing, sprang aboard the slab hovering a foot above the carpet, jabbed the red button marked LIFT. The cot shot ceiling-ward, slammed him hard against the flowered wallpaper. He groped, pushed a stud at random. The stretcher shot backward, raking Lafayette across a rank of fluorescent lights. He fumbled again, dropped the cot to head height and shot forward in time to clip an oncoming security man full in the mouth, sending him bounding back against his partner. Full tilt, the cot rushed along the passage; Lafayette closed his eyes and hung on as it hurtled toward the intersection; at the last possible instant it banked, whipped around the turn, and shot at high speed through a pair of double doors—fortunately open.

The runaway steed made three swift circuits of the large green-walled room before Lafayette found a control that brought it to a shuddering halt, sending him tumbling to the rug. He rolled to hands and knees, saw that he was in the room where he had first arrived. The green-haired woman behind the desk was stabbing hysterically at her console, yelping for help.

"Here, I'll help you," Lafayette said. He scrambled up, jumped on the desk, and pushed two palmfuls of buttons, jabbed half a dozen of the keys, flipped an entire rank of switches. A siren sounded; the lights brightened and dimmed. From wall apertures, a pale-pink gas began hissing into the room. The receptionist screeched.

"Don't worry, I'm not violent," Lafayette yelled. "All I want is out! Which way?"

"Don't come near me, you maniac!"

Lafayette dashed to the section of wall through which he had entered, began feeling over it frantically as alarm horns hooted behind him. Abruptly, a panel rotated open on a dimly glowing chamber. Lafayette stepped through;

the panel slammed behind him. A green light glowed on the opposite wall. There was a momentary sensation as if his brain had come loose from its moorings and was whirling at high speed inside his skull. Then darkness exploded around him.

2

He drifted among luminous flotsam and jetsam, straining every sense . . .

. . . tinky-tinky-tinky . . .

. . . you think you're the only bird in town with a pair o' them—

. . . where are you? Come in, dear boy, if you hear me. Come in, come in . . .

A vast, softly glowing construction of puce and magenta noodles swept grandly past, rotating slowly; a swarm of luminous blue-green BB shot veered close, passed him by; something vast and insubstantial as glowing smoke swelled before him, swirled around him with a crackle of static, was gone. A jittering assemblage of red-hot wires came tumbling from dark distances, swerved to intercept him. He back-pedaled, making frantic swimming motions, but it closed on him, was all about him, clinging, penetrating.

It was as though a hundred and seventy pounds of warm wax were being injected into his skin, painlessly squeezing him out through the pores.

Aha! Got you, you bodynapper! a silent voice yelled in both ears at once.

"Hey—wait!" O'Leary shouted. "Can't we discuss this?"

Wait, nothing! Out! Out!

For a moment O'Leary saw a vengeful face—the same face he had seen in the glass in Belarius' office—glaring at him. Then he was sliding away into emptiness.

"Wait! Help! I have to get word to Nicodaeus!"

"Leave me drifting in Limbo, will you . . . " the voice came back faintly.

"Raunchini! Don't leave me here! I've got to get back . . . "

"How . . . " the voice came faintly, receding, *"do you know my name—"* The voice was gone. Lafayette shouted—or not shouted, he realized; *transmitted*, in some way he would figure out later, after he was safe back home. But there was no answer; only faint, ghostly voices all around:

. . . told him no, but you know how men are . . .

. . . oopy-toopy-foopy-foom . . .

Nine . . . eight . . . seven . . .

DEAR BOY! IS IT REALLY YOU? I'D ABOUT GIVEN UP HOPE!

"Help!" Lafayette yelled. He was rotating end over end now—or was it the other way around? He could feel his sense of identity draining away like oil from a broken pot; his thoughts were growing weaker, vaguer, the voices fainter . . . *HOLD ON, LAD . . . JUST A FEW SECONDS LONGER . . . DON'T GIVE UP THE SHIP . . .*

Something as intangible as smoke brushed over him; a vague fog-shape loomed, enveloped him like a shadowy fist. A sense of pressure, a burst of light—then darkness . . .

3

He was lying on a hard, lumpy surface, itching furiously. He made a move to scratch, and discovered that both knees were bandaged, as well as both elbows and his chin.

He struggled to a sitting position. In the faint moonlight that filtered down through the leaves overhead, he saw that he was neatly enclosed in a cage made of lashed poles. He had been lying, he saw, on an ancient mattress with a stained striped ticking; there was a bowl of water beside him, and what appeared to be gnawed crusts of bread. He sniffed; the odors hanging in the air—of unwashed laundry, goat cheese, and wood-smoke—were somehow familiar. His legs and arms ached, his back ached, his neck ached.

"I must be black-and-blue all over," he grunted. "Where am I? What's happened to me?"

There was a soft sound of footsteps; a familiar figure approached.

"Gizelle!" O'Leary's voice broke with relief. "Am I glad to see you! Get me out of here!"

The girl stood with hands on hips, looking down at him with an unreadable expression. "Zorro?" she said doubtfully.

O'Leary groaned. "I know, I look like a fellow named Raunchini. But it's really me—not really Zorro, but the fellow you thought was Zorro—only I was actually Lafayette O'Leary, of course. But I'll explain all that later."

"You don't theenk you're a beeg bird anymore? You don't try to jump off cleef, flapping your arms?"

"What? I didn't jump off the cliff, I fell—and—"

Gizelle smiled; she turned, whistled shrilly. Voices responded. A moment later Luppo's hulking figure appeared. He stared at O'Leary with an expression like a Doberman awaiting the kill order.

"Why deed you wheestle?" he grunted. "Ees he—"

"He said he ees heemself—Zorro!"

"Of course I'm myself—in a manner of speaking," Lafayette snapped. "But—oh, well, never mind. You wouldn't understand. Just let me out of here, pronto!"

"Uh-huh—that's heem," Luppo said.

"Good! Een that case—when the sun rises—we can proceed!" Gizelle cried ecstatically.

"Oh, look here, Gizelle—you're not going to start that wedding business all over again?" Lafayette protested.

Luppo looked at him, a gold tooth shining in his crooked grin. "Not quite," he said. "Would you believe . . . the Death of the Thousand Hooks?"

4

"Eet weel be very exciting, Zorito," Gizelle informed Lafayette, leaning close to his cage to hiss the words in his face. "First weel be the feexing of the hooks. Een the old days, there was just one beeg hook, you know—but naturally we've been making progress. Now we use leetle beety feesh hooks—hundreds and hundreds of theem. We steeck theem een—slowly—all over you. Then we tie a streeng to each one, and leeft you up eento the air weeth theem—"

"Gizelle—spare me the details!" O'Leary groaned. "If I'm Zorro, I already know all this—and if I'm not, I'm innocent, and you ought to free me. You ought to free me anyway; what's a nice girl like you doing mixed up in a dirty business like this, anyway?"

"Free you? A feelthy peeg who takes advantage of a poor girl who ees fool enough to love heem?"

"I've told you—I'm not myself! I mean I'm not really Zorro! I mean—I *am* Zorro—physically—but actually I'm Lafayette O'Leary! I'm just occupying Zorro's body for the moment! Under the circumstances it wouldn't be ethical for me to marry you. Can't you see that?"

"First you made me streep; theen you sneaked out like a policeman een the night, and locked me een my own boudoir! A meellion feesh hooks could not repay me for the pangs I have suffered for you, you . . . sheep een wolf's clothing!"

"Why didn't you do the job while I was out of my mind? Then I wouldn't have known anything about it."

"What? Mistreat a holy man affleected of Dumballa? You theenk we are barbarians?"

"Yeah—it would have been pretty tough on Tazlo Haz. The poor boob wouldn't have had a clue what was going on."

"Tazlo Haz—that's what you kept screeching wheen you were trying to fly," Gizelle said. "What does eet mean?"

"It's my name. I mean it was Zorro's name—or the name of the ego that shifted into Zorro's body when I shifted into his. He's a birdman—with wings, you know." Lafayette fingered his skinned knees gingerly. "I guess it was as hard for him to realize his wings were gone as it was for me to walk through walls."

"Zorito—you are a beeg liar—for theese I geeve you credit," Gizelle said. "But eet's not enough. Now I'm going to get a leettle beauty sleep; I want to look my best for you tomorrow—while you're hanging from the hooks." She turned and hurried away; O'Leary wasn't sure whether there had been a break in her voice on the last words or not.

5

Lafayette slumped in the corner of the cage, his aching head resting on his bandaged knees.

"I must be getting old," he thought drearily. "I used to be able to land on my feet—but now I just stumble from one disaster to the next. If I could just explain to somebody, just once, what's actually going on—but somehow, nobody will listen. Everybody seems to hear what they want to hear—or what they expect to hear."

He shifted position. The moon was low in the sky now. It would be daylight in another couple of hours. He might last for a few more hours after that, but by lunchtime it would be all over—if he was lucky. The trestle tables set up under the trees would be laden with roast turkey and hams and nine-layer chocolate cakes, and pitchers of foaming ale; the holiday crowd would feast merrily, with his dangling body as the principal object of merriment. And back in Artesia City, Daphne would be snuggling up with . . .

"Oh, no, she's not," he reminded himself. "That's one consolation anyway. She's in Central, being trained as a rookie agent."

Yeah—but why?

"Well—maybe she got worried and dialed Central, reported that I was missing—"

Uh-uh. There was nothing in the record about that. Belarius checked.

"Maybe—" Lafayette felt cold fingers clutch at his chest. "Maybe that wasn't really Daphne! Maybe somebody's stolen *her* body, too!"

Guesswork! That won't get you anywhere. Stick to the point!

"Great! What *is* the point?"

The point is you've got about two hours to live unless you do something fast!

"But what?" he groaned between gritted teeth. "So far I've been a leaf in the storm, tossed this way and that by events that have been running wild, out of control. I've got to take over and start running things *my* way for a change. And the first item is to get out of here . . .

He prowled the cage for the fiftieth time, inspecting every joint—and found them all as securely lashed with rawhide as the last time. He checked each stout rail; the smallest was as big as his arm at the elbow, with room between them barely sufficient to pass a water cup. He tried again to rock the cage, on the chance that tipping it would open a seam; it was like rocking a bank vault.

"All right, without a knife, direct measures are out. What about more sophisticated techniques? Like focusing the Psychical Energies, for example . . . "

O'Leary closed his eyes, marshaled his thoughts.

It's worked before. It's how you got to Artesia in the first place, remember? And how you met Daphne. Remember how you wished for a bathtub, and got one—complete with occupant? She certainly looked charming, wearing nothing but soapsuds and a pretty smile. And later, in the pink and silver gown, facing the duchess . . . and later yet, snuggling up in the dark . . .

"But this isn't getting me out of this cage," he reminded himself sternly. "Think about the time you produced a Coke machine when you were dying of thirst in the desert, on your way to Lod's stronghold. Or about conjuring up Dinny, when I needed a ride. I got a dinosaur instead of a horse, true, but as it turned out, that was a lucky break . . ."

Stop reminiscing! He commanded himself. *You were going to focus your Psychical Energies, remember?*

"I can't," he muttered. "Central put an end to all that with their blasted Suppressor. Let's face it, I'm stuck."

That's what you thought when you were in Melange, too—but you were wrong!

"Sure—but that was a special case. I was in another Locus, the rules were changed . . ."

Try! This is no time to give up!

"Well . . ." Lafayette closed his eyes, pictured a sharp-bladed pocket knife lying in the corner of the cage. *Under some litter,* he specified, *in a spot where I wouldn't have seen it. I haven't actually scraped around over there; I don't KNOW there isn't a knife . . . So BE there, knife! A nice little Barlow with a bone handle . . .*

If there was a small quiver in the even flow of entropy, he failed to detect it.

"But that doesn't mean it didn't work," he said bravely. "Take a look . . ." He went to the corner in question, scraped away the drifted leaves and bird droppings and straw, exposing bare planks.

"No knife," he mumbled. "It figures. My luck's run out. I didn't have a chance from the beginning. I can see that now."

Sure. But why? Maybe if you could figure out why, you'd have a chance of fighting back.

"Why? How do I know? Because somebody wanted me out of the way, I suppose."

Why not just knock you in the head, in that case? Why all this business of turning you into Zorro?

"Maybe . . . maybe that was just a side effect. If it wasn't just you that was turned into Zorro; if Zorro was also turned into *you*—and it seems like a logical assumption—if you can call any part of this insanity logical . . ."

Then—the whole idea might have been to get Zorro into my body—and I was just dumped into his to get me out of the way.

"It's a possibility."

But why? What would that accomplish?

"For one thing—assuming Zorro's the culprit—it would put him in the palace right now, occupying your place, using your clothes, your toothbrush, your bed—"

Let's drop that line of thought for the moment! OK, so Zorro found a way to steal bodies. He conned the Red Bull into handing me the Mark III Shape Changer, and I was boob enough to push the button. Then what? It still doesn't explain things like the Stasis Pod, and the old geezer in blue robes . . .

"Ye gods!" O'Leary blurted. "That's who the photo was, back in Belarius' office! The old man in the tank—but without the beard!"

6

Now we're getting somewhere, Lafayette assured himself. *We've established a connection between Central and Artesia—that Central, or at least Belarius—doesn't seem to know anything about.*

"Right—and if you recall, he got a bit paranoid as soon as he caught you staring at the photo of . . . what did he call him? Jorlemagne. Wanted you to rat on him, spill the beans—implying you were in it with him—whatever 'it' is."

But that doesn't explain why this Jorlemagne was lying around in a cave like Sleeping Beauty in an electronic bunk bed making strange noises at anybody who disturbs him.

"Wait a minute; let's see what we've got: Back at Central, there's been some skullduggery. Belarius is upset about something done by Jorlemagne, who's dropped out of sight. This may or may not tie in with the Focal Referent, which Belarius may not know anything about, probably the latter, since he's under the impression it weighs umpteen tons . . . "

Wait a minute. It seems I remember him correcting me when I called it a Mark III. He insisted it was a Mark II. So . . .

"So—maybe what you had was a new model, miniaturized. But—why wouldn't Belarius know that? After all, he's Chief of Research, and the Focal Referent was his baby."

I don't know. But at the same time he's having trouble with this Jorlemagne absconding—presumably with a newer model FR than even Belarius knows about—funny things started happening in Artesia. And Artesia is where Jorlemagne is. So—

"So all I have to do is get to a phone and dial my special number, and tell them where to pick up their boy!"

Fine—except you'll still be Zorro—and somebody else with your face will be filling in for you at home!

"Maybe Central can fix that, too.

"I can't wait that long! I have to get back and see what's going on! There's got to be a reason for that sneaking phony to have stolen my body! I want to know what it is!"

Meanwhile—how do you get out of this cage?

"Yeah—there *is* that," O'Leary muttered. "I can't cut my way out—and I can't wish myself out. It looks like the end of the trail. Damn! And just when I was beginning to see a little light."

There's still a lot of loose ends. What about Lom—the kindly old geezer who picked you up and fed you—and then picked your pocket?

"Yeah—what about him? Bavarian ham, yet. And Danish butter. Nobody in Artesia ever heard of Denmark or Bavaria. Or New Orleans, either!" O'Leary smacked his fist into his palm. "It's obvious! Lom's a Central agent, too."

And when he found the Focal Referent on you—he naturally assumed you were the thief—or that you were in it with Jorlemagne—

"So he took steps to get rid of you. Dumped you in Thallathlone."

Uh-huh. But I got away—by a fluke—and wound up back here. Nice work, O'Leary. Which is better—a nice cool cell in Thallathlone, or the Death of the Thousand Hooks?

"In another few hours it won't matter, one way or another," O'Leary sighed. "Well, I've had a nice run, while it lasted, but it had to end. I parlayed it from a dull job in a foundry to six years of high living in a palace; I guess I should be satisfied with that. Even if I'd known how it would end, I wouldn't want to change it. Except maybe this last part. It seems like a dirty way to go. This is one time the miracle isn't going to happen. But since there's no hope the least I can do is pull myself together and die like a man."

The moon had set; through the inky black, Lafayette could see nothing except the glow of the guard fire a hundred yards away, and a single candle in a wagon window.

Something passed between Lafayette and the light. Stealthy footsteps sounded from the darkness, coming toward him.

"Hey," he protested, discovering a sudden obstruction in his throat. "It's not time yet."

"Hssst!" Someone was at the bars—a small, silvery-haired figure.

"Lom!"

"Quite right, my boy. Sorry I took so long." There was a rasp of steel against hard leather; a knifeblade threw back a glint from the distant fire. Lashings parted; bars were pulled aside. Lafayette crawled through, ignoring the pain in his scraped knees.

"Let's be off," Lom whispered. "You and I have things to discuss, my lad."

Chapter Eight

1

The stars were fading in the first gray paling of the dawn. Lafayette huddled, shivering, beside the tiny fire Lom had built under a sheltering rock ledge.

"Sorry there's no coffee this time," the old gentleman said. "You look as though you need it, indeed."

"New Orleans style?" O'Leary queried.

"Umm. Rather good, wasn't it? Never fear, we'll soon be back at my digs, and—"

"They don't have New Orleans coffee in Artesia, Lom—or German ham, either."

"I'm afraid I don't quite understand . . . " Lom looked genuinely puzzled.

"New Orleans is in Locus Alpha Nine-three. So is Bavaria—and Denmark."

Lom shook his head. "Dear lad, I merely read what it said on the labels. I don't even know what an old Orleans is, to say nothing of a New one."

"Where did you get the stuff, Lom? There's no handy supermarket around the corner from that peak of yours."

There was a pause.

"Oh, dear," Lom said.

"Well?"

"I . . . I should have known it was wrong. But after all—there seemed to be no owner. There it was, piled in the cave—and—and I—well, I appropriated it. My only defense is . . . I was hungry."

"You *found* it?"

"Please believe me. It would be dreadful if you got the wrong impression."

"Yes—wouldn't it . . . "

"Are you hinting at something?"

"Not hinting, Lom. I want to know where you fit into all this."

"You're being frightfully obscure, my boy—"

"I'm not your boy—in spite of your rescuing me. Come clean, Lom: what do you want from me?"

"I? Why, nothing at all. I felt responsible for you, in a way, and did my best to help you—"

"How did you find me?" Lafayette cut in.

"Ah—as to that, I employed a simple device called a Homer. It makes bipping sounds, you see, and—"

"More electronic gadgets, eh? Where'd you get it?"

"Concealed in a small grotto."

"Grotto?"

"Cave. I hope I didn't do wrong by using it to save you from a horrible death—"

"Another lucky find, eh? That's your answer to everything. Well, I suppose it's possible. Every cave in Artesia seems to be stuffed full of loot. But that still doesn't explain how you carried me from wherever I landed up to that eagle's nest. A mountain goat couldn't have climbed those cliffs, even without me on his back."

"Climb—Oh, I see what you were thinking! No, no, I should have explained. You see—there's a stairway. An escalator, as a matter of fact. No trick at all, just had to drag you a few feet and push the button." Lom beamed.

"Oh, that clears everything up," Lafayette said. "Swell. You didn't climb, you used the escalator. How stupid of me not to have figured that one out."

"You—you sound dubious."

"Who are you, Lom!" O'Leary demanded. "Where do you come from? Why did you cut me out of that cage?"

Lom drew a breath, hesitated, let it out in a sigh. "I," he said in a dismal tone, "am a failure." He looked across the flickering fire at Lafayette. "Once, I occupied a . . . a position of considerable trust. Then . . . things went badly for me. There was a robbery, so arranged as to make it appear that I—that I was the thief. I escaped barely ahead of the authorities."

"And?"

"I . . . made my way here. Foraging, I stumbled on the, er, supplies of which you know; I found the route to my isolated hideaway. Then—*you* dropped from the skies. I naturally did what I could for you."

"Then?"

"Then you disappeared. Poof! I searched for you—and at last I found you, as you know. And here we are."

"You left out one small item. What did you do with the Mark III?"

"Mark who?"

"Maybe you didn't make off with the till, back where you came from," O'Leary said. "But there was a gadget concealed in a secret pocket of my coat. You took it while I was unconscious. I want it back."

Lom was shaking his head emphatically. "You wrong me, my boy—"

"Just call me O'Leary."

"Is that your name?" Lom asked quickly.

"Certainly—"

"Then why did you tell the young woman—the one who seemed to dislike you so—that it was Zorro?"

"Because it is. I mean, she knows me as Zorro—"

"But that's not your real name? Curious that you have the letter Z embroidered on your shirt pocket—and on your handkerchief—and your socks."

"I'm in disguise," Lafayette said. "Don't try to change the subject. Where's the Mark III?"

"Tell me about it," Lom suggested.

"I'll tell you this much," Lafayette snapped. "It's the most dangerous object in the country! I don't know why you wanted it; maybe you thought you could pawn it; but—"

"Mr. O'Leary—I took nothing from your person, while you were asleep or any other time!"

"Don't stall, Lom! I want it back!"

"You may search me if you wish; you're considerably larger and stronger than I. I can't stop you."

"What good would that do? You could have hidden it."

"Indeed! And why, if I had robbed you, would I have returned to preserve you from what, it appeared, would have been a peculiarly unpleasant fate?"

"Maybe you needed me to show you how to operate it."

"I see. Without letting on I had it, I suppose."

"Well, blast it," O'Leary snarled. "If you didn't take it, where is it?"

"Possibly," Lom said thoughtfully, "it dropped from your pocket when you fell . . . "

There was a momentary silence, while Lafayette stared across the fire at the small, indignant figure, who returned the look defiantly.

"All right," O'Leary sighed. "I can't prove you took it. I guess I ought to apologize. And to thank you for getting me out of that cage."

"Perhaps," Lom said, "if you told me a bit more about the missing item?"

"Forget it, Lom. The less anybody knows about it, the better."

"This Mark III; was it your property? Or were you keeping it for someone else?"

"Don't pry, Lom! Tell me: in your explorations, did you come across a cave with, ah, with anything, oh, like a sort of box in it?"

"Since you won't answer my questions, O'Leary, why should I answer yours?"

"Because I need to get to the bottom of this, that's why! There's a plot afoot, Lom! Bigger than anything you could imagine! And I'm mixed up in it! And I want out!"

"Oh? In that case, why not tell me all you know—"

"Never mind." O'Leary got painfully to his feet. "I've got to get going, Lom. Time's a-wasting. I have to make contact with—" He broke off. "With some friends of mine," he finished.

"Suppose I go with you," Lom suggested, jumping up.

"Out of the question," Lafayette said. "I don't mean to be rude, but I can't afford to be slowed down. Beside which it might be dangerous."

"I don't mind. And I'll do my best to keep to the pace."

"Look, Lom, you're far better off right here. You have your hut, and you can live on leaves and berries and Bavarian ham, in peace and quiet—"

"I still have hopes," Lom cut in, "of clearing my name. Possibly these friends you mentioned could help me."

"King Shosto and his boys will be combing the woods for me. If they catch you in my company they'll probably allocate five hundred of those hooks to you."

"I doubt it, lad. I know the trails through these hills quite well. In fact, without me to guide you, I doubt if you'll ever reach the city."

"Well—come on then. I can't stop you. But don't expect me to wait for you." He turned away.

"Wait!" Lom said sharply. "Not that way, Mr. O'Leary." He stepped forward and parted the bushes to reveal a narrow path leading down the rocky slope. "Shall we go?"

2

Twice in the hour before sunrise, O'Leary and Lom were forced to take refuge in deep shrubbery while a party of Wayfarers thrashed their way through the under-brush close at hand. From their conversation it was apparent that there would be plenty of hooks to go around when the owner of the footprints near the broached cage was apprehended along with the escaped prisoner.

"Tsk. Such an uncharitable attitude," Lom commented as they emerged from their last concealment.

"Just wait until I get my hands on this Zorro character," Lafayette said. "He's the one at the bottom of this—"

"I thought *you* were Zorro?" Lom said sharply.

"Not really. I just look like him. I mean—well, never mind. It's too complicated."

He turned to see Lom staring hard at his thumb, which he was solemnly waggling.

"Playing with your fingers?" O'Leary snapped.

"Ah—not at all, my boy," Lom said, thrusting both hands into his pockets. "Tell me—what will you do when we reach the city?"

"I'll have to play it by ear. Once inside the palace, if I can just get a word with Adoranne . . ."

"Frankly, my boy—you look a trifle disreputable. Your garments are somewhat the worse for wear, and it appears you haven't shaved of late, and that gold earring in your left ear is hardly calculated to inspire confidence."

"I'll think of something. I'll have to."

As the sun cleared the treetops, they emerged from the woods onto a stretch of sloping pastureland dotted with peaceful cows, which gazed placidly at them as they tramped down to the road. A passing steam-powered wain gave them a lift to the city limits. As they walked through the cobbled street, redolent of early-morning odors of roasting coffee and fresh-baked bread, a few early risers gave them curious looks. They paused at a sidewalk stall within sight of the palace towers, rosy-tinted in the early light, for a quick breakfast of eggs, bacon, toast and jam, which seemed to Lafayette to drop into an empty cavern the size of a municipal car-barn.

"It's amazing what a little food will do," he commented, as he finished off his second cup of coffee. "Suddenly, everything seems simpler. I'll go to the palace gates, explain that I have important information, and request an audience. Then, after I've told Adoranne a few things that could only be known to me—I'll explain who I am. After that it will be routine. By this time tomorrow, everything will be straightened out."

"I take it you know this Princess Adoranne personally?"

"Certainly. We're old friends. In fact, I was engaged to her once; but I realized in the nick of time that it was really Daphne I was in love with—"

"You—engaged to a princess?" Lom was looking highly skeptical.

"Sure—why not?"

Lom's mouth tightened. "Mr. O'Leary—this is hardly the time for leg-pulling. After all, if we've joined forces—"

"Who says we've joined forces? I let you come along for the ride, that's all, Lom. I still have no reason to trust you. In fact, I think this is where our paths should part. You go your way and I'll go mine."

"You promised to introduce me to your, ah, influential friends," Lom said quickly.

"Oh, no, I didn't." O'Leary shook his head. "That was *your* idea."

"See here, O'Leary—or Zorro—or whatever your name might be," Lom said testily. "I can be of help to you; suppose you have difficulty in gaining entrance to the palace—"

"Don't worry about that; I'll manage."

"Then you intend to—to repay my efforts on your behalf by abandoning me here?"

"Why put it like that? I'll tell you what, Lom: if everything goes well, I'll look you up afterward, and see what I can do for you, all right?"

"I want to do something—something positive, to demonstrate my usefulness. Now, if I go with you to the palace—"

"Out of the question. I might be able to talk myself inside, but you . . . well, candidly, Lom, you don't look particularly impressive, you know, in those tattered clothes and needing a haircut."

"Surely there's *something* I can do?"

"Well—all right, if you insist. Go find the Red Bull. Bring him to the palace. No, on second thought, make it the Axe and Dragon. If I flunk out at the palace, I'll meet you there. And if I make it—I'll send for you. OK?"

"Well . . . I'll do my best. The Red Bull, you say?"

"Sure. Ask around. Any pickpocket in town can help you. Now I've got to be off." Lafayette rose, paid for their breakfast with the lone silver dollar he had found in Zorro's pocket, and set off at a purposeful stride toward the palace.

3

The brass-helmeted guard, resplendent in baggy blue knee pants and a yellow-and-blue striped coat, gave O'Leary a lazy up-and-down look.

"Get hence, Jack, before I run you in for loitering," he suggested curtly.

"I'm here on business," Lafayette said. "I have important news for Princess Adoranne."

"Oh yeah?" The man shifted his harquebus casually. "What about?"

"Classified," O'Leary said. "Look here, we're wasting time. Just pass my request along to the sergeant of the guard."

"Oh, a wise one, eh?" the sentry growled. "Beat it, Greaser, while you still got the chanst."

"Like that, huh?" Lafayette said. He cupped his hands to his mouth:

"Sergeant of the Guard, post number one—on the double!"

"Why, you—"

"Ah-ah—don't do anything rash," O'Leary cautioned as the enraged man raised his bell-mouthed gun. "Witnesses, remember?"

"All right, what's this all about?" a short, plump noncom with a handlebar mustache swaggered into view. He halted, looked Lafayette up and down. His face turned an alarming shade of purple.

"Shorty!" Lafayette cried. "Am I glad to see you!"

"Grab that bum!" the sergeant roared. "That's the lousy punk that clobbered three o' my boys here Monday a week!"

4

It was difficult, Lafayette conceded, to keep his voice cool, calm, and reasonable with three large men clamping his arms in pretzel-like positions behind his back, while dragging him across the cobbled courtyard. Still, it was no time to give way to intemperate language.

"If you'd just—*ow!*—listen to what I have to say—*ouch!*—I'm sure you'll agree that what I have to report—*unh!*—is worth listening to."

"Yeah? Give him another quarter turn, LaVerne!"

"Shorty—at least give me a hearing—"

"That's Sergeant to you, crum-bum!" the five-foot-three harquebusier bellowed. "You can tell it to the judge—next month, when he gets back from his vacation!"

"I can't wait a month! It's an emergency!"

"If he says anything else, LaVerne—stick a bandanna in his mouth. The one you use to mop off the back o' your neck on hot afternoons!"

They passed the stables and the harness room, turned into the serviceway that ran beside the royal pigpen. The guards recoiled as the imprisoned boar emitted a loud snort and threw his quarter-ton bulk against the fence.

"What's got into George?" LaVerne inquired. "He ain't been hisself for a couple weeks now."

"Maybe he knows we got a barbecue planned for next month," someone suggested.

"Nothing ain't been normal lately," LaVerne mourned. "Not since—"

"Belay that!" Shorty yelled. "You slobs are at attention!"

Lafayette's escort hustled him up three steps into a small squad-room lit even at this hour by a forty-watt bulb dangling from a kinked cord. An unshaven man in shirt sleeves sat with a boot propped on a battered desk, picking his teeth with a short dagger. He raised a sardonic eyebrow and reached for a form.

"Book this mug on suspicion, Sarge," Shorty said.

"Suspicion o' what?"

"Suit yourself. Forgery, maybe. Or Peeping Tom. Or watering wine. Just hold him while I work up a file on him that'll keep him on ice until they pension me off."

"This has gone far enough," Lafayette spoke up. "While you flatfoots jabber, the kingdom may be lost. I have to see Princess Adoranne, right now!"

The desk sergeant listened with his mouth slightly open. He looked Lafayette up and down, then turned an unfriendly eye on the mustachioed noncom who had arrested him.

"What's the idea bringing a loony in here?" he demanded. "You know all them nut cases go directly to the filbert factory—"

"Call Princess Adoranne," Lafayette said in a voice which cracked slightly in spite of his efforts. "Just request her Highness to come down for a moment, all right?" He tried a friendly smile, which caused the desk sergeant to edge backward.

"Hold him, boys," he muttered. "He's getting ready to go violent." He dinged a bell on the desk; a door opened and an uncombed head of shaggy pale hair appeared, surmounting the thick-lipped, puffy-eyed face of a deputy.

"Oglethorpe, slap a set of irons on this pigeon," he said. "Throw him in dungeon number twelve, at the back. We don't want him yelling and getting everybody upset—"

"Irons?" Lafayette yelled. "I'll have the lot of you pounding beats on the graveyard shift!" He jerked free, eluded a grab, made a dive for the door, hooked a foot over an outthrust ankle and witnessed the finest display of pyrotechnics since the previous Third of October: Artesian Independence Day.

Hard hands were clamped on his arms, hauling him upright. He tried to move his legs, then let them drag. He was aware of descending stairs, of tottering along a dark, evil-smelling corridor, of a heavy iron gate being lifted. A shove sent him stumbling into a low-ceiling room that stank of burning kerosene from the flambeaux mounted in brackets along the wall.

"I'm S'Laf'yet 'Leary," he mumbled, shaking his head to clear it. "I demand a lawyer. I demand to see Adoranne. I demand to send a message to my wife, Countess Daphne—" He broke off as his arms were twisted up behind him and held in a double come-along grip.

"Looks like the booze has rotted his wits out," the blond turnkey said, exhaling a whiskey breath into O'Leary's ear.

"Stick him in number twelve, Percy. All the way in the back."

"Sure, Oglethorpe—but, geez, I ain't swept twelve out in a while, an'—"

"Never mind coddling the slob. He's one o' them Peeping Irvings."

"Yeah? Geez, Oglethorpe, is he the one they spotted last month, climbing the ivy fer a glimpse o' Princess Adoranne taking a shower?"

"Never mind that, Percy! Lock him up, and get back to yer comic book!"

Percy, Lafayette noted vaguely, was even larger and less intellectual-looking than Oglethorpe. He allowed himself to be prodded along to the end of the dark passage, stood leaning dizzily against the wall as the jailer selected an oversized key from the ring at his belt.

"Say, pal . . . uh . . . how was it?" the lout inquired in confidential tones as he removed the handcuffs. "I mean . . . does her Highness look as neat in the nood as a guy would figger?"

"Neater," Lafayette said blurrily, rubbing his head. "That is . . . it's none of your business. But listen—this is all an error, you understand? A case of mistaken identity. I have to get a message to Countess Daphne or the Princess, and—"

"Yeah." The jailer nodded. As he thrust Lafayette into the tiny cell, from which a goaty odor wafted, O'Leary hardly noticed his hand brushing the other's side, his fingers nimbly plucking something away, palming it . . .

"That's why you was climbing the ivy, sure," Percy rambled on sardonically. "It's as good of a alibi as any, punk. I bet you never even glommed nothing."

"That's what you think!" Lafayette yelled, as the door slammed. He pressed his face against the bars set in the foot-square opening in the metal slab. "I'll make a deal: you deliver my message, and I'll tell you all about it!"

"Yeah?" Percy replied, somewhat doubtfully. "How do I know you ain't lying?"

"Even if I make it up, it'll be better than a comic book," Lafayette snapped.

"Nuts," Percy said loftily. "And anyway—the whole conversation is in lousy taste, considering."

"Considering what?"

"Considering the shape her Highness is in." The jailer's lower lip thrust out. "Ain't it a crying shame?"

"Ain't what—I mean isn't what a crying shame?"

"That the Princess is laying at death's door—down wit' a fever which nobody don't know how to cure it—that's what! And Count Alain and the Lady Daphne along wit' her!"

"Did you say—at death's door?" O'Leary choked.

"Right, Bub. They say all took sick at once—a fortnight since—and they ain't expected to recover. That's how come King Lafayette had to take over."

"K-King Lafayette?"

"Sure. And the first thing he done was to beef up the guard force, which I was one o' the first hired. Where you been, anyways?"

"But . . . but . . . but . . . "

"Yeah—so don't crack wise," Percy said with dignity. "So long, hotshot. See you in death Row."

5

Lafayette sat on the heap of damp straw that was the cell's only furnishing, numbly fingering the knobs on his skull.

"Things couldn't go this wrong," he mumbled. "I must be the one who's feverish. I'm delirious, imagining all this. Actually, I'm in bed, being tended by Daphne—"

He broke off. "Hey," he said thoughtfully. "Daphne can't be sick in bed—I saw her at Central, going through rookie training, yesterday!" He jumped up, banged on the bars until Percy appeared with a napkin tucked in his collar, wiping his chin.

"You said that Countess Daphne's been sick in bed for two weeks?"

"Yeah, that's right."

"And she hasn't recovered?"

"Nope. Nor likely to, poor kid."

"How do you know? Did you see her?"

"Now I know you're loopy, Rube. I'll get a squint at her Ladyship in bed right after I get my promotion to Buck Admiral."

"Who says she's sick?"

Percy spread his thick hands. "It's what they call common knowledge. King Lafayette kept it quiet for a couple days, but then he had to let the word out, on account of everybody was getting a little uptight on account of they didn't see the Princess around and about, like." Percy took out a bone toothpick and gouged at a back tooth.

"Have you seen this King Lafayette?" O'Leary asked.

"Sure; I seen him yesterday, reviewing the guard. The poor guy looked pretty bad off, and I guess it figgers, wit' that snazzy little piece Countess Daphne about to croak, an' all—"

"What did he look like?"

"You know—kind of a skinny long-legged kid wit' a bunch o' curly brown hair and sort o' sappy smile—only he wasn't smiling yesterday. Boy, what a temper!" Percy shook his head admiringly. "The boys tell me it's the first time he ever had anybody horsewhipped, too."

"He's horsewhipping people?"

"Sure. Well, the poor slob's got a lot on his mind, like. I guess that's why he kicked the cat—"

"He kicked a cat?"

"Uh-huh. Tried to, anyways. I always heard he was a good natured bozo, but I guess having your frail croak on you is enough to kind of give anybody a little edge on. That, and the war." Percy inspected his toothpick gravely.

"What war?"

"Geez, Bub, you're really out of it, ain't you? The war wit' the Vandals, natcherly."

"You mean—Artesia's at war?"

"Naw—not yet. But any day now. See, these Vandals, they got this invasion planned, which they want to take over the country so's they can loot and rob and all. What they'll do, they'll kill off all the men, and capture all the broads—"

"Who says so?"

"Huh? King Lafayette said so—the first day after he had hisself coronated on account of the Princess being laid up—"

"When is all this supposed to happen?"

"Any day now. That's why everybody's got to turn in their cash and jewels, for the like war effort. Boy, you should of seen some o' the rich merchants howl when us boys was sent out to make some collections." Percy wagged his head. "Some o' them bums got no patriotism."

Lafayette groaned.

"Yeah, it's a heartbreaker, ain't it, pal?" Percy belched comfortably. "Well, it's about time fer my relief, Rube.

Hang loose—as the executioner said to the customer just before he sprang the trap." Percy sauntered off, whistling. Lafayette tottered to a corner and sank down. Things were beginning to come into focus now. The plot was bigger and better organized than anything he'd imagined. There was an invasion, all right—but not from outside. The invader had saved a lot of time and effort by going right to the heart of things; it was a neat switch: invade the palace first, and take over the country at leisure.

"But how did he do it?" Lafayette got to his feet and paced.

"Let's say this Zorro stumbled onto some loot stashed by Goruble; Lom said the hills are full of caves full of the stuff. So—he got his hands on the Mark III, discovered what it would do. He got to the Red Bull, and planted the infernal thing on me, knowing I'd be boob enough to push the button. When I did, he hurried off to the palace and took up where I left off. Only—" He paused at a thought.

"Only he didn't fool Daphne. Good girl! She smelled a rat, went to the secret phone in Nicodaeus' old lab, and called Central. They picked her up, and she reported . . . reported . . . " Lafayette paused, scratching his chin.

"What could she report? She noticed something wrong; she knows I never kick cats. But she had no way of knowing I was really this Zorro, masquerading as me. She'd just think that somebody had hypnotized me, or something. Whatever she said, she'd have a hard time getting those bureaucrats to listen. Their policy is minimum interference. If they checked, they'd find everything apparently normal. The most they'd do would be to send an agent in to look over the situation . . . " Lafayette halted and smacked a fist into his palm.

"Of course! What an idiot I was not to have spotted it sooner! Lom! He's a Central agent! That's why he knows all those things he shouldn't know! And no wonder he was suspicious of me! I claimed to be Lafayette O'Leary—the man he was sent here to investigate! No wonder he wanted to come into the city with me! He had to keep an eye on me! Only . . . only why did he let me talk him into splitting to go off on a wild-goose chase after the Red Bull—"

Well, after all, the Red Bull was involved in this, right? Maybe he saw the chance to get filled in on the details of my story, figuring I'd be available whenever he wanted to get back to me. Or maybe—maybe he'd already become convinced of my innocence—or at least that things were more complicated than they looked—and he had to get off by himself to report back to HQ. That's probably it! He's made his report by now; he ought to show up any minute with a Central Enforcer squad to spring me, and get this whole mess straightened out!

At that moment there was a clump of boots in the passage. O'Leary struggled to his feet, blinking at the glare of a lantern.

"Whatta ya mean, lost it?" said the heavy voice of Oglethorpe. "OK, OK, I'll use mine . . . "

An iron key clattered in the lock; the door swung wide. Beyond it, beside the hulking guard, Lafayette saw a small, silver-haired figure.

"OK, OK, let's go, chum," Oglethorpe rasped.

"Lom! You finally made it!" Lafayette started forward. A large hand against his chest stopped him in his tracks.

"Don't try nothing dumb, Clyde," Oglethorpe advised him in a patient tone, and administered a shove which sent O'Leary staggering back to rebound from the far wall, just in time to collide with Lom as he was pitched through the door. The heavy gate clanged shut.

"Well, we meet again, my boy," the old fellow said apologetically.

Chapter Nine

1

"You mean," Lafayette said in a sagging voice, "you're *not* a Central agent? You weren't sent here to investigate Daphne's report? You don't have an Enforcer squad standing by to put the arm on this bogus King Lafayette?"

Lom frowned at O'Leary. "You almost sound," he said, "as if you hoped I *was* a Central agent . . . "

"You don't deny you know about Central, then?" Lafayette leaped into the breach. "I guess that's something. Look here, Lom—just who *are* you? How do you figure in all this?"

"Just the question I was about to ask you," Lom countered. "Frankly—my previous theories seem somewhat untenable in light of the present contretemps."

"What theories?"

"Not so fast, young fellow," Lom said in an entirely new tone. "I didn't say I was satisfied with your *bona fides*; far from it. As a matter of fact, it's obvious to me now that you're either innocent—a hapless victim—or more deeply involved than I'd thought. I sincerely hope you can establish that the former is the case . . . "

"Wait a minute. You sound as if I was expected to make excuses to *you*! If you're not a Central agent, then you must be in this mess up to your ears!"

"How does it happen," Lom demanded in a no-nonsense voice, "that you seem familiar with a device—the Mark III Focal Referent—which is a secret I had supposed to be known only to its inventor, and one other?"

"Easy; the Red Bull handed it to me—"

"A facile explanation, but hardly satisfying."

"I don't know why I'm alibiing in the first place," O'Leary snapped. "You're the one with some explanations to give. And don't try to snow me with that story about just happening to stumble on a cave full of just what you needed. If Central sent you here, well and good. They'd have supplied you, naturally. If not—then you must know a lot more than you're telling."

"Possibly," Lom said crisply. "Now, tell me: why were you roaming the hills in the first place?"

"What were you doing on the mountaintop?" Lafayette came back.

"Why did you come here to Artesia City? Whom were you expecting to meet?"

"How do you know about Central? Nobody in Artesia ever heard of it, but me, and Daphne!"

"What's *your* connection with Central?"

"I asked you first!"

"What's he paying you?"

"What's who paying me?"

"*Him*, that's who!"

"I don't know what you're talking about!"

"I'll double his offer!"

"Talk or I'll twist that skinny neck of yours!"

"Lay a hand on me and I'll visit you with a plague of cramps!"

"Aha! Now you're a warlock!" Lafayette took a step toward the old man—and doubled up at a stab of pain under the ribs. He made a desperate grab, and yelped as his left calf knotted in a Charley horse.

"I warned you," Lom said calmly.

Lafayette made one more try, was rewarded by a stitch in his side. He lurched back against the bars.

"Now talk," Lom snapped. "I want the whole story. What was your role supposed to be? How did you happen to fall out with him? That's why you fled to the hills, eh? But why did you come back?"

"You're babbling," Lafayette gasped, clutching his ribs. "I'm Lafayette O'Leary. Somebody tricked me . . . into this Zorro routine . . . so they could take my place . . . "

"Anyone who wanted to masquerade as O'Leary would simply have disposed of his person, not set him free to confuse the issue. No, my lad, it won't do. Now talk! The truth, this time! Or I'll give you a spasm of the eyeballs, a sensation you'll not soon forget!"

"You talk as if . . . you really didn't know," Lafayette managed, between pangs resembling, he suspected, those of imminent childbirth. His fingers encountered an object in an inside pocket, felt over it. He had a sudden, vivid recollection of those same fingers—Zorro's trained fingers—darting out deftly as Percy thrust him into the cell, lifting something from Percy's belt. He drew the object out, focused watery eyes on it.

" . . . don't know," Lom was still talking. "Even if I were convinced you were a mere dupe—which I'm not—"

"How," Lafayette cut in, "would you like to escape from this cell?"

"I should like that very well indeed," Lom spat. "But don't change the subject! I—"

"Take this whammy off me . . . " O'Leary panted, "and we'll talk about it."

"Not until you've made a clean breast of it!"

"Did you notice what I'm holding in my hand?"

"No. What difference would—" Lom paused. "It . . . it appears to be a large key of some sort. It's not—it's not the key to this door—"

"It better be—or Zorro's fingers have lost their touch." Lafayette thrust the key out between the bars.

"Careful, my boy! Don't drop it! Bring it back inside, carefully!"

"Untie this knot in my duodenum!"

"I . . . I . . . very well!"

Lafayette staggered at the sudden relief of the stomach cramp. "That was a neat trick," he said. "How did you do it?"

"With this." Lom showed an artifact resembling a ball-point pen. "A simple invention of mine. It projects a sound beam of the proper frequency to induce muscular contraction. You see, I confide in you. Now . . . the key, dear boy!"

"Deal," Lafayette said. "A truce between us. We join forces until we find out what's going on."

"Why should I trust you?"

"Because if you don't I'll pitch this key out of reach, and we'll both be stuck here. I won't be able to help Adoranne, maybe—but you won't be free to do her any more harm!"

"I assure you, that's the last thing I desire, lad!"

"Deal?" Lafayette persisted.

"Deal, then. But at the first false move—"

"Let's not waste time," Lafayette said, tossing the key to Lom. "We have some plans to make."

2

"Geez, don't you ever sleep?" Percy inquired aggrievedly as he halted before the cell door. "What you want this time? I told you already chow ain't till one pee em—" He broke off, peering between the bars into the gloomy cell. "Hey—it seems to me like there was another mug in here wit' youse. A little geezer—" He broke off with a grunt, doubled over, and went down. Lafayette thrust the door open and stepped over the prostrate turn-key as Lom came forward from the dark corner where he had lain in wait.

"He'll be all right, won't he?"

"Ummm. I just gave him a touch of *angina*," Lom said offhandedly. "He'll be as good as new in half an hour. Now what?"

"There's still Oglethorpe to deal with. Come on." Stealthily, the escapees moved along the corridor, past empty cells, to the archway beyond which the corner of the warden's desk was visible, supporting a pair of size-fourteen boots with well-worn soles.

"Give him a shot in the ankle," Lafayette murmured. Lom eased forward, focused his sound projector, pressed the stud. There was a muffled exclamation; a large, hairy hand came down to massage the foot. Lom administered a second dose; with a yelp, Oglethorpe swiveled in his chair, swinging his feet out of sight as his head and shoulders rotated into view. Lom took careful aim and zapped him again. The big man roared and slapped his own jaw with a report like a pistol shot. As he jumped up, the old gentleman sighted on his lumbar area and gave him yet another blast. Oglethorpe arched backward, lost his balance, and cracked his head on the desk on the way down.

"Got him," Lom stated with satisfaction.

"You're going to have to simplify that procedure before it replaces a sock full of sand," O'Leary told him. "He made more noise than a rumble between rival gangs armed with garbage can lids."

"Still, we seem to have occasioned no alarm. After all, who would expect a jailbreak at this hour of the day?"

"Well, let's not just stand here congratulating ourselves. We've got ground to cover. Let's take in those lockers and see what's available in the way of disguises."

Five minutes of rummaging turned up a pair of shabby cloaks and a worn canvas pouch full of battered tools.

"We're plumbers," O'Leary said. "I'm the master pipefitter, and you're my assistant—"

"Quite the contrary," Lom interrupted. "A silver-haired apprentice would hardly carry conviction."

"All right—let's not fall out over a jurisdictional dispute." Lafayette adjusted the cloak to cover as much as possible of his grimy silk shirt and baggy satin trousers. In a desk drawer he found the keys to the heavy grate that barred the passage. They lifted it, occasioning a dismal groan of rusty metal, eased under, lowered it back in position. Ten feet farther, the passage branched.

"Which way?" Lom wondered aloud. "I confess I have no sense of direction."

"Come on," O'Leary said, leading the way toward a steep flight of stone stairs. At the top, a cross passage led two ways.

"To the left," Lafayette hissed. "We have to pass the squad room, so take it easy."

"How does it happen," Lom whispered, "that you know your way well?"

"I did time down here the first week I was in Artesia. And since then I've been down a few times to visit friends."

"Hmmm. You know, my boy, at times I'm tempted to believe your story . . . "

"Whether you believe it or not, we're in this together. Now let's go before we're arrested for loitering." Lafayette advanced stealthily, risked a peek into the room. Three harquebusiers were seated around a table spooning up beans, their shirts unbuttoned, their floppy hats laid aside, their rapiers dangling from wooden pegs on the wall. One of the trio looked up; his eyes met O'Leary's.

"Yeah," he barked. "Who youse looking for?"

"Roy," Lafayette said promptly. "He said it was a hurry-up call."

"Shorty ain't on until six pee em. A hurry up call, hey? You must be the vet."

"Right," Lafayette improvised as the man rose and sauntered toward him, hitching at his purple-and-green suspenders. The cop eyed O'Leary's tool bag, prodded it with a thick finger.

"What's a vet doing wit' a bunch o' pipe wrenches?" he demanded. "And hack saws, yet. Youse ain't planning a jail break?" He grinned widely at the jape.

"Actually, we do a bit of plumbing on the side," O'Leary said. "We're combination animal doctors and plumbers, you see."

"Yeah?" the cop scratched the back of his thick neck. He yawned. "Well, if you can fix old George's plumbing, Jemimiah'll be your friend fer life." He guffawed, cleared his throat, spat, and gave Lom a suspicious look.

"Ain't I see youse before, Pops?"

"Not unless you've been down with an attack of goat fever, Junior," the old man snapped. "And don't call me Pops."

"Well, we'd better be getting along," Lafayette said hastily. "Actually, it was a leaky faucet we were after. In the tower, Roy said. So—"

"Nix, Bub. Nobody goes up inna tower. Off limits, like. Quarantine."

"Yes. Well, Roy's point was that the drip was annoying the patient—"

"What patient? There ain't no patient inna tower. They're all in the Royal Apartment wing."

"The patient fellows on duty there, I was about to say," O'Leary recovered nimbly. "Just imagine pulling four on and four off with a leaky faucet going drip, drip, drip, drip, drip, drip . . . "

"Yeah, yeah—I get the idear. Well—as long as it's fer the boys. I'll send Clarence here along wit' youse." The NCO beckoned to a slack-faced loon with unevenly focused eyes.

"That's all right, Lieutenant, we can find it—" Lafayette started; but the cop cut him off with a curt gesture.

"Nobody don't go inna tower wit'out he got a escort," he stated firmly.

"Well—in that case," O'Leary conceded the point. Clarence pulled on his coat, strapped on his sword, gave O'Leary a vague look and stood waiting.

"You, uh, kind of got to tell Clarence what to do," the NCO said to Lafayette behind his hand. "Like, in detail, if you know what I mean."

"Let's go, Clarence," Lafayette said. "To the tower."

3

In the courtyard, bright with the late-afternoon sun, Lom overtook O'Leary. "When are we going to dispose of this cretin and make our escape?" he whispered.

"Change of plan," Lafayette murmured. "Getting Clarence was a big break. With an escort we can go where we want to."

"Have you lost your wits? Our only chance is to get clear of this place, and regroup!"

"Let's face it: we'd never get past the gate."

"But—what can you hope to accomplish, skulking about inside the lion's den?"

"Just as I told the gendarmes—the tower—up there." Lafayette pointed to a lofty spire soaring high in the blue sky, a pennant snapping from the flagstaff at its peak.

"Whatever for?" Lom gasped. "We'll be trapped!"

"Classified," Lafayette said.

"Hey," Clarence spoke suddenly in a hoarse whisper. "Hows come we're whispering?"

"It's a secret mission," O'Leary replied. "We're counting on you, Clarence."

"Oh, boy," Clarence said happily. Lom snorted.

Lafayette led the way into the palace proper via a side door—the same door through which he had left that night—only two weeks before, but seeming like a lifetime—for his ill-fated rendezvous with the Red Bull. Inside, he motioned Lom and Clarence along a narrow corridor that passed behind the State Dining Room. Through a half-open door he saw the long tables spread with dazzling linen, adorned with colorful floral centerpieces—a glimpse of another life.

"Looks like they're making ready for a celebration," Lom observed.

"Yeah," Clarence nodded vigorously. "A big blowout scheduled fer tonight. Duh woid is, duh king, he's gonna make a speech, which all duh notables dey'll be dere."

"Keep moving!" Lom hissed. "We'll be seen—and I doubt if the household majordomos will be as readily satisfied with explanations involving medical ministrations to sick pipes as those flatfoots!"

"Hey—dat sounded like it could grow up tuh be a doity crack at us cops," Clarence muttered.

"No offense," Lom reassured him.

They resumed their cautious progress, paused at a brocaded hanging through which Lafayette poked his head to survey the mirrored grand hall. "Come on—the coast is clear."

"Where is everybody?" Lom queried. "The place is like a mausoleum."

"Never mind questioning our good fortune. Let's just take advantage of it."

They reached the back stairs without incident. On the second floor, they passed a red-eyed maid-servant with a mop and bucket, who gave them a tearful look and hurried on. Three flights higher a guard lounged on the landing, reading a newspaper with the aid of a blunt forefinger.

"Whazzis?" he inquired, looking suspiciously at the two adventurers. "Who's these mugs, Clarence?"

"Dat's uh like secret," Clarence whispered. "Shhhh."

"Special mission," O'Leary amplified, "under the personal supervision of Sir Lafayette—"

"You mean King Lafayette, don't you, pal?"

"Right. Now his Majesty has his eye on you, corporal—"

"Corporal, my grandma's pickled bananas," the fellow growled. "I been in this outfit nine years and I ain't got stripe one yet."

"You'll have two, as soon as this job is over," O'Leary said. "I personally guarantee it."

"Yeah? Whom did you say you was, sir?"

"A . . . a person in whom his Majesty resides special confidence."

"And where do you think you're going?" the guard inquired as O'Leary started past him.

"Up there," O'Leary pointed.

"Uh-uh," the man planted himself in Lafayette's path. "Not without a OK from the sergeant, chum."

"Don't you think a king outweighs a sergeant, corporal?"

"Could be—but I work for the sergeant. He works for the lieutenant; *he* works for the captain; *he* works for the colonel—"

"I'm familiar with the intricacies of the military hierarchy," O'Leary snapped. "But we don't have time to waste right now going through channels."

"Nobody goes up without a pass," the guard said.

"Will this do?" Lom inquired at O'Leary's elbow. There was a soft *bzapp!* The unfortunate sentry stiffened, staggered two steps, and fell heavily on the purple carpet.

"Tsk. Drunk on duty," Lafayette said. "Make a note of that, Clarence."

They hurried on, Lom puffing hard, Clarence bringing up the rear, around and around the winding staircase. The steps narrowed, steepened between bare stone walls. The climb ended on a small landing before a massive wood-plank door.

"Wh-what's this?" Lom panted.

"This is as far as we go—without an understanding," O'Leary said. "Note the lock on the door. I know the combination. You don't."

"So?"

"Give me that trick ball-point, and I'll unlock it."

"Not likely," Lom snapped. "Why should I give a rap whether you unlock it or not?"

"Listen," O'Leary invited. From the stairwell, sounds were rising: sounds of alarm.

"They've found that chap we dealt with down below," Lom said. "We should have hidden him—"

"They'd have noticed he was missing. They'll be here in a minute or two."

"Trapped! You treacher, I should have known better—"

"Shhh! Clarence won't understand," Lafayette said softly as the guardsman arrived, breathing hard. "Anyway, we're not trapped—not if we hide in there." He hooked a thumb at the door.

"What's in there? Why did you lead me into a cul-de-sac—"

"It's Nicodaeus' old lab. He was an Inspector, sent in here by Central to investigate a Probability Stress. It's full of special equipment. We'll find everything we need—"

"Well, for heaven's sake, get it open, man!" Lom cut in as the sounds of ascending feet rang clearly from below.

"First, the zap gun, Lom. Just so you aren't tempted to use it on me."

"And what's to keep *you* from using it on *me*?"

"I won't—unless you make a false move. Make up your mind. We have about thirty seconds."

"Blackmail," Lom muttered, and handed over the weapon.

"Once inside we're home safe," O'Leary said. "Let's see, now. It's been a long time since I used this combination . . . " He twirled the dial; the feet pounding below came closer. The lock snicked and opened. O'Leary pushed the door wide.

"Clarence—inside, quick!"

The harquebusier stepped through hesitantly; Lom ducked after him. O'Leary followed, closed the door and set the lock.

"Full of equipment, eh?" Lom rasped behind him.

He turned; in the dim light filtering down through dusty clerestory windows, Lafayette stared in dismay at blank stone walls and a bare stone floor.

"Stripped!" he groaned.

"Just as I thought," Lom said in a deadly tone. "Betrayal. But I'm afraid you won't live to complete your plans, traitor!" Lafayette turned, was looking down the barrel of a slim, deadly-looking pistol.

"Another of your inventions?" he inquired, backing away.

"Quite correct. I call it a disaster gun, for reasons which you'll, alas, not survive to observe. Say your prayers, my boy. At the count of three, you die."

4

Outside, boots clumped on the landing. Someone rattled the door.

"Geez, where could they of went?" a querulous voice inquired.

"Maybe t'rough duh door," another replied.

"Negative, it's locked, and nobody but King Lafayette don't know the combination."

"Nuts, Morton. Let's bust it down—"

"I say negative, Irving! They didn't go that way! You must of give us a bum steer. They never come up here—"

"Where else could they of went? They gotta of went t'rough duh door!"

"They din't!"

"How do you know?"

"They din't because they cun't, rum-dum!"

The door rattled again. "Yeah—I guess yez'r right. Like you said, nobody but King Lafayette could spring dat latch."

The booted feet withdrew.

Lafayette swallowed hard, his eyes on the gun. "Well—what are you waiting for? They're gone. Nobody will hear you killing me. And I deserve whatever happens for being dumb enough to forget to search you."

Lom was frowning thoughtfully. "That fellow said . . . that only King Lafayette knew the combination. That being the case—how did *you* open it—"

"We've been all over that, remember? You didn't believe me."

"You could have shouted whilst the men were outside. It might not have saved your life, but it would have cooked my goose. Yet—you failed to. Why?"

"Maybe I have a goose of my own."

"Hmmm. My boy, I'm inclined to give you one more chance—in spite of your having led me into this dead end. Just what did you intend to accomplish in this vacant chamber?"

"It shouldn't have been vacant," O'Leary snapped. "That lock is a special Probability Lab model, unpick-able. But—somebody picked it." He frowned in deep thought. "I've noticed that there are residual traits that seem to stay with the flesh, even when the minds are switched. As Tazlo Haz, I could almost fly. And I mastered merging, with a little concentration." He looked at his hands. "And it would never have occurred to *me* to lift that key from Percy's belt—Zorro's fingers did it on their own. So—the fellow who's wearing my body must have gotten certain skills along with it—including the combination."

"Very well . . . " Lom half-lowered the gun. "Assuming I accept that rather dubious explanation: what do you propose we do now?"

"Are we partners again?"

"Of sorts. By the way, you'd better return the sonic projector."

Lom jumped as Clarence spoke at his elbow. "Hey—you guys gonna chin all day? Let's get duh secret pipes fixed and blow outa here. Duh joint gives me duh willies."

"Don't creep up on me like that!" Lom snapped. "As for you, O'Leary—or whoever you are: you've brought me here—now do something!"

Lafayette looked around the gloomy chamber. The last time he had seen it, the wall cabinets which now gaped empty had been crowded with cryptic gear. The Court Magician's workbench, once littered with alembics and retorts and arcane assemblies, was now a bare slab of stained marble. Above, where the black crackle-finish panel with its ranked dials had been, snarled wires protruded from the bare wall.

"Even the skeleton's gone," he lamented. "It was gilded. It used to hang from a wire in the middle of the room. Very atmospheric."

"Skeletons?" Lom rapped. "What sort of mumbo jumbo is this? You said this fellow Nicodaeus was an Inspector of Continua, working out of Central—"

"Right—the skeleton and the stuffed owls and the bottled eye of newt were just window dressing, in case anybody stumbled in here."

"How did *you* happen to stumble in here? No self-respecting Inspector would allow a local in his operations room."

"I wasn't a local. And he didn't exactly allow me in. I came up here to find out what he knew about Princess Adoranne's disappearance. Frankly, I was ready to slit his weasand, but he talked me out of it."

"Indeed? And how, may I ask? You seem remarkably pertinacious of erroneous theories."

"Your vocabulary gets more portentous all the time," O'Leary said. "He convinced me he was what he said he was—which is more than you've done."

"And how did he accomplish that feat?"

"He made a phone call."

"Oh? I was unaware that telephones were known in this Locus."

"They aren't. Just the one, a hot-line direct to Central. It used to be over there"—O'Leary gestured—"in a cabinet behind the door."

"This is all very nostalgic, I'm sure—but it isn't resolving the present contretemps," Lom said.

"Hey, gents," Clarence called from across the room. "What is—"

"Not now, Clarence," O'Leary said. "Look here, Lom, it's not my fault the lab's been cleaned out. And it's not doing us any good to stand here and carp about it. We still have our freedom; what are we going to do with it?"

"You were the mastermind who had everything in hand!" Lom said testily. "What do *you* propose?"

"We have to put our heads together, Lom. What do *you* think we ought to do?"

"Hey, fellas," Clarence spoke up. "What's—"

"Not now, Clarence," Lom said over his shoulder. "Frankly, it looks to me as if we have no choice in the matter. We'll have to simply confront this King Lafayette—this false King Lafayette if your tale is to be credited—and . . . and . . . "

"And what? Invite him to hang us in chains from the palace walls?"

"Blast it, if I could only get my hands on my hands . . . " Lom muttered.

"What's that supposed to mean?"

"Nothing. Forget I said it."

"You've got a thing about hands, haven't you?" O'Leary snarled. "Don't think I haven't seen you playing with your fingers when you thought I wasn't looking."

"I wasn't playing, you impertinent upstart! I was . . . oh, never mind."

"Go ahead," O'Leary said, and slumped against the wall. "You might as well snap your lid in your own way. Let's face it: we're at the end of our tether."

Lom laughed hollowly. "You know—I'm almost convinced, at last, that you're what you say you are. What a pity it's too late to do any good."

"Hey," Clarence said. "Pardon duh inneruption—but what's dis funny-looking contraption, which I found inna cupboard behind duh door?"

Lafayette looked dully toward the man. He went rigid.

"The telephone!" he yelled. "Don't drop it, Clarence!"

5

"Clarence, my lad, you're a genius," Lom chortled, hurrying forward. "Here, just hand me that—"

"Not on your life," O'Leary said, and elbowed the old man aside to grab the old-fashioned, brass-trimmed instrument from Clarence. "Anyway, I'm the only one who knows the number!" He held the receiver to his ear, jiggled the hook.

"Hello? Hello, Central—"

There was a sharp *ping!* and a hum that went on and on.

"Come on! Answer!" Lafayette enjoined.

"Central," a tinny voice said brightly in his ear. "Number, please."

"It's—let's see . . . nine, five, three . . . four, nine, oh . . . oh, two, one-one."

"That is a restricted number, sir. Kindly refer to your directory for an alternate—"

"I don't have a directory! Please! This is an emergency!"

"Well—I'll speak to my supervisor. Hold the line, please."

"What do they say?" Lom asked breathlessly.

"She's speaking to her supervisor."

"What about?"

"I don't know—"

"Here—give me that telephone!" Lom made a grab; Lafayette bumbled the instrument, bobbled it, missed as Lom plunged for it. Clarence made a brilliant save an inch from the floor as the two staggered back in an off-balance embrace.

"Uh, no'm, it ain't," Clarence was saying into the mouthpiece as Lafayette extricated himself. "Name of Clarence: K...L...A...R...I...N...T...S..." He gave O'Leary an aggrieved look as the latter snatched the phone away.

"Yes? To whom did you wish to speak, sir?" a brisk voice said.

"Inspector Nicodaeus—only I understand he's on a field job somewhere—so just give me whoever's taking his place! I have vital information to report!"

"From where are you calling, sir?"

"Artesia—but never mind that—just give me somebody who can do something about—"

"Hold the line, please."

"Wait minute! Hello! Hello?"

"What do they say?" Lom demanded.

"Nothing. I'm holding the line."

"O'Leary—if you lose that connection—"

"I know; it might be fifty years before I get through again."

"Ah, there, O'Leary?" A hearty voice came on the line. "Good to hear from you. All's now well, I take it?"

"Well? Are you kidding? It couldn't be worse! Adoranne and Alain are dying of some unknown disease, there's a phony king going around kicking cats, and I'm trapped in the tower!"

"Here, who is this? I know O'Leary's voice, and this isn't it!"

"I've been all over that! I'm temporarily a fellow named Zorro, but actually I'm O'Leary, only somebody else is me, and he's running amok, and—"

"Look here, whoever you are—unauthorized use of the Central Comm Net is an offense punishable by fine, brain-scrape, and imprisonment, or any combination thereof! Now, get off the line, and—"

"You're not listening! I'm in trouble! Artesia's in trouble! We need help!"

"I'm sure," the strange voice said icily, "that matters are now well in hand. You needn't trouble yourself further—"

"Trouble myself—are you out of your hairpiece? If those trigger-happy guards get their hands on me, it'll be the firing squad!"

"See here, fellow: just take your grievances to the agent on the scene. If you have a legitimate case, it will be looked into. Now—"

"Agent? What agent? *I'm* the Central agent here, and I've been faked out of position and—"

"The regular man, Mr. O'Leary, is incapacitated, it appears. However, a Special Field Agent was dispatched to the Locus some hours ago, with instructions to proceed direct to the palace and make contact with one Princess Adoranne. That being the case—"

"You've sent a special agent in? Here? To Artesia?"

"That's what I said," the voice snapped. "Now if you'll excuse me—"

"Where is he? How will I recognize him? What—"

There was a sharp click, and the wavering hum of a dead line. Lafayette jiggled and yelled, but to no avail.

"Well? Well?" Lom was fairly dancing with impatience.

"He hung up on me. But I managed to pry some good news out of him: they've sent another agent in, probably one of their best men, with full powers. He'll have things straightened out in a hurry."

"Oh? Indeed. I see. Ha-hum."

"You don't seem overjoyed."

Lom pulled at his lower lip, frowning intently. "Actually," he said, "I'm not at all sure this is a desirable development at just this point."

"What's *that* remark supposed to mean?"

"Our antagonist, my boy, is a man of fiendish cleverness. At this moment he holds all the cards. Against him, a lone Agent hasn't a chance."

"Nonsense. I admit the fellow may not know the score—having me not be me is a bit confusing. But all I have to do is make contact with this new Agent, fill him in on a few facts, and make the pinch—"

"But that may not be so easy. Remember: I have one vital datum that you lack."

"Oh? What's that?"

"I," said Lom, "know who the villain is."

Chapter Ten

1

"You could have saved some time," Lafayette said, "if you'd mentioned this a little earlier."

"How could I? I thought you were his partner in the scheme."

"All right—who is he? Zorro?"

"Good heavens, no—"

"Not the Red Bull?"

"Nothing like that. You've never met him. The fact is, he's a renegade Commissioner of the Central Authority, by the name of Quelius."

"A commissioner? Ye gods—one of the top men—"

"Precisely. Now you can see the seriousness of his defection. I was his first victim. Then you. Now he's gobbling up an entire kingdom—and it will require a good deal more than honest intentions to topple the madman."

"All right—what's your suggestion?"

"First, we must make contact with this new chap Central's sent in, before he comes to grief. Presumably he's here in the palace by now, possibly in disguise. We'll attempt to intercept him when he calls on the princess."

"How are we going to recognize him?"

"I have," Lom said, patting his pockets, "a small ID device. When within fifty feet of a Central Authority ID card, it emits a warning buzz. Its failure to react to you was one of the principal reasons for my suspicions of you."

"Ummp. My ID is in a dresser drawer, downstairs."

"Quite. Now, at this point I suggest we divide forces. In that way, if one of us is caught the other may still get by in the confusion."

"Ummm. Shall we flip a coin?"

"I'll go first, dear boy. Now—what is the most direct route to the royal apartments?"

Lafayette told him. "Be careful," he finished. "There'll be guards six deep around the whole wing."

"Never fear, I shall make judicious use of the sonic projector. And I suppose you may as well have the disaster gun. But I'd suggest using it only in emergency. It's never been tested, you know."

"Thanks a lot." O'Leary accepted the weapon gingerly.

"Well—no point in waiting, I suppose. You follow in, oh, ten minutes, eh?" Lom moved to the door.

"Wait a minute," Lafayette said. "You've got your buzzer to identify the agent—but what do *I* use?"

"I should think any stranger might be a likely prospect. Ta-ta, my lad. I'll see you in court." The old fellow opened the door and slipped out. Lafayette listened. Two minutes passed with no audible alarm.

"So far so good," Lafayette murmured. "Now it's my turn."

Clarence was sound asleep, sitting in a corner with his head tilted on one shoulder. He opened his eyes, blinking in a bewildered way when Lafayette tapped him on the knee.

"I'm going now, Clarence. You can go back to the squad room. If anybody asks, tell them we went home. And thanks a lot."

"Geez," Clarence said, rubbing his eyes. He yawned prodigiously. "I wanna stay on duh job, boss. Dis cloak and dagger game is loads o' fun."

"Sure—but we need you back with the troops—someone who knows the score in case things go wrong."

"Yeah! Wow! Duh fellers won't never know I'm on a secret lay, which I'm woiking as usual wit' every appearance o' normality, an' all."

"That's the idea—" Lafayette jumped fourteen inches as a sharp ring sounded from the cabinet beside the door.

"Hey—dat sounds like duh doorbell," Clarence said. "OK if I answer it, boss?"

"It's the phone," O'Leary said, and grabbed it up. "Hello?"

"Oh, is that you?" It was the same voice he had last spoken to. "I say, look here, it appears something has come up; a Very Important Person wishes a word with you. Just hang on."

There was an electrical chatter, and a new voice spoke:

"Hello? This is Inspector Nicodaeus. To whom am I speaking, please?"

"Nicodaeus! Am I glad to hear from you! When did you get back?"

"Kindly identify yourself!"

"Identify myself? Oh, you mean because of the voice. Don't let that bother you—it's Lafayette. Just think of me as a little hoarse—"

"A little *what*? Look here, they told me there was a chap claiming to be O'Leary in another form, but nothing was said about *this*!"

"My voice," O'Leary said, striving for calm. "Not me. Listen, Nicodaeus—there's a serious emergency here in Artesia—"

"One moment," interrupted the voice on the line. "Tell me: what were the first words you ever said to me—assuming you are, as you claim, Sir Lafayette?"

"Look, is this necessary—"

"It is," Nicodaeus said in a tone of finality.

"Well—ah—I think you asked me where I was from, and I told you."

"Eh? Hmmm. Maybe you're right. I was thinking—but never mind. Now then: what was the object I showed you which first aroused your suspicions that I might be more than a mere Court magician?"

"Let's see. A . . . a Ronson lighter?"

"By Jove, I believe you're right! Is that really you, Lafayette?"

"Of course! Let's stop wasting time! How soon can you have a couple of platoons of Special Fields Agents in here to arrest this imposter who's rampaging around kicking cats and sleeping in my bed?"

"That's what I'm calling about, Lafayette. When I heard someone representing himself as you had been here at Central, I immediately looked into the situation—and what I've turned up isn't good—"

"I already knew that! The question is—"

"The question is more complicated than you know, Lafayette. Have you ever heard of a man named Quelius?"

"Quelius? Commissioner Quelius?"

"The same. Well, it seems that Quelius has run amok. He was Chief of Research, you know—"

"No, I didn't know—but I've already heard about him. Glad you confirmed what my friend Lom told me about him. But can't this discussion wait until after we've cleaned up this mess?"

"That's what I'm trying to tell you, Lafayette! Quelius, it now appears, has absconded with the entire contents of the Top Cosmic Lab, including our top researcher, Jorlemagne. From bits and pieces of evidence, we've learned that he has perfected a device with which he plans to seal off the Artesia continuum from any further contact with Central—to shift the entire Locus, in effect, into a new alignment, rendering himself forever safe from apprehension—and placing Artesia forever under his domination!"

"I never heard of any such gadget! That's impossible!"

"Not at all; in fact, it's quite easy, it appears, once given the basic theory. You remember a device called a Suppressor?"

"How could I forget? If it hadn't been for that, I wouldn't be in the fix I'm in now! How about lifting it, so I can go into action?"

"I'm afraid that's already been taken out of our hands," Nicodaeus said grimly. "Phase one of Quelius' plan has already gone into effect. The first step was to erect a Suppressor barrier around the entire Locus, cutting off all physical contact. This went into action only minutes ago. Our sole link is now this telephone connection—"

"You mean—you can't send any more men in?"

"Or out. Now it's up to you, Lafayette. Somehow, you must locate this man Quelius and lay him by the heels before his second phase is activated and Artesia is cut off forever!"

"How . . . how much time have I got?"

"Not much, I fear. Minutes, perhaps; hours at best. I suggest you go into action with all haste. I needn't remind you what's at stake!"

"And there's *nothing* Central can do to help?"

"Candidly, Lafayette—if more than a single obscure Locus were involved—if there were an actual threat to Central—certain extraordinary measures *might* be taken. But as it is, only my personal, sentimental interest in Artesia caused me to attempt this call. The simplest solution for Central, you must understand, is to let the matter solve itself. No doubt that's precisely the policy on which Quelius is counting for immunity. Well, perhaps we'll surprise him."

"Me—single-handed—plus one Field Agent you're apparently ready to abandon? What can we do?"

"I'm afraid that's up to you, Lafayette," Nicodaeus said, his voice fainter now as the crackling on the line increased. "I have great confidence in you, you know."

"What does this Quelius look like?" Lafayette shouted.

"He's an elderly man—about five three—bald as an egg."

"Did you say five three, elderly—and bald as an egg?"

"Correct. Not very formidable in appearance, but a deadly antagonist—"

"With a squeaky voice?"

"Why—yes! Have you seen him?"

"Oh, yes, I've seen him," Lafayette said, and uttered a hollow laugh. "I got him into the palace, past the guards, hid him until they were gone, gave him explicit directions for reaching Adoranne's apartment, patted him on the head, and sent him on his way . . ."

" . . . fayette—what's that . . . hear you . . . fading . . ." The static rose to drown the faint voice.

"Chee, boss, what's duh matter?" Clarence inquired as O'Leary hung up the phone. "Youse are as white as a tombstone!"

"Under the circumstances, that's an apt simile." Lafayette chewed his lower lip, thinking hard. Lom—or Quelius—at least hadn't lied when he named the villain of the piece—had used him like a paper towel. He'd gotten himself thrown in the same dungeon, pumped him dry of information, and then removed himself to a place of safety, leaving a gullible O'Leary to fare forth into the waiting arms of the enemy.

"Well, I'll fool him on that point, anyway," O'Leary said aloud. "Clarence—how would you like to have a *real* undercover assignment?"

"Chee, boss! Great!"

"All right, listen carefully . . ."

2

"Wait five minutes," O'Leary completed his instructions. "Then go into action. And remember: stick to your story, no matter what—until I give you the signal."

"Got it, Chief."

"Well—so long, and good luck." Lafayette opened the double glass doors that led onto the small balcony, stepped out into a drizzling rain under a sky the color of aged pewter.

"Splendid," he commented. "It fits right in with the overall picture." The iron railing was cold and slippery under his hands as he climbed over, lowered himself to find a foothold in the dense growth of vines below.

"Hey," Clarence said, leaning over to stare down at him. "A guy could like get hurt iff'n he was to fall offa dere."

"I've made this climb before," O'Leary reassured him. "In the dark. Now go back inside before you catch cold." He started down, wet leaves slapping at his face, icy water running down inside his sleeves. By the time he reached the stone coping twenty feet below, he was soaking wet. Carefully not looking down at the paved court a hundred feet beneath him, he made his way around the tower to a point above the slanting, copper-shingled roof of the residential wing. It was another fifteen-foot climb down to a point where he could plant a foot on the gable, which looked far steeper and more slippery than he had remembered.

No time now for second thoughts, he told himself firmly, and leaped, throwing himself flat. His hands scrabbled at the wet surface; he slid down until his feet went over the edge, his shins, his knees—and stopped.

All right, heart; slow down. The heavy copper gutter was under his belt buckle. He hitched himself sideways to a point which he estimated was approximately opposite the window to a small storeroom, then lowered himself over the edge. The window was there, directly before him, three feet away under the overhanging eave. Lafayette swung a toe at the latch securing the shutters; they sprang open, banging in the wind. A second kick, lightly administered, shattered the glass. He tapped with his boot, clearing the shards away.

"All right, O'Leary," he whispered, eyeing the dark opening. "Here's where that book you read on acrobatics will come in handy."

He swung himself forward, back, forward, back—

On the forward swing he let go, shot feetfirst through the window to slam the floor of the room rump-first.

3

"Nothing broken," O'Leary concluded after struggling to his feet and hobbling a few steps. He paused to listen to absolute silence. "No alarm. So far so good." He opened the hall door an inch; the passage was empty; not even the usual ceremonial sentries were on duty at the far end. Lafayette slipped out, moved silently along to the gilt and white door to the suite formerly occupied by a favorite courtier of Goruble's. There were no sounds from inside. He tried the latch; it opened and he stepped inside, closing the door behind him.

The room was obviously unused now; dust covers were draped over the furniture; the drapes were drawn, the window shuttered. Lafayette went to the far wall, tapped the oak panels, pressed at the precise point in the upper left-hand corner that Yokabump had pointed out to him, long ago. The panel swung inward with a faint squeak, and O'Leary stepped through into the musty passage.

"This is one ace Lom didn't know I was holding," he congratulated himself. "Now, if I can get to Adoranne before *he* does . . ."

It was a difficult fifteen-minute trip through the roughly mortared secret passage system, up narrow ladders, under low-clearance beams, which O'Leary located with his skull, to the black wall behind which lay the royal apartment. Lafayette listened, heard nothing. At his touch the inconspicuous latch clicked open and the panel slid smoothly aside.

Across the deep pile rug he could see the corner of Adoranne's big, canopied four-poster bed. No on was visible in the room. He stepped out—and whirled at the sudden whistle of steel clearing a sheath. A sharp point prodded his throat, and he was looking down the length of a sword blade into the square-jawed and hostile face of Count Alain.

4

"Hold it, Alain!" O'Leary said with some difficulty, owing to the angle at which his head was tilted. "I'm friendly."

"You have a curious manner of approach for one who means no ill, rascal!" Alain said. "Who are you? What would ye here?"

"I think I'd better let my identity ride for a moment; it would only complicate matters. Just think of me as a friend of Yokabump. He showered me the route here."

"Yokabump? What mare's tail's this? He lies in the palace dungeons, banished there by the madness of the usurper."

"Yes. Well, as it happens, I just escaped from the dungeon myself. Ah—would you mind putting the sword down, Alain? You'll break the skin."

"Aye—and a few bones beside! Speak, varlet! Who sent you here? What's your errand? Assassination, I doubt not!"

"Nonsense! I'm on your side, get it?"

A door across the room opened; a slim figure with golden hair and immense blue eyes appeared, clad in a flowing sky-blue gown.

"Adoranne—tell this clown to put the sword down before he gets into trouble with it," O'Leary called.

"Alain—who—"

"A would-be assassin," Alain growled.

"A friend of Yokabump; I came to help!" O'Leary countered.

"Alain—lower your blade. Let's hear what the poor man has to say."

"Well, then: speak. But at the first false move . . . " Alain stepped back and lowered the sword. O'Leary fingered his throat and let out a long breath.

"Listen," he said. "There's no time for formalities. I'm glad to see you two in good shape. The story is you're dying of a mysterious fever—"

"Aye, 'tis the lie spread by that treacher I once named as friend," Alain rumbled.

"There's a fellow on his way here—a man named Quelius, alias Lom." Lafayette described his former ally. "Have you seen him?"

Both Alain and Adoranne shook their heads.

"Good. He's the one who's at the bottom of this whole fiasco. Now, suppose you kids start by filling me in on the picture from your end?"

"Fellow, you're overfamiliar—" Alain started; but Adoranne put a hand on his arm.

"Hush," she said softly. "As you wish, friend of Yokabump. We, as you see, are held prisoner in our own apartments. His Majesty assures us that it's but a temporary measure—"

"Majesty, my left elbow!" Alain cut in. "I knew the first time I laid eyes on the miscreant no good would come of him! King Lafayette indeed! Wait 'til I lay hands on the treacher's neck!"

"As I remember, you didn't do so well the last time you two had a run-in," O'Leary observed. "Anyway, maybe you ought to make a few allowances. Maybe it's not really Lafayette O'Leary at all, who from all reports is a prince of a fellow, and—"

"Think you not I know the oil-tongued wretch who once forced his way into her Highness's good graces with his trickery, and—"

"Trickery! That was no trick, just superior personal magnetism. And killing Lod was a pretty hard thing even for you to brush off as sleight-of-hand—and how about killing the dragon? I suppose you could have done better?"

"Enough, sirrah!" Adoranne cut in. "Alain—stay to the subject."

"All right. So this blackguard, having lulled us into a false sense of security by lying low for a time, suddenly revealed his true colors. First, he came to her Highness with tales of an invading army. When, at my advice, she asked for evidence, he put us off with lies, meantime assuming what he termed emergency powers—which her Highness had not authorized. When I complained —we found ourselves one morning locked in, under guard by coarse fellows, new recruited, in the pay of O'Leary. When next we had tidings, whispered through a keyhole by a loyal housemaid, the scoundrel had in sooth declared himself to be regent!"

"All right—it's about as bad as it could be," O'Leary said. "Now, there are angles to this that I can't explain right now—you wouldn't believe me if I did—but what it boils down to is that we have to nail this fellow Quelius. He's the real power behind the throne. The imposter who's claiming to be O'Leary is working for him—"

" 'Tis no imposter, but O'Leary's self!" Alain rasped.

"What makes you so sure? Did Lafayette O'Leary ever do anything before to make you doubt him? Hasn't he always been true-blue, loyal, brave, honest—"

"I never trusted the varlet," Alain said flatly. "His present demeanor but confirms my reservations."

"Speaking of confirmed reservations, we'd better travel," Lafayette snapped. "I can see there's no point in trying to explain anything to you, you fair-weather chum."

"Mind your tongue, lackwit, else I'll probe for your jugular with my point!"

"Yeah, sure. All right, let's stop wasting time. You two can make your escape via the secret passages. I'll wait here for Quelius to show. When he does I'll give him a shot from his own shooter." He patted the disaster gun in his belt.

"What? You think I'd flee and leave even a scurvy knave like you to face the foe alone? Hah! Adoranne, you go, and—"

"Don't prattle nonsense," the princess cut him off coolly. "I stay, of course."

"If this were an ordinary situation, I'd argue with you," Lafayette said. "But under the circumstances, you may as well. If I miss, it's all over for Artesia."

"How is't, sirrah, that you seem to be privy to information unknown to the general public—or even to her Highness?" Alain demanded.

"I'll explain all that later—if there *is* a later."

"Not so," Alain barked. "Who else but a lackey of the tyrant would know his plans?" The sword leaped out to prod O'Leary's chest.

"If you must know, I got the information from a place called Central!"

Alain and Adoranne looked at each other.

"Indeed?" the count murmured. "That being the case, I suppose you'd be pleased to meet a fellow minion of this Central you speak of?"

"Certainly—but you're not supposed to know anything about Central. Its existence is a secret from everybody but accredited Central agents."

"Even so," Alain said. "And it happens, an emissary from Central arrived before you."

"That's right! I'd forgotten! Where is he?"

"Lying down in the next room. Adoranne—wilt summon the agent?"

The princess left the room. Lafayette heard low voices, then soft foot falls on the carpet. A slim, girlish figure in a trim gray uniform appeared in the doorway.

"Daphne!" Lafayette gasped. "What are *you* doing here?"

5

"You know her?" Alain said in an amazed tone.

"I thought you were safe at Central Casting," Lafayette said, starting forward. "You poor kid, I knew they'd sent someone, but it never occurred to me they'd be idiots enough to—"

Daphne jerked a pistol from the holster at her waist, aimed it at O'Leary.

"I don't know how you know my name," she said in a voice with only the faintest quaver, "but if you take another step, I'll fire!"

"Daphne—it's me—Lafayette! Don't you know me?"

"What, you too? Does everybody think I'm so addled I don't know my own husband?"

Lafayette moistened his lips and took a deep breath. "Look, Daphne—try to understand. I don't look like myself, I know. I look like a Wayfarer named Zorro. But actually I'm me, you see?"

"I see you're out of your mind! Stand back!"

"Daphne—listen to me! I stepped out that night—Wednesday, I think it was, two weeks ago—to, er, drop down to the A & D—and *this* happened to me!

It's all because of a thing called a Focal Referent. A fellow named Quelius is responsible. He paid the Red Bull to entice me down there, and—"

"Stop it! You're not Lafayette! He's tall, and handsome, in a baby-faced sort of way, and he has curly hair and the sweetest smile, especially when he's done something foolish—"

"Like this!" Lafayette smiled his most sheepish smile. "See?" he said between his teeth. Daphne yipped and jumped back.

"Not anything like that, you oily, leering monster!"

"Look, Zorro can't help it if he has close-set eyes!"

"Enough of this, varlet!" Alain roared. "Art daft, lout? Think you the Countess Daphne—and her Highness and myself as well—know not this turncoat O'Leary on sight?"

"He's not a turncoat!" Daphne cried, whirling on Alain. "He's just . . . just . . . sick . . . or something." She sniffled suddenly, and blinked back a tear.

"Look, we can't have a falling-out now over a little misunderstanding," Lafayette appealed. "Forget my identity; the important thing is that we stop Quelius—fast! He's got some sort of probability engine set up that will rotate Artesia right out of the Continuum! Once he does that, he's safe forever from outside interference from Central!"

"What do *you* know about Central?"

"Don't you remember? You saw me there, yesterday! You even helped me—"

"I saw another crazy man there who tried to convince me he was Lafayette O'Leary. I never saw you before in my life—or him, either!"

"Daphne—they were both me! I mean, I was both of them! I mean—oh, never mind. The point is—I'm on your side—and Adoranne's side. I just talked to Nicodaeus. He was the one who warned me about Lom—I mean Quelius!"

"Do you have any proof?"

"Well—nothing documentary—but Daphne—listen: close your eyes, and imagine I've got a bad cold, or got hit in the larynx by a polo ball, or something. Now . . . remember the night I met you? You were wearing nothing but soapsuds, remember? So I ordered up a nice dress for you to wear to the ball—a pink and silver one. And later that evening you saved my life for the first time by dropping the chamber pot on Count Alain's head! And—"

"Who told you all this!"

"Nobody! It's me, I remember it! Just pretend I'm . . . I'm enchanted or something, like the frog prince. Inside this unwashed exterior is the same old Lafayette who wooed you and won you!"

"There *is* something . . . it's almost as if . . . "

"Then you *do* recognize me?"

"No! But . . . but I suppose there's no harm in listening to what you have to say—even if you *are* crazy."

"Well, that's something . . . "

"We've heard enough madman's raving," Alain said. "The question remains—what to do? We know the false king plans some great coup for this evening: the rumors make that plain. We must make our move before then—or not at all. I say the time has come for me to fare forth, beat my way through the usurper's hirelings who guard us here, and slay their master as he takes his place in the banquet hall!"

"You'd never make it, Al," O'Leary said flatly. "Anyway, there's no need for a grandstand play. We can use the secret passages and pop up in the ballroom, surprise, surprise."

"If we can trust this intelligence of hidden ways . . . "

"Alain—he's our friend; I feel it. It almost seem I know him . . . " Adoranne looked searchingly at O'Leary.

He sighed. "Let's not get me started on that again," he said. "What time is this big affair scheduled for?"

"Eight p.m.—about an hour from now."

"Unless I'm badly mistaken, you'll have callers before then—bound on the errand you thought I was on. Quelius can't afford to have you alive when his puppet springs his big announcement this evening. He probably figures on the confusion of the big dance to cover sneaking the bodies out of the palace. Later he'll make the sad announcement that you've fallen victims to the fever. Your showing up in good health will blow that plan off the map. After that we'll have to play it by ear."

"Once in the ballroom, in full sight of the people," Alain mused, "we'll be safe—for the moment. He'd not dare to cut us down before our subjects."

"And our very presence there," Adoranne added, "will give the lie to his claims of our indisposition."

Alain smacked a fist into his palm.

" 'Tis possible—but if this secret way leads into a trap . . . " Alain gave Lafayette a fierce look. "I know who will be first to die."

"Don't be nervous, Al—you'll get through all right," O'Leary assured him. "Now, I think you both ought to look your best, to properly impress the public. Medals, orders, jewels, tiaras—the works."

"You could do with a wash yourself, fellow," Alain addressed O'Leary. "There's a distinct odor of goat about you."

"A bath?" Lafayette said wonderingly. "I'd forgotten such things existed."

"In there." Alain motioned along a short passage toward a door through which were visible pale-green tiles and golden fittings. "And you may burn those garish rags; I think my footman's attire will fit you well enough."

"I guess I can spare the time," Lafayette said, heading for the bathroom.

For a quarter of an hour O'Leary luxuriated in hot, scented water, scrubbing his skin with violet soap until it tingled.

"Easy, boy," he advised himself. "You'll wash all the hide off. Some of that dark shade is permanent . . . "

Afterward, he shaved, deciding to retain Zorro's mustache, trimmed drastically to an Errol Flynn effect with a pair of fingernail scissors, which he also employed on his fingernails. His glossy blue-black hair was also trimmed lightly and toweled dry, after which, with a minimum of brushing, it fell into a rather dashing natural coif.

Alain had laid out clothing in the anteroom. Lafayette put on clean underwear, tight black pants, a white shirt with baggy sleeves and an open collar. Before adding the black coat provided, he donned the scarlet cummerbund from his former outfit—a recent acquisition, apparently, almost unsoiled. Of necessity he also retained the gold rings on his fingers, as well as the one in his left ear, since they seemed to be permanently attached.

He strolled back along the passage into the drawing room; Daphne turned with a startled expression.

"Oh—it's you. You look—different."

"Where are Adoranne and Alain?"

"In their boudoir, dressing."

"You look pretty cute in that uniform, Daphne," O'Leary said. "But I liked you better in soapsuds."

"Please—spare me these fanciful reminiscences, sir! I have no choice but to work with you. But it's silly for somebody who doesn't have the remotest resemblance to Lafayette to attempt to impersonate him!"

"Well—I guess I'll have to settle for a platonic relationship. But it's hard, Daphne. You'll never know how I've missed you these past two weeks, how I've wanted to take you in my arms, and—"

"Don't be impertinent," Daphne said mildly. "You'd best fill me in on the plan."

"Oh, the plan. Well, frankly, the plan needs work. Daphne, did you know you have the most beautiful eyes in the world?"

"Do you really think so? But never mind that. We must talk of what we'll do when we reach the ballroom."

"Well, this fellow Quelius is a potent operator. Our only chance is to sneak up on him and nail him before he can use his sonic projector. Do you know, your hair is like spun onyx. And even in that uniform, your figure is enough to break a man's heart at a hundred yards."

"Silly boy," Daphne murmured. "I must say you look better with a shave. But we really can't stand here chattering all day . . . " She looked up into Lafayette's face as he came up to her. His arms went around her. She sighed and closed her eyes, her lips upturned . . .

"Hey! What are you doing!" he said suddenly. "Kissing a stranger, eh? I'm surprised at you, Daphne!"

She stiffened, then stepped back and swung an open-handed slap that sent him staggering.

"Here—what's this?" Alain spoke up from behind O'Leary. He stood in the doorway, resplendent in a dashing costume of blue and scarlet.

"It's quite all right," Daphne said haughtily, turning her back on O'Leary. "I've dealt with the matter."

Alain gave O'Leary a crooked smile. "The lady is abominably true to her marriage vows," he commented, rubbing his cheek reminiscently.

Adoranne appeared, regal as a fairy queen in silver gown and diamonds. She turned from Alain to O'Leary to Daphne, standing at the window with her back to the room. She went to her, put an arm around her waist.

"Never mind, Daph," she whispered. "I know someday Lafayette will come to his senses."

Daphne sobbed once, dabbed at her eyes, then turned, straight-backed. At that moment there was a peremptory knock at the outer door.

"I think it's time to go," she said.

Chapter Eleven

1

Ten minutes later they were crowded in the stuffy chamber scarcely a yard deep, ten feet long, concealed in the thickness of the wall behind the ballroom.

"Now, remember," Lafayette said. "Adoranne, you and Alain give me time to get in position. Then wait until this phony's just about to make his big announcement —then spring it on him. Just behave as if everything were normal: this is just a delightful surprise, you recovered unexpectedly, and here you are to join the fun. He'll have to play up to it. And while he's busy trying to regroup, I'll have my chance to take a crack at him."

"But—that will be dangerous for you!" Daphne said. "Why don't we draw lots—or something."

"He knows all of you; I'll be a stranger to him, a nobody. He won't be watching me."

"He's right, girl," Alain muttered. "But I'll stand ready to join in as opportunity offers."

"All right—here I go." Lafayette pressed the latch, the panel rolled aside, and he slipped through into the dazzle of light and the babble of conversation. The football-field-sized white marble floor was crowded with guests in laces and satins, gold braid and glittering jewels, aglow in the polychrome light from the great chandeliers suspended from the gold-ribbed vault of the high ceiling.

Solemn-looking guards in uniforms with unfamiliar armbands were posted at twenty-foot intervals against the brocaded walls, he noted. By sheer luck he had emerged midway between two of them. A few familiar faces turned casually to glance his way; but most of those present kept their eyes fixed firmly on the great golden chair set up at the far end of the room. And in spite of the superficial appearance of casual gaiety, there was an air of tension, a note of anxiety in the laughter and chatter.

Lafayette moved along the fringes of the crowd unchallenged. He took a drink from a passing tray and downed it at a gulp.

Abruptly, horns sounded. Silence fell, broken by a few nervous coughs. The wide doors at the opposite end of the room swung wide. A second fanfare blared. Then a tall, slender, fair-haired man appeared, strolling through the archway with an air of negligent authority. He was dressed in yellow silks adorned with white ermine, and a lightweight sport-model crown was cocked at a jaunty angle on his head.

"Why, the poor stumble-bum looks like a complete nincompoop!" O'Leary muttered aloud. "Doesn't he know yellow takes all the color out of my complexion?"

"Shhh!" hissed a stout nobleman in purple at Lafayette's elbow. "His spies are everywhere!"

"Listen," O'Leary said urgently. "That popinjay isn't the real—"

"Oh, I know, I know! Hold your tongue, sir! Do you want to get us all hanged?" The man in purple moved off quickly.

The regent sauntered across to the dais, stepped up, assisted by a cluster of courtiers, and seated himself grandly in the ornate chair. He tucked one foot back, thrust out the other, and leaned forward, resting his chin on one fist.

"Ha! Just like Henry the Eighth in a grade-B movie," O'Leary murmured, netting several apprehensive looks from those about him. As he made his way closer a functionary—a former second assistant stock room tallier, Lafayette saw, now decked out in full ceremonial garb—stepped forward, cleared his throat, unrolled a scroll with a flourish.

"Milords and ladies, his Royal Highness, Prince Lafayette, will graciously address the assemblage," he piped in a thin voice.

There was a patter of applause. The man in the golden chair shifted his chin to the other fist.

"Loyal subjects," he said in a mellow tenor, "how I admire your brave spirits—your undaunted gallantry in joining me here this evening—defying gloom, rejecting the melancholy counsels of those who would have us quail before the grim specter now hovering over our beloved Princess and her esteemed consort. If they could join us this evening, they would be the first to applaud you, carrying on in the gala mood they loved—love, that is—so well." The regent paused to shift position again.

"Look at that dumbbell, trying to talk with his jaw on his fist," Lafayette whispered to no one in particular. "He looks like a terminal paresis case."

Several people moved away from him; but one wizened little fellow in scarlet velvet muttered, "Hear! Hear!"

"Why is everybody standing around listening to this clown?" Lafayette asked the old gentleman. "Why don't they do something?"

"Eh? You ask a question like that? Have you forgotten Sir Lafayette's many services to the crown—and the squads of armed bravos he's lately hired to help secure his continued popularity, the while he so unselfishly volunteers his services during our ruler's indisposition?"

"Lord Archibald—what would you say if I said Adoranne's not really sick at all?" Lafayette inquired, *sotto voce*.

"Say? Why, I'd say you were prey to wishful thinking. And have we met, sir?"

"No—not exactly. But if she *were* actually well—just being held incommunicado—"

"Then all the cut-necks in Hell wouldn't restrain my sword from her service, sir!"

"Shhh! Good boy, Lord Archie—and keep your eyes peeled." O'Leary moved off as the regent droned on, took up a position some ten yards from the speaker, in the front rank of the crowd.

" . . . it is therefore incumbent on me—a realization to which I come with inexpressible reluctance—to formally assume a title commensurate with the dignities residing in the *de facto* Chief of the Artesian state. Accordingly—and with a heavy heart—" The regent broke off as his eye fell on O'Leary. For a long moment he gazed blankly at him. Suddenly he jerked upright, his eyes blazing, pointed a finger at O'Leary.

"Seize me that traitor!" he roared.

2

There were small shrieks and muttered exclamations as a squad of strong-arm men jostled their way through the press to grab Lafayette by both arms and the back of the neck. He landed one solid kick to a uniformed kneecap before a double wrist lock immobilized him.

"Don't kill him yet!" the regent yelled; then, as startled faces jerked around to stare at him, he managed an undernourished smile. "I mean to say, remember the prisoner's constitutional rights, lads, and treat him with all due gentility."

"What's the charge?" O'Leary croaked, speaking with difficulty because of the awkward angle at which his chin was being crushed against his sternum.

"Take him away," the regent snapped. "I'll question him later."

"One moment, if you please," a cracked voice piped up. Lord Archibald pushed his way forward to stand before the golden chair.

"I, too, would like to know the nature of the charge," he said.

"What's this? You dare to question me—that is, ah, why, my dear Archie—suppose we discuss the matter later—in private. Security of the realm involved and all that—"

"Sire, the security of the realm is involved at any time that one of her citizens is arrested arbitrarily!"

There was a small murmur of assent that faded swiftly as the man in the chair thrust out his lower lip and frowned down at the crowd.

"I perceive," he said in a lowered tone, "that the time has come for the enforcement of more stringent wartime regulations regarding free speech—or more properly—treason!"

"Treason against what, Messire?" Archibald persisted.

"Against me, your sovereign!"

"Princess Adoranne, sire, is *my* sovereign!" the old nobleman said loudly.

"I may as well tell you—your Princess is dead!"

There was an instant, dead silence. And in the silence, a clear feminine voice spoke:

"Liar!"

All heads whirled; Adoranne, radiant in silver and pearls, her long hair floating like a golden fog behind her, advanced through an aisle that opened magically before her. Behind her, Count Alain strode, tall and impressively handsome in tailcoat and spurs. Daphne followed, trim and beautiful, her face rigid with tortured emotions.

Bedlam broke out. Cheers, laughter, shouts of joy; elderly nobles went to one knee to kiss their princess' hand; younger ones brandished their dress swords over-head; ladies curtseyed until their wimples swept the floor, and rose, wet-eyed to embrace the person nearest. Lafayette jerked free of the suddenly nerveless grips on his arms to see the regent leap to his feet, his face twisted with rage.

"Imposters!" he roared. "Mummers, tricked out to resemble the dead! I myself witnessed the demise of her Highness but an hour since, and with her last breath she charged me with the solemn duty of assuming the crown—"

"Let me at the conscienceless swine!" Alain roared, leaping onto the dais.

"No!" Daphne shrieked, and threw herself at him, impeding his draw as the pretender scuttled backward. "He's not a traitor, Alain. He's just temporarily lost his wits!"

"Grab him!" O'Leary yelled. "But don't hurt him," he added.

"Right!" Lord Archibald chirped as he bounded for-ward, chrome-plated blade bared. "We need the scoun-drel in one piece for trial!"

There was a sudden disturbance behind Lafayette; he turned to see a familiar figure thrusting toward him.

"Lom!" he blurted. "Or should I say Quelius?" He reached for the little man—and froze as the sonic projec-tor swung to cover him.

"Wait!" Lom shouted. "Don't do anything foolish! You don't know—"

"I know I want to get my hands on your skinny neck!" O'Leary yelled, and charged.

"No! You don't understand! We have to—" Lom broke off, ducked under O'Leary's clutch, whirled to face the dais.

"Quelius!" Lom roared. "Stand where you are! It's all over!"

Lafayette checked in midstride as the usurper spun to face Lom.

"You!" the regent said in a strangled tone. "But—but—but—"

"That's right—me!" Lom yelled, as the man on the dais fumbled in his robes, drew out an object the size of an electric can opener, fumbled with it—

A soundless detonation sent O'Leary whirling off into lightless depths.

3

The stars were rushed toward him; they struck with a ghostly impact, blasting him outward in the form of an expanding shell of thin gas. Gazing inward from all points of the compass at once, he saw all the matter in the universe, gathered at his exact center, dwindle to a single glowing point and wink out. At once he was collapsing inward, shrinking, compressing. There was a momentary sensation of searing heat and crushing weight—

He was stumbling backward, to fetch up hard against folds of a velvet hanging against the wall. Something heavy slid down over his right eye, clanged to the floor and rolled. Below him, the man he had known as Lom looked swiftly up; his eye—as piercing as a red-hot needle—fell on O'Leary. His mouth quirked in a smile of ferocity; he raised the sonic projector—and uttered a yell as Sir Archibald brought the dull edge of his sword down on his wrist, knocking the weapon across the floor.

"I said he'll live to stand trial, you old goat!" the elderly courtier snapped. "Seize him, gentlemen! And the false regent as well!"

Eager hands grabbed Lom, who kicked and cursed in vain. And elegantly manicured hands fell on O'Leary, dragged him forward and held him, as the crowd stared up at him, wide-eyed.

"Alain," Lafayette barked. "Let go, you big oaf! It's all right now! I've got my own shape back—"

"Have done, false rogue, or I'll take pleasure in snapping your spine!"

Below, a swarthily handsome fellow in tight-fitting black with a red cummerbund stood gaping about him with an expression of total wonder.

"Zorro!" O'Leary yelled. "Tell them you're you! That you're not me anymore! I mean, that I'm not you anymore!"

"Think not to cop a plea of insanity!" Alain growled in O'Leary's ear. "There's a VIP dungeon ready and waiting for you, turncoat rebel!"

"I'm not insane! I'm Lafayette O'Leary! I was somebody else, but now I'm me again, can't you understand, you numbskull? And we're not out of trouble yet—"

"How could you?" a tearful feminine voice spoke near at hand. Daphne stood there, looking up into his face. "Is it really *you*, Lafayette—or was that man telling the truth! That somehow you aren't really you, and—"

"Daphne—before I wasn't me—but now I am, don't you see? I'm Lafayette O'Leary, nobody else—"

"Did somebody call fer Sir Lafayette?" a deep voice boomed. Clarence appeared, making his way through the crowd with a pleased smile on his face. "Dat's me," he announced, indicating himself with a thumb. "Anybody want to make sumpin of it?"

"No, Clarence, not now!" O'Leary shouted. "Cornmeal mush!"

"Don't pay no never mind to dat bozo," Clarence exhorted the crowd. "He's a ringer. Me, I'm duh McCoy."

"Zorro!" O'Leary appealed to the Wayfarer. "I told Clarence to stick to his story until I said 'cornmeal mush.' I mean until *you* said 'cornmeal mush.' That is, I was you then, and what I meant was—"

"I'm duh real O'Leary!" Clarence roared.

"No, he's not!" Daphne cried. "*He* is!" She pointed at Zorro, who goggled at her in astonishment. Daphne rushed to him, threw her arms around his neck.

"I recognized you in spite of your—your disguise—as soon as you laid hands on me," she sobbed.

Zorro stared over her head; his look of amazement gave way to a delighted smile.

"You bet, keed," he said.

"Daphne!" O'Leary yelled, "get away from that degenerate! Clarence—" A loud screech cut across the room. There was a stir in the crowd, cries of outrage as a small, furious figure in a scarlet skirt, a shiny black blouse, and jingling earrings forced her way through the press, followed by half a dozen olive-hued, black-haired barbarously attired Wayfarers.

"Gizelle! Luppo! What are *you* doing here?" O'Leary cried. The girl burst through the front rank and threw herself at Zorro, who leaped from Daphne's embrace to dive for cover as his enamorata's knife whistled past his ribs.

"Peeg! Lecher! Philanderer!" Gizelle shrieked as her arms were seized and the knife clattered away. "Wait unteel I get my hands on you, you sneaky, feelthy worm in the weeds, you!"

"Hey! Watch him!" Lafayette shouted—too late. Lom, his captor's attention distracted by the disturbance, wrenched free, ducked to catch up Gizelle's knife, darted to Daphne, now standing alone, seized her by the arm and whirled to face the crowd, holding the point of the stiletto at his captive's throat.

"Back!" he barked. "Or I slit it from ear to ear!"

Women screamed; men uttered oaths and grabbed for their sword hilts; but they fell back.

All but one man. O'Leary stared in horror as a tall, white-bearded patriarch in a glowing blue robe circled behind Lom, unseen.

The latter backed slowly, his eyes darting from face to face; he stooped, scooped up the object that the regent had been holding at the moment of O'Leary's transfer back into his original body.

"No!" Lafayette yelled, and plunged against the men holding him. "Don't let him—"

Lom uttered a shrill laugh. "Don't *let* me? Ha! Who can stop me?"

The tall man in blue tapped Lom on the shoulder.

"I can," he said in a tone like the tolling of a bell.

Lom whirled to goggle at the tall apparition that had appeared so suddenly behind him.

"Jorlemagne!" he gasped. He dropped the knife, clutched Daphne to him, thumbed a control on the button of the device in his hands—and with a sharp *whop!* of imploding air, vanished.

4

For the next two minutes, bedlam reigned. Lafayette made a frantic try for freedom, received a stunning blow on the skull, then hung dazedly in the grasp of the vigilantes. Confused images whirled in his brain, blended with the cacophony of a hundred voices raised in simultaneous hysteria.

"Quiet!" a thunderous tone broke through the hubbub. "Ladies and gentlemen—quiet! I must have silence in order to think!"

"Who might you be, sir?" "Where did he go?" "What's happened to Countess Daphne?" The clamor broke out again at once.

"I said QUIET!" the old man roared: he made a curt gesture—and sudden, total silence fell. O'Leary could see lips moving feebly, but not a sound was audible. The crowd stood as if bemused, staring at nothing.

"Well, that's better," the old man in blue said, his voice alone audible. "Now . . . " He half closed his eyes. "Hmmm. Quelius is a tricky devil. Who'd have thought *he'd* have thought of using the Mark III in that fashion? And where would he have fled? Not the caves . . . He knows I know . . . "

Lafayette! Help! a silent voice rang in O'Leary's ears—or no—not in his ears. Inside his head.

Daphne! Where are you? he cried silently.

It's dark, Lafayette! Lafayette . . . !

The elder in blue was standing before him.

"Lafayette—it is *you*, isn't it? Oh, it's all right; you may speak."

"I've got to get out of here," O'Leary said. "Daphne needs me—"

"Lafayette—don't you know me?"

"Sure—I saw you in a cave, you climbed out of a coffin and tried to bite me!"

"Lafayette—I'm your ally! You knew me as Lom, an assumed name, true, but then I was hardly in a position to trust you, eh? My real name is Jorlemagne."

"*You're* Lom? Are you out of your mind? Lom is a little shrimp under five six with a bald head and—"

"Surely you, of all people, can understand, Lafayette! Your description is of Quelius! I was caught by surprise, or he'd never have succeeded in exchanging identities with me!"

"You mean—you were Lom? And Lom was—"

"You! Simple enough, eh, now that I've explained it?"

"Wait a minute: even if you *are* Lom—or Jorelwhat-sit—or whoever that was I made the jailbreak with—what makes you think I think you're any friend of mine? The way I analyzed the situation, you conned me into sneaking you into the palace so you could join forces with your sidekick, played by me—"

"But you were wrong, my boy, eh? What need to enter the palace by subterfuge if I were in fact in league with Quelius? Actually, on leaving the tower, I was trapped in a broom closet for the better part of half an hour by four palace guardsmen playing a surreptitious game of chance. When they were called away to attend a disturbance in the ballroom, I followed."

"And another thing: I've been thinking about that sudden trip to Thallathlone—wings and all. Not your doing, I suppose?"

"Oh, that. Pray forgive me, lad. At that point I was under the not unwarranted impression that *you* were Quelius' dupe. I employed a sophisticated little device which should have phased you back into what I assumed was your natural Locus—namely, Central. But naturally, since you were in fact the O'Leary ego, from Colby Corners, occupying the Zorro body—native to Artesia—the coordinates I used had the effect of switching you right out of the base-plane of the continuum. But I did keep tabs on you, and make contact as soon as you phased back in, you must concede that."

"All right—that's all gravy over the tablecloth now. What about this Quelius?"

"Ah, yes. Quelius. He planned his operation with care—but right at the beginning he made a slip. His original intention was to displace my ego into the body of a prize hog, and store my body—as well as his own—the Lom body, occupied by the mind of a pig—in a stasis tank for future use; but I was able to effect a last-second baffle and shunt my ego into his corpus, while the pig-mind occupied my unconscious body. You see?"

"No. And where was he in the meantime?"

"Oh, Quelius assumed the identity of a chap who happened along. Just as a stopgap, you understand. His real objective was to exchange identities with you."

"You mean—that wasn't really the Red Bull I met at the Axe and Dragon?"

"A large chap with bristly hair? That sounds like him. Then, after you'd been finessed into activating the Mark III, he would take over in your place, whilst you were gathered in by the local constabulary. The first part of the plan succeeded—but you slipped out of his hands somehow."

"Well—I guess I should be grateful to Luppo for that. But how did you get your own shape back?"

Jorlemagne chuckled. "I put Quelius on the spot—with your help, of course. When I pointed the sonic gun at him, he panicked and shifted back into his own body—which of course displaced me from it, to resume my own. Which in turn forced the pig personality back into its pig-body, etc, etc." Jorlemagne wagged his head. "I came to myself leaning against the royal pigsty, looking yearningly at a prize sow."

"Well—this isn't finding Quelius," O'Leary said. "How did he do that disappearing act? One second they were here, and the next—phhtt!"

"The Mark III is a more versatile device than you suspect." Jorlemagne looked grave. "Now—the next problem is to deduce where he's taken her."

"That way," O'Leary said, closing his eyes and pointing. "About ten and a half miles."

"Eh? How do you know, my boy?"

"It's just a little trick I picked up from Tazlo Haz. Now let's call out the guard and—"

"A crowd of locals would merely complicate matters," Jorlemagne cut in. "You and I, lad—we'll have to tackle him alone."

"Then what are we waiting for?"

At the door the sage paused, motioned with his left forefinger; at once, the clamor in the room broke out in full force.

"Magic?" Lafayette gulped.

"Don't be silly," Jorlemagne snorted. "Microhypnotics, nothing more."

"So that's why you were always playing with your fingers—I mean, Lom's fingers."

"Quelius' fingers, to be precise. He's a clever man, but he lacks the necessary digital dexterity for microhypnotics and manipulation. Pity. It would have saved a spot of bother."

"Well, we still have a spot of bother ahead. It's a hard half hour's ride, and we're wasting time."

The stable attendants stumbled over each other to accommodate them; five minutes later, mounted on stout Arabian stallions, they cantered out through the gates, galloped full tilt through the echoing street, and out along the dark road to the north.

5

The peak loomed like a giant shard of black glass into the night sky.

"High Tor, it's called," O'Leary said. "They're up there—I'm sure of it. But why there?"

"The entire formation is riddled with passages," Jorlemagne said, as the horses, winded by the run, picked their way up the slope of rubble that led to the base of the mesa. "It's a natural volcanic core, left standing after the cone weathered away. Quelius spent considerable time and effort tunneling it out, under the pretext that it was to be an undercover observation station. I'll wager the Distorter gear is installed somewhere inside it. And he won't waste any time getting it in full operation, if I know Quelius—and I do."

"Well—produce one of those gadgets of yours," O'Leary urged impatiently. "I want to feel that stringy neck in my hands!"

"It's not to be quite so simple as that, my lad. My pockets are empty, I fear."

"Climbing that would be like going up the side of an apartment house," O'Leary said as he stared up at the vertical wall rising before him. He dismounted, scanned the rockface, picked a spot, hoisted himself up a few feet—and came tumbling back as his grip slipped on the smooth stone.

"A human fly couldn't go up that," he said. "We should have brought the field artillery along, and blasted a hole through it!"

"Well—we didn't," Jorlemagne said. "And since we can't walk through solid walls, we'll have to think of something else . . . "

"Hey!" O'Leary said. "You may have given me an idea." He closed his eyes, willed his thoughts back to the moment in Thallathlone when he had stood in the sealed chamber hollowed from the giant tree, abandoned there to merge—or die. He remembered the smell of the waxed, resinous wood, the sensation as he had stepped forward, pressed against and *through* the iron-hard wood . . .

It was like wading through dense fog; a fog so thick as to drag him as he pressed forward. He felt it touch his skin, interpenetrating, swirling about his interior arrangements—and then the breaking-bubble sensation as he emerged on the far side . . .

He opened his eyes. He was standing in a low, stone-walled passage before a flight of rudely chipped stone steps.

6

"It's too bad about you, young woman," the cracked old voice was saying as Lafayette crept up the last few steps and poked his head over the threshold to the circular room, which, to judge from the ache in O'Leary's knees, occupied the topmost level of the Tor. Across the small chamber, Daphne, looking more beautiful than ever with a lock of black hair over one eye and three buttons missing from her jacket, was tugging at the handcuffs that secured her to a massive oak chair. Quelius stood looking down at her with an expression of mild reproof.

"You've caused me no end of trouble, you know—first by behaving in a most unwifely manner in refusing to espouse my regency, then by running off like a little fool, and now by saddling me with your person. Still, you'll make a useful hostage, once I've completed certain arrangements against interference."

"I never saw you before, you nasty little man," she said coolly.

"Tsk. What a pity you don't appreciate the true symmetry of the situation. As O'Leary, I paved the way for the deposition of your little featherweight princess and her lout of a consort, while at the same time destroying O'Leary's popularity with the mob—and simultaneously, established a workable police apparatus with an adequate war chest. The stage is now set for me to step in and set matters right."

"When Lafayette catches you," Daphne said defiantly, "he'll fold you double and throw you away."

"Aha! But that's just it, my child. Lafayette will never catch me! At this moment the poor imbecile is no doubt suffering the penalty for *my* outrageous behavior!"

"Wrong!" O'Leary yelled, and launched himself at Quelius. The little old man whirled with astonishing agility, bounded to the wall, and jerked a rope dangling from above. Too late Lafayette saw the entire section of the floor before him drop like a hangman's trap. He made a wild clutch, missed, went over the edge and fell ten feet into a net that snapped shut around him like a closing fist.

7

Quelius lounged on the landing, smiling cheerfully at Lafayette, suspended in the open stairwell with his head in fetal position between his knees.

"And you were going to fold *me* double," the old fellow said good-humoredly. "Or so your bride predicted. Ah, well, we must excuse the ladies their predictable misconceptions, eh?"

"You're not going to get away with this, Quelius," Lafayette said as clearly as he could with a mouthful of kneecap. "Jorlemagne will slice you into pastrami—"

"Permit me to contradict you, Mr. O'Leary. Jorlemagne will do nothing. I'm quite immune to his digital trickery—and although he is indeed a clever chap, I happen to be in possession of the contents of his laboratory—so you see—I hold not merely the aces, but the entire deck."

"I noticed you left the ballroom in something of a hurry," O'Leary countered. "I suppose being in your burrow makes you feel brave. But I got inside without much trouble, you notice."

"So you did," Quelius nodded imperturbably. "My instruments indicate that you employed a rather interesting molecular polarization technique to pull off the trick. I invite you to use the same method to extricate yourself from your present situation." He cackled merrily. "You've been a sore trial to me, O'Leary. Bad stroke of luck, encountering Hymie the Ferocious, I believe he called himself, when I stepped outside the tavern that night. My, I'll warrant the red-headed ruffian whose shape I was using had skinned knuckles when he came to himself. But for that interruption you'd have been safely tucked away in the palace brig, ready to assist me in my impersonation. But then, all's well that ends well."

"Why go to so much trouble to strand yourself in a backward Locus like Artesia?" Lafayette inquired.

"Just making conversation, O'Leary? But I may as well oblige you; the Distorter won't be up to full charge for another half hour or so. Why Artesia, you ask? Well, I find it ideally suited to my purposes. Too backward to possess adequate techniques of self-defense, but sufficiently advanced to offer the industrial base I require to construct the masterwork of my career."

"So what? Nobody here will be able to appreciate it—and you're cutting off all contact with Central, so no one there will ever know."

"Correction," Quelius beamed. He rubbed his hands together with a sound like sand blocks in a kindergarten orchestra. "I estimate it will require no more than a year to assemble a high-capacity Distorter capable of acting effectively, against the Probability gradient. My, won't the pompous officials of Central—those self-appointed monitors of continuum morality—be surprised when they discover that it's their own bureaucratic beehive that's cut off from all outside contact? And then, O'Leary—then I can set about rearranging matters in a manner more to my liking!"

"Quelius—you're nuts—did you know that?"

"Of course. That's quite all right. Better embarked on an exciting insanity than moldering away in dull normality. One thing you can't deny: we psychotics lead interesting lives." Quelius dropped his bantering tone. "Now," he said briskly, "it's time to make disposition of you, Mr. O'Leary, and see to my equipment. Now, I could merely cut the rope and allow you to continue your interrupted descent—or I might lower you to a point six feet above the cellar floor and build a small fire to keep the chill off your bones. Any preference, Mr. O'Leary?"

"Sure. I'd prefer to die of old age."

"To be sure, so would we all—all but myself, of course. I'll have available to me an endless series of fresh young vessels to contain the vital essence of my personality.

Possibly I'll begin with Mrs. O'Leary, eh? It might be quite a lark to be a female—until I tired of the game; but this isn't solving the problem of your brief future. Hmm. I may have an idea—if you'll excuse me a moment. Now don't go 'way." Quelius cackled and hurried off.

The stoutly woven net, of quarter-inch hemp, rotated slowly, affording O'Leary an ever-changing aspect of damp stone walls. Hanging head-down as he was, he had an equally clear view of the floor a hundred feet below. He imagined how it would feel when the knife blade began sawing through the rope. First one strand would break, and the net would drop a few inches; then another—and another—and at last the final popping sound and the downward plunge—

"That kind of thinking won't help any, O'Leary," he told himself sternly. "Maybe Jorlemagne has a trick or two up his sleeve. Maybe a regiment of Royal Cavalry are riding to the rescue right now; maybe Daphne will free the cuffs and bean the old devil when he pokes his head in the room . . . "

"Maybe you'd like to take part in an experiment?" Quelius called as he came pattering back down the stairs. "Actually, it's wasteful to merely cast aside a valuable experimental animal—and as it happens, I have a new modification on one of Jorlemagne's little trinkets I'd like to put to trial. It will take a few moments to set things up, but please be patient."

By rolling his eyes, Lafayette could see the renegade Commissioner setting out an armload of equipment on the landing. There was a tripod, a spherical, green-painted object the size of a softball, wires, pipes, a heavy black box.

"Jorlemagne intended the device as an aid to medical examination," Quelius confided as he worked. "Gives the surgeons a superb view of one's insides, eh? It required only a slight shifting about of components to improve it, however. My version simply turns the subject inside out, with no nonsense. Liver and lights right there for handy inspection. Of course, there's a bit of difficulty when it comes to getting you put back in the original order afterward, but after all, we can't expect the pilot model to be without bugs, eh?"

Lafayette closed his eyes. No point in spending his last moments listening to the raving of a madman when he could be remembering pleasant scenes of the past for the last time. He pictured Daphne's smiling face . . . but the vision of her chained to a chair rose to blot out the image. He thought of Adoranne and Alain—and pictured them humbled before Quelius as he lolled on his stolen throne flanked by his secret police. Jorlemagne's towering figure was there—shaking his head futilely. Luppo rose up; Gizelle looked at him tearfully. Belarius stared at him accusingly; Agent Raunchini shook a fist at him, mouthing reproaches. The lean visage of Wizner Hiz was there, alight with triumph as he led his choral group in song . . .

Lafayette opened his eyes. Quelius was busily stringing wires.

"Won't be a moment, O'Leary. Don't be impatient," he called.

Lafayette cleared his throat, and started to sing:

> *Out of the world*
> > *Away and beyond*
> *Back through the veil*
> > *Quelius begone . . .*

"What's this?" the oldster looked around in surprise. "Vocal renditions in the face of eternity? A notable display of pluck. Pity your bride will never know. I intend to tell her that you kicked and screamed, offered to trade her for your life, volunteered to cut her ears off and all that sort of thing. Most amusing to watch her attempting to keep a stiff upper lip."

> *Afloat on a sea*
> > *Wider than night*
> *Deeper and deeper*
> > *Sinking from sight*

"Catchy tune," Quelius said. "Interesting rhythm. Seems to be a variation on the natural reality harmonic. Curious. Where did you learn it?"

> *Back where you came from,*
> > *Stealer of thrones*
> *Back to the depths*
> > *Far under the stones . . .*

"You're annoying me, O'Leary," Quelius snapped. He had stopped work to glare at his captive. "Stop that caterwauling at once!"

Out of the world,
Far from the sun
Begone from Artesia
Forever begone.

"Stop it at once, do you hear?" Quelius shrieked, covering his ears. "You're making me dizzy!" Suddenly he snatched up the knife from the heap of tools at his feet, leaned far out and slashed at the rope supporting the net.

Borne on the wings
Of the magic song
From fair Artesia
Forever begone!

There was a sharp *pop!* The rasping of the knife against the rope ceased abruptly. In the sudden silence, O'Leary thought he heard a faint, faraway cry, that trailed off into silence . . .

Footsteps rasped on the stone steps. O'Leary pried an eye open, saw Jorlemagne leaning out to pull the net in to the landing.

" . . . found the entry . . . few minutes to discover trick . . . Quelius . . . where is he—" the scientist's voice boomed and faded.

"Daphne—upstairs . . . " Lafayette managed; and then the darkness folded in like a black comforter.

3

Lafayette awoke lying on his back in a narrow white bed. An anxious-looking old fellow whom he recognized as the royal physician was hovering over him.

"Ah, awake at last, are we, sir? Now, just rest quietly—"

"Where's Daphne?" O'Leary sat up, threw off the covers.

"Sir Lafayette! I must insist! You've been unconscious for two days—"

"Nonsense! I've never felt better. Where is she?"

"Why—ah—as to that—Countess Daphne is in her apartments—in seclusion. She, er, doesn't wish to be disturbed—"

"Don't be silly, I don't want to disturb her." Lafayette leaped up, staggering only slightly, and grabbed a robe from the chair beside the bed.

"But Sir Lafayette—you can't—"

"Just watch me!"

Two minutes later, O'Leary rapped on Daphne's door.

"It's me, Lafayette!" he called. "Open up, Daphne!"

"Go away," came a muffled reply.

"Lafayette—what seems to be the trouble?" Jorlemagne called, arriving at a trot. "Dr. Ginsbag told me you'd leaped up and dashed off in a frenzy!"

"What's the matter with Daphne? She won't open the door!"

The old gentleman spread his hands. "Poor child, she's been through so much. I suggest you give her a few weeks to recover from the shock—"

"A few weeks! Are you out of your beanie? I want to see her *now!*" He pounded on the door again. "Daphne! Open this door!"

"Go away, you imposter!"

"Imposter—" Lafayette whirled to the startled sentries flanking the door. "All right, boys—break it down!"

As they hesitated, shuffling their feet and exchanging anxious glances, the door was flung open. Daphne stood there, dabbing at tear-reddened eyes. She jumped back as Lafayette reached for her.

"Leave me alone, you . . . you makeup artist," she wailed. "I knew you weren't really Lafayette the minute you threw the soup tureen at the Second cook!"

"Daphne—that was all a mistake! I wasn't really me then, but I am now!"

"No, you're not; you're a stranger! And Lafayette is a horrid man with a gold ring in his ear and the whitest teeth, and the most immense black eyes, and . . . "

"That's Zorro, the crook!" O'Leary yelled. "I was him for a while, while Quelius was me, but now I'm me again, and so is he!"

"I recognized him when he kissed me—"

"Almost kissed you," Lafayette corrected. "I stopped in time, remember?"

"I mean the next time. And then . . . and then he went away with that little dark-eyed creature with the knife—and he . . . he stole my gold bracelet before he left!"

"Daphne! What's been going on here? Don't tell me! Zorro is Zorro—and I'm me! Lafayette! Look at me! Don't you know me, Daphne?"

"My dear Countess," Jorlemagne started, "I assure you—"

"Stay out of this!" O'Leary yelled. "Daphne! Remember the fountain in the gardens where we used to sit and feed the goldfish? Remember the time you dropped the chamber pot on Alain's head? Remember the dress—the rose-colored silk one? Remember the time you saved me when I was falling off the roof?"

"If . . . if you're actually Lafayette," Daphne said, facing him, "when is my mother's birthday?"

"Your mother's birthday? Ah . . . let's see . . . uh . . . in October?"

"Wrong! What night are we supposed to play bridge with the duchess?"

"Er . . . Wednesday?"

"Wrong! When is our anniversary?"

"I know that one," Lafayette cried in relief. "The third of next month!"

"He's an imposter," Daphne wailed. "Lafayette never remembered our anniversary!" She turned and fled into the room, threw herself facedown on the bed, weeping. Lafayette hurried after her.

"Don't touch me!" she cried as he bent over her.

"Oh, this is fine," O'Leary groaned. "Just perfect! Why did I have to do such a convincing job of selling you on my identity when I was Zorro?"

"It wasn't so much what he said," Daphne wept, "it was the way he made love that convinced me . . . and now he's gone . . . "

"Daphne! I keep telling you—you—what?" O'Leary's voice rose to a squeak. "Give me air!" he yelped, and plunged through the doors to the balcony—

And fell twenty feet into a rhododendron bush.

4

Daphne was sitting on the ground, cradling his head in her lap.

"Lafayette—is it really you—"

"I . . . I've been telling you . . . "

"But it has to be. The false Lafayette was the one who ordered the balcony removed, when he tried to lock me in our apartments. *He* would have known it wasn't there. And besides—nobody but my very own Lafayette falls down quite the way you do!"

"Daphne," O'Leary murmured, and drew her down to him . . .

"I just happened to think," Daphne said later. "If you were Zorro—just what was your relationship with that little brunette baggage named Gizelle?"

"*I* was wondering what *your* sleeping arrangements were—up until that four-flusher showed his true colors—"

"But then," Daphne went on as if he hadn't spoken, "I decided there are some questions best left unasked."

HONORVERSE VOLUMES:

Crown of Slaves (with Eric Flint) 0-7434-9899-2 • $7.99
Sent on a mission to keep Erewhon from breaking with Manticore, the Star Kingdom's most able agent and the Queen's niece may not even be able to escape with their lives....

The Shadow of Saganami 0-7434-8852-0 • $26.00
1-4165-0929-1 • $7.99
A new generation of officers, trained by Honor Harrington, are ready to hit the front lines as war erupts again.

ANTHOLOGIES EDITED BY DAVID WEBER:

More Than Honor 0-671-87857-3 • $6.99

Worlds of Honor 0-671-57855-3 • $7.99

Changer of Worlds 0-7434-3520-6 • $7.99

The Service of the Sword 0-7434-8836-9 • $7.99

THE DAHAK SERIES:

Mutineers' Moon 0-671-72085-6 • $7.99

The Armageddon Inheritance 0-671-72197-6 • $6.99

Heirs of Empire 0-671-87707-0 • $7.99

Empire from the Ashes trade pb • 1-4165-0993-X • $15.00
Contains *Mutineers' Moon*, *The Armageddon Inheritance* and *Heirs of Empire* in one volume.

THE BAHZELL SAGA:

Oath of Swords   0-671-87642-2 • $7.99

The War God's Own   hc • 0-671-87873-5 • $22.00
                              pb • 0-671-57792-1 • $7.99
Wind Rider's Oath   hc • 0-7434-8821-0 • $26.00
                              pb • 1-4165-0895-3 • $7.99

Bahzell Bahnakson of the hradani is no knight in shining armor and doesn't want to deal with anybody else's problems, let alone the War God's. The War God thinks otherwise.

BOLO VOLUMES:

Bolo!   hc • 0-7434-9872-0 • $25.00
                              pb • 1-4165-2062-7 • $7.99

Keith Laumer's popular saga of the Bolos continues.

Old Soldiers   hc • 1-4165-0898-8 • $26.00
                              pb • 1-4165-2104-6 • $7.99

A new Bolo novel.

OTHER NOVELS:

The Excalibur Alternative hc • 0-671-31860-8 • $21.00
                               pb • 0-7434-3584-2 • $7.99

An English knight and an alien dragon join forces to overthrow the alien slavers who captured them. Set in the world of David Drake's *Ranks of Bronze*.

In Fury Born   pb • 1-4165-2131-3 • $7.99

A greatly expanded new version of *Path of the Fury*, with almost twice the original wordage.

1633 with Eric Flint   hc • 0-7434-3542-7 • $26.00
                                         pb • 0-7434-7155-5 • $7.99
1634: *The Baltic War* with Eric Flint   hc • 1-4165-2102-X • $26.00
American freedom and justice versus the tyrannies of the 17th century. Set in Flint's *1632* universe.

THE STARFIRE SERIES WITH STEVE WHITE:

The Stars at War I   0-7434-8841-5 • $25.00
Rewritten *Insurrection* and *In Death Ground* in one massive volume.

The Stars at War II   0-7434-9912-3 • $27.00
The Shiva Option and *Crusade* in one massive volume.

PRINCE ROGER NOVELS WITH JOHN RINGO:

March Upcountry   0-7434-3538-9 • $7.99

March to the Sea   0-7434-3580-X • $7.99

March to the Stars   0-7434-8818-0 • $7.99

We Few   1-4165-2084-8 • $7.99
"This is as good as military sf gets." *—Booklist*